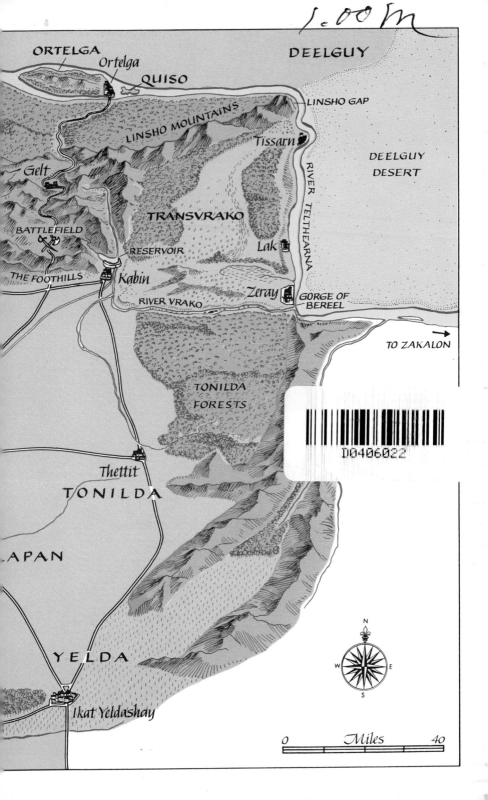

Shardik

Richard Adams

SIMON AND SCHUSTER
NEW YORK

Designed by Irving Perkins
Endpaper map by Rafael Palacios
Manufactured in the United States of America
Printed by The Murray Printing Company
Bound by American Book-Stratford Press, Inc.

1   2   3   4   5   6   7   8   9   10

Library of Congress Cataloging in Publication Data

Adams, Richard
Shardik.
I.   Title.
PZ4.A2163Sh3   [PS3551.D394]   813'.5'4   74-32031
ISBN 0-671-22015-2

ACKNOWLEDGMENTS

I acknowledge with gratitude the help I have received from my friends Reg. Sones and John Apps, who read the book before publication and made valuable criticisms and suggestions.

The manuscript was typed by Mrs. Margaret Apps and Mrs. Barbara Cheeseman. I thank them warmly for their patience and accuracy.

The interior maps were drawn by Mrs. Marilyn Hemmett and need no praise from me. The services of a qualified cartographer are a great asset.

NOTE

Lest any should suppose that I set my wits to work to invent the cruelties of Genshed, I say here that all lie within my knowledge and some —would they did not—within my experience.

To my onetime Ward in Chancery
ALICE PINTO
with sincere affection, always

οἴκτιστον δὴ κεῖνο ἐμοῖς ἴδον ὀφθαλμοῖσι
πάντων ὅσσ' ἐμόγησα πόρους ἁλὸς ἐξερεείνων.

ODYSSEY XII 258

Contents

BOOK VII

The Power of God

*Behold, I will send my messenger. . . . But
who may abide the day of his coming?
And who shall stand when he appeareth?
For he is like a refiner's fire. . . .*

MAL. 3:1–2

*Superstition and accident manifest the will
of God.*

C. G. Jung

BOOK I

Ortelga

1 *The Fire*

EVEN IN THE DRY HEAT of summer's end, the great forest was never silent. Along the ground—soft, bare soil, twigs and fallen branches, decaying leaves black as ashes—there ran a continuous flow of sound. As a fire burns with a murmur of flames, with the intermittent crack of exploding knots in the logs and the falling and settling of coal, so on the forest floor the hours of dusky light consumed away with rustlings, patterings, sighing and dying of breeze, scuttlings of rodents, snakes, lizards and now and then the padding of some larger animal on the move. Above, the green dusk of creepers and branches formed another realm, inhabited by the monkeys and sloths, by hunting spiders and birds innumerable—creatures passing all their lives high above the ground. Here the noises were louder and harsher —chatterings, sudden cacklings and screams, hollow knockings, bell-like calls and the swish of disturbed leaves and branches. Higher still, in the topmost tiers, where the sunlight fell upon the outer surface of the forest as upon the upper side of an expanse of green clouds, the raucous gloom gave place to a silent brightness, the province of great butterflies flitting across the sprays in a solitude where no eye admired nor any ear caught the minute sounds made by those marvelous wings.

The creatures of the forest floor—like the blind, grotesque fish that dwell in the ocean depths—inhabited, all unaware, the lowest tier of a world extending vertically from shadowless twilight to shadeless, dazzling brilliance. Creeping or scampering upon their furtive ways, they seldom went far and saw little of sun and moon. A thicket of thorn, a maze of burrows among tree trunks, a slope littered with rocks and stones—such places were almost all that their inhabitants ever knew of the earth where they lived and died. Born there, they survived for a while, coming to know every inch within their narrow bounds. From time to time a few might stray farther—when prey or forage failed, or more rarely, through the irruption of some uncomprehended force from beyond their daily lives.

Between the trees the air seemed scarcely to move. The heat had thickened it, so that the winged insects sat torpid on the very leaves beneath which crouched the mantis and spider, too drowsy to strike. Along the foot of a tilted red rock a porcupine came nosing and grubbing. It broke open a tiny shelter of sticks and some meager, round-eared little creature, all eyes and bony limbs, fled across the stones. The porcupine, ignoring it, was about to devour the beetles scurrying among the sticks when suddenly it paused, raised its head and listened. As it remained motionless a brown, mongoose-like creature broke quickly through the bushes and disappeared down its hole. From farther away came a sound of scolding birds.

A moment later the porcupine too had vanished. It had felt not only the fear of other creatures nearby, but also something of the cause—a disturbance, a vibration along the forest floor. A little distance away, something unimaginably heavy was moving, and this movement was beating the ground like a drum. The vibration grew until even a human ear could have heard the irregular sounds of ponderous movement in the gloom. A stone rolled downhill through fallen leaves and was followed by a crashing of undergrowth. Then, at the top of the slope beyond the red rock, the thick mass of branches and creepers began to shake. A young tree tilted outward, snapped, splintered and pitched its length to the ground, springing up and down in diminishing bounds on its pliant branches, as though not only the sound but also the movement of the fall had set up echoes in the solitude.

In the gap, half-concealed by a confused tangle of creepers, leaves and broken flowers, appeared a figure of terror, monstrous beyond the nature even of that dark, savage place. Huge it was—gigantic—standing on its hind legs more than twice as high as a man. Its shaggy feet carried great, curved claws as thick as a man's fingers, from which were hanging fragments of torn fern and strips of bark. The mouth gaped open, a steaming pit set with white stakes. The muzzle was thrust forward, sniffing, while the bloodshot eyes peered shortsightedly over the unfamiliar ground below. For long moments it remained erect, breathing heavily and growling. Then it sank clumsily upon all fours, pushed into the undergrowth, the round claws scraping against the stones—for they could not be retracted—and smashed its way down the slope toward the red rock. It was a bear—such a bear as is not seen in a thousand years—more powerful than a rhinoceros and heavy as eight strong men. It reached the open ground by the rock and paused, throwing its head uneasily to one side and the other. Then once more it reared up on its hind legs, sniffed the air and on the instant gave a deep, coughing bark. It was afraid.

Afraid—this breaker of trees, whose tread shook the ground —of what could it be afraid? The porcupine, cowering in its shallow burrow beneath the rock, sensed its fear with bewilderment. What had driven it wandering through strange country, through deep forest not its own? Behind it there followed a strange smell—an acrid, powdery smell, a drifting fear.

A band of yellow gibbons swung overhead, hand over hand, whooping and ululating as they disappeared down their tree-roads. Then a pair of genets came trotting down from the undergrowth, passed close to the bear without a glance and were gone as quickly as they had come. A strange, unnatural wind was moving, stirring the dense mass of foliage at the top of the slope, and out of it the birds came flying—parrots, barbets and colored finches, brilliant blue and green honeycreepers and purple jackdaws, gentuas, and forest kingfishers—all screaming and chattering down the wind. The forest began to be filled with the sounds of hasty, pattering movement. An armadillo, apparently injured, dragged itself past; a peccary and the flash of a long, green snake. The porcupine broke from its hole, almost under the bear's feet, and vanished. Still the bear stood upright, towering over the flat rock, sniffing and hesitating. Then the wind strengthened, bringing a sound that seemed to stretch across the forest from end to end—a sound like a dry waterfall or the breathing of a giant—the sound of the smell of the fear. The bear turned and shambled away between the tree trunks.

The sound grew to a roaring and the creatures flying before it became innumerable. Many were almost spent, yet still stumbled forward with open mouths set in snarls and staring eyes that saw nothing. Some tripped and were trampled down. Drifts of green smoke appeared through gaps in the undergrowth. Soon the glaucous leaves, big as human hands, began to shine

19

here and there with the reflection of an intermittent, leaping light, brighter than any that had penetrated that forest twilight. The heat increased until no living thing—not a lizard, not a fly —remained in the glade about the rock. And then at last appeared a visitant yet more terrible than the giant bear. A single flame darted through the curtain of creepers, disappeared, returned and flickered in and out like a snake's tongue. A spray of dry, sharp-toothed leaves on a *zeltazla* bush caught fire and flared brightly, throwing a dismal shine on the smoke that was now filling the glade like fog. Immediately after, the whole wall of foliage at the top of the slope was ripped from the bottom as though by a knife of flame and at once the fire ran forward down the length of the tree that the bear had felled. Within moments the place, with all its features, all that had made a locality of smell, touch and sight, was destroyed forever. A dead tree, which had leaned supported by the undergrowth for half a year, fell burning across the red rock, splintering its cusps and outcrops, barring it with black like a tiger's skin. The glade burned in its turn, as miles of forest had burned to bring the fire so far. And when it had done burning, the foremost flames were already a mile downwind as the fire pursued its way.

2 *The River*

THE ENORMOUS BEAR wandered irresolutely on through the forest, now stopping to glare about at its unknown surroundings, now breaking once more into a shambling trot as it found itself still pursued by the hiss and stench of burning creepers and the approach of the fire. It was sullen with fear and bewilderment. Since nightfall of the previous day it had been driven, always reluctant yet always unable to find any escape from danger. Never before had it been forced to flight. For years past no living creature had stood against it. Now, with a kind of angry shame, it slunk on and on, stumbling over half-seen roots, tormented with thirst and desperate for a chance to turn and fight against this flickering enemy that nothing could dismay. Once it stood its ground at the far end of a patch of marsh, deceived by what seemed a faltering at last in the enemy's advance, and fled just in time to save itself from being encircled as the fire ran forward on either side. Once, in a kind of madness, it rushed back on its tracks and actually struck and beat at the flames, until its pads were scorched and black, singed streaks showed along its pelt. Yet still it paused and paced about, looking for an opportunity to fight, and as often as it turned and went on, slashed the tree trunks and tore up the bushes with heavy blows of its claws.

Slower and slower it went, panting now, tongue protruding and eyes half-shut against the smoke that followed closer and closer. It struck one scorched foot against a sharpened boulder, fell and rolled on its side, and when it got up, became confused, made a half-turn and began to wander up and down, parallel to the line of the oncoming flames. It was exhausted and had lost the sense of direction. Choking in the enveloping smoke, it could no longer tell even from which side the fire was coming. The nearest flames caught a dry tangle of *quian* roots and raced along them, licking across one forepaw. Then from all sides there sounded a roaring, as though at last the enemy were coming to grips. But louder still rose the frenzied, angry roaring of the bear itself as it turned at last to fight. Swinging its head from side to side and dealing tremendous, spark-showering blows upon the blaze around it, it reared up to its full height, trampling back and forth until the soft earth was flattened under its feet and it seemed to be actually sinking into the ground beneath its own weight. A long flame crackled up the thick pelt and in a moment the creature blazed, all covered with fire, rocking and nodding in a grotesque and horrible rhythm. In its rage and pain it had staggered to the edge of a steep bank. Swaying forward, it suddenly saw below, in a lurid flash, another bear, shimmering and grimacing, raising burning paws toward itself. Then it plunged forward and was gone. A moment later there rose the sound of a heavy splash and a hissing, quenching after-surge of deep water.

In one place and another, along the bank, the fire checked, diminished and died, until only patches of thicker scrub were left burning or smoldering in isolation. Through the miles of dry forest the fire had burned its way to the northern shore of the Telthearna River and now, at last, it could burn no farther.

Struggling for a foothold but finding none, the bear rose to the surface. The dazzling light was gone and it found itself in shadow, the shadow of the steep bank and the foliage above, which arched over, forming a long tunnel down the river's marge. The bear splashed and rolled against the bank but could get no purchase, partly for the steepness and the crumbling of the soft earth under its claws, and partly for the current which continually dislodged it and carried it farther downstream. Then, as it clutched and panted, the canopy above began to fill with the jumping light of the fire as it caught the last branches, the roof of the tunnel. Sparks, burning fragments and cinders dropped hissing into the river. Assailed by this dreadful rain, the bear thrust itself away from the bank and began to swim clumsily out from under the burning trees toward the open water.

The sun had begun to set and was shining straight down the river, tingeing to a dull red the clouds of smoke that rolled over the surface. Blackened tree trunks were floating down, heavy as battering rams, driving their way through the lesser flotsam, the clotted masses of ash and floating creeper. Everywhere was plunging, grinding and the thump and check of heavy masses, striking one another. Out into this foggy chaos swam the bear, laboring, submerging, choking, heaving up again and struggling across and down the stream. A log struck its side with a blow that would have stove in the ribs of a horse and it turned and brought both forepaws down upon it, half clutching in desperation, half striking in anger. The log dipped under the weight and then rolled over, entangling the bear in a still-smoldering branch that came slowly down like a hand with fingers. Below the surface, something unseen caught its hind paws and the log drifted away as it kicked downward and broke free. It fought for breath, swallowing water, ashy foam and swirling leaves. Dead animals were sweeping by—a striped makati with bared teeth and closed eyes, a terrian floating belly uppermost, an anteater whose long tail washed to and fro in the current. The bear had formed some cloudy purpose of swimming to the farther shore—a far-off glimpse of trees visible across the water. But in the bubbling, tumbling midstream this, like all else, was swept away and once more it became, as in the forest, a creature merely driven on, in fear of its life.

Time passed and its efforts grew weaker. Fatigue, hunger, the shock of its burns, the weight of its thick, sodden pelt and the continual buffeting of the driftwood were at last breaking it down, as the weather wears out mountains. Night was falling and the smoke clouds were dispersing from the miles of lonely, turbid water. At first the bear's great back had risen clear above the surface and it had looked about it as it swam. Now only its head protruded, the neck bent sharply backward to lift the muzzle high enough to breathe. It was drifting, almost unconscious and unaware of anything around it. It did not see the dark line of land looming out of the twilight ahead. The current parted, sweeping strongly away in one direction and more gently in the other. The bear's hind feet touched ground but it made no response, only drifting and tripping forward like a derelict until at length it came to rest against a tall, narrow rock sticking out of the water; and this it embraced clumsily, grotesquely, as an insect might grasp a stick.

Here it remained a long time in the darkness, upright like some tilted monolith, until at last, slowly relaxing its hold and slipping down upon all fours in the water, it splashed through the shallows, stumbling into the forest beyond and sank unconscious among the dry, fibrous roots of a grove of quian trees.

3 *The Hunter*

THE ISLAND, some twenty-five miles long, divided the river into two channels, its upstream point breaking the central current, while that downstream lay close to the unburned shore which the bear had failed to reach. Tapering to this narrow, eastern end, the strait flowed out through the remains of a causeway— a rippling shallow, dangerously interspersed with deep holes—

built by long-vanished people in days gone by. Belts of reeds surrounded most of the island, so that in wind or storm the waves, instead of breaking directly upon the stones, would diminish landward, spending their force invisibly among the shaking reed beds. A little way inland from the upstream point a rocky ridge rose clear of the jungle, running half the length of the island like a spine.

At the foot of this ridge, among the green-flowering quian, the bear slept as though it would never wake. Below it and above, the reed beds and lower slopes were crowded with fugitive creatures that had come down upon the current. Some were dead—burned or drowned—but many, especially those accustomed to swim—otters, frogs and snakes—had survived and were already recovering and beginning to search for food. The trees were full of birds which had flown across from the burning shore and these, disturbed from their natural rhythms, kept up a continual movement and chatter in the dark. Despite fatigue and hunger, every creature that knew what it was to be preyed upon, to fear a hunting enemy, was on the alert. The surroundings were strange. None knew where to look for a place of safety, and as a cold surface gives off mist, so this lostness gave off everywhere a palpable tension—sharp cries of fear, sounds of blundering movement and sudden flight—much unlike the normal, stealthy night-rhythms of the forest. Only the bear slept on, unmoved as a rock in the sea, hearing nothing, scenting nothing, not feeling even the burns which had destroyed great patches of its pelt and shriveled the flesh beneath.

With dawn the light wind returned and brought with it from across the river the smell of mile upon mile of ashes and smoldering jungle. The sun, rising behind the ridge, left in shadow the forest below the western slope. Here the fugitive animals remained, skulking and confused, afraid to venture into the brilliant light now glittering along the shores of the island.

It was this sunshine, and the all-pervading smell of the charred trees, which covered the approach of the man. He came wading knee-deep through the shallows, ducking his head to remain concealed below the feathery plumes of the reeds. He was dressed in breeches of coarse cloth and a skin jerkin roughly stitched together down the sides and across the shoulders. His feet were laced round the ankles into bags of skin resembling ill-shaped boots. He wore a necklace of curved, pointed teeth, and from his belt hung a long knife and a quiver of arrows. His bow, bent and strung, was carried round his neck to keep the butt from trailing in the water. In one hand he was holding a stick on which three dead birds—a crane and two pheasants—were threaded by the legs.

As he reached the shadowed, western end of the island he paused, raised his head cautiously and peered over the reeds into the woods beyond. Then he began to make his way to shore, the reeds parting before him with a hissing sound like that of a scythe in long grass. A pair of ducks flew up but he ignored them, for he seldom or never risked the loss of an arrow by shooting at birds on the wing. Reaching dry ground, he at once crouched down in a tall clump of hemlock.

Here he remained for two hours, motionless and watchful, while the sun rose higher and began to move around the shoulder of the hill. Twice he shot, and both arrows found their mark —the one a goose, the other a *ketlana,* or small forest deer. Each time he left the quarry lying where it fell and remained in his hiding place. Sensing the disturbance all around him and himself smelling the ashes on the wind, he judged it best to keep still and wait for other lost and uprooted creatures to come wandering near. So he crouched and watched, vigilant as an Eskimo at a seal hole, moving only now and then to brush away the flies.

When he saw the leopard, his first movements were no more than a quick biting of the lip and a tightening of his grasp on his bow. It was coming straight toward him through the trees, pacing slowly and looking from side to side. Plainly it was not only uneasy, but also hungry and alert—as dangerous a creature as any solitary hunter might pray to avoid. It came nearer, stopped, stared for some moments straight toward his hiding place and then turned and padded across to where the ketlana lay with the feathered arrow in its neck. As it thrust its head forward, sniffing at the blood, the man, without a sound, crept out of concealment and made his way around it in a half-circle, stopping behind each tree to observe whether it had moved. He turned his head away to breathe and carefully placed each footstep clear of twigs and loose pebbles.

He was already half a bowshot away from the leopard when

suddenly a wild pig trotted out of the scrub, blundered against him and ran squealing back into the shadows. The leopard turned, gazed intently and began to pace toward him.

He turned and walked steadily away, fighting against the panic impulse to go faster. Looking around, he saw that the leopard had broken into a padding trot and was overtaking him. At this he began to run, flinging down his birds and making toward the ridge in the hope of losing his terrible pursuer in the undergrowth on the lower slopes. At the foot of the ridge, on the edge of a grove of quian, he turned and raised his bow. Although he knew well what was likely to come of wounding the leopard, it seemed to him now that his only, desperate chance was to try, among the bushes and creepers, to evade it long enough to succeed in shooting it several times and thus either disable it or drive it away. He aimed and loosed, but his hand was unsteady with fear. The arrow grazed the leopard's flank, hung there for a moment and fell out. The leopard bared its teeth and charged, snarling, and the hunter fled blindly along the hillside. A stone turned beneath his foot and he pitched downward, rolling over and over. He felt a sharp pain as a branch pierced his left shoulder and then the breath was knocked out of him. His body struck heavily against some great, shaggy mass and he lay on the ground, gasping and witless with terror, looking back in the direction from which he had fallen. His bow was gone, and as he struggled to his knees, he saw that his left arm and hand were red with blood.

The leopard appeared at the top of the steep bank from which he had fallen. He tried to keep silent, but a gasp came from his spent lungs and quick as a bird its head turned toward him. Ears flat, tail lashing, it crouched above him, preparing to spring. He could see its eyeteeth curving downward, and for long moments hung over his death as though over some frightful drop, at the foot of which his life would be broken to nothing.

Suddenly he felt himself pushed to one side and found that he was lying on his back, looking upward. Standing over him like a cypress tree, one haunch so close to his face that he could smell the shaggy pelt, was a creature—a creature so enormous that in his distracted state of mind he could not comprehend it. As a man carried unconscious from a battlefield might wake

26

bemused, and glimpsing first a heap of refuse, then a cooking-fire, then two women carrying bundles, might tell that he was in a village, so the hunter saw a clawed foot bigger than his own head; a wall of coarse hair, burned and half-stripped to the raw flesh, as it seemed; a great, wedge-shaped muzzle outlined against the sky; and knew that he must be in the presence of an animal. The leopard was still at the top of the bank, cringing now, looking upward into a face that must be glaring terribly down upon it. Then the giant animal, with a single blow, struck it bodily from the bank, so that it was borne altogether clear, turning over in the air and crashing down among the quian. With a growling roar that sent up a cloud of birds, the animal turned to attack again. It dropped on all fours and as it did so its left side scraped against a tree. At this it snarled and shrank away, wincing with pain. Then, hearing the leopard struggling in the undergrowth, it made toward the sound and was gone.

The hunter rose slowly to his feet, clutching his wounded shoulder. However terrible the transport of fear, the return can be swift, just as one may awaken instantly from deep sleep. He found his bow and crept up the bank. Though he knew what he had seen, yet his mind still whirled incredulously round the center of certainty, like a boat in a maelstrom. He had seen a bear. But in God's name, what kind of bear? Whence had it come? Had it in truth been already on the island when he had come wading through the shallows that morning; or had it sprung into existence out of his own terror, in answer to prayer? Had he himself perhaps, as he crouched almost senseless at the foot of the bank, made some desperate, phantom journey to summon it from the world beyond? Whether or not, one thing was sure. Whencesoever it had come, this beast, that had knocked a full-grown leopard flying through the air, was now of this world, was flesh and blood. It would no more vanish than the sparrow on the branch.

He limped slowly back toward the river. The goose was gone and his arrow with it, but the ketlana was still lying where it had fallen and he pulled out the arrow, heaved it under his good arm and made for the reeds. It was here that the delayed shock overtook him. He sank down, trembling and silently weeping by the water's edge. For a long time he lay prone, oblivious of his own safety. And slowly there came to him—not all at once, but brightening and burning up, little by little, like a new-lit fire—the realization of what—of who—it must truly be that he had seen.

As a traveler in some far wilderness might by chance pick up a handful of stones from the ground, examine them idly and then, with mounting excitement, first surmise, next think it probable and finally feel certain that they must be diamonds; or as a sea captain, voyaging in distant waters, might round an unknown cape, busy himself for an hour with the handling of the ship and only then, and gradually, realize that he—he himself—must have sailed into none other than that undiscovered, fabled ocean known to his forebears by nothing but legend and rumor; so now, little by little, there stole upon this hunter the stupefying, all-but-incredible knowledge of what it must be that he had seen. He became calm then, got up and fell to pacing back and forth among the trees by the shore. At last he stood still, faced the sun across the strait and, raising his unwounded arm, prayed for a long time—a wordless prayer of silence and trembling awe. Then, still dazed, he once more took up the ketlana and waded through the reeds. Making his way back along the shallows, he found the raft which he had moored that morning, loosed it and drifted away downstream.

4 *The High Baron*

IT WAS LATE IN THE AFTERNOON when the hunter, Kelderek, came at last in sight of the landmark he was seeking, a tall *zoan* tree some distance above the downstream point of the island. The boughs, with their silver-backed, fernlike leaves, hung down over the river, forming an enclosed, watery arbor inshore. In front of this the reeds had been cut to afford to one seated within a clear view across the strait. Kelderek, with some difficulty, steered his raft to the mouth of the channel, looked toward the zoan and raised his paddle as though in greeting. There was no response, but he expected none. Guiding the raft up to a stout post in the water, he felt down its length, found the rope running shoreward below the surface and drew himself toward land.

Reaching the tree, he pulled the raft through the curtain of pendent branches. Inside, a short, wooden pier projected from the bank and on this a man was seated, staring out between the leaves at the river beyond. Behind him a second man sat mending a net. Four or five other rafts were moored to the hidden quay. The lookout's glance, having taken in the single ketlana and the few fish lying beside Kelderek, came to rest upon the weary, blood-smeared hunter himself.

"So, Kelderek Play-with-the-Children. You have little to show and less than usual. Where are you hurt?"

"The shoulder, shendron—and the arm is stiff and painful."

"You look like a man in a stupor. Are you feverish?"

The hunter made no reply.

"I asked, 'Are you feverish?' "

He shook his head.

"What caused the wound?"

Kelderek hesitated, then shook his head once more and remained silent.

"You simpleton, do you suppose I am asking you for the sake of gossip? I have to learn everything—you know that. Was it a man or an animal that gave you that wound?"

"I fell and injured myself."

The shendron waited.

"A leopard pursued me," added Kelderek.

The shendron burst out impatiently, "Do you think you are telling tales now to children on the shore? Am I to keep asking, 'And what came next?' Tell me what happened. Or would you prefer to be sent to the High Baron, to say that you refused to tell?"

Kelderek sat on the edge of the wooden pier, looking down and stirring a stick in the dark green water below. At last the shendron said, "Kelderek, I know you are considered a simple fellow, with your 'Cat Catch a Fish' and all the rest of it. Whether you are indeed so simple, I cannot tell. But whether or not, you know well enough that every hunter who goes out has to tell all he knows upon return. Those are Bel-ka-Trazet's orders. Has the fire driven a leopard to Ortelga? Did you meet with strangers? What is the state of the western end of the island? These are the things I have to learn."

Kelderek trembled where he sat but still said nothing.

"Why," said the net mender, speaking for the first time, "you know he's a simpleton—Kelderek Zenzuata—Kelderek Play-with-the-Children. He went hunting—he hurt himself—he's returned with little to show. Can't we leave it at that? Who wants the bother of taking him up to the High Baron?"

The shendron, an older man, frowned. "I am not here to be trifled with. The island may be full of all manner of savage beasts—of men, too, perhaps. Why not? And this man you believe to be a simpleton—he may be deceiving us. With whom has he spoken today? And did they pay him to keep silent?"

"But if he were deceiving us," said the net mender, "would he not come with a tale prepared? Depend upon it, he—"

The hunter stood up, looking tensely from one to the other.

"I am deceiving no one: but I cannot tell you what I have seen today."

The shendron and his companion exchanged glances. In the evening quiet, a light breeze set the water *clop-clopping* under the platform and from somewhere inland sounded a faint call, "Yasta! The firewood!"

"What is this?" said the shendron. "You are making difficulties for me, Kelderek, but worse—far worse—for yourself."

"I cannot tell you what I have seen," repeated the hunter, with a kind of desperation.

The shendron shrugged his shoulders. "Well, Taphro, since it seems there's no curing this foolishness, you'd better take him up to the Sindrad. But you are a great fool, Kelderek. The High Baron's anger is a storm that many men have failed to survive before now."

"This I know. God's will must be done."

The shendron shook his head. Kelderek, as though in an attempt to be reconciled with him, laid a hand on his shoulder, but the other shook it off impatiently and returned in silence to his watch over the river. Taphro, scowling now, motioned the hunter to follow him up the bank.

The town that covered the narrow, eastern end of the island

was fortified on the landward side by an intricate defensive system, part natural and part artificial, that ran from shore to shore. West of the zoan tree, on the further side from the town, four lines of pointed stakes extended from the waterside into the woods. Inland, the patches of thicker jungle formed obstacles capable of little improvement, though even here the living creepers had been pruned and trained into almost impenetrable screens, one behind another. In the more open parts thornbushes had been planted—*trazada,* curlspike and the terrible *ancottlia,* whose poison burns and irritates until men tear their own flesh with their nails. Steep places had been made steeper and at one point the outfall of a marsh had been dammed to form a shallow lake—shrunk at this time of year—in which small alligators, caught on the mainland, had been set free to grow and become dangerous. Along the outer edge of the line lay the so-called "Dead Belt," about eighty yards broad, which was never entered except by those whose task it was to maintain it. Here were hidden trip-ropes fastened to props holding up great logs; concealed pits filled with pointed stakes—one contained snakes; spikes in the grass; and one or two open, smooth-looking paths leading to enclosed places, into which arrows and other missiles could be poured from platforms constructed among the trees above. The Belt was divided by rough palisades, so that advancing enemies would find lateral movement difficult and discover themselves committed to emerge at points where they could be awaited. The entire line and its features blended so naturally with the surrounding jungle that a stranger, though he might, here and there, perceive that men had been at work, could form little idea of its full extent. This remarkable closure of an open flank, devised and carried out during several years by the High Baron, Bel-ka-Trazet, had never yet been put to the proof. But, as Bel-ka-Trazet himself had perhaps foreseen, the labor of making it and the knowledge that it was there had created among the Ortelgans a sense of confidence and security that was probably worth as much as the works themselves. The line not only protected the town but made it a great deal harder for anyone to leave it without the High Baron's knowledge.

Kelderek and Taphro, turning their backs on the Belt, made

their way toward the town along a narrow path between the hemp fields. Here and there women were carrying up water from among the reeds, or manuring ground already harvested and gleaned. At this hour there were few workers, however, for it was nearly supper time. Not far away, beyond the trees, threads of smoke were curling into the evening sky and with them, from somewhere on the edge of the huts, rose the song of a woman:

> He came, he came by night.
> I wore red flowers in my hair.
> I have left my lamp alight, my lamp is burning.
> *Senandril na kora, senandril na ro.*

There was an undisguised warmth and satisfaction in the voice. Kelderek glanced at Taphro, jerked his head in the direction of the song and smiled.

"Aren't you afraid?" asked Taphro in a surly tone.

The grave, preoccupied look returned to Kelderek's eyes.

"To go before the High Baron and say that you persisted in refusing to tell the shendron what you know? You must be mad! Why be such a fool?"

"Because this is no matter for concealment or lying. God—" he broke off.

Taphro made no reply, but merely held out his hand for Kelderek's weapons—knife and bow. The hunter handed them to him without a word.

They came to the first huts, with their cooking, smoke and refuse smells. Men were returning from the day's work and women, standing at their doors, were calling to children or gossiping with neighbors. Though one or two looked curiously at Kelderek trudging acquiescently beside the shendron's messenger, none spoke to him or called out to ask where they were going. Suddenly a child, a boy perhaps seven or eight years old, ran up and took his hand. The hunter stopped.

"Kelderek," asked the child, "are you coming to play this evening?"

Kelderek hesitated. "Why—I can't say. No, Sarin, I don't think I shall be able to come this evening."

"Why not?" said the child, plainly disappointed. "You've hurt your shoulder—is that it?"

"There's something I've got to go and tell the High Baron," replied Kelderek simply.

Another, older boy, who had joined them, burst out laughing. "And I have to see the Lord of Bekla before dawn—a matter of life and death. Kelderek, don't tease us. Don't you want to play tonight?"

"Come on, can't you?" said Taphro impatiently, shuffling his feet in the dust.

"No, it's the truth," said Kelderek, ignoring him. "I'm on my way to see the High Baron. But I'll be back: either tonight or—well, another night, I suppose."

He turned away, but the boys trotted beside him as he walked on.

"We were playing this afternoon," said the little boy. We were playing 'Cat Catch a Fish.' I got the fish home twice."

"Well done!" said the hunter, smiling down at him.

"Be off with you!" cried Taphro, making as though to strike at them. "Come on—get out! You great dunderheaded fool," he added to Kelderek, as the boys ran off. "Playing games with children at your age!"

"Good night!" called Kelderek after them. "The good night you pray for—who knows?"

They waved to him and were gone among the smoky huts. A man passing by spoke to Kelderek but he made no reply, only walking on abstractedly, his eyes on the ground.

At length, after crossing a wide area of ropewalks, the two approached a group of larger huts standing in a rough semicircle not far from the eastern point and its broken causeway. Between these, trees had been planted, and the sound of the river mingled with the evening breeze and the movement of the leaves to give a sense of refreshing coolness after the hot, dry day. Here, not only women were at work. A number of men, who seemed by their appearance and occupations to be both servants and crafts-men, were trimming arrows, sharpening stakes and repairing bows, spears and axes. A burly smith, who had just finished for the day, was climbing out of his forge in a shallow, open pit, while his two boys quenched the fire and tidied up after him.

Kelderek stopped and turned once more to Taphro.

"Badly aimed arrows can wound innocent men. There's no need for you to be hinting and gossiping about me to these fellows."

"Why should you care?"

"I don't want them to know I'm keeping a secret," said Kelderek.

Taphro nodded curtly and went up to a man who was cleaning a grindstone, the water flying off in a spiral as he spun the wheel.

"Sheldron's messenger. Where is Bel-ka Trazet?"

"He? Eating." The man jerked his thumb toward the largest of the huts.

"I have to speak to him."

"If it'll wait," replied the man, "you'd do better to wait. Ask Numiss—the red-haired fellow—when he comes out. He'll let you know when Bel-ka-Trazet's ready."

Neolithic man, the bearded Assyrian, the wise Greeks, the howling Vikings, the Tartars, the Aztecs, the samurai, the cavaliers, the anthropophagi and men whose heads do grow beneath their shoulders: there is one thing at least that all have in common—waiting until someone of importance has been ready to see them. Numiss, chewing a piece of fat as he listened to Taphro, cut him short, pointing him and Kelderek to a bench against the wall. There they sat. The sun sank until its rim touched the horizon upstream. The flies buzzed. Most of the craftsmen went away. Taphro dozed. The place became almost deserted, until the only sound above that of the water was the murmur of voices from inside the big hut. At last Numiss came out and shook Taphro by the shoulder. The two rose and followed the servant through the door, on which was painted Bel-ka-Trazet's emblem, a golden snake.

The hut was divided into two parts. At the back were Bel-ka-Trazet's private quarters. The larger part, known as the Sindrad, served as both council chamber and mess hall for the barons. Except when a full council was summoned, it was seldom that all the barons were assembled at once. There were continual journeys to the mainland for hunting expeditions and trade, for the island had no iron or other metal except what could be imported from the Gelt Mountains in exchange for skins, feathers, semi-precious stones and such artifacts as arrows and rope—whatever, in fact, had any exchange value. Apart from the barons and those who attended upon them, all hunters and traders had to obtain leave to come and go. The barons, as often as they returned, were required to report their news like anyone else and while living on the island usually ate the evening meal with Bel-ka-Trazet in the Sindrad.

Some five or six faces turned toward Taphro and Kelderek as they entered. The meal was over and a debris of bones, rinds and skins littered the floor. A boy was collecting this refuse into a basket, while another sprinkled fresh sand. Four of the barons were still sitting on the benches, holding their drinking horns and leaning their elbows on the table. Two, however, stood apart near the doorway—evidently to get the last of the daylight, for they were talking in low tones over an abacus of beads and a piece of smooth bark covered with writing. This seemed to be some kind of list or inventory, for as Kelderek passed, one of the two barons, looking at it, said, "No, twenty-five ropes, no more," whereupon the other moved back a bead with his forefinger and replied, "And you have twenty-five ropes fit to go, have you?"

Kelderek and Taphro came to a stop before a young, very tall man with a silver torque on his left arm. When they entered he had had his back to the door, but now he turned to look at them, holding his horn in one hand and sitting somewhat unsteadily on the table with his feet on the bench below. He looked Kelderek up and down with a bland smile but said nothing. Confused, Kelderek lowered his eyes. The young baron's silence continued, and the hunter, by way of keeping himself in countenance, tried to fix his attention on the great table, which he had heard described but never before seen. It was old, carved with a craftsmanship beyond the skill of any carpenter or woodworker now alive on Ortelga. Each of the eight legs was pyramidal in shape, its steeply tapering sides forming a series of steps or ledges, one above another to the apex. The two corners of the board that he could see had the likeness of bears' heads, snarling, with open jaws and muzzles thrust forward. They were most lifelike. Kelderek trembled and looked quickly up again.

"And what ekshtra work you come give us?" asked the young baron cheerfully. "Want fellows repair causeway, zattit?"

"No, my lord," said Numiss in a low voice. "This is the man who refused to tell his news to the shendron."

"Eh?" asked the young baron, emptying his horn and beckoning to a boy to refill it. "Man with shensh, then. No ushe talking shendrons. Shtupid fellowsh. All shendrons shtupid fellowsh, eh?" he said to Kelderek.

"My lord," replied Kelderek, "believe me, I have nothing against the shendron, but—but the matter—"

"Can you read?" interrupted the young baron.

"Read? No, my lord."

"Neither c'n I. Look at old Fassel-Hasta there. What's he reading? Who knows? You watch out, he'll bewitch you."

The baron with the piece of bark turned with a frown and stared at the young man, as much as to say that he at any rate was not one to act the fool in his cups.

"I'll tell you," said the young baron, sliding forward from the table and landing with a jolt on the bench, "*all* 'bout writing— one word—"

"Ta-Kominion," called a harsh voice from the further room, "I want to speak with those men. Zelda, bring them."

Another baron rose from the bench opposite, beckoning to Kelderek and Taphro. They followed him out of the Sindrad and into the room beyond, where the High Baron was sitting alone. Both, in token of submission and respect, bent their heads, raised the palms of their hands to their brows, lowered their eyes and waited.

Kelderek, who had never previously come before Bel-ka-Trazet, had been trying to prepare himself for the moment when he would have to do so. To confront him was in itself an ordeal, for the High Baron was sickeningly disfigured. His face—if face it could still be called—looked as though it had once been melted and left to set again. Below the white-seamed forehead the left eye, askew and fallen horribly down the cheek, was half-buried under a great, humped ridge of flesh running from the bridge of the nose to the neck. The jaw was twisted to the right, so that the lips closed crookedly, while across the chin stretched a livid scar, in shape roughly resembling a hammer. Such expression

36

as there was upon this terrible mask was sardonic, penetrating, proud and detached—that of a man indestructible, a man to survive treachery, siege, desert and flood.

The High Baron, seated on a round stool like a drum, stared up at the hunter. In spite of the heat he was wearing a heavy fur cloak, fastened at the neck with a brass chain, so that his ghastly head resembled that of an enemy severed and fixed on top of a black tent. For some moments there was silence—a silence like a drawn bowstring. Then Bel-ka-Trazet said, "What is your name?"

His voice, too, was distorted—harsh and low, with an odd ring, like the sound of a stone bounding over a sheet of ice.

"Kelderek, my lord."

"Why are you here?"

"The shendron at the zoan sent me."

"That I know. Why did he send you?"

"Because I did not think it right to tell him what befell me today."

"Why does your shendron waste my time?" said Bel-ka-Trazet to Taphro. "Could he not make this man speak? Are you telling me he defied you both?"

"He—the hunter—this man, my lord," stammered Taphro. "He told us—that is, he would not tell us. The shendron—he asked him about—about his injury. He replied that a leopard pursued him, but he would tell us no more. When we demanded to know, he said he could tell us nothing."

There was a pause.

"He refused us, my lord," persisted Taphro. "We said to him—"

"Be silent."

Bel-ka-Trazet paused, frowning abstractedly and pressing two fingers against the ridge beneath his eye. At length he looked up.

"You are a clumsy liar, Kelderek, it seems. Why trouble to speak of a leopard? Why not say you fell out of a tree?"

"I told the truth, my lord. There was a leopard."

"And this injury," went on Bel-ka-Trazet, reaching out his hand to grasp Kelderek's left wrist and gently moving his arm in a way that suggested that he might pull it a good deal harder

37

if he chose, "this trifling injury. You had it, perhaps, from someone who was disappointed that you had not brought him better
news? Perhaps you told him, 'The shendrons are alert, surprise
would be difficult,' and he was displeased?"

"No, my lord."

"Well, we shall see. There was a leopard, then, and you fell.
What happened then?"

Kelderek said nothing.

"Is this man a half-wit?" asked Bel-ka-Trazet, turning to
Zelda.

"Why, my lord," replied Zelda, "I know little of him, but I
believe he is known for something of a simple fellow. They
laugh at him—he plays with the children—"

"He does what?"

"He plays with children, my lord, on the shore."

"What else?"

"Otherwise he is solitary, as hunters often are. He lives alone
and harms no one, as far as I know. His father had hunter's
rights to come and go and he has been allowed to inherit them.
If you wish, we can send to find out more."

"Do so," said Bel-ka-Trazet, and then to Taphro, "You may
go."

Taphro snatched his palm to his forehead and was gone like a
candle flame in the wind. Zelda followed him with more dignity.

"Now, Kelderek," said the twisted mouth, slowly, "you are
an honest man, you say, and we are alone, so there is nothing
to hinder you from telling your story."

Sweat broke out on Kelderek's face. He tried to speak, but no
words came.

"Why did you tell the shendron a few words and then refuse
to tell more?" said the High Baron. "What foolishness was that?
A rogue should know how to cover his tracks. If there was
something you wished to conceal, why did you not invent some
tale that would satisfy the shendron?"

"Because—because the truth—" The hunter hesitated. "Because I was afraid and I am still afraid." He stopped, but then
burst out suddenly, "Who can lie to God—?"

Bel-ka-Trazet watched him as a lizard watches a fly.

"Zelda!" he called suddenly. The baron returned.

"Take this man out, put his arm in a sling and let him eat.

Bring him back in half an hour—and then, by this knife, Kelderek—" and he drove the point of his dagger into the golden snake painted on the lid of the chest beside him "—you shall tell me what you know."

The unpredictable nature of dealings with Bel-ka-Trazet was the subject of many a tale. With Zelda's hand under his shoulder, Kelderek stumbled out into the Sindrad and sat huddled on a bench while the boys brought him food and a leather sling.

When next he faced Bel-ka-Trazet night had fallen. The Sindrad outside was quiet, for all but two of the barons had gone to their own quarters. Zelda sat in the firelight, looking over some arrows which the fletcher had brought. Fassel-Hasta was hunched on another bench at a table, slowly writing with an inked brush on bark, by the light of a smoky earthenware lamp. A lamp was burning also on the lid of Bel-ka-Trazet's chest. In the shadows beyond, two fireflies went winking about the room. A curtain of wooden beads had been let fall over the doorway and from time to time these clicked quietly in the night breeze.

The distortion of Bel-ka-Trazet's face seemed like a trick of the lamplight, the features monstrous as a devil mask in a play, the nose appearing to extend to the neck in a single, unbroken line, the shadows under the jaw pulsing slightly and rhythmically, like the throat of a toad. And indeed it was a play they were now to act, thought Kelderek, for it accorded with nothing in life as he had known it. A plain man, seeking only his living and neither wealth nor power, had been mysteriously singled out and made an instrument to cross the will of Bel-ka-Trazet.

"Well, Kelderek," said the High Baron, pronouncing his name with a slight emphasis that somehow conveyed contempt, "while you have been filling your belly, I have learned as much as there is to be known about a man like you—all, that is, but what you are going to tell me now, Kelderek Zenzuata. Do you know they call you that?"

"Yes, my lord."

"Kelderek Play-with-the-Children. A solitary young man, with no taste for taverns, it seems, and an unnatural indifference toward girls, but known nevertheless for a skillful hunter who often brings in game and rarities for the factors trading with Gelt and Bekla."

"If you have heard so much, my lord—"

"So that he is allowed to come and go alone, much as he pleases, with no questions asked. Sometimes he is gone for several days at a time, is he not?"

"It is necessary, my lord, if the game—"

"Why do you play with the children? A young man unmarried —what sort of nonsense is that?"

Kelderek considered.

"Children often need friends," he said. "Some of the children I play with are unhappy. Some have been left with no parents— their parents have deserted them—"

He broke off in confusion, meeting the gaze of Bel-ka-Trazet's distorted eye over the ridge. After some minutes he muttered uncertainly, "The flames of God—"

"What? What did you say?"

"The flames of God, my lord. Children—their eyes and ears are still open—they speak the truth—"

"And so shall you, Kelderek, before you are done. You'd be thought a simple fellow, then, soft in the head perhaps, a stranger to drink and wenches, playing with children and given to talk of God—for no one would suspect such a man, would he, of spying, of treachery, of carrying messages or treating with enemies on his lonely hunting expeditions—"

"My lord—"

"Until one day he returns injured and almost empty-handed from a place believed to be full of game, too much confused to have been able to invent a tale—"

"My lord!" The hunter fell on his knees.

"Did you displease the man, Kelderek, was that it? Some brigand from Deelguy, perhaps, or slimy slave trader from Terekenalt out to make a little extra money by carrying messages during his dirty travels? Your information was displeasing, perhaps, or the pay was not enough?"

"No, my lord, no!"

"Stand up!"

The beads clicked in a gust that flattened the lamp flame and made the shadows dart on the wall like fish startled in a deep pool. The High Baron was silent, collecting himself with the air of a man repulsed by an obstacle but still determined to overcome it by one means or another. When he spoke again it was in a quieter tone.

"Well, so far as I am any judge, Kelderek, you may be an honest man, though you are a great fool with your talk of children and God. Could you not have asked for one single friend to come here, to testify to your honesty?"

"My lord—"

"No, you could not, it seems, or else it never occurred to you. But let us assume that you are honest, and that something took place today which for some reason you have neither concealed nor revealed. If you had gone about with cunning to conceal it altogether, I suppose you would not have been compelled to come here—you would not be standing here now. No doubt, then, you know very well that it is something that is bound to come to light sooner or later, so that it would have been foolish for you to try to hide it."

"Yes, I am sure enough of that, my lord," replied Kelderek without hesitation.

Bel-ka-Trazet drew his knife and, like a man idly passing the time while waiting for supper or a friend, began to heat the point in the lamp flame.

"My lord," said Kelderek suddenly, "if a man were to return from hunting and say to the shendron, or to his friends, 'I have found a star, fallen from the sky to the earth,' who would believe him?"

Bel-ka-Trazet made no reply but went on turning the point of the knife in the flame.

"But if that man had indeed found a star, my lord, what then? What should he do and to whom should he bring it?"

"You question me, and in riddles, Kelderek, do you? I have no love for visionaries or their talk, so be careful."

The High Baron clenched his fist but then, like a man determined to exercise patience, let it fall open and remained staring at Kelderek with a skeptical look.

"Well?" he said at length.

"I fear you, my lord. I fear your power and your anger. But the star that I found—it is from God, and this, too, I fear. I fear it more. I know to whom it must be revealed—" his voice came in a strangled gasp—"I can reveal it—only to the Tuginda!"

In an instant Bel-ka-Trazet had seized him by the throat and forced him to the floor. The hunter's head bent sharply backward, away from the hot knife point thrust close to his face.

41

"I will do this—I can do only that! By the Bear, you will no longer choose what you will do when your bow eye is out! You'll end in Zeray, my child!"

Kelderek's hands stretched upward, clutching at the black cloak bending over him and pressing him backward from knee to wounded shoulder. His eyes were closed against the heat of the knife and he seemed about to faint in the High Baron's grasp. Yet when at length he spoke—Bel-ka-Trazet stooping close to catch the words—he whispered,

"It can be only as God wills, my lord. The matter is great—greater, even, than your hot knife."

The beads clashed in the doorway. Without relinquishing his hold, the Baron peered over his shoulder into the gloom beyond the lamp. Zelda's voice said,

"My lord, there are messengers from the Tuginda. She would speak with you urgently, she says. She requests that you go to Quiso tonight."

Bel-ka-Trazet drew in his breath with a hiss and stood straight, shaking off Kelderek, who fell his length and lay without moving. The knife slipped from the High Baron's hand and stuck in the floor, transfixing a fragment of some greasy rubbish, which began to smolder with an evil smell. He stooped quickly, recovered the knife and trod out the fragment. Then he said quietly,

"To Quiso, tonight? What can this mean? God protect us! Are you sure?"

"Yes, my lord. Would you speak yourself with the girls who brought the message?"

"Yes—no, let it be. She would not send such a message unless — Go and tell Ankray and Faron to get a canoe ready. And see that this man is put aboard."

"This man, my lord?"

"Put aboard."

The bead curtain clashed once more as the High Baron passed through it, across the Sindrad and out among the trees beyond. Zelda, hurrying across to the servants' quarters, could see in the light of the quarter moon the conical shape of the great fur cloak striding impatiently up and down the shore.

42

5 To Quiso by Night

KELDEREK KNELT IN THE BOW, now peering into the speckled gloom
ahead, now shutting his eyes and dropping his chin on his chest
in a fresh spasm of fear. At his back the enormous Ankray,
Bel-ka-Trazet's servant and bodyguard, sat silent as the canoe
drifted with the current along the south bank of the Telthearna.
From time to time Ankray's paddle would drop to arrest or
change their course, and at the sound Kelderek started as though
the loud stir of the water were about to reveal them to enemies
in the dark. Since giving the order to set out Bel-ka-Trazet had
said not a word, sitting hunched in the narrow stern, hands
clasped about his knees.

More than once, as the paddles fell, the swirl and seethe of
bubbles alarmed some nearby creature, and Kelderek jerked his
head toward the clatter of wings, the splash of a dive or the
crackle of undergrowth on the bank. Biting his lip and clutching
at the side of the canoe, he tried to recall that these were nothing
but birds and animals with which he was familiar—that by day
he would recognize each one. Yet beyond these noises he was
listening always for another, more terrible sound and dreading
the second appearance of that animal to whom, as he believed,
the miles of jungle and river presented no obstacle. And again,
shrinking from this, his mind confronted dismally another life-
long fear—the fear of the island for which they were bound.
Why had the Baron been summoned thither and what had that
summons to do with the news which he himself had refused to
tell?

They had already traveled a long way beneath the trees overhanging the water when the servants evidently recognized some
landmark. The left paddle dropped once more and the canoe
checked, turning toward the center of the river. Upstream, a few
faint lights on Ortelga were just visible, while to their right, far
out in the darkness, there now appeared another light, high up
—a flickering red glow that vanished and re-emerged as they
moved on. The servants were working now, driving the canoe

across the stream while the current, flowing more strongly at this distance from the bank, carried them down. Kelderek could sense in those behind him a growing uneasiness. The paddlers' rhythm became short and broken. The bow struck against something floating in the dark, and at the jolt Bel-ka-Trazet grunted sharply, like a man on edge. "My lord—" said Ankray. "Be silent!" replied Bel-ka-Trazet instantly.

Like children in a dark room, like wayfarers passing a graveyard at night, the four men in the canoe filled the surrounding darkness with the fear from their own hearts. They were approaching the island of Quiso, domain of the Tuginda and the cult over which she ruled, a place where men retained no names —or so it was believed—weapons had no effect and the greatest strength could spend itself in vain against incomprehensible power. On each fell a mounting sense of solitude and exposure. To Kelderek it seemed that he lay upon the black water helpless as the diaphanous *gylon* fly, whose fragile myriads clotted the surface of the river each spring; inert as a felled tree in the forest, as a log in the timber yard. All about them, in the night, stood the malignant, invisible woodmen, disintegrators armed with axe and fire. Now the log was burning, breaking up into sparks and ashes, drifting away beyond the familiar world of day and night, of hunger, work and rest. The red light seemed close now, and as it drew nearer still and higher above them he fell forward, striking his forehead against the bow.

He felt no pain from the blow, and to himself he seemed to have become deaf, for he could no longer hear the lapping of the water. Bereft of perceptions, of will and identity, he knew himself to have become no more than the fragments of a man. He was no one; and yet he remained conscious. As though in obedience to a command, he closed his eyes. At the same moment, the paddlers ceased their stroke, bowing their heads upon their arms, and the canoe, losing way entirely, drifted with the current toward the unseen island.

Now into the remnants of Kelderek's mind began to return all that, since childhood, he had seen and learned of the Tuginda. Twice a year she came to Ortelga by water, the far-off gongs sounding through the mists of early morning, the people waiting silent on the shore. The men lay flat on their faces as she and

44

her women were met and escorted to a new hut built for her coming. There were dances and a ceremony of flowers; but her real business was, first, to confer with the barons and, secondly, in a session secret to the women, to speak of their mysteries and to select, from among those put forward, one or two to return with her to perpetual service on Quiso. At the end of the day, when she left in torchlight and darkness, the hut was burned and the ashes scattered on the water.

When she stepped ashore she was veiled, but in speaking with the barons she wore the mask of a bear. None knew the face of the Tuginda, or who she might once have been. The women chosen to go to her island never returned. It was believed that there they received new names; at all events their old names were never spoken again in Ortelga. It was not known whether the Tuginda died or abdicated, who succeeded her, how her successor was chosen, or even, on each occasion of her visit, whether she was, in fact, the same woman as before. Once, when a boy, Kelderek had questioned his father with impatience, such as the young often feel for matters which they perceive that their elders regard seriously and discuss little. For reply his father had moistened a lump of bread, molded it to the rough shape of a man and put it to stand on the edge of the fire. "Keep away from the women's mysteries, lad," he said, "and fear them in your heart, for they can consume you. Look—" the bread dried, browned, blackened and shriveled to a cinder "—do you understand?" Kelderek, silenced by his father's gravity, had nodded and said no more. But he had remembered.

What had possessed him, tonight, in the room behind the Sindrad? What had prompted him to defy the High Baron? How had those words passed his lips and why had not Bel-ka-Trazet killed him instantly? One thing he knew—since he had seen the bear, he had not been his own master. At first he had thought himself driven by the power of God, but now chaos was his master. His mind and body were unseamed like an old garment and whatever was left of himself lay in the power of the numinous, night-covered island.

His head was still resting on the bow and one arm trailed over the side in the water. Behind him, the paddle dropped from Ankray's hands and drifted away, as the canoe grounded on the upstream shore, its occupants slumped where they sat, tranced and spell-stopped, not a will, not a mind intact. And thus they stayed, driftwood, flotsam and foam, while the quarter moon set far upstream and darkness fell, broken only by the gleam of the fire still burning inland, high among the trees.

Time passed—a time marked only by the turning of the stars. Small, choppy river-waves chattered along the sides of the canoe and once or twice, with a rising susurration, the night wind tossed the branches of the nearest trees: but never the least stir made the four men in the canoe, huddled in the dark like birds on a perch.

At length a nearer, smaller light appeared, green and swaying, descending toward the water. As it reached the pebbly shore there sounded a crunching of footsteps and a low murmur of voices. Two cloaked women were approaching, carrying between them, on a pole, a round, flat lantern as big as a grindstone. The frame was of iron and the spaces between the bars were paneled with plaited rushes, translucent yet stout enough to shield and protect the candles fixed within.

The two women reached the edge of the water and stood listening. After a little they perceived in the dark the knock of the water against the canoe—a sound distinguishable only by ears familiar with every cadence of wind and wave along the shore. They set down the lantern then, and one, drawing out the pole from the ring and splashing it back and forth in the shallows, called in a harsh voice, "Wake!"

The sound came to Kelderek sharp as the cry of a moorhen. Looking up, he saw the wavering green light reflected in the splashed water inshore. He was no longer afraid. As the weaker of two dogs presses itself to the wall and remains motionless, knowing that in this lies its safety, so Kelderek, through total subjection to the power of the island, had lost his fear.

He could hear the High Baron stirring behind him. Bel-ka-Trazet muttered some inaudible words and dashed a handful of water across his face, yet made no move to wade ashore. Turning his head for a moment, Kelderek saw him staring, as though still bemused, toward the dimly shining turbulence in the shallows.

The woman's voice called again, "Come!" Slowly, Bel-ka-

QUISO

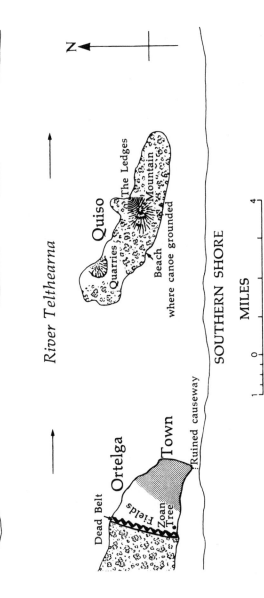

NORTHERN SHORE

River Telthearna

Quiso

The Ledges

Mountain

Quarries

Beach
where canoe grounded

Dead Belt

Ortelga

Zoan
Tree

Fields

Town

Ruined causeway

SOUTHERN SHORE

N

MILES

1   0   4

Trazet climbed over the side of the canoe into the water, which reached scarcely to his knees, and waded toward the light. Kelderek followed, splashing clumsily through the slippery pools. Reaching the shore, he found confronting him a tall, cloaked woman standing motionless, her face hidden in her cowl. He too stood still, not daring to question her silence. He heard the servants come ashore behind him, but the tall woman paid them no heed, only continuing to gaze at him as though to perceive the very beating of his heart. At last—or so he thought —she nodded, and thereupon at once turned about, stooped and passed the pole through the iron ring on the lantern. Then she and her companion took it up between them and began to walk away, unstumbling over the loose, yielding stones. Not a man moved until, when she had gone perhaps ten paces, the tall woman, without turning her head, called, "Follow!" Kelderek obeyed, keeping his distance behind them like a servant.

Soon they began to climb a steep path into the woods. He was forced to grope among the rocks for handholds, yet the women went up easily, one behind the other, the taller raising the pole above her head to keep the lantern level. Still they climbed and still he followed breathlessly in the dark until, the way growing less steep and at last level, he thought that they could not be far below the very summit of the island. The trees grew thickly and he could no longer see the light ahead. Groping among the ferns and drifts of leaves he could hear—louder as he went on —the sound of cascading water and suddenly found himself standing on a spur of rock overlooking a ravine. On the opposite side lay a stone-paved terrace, in the middle of which were glowing the embers of a fire. This, he felt sure, must be the source of that light, high up, which he had seen from the river —a beacon lit to guide them. Beyond, a wall of rock rose into the dark, and this he could see plainly, for around the edges of the terrace stood five tripods, each supporting a bronze bowl from which rose translucent flames, yellow, green and blue. There was little smoke, but the air was filled with a resinous, sweet scent.

More disturbing and awe-inspiring than the empty terrace, with its basins of flame, was the square opening cut in the rock wall behind. A carved pediment overhung it, supported by a pillar on either side, and to him it seemed that the black space between was gazing upon him inscrutably, like the unseen face of the cowled woman on the shore. Disturbed, he turned his eyes away, yet still, like a prisoner standing in a crowded court, felt himself watched, and, looking back once more, saw again only the flame-lit terrace and the opening beyond.

He stared downward into the ravine. A little to his right, scarcely visible in the flickering darkness, he could make out a waterfall, not sheer, but cascading steeply over rocks until lost in the deep cleft below. In front of this, close to the falling water and gleaming wet with spray, a felled tree trunk, no thicker than a man's thigh, spanned the ravine from bank to bank. The upper side had been roughly planed, and upon this, with no handrail, the two women were now crossing as easily as they had walked over the shore. The pliant trunk sprang beneath their weight and the lantern tossed upon its pole, yet they moved with an unhurried grace, like village girls at evening carrying their pitchers from the well.

Slowly Kelderek descended from the spur. Coming to the nearer end of the bridge he began, fearfully, to put one foot before the other. The cascade at his elbow showered him with its cold spray; the invisible water below sent up its echoes about him; after a few steps he crouched upon his knees, fumbling one-handed along the undulating tree trunk. He dared not raise his eyes to look ahead. Staring down at his own hand, he could see nothing besides but the grain of the wood, knot after knot coming into his circle of vision and disappearing under his chin as he edged forward. Twice he stopped, panting and digging his nails into the curved underside as the trunk swayed up and down.

When at last he reached the farther end, he continued groping blindly along the ground on his hands and knees, until by chance he caught and crushed a handful of creeping *locatalanga* and with that pungent scent about him, came to himself and realized that he was no longer clutching and tossing above the water. He stood up. Ahead, the women were crossing the center of the terrace, one behind the other as before. Watching, he saw them reach the edge of the heap of embers within their fleece of ash. Without a pause they stepped into it, lifting the hems of their cloaks exactly as though wading a ford. As the hindmost raised her hem he glimpsed for a moment her bare feet. Ash and sparks rose in a fine dust, as chaff rises about the feet of a miller. Then they were pacing on beyond, leaving behind them an exposed, dull-red track across the circle of the dying fire.

Kelderek, moaning, sank to the ground and buried his face in the crook of his arm.

This, then, was the manner of his coming to the Upper Temple upon Quiso of the Ledges—this bringer of the tidings that generations had awaited but never heard: injured, drenched, groveling and half-hysterical, shutting out what lay before his eyes, determined—strange determination—only upon the surrender of whatever shreds of will power the island had left him. When at length the High Baron and his servants came to the edge of the ravine and in their turn tottered like cripples along the leaping tree, they found him lying prone on the edge of the terrace, cackling and gasping with a sound more dreadful than the laughter of the deaf and dumb.

6 *The Priestess*

As KELDEREK BECAME QUIET and seemed to fall asleep where he lay, a light appeared within the opening in the rock wall. It grew brighter and two young women came out, each carrying a burning torch. They were sturdy, rough-looking girls, barefooted and dressed in coarse tunics, but no baron's wife could have matched the half of their ornaments. Their long earrings, which swung and clicked as they walked, were formed of separate pieces of carved bone, strung together in pendants. Their triple necklaces, of alternate *penapa* and *ziltate,* shone rose and tawny in the firelight. On their fingers were wooden rings, carved to resemble plaiting and stained crimson. Each wore a broad belt of bronze plates with a clasp fashioned like the head of a bear, and on the left hip an empty dagger sheath of green leather, whorled like a shell, in token of perpetual virginity.

On their backs they carried wicker baskets filled with fragments of a resinous gum and a black fuel hard and fine as gravel. At each tripod they stopped and, taking handfuls from each other's panniers, threw them into the bowls. The fuel fell with a faint, ringing sound, lingering and overtoned; and the girls, as they worked, paid no more attention to the waiting men than if they had been tethered beasts.

They had almost finished their task and the terrace was bright with fresh light, when a third young woman came pacing slowly from the darkness of the cave. She was dressed in a pleated, sheathlike robe of white cloth, finer than any woven in Ortelga, and her long black hair hung loose at her back. Her arms were bare and her only ornament was a great collar of fine links, more than a span broad, which completely covered her shoulders like a vestment. As she appeared the two girls slipped their baskets from their backs and took up places side by side upon the edge of the ashes.

Bel-ka-Trazet raised his eyes to meet those of the young woman. He said nothing, however, as she returned his look with an impassive air of authority, as though every man had a face like his and they were all one to her. After a few moments she jerked her head over her shoulder and one of the girls, coming forward, led the servants away, disappearing into the darkness under the trees near the bridge. At the same moment the hunter stirred and rose slowly to his feet. Ragged and dirty, he stood before the beautiful priestess with an air less of callowness than of simple unawareness either of his appearance or his surroundings.

Like the tall woman on the beach, the priestess stared intently at Kelderek, as though weighing him in some balance of her mind. At length she nodded her head two or three times with a kind of grave, comprehending recognition, and turned once more toward the High Baron.

"It is meant, then," she said, "that this man should be here. Who is he?"

"One whom I have brought, säiyett," replied Bel-ka-Trazet briefly, as though to remind her that he too was a person of authority.

The priestess frowned. Then she stepped close to the High

Baron, put her hand upon his shoulder and, assuming the air of a wondering and inquisitive child, drew his sword from the scabbard and examined it, the Baron making no attempt to stop her.

"What is this?" she asked, moving it so that the light of the flames flashed along the blade.

"My sword, säiyett," he answered, with a touch of impatience.

"Ah, your—" she paused, hesitating a moment, as though the word were new to her "—sword. A pretty thing, this—this sword. So—so—so—" and, pressing hard, she drew the edge three or four times across her forearm. It made no cut and left no mark whatever. "Sheldra," she called to the remaining girl, "the High Baron has brought us a—a sword." The girl approached, took the sword in both hands and held it out horizontally at the height of her eyes, as though admiring the sharpness of the edge.

"Ah, now I see," said the priestess lightly. Drawing the flat of the blade against her throat and motioning the girl to hold it firmly, she made a little jump, swung a few moments by her chin on the sharp edge and then, dropping to the ground, turned back to Bel-ka-Trazet.

"And this?" she asked, plucking his knife from his belt. This time he made no reply. Assuming a puzzled look, she drove the point into her left arm, twisted it, drew it out bloodless, shook her head and handed it to the girl.

"Well—well—toys." She stared coldly at him.

"What is your name?" she asked.

The Baron opened his mouth to speak, but after a moment the twisted lips closed askew and he remained looking at her as though she had not yet spoken.

"What is your name?" she said to Kelderek in the same tone.

As though in a dream, the hunter found himself perceiving on two planes. A man may dream that he is doing something— flying, perhaps—which, even in the dream, he knows that he cannot do. Yet he accepts and lives the illusion, and thus experiences as real the effects following from the discounted cause. In the same way Kelderek heard and understood the priestess's words and yet knew that they had no meaning. She might as well have asked him "What is the sound of the moon?" More-

52

over, he knew that she knew this and would be satisfied with silence for an answer.

"Come!" she said, after a pause, and turned on her heel.

Walking before them—the grim, mutilated Baron and the bewildered hunter—she led them out of the circle of blue-flaming bowls and through the opening in the rock.

7 The Ledges

THE DARKNESS WAS BROKEN only by the indirect flame-light from the terrace outside; but this was sufficient to show Kelderek that they were in a square chamber apparently cut out of the living rock. The floor beneath his feet was stone and the shadows of himself and his companions moved and wavered against a smooth wall. On this he glimpsed a painting which seemed, as he thought, to represent some gigantic creature standing upright. Then they were going on into the dark.

Feeling his way after the priestess, he touched the squared jamb of an opening in the wall and, groping upward, for he feared to strike his head, could find no transom above. Yet the cleft, if tall, was narrow enough—scarcely as wide as a man— and to save his injured shoulder he turned sideways and edged into it, right arm first. He could see nothing—only those mysterious, faintly colored clouds and vaporous screens that swim before our eyes in darkness, seeming exhaled, as it were, from our own sightlessness as mists rise from a marsh.

The floor sloped steeply downward underfoot. He stumbled on, groping against the wall as it curved away to the right. At last he could make out, ahead, the night sky and, outlined against it, the figure of the waiting priestess. He reached her side, stopped and looked about him.

It was not long after midnight by the stars. He was high up in some spacious, empty place, standing on a broad ledge of stone, its surface level but the texture so rough that he could feel the grains and nodules under the soles of his feet. On either side were wooded slopes. The ledge stretched away to the left in a long, regular curve, a quarter-circle a stone's throw across, ending among banks of ivy and the trunks of trees. Immediately below it extended another, similar ledge and below that fell away many more, resembling a staircase for giants or gods. The pitch was steep—steep enough for a fall to be dangerous. The faintly shining concentric tiers receded downward until the hunter could no longer distinguish them in the starlight. Far below, he could just perceive a glimmering of water, as though from the bottom of a well, and this, it seemed to him, must be some landlocked bay of the island. All around, on either side, great trees towered, an orderly forest, the spaces between them free from the creepers and choking jungle of the mainland. As he gazed up, the night wind freshened and the rustling of leaves became louder and higher, with a semblance of urgent repetition —"Yess! Yess, yess!" followed by a dying fall—"Sshow!— Sssh-ow!" Mingled with this whispering came another sound, also liquid and continuous, but unaltering in pitch, lower and lightly plangent. Listening, he recognized it for the trickling and dropping of water, filling all the place no less than the sound of the leaves. Whence might this come? He looked about.

They were standing near one end of the uppermost tier. Further along its length a shallow stream—perhaps that of the ravine he had crossed earlier that night—came whelming smoothly out of the hillside and across the ledge. Here, no doubt because of some tilting of the stones, it spread in either direction, to become at the edges a mere film of water trickling over the rough, level surface. Thence it oozed and dripped and splashed its way downward, passing over one terrace after another, spreading all abroad, shallow as rain on the pitch of a roof. This was the cause of the faint shining of the ledges in the starlight and of the minute, liquid sounds sparkling faintly about them, myriad as windy heather on a moor or crickets in a meadow.

Struck with amazement, Kelderek realized that this vast place was an artifact. He stood trembling—with awe indeed, but not with fear. Rather, he was filled with a kind of wild and expansive joy, like that of dance or festival, seeming to himself to be floating above his own exhaustion and the pain in his shoulder.

"You have never seen the Ledges?" said the priestess at his elbow. "We have to descend them—are you able?"

At once, as though she had commanded him, he set off down the wet slabs as confidently as though upon level ground. The Baron called to him sharply and he stayed himself against the solitary island of a bank of ivy, smiling back at the two still above him for all the world as though they were comrades in some children's game. As the priestess and the Baron approached carefully, picking their way down the wet stones, he heard the latter say, "He is light-headed, säiyett—a simple, foolish fellow, as I am told. He may fall, or even fling himself down."

"No, the place means him no harm, Baron," she replied.

"Since you brought him here, perhaps you can tell why."

"No," replied the Baron shortly.

"Let him go," she said. "On the Ledges, they say, the heart is the foot's best guide."

At this, Kelderek turned once more and bounded away, splashing sure-footed down and down. The dangerous descent seemed a sport, exhilarating as diving into deep water. The pale shape of the inlet below grew larger and larger and now he could see a fire twinkling beside it. He felt the steep hillside ever higher at his back. The curves of the ledges grew shorter, narrowing at last to little more than a broad path between the trees. He reached the very foot and stood looking round him in the enclosed gloom. It was indeed, he thought, like the bottom of a well—except that the air was warm and the stones now seemed dry underfoot. From above he could hear no sound of his companions and after a little began to make his way toward the glow of the fire and the lapping water beyond.

It was irregular, this shore among the trees, and paved with the same stone as the ledges above. As far as he could discern, it was laid out as a garden. Patches of ground between the paving had been planted with bushes, fruit trees and flowering plants. He came upon a clustering *tendriona*, trained on trellises to form an arbor, and could smell the ripe fruit among the leaves above him. Reaching up, he pulled one down, split the thin rind and ate as he wandered on.

Scrambling over a low wall, he found himself on the brink of a channel perhaps six or seven paces across. Water lilies and arrowhead were blooming in the scarcely moving water at his feet, but in the middle there was a smooth flow and this, he guessed, must be the regathered stream from the Ledges. He crossed a narrow footbridge and saw before him a circular space, paved in a symmetrical pattern of dark and light. In the center stood a flat-topped stone, roughly ovoid and carved with a star-like symbol. Beyond, the fire was glowing red in an iron brazier. His weariness and dread returned upon him. Unconsciously, he had thought of the waterside and the fire as the end of the night's journey. What end he did not know; but where there was a fire, might one not have expected to find people—and rest? His impulse on the Ledges had been both foolish and impertinent. The priestess had not told him to come here; her destination might be elsewhere. Now there were only the starlit solitude and the pain in his shoulder. He thought of returning, but could not face it. Perhaps, after all, they would come soon. Limping across to the stone, he sat down, elbow on knee, rested his head on his hand and closed his eyes.

He fell into an uneasy, slightly feverish doze in which the happenings of the long day began to recur, dreamlike and confused. He imagined himself to be crouching once more in the canoe, listening to the knock and slap of water in the dark. But it was on the shendron's platform that he landed, and once again refused to tell what he had seen. The shendron grew angry and forced him to his knees, threatening him with his hot knife as the folds of his fur cloak rippled and became a huge, shaggy pelt, dark and undulant as a cypress tree.

"By the Bear!" hissed the Baron. "You will no longer choose!"

"I can speak only to the Tuginda!" cried the hunter aloud.

He started to his feet, open-eyed. Before him on the checkered pavement was standing a woman of perhaps forty-five years of age. She had a strong, shrewd face and was dressed like a servant or a peasant's wife. Her arms were bare to the elbow and in one hand she was carrying a wooden ladle. Looking at her in the starlight, he felt reassured by her homely, sensible appearance. At least there was evidently cooking in this island of sorcery, and a straightforward, familiar sort of person to do it. Perhaps she might have some food to spare.

"*Crendro*" (I see you), said the woman, using the colloquial greeting of Ortelga.

"Crendro," replied the hunter.

"You have come down the Ledges?" asked the woman.

"Yes."

"Alone?"

"The priestess and the High Baron of Ortelga are following—at least, so I hope." He raised one hand to his head. "Forgive me. I'm tired out and my shoulder's painful."

"Sit down again." He did so.

"Why are you here—on Quiso?"

"That I must not tell you. I have a message—a message for the Tuginda. I can tell it only to the Tuginda."

"Yourself? Is it not for your High Baron, then, to tell the Tuginda?"

"No. It is for myself to do so." To avoid saying more, he asked, "What is this stone?"

"It's very old. It fell from the sky. Would you like some food? Perhaps I can make your shoulder more comfortable."

"It's good of you. I'd like to eat, and to rest too. But the Tuginda—my message—"

"It will be all right. Come this way, with me."

She took him by the hand and at the same moment he saw the priestess and Bel-ka-Trazet approaching over the bridge. At the sight of his companion the High Baron stopped, bent his head and raised his palm to his brow.

8 *The Tuginda*

IN SILENCE THE HUNTER allowed himself to be led across the circle and past the iron brazier, in which the fire had sunk low. He wondered whether it too had been lit for a signal and had now served its turn, for there seemed to be none to keep it burning. Overtaking them, the Baron spoke no word, but again raised his hand to his forehead. It shook slightly and his breathing, though he controlled it, was short and unsteady. The hunter guessed that the descent of the steep, slippery Ledges had taxed him more than he cared to show.

They left the fire, ascended a flight of steps and stopped before the door of a stone building, its handle a pendent iron ring made like two bears grappling each with the other. Kelderek had never before seen workmanship of this kind and watched in wonder as the handle was turned and the weight of the door swung inward without sagging or scraping against the floor within.

Crossing the threshold, they were met by a girl dressed like those who had tended the cressets on the terrace. She was carrying three or four lighted lamps on a wooden tray which she offered to each of them in turn. He took a lamp but still saw little of what was around him, being too fearful to pause or stare about. From somewhere not far away came a smell of cooking and he realized once again that he was hungry.

They entered a firelit, stone-floored room, furnished like a kitchen with benches and a long, rough table. The hearth, set in the wall, had a cowled chimney above and an ash pit below, and here a second girl was tending three or four cooking pots. The two exchanged a few words in low voices and began to busy themselves about the hearth and table, from time to time glancing sideways at the Baron with a kind of shrinking fascination.

Since they had left the paved circle the hunter had been overcome by the knowledge that he had committed sacrilege. Clearly, the stone on which he had sat was sacred. Had he not indeed been told that it had fallen from the sky? And the woman— the homely woman with the ladle—she could be only—

As she approached him in the firelight he turned, trembling, and fell upon his knees.

"Säiyett—I—I was not to know—"

"Don't be afraid," she said. "Lie down here, on the table. I want to look at your shoulder. Melathys, bring some warm water; and, Baron, will you please hold one of the lamps close?"

As they obeyed her, the Tuginda unlaced the hunter's jerkin and began to wash the clotted blood from the gash in his shoulder. She worked carefully and deliberately, cleaned the wound, dressed it with a stinging, bitter-scented ointment and finally bound his shoulder with a clean cloth. From behind the lamp the Baron's disfigured face looked down at him with an expression which made him prefer to keep his eyes shut.

"Now we will eat—and drink too," said the Tuginda at last, helping him to his feet, "and you girls may go. Yes, yes," she added impatiently to one who was lifting the lid from the stew pot and lingering by the fire, "I can ladle stew into bowls, believe it or not."

The girls scurried out and the Tuginda, picking up her ladle, stirred the various pots and filled four bowls from them. Kelderek ate apart, standing up, and she did nothing to dissuade him, herself sitting on a bench by the hearth and eating slowly and little, as though to make sure that she would finish no sooner and no later than the rest. The bowls were wooden, but the cups into which Melathys poured wine were of thin bronze, six-sided and flat-based, so that, unlike drinking horns, they stood unsupported without spilling. The cold metal felt strange to the hunter's lips.

When the two men had finished, Melanthys brought water for their hands, took away the bowls and cups and made up the fire. The Baron, with his back against the table, sat facing the Tuginda, while the hunter remained standing in the shadows beyond.

"I sent for you, Baron," began the Tuginda. "As you know, I asked you to come here tonight."

"You have put me to indignity, säiyett," replied the Baron. "Why was the fear of Quiso unloosed upon us? Why must we have lain bemused in darkness upon the shore? Why—"

"Was there not a stranger with you?" she answered, in a tone which checked him instantly, though his eyes remained fixed upon hers. "Why do you suppose you could not reach the landing place? And were you not armed?"

"I came in haste. The matter escaped me. But in any case, how could you have known these things, säiyett?"

"No matter how. Well, the indignity, as you call it, is ended now. We will not quarrel. The girls who carried my message to Ortelga—they have been looked after?"

"It is hard to reach Ortelga against the current. They were tired. I said they should remain there to sleep."

She nodded.

"My message, as I suppose, was unexpected, and you have made me an unexpected reply, bringing me a wounded man whom I find sitting alone and exhausted on the Tereth stone."

"Säiyett, this man is a hunter—a simple fellow whom they call—"

He stopped, frowning.

"I know of him," she said. "On Ortelga they called him Kelderek Play-with-the-Children. Here he has no name, until I choose."

Bel-ka-Trazet resumed.

"He was brought to me tonight on his return from a hunting expedition, having refused to tell one of the shendrons whatever it was that he had seen. At first I treated him with forbearance, but still he would say nothing. I questioned him and he answered me like a child. He said, 'I have found a star. Who will believe that I have found a star?' Then he said, 'I will speak only to the Tuginda.' At this I threatened him with a heated knife, but he answered only, 'It must be as God wills.' And then, in this very moment, säiyett, arrived your message. 'So,' thought I, 'this man, who has said that he will speak only to you—who ever heard a man say this before?—let us take him at his word, if only to make him speak. He had better come to Quiso too— to his death, as I suppose, which he has brought upon himself.' And then he sits down upon the Tereth stone, God help us! And we find him face to face and alone with yourself. How can he return to Ortelga? He must die."

"That is for me to say, while he remains on Quiso. You see much, Baron, and you guard the people as an eagle her brood. You have seen this hunter and you are angry and suspicious because he has defied you. Have you seen nothing else from your eyrie on Ortelga this two days past?"

It was plain that Bel-ka-Trazet resented being questioned, but he answered civilly enough.

"The burning, säiyett. There has been a great burning."

"For leagues beyond the Telthearna the jungle has burned. All yesterday it rained ashes in Quiso. During the night, animals came ashore from the river—some of kinds never seen here before. A makati comes tame as a cat to Melathys, begging for food. She feeds it and then, following it to the water, finds a green snake coiled about the Tereth. Of whom are these the forerunners? At dawn, the brook in the high ravine left its course and streamed down over the Ledges: but at the foot it gathered itself, flowed back into its channel and did no harm. Why? Why were the Ledges washed, Baron? For the coming of your feet, or my feet? Or was it for the coming of some other feet? What messages, what signs were these?"

The Baron slid his tongue along the jagged edge of one lip and plucked the fur of his cape between his fingers, but answered nothing. The Tuginda turned to face the firelight and remained silent for some time. She sat perfectly still, her hands at rest in her lap, her composure like that of a tree when the wind has dropped. At length she said,

"So I ponder and pray and call upon such little wisdom as I may have acquired over the years, for I know no more than Melathys, or Rantzay or the girls what these things may mean. At last I send for you. Perhaps, it seems to me, *you* may be able to tell me something that you have seen or heard. Perhaps *you* may give me some clue.

"Meanwhile, if he should come, how should I receive him— he whom God means to send? Not with power or display, no, but as a servant. What else am I? So in case he should come, I dress myself like the ignorant, poor woman that God sees me to be. I know nothing, but at least I can cook a meal. And when the meal is ready I go out to the Tereth, to wait and pray."

Again she was silent. Melathys murmured,

"Perhaps the High Baron knows more than he has told us."

"I know nothing, säiyett."

"But it did not occur to me," went on the Tuginda, "that the stranger whom I knew to be with you—"

She broke off and looked across the room to where Kelderek was still standing by himself, away from the light. "So, hunter, you maintained to the High Baron's hot knife, did you, that you had a message for my ears alone?"

"It is true, säiyett," he answered, "and it is true also, as the High Baron says, that I am a man of no rank—one who gets his living as a hunter. Yet I knew—and know now—beyond doubt or gainsaying, that none must hear this news before yourself."

"Tell me, then, what you could not tell to the shendron or the High Baron."

He began to speak of his hunting expedition that morning and of the undergrowth full of bewildered, fugitive animals. Then

61

he told of the leopard and of his foolhardy attempt to pass it and escape inland. As he spoke of his ill-aimed arrow, his panic flight and fall from the bank, he trembled and gripped the table to steady himself. One of the lamps had burned dry, but the priestess made no move and the wick remained smoking until it died.

"And then," said the hunter, "then there stood over me, where I lay, säiyett, a bear—such a bear as never was, a bear tall as a dwelling-hut, his pelt like a waterfall, his muzzle a wedge across the sky. The leopard was as iron on his anvil. Iron —no—ah, believe me!—when the bear struck him he became like a chip of wood when the axe falls. He spun through the air and tumbled like a pierced bird. It was the bear—the bear who saved me. He struck once and then he was gone."

The hunter paused and came slowly forward to the fire.

"He was no vision, säiyett, no fancy of my fear. He is flesh and bone—he is real. I saw the burns on his side—I saw that they hurt him. A bear, säiyett, on Ortelga—a bear more than twice as tall as a man!" He hesitated, and then added, almost inaudibly, "If God were a bear—"

The priestess caught her breath. The Baron stood up, tipping back the bench against the table as his hand clutched at his empty scabbard.

"You had better be plain," said the Tuginda in a calm, matter-of-fact tone. "What do you mean, and what is it that you are thinking about the bear?"

To himself the hunter seemed like a man setting down at last a heavy burden which he has carried for miles, through darkness and solitude, to the place where it must go. But more strongly still, he felt once again the incredulity which had filled him that morning on the lonely, upstream shore of Ortelga. How could it be that this was the appointed time, here the place and himself the man? Yet it was so. It could not be otherwise. His eyes met the shrewd, intent gaze of the Tuginda.

"Säiyett," he replied, "it is Lord Shardik."

There was dead silence. Then the Tuginda answered carefully, "You understand that to be wrong—to deceive yourself and others—would be a sacrilegious and terrible thing? Any man can see a bear. If what you saw was a bear, O hunter who plays with children, for God's sake say so now and return home unharmed and in peace."

"Säiyett, I am nothing but a common man. It is you that must weigh my tale, not I. Yet as I live, I myself feel certain that the bear that saved me was none other than Lord Shardik."

"Then," replied the Tuginda, "whether you are proved wrong or right, it is plain what we have to do."

The priestess was standing with palms outstretched and closed eyes, praying silently. The Baron, frowning, paced slowly across to the farther wall, turned and paced back, gazing down at the floor. As he reached the Tuginda she laid her hand upon his wrist and he stopped, looking at her from one half-closed and one staring eye. She smiled up at him, for all the world as though no prospect lay before them but what was safe and easy.

"I'll tell you a story," she said. "There was once a wise, crafty baron who pledged himself to guard Ortelga and its people and to keep out all that could harm them: a setter of traps, a digger of pits. He perceived enemies almost before they knew their own intents and taught himself to distrust the very lizards on the walls. To make sure that he was not deceived, he disbelieved everything—and he was right. A ruler, like a merchant, must be full of craft, must disbelieve more than half he hears, or he will be a ruined man.

"But here the task is more difficult. The hunter says, 'It is Lord Shardik,' and the ruler, who has learned to be a skeptical man and no fool, replies, 'Absurd.' Yet we all know that one day Lord Shardik is to return. Suppose it *were* today and the ruler were in error, then what an error that would be! All the patient work of his life could not atone for it."

Bel-ka-Trazet said nothing.

"We cannot take the risk of being wrong. To do nothing might well be the greatest sacrilege. There is only one thing we can do. We must discover beyond doubt whether this news is true or false; and if we lose our lives, then God's will be done. After all, there are other barons and the Tuginda does not die."

"You speak calmly, säiyett," replied the Baron, "as though of the tendriona crop or the coming of the rains. But how can it be true—"

"You have lived long years, Baron, with the Dead Belt to

63

strengthen today and the tax to collect tomorrow. That has been your work. And I—I too have lived long years with my work—with the prophecies of Shardik and the rites of the Ledges. Many times I have imagined the news coming and pondered on what I should do if ever it were to come indeed. *That* is why I can say to you now, 'The hunter's tale may be true,' and yet speak calmly."

The Baron shook his head and shrugged his shoulders, as though unwilling to argue.

"Well, and what are we to do?" he asked.

"Sleep," she replied unexpectedly, going to the door. "I will call the girls to show you where."

"And tomorrow?"

"Tomorrow we will go upstream."

She opened the door and struck once upon a bronze gong. Then she returned and, going across to Kelderek, laid her hand on his sound shoulder.

"Good night," she said, "and let us trust that it may indeed be that good night that the children are taught to pray for."

9 *The Tuginda's Story*

THE NARROW PASSAGE from the landlocked inlet to the Telthearna bent so sharply that it was only just possible for a canoe to negotiate it. The rocky spurs on either side overlapped, closing the inlet like a wall, so that from within nothing could be seen of the river beyond.

The little bay, running inland between its paved shores, ended among colored water lilies at the outfall of the channel by the Tereth stone. Waiting with Melathys while the servants loaded the canoes, Kelderek gazed upward, past the bridge which he had crossed the night before, to where the Ledges opened above, their shape like that of a great arrowhead lying point downward on the hillside between the woods. The stream, he saw, was no longer flowing over them: it must have returned, during the night, to its normal course. High up, he could make out the figures of girls stooping over hoes and baskets, weeding and scouring among the stones.

When the loading of the canoes had begun, the sun had not yet reached this north-facing shore, but now it rose over the Ledges and shone down upon the inlet, changing the opaque gray water to a depth of slow-moving, luminous green. Sharp shadows fell across the pavements from the small stone buildings standing here and there along the edges, some secluded among the trees, others in the open among grass and flowers.

He wondered how old these buildings might be. There was none such on Ortelga. The whole place could be the work only of people long ago. What sort of people could they have been, who had constructed the Ledges?

Blinking, he turned away from the sun to watch the grave, silent girls loading the canoes. On Ortelga there would have been gossip, banter, songs to lighten the work. These women moved deliberately and spoke only such few words as were needed. They were silent, he supposed, by custom and the rule of the island. What a release it would be to leave this shady, mind-bemusing place of secrets and sorcery! Then he recalled whither they were bound and felt again the clutch of fear in his stomach.

An elderly, gray-haired woman, who had been directing the girls at their work, left the waterside and approached Melathys.

"The loading is done, säiyett," she said. "Do you wish to check that all is there?"

"No, I will trust you, Thula," replied the priestess absently.

The old woman laid a hand on her arm.

"We do not know where you are going, my dear, or for how long," she said. "Will you not tell me? Do you remember how I comforted you as a child, when you used to dream of the slave traders and the war?"

"I know all too well where we are going," replied Melathys, "but not when I shall return."

"A long journey?" persisted the old woman.

"Long or short," answered Melathys, with a quick, nervous laugh, "I promise you that whoever may die, I will take good care that I do not." She stooped, plucked a red flower, held it for a moment to the other's nostrils and then tossed it into the water.

The old woman made a restrained gesture of impatience, like a trusted servant who is privileged to express her feelings. "There is danger, then, my child?" she whispered. "Why do you speak of death?"

Melathys stared a moment, biting her lip. Then she unclasped the broad, golden collar from her neck and put it into the old woman's hands.

"At all events I shall not need this," she said, "and if there is danger I shall run faster without the weight of it. Ask me no more, Thula. It is time for us to set out. Where are the Baron's servants?"

"He said that they were to return to Ortelga," replied the old woman. "They have already taken their canoe and gone."

"Then go yourself now and tell the Baron that we are ready. Goodbye, Thula. Remember me in your prayers."

She made her way across the pavement, stepped down into the nearest of the four canoes and motioned to the hunter to take his place behind her. The two girls in the stern dipped their paddles and the canoe drew away from the shore. They crossed the inlet and began to edge their way out through the narrow cleft between the rock spurs.

The bow skirted a curtain of trailing, purple-leaved trazada and Kelderek, knowing how the little thorns tear and smart, dropped his head, shielding his face with his good arm. He heard the stiff leaves clashing against the side of the canoe, then felt a freshness of wind and opened his eyes. They were outside and rocking in a bay of slack water under the northern shore. The green shadow of the woods above them stretched upstream and across the river. Beyond, the water was blue and choppy, glittering in the sun and broken, here and there, into small, white-topped waves. Far off lay the blackened, desolate line of the left bank. He looked back over his shoulder but could no longer discern, among the tangle of green, the cleft from which they had emerged. Then the bow of the second canoe appeared, thrusting through the foliage. Melathys, following his gaze, smiled coldly.

"There is no other landing place on the island where a canoe can come to shore. All else is cliff or shoal, like the place where you landed last night."

"The Tuginda, then?" he asked. "Is she not coming with us?"

The priestess, watching the two remaining canoes as they came out, made no immediate reply, but after a while said, "Do you know the tale of Inanna?"

"Why, yes, säiyett. She went to the underworld to beg for a life and as she passed each gate they took from her her clothes, her jewels and all that she had."

"Long ago, whenever the Tuginda set out from Quiso to seek Lord Shardik, it was the custom that she should have nothing whatever upon her when she left the island." She paused and then added, "The Tuginda does not wish it to be known on Quiso that is leaving. By the time they learn that she is gone—"

"But if there is no other landing place?" he blurted out, interrupting her.

She spoke to the girls at the paddles.

"Nito! Neelith! We will go up the shore now, as far as the quarries."

At the westward end of the bay the shore extended to form a point. Below this the sheltered water was smooth, but once they had rounded it their progress became laborious, for the head wind was troublesome and on this side of the island the current ran strongly. They moved slowly upstream, the canoes jumping and bouncing in the choppy water. At length Kelderek could see that some way ahead the steep, green slopes gave place to cliffs of gray rock. The face of these cliffs appeared to have been cut and broken into. There were several straight-sided openings, like great windows, and at the foot of the lowest he noticed a kind of sill—a flat, projecting shelf of rock, perhaps three or four times the height of a man above the water. Through these openings, as they neared, he could catch glimpses of a deep, rock-sided excavation, on the floor of which, here and there, were lying boulders and a few squared slabs of stone; but all seemed neglected and desolate.

Melathys turned her head. "That is where they quarried the stone for the Ledges."

"Who, säiyett? When?"

Again she made no answer, merely gazing across at the little waves slap-slapping against the foot of the cliff. Suddenly Kelderek started, so that the canoe rocked sideways and one of the girls struck the water sharply with the flat of her paddle to recover its balance. On the flat shelf above them stood a naked woman, her hair flowing loose over her shoulders. She stepped forward to the edge and for a few moments stood looking down, moving her feet for a firm hold. Then, without hesitation, she dived into the deep water.

As she came to the surface, the hunter realized that this was none other than the Tuginda. She began swimming gently toward the third canoe, which was already cutting across to meet her. The Baron's canoe had turned away. Confused, the hunter first closed his eyes and then, to make sure that the priestess should not rebuke him, buried his face in his hands.

"Crendro, Melathys!" called the Tuginda, whom Kelderek could hear laughing as she climbed into the canoe. "I thought I had brought nothing with me but a light heart, but now I remember that I have two things more—their names, to be restored to our guests. Bel-ka-Trazet, can you hear me, or are you hastening out of earshot as well as out of sight?"

"Why, säiyett," answered the Baron gruffly, "you startled us. And am I not to respect you as a woman?"

"The breadth of the Telthearna is respect indeed. Are your servants not here?"

"No, säiyett. I have sent them back to Ortelga."

"God be with them. And with Melathys, for her pretty arms have been scratched by the trazada. Hunter—shy, pondering hunter—what is your name?"

"Kelderek, säiyett," he replied, "Kelderek Zenzuata."

"Well, now we can be sure that we have left Quiso. The girls will enjoy this unexpected trip. Who is with us? Sheldra, Nito, Neelith—"

She began chatting and joking with the girls, who from their answers were clearly convinced that she was in excellent spirits. After a time her canoe drew alongside and she touched Kelderek's arm.

"Your shoulder?" she asked.

"Better, säiyett," he answered. "The pain is much less."

"Good, for we are going to need you."

Although the Tuginda had kept her departure secret, some-one besides Melathys had evidently known what she meant to do and loaded her canoe accordingly, for she was now dressed, as though for hunting, in a tunic of stitched and overlapping leather panels, with leather greaves and sandals, and her wet hair, coiled about her head, was bound with a light silver chain. Like the girls, she was carrying a knife at her belt.

"We will not go up the shore of Ortelga, Melathys," she said. "The shendrons would see us and the whole town would be talking within the hour."

"How then, säiyett? Are we not making for the western end of the island?"

"Certainly. But we will cross to the farther side of the river and then return."

Their journey, thus extended, lasted almost until evening. As they crossed, the current carried them downstream, especially when they were obliged to give way to avoid the heavy, floating debris still drifting here and there. By the time they had reached the desert of the farther bank, with its scorched, ashen smell, the girls were tired. There was little or no true shade and they were forced to rest as best they could, partly in the canoes and partly in the river itself—for they could all swim like otters. Only Melathys, preoccupied and silent, remained in her place, apparently indifferent to the heat. They ate *selta* nuts, goat's cheese and rose-pale tendrionas. The long afternoon was spent in working slowly upstream along the dead bank. It was hard going, for every reach was obstructed inshore with half-burned trees and branches, some submerged, others spreading tangles of twigs and leaves across the surface. There was a continual drift of fine, black grit through the air and the sides of the canoes above the waterline became coated with a froth of ash suspended in the slack water.

The sun was nearing the horizon when the Tuginda at last gave the word to turn left and head out once more across the current. Kelderek, who knew the difficulty of judging the ever-changing currents of the Telthearna, realized that she was evidently an experienced and skillful waterman. At all events her judgment now was excellent, for with little further effort on the part of the weary girls, the river carried them across and down so that they drifted almost exactly upon the tall, narrow rock at the western point of Ortelga.

They waded ashore, dragging the canoes between them through the reeds, and made camp on dry ground among the soft, fibrous root tangles of a grove of quian. It was a wild shore, and as their fire burned up—so that the shapes of the tree trunks seemed to waver in its heat—and outside, the sunset faded from the expanse of the river, Kelderek felt again, as he had felt two days before, the unusual restlessness and disturbance of the forest around them.

"Säiyett," he ventured at last, "and you, my lord Baron, if I may be allowed to advise you, we should let no one wander away from the fire tonight. If any must do so, let them go to the shore but nowhere else. This place is full of creatures that are themselves strangers, lost and savage with fear."

Bel-ka-Trazet merely nodded and Kelderek, afraid of having said too much, busied himself in rolling a log to one side of the fire and scraping it clean to make a seat for the Tuginda. On the farther side the girl Sheldra was setting up the servants' quarters and allotting them their duties. She had said nothing whatever to Kelderek throughout the day and he, unsure what his place might be, was about to ask her whether he could be of use when the Tuginda called him and asked him to take the first watch.

As it fell out, he remained on guard half the night. He felt no desire to sleep. What sort of sentries would they make, he asked himself—these silent, self-contained girls, whose lives had been enclosed so long by the solitude of Quiso? Yet he knew that he was merely trying—and failing—to deceive himself; they were reliable enough and this was not the reason for his wakefulness. The truth was that he could not be free—had not been free all day—from the fear of death and the dread of Shardik.

Brooding in the darkness, fresh misgivings came upon him as he thought first of the High Baron and then of Melathys. Both felt fear—of this he was sure: fear of death no doubt, but also—and it was in this that they differed from himself—fear of losing what each already possessed. And because of this fear there lay in both their hearts an actual hope, of which neither would speak before the Tuginda, that he had told them false and that this search would end in nothing: for to each it seemed that even if what he had told them were the truth, he or she stood to gain nothing from it.

It occurred to him—troubling his heart and heightening still further his sense of loneliness—that the High Baron was actually unable to grasp what to himself was plain as flame. There came into his mind the recollection of an old, miserly trader who had lived near his home some years before. This man had amassed a competence by a lifetime of petty, hard bargaining. One night some swaggering young mercenaries, returned to Ortelga from a campaign in the service of Bekla and reluctant to call an end to a drunken frolic, had offered him three great emeralds in return for a jar of wine. The old man, convinced of some trick, had refused them and later had actually boasted of how he had shown himself too sharp for such rogues.

Bel-ka-Trazet, thought Kelderek, had spent years in making Ortelga a fortress, and looked now to reap his harvest—to grow old in safety behind his pits and stakes, his river moat and his shendrons along the shore. In his world, the proper place for anything strange or unknown was outside. Of all hearts on Ortelga, perhaps, his was the least likely to leap and blaze at news of the return of Shardik, the Power of God. As for Melathys, she was already content with her role as priestess and her island sorcery. Perhaps she hoped to become Tuginda herself in time. She was obeying the Tuginda now merely because she could not disobey her. Her heart, he felt sure, shared neither the Tuginda's passionate hope nor the Tuginda's deep sense of responsibility. It was natural, perhaps, that she should be afraid. She was a woman, quick-witted and young, who had already attained to a position of authority and trust. She had much to lose if a violent death should strike her down. He recalled how he had first seen her the night before, asserting her dismaying power on the flame-lit terrace, discerning, among the night travelers from Ortelga, the presence of the secret lying unspoken in his heart and in none other. At the memory he was overcome by a keen pang of disappointment. The truth was that the incomparable news which he had brought she would have preferred not to learn.

"They are both far above me," he thought, pacing slowly

across the grove, his ears full of the incessant croaking of the frogs along the shore. "Yet I—a common man—can see plainly that each is clinging—or trying to cling—to that which they fear may now be changed or swept away. I have no such thoughts, for I have nothing to lose; and besides, I have seen Lord Shardik and they have not. Yet even if we find him again and do not die, still, I believe, they will try by some means or other to deny him. And that I could never do, come of it what might."

The sudden, harsh cry of some creature in the forest recalled him to the duty he had undertaken, and he turned back to his watch. Crossing the clearing once more, he threaded his way among the sleeping girls.

The Tuginda was standing beside the fire. She beckoned, and as he approached, looked at him with the same shrewd, honest smile which he had first seen at the Tereth stone, before he had known who she was.

"Surely, Kelderek, your watch is long over?" she asked.

"If another were to take my place, säiyett, I could not sleep, so why should I not watch?"

"Your shoulder hurts?"

"No—my heart, säiyett." He smiled back at her. "I'm ill at ease. There's good cause."

"Well, I'm glad you're awake, Kelderek Play-with-the-Children, for we need to talk, you and I." She moved away from the sleepers and he followed her until she stopped and faced him in the gloom, leaning against a quian trunk. The frogs croaked on and now he could hear the waves lapping in the reeds.

"You heard me say to Melathys and the Baron that we ought to act as though your news were true. That was what I said to them: but you yourself, Kelderek, must know this. If I were unable to perceive the truth that flows from a man's heart into his words, I would not be the Tuginda of Quiso. I am in no doubt that it is indeed Lord Shardik that you have seen."

He could find no reply and after a little she went on, "So— of all those countless thousands who have waited, we are the ones, you and I."

"Yes. But you seem so calm, säiyett, and I—I am full of fear —ordinary coward's fear. Awe and dread I feel indeed, but most, I am afraid simply of being torn to pieces by a bear. They are very dangerous creatures. Are you not afraid too?"

She replied to his question with another.

"What do you know of Lord Shardik?"

He thought for a time and then answered, "He is from God—God is in him—he is the Power of God—he departed and he is to return. Nay, säiyett, one thinks he knows until another calls for the words. Like all children, I learned to pray for that good night when Shardik will return."

"But there is such a thing as getting more than we bargain for. Many pray. How many have really considered what it would mean if the prayers were granted?"

"Whatever may come of it, säiyett, I could never wish that he had not returned. For all my fear, I could not wish that I had never seen him."

"Nor I, for all mine. Yes, I am afraid too; but at least I can thank God that I have never forgotten the real, the true work of the Tuginda—to be ready, in all sober reality, night and day, for the return of Shardik. How often, by night, have I walked alone on the Ledges and thought, "If this were the night—if Shardik were to come now—what should I do?" I knew I could not but fear, but the fear is less—" she smiled again—"less than I feared. Now you must know more, for we are the Vessels, you and I." She nodded slowly, holding his eyes among the shadows. "And what that means we shall learn, God help us, and in His good time."

Kelderek said nothing. The Tuginda folded her arms, leaned back once more against the tree and went on.

"It is more than a matter of the people falling flat on their faces—much, much more." Still he said nothing.

"Do you know of Bekla, that great city?"

"Of course, säiyett."

"Have you ever been there?"

"I? Oh no, säiyett. How should a man like me go to Bekla? Yet many of my skins and feathers have been brought by the factors for the market there. It is four or five days' journey to the south, that I know."

"Did you know that long ago—no one knows how long—the people of Ortelga ruled in Bekla?"

"*We* were the rulers of Bekla?"

"We were. Of that empire which stretched north to the shores of the Telthearna, west to Paltesh and south to Sarkid and Ikat-Yeldashay. We were a great people—fighters, traders and, above all, builders and craftsmen—yes, we who now skulk on an island in thatched sheds and scratch for a living with ploughs and mattocks on a few pebbly miles of the mainland.

"It was we who built Bekla. To this day it is like a garden of sculpted and dancing stone. The Palace of the Barons is more beautiful than a lily pool when the dragonflies hover over it. The street of the builders was full then of rich men's messengers from far and near, offering fortunes to craftsmen to come and work for them. And those who condescended to go traveled swiftly, for there were broad, safe roads to the frontiers.

"In those days, Shardik was with us. He was with us as the Tuginda is with us now. He did not die. He passed from one bodily home to another."

"Shardik ruled in Bekla?"

"No, not in Bekla. Shardik was worshiped and Shardik blessed us from a lonely, sacred place on the borders of the empire, to which his suppliants journeyed in humility. Where was that, do you think?"

"I cannot tell, säiyett."

"It was Quiso, where the shreds of Shardik's power still cling like rags on a windy hedge. And it was the craftsmen of Bekla who made of the whole island a temple for Shardik. They built the causeway from the mainland to Ortelga—the causeway that is now broken—for the bands of pilgrims, after they had assembled on the mainland shore among the Two-Sided Stones, would be brought first to Ortelga and thence make the night journey to Quiso, just as you made it last night. Our craftsmen, too, leveled and paved the terrace where Melathys met you; and over the ravine in front of it they made the Bridge of the Suppliants, a span of iron slender as a rope, by which all strangers had to cross or else go back. But that bridge is fallen this many a year—fallen long before we were born, you and I. Behind the terrace, as you know, lies the Upper Temple, which they cut out of the rock. You did not see the interior, for you were in darkness. It is a high chamber, twenty paces square, hewn throughout thirty years, flake by flake out of the living rock. And more than all this, they made—"

"The Ledges!"

"The Ledges: the greatest artifact in the world. Four generations of stonemasons and builders worked for more than a hundred years to complete the Ledges. Those who began it never saw the end. And they paved the shores of the bay below and built the dwellings for the priestesses and the women."

"And Shardik, säiyett? How was he housed?"

"He was not. He went where he would. He roamed free—sometimes among the woods, sometimes on the Ledges. But the priestesses hunted for him, fed him and looked after him. That was their mystery."

"But did he never kill?"

"Yes, sometimes he would kill—a priestess in the Singing, if such was God's will, or perhaps some over-bold suppliant who had approached him rashly or provoked him in some way. Also, he knew the truth in men's hearts and could tell when one was secretly his enemy. When he killed he did so out of his own divining—we did not set him on to kill. Rather it was our mystery and our skill to tend him so that he did not. The Tuginda and her priestesses walked and slept near Shardik—this was their art, the wonder that men came to see, the wonder that gave Bekla its luck and mastery."

"And was he mated?"

"Sometimes he was mated, but it did not have to be so. Whom God made Shardik was a matter of signs and omens, of His will rather than of human intent. Sometimes, indeed, the Tuginda would know that she must leave Quiso and go into the hills or the forest with her girls, to find and bring back a mate for Shardik. But again, he might live until he seemed to die, and then they would go to find him reborn and bring him home."

"How?"

"They had ways of which we still know—or hope that we know, for they have been long unused—both drugs and other arts by which he could be controlled, though only for a little time. Yet none of these was sure. When the Power of God appears in earthly form, he cannot be driven here and there like a cow, or where would be the wonder and the awe? Always, with Shardik, there was uncertainty, danger and the risk of death: and that at least is one thing of which we can still be sure. Shardik requires of us all that we have, and from those who cannot offer so much freely, he may well take it by force."

She paused, gazing unseeingly into the dark jungle, as though remembering the power and majesty of Shardik of the Ledges and his Tuginda long ago. At last Kelderek asked, "But—those days came to an end, säiyett?"

"They came to an end. The full story I do not know. It was a sacrilege too vile to be fully known or spoken. All I can tell is that the Tuginda of that time betrayed Shardik and betrayed the people and herself. There was a man—no, not fit to be called a man, for who but one lost to God would dare to contrive such a thing?—a wandering slave trader. She became—with him— ah!" and here the Tuginda, overcome, stood silent, her body pressed back against the trunk of the quian, shuddering with disgust and horror. At length, recovering herself, she went on,

"He—he slew Shardik, and many of the sacred women also. The rest he and his men took for slaves, and she who had once been called Tuginda fled with him down the Telthearna. Perhaps they came to Zeray—perhaps to some other place—I cannot say—it does not greatly matter. God knew what they had done and He can always afford to wait.

"Then the enemies of Bekla rose up and attacked it and we were left without heart or courage to fight them. They took the city. The High Baron died at their hands and what was left of the people fled over the plain and the Gelt Mountains to the shores of the Telthearna, for they hoped that if they fled as suppliants to these islands, they might save at least their lives. So they crossed to Ortelga and broke up the causeway behind them. And their enemies left them there, to scratch in the earth and scavenge in the forest, for they had taken their city and their empire and it was not worth their while to attack desperate men in their last stronghold. Quiso too they left them, for they feared Quiso, even though it had become an empty, defiled place. Yet one thing they forbade. Shardik was never to return; and for a long time, until there was no more need, they kept watch to make sure of this.

"The years passed and we became an ignorant, impoverished

people. Many Ortelgan craftsmen drifted away to sell their skill in richer places; and those who were left lost their cunning for lack of fine materials and wealthy custom. Now we venture as far on the mainland as we dare and trade what resources we have—rope and skins—for what we can get from beyond. And the barons dig pits and post shendrons to keep themselves alive on a spit of jungle that no one else requires. Yet still the Tuginda, on her empty island, has work—believe me, Kelderek, she has work—the hardest. Her work is to wait. To be ready, always, for Shardik's return. For one thing has been plainly foretold, again and again, by every sign and portent known to the Tuginda and the priestesses—that one day Shardik will return."

Kelderek stood for some time looking out toward the moonlit reeds. At length he said,

"And the Vessels, säiyett? You said that we were the Vessels."

"I was taught long ago that God will bless all men by revealing a great truth through Shardik and through two chosen vessels, a man and a woman. But those vessels He will first shatter to fragments and then Himself fashion them again to His purpose."

"What does this mean?"

"I don't know," answered the Tuginda. "But of this you can be sure, Kelderek Zenzuata. If this is indeed Lord Shardik, as I, like you, believe, then there will be good reason why you and none other have been chosen to find and to serve him—yes, even though you yourself cannot guess what that reason may be."

"I am no warrior, säiyett. I—"

"It has never been foretold that Shardik's return will necessarily mean that power and rule is to be restored to the Ortelgans. Indeed, there is a saying, 'God does not do the same thing twice.'"

"Then, säiyett, if we find him, what are we to do?"

"Simply wait upon God," she replied. "If our eyes and ears are open in all humility, it will be shown us what we are to do. And you had better be ready, Kelderek, and submit yourself with a humble and honest heart, for the accomplishment of God's purpose may well depend upon that. He can tell us nothing if we will not hear. If you and I are right, our lives will soon cease to be our own to do with as we will."

She began to walk slowly back toward the fire and Kelderek walked beside her. As they reached it she clasped his hand. "Have you the skill to track a bear?"

"It is very dangerous, säiyett, believe me. The risk—"

"We can only have faith. Your task will be to find the bear. As for me, I have learned in long years the mysteries of the Tuginda, but neither I nor any woman alive has ever performed them, nor even seen them performed, in the presence of Lord Shardik. God's will be done."

She was whispering, for they had passed the fire and were standing among the sleeping women.

"You must get some rest now, Kelderek," she said, "for we have much to do tomorrow."

"As you say, säiyett. Shall I wake two of the girls? One alone may give way to fear."

The Tuginda looked down at the breathing figures, their tranquillity seeming as light, remote and precarious as that of fish poised in deep water.

"Let the poor lasses rest," she said. "I will take the watch myself."

10   *The Finding of Shardik*

As THE SUN ROSE HIGHER and moved southward round the hill, the watery glitter from the reed beds, reflected into the trees along the shore, was sifted upward through the translucent leaves, to encounter at last and be dimmed by the direct rays penetrating among the higher branches. A green, faint light, twice reflected, shone down from the undersides of the leaves, speckling the bare ground between the tree trunks, placing the faintest of shadows beside fallen twigs, glistening in tiny points upon the domes of pebbles. Dappled by the continual movement of the sunlit water, the leaves seemed stirred as though by a breeze. Yet this apparent disturbance was an illusion: there was no wind, the trees were still in the heat and nothing moved except the river flowing outside.

Kelderek was standing near the shore, listening to the sounds from the jungle inland. He could tell that since his adventure of two days before—even since their landing the previous night—the confusion in the forest had lessened and the agitation of movement subsided. There were fewer cries of alarm, fewer startlings of birds and flights of monkeys through the trees. No doubt many of the fugitive creatures had already fallen prey to others. Of those surviving, most must have begun to move eastward down the island in search of food and safety. Some, probably, had taken to the water again, making for the Telthearna's southern bank on the opposite side of the strait. He had seen prints here and there in the mud and narrow passages broken through the reeds. The thought came to him, "Suppose *he* should be gone? Suppose *he* is no longer on the island?"

"We would be safe then," he thought, "and my life, like a stream after a cloudburst, would return between the banks where it ran two days ago." He turned his head toward the Tuginda who, with Bel-ka-Trazet, was standing a little way off among the trees. "But I could not become once more the man who fled from the leopard. Two days—I have lived two years! Even if I were to know that Shardik will kill me—and like enough he will—still I could not find it in my heart to pray that we should find him gone."

The more he considered, however, the more he felt it probable that the bear was not far away. He recalled its clumsy, weary gait as it made off through the bushes and how it had winced in pain when it scraped its side against the tree. Huge and fearsome though it was, there had been something pitiable about the creature he had seen. If he were right and it had been hurt in some way, it would be more than dangerous to approach. He had better put out of his mind for the moment all thought of Shardik the Power of God, and address himself to the daunting task—surely sufficient to the day, if ever a task was—of finding Shardik the bear.

Returning to the Tuginda and the Baron, he told them how he read the signs of the forest. Then he suggested that for a start, they might go over the ground which he had covered two days before, and so come to the place where he had first seen the bear. He showed them where he had come ashore and how he had tried to slip unseen past the leopard and then to walk away from it. They made their way inland among the bushes, followed by Melathys and the girl Sheldra.

Since they had left the camp Melathys had spoken scarcely a word. Glancing behind him, Kelderek saw her drawn face, very pale in the heat, as she lifted a trembling hand to wipe the sweat from her temples. He felt full of pity for her. What work was this for a beautiful young woman, to take part in tracking an injured bear? It would have been better to have left her in the camp and to have brought a second girl from among the servants; one dour and stolid as Sheldra, who looked as though she would not notice a bear if it stood on her toe.

As they approached the foot of the hill he led the way through the thicker undergrowth to the place where he had wounded the leopard. By chance he came upon his arrow and, picking it up, fitted the notch to the string of the bow he was carrying. He drew the bow a little, frowning uneasily, for he disliked it and missed his own. This was the bow of one of the girls—too light and pliant: he might have saved himself the trouble of bringing it. He wondered what that surly fool Taphro had done with his bow. "If ever we get back," he thought, "I'll ask the Baron to order it to be restored to me."

They went on cautiously. "This is where I fell, säiyett," he whispered, "and see, here are the marks the leopard made."

"And the bear?" asked the Tuginda, speaking as quietly as he.

"He stood below, säiyett," replied Kelderek, pointing down the bank, "but he did not need to reach up to strike the leopard. He struck sideways—thus."

The Tuginda gazed down the extent of the steep bank, drew in her breath and looked first at Bel-ka-Trazet and then back at the hunter.

"Are you sure?" she asked.

"The leopard, as it crouched, was looking upward into the bear's face, säiyett," replied Kelderek. "I can see it still, and the white fur beneath its chin."

The Tuginda was silent as though trying to imagine more

clearly the gigantic figure that had reared itself, bristling and snarling, above the level of the bank on which they stood. At length she said to Bel-ka-Trazet,

"Is it possible?"

"I would think not, säiyett," replied the Baron, shrugging his shoulders.

"Well, let us go down," she said. Kelderek offered her his arm, but she gestured to him to turn back for Melathys. The priestess's breathing was quick and irregular and she leaned hard on him, hesitating at every step. When they reached the foot of the bank she set her back against a tree, bit her lip and closed her eyes. He was about to speak to her when the Tuginda laid a hand on his shoulder.

"You did not see the bear again after it left you here?"

"No, säiyett," he replied. "That's the way it went—through those bushes," he went across to the tree against which the bear had scraped its injured side. "It has not returned this way." He paused a few moments and then, trying to speak calmly, asked, "Am I to track it now?"

"We must find the bear if we can, Kelderek. Why else have we come?"

"Then, säiyett, it will be best if I go alone. The bear may be close and above all I must be silent."

"I will come with you," said Bel-ka-Trazet.

He unclasped the chain at his throat, took off his fur cloak and laid it on the ground. His left shoulder, like his face, was mutilated—humped and knotted as the exposed root of a tree. Kelderek thought, "He wears the cloak to conceal it."

They had gone only a few yards when the hunter perceived the tracks of the leopard, partly trodden out by those of the bear. The leopard, he supposed, had been injured but had tried to escape, and the bear had pursued it. Soon they came upon the leopard's body, already half-devoured by vermin and insects. There were no signs of a struggle and the bear's trail led on through the bushes to emerge in open, stone-strewn woodland. Here, for the first time, it was possible to see some distance ahead between the trees. They halted on the edge of the undergrowth, listening and watching, but nothing moved and all was quiet save for the chittering of parakeets in the branches.

"No harm in the women coming this far," said Bel-ka-Trazet in his ear; and a moment later he had slipped noiselessly back into the undergrowth.

Kelderek, left alone, tried to guess which way the bear might have taken. The stony ground showed no tracks, however, and he felt himself at a loss. The Baron did not return and he wondered whether perhaps Melathys might have fainted or been taken ill. At last, growing weary of waiting, he counted a hundred paces to his right and then began to move slowly in a wide half-circle, examining the ground for the least sign—tracks, claw marks, droppings or shreds of hair.

He had completed perhaps half this task without success when he came once more to the edge of a belt of undergrowth. It did not extend far, for he could glimpse open ground beyond. On impulse he crept through it and came out at the top of a grassy slope, bordered on each side by forest and stretching away to the northern shore of the island and the Telthearna beyond. Some little way from where he stood was a hollow—a kind of pit about a stone's throw across. It was surrounded by bushes and tall weeds, and from somewhere in the same direction came a faint sound of water. He might as well go and drink, he thought, before returning. To recover the bear's tracks, now that they had lost them, would probably prove a long and arduous business.

Setting off across the open ground, he saw that there was indeed a brook running down the slope beyond the hollow. The hollow was not directly in his way, but out of mere curiosity he turned aside and looked down into it. Instantly he dropped on his hands and knees, concealing himself behind a thick clump of weeds near the verge.

He could feel the pulse behind his knee like a finger plucking the tendon and his heart was beating so violently that he seemed to hear it. He waited, but there was no other sound. Cautiously he raised his head and looked down once more.

In contrast to the heat-parched forest all about, the ground below was fresh and verdant. On one side grew an oak, its lower branches level with the top of the pit and spreading over the ground near the brink. The foot of the trunk was surrounded by short, smooth turf and close by, in its shade, lay a shallow pool. There was no outfall and, as he watched, the water, still as glass, reflected two ducks, which flew across a shield-shaped cloud, wheeled in the blue and passed out of sight. Along the further edge rose a bank and over this grew a tangle of *trepsis* vine—a kind of wild marrow, with rough leaves and trumpet-shaped scarlet flowers.

Among the trepsis the bear was lying on its side, its head drooping toward the water. The eyes were closed, the jaws a little open and the tongue protruding. Seeing for the second time its enormous shoulders and the unbelievable size of its body, the hunter was possessed by the same trancelike sense of unreality that he had felt two days before: yet now, with this, there came a sense of being magnified, of being elevated to a plane higher than that of his own everyday life. It was impossible that there should be such a bear—and yet it lay before him. He had not deceived himself. This could indeed be none other than Shardik, the Power of God.

There was no more room for the least doubt and all that he had done had been right. In an anguish of relief, in fear and awe, he prayed, "O Shardik, O my lord, accept my life. I, Kelderek Zenzuata—I am yours to command forever, Shardik my lord!"

As his first shock began to subside, he saw that he had also been right in guessing that the bear was sick or injured. It was clearly sunk in a coma altogether different from the sleep of a healthy animal. And there was something else—something un-natural and disturbing—what? It was lying in the open cer-tainly, but that was not all. Then he perceived. The trepsis vine grows quickly: it will grow across a doorway between sunrise and sunset. The bear's body was covered here and there with trailing stems, with leaves and scarlet flowers. How long, then, had Shardik lain beside the pool without moving? A day? Two days? The hunter looked more closely, his fear turning to pity. Along the exposed flank, bare patches showed in the shaggy pelt. The flesh appeared dark and discolored. But surely even dried blood was never so dark? He went a little forward down the slope of the pit. There was blood, certainly; but the wounds appeared dark because they were covered—crawling—with tor-pid flies. He cried out in disgust and horror. Shardik the leopard-slayer, Shardik of the Ledges, Lord Shardik returned to his people after untold years—was lying flyblown and dying of filth in a jungle pit of weeds!

"He will die," he thought. "He will die before tomorrow—unless we can prevent it. As for me, I will go down to help him no matter what the danger."

He turned and ran back across the open ground, smashed his way noisily through the belt of undergrowth and raced on between the trees toward the place where the Baron had left him. Suddenly he felt himself tripped and fell sprawling with a jolt that left him dazed and winded. As he rolled over, gasping for breath, the floating lights before his eyes cleared to reveal the face of Bel-ka-Trazet, awry as a guttering candle with one staring eye for flame.

"What now?" said the twisted mouth. "Why do you run about making a noise like a goat in a market pen, you coward?"

". . . tripped . . . my lord . . ." gasped Kelderek.

"It was I who tripped you, you craven fool! Have you led the bear upon us? Quick, man, where is it?"

Kelderek stood up. His face was cut and he had twisted his knee, but mercifully his wounded shoulder had escaped.

"I was not running from the bear, my lord. I have found him —I have found Lord Shardik—but he may well be in the sleep of death. Where is the Tuginda?"

"I am here," she said, from behind him. "How far away, Kelderek?"

"He is close, säiyett—injured and very ill, so far as I can judge. He cannot have moved for over a day. He will die—"

"He will not," replied the Tuginda briskly. "If it is indeed Lord Shardik, he will not die. Come, lead us there."

Halting on the edge of the pit, Kelderek pointed in silence. As each of his four companions reached the verge he watched them closely. Bel-ka-Trazet started involuntarily and then—or so it seemed—averted his eyes, as though actually fearful of what he saw. If fear it was, he had recovered himself in an instant and dropped, like Kelderek, behind the cover of the weeds, whence he stared down into the pit with an intent, wary look, like that of a boatman scanning rough water ahead.

Melathys barely looked down before raising her hands to

84

either bloodless cheek and closing her eyes. Then she turned her back and sank to her knees like a woman stricken to the heart by dreadful tidings.

Sheldra and the Tuginda remained standing on the verge. Neither appeared startled or made any move to conceal herself. The girl, impassive, had halted behind and a little to the left of her mistress, her feet apart, her weight on her heels, her arms hanging loosely at her sides. It was certainly not the posture of one who was afraid. For a few moments she stood looking down without moving. Then, raising her head with the air of one recalling herself to her proper business, she looked toward the Tuginda and waited.

The Tuginda's hands were clasped together at her waist and her shoulders rose and slowly fell as she breathed. Her stance gave a curious impression of weightlessness, as though she might actually be about to float down into the hollow. The poise of her head was alert as a bird's; yet for all her eager tension she seemed no more afraid than the servant standing at her elbow.

Bel-ka-Trazet rose to his feet and the Tuginda turned and stared at him gravely. Kelderek remembered yet again how Melathys, two nights before, had gazed silently into the faces of the men who had stumbled their way to the Upper Temple; and how he himself had been in some way divined and selected. No doubt the Tuginda too possessed the power to perceive without asking questions.

After a few moments, turning away from Bel-ka-Trazet, the Tuginda said calmly, "Sheldra, you see that it is Lord Shardik?"

"It is Lord Shardik, säiyett," replied the girl in the level tone of liturgical response.

"I am going down and I wish you to come with me," said the Tuginda.

The two women had already descended some yards when Kelderek, coming to himself, started after them. As he did so Bel-ka-Trazet caught him by the arm.

"Don't be a fool, Kelderek," he said. "They'll be killed. Even if they're not, this nonsense need be no business of yours."

Kelderek stared at him in astonishment. Then, without contempt, certainly, for this gray and ravaged warrior, but with a

8 5

new and strange sense of having traveled beyond his authority, he answered, "Sir, Lord Shardik is close to death." Quickly inclining his head and raising his palm to his forehead, he turned and followed the two women down the steep slope.

The Tuginda and her companion had reached the floor of the hollow and were walking swiftly, with as little hesitation as the women with the lantern had walked into the fire; and Kelderek, since he judged it better not to leap or run for fear of rousing the bear, had not overtaken them before they stopped on the nearer side of the pool. The grass was damp underfoot and he guessed that it must be watered and the pool filled from the same underground source as that which fed the brook on the open slope beyond.

The pool, knee-deep and perhaps a little broader than a man could jump, was fringed all along the farther side by the scarlet trumpet-flowers, half-hidden among their masses of palmate, hairy leaves. There was a fetid smell of filth and sickness and a buzzing of flies. The bear had not moved and they could hear its labored breathing—a sodden, injured sound. The muzzle was dry, the pelt staring and lusterless. A glimpse of the bloodshot white of one eye showed beneath the half-closed lid. At close quarters its size was overwhelming. The shoulder rose above Kelderek like a wall, beyond which could be seen only the sky. As he stood uncertain the bear, without opening its eyes, lifted its head for a moment and then wearily let it fall again. Even so, a man in grave illness tosses and moves, seeking relief, but then, finding in movement nothing but wretchedness and futility, desists.

Without thought of danger, Kelderek took half a dozen splashing steps across the pool, plucked the cloth from his wounded shoulder and, soaking it in the water, held it to the bear's muzzle and moistened its tongue and lips. The jaws moved convulsively and he, seeing that the great beast was trying to chew the cloth, soaked it once more and squeezed the water into the side of its mouth.

The Tuginda, bending over the bear's flank with a frond of green fern in one hand, had evidently got rid of the flies in one of the wounds and was examining it. This done, she began searching over the whole body, sometimes parting the pelt with her fingers, sometimes using the stalk of the frond as a probe;

Kelderek guessed that she was removing flies' eggs and maggots, but her face showed no disgust, only the same care and deliberation that he had seen while she dressed his shoulder.

At length she paused and beckoned to him where he stood in the pool. He scrambled up the bank, the hollow stems of the trepsis bursting under his feet with a soft "Nop! Nop!" Feeling for a hold, he inadvertently grasped for a moment the curved claws of the off forepaw, each as long as his hand and thick as his finger. He reached the top, stood beside Sheldra and looked down at the body.

The bear's belly and flank were marked with long, singed streaks, black or dirty gray in color, as though scored with a burning torch or hot iron bar. In several places the pelt, four fingers thick, had been burned away altogether and the bare flesh, withered and contracted into furrows and proud ridges, was split by cracks and open sores. Here and there hung a cluster of bluebottles' eggs or a maggot that the Tuginda had overlooked. Several of the wounds were putrescent, oozing a glistening green matter that had discolored the shaggy hair and clotted it into stiff, dry spikes. A pulpy mess of yellow, withering trepsis showed that the helpless creature had urinated where it lay. No doubt, thought Kelderek, the hindquarters too were fouled and full of maggots. But he felt no revulsion—only pity and a determination at all costs to play his part in saving Shardik's life.

"There is much to be done," said the Tuginda, "if he is not to die. We must work quickly. But first, we will go back and speak with the Baron and I will tell the priestess what we require."

As they made their way up the side of the pit she said to Kelderek, "Take heart, clever hunter. You had the skill to find him and God will grant us the skill to save him, never fear."

"It was no skill of mine, säiyett—" he began, but she motioned him to silence and, turning her head, began speaking in low tones to Sheldra. "—need both *tessik* and *theltocarna*," he heard, and a few moments later, "if he recovers we must attempt the Singing."

Bel-ka-Trazet was standing where Kelderek had left him. Melathys, white as the moon, had risen to her feet and was standing with eyes fixed on the ground.

"There are many wounds," said the Tuginda, "and several

are flyblown and poisoned. He must have fled from the fire across the river—but of that I was already sure when Kelderek first told us his tale."

Bel-ka-Trazet paused as though deliberating with himself. Then, with the air of one resolved, he looked up and said, "Säiyett, let us understand one another, you and I. You are the Tuginda and I am the High Baron of Ortelga—until someone kills me. The people consent to obey us because they believe that each of us, by one means or another, can keep them safe. Old tales, old dreams—people can be ruled and led by these, as long as they believe in them and in those who draw from them power and mystery. Your women walk on fire, take away men's names out of their minds, plunge knives into their arms and take no hurt. That is good, for the people fear and obey. But of what help to us is this business of the bear, and what use do you mean to make of it?"

"I don't know," answered the Tuginda, "and this is no time to be discussing such things. At all costs we have to act quickly."

"Nevertheless, hear me, säiyett, for you will need my help and I have learned from long experience what is most likely to follow from this deed and that. We have found a large bear—possibly the largest bear that has ever lived. Certainly I would not have believed that there could be such a bear—that I grant you. But if you heal it, what will follow? If you remain near it, it will kill you and your women and then become a terror to the whole of Ortelga, until men are forced to hunt and destroy it at the risk of their lives. Even supposing that it does not kill you, at the best it will leave the island and then you, having tried to make use of it and failed, will lose influence over the people. Believe me, säiyett, you have nothing to gain. As a memory and a legend, Shardik has power and that power is ours, but to try to make the people believe that he has returned can end in nothing but harm. Be advised by me and go back, now, to your island."

The Tuginda waited in silence until he had finished speaking. Then, beckoning to the priestess, she said,

"Melathys, go at once to the camp and tell the girls to bring here everything we are going to need. It will be best if they paddle the canoes around the shore and land down there," She pointed across the pit to the distant, northern shore at the foot of the long slope.

The priestess hurried away without a word and the Tuginda turned back to the hunter.

"Now, Kelderek," she said, "you must tell me. Is Lord Shardik too sick to eat?"

"I am sure of that, säiyett. But he will drink, and he might perhaps drink blood, or even take food which has been chewed small, as they sometimes do for babies."

"If he will, so much the better. There is a medicine which he needs, but it is an herb and must not be weakened by being mixed with water."

"I will go at once, säiyett, and kill some game. I only wish I had my own bow."

"Was it taken from you at the Upper Temple?"

"No, säiyett." He explained.

"We can see to that," she said. "I shall need to send to Ortelga on several matters. But go now and do the best you can."

He turned away, half-expecting Bel-ka-Trazet to call him back. But the Baron remained silent and Kelderek, walking around the pit, made his way to the brook and at last drank his fill before setting out.

His hunting lasted several hours, partly because, remembering the leopard, he moved through the woods very cautiously, but mainly because the game was shy and he himself nervous and disturbed. He had trouble with the bow and more than once missed an easy mark. It was late in the afternoon before he returned with two brace of duck and a paca—a poor bag by his usual standards, but one for which he had worked hard.

The girls had lit a fire downwind of the pit. Three or four were bringing in wood, while others were making shelters from branches bound with creeper. Melathys, seated by the fire with a pestle and mortar, was pounding some aromatic herb. He gave the duck to Neelith, who was baking on a hot stone, and laid the paca aside to draw and skin himself. But first he went across to the pit.

The bear was still lying among the scarlet trepsis, but already it looked less foul and wretched. Its great wounds had been dressed with some kind of yellow ointment. One girl was keeping the flies from its eyes and ears with a fan of fern fronds, while another, with a jar of the ointment, was working along its back and as much as she could reach of the flank on which it was lying. Two others had brought sand to cover patches of soiled ground which they had already cleaned and hoed with pointed sticks. The Tuginda was holding a soaked cloth to the bear's mouth, as he himself had done, but was dipping it not in the pool but in a water jar at her feet. The unhurried bearing of the girls contrasted strangely with the gashed and monstrous body of the terrible creature they were tending. Kelderek watched them pause in their work, waiting as the bear stirred restlessly. Its mouth gaped open and one hind leg kicked weakly before coming to rest once more among the trepsis. Recalling what the Baron had said, Kelderek thought for the first time, "If we do succeed in healing it, what, indeed, will happen then?"

11 Bel-ka-Trazet's Story

WAKING SUDDENLY, Kelderek was aware first of the expanse of stars and then of a black, shaggy shape against the sky. A man was standing over him. He raised himself quickly on one arm.

"At last!" said Bel-ka-Trazet, thrusting his foot once more into his ribs. "Well, before long you will be sleeping sounder, I dare say."

Kelderek clambered to his feet. "My lord?" He now caught sight of one of the girls standing, bow in hand, a little behind the Baron.

"You took the first watch, Kelderek," said Bel-ka-Trazet. "Who took the second?"

"The priestess Melathys, my lord. I woke her, as I was told."

"How did she strike you? What did she say?"

"Nothing, my lord; that is, nothing that I remember. She seemed—as she seemed yesterday; I think she may be afraid."

Bel-ka-Trazet nodded. "It is past the third watch."

Again Kelderek looked up at the stars. "So I see, my lord."

"This girl here woke of her own accord and went to take her watch, but found no one else awake except the two girls with the bear. The girl who was supposed to have the watch before her had not been woken and the priestess is nowhere to be found."

Kelderek scratched an insect bite on his arm and said nothing.

"Well?" snarled the Baron. "Am I to stand here and watch you scratch yourself like a mangy ape?"

"Perhaps we should go down to the river, my lord?"

"I had thought as much myself," replied the Baron. He turned to the girl. "Where did you leave the canoes yesterday afternoon?"

"When we had unloaded them, my lord, we pulled them out of the water and laid them up among some trees nearby."

"You need not wake your mistress," said Bel-ka-Trazet. "Take your watch now and be ready for us to return."

"Should we not be armed, my lord?" asked Kelderek. "Shall I get a bow?"

"This will do," replied the Baron, plucking the girl's knife from her belt and striding away into the starlight.

It was easy going to the river, following the course of the brook over the dry, open grass. Bel-ka-Trazet walked with the help of a long thumb-stick which Kelderek remembered to have seen him trimming the evening before. Soon they could hear the night-breeze hissing faintly in the reeds. The Baron paused, gazing about him. Near the water the grass grew long and the girls, in dragging the canoes, had trampled a path through it. This Bel-ka-Trazet and Kelderek followed from the shore to the trees. They found only three canoes, each stowed carefully and covered by the low branches. Near them, a single furrow ran back toward the river. Kelderek crouched down over it. The torn earth and crushed grass smelled fresh and some of the weeds were still slowly moving as they re-erected their flattened leaves.

Bel-ka-Trazet, leaning on his stick like a goatherd, stood looking out over the river. There was a smell of ashes on the breeze but nothing to be·seen.

"That girl had some sense," he said at length. "No bear for her."

Kelderek, who had been hoping against hope that he might be proved wrong, felt a dreary disappointment, an anguish like that of a man who, having been robbed, reflects how easily all might have been prevented; and a sense of personal betrayal by one whom he had admired and honored, which he knew better than to try to express to the Baron. Why could Melathys not have asked him to help her? She had turned out, he thought sorrowfully, like some beautiful, ceremonial weapon, all fine inlay and jewels, which proved to have neither balance nor cut.

"But where has she gone, my lord? Back to Quiso?"

"No, nor to Ortelga, for she knows they would kill her. We'll never see her again. She'll end in Zeray. A pity, for she could have done more than I to persuade the girls to go home. As it is, we've simply lost a canoe; and one or two other things as well, I dare say."

They began to make their way back beside the brook. The Baron walked slowly, jabbing with his stick at the turf, like one turning something over in his mind. After a time he said, "Kelderek, you were watching me when I first looked down into the pit yesterday. No doubt you saw that I was afraid."

Kelderek thought, "Does he mean to kill me?" "When *I* first saw the bear, my lord," he answered, "I threw myself on the ground for fear. I—"

Bel-ka-Trazet raised a hand to silence him.

"I *was* afraid, and I am afraid now. Yes, afraid for myself—to be dead may be nothing, yet who relishes the business of dying?—but afraid for the people also, for there will be many fools like you; and women, too, perhaps, as foolish as those up there," and he swung the point of his stick toward the camp.

After a little, "Do you know how I came by my pretty looks?" he asked suddenly. And then, as Kelderek said nothing, "Well, do you know or not?"

"Your disfigurement, my lord? No—how should I know?"

"How should *I* know what tales are told in the pothouses of Ortelga?"

"I'm something of a stranger to those, my lord, as you know, and if there is a tale, I never heard it."

"You shall hear it now. Long ago, while I was still little more than a lad, I used to go out with the Ortelgan hunters—now with one and now with another, for my father was powerful and could require it of them. He wanted me to learn both what hunting teaches lads and what hunters can teach them; and I was ready enough to learn on my own account. I traveled far from Ortelga. I have crossed the mountains of Gelt and hunted the long-horned buck on the plains southwest of Kabin. And I have crossed to Deelguy and stood two hours up to my neck in the Lake of Klamsid to net the golden cranes at dawn."

They had reached the lower end of a pool into which the brook came down in a little fall something higher than a man. On either side extended a steep bank, and beside the pool a *melikon* stretched its trim, crisp-leaved branches over the water. This is the tree that the peasants call "False Lasses." The bright, pretty berries that follow the flowers are unfit to eat and of no use, but toward summer's end their color turns to a glinting, powdery gold and they fall of their own accord in the stillest of air. Bel-ka-Trazet stooped, drank from his hands and then sat down with his back against the bank and the long stick upright between his raised knees. Kelderek sat uneasily beside him. Afterward, he remembered the harsh voice, the slow turning of the stars, the sound of the water and now and again the light plop as a berry fell into the pool.

"I have hunted with Durakkon, and with Senda-na-Say. I was with the Barons of Ortelga thirty years ago, when we hunted the Blue Forest of Katria as the guests of the king of Terekenalt and killed the leopard they called the Blacksmith. That was King Karnat, who was almost a giant. We were merry after the hunt and we weighed him against the Blacksmith; but the Blacksmith turned the scale. The Barons were pleased with the part I had played in the hunt and they gave me the Blacksmith's eyeteeth, but I gave them to a girl later. Yes," said Bel-ka-Trazet reflectively, "I gave them to a girl who used to be glad to see my face.

"Well, it's no matter, lad, what I've seen or known, though I sit here bragging to the stars that saw it long ago and can tell the truth from the lies. By the time I had become a young man there was not a baron or a hunter in Ortelga who was not eager and proud to hunt with me. I hunted with whom I would and declined company that I thought too poor for the name I had made for myself. I was—ah!" He broke off, thumping the butt of his stick on the grass—"You have heard old, wrinkled women round a fire, have you, talking of their lovers and their beauty?

"One day a lord from Bekla, one Zilkron of the Arrows, came to visit my father with presents. This Zilkron had heard of my

9 3

father in Bekla—how he drew the best hunters about him, and of the skill and courage of his son. He gave my father gold and fine cloth; and the heart of it was that he wanted us to take him hunting. My father did not fancy this soap-using lord from Bekla but, like all the flea-bitten barons of Ortelga, he could not afford to refuse gold; so he said to me, 'Come, my lad, we'll take him across the Telthearna and find him one of the great, savage cats. That should send him home with a tale or two.'

"Now the truth was that my father knew less than he supposed about the great cats—the cats that weigh twice as much as a man, kill cattle and alligators and rip open the shells of turtles when they come ashore to lay their eggs. The plain truth is that they are too dangerous to hunt, unless one traps them. By this time I knew what could and could not be done and did not need to prove to myself that I was no coward. But I did not want to tell my father that I knew better than he. So I began to think how I could best go to work behind his back to save our lives.

"We crossed the Telthearna and began by hunting the green-and-black water serpents, the leopard killers that grow to four or five times the length of a man. Have you hunted them?"

"Never, my lord," replied Kelderek.

"They are found by night, near rivers, and they are fierce and dangerous. They have no poison, but kill by crushing. We were resting by day, so that I spent much idle time with Zilkron. I came to know him well, his pride and vanity, his splendid weapons and equipment which he did not know how to use, and his trick of capping hunters' talk with tales he had heard elsewhere. And always I worked on him to make him think that the great cats were not worth his while and that he would do better to hunt some other beast. But he was no coward and no fool and soon I saw that I would have to pay some real price to change his mind, for he had come of set purpose to buy danger of which he could go home and boast in Bekla. At last I spoke of bears. What trophy, I asked, could compare with a bearskin, head and claws and all? Inwardly I knew that the danger would still be great, but at least I knew of bears that they are not constantly savage and that they have poor sight and can sometimes be confused. Also, in rocky or hilly country you can sometimes get

94

above them and so use a spear or an arrow before they have seen you. The long and short of it was that Zilkron decided that what he wanted was a bear and he spoke to my father.

"My father was of two minds, for as Ortelgans we had no business to be killing bears. At first he was afraid of the idea, but we were far from home, the Tuginda would never get to hear and none of us was pious or devout. At length we set off for the Shardra-Main, the Bear Hills, and reached them in three days.

"We went up into the hills and hired some villagers as trackers and guides. They led us higher, on to a rocky plateau, very cold. The bears, they said, lived there but often came down to raid farms and hunt in the woods below. No doubt the villagers had learned something from the bears, for they too stole all they could. One of them stole a tortoiseshell comb that Zilkron had given me, but I never found out which was the thief.

"On the second day we found a bear—a big bear that made Zilkron point and chatter foolishly when he saw it moving far off against the sky. We followed it carefully, for I was sure that if it came to feel that it was being driven, it would slip away down one or another side of the mountain, and we would lose it altogether. When we reached the place where we had seen it, it had disappeared, and there was nothing to do but to go higher and hope to get a sight of it from above. We did not see it again all that day. We camped high up, in the best shelter we could find; and very cold it was.

"The next morning, just as it was getting light, I woke to hear strange noises—breaking sticks, a sack dragged, a pot rolling on its side. It was not like fighting, but more like some drunken fellow stumbling about to find his bed. I was lying in a little cleft like a passage, out of the wind, and I got up and went outside to see what was amiss.

"What was amiss was the bear. The Beklan lout on guard had fallen asleep, the fire had burned low and no one had seen the bear come shambling into the camp. He was going through our rations, such as they were, and helping himself. He had got hold of a bag of dried tendriona and was dragging it about. The village fellows were all lying flat, and still as stones. As I watched, he patted one of them with his paw, as much as to tell him not to be afraid. I thought, 'If I can get up on some high spot, where he can't reach me, I can wait until he is clear of the camp and then put an arrow in him'—for I was not going to wound him in the camp, among men who had had no warning. I slipped back for my bow and climbed up the side of the little cleft where I had been sleeping. I came out on top of the rock and there was our fine friend just below me, with his head buried in the bag, munching away and wagging his tail like a lamb at the ewe. I could have leaned down and touched his back. He heard me, pulled his head out and stood up on his hind legs; and then—you may believe this or not, Kelderek, just as you please—he looked me in the face and bowed to me, with his front paws folded together. Then he dropped on all fours and trotted away.

"While I was staring after him, up comes Zilkron and two of his servants, all set to follow. I put them off with some excuse or other—a lame one it must have been, for Zilkron shrugged his shoulders without a word and I saw his men catch each other's eye. I left them to make what they cared out of it. I was like you, Kelderek—and like every man in Ortelga, I dare say. Now that I had come face to face with a bear, I was not going to kill him and I was not going to let Zilkron kill him either. But I did not know what to do, for I could not say, 'Now let us all turn round and go home.'

"My father, after he had heard Zilkron's story, asked me privately whether I had been afraid. I tried to tell him something of what I felt, but he had never actually encountered a bear and merely looked perplexed.

"That day I bribed the leader of the villagers to guide us in such a way that it would look as though we were after the bear, but actually to take us where we were unlikely to find it. It was nothing to him—he merely grinned and took the price. By night-fall we had seen nothing more and I fell asleep wondering what I should do next.

"I was woken by Zilkron. A full moon was setting and frost was glittering on the rocks. His face was full of triumph—and mockery too, I fancied. He whispered, 'He's here again, my lad!' He was holding his big, painted bow with the green silk tassels and hand grip of polished jet. As soon as he was sure I was awake, he left me. I got up and stumbled after him. The villagers were huddled behind a rock but my father and Zilkron's two servants were standing out in the open.

"The bear was certainly coming. He was coming like a fellow on his way to the fair—trotting along and licking his lips. He'd seen our fire and smelled the food. I thought, 'He has never come across men until yesterday. He does not know we mean to kill him.' The fire was burning bright enough but he did not seem afraid of it. He came clambering over a little pile of rocks and began nosing round the foot. I suppose the cooks had left some food there.

"Zilkron laid a hand on my shoulder and I could feel his gold rings against my collarbone. 'Don't be afraid,' he said. 'Don't be afraid, my lad. I'll have three arrows in him before he has time even to think of charging.' He went closer. I followed him and the bear turned and saw us.

"One of Zilkron's men—an old fellow who had looked after him since he was a child—called out, 'No nearer, my lord.' Zilkron flapped his hand behind him without looking back and then drew his bow.

"At that moment the bear stood up once more on his hind legs and looked straight at me, his head inclined and his front paws one over the other, and gave two little grunts, 'Ah! Ah!' As Zilkron loosed the string I struck his arm. The arrow split a branch in the fire and the sparks flew up in a shower.

"Zilkron turned on me very quietly, as though he had been half-expecting something of the sort. 'You stupid little coward,' he said, 'get back over there.' I stepped in front of him and walked toward the bear—my bear, who was begging a man of Ortelga to save him from this golden oaf.

"'Get out of the way!' shouted Zilkron. I looked round to answer him and in that instant the bear was down upon me. I felt a heavy blow on my left shoulder and then he had wrapped me about and was clutching me against him, gnawing and biting at my face. The wetness and sweetness of his breath was the last thing I felt.

"When I came to myself, it was three days later and we were back in the hill village. Zilkron had left us, for my father had heard him call me coward and they had quarreled bitterly. We stayed there two months. My father used to sit by my bed and talk, and hold my hand, and tell old tales, and then fall silent, the tears standing in his eyes as he looked at what was left of his splendid son."

Bel-ka-Trazet gave a short laugh. "He took it hard. He'd learned less of life than I, now I'm his age. But that's no matter. Why do you think I sent my servants back from Quiso and came here unattended? I will tell you, Kelderek, and mark me well. As you are a man of Ortelga, so you cannot help feeling the power of the bear. And every man in Ortelga will feel it, unless we see to it—you and I—that things go otherwise. If we cannot, then in one way or another all Ortelga will be set awry and smashed, just as my face and body have been smashed. The bear is a folly, a madness, treacherous, unpredictable, a storm to wreck and drown you when you think yourself in calm water. Believe me, Kelderek, never trust the bear. He'll promise you the power of God and betray you to ruin and misery."

Bel-ka-Trazet stopped and looked up sharply. From beyond the top of the bank a heavy, stumbling tread shook the branches of the melikon so that a perfect cascade of berries tumbled into the pool. Then, immediately above them, there appeared against the brilliant stars a huge, hunched shape. Kelderek, springing to his feet, found himself looking up into the bleared and peering eyes of Shardik.

12 *The Baron's Departure*

WITHOUT GETTING UP or taking his eyes from the bear, Bel-ka-Trazet groped in the water behind him, picked up a stone and tossed it into the darkness beyond the bank. As it fell the bear turned its head and the Baron stepped quickly into the pool, wading under the cascade and into the narrow space between the curtain of falling water and the bank behind. Kelderek remained where he was as the bear once more looked down at him. Its eyes were dull and there was a trembling, now in the front legs and now in the head itself. Suddenly the creature's massive shoulders convulsed. In a low, sharp voice, Bel-ka-Trazet said, "Kelderek, come back here!"

Once more the hunter found himself without fear, sharing, with spontaneous insight at which he had no time to wonder, the bear's own perceptions. They, he knew, were dulled with pain. Feeling that pain, he felt also the impulse to wander blindly away, to seek relief in restlessness and movement. To strike, to kill would have been a still greater relief, but the pain had induced an insuperable feebleness and confusion. He realized now that the bear had not seen him. It was peering, not at him but at the slope of the bank and hesitating, in its weakness, to descend it. As he still stood motionless, it sank slowly down until he could feel upon his face the moisture of its breath. Again Bel-ka-Trazet called, "Kelderek!"

The bear was sliding, toppling forward. Its fall was like the collapse of a bridge in a flood. As though through the creature's own dimmed eyes, Kelderek saw the ground at the foot of the bank rising to meet him and lurched aside from the suddenly perceived figure of a man—himself. He was standing in the water as Shardik, with a commotion like that of shipwreck, clawed, fell and rolled to the edge of the pool. He watched him as a child watches grown men fighting—intensely, shockingly aware, yet at the same time unafraid for himself. At length the bear lay still. Its eyes were closed and one of the wounds along its flank had begun to bleed, slow and thick as cream, upon the grass.

It was growing light and Kelderek could hear from behind him the first raucous cries in the awakening forest. Without a word Bel-ka-Trazet stepped through the waterfall, drew his knife and dropped on one knee in front of the motionless bulk. The bear's head was sunk on its chest, so that the long jaw covered the slack of the throat. The Baron was moving to one side for his blow when Kelderek stepped forward and twisted the knife out of his hand.

Bel-ka-Trazet turned on him with a cold rage so terrible that the hunter's words froze on his lips.

"You dare to lay your hands on *me!*" whispered the Baron through his teeth. "Give me that knife!"

Confronted, for the second time, by the anger and authority of the High Baron of Ortelga, Kelderek actually staggered, as though he had been struck. To himself, a man of no rank or position, obedience to authority was almost second nature. He dropped his eyes, shuffled his feet and began to mutter unintelligibly.

"Give me that knife," repeated Bel-ka-Trazet quietly.

Suddenly Kelderek turned and fled. Clutching the knife, he stumbled through the pool and clambered to the top of the bank. Looking back, he saw that Bel-ka-Trazet was not pursuing him, but had lifted a heavy rock in both hands and was standing beside the bear, holding it above his head.

With a hysterical feeling like that of a man leaping for his life from a high place, Kelderek picked up a stone and threw it. It struck Bel-ka-Trazet on the back of the neck. As he flung back his head and sank to his knees, the rock slipped from between his hands and fell across the calf of his right leg. For a few moments he knelt quite still, head thrown upward and mouth gaping wide; then, without haste, he released his leg, stood up and looked at Kelderek with an air of purposeful intent more frightening even than his anger.

The hunter knew that if he were not himself to die, he must now go down and kill Bel-ka-Trazet—and that he could not do it. With a low cry he raised his hands to his face and ran blindly up the course of the brook.

He had gone perhaps fifty yards when someone gripped his arm. "Kelderek," said the Tuginda's voice, "what has happened?"

Unable to answer, bemused as the bear itself, he could only point, with a shaking arm, back toward the fall. At once she hastened away, followed by Sheldra and four or five of the girls carrying their bows.

He listened but could hear nothing. Still full of fear and irresolution, he wondered whether he might yet escape Bel-ka-Trazet by hiding in the forest and later, somehow, contriving to cross to the mainland. He was about to resume his flight when suddenly it occurred to him that he was no longer alone and defenseless against the Baron, as he had been three days before. He was the messenger of Shardik, the bringer of God's tidings to Quiso. Certainly the Tuginda, if she knew what had been attempted and prevented by the pool that morning, would never stand by and allow Bel-ka-Trazet to kill him.

"We are the Vessels, she and I," he thought. "She will save me. Shardik himself will save me; not for love, or because I have done him any service, but simply because he has need of me and therefore it is ordained that I am to live. God is to shatter the Vessels to fragments and Himself fashion them again to His purpose. Whatever that may mean, it cannot mean my death at the hands of Bel-ka-Trazet."

He rose to his feet, splashed through the brook and made his way back to the fall. Below him the High Baron, leaning on his staff, was deep in talk with the Tuginda. Neither looked up as he appeared above them. One of the girls had stripped herself to the waist and, on her knees, was staunching with her own garments the flow of blood from the bear's opened wound. The rest were standing together a little distance away, silent and watchful as cattle round a gate.

"Well, I have done what I could, säiyett," said the Baron grimly. "Yes, if I could I would have killed your bear sure enough, but it was not to be."

"That in itself should make you think again," she answered.

"What I think of this business will not change," said he. "I do not know what you intend, säiyett, but I will tell you what I intend. The first has brought a large bear to this island. Bears are mischievous, dangerous creatures, and people who think otherwise come to loss and harm through them. As long as it remains in this lonely place, to risk lives is not worthwhile, but if it moves down the island and begins to plague Ortelga, I promise you I will have it killed."

"And I intend nothing but to wait upon the will of God," replied the Tuginda.

Bel-ka-Trazet shrugged again. "I only hope the will of God will not turn out to be your own death, säiyett. But now that you know what I intended, perhaps you have it in mind to tell your women to put *me* to death? Certainly I am in your power."

"Since I have no plans and you have been prevented from killing Lord Shardik, you are doing us no harm." She turned away with an air of indifference, but he strode after her.

"Then two things more, säiyett. First, since I am to live, perhaps you will permit me now to return to Ortelga. If you will give me a canoe, I will see that it returns to you. Then, as for the hunter fellow, I have already told you what he has just done. He is my subject, not yours. I trust you will not hinder me from finding and killing him."

"I am sending two of the girls to Quiso with a canoe. They will put you off at Ortelga. I cannot spare the hunter. He is necessary to me."

With this the Tuginda walked away and began speaking to the girls with complete absorption, pointing first up the slope and then down toward the river as she gave her instructions. For a moment the Baron seemed about to follow her again. Then he shrugged his shoulders, turned and climbed the bank, passed Kelderek without a glance and walked on in the direction of the camp. He was suppressing a limp and his terrible face appeared so gray and haggard that Kelderek, who had been preparing to defend himself as best he could, trembled and averted his eyes as though from some fearful apparition. "He is afraid!" he thought. "He knows now that he cannot prevail against Lord Shardik, and he is afraid!"

Suddenly he sprang forward, calling, "My lord! O my lord, forgive me!" But the Baron, as though he had heard nothing, stalked on and Kelderek stood looking after him—at the livid bruise across the back of his neck and the heavy black pelt swinging from side to side above the grass.

He never saw Bel-ka-Trazet again.

13 *The Singing*

ALL THAT DAY Shardik lay beside the brook, shaded, as the sun crossed the meridian, by the bank above and the boughs of the melikon. The two girls who had been watching in the pit during the night had acted prudently enough when the bear first struggled to its feet and wandered up the slope. At first they had thought that it was too weak to reach the top, but when it had actually done so and then, though almost exhausted, had begun to make its way downhill toward the brook, the older girl, Muni, had followed it, while her comrade went to wake the Tuginda. In fact, Muni had been only a short distance away when Shardik collapsed beside the pool, but had not seen Kelderek in her haste to return and bring the Tuginda to the place.

The girls sent to Quiso were back before midnight, for without the long detour across the river their upstream journey was much shorter than the first. They brought fresh supplies of the cleansing ointment, together with other medicines and an herbal narcotic. This the Tuginda immediately administered to the bear herself, soaked in thin segments of tendriona. For some hours the drug had little effect, but by morning Shardik was sleeping heavily and did not stir while the burns were cleaned once more.

On the afternoon of the following day, as Kelderek was returning from the forest, where he had been setting snares, he came upon Sheldra standing on the open grass a little way from the camp. Following her gaze he saw, some distance off, the figure of an unusually tall woman, cloaked and cowled, striding up the slope beside the brook. He recognized her as the lantern-bearer whom he had met by night upon the shore of Quiso. Still further away, by the river, six or seven other women were evidently setting out for the camp, each carrying a load.

"Who is that?" asked Kelderek, pointing.

"Rantzay," replied Sheldra, without turning her eyes toward him.

There was still not one of the girls with whom Kelderek felt at ease. Even among themselves they spoke little, using words as they used knives or thread, simply as a means to complete their tasks. There was no contempt for him, however, in their somber reticence, which in fact he found daunting for precisely the opposite reason—because it suggested respect and seemed to confer upon him a dignity, even an authority, to which he was unused. They saw him, not as the girls in Ortelga saw a young man but, as they saw everything else, in the light of the cult to which their lives were devoted. Their manner showed that they felt him to be a person of importance, the one who had first seen and recognized Lord Shardik and had then come, at the risk of his life, to bring the news to the Tuginda. Sheldra's present reply was not intended contemptuously. She had answered him as briefly as she would have answered any of her companions and had even, perhaps, forgotten that he, unlike them, did not know the island priestesses by name. He felt it an omission rather than a slight that she should in effect have told him nothing. She had not used as many words as were necessary for informing him, just as she might (though practical and competent) have put too little water in a pail or not enough wood on the fire. Sure of this at least, he summoned the confidence to speak firmly.

"Tell me who Rantzay is," he said, "and why she and those other women have been brought here."

For a few moments Sheldra did not answer and he thought, "She is going to ignore me." Then she replied, "Of those who came with the Tuginda, Melathys was the only priestess. The rest of us are novices or servants."

"But Melathys must have been almost as young as any," said Kelderek.

"Melathys was not an Ortelgan. She was rescued from a slave camp during the Beklan civil wars—the wars of the Heldril—and brought to the Ledges when she was a child. She learned many of the mysteries very early."

"Well?" demanded Kelderek, as the girl said no more.

"When the Tuginda knew that Lord Shardik had indeed returned and that we must remain here to tend and cure him, she sent for the priestesses Anthred and Rantzay, together with the girls whom they are instructing. When Shardik recovers they will be needed for the Singing."

She fell silent again, but then broke out suddenly, "Those who served Lord Shardik long ago had need of all their courage and resolution."

"I believe you," answered Kelderek, looking down to where the bear, like a crag beside the pool, still lay in drugged sleep. Yet in the same moment there rose in his heart an abandoned elation and the conviction that to none but the Tuginda herself had it been given to feel so intensely as he the fierce and mysterious divinity of Shardik. Shardik was more than life to him, a fire in which he was ready—nay, eager—to be consumed. And for that very reason Shardik would transform but not destroy him—this he knew. As though with foreboding, he trembled for an instant in the sultry air, turned and made his way back to the camp.

That night the Tuginda talked with him again, walking slowly back and forth along the bank above the fall, where stood burning that safe flat, green-rush-shaded lantern that he had followed across the leaping tree trunk in the dark. Rantzay, a head taller than himself, kept pace with them on the Tuginda's other side, and as he saw her checking her long stride out of deference to the Tuginda and himself, he remembered with a certain wry amusement how he had groped and clambered after her through the steep woods. They spoke of Shardik, and the gaunt, silent priestess listened attentively.

"His wounds are clean," said the Tuginda. "The poison has almost left them. The drugs and medicines always work strongly on any creature, whether human or animal, that has never known them before. We can be almost certain now that he will recover. If you had found him only a few hours later, Kelderek, he would have been past our help."

Kelderek felt that now at last was the time to ask her the question that had been flickering in his mind for the past three days, vanishing and reappearing like a firefly in a dark room.

"What are we going to do, säiyett, when he recovers?"

"I do not know any more than you. We must wait until we are shown."

He blundered on. "But do you mean to take him to Quiso— to the Ledges?"

"*I* mean?" For a moment she looked at him coldly, as she had looked at Bel-ka-Trazet, but then answered in a brisk, matter-of-fact tone, "You must understand, Kelderek, that it is not for us to make schemes and put them into practice upon Lord Shardik. It is true, as I told you, that sometimes, long ago, it was the Tuginda's task to bring Shardik home to the Ledges. But those were days when we ruled in Bekla and all was ordered and sure. Now, at this moment, we know nothing, except that Lord Shardik has returned to his people. His message and his purpose we cannot yet discern. Our work is simply to wait, to be ready to perceive and to carry out God's will, whatever it may be."

They turned and began to walk back toward the fall.

"But that does not mean that we are not to think shrewdly and act prudently," she went on. "By the day after tomorrow the bear will no longer be drugged and will begin to recover its strength. You are a hunter. What do you think it will do then?"

Kelderek felt perplexed. His question had been returned to him without an answer. In spite of what he had heard her say to Bel-ka-Trazet, it had never occurred to him that the Tuginda had not in her mind some plan for bringing Shardik to the Ledges. What had been puzzling him was how it was to be done, for even if the bear were to remain drugged the difficulties seemed formidable. Now he realized, with a shock, that she intended simply to stand by while this enormous wild animal regained its natural strength. If this was indeed—as she evidently believed—the course of humility and faith in God, it was of a kind beyond his experience or understanding. For the first time his trust in her began to waver.

She read his thoughts. "We are not buying rope in the market, Kelderek, or selling skins to the factor. Nor are we laboring for the High Baron by digging a pit in the forest, or even choosing a wife. We are offering our lives to God and Lord Shardik in pledging ourselves humbly to accept whatever He may vouchsafe to give in return. I asked you—what is the bear likely to do?"

"It is in a strange place that it does not know, säiyett, and will be hungry after its illness. It will look for food and may well be savage."

"Will it wander?"

"I have been thinking that soon we shall all be forced to wander. We have little food left and I cannot hunt alone for so many."

"Since we can be sure that the High Baron would refuse to send us food from Ortelga, we must do the best we can. There are fish in the river and ducks in the reeds, and we have nets and bows. Choose six of the girls and take them out to hunt with you. There may be little enough to share at first, but there will be more as they learn their business."

"It can be done for a time, säiyett—"

"Kelderek, are you impatient? Whom have you left in Ortelga?"

"No one, säiyett. My parents are dead and I am not married."

"A girl?"

He shook his head, but she continued to gaze at him gravely. "There are girls here. Commit no sacrilege, now of all times, for the least ill to follow would be our death."

He broke out indignantly, "Säiyett, how can you think—"

She only looked steadily at him, holding his eyes, as they paced on and turned about once more under the stars. And before his inward sight rose the figure of Melathys on the terrace; Melathys, dark-haired, white-robed, with the golden collar covering her neck and shoulders; Melathys laughing as she played with the arrow and the sword; trembling and sweating with fear on the edge of the pit. Where was she now? What had become of her? His protest faltered and ceased.

Next day began a life which he was often to recall in after years—a life as clear, as simple and immediate as rain. If he had ever doubted the Tuginda or wondered what was to come of her humility and faith, he had no time to remember it. At first the girls were so awkward and stupid that he was in despair and more than once on the point of telling the Tuginda that the task was beyond him. On the first day, while they were driving a ketlana toward open ground, Zilthé, a mere child and the youngest of his huntresses, whom he had picked for her quickness and energy, mistook his movement in a thicket for that of the quarry and loosed an arrow that passed between his arm and body. They killed so little all day that he felt compelled to spend the night fishing. In the starlit shallows they netted a great *bramba*, spine-finned and luminous as an opal. He was about to spear it when the ill-fixed anchor stake carried away and the fish, plunging heavily, took half the net down with it into the deep water. Nito bit her lip and said nothing.

By the second evening the whole camp was hungry and the thin, ragged bear was kept half-drugged and fed with scraps of fish and ill-spared flour-cakes baked in the ashes.

But necessity brings out a desperate skill in the clumsiest. Several of the girls were at least passable shots and on the third day they were lucky enough to kill five or six geese. They feasted that night by the fire, telling old stories of Bekla long ago, of the hero Deparioth, liberator of Yelda and founder of

Sarkid, and of Fleitil, immortal craftsman of the Tamarrik Gate; and singing together in strange harmonies unknown to Kelderek, who listened with a kind of tremulous unease as their voices followed each other round and down, like the fall of the Ledges themselves between the woods of Quiso.

Soon, indeed, he had forgotten everything but the life of the moment—the wet grass of early morning, when he stood to pray with hands raised toward the distant river; the smell of the trepsis as they searched beneath its leaves for the little gourds that had ripened since the day before; the green light and heat of the forest and the tense glances between the girls as they waited in ambush with arrows on the string; the scent of jasmine at evening and the *chunk, chunk*, regular as a mill wheel, of the paddles as they made their way upstream to net some likely pool. After the first few days the girls learned quickly and he was able to send them out by twos and threes, some to fish, some to follow a trail in the forest or hide in the reeds for wildfowl. He was kept busy making arrows—for they lost far too many—until he had taught Muni to make them better than he could himself. Ortelga he put from his mind, and his fear of Bel-ka-Trazet's revenge. At first he dreamed vividly of the Baron, who rose out of the ground with a face of broken stones and beckoned him to follow into the forest, where the bear was waiting, or walked upon the shore and threw back his cowl to reveal a face of flickering heat, half-consumed, red and gray as the glowing surface of a log flaking in the fire. But soon his dreams changed, turning to vaporous, elusive impressions of stars and flowers reflected in dark water, or of clouds drifting over ruined walls far off upon an empty plain; or he would seem to hear the Tuginda speaking sorrowfully, accusing him, in words that he could never recall, of some ill deed as yet unperformed. It was not that he had ceased either to fear for his life or to believe that the future held danger. He had simply put these things aside, living, like the other creatures of forest and river, from hour to hour, his senses full of sounds and smells, his mind concerned only with his craft. Often he snatched sleep as a beast snatches it, by night or day wherever he found himself, and would be roused by a grave, breathless girl with news of a flight of ducks off-shore or a band of monkeys approaching through the trees a mile away. All quarry brought in was accepted without question; and often, when Neelith gave him his share out of the iron pot hanging over the fire, he could not imagine what meat it might be, only feeling glad that some of the girls had evidently been successful without his help.

It was on the fifth or sixth day after Sheldra had returned from Ortelga with his bow (which she had apparently been able to recover without troubling Bel-ka-Trazet) that Kelderek was standing with Zilthé a little inside the forest, about half a mile from the camp. They were in hiding beside a barely visible track that led to the shore, waiting for whatever animal might appear. It was evening and the sunlight had begun to redden the branches above him. Suddenly he heard at a distance the sound of women's voices singing. As he listened, the hair rose on his neck. He remembered the wordless songs by the fire. To his mind those had suggested, transmuted indeed yet still familiar, the sound of wind in leaves, of waves on the river, of the pitching of canoes in choppy water and the falling of rain. What he heard now resembled the movement, over centuries, of things that to men seem motionless only because their own lives are short: the movement of trees as they grow and die, of stars altering their relative places in the heavens, of mountains slowly ground away through millennia of heat, frost and storm. It was like the building of a city. Great, squared blocks of antiphonal sound were sung and lowered into place, one upon another, until the heart stood far below, gazing up at the clouds marching endlessly across the dark line of the completed ramparts. Zilthé was standing with closed eyes and outstretched palms. Kelderek, though he saw nothing and felt afraid, seemed to himself to have been lifted to some plane on which there was no more need of prayer, since the harmony that is continually present to the mind of God had been made audible to his own prostrate, worshiping soul. He had sunk to his knees and his mouth was twisted like that of a man in agony. Still listening, he heard the singing diminish and then slide quickly into silence, like a diver into deep water.

He rose and began to walk slowly toward the edge of the forest. Yet it was as though he, awake, observed himself mov-

ing in a dream. The dream was his own life of time and sensation, of hunger and thirst, which he now watched from a
pinnacle of shining silence. He saw his forearm scratched by a
spray of trazada and felt, far-off in his flesh, an echo of pain.
Slowly, very slowly, he floated down to rejoin his body. They
came together as broken reflections resolve on the surface of a
pool returning to stillness; and he found himself looking out
across the open grass and scratching his arm.

Shardik, the sun sinking behind him, was approaching down
the slope, now rambling uncertainly here and there, now halting
to gaze about at the trees and the distant river. At some distance
from him, in a wide half-circle, moved eight or nine of the
women, among them Rantzay and the Tuginda. When he hesitated they too paused, swaying in the rhythm of their chant,
equidistant one from another, the evening wind stirring their
hair and the fringes of their tunics. As he went on they moved
with him, so that he remained always central and ahead of them.
None showed haste or fear. Watching, Kelderek was reminded
of the instinctive, simultaneous turning of a flock of birds in
the air, or a shoal of fish in clear water.

It was plain that Shardik was half-bemused, though whether
from the continuing effect of the drug or the hypnotic sound of
the singing the hunter could not tell. The women pivoted about
him like wind-tossed branches radiating from the trunk of a
tree. Suddenly Kelderek felt a longing to join in their dangerous
and beautiful dance, to offer his life to Shardik, to prove himself
one among those to whom the power of Shardik had been revealed and through whom that power could flow into the world.
And with this longing came a conviction—though if he were
wrong it mattered nothing—that Shardik would not harm him.
He stepped out from beneath the trees and made his way up
the slope.

Until he was less than a stone's throw off, neither the women
nor the bear gave any sign of having seen him. Then the bear,
which had been moving toward the river rather than the forest,
stopped, turning its lowered head toward him. The hunter also
stopped and stood waiting, one hand raised in greeting. The
setting sun was dazzling him, but of this he was unaware.
Through the bear's eyes, he saw himself standing alone on the
hillside.

The bear peered uncertainly across the sunlit grass. Then it came toward the solitary figure of the hunter, approaching until it appeared as a dark mass before his light-blinded eyes and he could hear its breathing and the dry, clashing sound of its claws. Its rank smell was all about him, yet he was aware only of the smell of himself to Shardik, puzzled and uncertain in his awakening from illness and drugged sleep, afraid because of his own weakness and his unfamiliar surroundings. He sniffed suspiciously at the human creature standing before him, but remained unstartled by any sudden movement or act of fear on its part. He could hear once more the voices, now on one side of him, now on the other, answering each other in layers of sound, bewildering him and confusing his savagery. He went forward again, in the only direction from which they did not come, and as he did so the human creature, toward whom he felt no enmity, turned and moved with him toward the twilight and safety of the woods.

At a signal from the Tuginda the women stood still, each in her place, as Shardik, with the hunter walking beside him, entered the outskirts of the forest and disappeared among the trees.

14 *Lord Kelderek*

THAT NIGHT KELDEREK SLEPT on the bare ground beside Shardik, with no thought of fire or food, of leopards, snakes or other dangers of darkness. Nor did he think of Bel-ka-Trazet, of the Tuginda or of what might be taking place in the camp. As Melathys had laid the sword's edge to her neck, so Kelderek lay secure beside the bear. Waking in the night, he saw its back like a roof-ridge against the stars and returned at once into a sleep tranquil and reassured. When morning came, with a gray cold and the chittering of birds in the branches, he opened his eyes in time to catch sight of Shardik wandering away among the bushes. He rose stiffly to his feet and stood shivering in the chill, flexing his limbs and touching his face with his hands as though his wondering spirit had but newly entered this body for the first time. In some other place, he knew, in some other region, invisible yet not remote, insubstantial yet more real than the forest and the river, Shardik and Kelderek were one creature, the whole and the part, as the scarlet trumpet-flower is part of the rough-leaved, spreading stolon of the trepsis vine. Musing he made no attempt to follow the bear, but when it was gone turned back to seek his companions.

Almost at once he came upon Rantzay alone in a clearing, cloaked against the cold and leaning upon a staff. As he approached she bent her head, raising her palm to her brow. Her hand shook, but whether from cold or fear he could not tell.

"Why are you here?" he asked with quiet authority.

"Lord, one of us remained near you all night, for we did not know—we did not know what might befall. Are you leaving Lord Shardik now?"

"For a while. Tell three of the girls to follow him and try to keep him in sight. One should return at noon with news of where he is. Unless he can find it for himself he will need food."

She touched her forehead again, waited as he walked away and then followed behind him as he returned to the camp. The Tuginda had gone down to bathe in the river and he ate alone, Neelith bringing him food and drink and serving him in silence on one knee. When at last he saw the Tuginda returning he went to meet her. The girls with her at once fell back, and again he talked with her, alone beside the fall. Now, however, it was the hunter who questioned, the Tuginda paying him close heed and answering him carefully yet without reserve, as a woman answers a man whom she trusts to guide and help her.

"The Singing, säiyett," he began. "What is the Singing and what is its purpose?"

"It is one of the old secrets," she replied, "of the days when Lord Shardik dwelt upon the Ledges. It has been preserved from that time to this. Those long ago who offered the Singing showed, by that, that they offered their lives also. This is why no woman on Quiso has ever been ordered to become a singer. Each who determines to attain to it must do so of her own accord; and though we can teach her what we know ourselves, always there is a part which remains a matter of God's will and her own. The art cannot be sought for self-advancement or to please others, but only to satisfy the singer's own longing to offer all that she has. So if the will and devotion of the singers were to falter—or so I was taught—the power of the Singing would falter too. Before yesterday evening no woman now alive had ever taken part in offering the Singing to Lord Shardik. I thanked God when I saw that its power had not been lost."

"What is the power?"

She looked at him in surprise. "But you know what it is, Lord Kelderek Zenzuata. Why do you ask for words, to go on crutches, when you have felt it leaping and burning in your heart?"

"I know what the Singing did to me, säiyett. But it was not to me that it was offered last night."

"I cannot tell you what takes place in the heart of Lord Shardik. Indeed, I believe now that you know more of that than I. But as I learned long ago, it is a way by which we come nearer to him and to God. By worshiping him thus we put a narrow, swaying bridge across the ravine that separates his savage nature from our own; and so in time we become able to walk without stumbling through the fire of his presence."

Kelderek pondered this for some little time. At length he asked, "Can he be controlled, then—driven—by the Singing?"

She shook her head. "No—Lord Shardik can never be driven, for he is the Power of God. But the Singing, when it is offered devoutly, with sincerity and courage, is like that power which we have over weapons. It overcomes for a time his savagery and as he grows accustomed to it, so he comes to accept it as the due worship which we offer to him. Nevertheless, Kelderek—" she smiled—"*Lord* Kelderek, do not think that any man or woman could have done what you did last night, simply because of the Singing. Shardik is always more dangerous than lightning, more uncertain than the Telthearna in the rains. You are his Vessel, or you would now be broken like the leopard."

"Säiyett, why did you let the Baron go? He hates Lord Shardik."

"Was I to murder him? To overcome his hard heart with a harder? What could have come of that? He is not a wicked man, and God sees all. Did I not hear you yourself begging him for forgiveness as he strode away?"

"But do you believe that he will be content to leave Lord Shardik unharmed?"

"I believe, as I have always believed, that neither he nor anyone can prevent Lord Shardik from performing that which he has come to perform and imparting that which he has come to impart. But I say yet again—what will ensue we can only await with humility. To devise some purpose of our own and try to make use of Lord Shardik for that end—that would be sacrilege and folly."

"So you have taught me, säiyett; but now I will dare to advise you also. We should perfect our service of Lord Shardik as a man prepares the weapons with which he knows he will have to fight for his life. Worship yields nothing to the slipshod and half-hearted. I have seen men's worship which, if it had been a roof they had built, would not have kept out half an hour's rain; nor had they even the wit to wonder why it left their hearts cold and yielded them neither strength nor comfort. Lord Shardik is in truth the Power of God, but his worshipers will reap only what they sow. How many women have we, both here and on Quiso, who are adept in the Singing and able to serve close to Lord Shardik without fear, as they did long ago?"

"I cannot yet tell—perhaps no more than ten or twelve. As I said, it is more than a matter of skill and brave hearts, for it may turn out that Lord Shardik himself will accept some but not others. You know how a child in Ortelga may train to be a dancer and dream of breaking hearts in Bekla; but she grows up unshapely or too tall and there's an end."

"All this we must search out and prove, säiyett—his singers must be sure as an Ortelgan rope in a storm, his hunting-girls observant and tireless. He will wander now; and as he wanders, so we can perfect our work, if only we are given time."

"Time?" she asked, standing still to face him—and he saw once more the shrewd, homely woman with the ladle who had met him below the Ledges. "Time, Kelderek?"

"Time, säiyett. For sooner or later, either Shardik will go to Ortelga, or Ortelga will come to him. On that day, he will either prevail or be extinguished; and whichever way it goes, the issue will come about through us alone."

114

15 *Ta-Kominion*

KELDEREK CROUCHED LISTENING in the dark. There was no moon and the forest overhead shut out the stars. He could hear the bear among the trees and tried once again to make out whether it was moving away. But silence returned, broken only by the vibrant *rarking* of the frogs on the distant shore. After some time his straining ears caught a low growl. He called, "Peace, Lord Shardik. Peace, my lord," and lay down, hoping that the bear might rest if it felt that he himself was tranquil. Soon he realized that his fingers were thrusting into the soft ground and that he was holding himself tense, ready to leap to his feet. He was afraid: not only of Lord Shardik in this uncertain, suspicious mood, but also because he knew that Shardik himself was uneasy—of what, he could not tell.

For days past the bear had been wandering through the woods and open places of the island, sometimes splashing among the reeds along the southern, landward shore, sometimes turning inland to climb the central ridge, yet always tending eastward, downstream, toward Ortelga behind its jungle wall of traps and palisades. Night and day his votaries followed him. In all their hearts burned the fear of violent death, overborne by a wild hope and faith—hope for they knew not what, faith in the power of Lord Shardik returned to his people through fire and water.

Kelderek himself remained constantly near the bear, observing all that it did, attentive to its moods and ways—its frightening habit of ramping from side to side in excitement or anger; its indolent curiosity; the slow-moving strength, like that of a great head of water, with which it would turn over a heavy stone, lift a fallen log or push down a young tree; the doglike snarling of its lip in suspicion, its shrinking from the heat of the rocks in the midday glare and its preference for sleeping near water. At each sunset the Singing was repeated, the women forming their wide half-circle about the bear, sometimes smoothly and symmetrically in open ground, often with more difficulty among trees or on rocky slopes. During the early days most of those in the camp, ecstatic in their wonder and joy at the return of Shardik, came forward to offer themselves, eager to show their devotion greater than their fear and to put to the proof the age-old skills they had learned on the Ledges but never envisaged that they would be required to practice in earnest. On the fourth evening, when the singers had formed a wide circle around a grove near the shore, the bear suddenly burst through the undergrowth and struck down the priestess Anthred with a blow that almost broke her body in two. She died at once. The Singing ceased, Shardik disappeared into the forest and it was not until noon of the following day that Kelderek, having tracked him with difficulty for many hours, found him at the foot of a rocky bank on the farther side of the island. When the Tuginda reached the place she walked forward alone and stood in prayer until it became plain that Shardik would not attack her. That evening she led the Singing herself, moving without haste and gracefully as a girl whenever the bear came toward her.

A day or two later Sheldra, stepping backward on a steep slope, stumbled and struck her head. Shardik, however, ignored her, shambling past as she lay dazed among the stones. When Kelderek raised her to her feet she resumed her place without a word.

At length, as the Tuginda had envisaged in speaking to Kelderek of the days gone by, Shardik seemed to become accustomed to the attendance of the women and at times almost to play his part—towering erect and gazing at them, or prowling back and forth as though to try whether they had their art at command. Three or four—Sheldra among them—proved able to carry themselves steadily in his presence. Others, including some who had spent years in the service of Quiso and acquired every inflection and cadence, after a few evenings could no longer control their fear. To these Kelderek allowed respites, calling in turn upon one or another to play her part as best she could. As the Singing began he would watch them closely, for Shardik was keen to perceive fear and seemed angered by it; glaring with a look half-intelligent, half-savage, until the victim, her last shreds of courage consumed, broke the circle and turned tail, weeping with shame. As often as he could Kelderek would forestall this anger, calling the girl out of the circle before the bear came down upon her. His own life he risked daily, but Shardik never so much as threatened him, lying quietly while the hunter approached to bring him food or examine his almost-healed wounds.

Indeed, as the days passed, returning thoughts of Ortelga and the High Baron came to cause him more fear than did Lord Shardik. Daily it grew harder to find and kill sufficient game, and he realized that in their eastward course down the island they must already have come close to exhausting its never-plentiful resources. As often as their wanderings brought them to the southern shore, the mainland bank of the Telthearna showed nearer across the tapering strait. How far were they now from Ortelga? What watch was Bel-ka-Trazet keeping upon them and what would happen when they came—as at last they must—to the Dead Belt, with its maze of concealed snares? Even if he were able in some way to induce Shardik to turn back, what could follow but starvation? Daily, with the women looking on, he and the Tuginda stood before the bear and prayed aloud. "Reveal your power, Lord Shardik! Show us what we are to do!" Alone with the Tuginda, he spoke of his anxieties but was met always by a calm, untroubled faith with which, had it come from anyone else, he would have lost patience.

Now, crouching in the dark, he was full of doubt and uncertainty. For the first time since he had found him in the pit, he knew himself afraid of Shardik. All day they had killed no game, and at sunset, such had been the bear's threatening ferocity that the Singing had faltered and ceased, ragged and unpropitious. As night fell, Shardik had wandered away into dense forest. Kelderek, taking Sheldra with him, had followed as best he could, expecting at any moment to find himself the quarry and the bear the hunter, until at last, after how long he could not tell (for he could not see the stars), he had suddenly caught the sounds of Shardik's rambling movement not far off. There was no telling whether the bear would return to attack them, settle to sleep or go further into the forest and Kelderek, already weary, set himself to remain alert and wait.

After a time Sheldra slept, but he himself lay listening intently to each minute noise in the dark. Sometimes he thought he could hear the bear's breathing or the rustle of leaves disturbed by its claws. As the hours wore on he became intuitively aware that its mood had changed. It was no longer surly and ready to attack, but uneasy. He had never known or imagined Lord Shardik afraid. What could be the cause? Might some dangerous creature be close at hand—a great cat swum from the north bank, or one of the giant, nocturnal snakes of which Bel-ka-Trazet had spoken? He rose to his feet and called once more, "Peace, Lord Shardik. Your power is of God."

At this moment, from somewhere in the darkness, a man whistled. Kelderek stood rigid. The blood pulsed in his head—five, six, seven, eight. Then, quietly but unmistakably, the whistler ran through the refrain of a song, *"Senandril na kora, senandril na ro."*

An instant later Sheldra grasped his wrist.

"Who is it, my lord?"

"I cannot tell," he whispered. "Wait."

The girl strung her bow with barely a sound and then guided his hand to the hilt of the knife at her belt. He drew it and crept forward. Close by, to his left, the bear growled and coughed. The thought of Lord Shardik pierced by the arrows of unseen enemies filled him with a desperate haste and anger. He began to push his way more quickly through the bushes. Immediately, from the darkness on his right, a low voice called, "Who's there?"

Whoever had spoken, at least he himself was now between him and Shardik. Peering, he could just make out the trunks of trees black against a paler darkness—the open sky above the river. A faint wind stirred the leaves and a star shone twinkling through.

Now came the sound of movement like his own—the snapping of sticks and rustle of foliage. Suddenly he saw what he had been waiting for—an instant's flicker between one tree and the next, so close that he was startled.

Ten paces—eight? He wondered whether Bal-ka-Trazet himself might be close at hand and in the same moment remembered the Baron's trick by the pool, when he had distracted the bear. His groping fingers could not find a stone, but he squeezed together a handful of moist earth and tossed it upward through the space between the tree trunks. It fell beyond with a disturbance of leaves, and as it did so he dashed forward. He blundered into a man's back—a tall man, for his head struck him between the shoulders. The man staggered and Kelderek, flinging one arm up and around his neck, jerked him backward. The man fell heavily on top of him and he twisted clear, raising Sheldra's knife.

The man had not uttered a sound and Kelderek thought, "He is alone." At this he felt less desperate, for Bel-ka-Trazet would have known better than to send one man to tackle Lord Shardik and his armed and devoted followers. He pressed the point of the knife against his throat and was about to call to Sheldra when the man spoke for the first time.

"Where is Lord Shardik?"

"What's that to you?" answered Kelderek, thrusting him back as he tried to sit up. "Who are you?"

The man, amazingly, laughed. "I? Oh, I'm a fellow who's come from Ortelga through the Dead Belt, with a fancy to be knocked half silly for whistling in the dark. Was it Lord Shardik that taught you to crush a man's throat from behind you like a Deelguy footpad?"

Whether really unafraid or only concealing his fear, he certainly seemed in no hurry to get away.

"Come through the Dead Belt by night?" said Kelderek, startled in spite of himself. "You're lying!"

"As you please," replied the other. "It's no matter now. But in case you don't know it, you're only a few yards from the Belt yourself. If the wind changes you'll smell the smoke of Ortelga. Shout loud and the nearest shendron will hear you."

This, then, was the cause of Shardik's uneasiness and sullen fear! He must already have smelled the town ahead. Suppose he should wander into the Dead Belt before morning? "God will protect him," thought Kelderek. "When daylight comes, he may turn back. But if he does not, I will follow him into the Belt myself."

It crossed his mind also that by morning the bear would be close to starving and therefore still more savage and dangerous; but he put the thought aside and spoke once more to the stranger.

"Why have you come?" he asked. "What are you seeking?"

"Are you the hunter, the man who first saw Lord Shardik?"

"My name is Kelderek, sometimes called Zenzuata. It was I who brought the news of Lord Shardik to the Tuginda."

"Then we have met already, in the Sindrad, on the night when you set out for Quiso. I am Ta-Kominion."

Kelderek remembered the tall young baron who had sat on the table and bantered him in his cups. He had felt confused and uncertain then, a common man among his betters, facing trouble alone. But matters had changed since.

"So Bel-ka-Trazet sent you to murder me," he said, "and you found me less helpless than you expected?"

"Well, you're right this far," replied Ta-Kominion. "It's true that Bel-ka-Trazet is seeking your death, and it's true that that's the reason why I'm here. But now listen to me, Kelderek Play-with-the-Children. If you suppose that I've come alone through the Dead Belt on the off chance of coming across one man in miles of forest and killing him, then you must believe I'm a sorcerer. No, I came to look for you because I want to talk to you; and I came by land and darkness because I didn't want Bel-ka-Trazet to know of it. I had no idea where you might be, but it seems I've been lucky—if what you call luck's a half-broken neck and a blow on the elbow. Now tell me, is Lord Shardik here?"

"He is not a bowshot away. Speak no ill of him, Ta-Kominion, if you want to live."

"You must understand me better, Kelderek. I'm here as Bel-ka-Trazet's enemy and the friend of Lord Shardik. Let me tell you something of what has been happening in Ortelga since you left."

"Wait!" Kelderek gripped the other's arm. Crouching together and listening, they could both hear Shardik moving in the forest.

"Sheldra!" called Kelderek. "Which way is he going?"

"He is returning, my lord, by the way he came. Shall I go back and warn the Tuginda?"

"Yes, but try not to lose him if he should wander further."

"So," said Ta-Kominion after a few moments, "they obey you, do they, Lord Kelderek? Well, if all I hear is true, you deserve it. Bel-ka-Trazet told the barons that you struck him down."

"I threw a stone. He was about to kill Lord Shardik while he lay helpless."

"So he said. He spoke to us of the folly and danger of allowing the people to believe that Lord Shardik had returned. 'Those women'll ruin us all,' he said, 'with that half-burnt bear they've got hold of. God knows what superstitious rubbish will come of it if they're not packed off where they belong. It'll be the end of all law and order.' He sent men out to look for you at the western end of the island, but you'd gone from there, it seems. One of them tracked you eastward almost as far as this; but when he came back, it was to me he spoke and not to Bel-ka-Trazet."

"Why?"

Ta-Kominion laid a hand on Kelderek's knee.

"The people know the truth," he said. "One of the Tuginda's girls came to Ortelga—but even if she had not, truth blows through the leaves and trickles between the stones. The people are weary of Bel-ka-Trazet's harshness. They are speaking secretly of Lord Shardik and waiting for him to come. If need be they are ready to die for him. In his heart, Bel-ka-Trazet knows this and he is afraid."

"Why," answered Kelderek, "that morning when he left the Tuginda, I saw the fear already in his eyes. I pitied him then and I still pity him, but he has set himself up against Lord Shardik. If a man chooses to stand in the path of a fire, can the fire take pity on him?"

"He thinks—"

Kelderek cut him short. "What do you want with me, then?"

"The people are not Bel-ka-Trazet. They know that Lord Shardik has returned to them. I have seen decent, simple men in Ortelga weeping for joy and hope. They are ready to rise against Bel-ka-Trazet and to follow me."

"To follow *you?* Follow you where?"

In the solitude of the forest, Ta-Kominion dropped his voice still lower.

"To Bekla, to regain what is ours."

1 2 1

Kelderek drew in his breath. "You're seriously planning to attack Bekla?"

"With the power of Lord Shardik we cannot fail. But Kelderek, will you join us? They say you have no fear of Shardik and can persuade him as you will. Is that true?"

"Only in part. God has made of me a vessel let down into Shardik's well and a brand lighted at his fire. He suffers me; nevertheless, to be near him is always to be in danger."

"Could you bring him to Ortelga?"

"Neither I nor anyone can drive Lord Shardik. He is the Power of God. If it is so ordained, he will come to Ortelga. Yet how can he pass the Dead Belt? And what is it that you mean to do?"

"My own men are ready to strike now. They will make him a path through the Belt: along this shore—that's the easiest place. Only let Lord Shardik come and every man will join us—yes, join you and me, Kelderek! As soon as we are sure of Ortelga, then we'll march at once on Bekla, before they can learn the news."

"You make it sound easy, but I tell you again—I cannot bring Lord Shardik here and there like an ox. He acts by the will of God, not by my will. If you had seen him—*faced* him—you would understand."

"Let me face him, then. I will stand before him and beg him to help us. I'm not afraid. I tell you, Kelderek, all Ortelga is eager only to serve him. If I entreat him, he will give me a sign."

"Very well. Come with me. You shall speak with the Tuginda and face Lord Shardik for yourself. But if he gives you death, Ta-Kominion—"

"He will give much where much is offered. I have come to offer my life. If he takes it, why then I shall not live to be disappointed. If he gives it back to me, I will spend it in his service."

For answer Kelderek got to his feet and began to lead the way through the undergrowth. The night was still so dark, however, that he found it all but impossible to tell in which direction the camp lay. Feeling before them, they stumbled repeatedly; once Ta-Kominion nearly put out his eye on a pointed branch that pierced him under the lower lid. Kelderek could not tell how far they had gone or whether they might not have wandered in a circle. At last he glimpsed, still some distance off, the glow of the fire. He made toward it cautiously, expecting at any moment to be challenged by one of the girls, or even to come upon Lord Shardik himself, prowling in his angry hunger. But they met no one and at length, looking about him in perplexity, he realized that they had already reached the outskirts of the camp. They walked on side by side over the open ground, strewn with cut branches and garments, where the women had been sleeping, and so up to the untended remains of the fire.

Kelderek's perplexity became bewilderment. The place was deserted. Apparently there was no one whatever in the camp. He called, "Rantzay! Sheldra!" Receiving no reply, he shouted, "Where are you?"

The echo died and for some moments he could hear only the frogs and the rustle of the leaves. Then he was answered.

"Lord Kelderek!" It was Rantzay's harsh voice from the direction of the shore. "Come quickly, my lord!"

He had never heard her so much excited. He began to run and as he did so realized that it was growing light—light enough, at all events, to enable them to see their way to the river. As they approached he could make out the canoes and closer at hand the cloaked shapes of the women crowding together, some apparently up to their knees in the water. All were pressing forward, pointing, moving their heads one way and another and peering through the reeds. Beside the tall figure of Rantzay he recognized that of the Tuginda and ran toward her.

"What is it, säiyett? What has happened?"

Without speaking she took his arm and led him down into the shallows, among the reeds taller than his head. Between these, something had smashed a path and down this narrow lane he gazed out toward the Telthearna beyond. Over it the light was increasing, a windless, twilit gray without shadows. The far trees were motionless, the flowing water smooth. Still the Tuginda waded forward and still he followed, wondering at her haste. Waist-deep, feet groping, they reached the outer edge of the reed belt and to right and left the extent of the river opened before them. The Tuginda, one hand on his shoulder, pointed downstream to where a wide ripple like an arrowhead was breaking the calm surface. At its apex, the only living thing to be seen in all the expanse of trees and water, Shardik was swimming, his muzzle thrust upward at the sky as the current carried him toward Ortelga.

16 The Point and the Causeway

WITHOUT AN INSTANT'S HESITATION Kelderek flung himself forward into the deep water. Immediately—almost before his shoulders had broken the surface—he felt the current turning him bodily and sweeping him downstream. For a few moments he struggled, afraid as he found himself helpless against it. Then, awkwardly, he began to swim, bending back his neck to keep his head above water, splashing with his arms and bobbing up and down. Looking ahead, his water-blurred eyes could still make out the shape of the bear like a rick swept away in a flood.

Soon he realized that some freak of the river was carrying him toward the center, where the flow was swifter yet. Even if he should happen to touch upon a random spit or submerged bank, such as formed and dissolved continually in the strait, he would not be able to stand up in a current of this strength. Already he was beginning to tire. He tried to look about him for a floating branch or anything to which he might cling, but could see nothing. His feet, trailing deep, encountered some tangled, loomlike thing, intersticed and pliant, and as he jerked himself free, pain flickered up his leg and was gone as quickly as a spurt of flame. An instant later he spun around in an eddy, swallowed water, sank and, as his head came up again, found that he was facing upstream and still drifting on. The women among the reeds were now far-off, indistinguishable figures, appearing and disappearing as his eyes rose and fell. He tried to turn and face ahead, and as he did so heard across the water a sputtering call —"Kelderek! Inshore!"

Ta-Kominion, swimming behind him, was about halfway between himself and the shore which they had left. Although he appeared to be holding his own more easily than Kelderek, it was nevertheless clear that he had little breath for talking. He flung up one arm and gestured sharply toward the reeds, then fell once more to his task. Kelderek saw that he was trying to overtake him, but could not because of the slower current inshore. Indeed, the gap between them was widening. Ta-Kominion raised his head and seemed to shout again, but Kelderek could hear nothing except his own hard breathing and the splash and gurgle of the water. Then, as he bobbed upward for a moment, he caught faintly the words, "—shore before the point!"

As he grasped the baron's meaning, fear overcame him. He was being carried along the southeastern shore of Ortelga at a speed as fast as that of a man walking. As long as he remained in midstream he could not count on drifting against the submerged causeway that ran from the eastern point to the mainland. More likely he would be carried over or through it, pummeled down by this very current in which he was now struggling for his life. And if he were carried below Ortelga, he could not hope to come ashore alive.

He began to kick out and to clutch at the surface, panting and tiring himself still further. How far was it now to the point? The right, mainland bank seemed actually closer than that of Ortelga: yet how could that be? Then he recognized the place. The reeds had been cut back, exposing a sheet of open water beyond which, on the island shore, stood the zoan tree. Tall and far-off it looked—much farther than when last he had sighted it, returning to Ortelga on his raft. He thought of the shendron, perhaps looking out at this very moment through the silvery fronds. But the shendron, for all his vigilance, would never catch sight of him. He was nothing but flotsam, a dot moving in the gray light and gray water of early morning.

By God, but there was something else, though, that the shendron could not have failed to see! A little behind, but directly between himself and the zoan tree, Shardik was drifting like a cloud through a pale sky. There was no commotion of the water around him and the long wedge of his jaw lay half-submerged, the nostrils just clear, like those of an alligator. As the hunter watched, the bear turned his head for a moment and seemed to be staring toward him.

At this, desperate though he was, Kelderek felt a return of that brave impulse upon which he had thrown himself into the river to follow Shardik. Shardik had called him for some purpose of his own. Shardik had power to preserve and raise up those who gave him all, doubting nothing. If only he could reach Shardik, Shardik would save him, Shardik would not let him drown. As the zoan tree dropped out of sight he set himself, with the last of his strength, to swim inshore across the current. Slowly, very slowly, he began to converge upon the bear. As he came by degrees into the slacker stream the distance between them lessened, until at last they were floating side by side and only a few yards apart.

He could do no more. He was exhausted, conscious of nothing but the deep water beneath him, the fear of drowning and, somewhere far out of reach, the presence of Shardik. He could see neither sky nor shore. "Accept my life, Lord Shardik. I regret nothing I did for you." Losing the power of thought, sinking, no longer breathing: arms flung upward, fingers clawing at the black, fainting dark; and now, in death, he felt once more the shaggy hair, the flank of Shardik, just as he had felt it when he walked beside him at nightfall into the forest and slept in the safety of his presence.

The darkness burst apart. He caught his breath and drew in the air. Sunlight was glittering on the water and sparkling in his eyes. He was clutching Shardik's flank, hanging by his clenched hands, tossing up and down, while beside him the great off-hind leg trod water as fast as mill wheels strike. Scarcely able at first to realize what had happened, he knew only that he was alive and that he could still get ashore before the town was left behind.

The bear had not turned its head or tried to shake him off, and indeed seemed unaware of him. He was puzzled by its in-difference. Then, as his head and sight grew clearer, he sensed that it was intent upon something else, some purpose of its own. It was turning shoreward, to the left, and swimming more strongly. He could not see over the ridge of its back, but as it turned still further, land appeared beyond its shoulder. A moment later it was wading. He let his feet drop, touched bottom and found himself standing, submerged almost to his shoulders, on firm stones.

They came ashore together, the bear and the man, close to the now-cold cooking fires, the cluster of storage huts and servants' quarters lying shoreward of the Sindrad. Shardik, in his eagerness, thrust the water aside, splashing and shouldering through the shallows as though in pursuit of prey. Suddenly Kelderek saw the way of it. The bear was hungry—famished—desperate for food at any cost. Something had turned it back from the Dead Belt, but nevertheless it must have smelled food while lying in the forest and this was why it had plunged into the river. He remembered what Bel-ka-Trazet had said before leaving the Tuginda, "If it begins to plague Ortelga, I promise you I will have it killed."

Stumbling and still half-drowned, he began to follow Shardik up the slope of the shore but tripped and fell his length. For some moments he lay inert, then raised himself on one elbow. As he did so two men appeared from behind the nearest hut, carrying an iron cauldron between them and making for the water. They were bleary-eyed and tousled, scullions routed out of bed to the first chores of the day. The bear was almost on top of them before they looked up and saw it. The cauldron fell to the stones with a booming sound and for an instant they stared, fixed in grotesque attitudes of shock and terror. Then, shrieking, they turned to run. One disappeared by the way he had come. The other, blind with fear, blundered into the wall of the hut, hit his head and stood dazed, swaying on his feet. Shardik, following, reared up and struck him. The blow knocked the poor wretch bodily through the wattle-and-daub of the hut wall, smashing it open in a ragged gap. Shardik struck a second time and the wall collapsed, bringing down part of the roof above. The air was filled with dust, and with smoke from the new-lit hearth buried beneath the ruins. Women were screaming, men running and shouting. A burly man in a leather apron, holding a hammer, appeared suddenly through the haze, stared a moment, petrified, and was gone. Above all the hubbub rose the growling roar of Shardik, a sound like the sliding of heavy stones down a hillside.

Kelderek, watching from where he had fallen, saw the bear

lumber away into the smoke and confusion. Suddenly he felt hands under his armpits and a voice shouted in his ear.

"Get up, Kelderek, get up, man! There's no time to lose! Follow me!"

Ta-Kominion was beside him, his long hair streaming water as he dragged Kelderek to his knees. In his left hand he was holding a long, sharp-pointed dagger.

"Come on, man! Have you got a weapon?"

"Only this." He drew Sheldra's knife.

"That'll do! You can soon grab yourself a better."

They dashed forward around the burning ruins. On the farther side was lying a man's body, the backbone like a snapped bow. Beyond, the bear was dragging the carcass of a sheep from beneath the debris of a second hut. A little farther off, four or five men, on the point of flight, stood staring back over their shoulders.

Ta-Kominion leapt to the top of a pile of logs, shouting, "Shardik! Lord Shardik is come!" Round him the tumult spread wider as the whole town woke to the alarm. It was clear that there were those who had been awaiting his return. Already men were gathering about him, some already armed, others, half-naked from their beds, clutching spits, axes, clubs, whatever had come first to hand.

Dragging the end of a burning roof-pole from the ruins behind him, Ta-Kominion brandished it above his head. The second hut had caught fire and smoke had begun to obscure the sunlight. As the heat and noise increased, Shardik, disturbed from the sheep's carcass, became uneasy. At first he had glared about him, defying the strange surroundings as he satisfied his hunger, crouching in the posture of a cat to rip and chew the bloody flesh. As the dusky air began to waver and cinders blew out toward the river, he winced and snarled, cuffing at a spark that fell on his ear. Then, as the center-post of the second hut fell its length with a crash like that of a felled tree, he turned, still clutching the haunch in his mouth, and made off toward the shore.

Ta-Kominion, surrounded now by a shouting crowd, pointed with his dagger and raised his voice above the din. "Now you have seen for yourselves! Lord Shardik has returned to his people! Follow me and fight for Shardik!"

"He is going!" cried a voice.

"Going? Of course he's going!" yelled Ta-Kominion. "Going where we shall follow him—to Bekla! He knows Ortelga's as good as taken for him already! He's trying to tell you there's no time to be lost! Follow me!"

"Shardik! Shardik!" shouted the crowd. Ta-Kominion led them forward at a run toward the Sindrad. Kelderek heard the shouting grow to a roar. Fresh smoke rose, followed by the unmistakable sounds of fighting—orders, the clashing of weapons, curses and the cries of wounded men. Picking up a stout, woven hurdle leaning against the log pile, he began to fasten it on his left arm for a shield. It was awkward, contrary work and he knelt down to it, fumbling and forcing at the wicker plaiting.

Looking up, he suddenly found the Tuginda standing beside him. Her clothes were dry, but the black, powdery ash blowing in the air had streaked her face and arms and lay grimy on her hair. Although she was carrying a bow, ready strung, and a quiver of arrows, she seemed indifferent to the fighting, which was now filling the entire town with its uproar. She said nothing, but, stood looking down at him.

"I must go and join in the fight, säiyett," he said. "The young baron will think me a coward. He may be hard-pressed—I cannot tell."

Still she said nothing and he paused, looking up at her and at the same time trying to thrust his left arm farther through the rent which he had made in the hurdle.

"Lord Shardik is leaving Ortelga," said the Tuginda at length.

"Säiyett, the fighting—"

"His work here is done—whatever it may have been."

"You can hear that it is not! Do not delay me, säiyett, I beg you!"

"That may be others' work. It is not our work."

He stared at her.

"Why, what then is our work, if not to fight for Lord Shardik?"

"To follow the one whom God has sent."

She turned and began to walk back toward the river. Still hesitating, he saw her stoop and pick something up from among the ashes of the burned hut. She stood a moment, weighing it in her hand, and as she moved he saw that it was a wooden ladle.

129

Then she was gone, through the smoke, down the sloping shore. Kelderek let fall his hurdle, thrust the knife into his belt and followed her.

On the bank, Rantzay and Sheldra were waiting beside a canoe drawn up on the pebbles. Staring out over the water, they paid him no attention. Following their gaze, he saw Shardik splashing toward the mainland, along the line of the broken causeway. Close by, shading her eyes against the glitter, the Tuginda was standing on a flat, squared block of stone in the shallows. He took her arm, and together they began to follow Shardik across the strait.

BOOK II

Gelt

17 *The Road to Gelt*

THAT EVENING THE ARMY OF ORTELGA, led by Ta-Kominion, began crossing the strait: a grimy, shouting horde a few thousand strong, some armed with spear, sword or bow, some carrying nothing but mattocks or sharpened stakes; some—mostly servants, these—moving in bands under their masters for officers, others mere gangs of drinking companions or ruffians slouching with club and bottle for company; but all eager to march and ready to fight, all convinced that Bekla was destined to fall to the revealed power of God, by whose will they were to have full stomachs and never toil again. Some wore crude armor—scooped-out caps of fire-hardened wood, or rough-edged plates of iron fastened across their chests—and most had, scratched or painted somewhere about them, the rough likeness of a bear's head.

At the dangerous points in the broken causeway Ta-Kominion had had ropes stretched between wedged stakes or anchored rafts and at these there was sousing and horseplay, until a man was swept downstream and drowned. As darkness came, those still gathering on the island shore fell to drinking and singing as they waited for moonrise; and Ta-Kominion's henchmen made a last search through the town, rousing up any who remained in two minds or seemed inclined to feel that they might be leaving more than they could gain.

On the mainland shore other groups were mustering from the outlying lands: a party of foresters and woodmen armed with their axes, mauls and crowbars; a baron named Ged-la-Dan, whose substance came from the colored quartz—topaz and aquamarine—for which his men dived in rocky bays downstream; and a factor and his porters, just returned from their trading post in Gelt with a load of iron ore, who were quick-witted enough to auction themselves as guides to the highest bidders among the leaders.

133

Women, too, made the crossing, laden with arms, clothes, arrows or bags of food got together at the last minute, beg borrow or steal. Some of these, confused by the crowd, wandered here and there in the torch-lit twilight, calling the names of their men and dealing as best they could with importuners and thieves.

Ta-Kominion, having asked Fassel-Hasta to count the numbers and do his best to organize the force into companies, himself set off to recross the causeway, ignoring the surly nod and grunt with which the older baron left him. For some hours past he had been drenched through, first standing up to his waist in midstream to see the ropes fixed and then remaining at the gaps, less to encourage the rabble, most of whom were in high spirits, than to establish his authority and make sure that they knew him and would know him again. Already wearied by the work of the previous night and day, he was not intending a second night without sleep. He waded ashore on Ortelga, commandeered the nearest hut, bolted the food that was brought to him and then slept for two hours. When his servant Numiss woke him, the moon was well risen and the stragglers were being guided and coaxed across. He sat impatiently while Numiss changed the dirty cloth bound round the deep, jagged wound in his forearm; and then made his way upstream the length of the town, until he came to the shendron's post under the zoan tree.

There was no shendron there now, not even a woman or an old man, for Ta-Kominion was not concerned to set guards around Ortelga. Waiting, however, under the tent of leaves he found, as he had expected, two of the Tuginda's girls with a canoe. Numiss and another had been dispatched that morning, as soon as the fight was over, to cross the strait, find the Tuginda and ask for guides to be sent to the zoan tree after moonrise.

As the canoe moved obliquely across the midstream current and on into the slack water under the far bank Ta-Kominion, sitting in the stern, could make out, away to his left, the dull glint of weapons held high out of the water, an occasional splash —the sound reaching him an instant after the quick glitter in the moon—and the onward creeping of the line of black shapes as the last of his followers made the crossing. Coming ashore he stumbled, struck his arm against a tree and stood biting his lip as the pain slowly subsided. All day he had made light of the wound but now, when one of the girls unfastened the leather strap of her quiver to make him a rough sling, he was ready enough to do as she bid, bending his head meekly to let her tie the knot behind his neck.

The girls had become adept at moving in the dark. Whether they were following any path or how they knew their way he could not tell and was beginning to feel too feverish to care. His arm throbbed and his hearing seemed continually to change, now magnified, now dulled. He walked behind them in silence, revolving in his mind all that still remained to be done. At length he saw, far off, the leaping of a fire between the trees. He went toward it, halting as his guides were challenged and answered with some password. Then he stepped into the firelight and Kelderek came forward to meet him.

For a few moments they stood looking at one another, each thinking how strange it was that in spite of all that had passed he should not yet be familiar with the other's face. Then Kelderek dropped his eyes to the fire, stooped and threw on a log, speaking diffidently as he did so.

"Crendro, Ta-Kominion. I am glad that you have won Ortelga, but sorry to see you wounded. I hope you found the girls waiting?"

Ta-Kominion nodded and sat down on a creeper-covered log. Kelderek remained standing, leaning on a long stake which the girls had been using to stir the fire.

"Is the wound serious?"

"It's of no importance. Others were luckier—others who won't be afraid to fight again."

"How long did the fight last?"

"I don't know. Longer than it took you to get across the strait, I dare say."

He pulled a splinter from the log. A turn of the breeze blew the smoke into his face but he ignored it. Kelderek stirred the fire and shifted his feet. At length he said, "Most of the Tuginda's stuff is still on the other side. The women left it this morning when they followed us across the river."

There was another silence.

"It puzzles me," said Kelderek, "that last night, in spite of his hunger, Lord Shardik would not go on through the forest. He must have caught the scent of food from Ortelga, yet he turned back from the Dead Belt and took to the river."

Ta-Kominion shook his head as though the matter were of little interest to him.

"What has happened to Bel-ka-Trazet?" asked Kelderek.

"Oh, he took to the water, like you; not quite so quickly."

Kelderek drew in his breath and clenched his hand on the stake. After some moments he said,

"Where has he gone?"

"Downstream."

"Do you mean to pursue him?"

"It's not necessary. *He* isn't a coward, but to us he can be no more dangerous now than if he were." He looked up. "Where is Lord Shardik?"

"Over there, not far from the road. He reached the road this afternoon but then went back into the forest. I was near him until moonrise, but I returned to meet you."

"What road?"

"The road to Gelt. We are not far from it here."

Ta-Kominion got up and stood squarely in front of Kelderek, looking down into his face. His back was to the fire and, with his long hair falling forward, he seemed to be wearing a mask of heavy shadows, through which his eyes burned cold and harsh. Without turning his head he said, "You may leave us, Numiss."

"But where are we to go, my lord?"

Ta-Kominion said nothing more and after a moment the red-haired fellow and his companion slipped away among the trees. Before Ta-Kominion could speak again Kelderek burst out,

"My place is with Lord Shardik, to follow and serve him! That is my task! I am no coward!"

"I did not say you were."

"I have walked beside Lord Shardik, slept beside him, laid my hands upon him. Is that work for a coward?"

Ta-Kominion closed his eyes and passed his hand once or twice across his forehead.

"I did not come here, Kelderek, either to accuse you or to quarrel with you. I have more important things to speak of."

"You think I'm a coward. You have as good as said so!"

"What I may have let slip is nothing to do with our affairs now. You'd do better to put such personal ideas out of your mind. Every man in Ortelga who can use a weapon is across the Telthearna and ready to march on Bekla. They'll start soon—before dawn. I shall join them from here—no need to return to the camp. We shall be at Bekla in five days—perhaps sooner. It's not only surprise we need. We've got no more than three days' food, but that's not the whole of it either. Our people have got to take Bekla before they can lose the power that's burning in their hearts. Whose, do you suppose, is that power?"

"My lord?" It had slipped out before Kelderek could check himself.

"It was the power of Shardik that took Ortelga today. We were lucky—there were many who saw him before he crossed the causeway. Bel-ka-Trazet was driven out because he was known to be Shardik's enemy. The people have seen for themselves that Shardik has returned. They believe there's nothing he won't give them—nothing they can't do in his name."

He took a few uncertain steps back to the log and sat rigid and frowning, fighting a sudden fit of giddiness. For an instant his teeth chattered and he pressed his chin upon his open hand.

"Shardik has been sent to restore us to Bekla, peasant and baron alike. The peasants need to know no more than that. But I—I have to find the right way, the way to bring about victory through Shardik. And this *is* the way—or so it seems to me. Either we take Bekla within seven days or not at all."

"Why?"

Ta-Kominion paused, as though choosing his words.

"Common people can sing a song only when they are dancing, drinking or about some occupation—then it rises to their lips without thought. Ask them to teach it to you and it's gone from their heads. While their hearts are full of Shardik our men will do the impossible—march without sleep, fly through the air, tear down the walls of Bekla. But in the hearts of common men such power is like mist. The wind or the sun—any unexpected adversity—may disperse it in an hour. It must be given no chance to disperse." He paused and then said deliberately, "But there is more besides. Out of sight, out of mind. You understand children, I'm told. So you'll know that children forget what is not kept before their eyes."

Kelderek stared, guessing at his meaning.

"Shardik must be with us when we come to fight," said Ta-Kominion. "It is all-important that the people should see him there."

"At Bekla—in five days? How?"

"You must tell me how."

"Lord Shardik cannot be driven a hundred paces and you are speaking of five days' journey!"

"Kelderek, Bekla is a city more rich and marvelous than a mountain made of jewels. It is ours by ancient right and Shardik has returned to restore it to us. But he can restore it only by means of ourselves. He needed my help to take Ortelga today. Now he needs your help to bring him to Bekla."

"But that is impossible! It was not *impossible* to take Ortelga."

"No, no, of course not—an easy matter, I dare say, to those who did not happen to be there. Never mind. Kelderek, do you want to cease to be a simpleton playing with fatherless children on the shore? To see Shardik come in power to Bekla? To bring to its right end the work you began on that night when you faced Bel-ka-Trazet's hot knife in the Sindrad? There *must* be a way! Either you find it or we are fast on a sheer cliff. You and I and Lord Shardik—it is we who are climbing, and there is no way back. If we do not take Bekla, do you think the Beklan rulers will let us alone? No—they will hunt us down. They will not be long in dealing with you and your bear."

"*My* bear?"

"Your bear. For that is what he will become, Lord Shardik of the Ledges, who is ready at this moment to give us a great city and all its wealth and power, if only we can find the means. He will shrink to a creature of superstition, over which some rough fellows on Ortelga have made trouble and turned out their High Baron. A stop will be put to him—and to you."

A great bat came hovering out of the darkness, flittered soundlessly along the edge of the fire, turned away from the crackling heat and vanished as it had come.

"Kelderek, you say I think you're a coward. Is it I that think it, or you? It's not too late for you to redeem yourself, Kelderek

Play-with-the-Children: to show yourself a man. Find a way to bring Lord Shardik to the plains of Bekla—fight for him there with your own hands. Think of the prize—a prize beyond reckoning! Do this, and no one will ever call you a coward again."

"I never was a coward. But the Tuginda—"

For the first time, Ta-Kominion smiled at him.

"I know you are not. When we have taken Bekla, what reward do you suppose there will be for him to whom Shardik first appeared, for him who brought the news to Quiso? Why, there is not a man on Ortelga who does not know your name and honor it already."

Kelderek hesitated, frowning.

"How soon must we begin?"

"At once—now. There is not a moment to lose. There are two things, Kelderek, that a rebel leader needs above all. First, his followers must be filled with a burning ardor—mere obedience is not enough—and secondly he himself must be all speed and resolution. The second I myself possess. The first only you can ensure."

"It may perhaps be possible—but I shall need every blacksmith, wheelwright and carpenter in Ortelga. Let us go and speak with the Tuginda."

As Ta-Kominion rose, Kelderek offered him the support of his arm, but the baron waved him aside, staggered a few steps, hesitated, then himself put his sound arm through Kelderek's and drew himself upright, leaning hard until he found his balance.

"Are you ill?"

"It's nothing—a touch of fever. It will pass off."

"You must be tired out. You ought to rest."

"Later."

Kelderek guided him away from the fire. In the close darkness under the trees they paused, sightless after the flame-light. A hand plucked Kelderek's sleeve and he turned, peering.

"Shall I guide you, my lord? Are you returning now to Lord Shardik?"

"Is it your watch, Neelith?"

"My watch is ended, my lord. I was coming to wake Sheldra, but it's no matter if you need me."

"No, get to sleep. Who is watching Lord Shardik?"

"Zilthé, my lord."

"Where is the Tuginda?"

The girl pointed, "Down yonder, among the ferns."

"Is she asleep?"

"Not yet, my lord; she has been praying this hour and more."

They left the girl and, their eyes becoming accustomed to the dark, moved on more easily. Soon the trees grew fewer and the close growth overhead opened here and there to reveal clouds and moonlight. The white beams faded and reappeared continually between the branches as the clouds drifted eastward across the moon. The turbid heat of the forest, a single block of dense air lying all about them, seemed now to begin to be assailed, whittled, rifted, encroached upon by gusts and momentary, cooler currents coming and going like the first wavelets of floodwater lapping around a dry shoal. As the leaves and light shifted in response to the breeze outside, the mass of the hot darkness on the ground stirred, slow and heavy as a bed of weed under water. As yet unpenetrated, it felt already on its outskirts the first impulse of that appointed, seasonal force that soon would grow to split it with lightning and storm.

Ta-Kominion stopped, lifting his head and sniffing the fresher air.

"The rains can't be long now."

"A day or two," replied Kelderek.

"That's the strongest reason of all for speed. It's now or never. We can't march or keep the field in the wet and nor can they. Even Bekla lies low in the rains. The last thing they'll be expecting is any sort of attack at this time of year. If they have no warning and we get there before the rains break we shall have complete surprise."

"Have they no spies?"

"We're not worth spying on, man. Ortelga? A bunch of scavengers perched on the butt-end of an overgrown spit."

"But the risk! If the rains come first, before we can fight, that will be the end of us. Are you sure there's time?"

"Lord Shardik will give us time."

As he spoke they came suddenly upon a broad slab of rock rising upright from the ground like a wall. It was flat, about as thick as a man's body, and rose irregularly to a blunt apex an arm's length above their heads. In the faint light the two sides appeared almost smooth, though as Kelderek groped wonderingly across one of the planes he could feel that it was rougher than it looked, flawed here and there and ridged with excrescent mosses and lichens. The rock was set deep in the soft earth of the forest like a wedge hurled down and hammered in by a giant long ago. Beyond, they could make out another, also flat but larger, slightly tilted and of a different shape. This, when they came to it, they saw was half-covered on one side with rusty-red lichen like a stain of dried blood. And now they found themselves peering and wandering between numbers of these tall, flat-sided masses—some, like fences, long and no higher than a man's shoulder, others rising in steep, conical blocks or cut, as it seemed, into flights of steps vanishing upward in the dark, but all worked to an even thickness and sheer-sided like gigantic axeheads, with never a broadening at the foot to anything resembling a base or plinth. Among them grew the ferns of which the girl had spoken—some huge, like trees, with moss hanging from the undersides of their fronds, others small and delicate, lace-fronded with tiny leaflets that trembled like aspen leaves in the still air. From hidden places among the rocks there came, even at this time of year, thin tricklings out of the peaty mold, scarcely enough to form anywhere a pool bigger than a man's cupped hands; though they shone, where the moonlight caught them, in faint streaks along the stones and the moist, dim fern-boughs. A snatch of breeze brought for an instant the minute pattering of drops blown across the shallowest of surfaces.

"Have you never been here before?" asked Ta-Kominion, as Kelderek stared up at the outline of a rock that seemed to be toppling forward between his eyes and the moving clouds above. "These are the Two-Sided Rocks."

"Once, many years ago, I came here; but I was not old enough then to wonder how the rocks were brought—or why."

"The rocks were here from the beginning, as I was told. But the men who made the Ledges on Quiso—they worked them, as others might trim a hedge or shape a tree, to strike wonder into the hearts of pilgrims approaching Ortelga. For it was here that the pilgrims used to assemble to be guided down to the causeway."

"This place is Lord Shardik's then, as Quiso is, and that is why he has led us here."

The Tuginda was standing a little way off, in an open place among the ferns. Her back was half-turned, her hands clasped at her waist and her head inclined as she gazed into the moonlit distance. Her bearing recalled to Kelderek the moment when she had stood on the edge of the pit, filled with the knowledge that it was none other than Shardik lying among the trepsis below. Plainly she was not withdrawn into contemplation, but seemed rather to have attained to some heightened state of alertness, in which she was aware with rapture of all that lay about her. Yet just as evidently, her eyes passed through the fern grove as they might have passed through water to perceive—or partly perceive—the moving life within it, the silence of the pool. For an instant Kelderek understood that not only now, but always, his own eye was filled with reflections from a surface through which her sight passed unimpeded. She seemed to be gazing into the sultry gloom as though at some marvelous spectacle, a dance of light and flowers. Yet still there remained about her that air of plain directness and shrewdness that had both deceived and reassured him by the Tereth stone on Quiso. If her prayer had had words, she might have been speaking of leather, wood and bread.

Ta-Kominion stopped, withdrew his arm from Kelderek's and leaned against one of the rock slabs, pressing his forehead against the cool stone.

"Is that the Tuginda?"

"Yes." He was surprised for a moment, before remembering that Ta-Kominion could never have seen her unmasked—might never, perhaps, have seen her at all.

"Are you sure?"

Kelderek made no reply.

"The girl said she was praying."

"She is praying."

Ta-Kominion shrugged his shoulders and pushed himself upright. They went on. While they were still a little distance away the Tuginda turned toward them. Her face, in the moonlight, was full of a calm, tranquil joy which seemed to embrace and sanctify rather than transcend the dark forest and the danger and uncertainty surrounding all Ortelga. To Kelderek's eye, faith streamed from her as light from a lantern.

"It is she," he thought, in a swift access of self-knowledge, "she, not I, through whom the power of Shardik will be transmuted and made a blessing to us all. Her acceptance and faith—his force and savagery—they are one and the same. He is weak as a dumb creature without knowledge. She is strong as the shoots of the lilies, which great stones cannot prevent from breaking through the earth."

They stood before her and Kelderek raised his palm to his forehead. Her smile in reply was like the answering step in some happy dance, an exchange of mutual respect and trust.

"We interrupted you, säiyett."

"No, we are all doing the same thing—whatever it is. I came here because it's cooler among the ferns. But we'll go back to the fire now, Kelderek, if you prefer."

"Säiyett, your wishes are mine, and always will be."

She smiled again.

"You're sure?"

He nodded, smiling back at her.

"This is the High Baron of Ortelga, Lord Ta-Kominion. He has come to talk about Lord Shardik."

"I am afraid you are not well," she said, reaching out her fingers to take his wrist. "What has happened?"

"It is nothing, säiyett. I have been telling Kelderek that time is very short. Lord Shardik must come—"

At that instant, from somewhere in the middle distance, an appalling scream pierced the forest—a cry of fear and agony, confounding the minds of its hearers as lightning dazzles and confounds the eyes. There was a moment's silence. Then followed another scream, which broke off as suddenly as though a man falling in terror from a height had struck the ground.

Kelderek's eye met Ta-Kominion's and without a word the thought passed between them, "That was a man's death-cry."

Numiss and his companion came running toward them through the trees, their swords drawn in their hands.

"Thank God, my lord! We thought—"

"Never mind," said Ta-Kominion. "Follow me, come on!"

He set off at a run, threading his way in and out of the ferns and tall rocks. The two servants followed. Kelderek, however, remained with the Tuginda, suiting his pace to hers as he tried to persuade her to remain out of danger.

"Be advised, säiyett! Wait here and let me send you word of what we find. You must not risk your life."

"There's no risk now," she answered. "Whatever has happened, it's past mending."

"But there may—"

"Give me your arm over these rocks. Which way did the young baron take? The undergrowth is thick on the edge of the forest, but with luck they will break a way through for us."

Soon they came upon Ta-Kominion and the servants hacking with their knives at a belt of creepers.

"Is there no easier way, my lord?" panted Numiss, picking the trazada thorns from his forearm and stifling his curses as he caught sight of the Tuginda.

"Very likely there is," replied Ta-Kominion, "but we must make straight toward where the cry came from, or we shall lose direction and never find the fellow until daylight."

Suddenly Kelderek's ear caught a sound somewhere between weeping and the whimpering of fear. It was a woman's voice, a little distance away.

"Zilthé!" he called.

"My lord!" replied the girl. "Oh, come quickly!"

As Numiss cut his way out through the farther side of the creepers, Kelderek followed Ta-Kominion through the gap. He found himself clear of the trees and looking across an open valley. Opposite, perhaps half a mile away, the edge of the forest in the moonlight showed black and dry as a hide hung to cure on a line. Down in the bottom he could just make out the dark cleft of a brook, while far to his right the Gelt Mountains showed dimly against the night sky.

Below the place where they were standing ran the road from Ortelga to Gelt—a track trodden along the hillside between scrub and bushes, with here and there the stump of a long-felled tree and here and there, to mend some muddy or broken place, a patch of stones carried up from the bed of the brook and laid haphazard, to settle to a level with use and time.

Down at the edge of the road Zilthé, her bow lying beside her, was bending on one knee over the dark shape of a body. As Kelderek watched she rose, turned her head and looked up toward him, but evidently could not perceive him among the trees and shadows.

The Tuginda came through the creepers. He pointed without speaking and together they began to make their way down. Ta-Kominion, motioning his servants to remain a little behind, muttered, "A dead man—but where's the killer?"

The others made no reply. As they approached, Zilthé stepped back from the body. It was lying in blood which glistened viscous, smooth and black in the moonlight. One side of the head had been smashed into a great wound and from below the left shoulder blood was still oozing through lacerated rents in the cloak. The eyes were staring wide, but the open mouth and bared teeth were partly hidden by one arm which the man must have flung up to try to defend himself. He was wearing heeled boots, the boots of a messenger, and beneath the heels were dents in the ground, which he must have kicked as he died.

The Tuginda put her arm around Zilthé's shoulders, led her a little distance away and sat down beside her. Kelderek followed. The girl was weeping and terrified but able to speak.

"Lord Shardik, säiyett—he was sleeping. Then he woke suddenly and began to return toward the road, the same way that he went this afternoon. One would have thought that he had some purpose of his own. I tried to follow him but after a little he went fast, as though he were hunting—pursuing. When I reached the edge of the trees"—she pointed up the slope—"he was already down here. He was waiting—crouching behind the rocks. And then, after only a little, I heard the man—I saw him coming up the road and I ran out of the trees to call out and warn him. But I caught my foot—I stumbled and fell and as I got up, Lord Shardik came out from behind the rocks. The man saw him and screamed. He turned and ran, but Lord Shardik followed him and struck him down. He—he—" In the vividness of her recollection the girl beat at the air with one arm held out stiffly, open-handed, the fingers apart, rigid and curved.

"I might have saved him, säiyett—" She began to weep once more.

Ta-Kominion came over to them, his tongue protruding between his bared teeth as he shifted the position of his wounded arm in its sling.

"Do you recognize that man, Kelderek?" he asked.

"No. Is he from Ortelga?"

"He is from Ortelga. His name was Naron and he was a servant."

"Whose?"

"He served Fassel-Hasta."

"Served Fassel-Hasta? Then what could he have been doing here?"

Ta-Kominion hesitated, looking back at Numiss and his fellow, who had lifted the body to the other side of the track and were doing what they could to make it decent. Then he held out a blood-spattered leather scrip, opened it and showed to the Tuginda two strips of bark inked with brush-written letters.

"Can you read this message, säiyett?" he asked.

The Tuginda took the stiff, curved sheets and held first one and then the other at arm's length in the moonlight. Kelderek and Ta-Kominion could learn nothing from her face. At last she stood up, returned the sheets to the scrip and without speaking gave it back to the baron.

"You have read it, säiyett?"

She nodded once, reluctantly it seemed, as though she would have preferred, if she could, to disown knowledge of the message.

"Does it tell us what this man was doing here?" persisted Ta-Kominion.

"He was carrying news to Bekla of what happened in Ortelga today." She turned aside and looked down into the valley.

Ta-Kominion cried out and the servants across the road looked up, staring.

"God! It tells that we have crossed the causeway and what we mean to do?"

She nodded again.

"I might have guessed it! Why didn't I post my own men to watch the road? That treacherous—"

"But the road was watched for us nevertheless," said Kelderek. "Surely it was no accident that Zilthé stumbled before she could warn the man. Lord Shardik—*he* knew what had to be done!"

They stared at each other as the long, moonset shadow of the forest crept lower down the hillside.

"But Fassel-Hasta—why did he do it?" asked Kelderek at last.

"Why? For wealth and power, of course. I should have guessed! It was always he who dealt with Bekla. 'Yes, my lord.' 'I'll write it for you, my lord.' By the Bear! I'll write on his face with a hot knife this morning. That for a start. Numiss, you can leave that body for the buzzards—if they'll touch it."

His loud words, echoing, startled three or four pigeons out of the cleft of the brook below. As they rose with a clatter of wings and flew across the road and up into the forest Ta-Kominion, watching their flight, suddenly pointed.

From the edge of the trees, Shardik was looking down into the valley. For a moment they saw him plainly, his shape, black against the line of the woods, like an opened gate in a city wall. Then, as Kelderek raised his arms in salutation and prayer, he turned and vanished into the darkness.

"God be thanked!" cried Ta-Kominion. "Lord Shardik saved us from that devil! There—there is your sign, Kelderek! Our will is Shardik's will—our plan will succeed! No more children's games on the shore for you, my lad! We'll rule in Bekla; you and I! What is it you need? Tell me, and you shall have it within an hour of daybreak."

"Hark!" said the Tuginda, laying a hand on his arm.

From the forest above came faint calls. "Säiyett!" "Lord Kelderek!"

"Neelith will have woken Rantzay when she heard the man scream," said Kelderek. "They're looking for us. Zilthé, go up and bring them down. You are not afraid?"

The girl smiled. "Not now, my lord."

As she set off up the slope, the Tuginda turned to Kelderek.

"What plan is he speaking of?" she asked.

"Lord Ta-Kominion is going to lead our people against Bekla, säiyett, to win back what is ours by ancient right. They have crossed the Telthearna—"

"By now they will already be on the march," said Ta-Kominion.

"And our part, säiyett," went on Kelderek eagerly, "is to take Lord Shardik there, you and I. The baron will give us craftsmen to make a wheeled cage and men to draw it—"

147

He stopped a moment, meeting her incredulous eyes; but she said nothing and he resumed.

"He will be drugged, säiyett, as he was in the first days. I know it will be difficult—dangerous too—but I am not afraid. For the sake of the people—"

"I never heard such nonsense in my life," said the Tuginda. "Säiyett!"

"It will not be attempted. It is plain that you know nothing either of Lord Shardik or the true nature of his power. He is not some weapon or tool to be used for men's worldly greed. No—" she held up her hand as Ta-Kominion was about to speak— "nor even for the material gain of Ortelga. What God is pleased to impart to us through Shardik, that we should be holding ourselves ready to receive with humility and thanks. If the people believe in Shardik, that is their blessing. But you and I— we neither determine nor confer that blessing. I drugged Lord Shardik to save his life. He will not be drugged in order that he may be taken in a cage to Bekla."

Ta-Kominion remained silent for a little, the fingers of his injured arm, in its sling, tapping gently against his left side. At length he said, "And long ago, säiyett, when Shardik was brought to the Ledges, how, may I ask, was he brought, if not drugged and restrained?"

"Means used for an end appointed by God, that his servants might serve him. *You* are intending to make him a weapon of bloodshed for your own power."

"Time is short, säiyett. I have no time for argument."

"There is nothing over which to argue."

"Nothing," replied Ta-Kominion in a low, hard voice.

Stepping forward, he grasped the Tuginda strongly by the wrist. "Kelderek, you shall have your craftsmen within two hours, though the iron and some of the heavy materials may take longer. Remember, everything depends on resolution. *We'll* not fail the people, you and I."

For an instant he looked at Kelderek and his look said, "Are you a man, as you maintain, or an overgrown child under the thumb of a woman?" Then, still gripping the Tuginda's wrist, he called to the servants, who approached hesitantly from the scrub on the other side of the track.

148

"Numiss," said Ta-Kominion, "the säiyett is returning with us to meet Lord Zelda and the army on the road." He slipped his arm out of the leather strap. "Take this and tie her wrists behind her back."

"My—my lord," stammered Numiss, "I am afraid—"

Without another word Ta-Kominion, setting his teeth against the pain in his arm, himself drew the Tuginda's hands behind her back and bound them tightly with the strap. Then he put the free end into Numiss's hand. He held his knife in his teeth the while and was clearly ready to use it, but she made no resistance, standing silent with closed eyes and only compressing her lips as the strap cut into her wrists.

"Now we will go," said Ta-Kominion. "Believe me, säiyett, I regret this affront to your dignity. I do not wish to be obliged to gag you, so no cries for help, I beg you."

In the near-darkness of moonset the Tuginda turned and looked at Kelderek. For a moment his eyes met hers; then they fell to the ground and he did not look up as he heard her footsteps begin to stumble away along the track. When at length he did so, both she and Ta-Kominion were already some distance off. He ran after them and Ta-Kominion turned quickly, knife in hand.

"Ta-Kominion!" He was panting. "Don't harm her! She must not be hurt or ill-treated! She is not to come to any harm! Promise me."

"I promise you, High Priest of Lord Shardik in Bekla!"

Kelderek stood hesitant, half-hoping that she might speak even now. But she said nothing and soon they were gone, sight and sound, into the dawn mist and gloom of the valley. Once he heard Ta-Kominion's voice. Then he was alone in the solitude.

He turned and walked slowly back, past the dead man shrouded in his bloody cloak, past the rock where Shardik had lain in wait. On his left, above the dreary forest, the first light was gathering in the sky. Not a blow had yet been struck in the war, and yet he was filled with a sense of loneliness and danger, of being already committed past recall on a desperate enterprise which, if it did not succeed, could end only in ruin and death. He looked about the empty, twilit valley with a kind of puzzled surprise, such as a malicious child might feel, on holding a burning torch to a rick or thatch, to find that it caught slowly and did not on the instant blaze up to match the idea he had formed in his mind. Was desperation, then, so slow a business?

From the hillside he heard his name called and, turning, saw the tall shape of Rantzay striding down, with six or seven of the girls. At once his apprehension left him and he went to meet them, clear in mind and purposeful.

"Zilthé has told us, my lord, how Lord Shardik struck down the traitor from Ortelga. Is all well? Where are the Tuginda and the young baron?"

"They—they have returned together down the valley. The army has already set out and they have gone to join it. It is Lord Shardik's will to join the march on Bekla. We have to carry out that will, you and I, and there is no time to be lost."

"What are we to do, my lord?"

"Have you still got the sleeping drug in the camp—the drug which was used to heal Lord Shardik?"

"We have that and other drugs, my lord, but none in great quantity."

"There may well be enough. You are to seek out Lord Shardik and drug him insensible. How can it best be done?"

"He may take it in food, my lord. If not, we shall have to wait until he sleeps and then pierce him. That would be very dangerous, though it could be attempted."

"You have until sunset. If by some means or other he can be brought near this place, so much the better. Indeed, he must not fall asleep in thick forest, or all may fail."

Rantzay frowned and shook her head at the difficulty of the task. She was about to speak again, but Kelderek forestalled her.

"It *must* be attempted, Rantzay. If it is God's will—and I know that it is—you will succeed. At all costs, Lord Shardik must be drugged insensible by sunset."

At that moment they became aware of a confused noise, far off and still so faint as to be audible only between the gusts of the dawn breeze. As they listened it grew louder, until they could discern metallic sounds and human voices, a shouted order, a snatch of song. At length in the growing light they saw,

150

far below them, a slowly moving, dusty line, creeping on like a thread of spilled water across a paved floor. The vanguard of Ta-Kominion's army was coming up the valley.

Kelderek spoke quickly. "Only put aside doubt, Rantzay, and act out of a true belief that this can be achieved, and all will be well. I am going down to meet Lord Ta-Kominion. I shall return later and you will find me here. Sheldra and Neelith, come with me."

As he strode downhill between the two silent girls, with the sound of the marching tumult coming up to meet him, he felt his inward prayers turned back upon himself. Whether or not he had been right could be revealed only by the outcome. Yet Ta-Kominion was certain that it was Shardik's divine purpose to lead the army to victory. "We'll rule in Bekla, you and I." "And when that day comes," Kelderek thought, "no doubt the Tuginda will understand that all was for the best."

18 Rantzay

ON THE EDGE OF THE FOREST, Rantzay knelt over the tracks showing faintly in the hard ground. They led westward, into thick undergrowth, and where they disappeared the bark of a kalmet tree had been slashed white, high up, by the bear's claws. She knew that it was not two hours since Shardik had deliberately lain in wait and killed a man. In this mood he might well kill again—might lie in wait for those who tracked him or steal, elusive and silent, through the woods until he was behind them and the pursuers became the pursued.

The strain of the past month had told increasingly on the priestess. She was the oldest of the women who had followed Shardik down Ortelga and across the Telthearna strait, and though her belief in his divine power was untouched by the least doubt, she had felt also—more and more as the days went by—the hardship of the life and the continual fear of death. The young risk their lives heedlessly—often actually for sport—

but their elders, even while they may grow in humility and self-lessness, grow also in prudence and in regard for their own lives, those little portions of time in which they hope to create something fit to be offered at last to God. Rantzay, novice mistress and warden of the Ledges, had not, like Melathys, been caught unawares by the sudden coming of Shardik like a thief in the night. From the moment when the Tuginda's message had reached Quiso, she had know what would be required of her. Since then, day after day, she had been driving her gaunt and aging body over the rocky hillsides and through the thickets of the island, struggling with her own fear even while she calmed some near-hysterical girl and persuaded her to take part once more in the Singing, or herself took the girl's place and felt yet again the slow response of her muscles to the bear's lithe, unpredictable movements. On Quiso, Anthred, the woman struck down and killed among the trees by the shore, had been first her servant, then her pupil and finally her closest friend. Once in a dream she had embraced her as her own child and together they had dug up and burned that day in the rains, long ago, when Rantzay's disappointed father, frightened at last by her waking fits, her swoons and the voices that spoke and babbled from her at these times, had gone to the High Baron to offer to the Ledges his ugly, unmarriageable tent-pole of a daughter. She had recalled the dream as she performed the traditional rite of burning Anthred's quiver, bow and wooden rings upon her grave by the Telthearna strait.

By what means was Shardik to be brought into the open and drugged insensible? And if the means she chose were faulty, how many lives would be lost with nothing to show? She returned to the girls, who were standing together a little way off, looking down into the valley.

"When did he last eat?"

"No one has seen him eat, madam, since he left Ortelga yesterday morning."

"Then he is likely to be looking for food now. The Tuginda and Lord Kelderek say that he is to be drugged."

"Can we not follow him, madam," said Nito, "and put down meat or fish with tessik hidden in it?"

"Lord Kelderek says he must not fall asleep in the thick forest. If it can be accomplished, he is to return here."

"He will hardly return here, madam," said Nito, nodding her head toward the road below.

At the foot of the slope fires were already burning and the sounds came up of many men at work: sudden cries of urgency or warning, the flat ringing of a hammer on iron, the gushing of flame fanned by a bellows, the rasp of a saw, the tap-tap-tap of a mallet and chisel. They could see Kelderek going from one group to another, conferring, pointing, nodding his head while he talked. As they watched, Sheldra left his side and came climbing quickly toward them. Impassive as usual, she showed no excitement or breathlessness as she stood before Rantzay and raised her palm to her forehead.

"Lord Kelderek asks whether Shardik has yet gone far and what is to be done?"

"He may well ask—and he a hunter. Does he think Shardik is likely to stay near that stinking smoke and tumult?"

"Lord Kelderek has ordered that some goats should be driven higher up the valley and tethered on the edge of the forest. He hopes that if Lord Shardik can be prevented from hunting or feeding elsewhere, he may perhaps make his way toward them and that you may find means, madam, to drug him there."

"Go back and tell Lord Kelderek that if it can be done we will find a way to do it, with God's help. Zilthé, Nito, go back to the camp and bring up what meat you can find and all the tessik that is there—the green leaves as well as the dried powder. And you are to bring the other drug too—the theltocarna."

"But theltocarna can be administered only in a wound, madam, and not in food: it must be mingled with the blood."

"I know that as well as you," snapped Rantzay, "and I have already told you to bring it. There are six or seven gallbladders packed with moss in a wooden box with a sealed lid. Handle it carefully—the bladders must not be broken. I will send back one of the other girls to meet you here and bring you on to join us, wherever we may be."

The long and dangerous search for Shardik, westward through the forest, continued until after noon, and when at last Zilthé came running between the trees to say that she had caught sight of the bear prowling along the bank of a stream not far away, Rantzay already felt herself on the point of collapse from strain and fatigue. She followed the girl slowly through a grove of myrtles and out into an expanse of tall, yellow grass buzzing with insects in the sun. Here Zilthé pointed to the bank of the stream.

Shardik gave no sign that he had seen them. He was fishing—splashing in and out of the water and every now and then scooping out a fish to flap and jump on the stony bank before he held it down and ate it in two or three bites. Watching him, Rantzay's heart sank. To approach him was more than she dared attempt. The girls, she knew, would not refuse to obey her if she ordered them to do it. But what end would it serve? Suppose they could, somehow, succeed in startling him from the brook, what then? How were they to drive or entice him to return in the direction from which he had come?

She went back to the trees and lay prone, her chin propped on her hands. The girls, gathering about her, waited for her to speak, but she said nothing. The shadows moved over the ground before her eyes and the flies settled at the corners of her mouth. The heat was intense but she gave no sign of discomfort, only now and then standing up to look at the bear and then lying down as before.

At length Shardik left the stream and stretched himself out in a patch of great hemlock plants not far from where the priestess was lying. She could hear the hollow sound of the stems as they snapped and see the white umbels of bloom toppling and falling as the bear rolled among them. The silence returned, and with it the weight of her impossible task and the agony of her determination. In her perplexed exhaustion she thought with envy of her friend, free at last from every burden —from the laborious dedication of the Ledges and the continual fatigue and fear of the last weeks. If one had power to change the past—it was a favorite fantasy with her, though one which she had never shared, even with Anthred. If she had power to change the past, at what point would she enter it to do so? At that night on the beach of Quiso, a month ago? This time she would not guide them inland, but turn them back, the night messengers, the heralds of Shardik.

It was dark. It was night. She and Anthred were standing once more on the stony beach with the flat, green lanterns between them, splashing the shallow water with their staves.

"Go back!" she cried into the darkness. "Go back, return whence you came! You should never have come here! I—yes, I myself—am the voice of God and that is the message I am sent to deliver to you!"

She felt Anthred clutch at her arm, but pushed her aside. The windless, moonless darkness was thick about them: only the sky retained a faint trace of light. Something was approaching, splashing slowly and heavily toward the shore. A huge, black shape loomed above her, its lowered head turning from side to side, the mouth open, the breath fetid and rank. She faced it imperiously. Once she and it had gone their several ways, then —ah! then she would return with Anthred to find her girlhood, to turn its course away from Quiso forever. She raised her arm and was about to speak again, but the presence, with a soft, shaggy slapping of wet feet on the shore, passed by her and was gone into the wooded island.

There was a blinding light and a noise of scolding birds. Rantzay looked about her in bewilderment. She was standing knee-deep in the dry, tawny grass. The sun was thinly covered with a fleece of cloud and suddenly a long, distant roll of thunder ran round the edge of the sky. Some insect had stung her on the neck and her fingers, as she drew them across the place, came away smeared with blood. She was alone. Anthred was dead and she herself was standing in the dried-up, bitter forest south of the Telthearna. The tears flowed silently down her haggard, dusty face as she bent forward, supporting herself upon her staff.

After a few moments she bit hard upon her hand, drew herself up and gazed about her. Some distance away, Nito looked out from among the trees and then approached, staring at her incredulously.

"Madam—what—the bear—what have you done? Are you unharmed? Wait—lean on me. I—oh, I was afraid—I am so much afraid—"

"The bear?" said Rantzay. "Where is the bear?"

As she spoke, she noticed for the first time a broad path flattened through the grass beside her and on it, here and there, the tracks of Shardik, broader than roof tiles. She bent down. The smell of the bear was plain. It could have passed only since she had last seen it among the hemlocks. Dazed, she raised her hands to her face and was about to ask Nito what had happened, when she became conscious of yet one more bodily affliction. Her tears fell again—tears of shame and degradation.

"Nito, I—I am going down to the stream. Go and tell the girls to follow Lord Shardik at once. Then wait for me here. You and I will overtake them."

In the water she stripped and washed her body and fouled clothes as well as she could. On Quiso it had been easier; often Anthred had been able to perceive when one of her fits was coming on and had contrived to help her to save her dignity and authority. Now there was not one of the girls whom she could think of as her friend. Looking back, she caught a glimpse of Nito loitering discreetly among the trees. She would know what had happened, of course, and tell others.

They must not be too long in catching up. Left to themselves the girls would not be steady, and if by some incredible stroke of fortune Shardik were indeed to return whence he had come, nevertheless without herself they could not be relied upon to do their utmost—to death if necessary—to carry out the Tuginda's instructions.

She and Nito had not gone far when she realized that the fit had left her dulled and stupefied. She longed to rest. Perhaps, she thought, Shardik would stop or turn aside before the evening, and Lord Kelderek would be forced to allow them another day. But each time they came up with one or other of the girls waiting to show them the direction, the news was that the bear was still wandering slowly southeastward, as though making for the hill country below Gelt.

Evening came on. Rantzay's pace had become a limping hobble from one tree trunk to the next; yet still she exhorted Nito to keep her eyes open, to make sure of the right way forward and to call from time to time in hope of hearing a reply from ahead. Vaguely, she was aware of twilight, of the fall of darkness and later of moonlight among the trees; of intermittent thunder, far off, and of swift, momentary gusts of wind. Once she saw Anthred standing among the trees and was about to speak to her when her friend smiled, laid a ringed finger to her lips and disappeared.

At last, in clear moonlight, at some mid hour of the night, she looked about her and realized that she had caught up with the girls. They were standing close together, in a whispering group; but as she approached, leaning on Nito's arm, they all turned toward her and fell silent. To her their silence seemed full of dislike and resentment. If she had hoped for comradeship or sympathy at the end of this bitter journey, she was clearly to be disappointed. Handing her staff to Nito she drew herself up, almost crying out as she put her full weight upon the broken-blistered soles of her feet.

"Where is Lord Shardik?"

"Close at hand, madam—not a bowshot away. He has been sleeping since moonrise."

"Who is that?" said Rantzay, peering. "Sheldra? I thought you were with Lord Kelderek. How do you come to be here? Where are we?"

"We are a little higher up the valley that you left this morning, madam, and on the edge of the forest. Zilthé came down to the camp to tell Lord Kelderek that Shardik had returned, but she was exhausted, so he sent me back instead of her. He says that Lord Shardik must be drugged tonight."

"Has any attempt been made to drug him?"

No one replied.

"Well?"

"We have done all we could, madam," said another of the girls. "We prepared two haunches of meat with tessik and placed them as close to him as we dared, but he would not touch them. There is no more tessik. We can only wait until he wakes."

"Before I left Lord Kelderek, madam," said Sheldra, "a messenger arrived from Gelt, from Lord Ta-Kominion. He sent word that he expected to fight the day after tomorrow and that Shardik must come no matter what the cost. His words were, 'The hours now are more precious than stars.' "

From the hills to the south the lightning flickered between the trees. Rantzay limped the few yards to the edge of the forest and looked out across the valley. The sound of the brook below wavered on the air. Away to her left she could see the fires of the camp where the Tuginda and Kelderek must at this moment be waiting for news. She thought of the black shape that had

157

passed her in the noonday night, through the watery shallows of the grass, and of Anthred smiling among the trees, her hands adorned with the plaited rings that she herself had burned by the shore. These signs were clear enough. The situation was, in fact, a simple one. All that was required was a priestess who knew her duty and was capable of carrying it out with resolution.

She returned to the girls. They drew back from her, staring silently in the dimness.

"You say Lord Shardik is close at hand. Where?"

Someone pointed. "Go and make sure that he is still sleeping," said Rantzay. "You should not have left him unwatched. You are all to blame."

"Madam—"

"Be silent!" said Rantzay. "Nito, bring me the box of theltocarna."

She drew her knife and tested it. The sharp edges sliced lightly through a leaf held between her finger and thumb, while the point, with the least pressure upon it, almost pierced the skin of her wrist. Nito was standing before her with the wooden box. Rantzay stared coldly down at the girl's trembling fingers and then at the knife held motionless in her own steady hand.

"Come with me. You too, Sheldra." She took the box.

She remembered the last time that she and Anthred had walked through fire, in the courtyard of the Upper Temple, on the night when they had led Kelderek to the Bridge of the Suppliants. There was an unreality about the memory, as though it were not hers but some other woman's. The night sounds seemed magnified about her. The dry forest echoed through caves of dripping water and her body felt like a mass of hot sand. These were symptoms she recognized. She would need to be quick. Her fear was somewhere behind her, searching for her, overtaking her among the trees.

The bear was stretched on its side in a thicket of *cenchulada* saplings, two of which he had pushed down and snapped in making a place to sleep. A few feet away lay one of the haunches of meat. Whoever had put it there had not lacked courage. The huge mass of the body was dappled with moonlight and leaf shadows. The shaggy flank, rising and falling in sleep and overlaid with the speckled, moving light, appeared like a dark plain of grass. Before the half-open, breathing mouth the leaves on one of the broken branches stirred and glistened. The claws of one extended forepaw were curved upward. Rantzay stood a few moments, gazing as though at a deep, swift river into which she must now plunge and drown. Then, motioning the girls away, she stepped forward.

She was standing against the ridge of Shardik's back, looking over his body, as though from behind an earthwork, at the restless, wind-moved forest. The thunder muttered in the hills and Shardik stirred, twitched one ear and then once more lay still.

Rantzay thrust her left hand deep into the pelt. She could not lay bare the skin and began cutting away the oily hair, matted and full of parasites as a sheep's fleece. Her own hands were trembling now and she worked faster, lifting each handful carefully, cutting and then drawing it away from under the sharp knife.

Soon she had cut a wide, bristling patch across the shoulder, almost baring the gray, salt-flaked skin. Two or three veins ran across it, one thick enough to reveal the slow beating of the pulse.

Rantzay turned and stooped for the box beside her. Taking out two of the little oiled bladders, she placed them between the fingertips of her left hand. Then she drove the point of the knife into the bear's shoulder and drew the blade back toward her, opening a gash half as long as her own forearm. Smoothly, without a pause, she pushed the bladders into it, drew the edges of the incision over them, pressed downward and felt them crush inside.

With a snarl, Shardik threw back his head and rose upon his hind legs. Rantzay, flung to the ground, got up and stood facing him. For a moment it seemed that he would strike her down. Then, lurching forward, he crushed her against his body. A few steps he carried her, hanging grotesquely in his grip. Then, letting her drop, limp as an old garment fallen from a line, he staggered out to the open slope beyond the trees. He rolled on the ground and froth flew from his mouth as he bit and tore at the grass.

Sheldra was the first to reach the priestess. Her left hand had been gashed by her own knife, her tongue protruded and her head lay grotesquely upon her shoulder, like that of a hanged man. When Sheldra put one arm beneath her and tried to raise her a terrible, crackling sound came from the broken body. The girl laid her back and for a moment she opened her eyes.

"Tell the Tuginda—did what she said—"

Blood gushed from her mouth and when it ceased her gaunt, bony body vibrated very lightly, like the surface of a pool fluttered by the wings of a trapped fly. The movement ceased and Sheldra, perceiving that she was dead, drew off her wooden rings, picked up the box of theltocarna and the fallen knife and made her way out to the slope where Shardik lay insensible.

19 *Night Messengers*

THE CAGE HAD TAKEN ALL DAY TO COMPLETE—if complete it were. On hearing his orders Baltis, the master smith, had shrugged his shoulders, making light of Kelderek, whom he had heard of as a simple young fellow with neither family, wealth nor craft— for in his eyes hunters were not craftsmen. He and his men, being armed with excellent weapons of their own making, had supposed that they were about to play their part in the sack of Bekla—or at any rate the sack of Gelt—and took it ill to be called out of the march and put back on their accustomed work. Kelderek, having tried in vain to bring home to the great, lumbering fellow the vital importance of what he had to do, went back to Ta-Kominion, catching him just as he was about to set out with the advance guard. Ta-Kominion, cursing with impatience, summoned Baltis to him under the tree that bore the body of Fassel-Hasta and promised him that if the cage were not complete by nightfall he should hang like the baron. This was talk that Baltis could understand clearly enough, and he immediately asked for double the number of men he expected to get. Ta-Kominion, being in too much haste to argue, allowed him fifty, including two rope makers, three wheelwrights and five carpenters. As the army wound away up the valley in the thickening, sultry morning, Kelderek and Baltis fell to their work.

Messengers were sent back to Ortelga and before midday all the stored fuel on the island, much of its stock of sawn timber and every piece of forged iron had been carried up to the camp by women and boys. The iron was of different lengths and thickness, much of it too short to be of use except as pieces for welding. Baltis set his men to make three axles and as many iron bars as possible, the latter to be of equal length and thickness, pointed and pierced at both ends. Meanwhile the carpenters and wheelwrights, using seasoned wood, some of which had until that morning formed part of the walls, roofs and tables of Ortelga, built a heavy platform of strutted planks, which they raised with levers and mounted upon six spokeless wheels, solid wood to the rims.

By evening Baltis's men had forged, welded or cut sixty bars—disparate, rough-edged things, yet serviceable enough to be driven point-first through the holes drilled round the edges of the platform and then secured with iron pins.

"The roof will have to be wooden too," said Baltis, looking at the poles sticking up out of the planks and pointing this way and that like a bed of reeds. "There's no more iron, young man, and none to be had, so no use to fret over it."

"A wooden roof will shake to pieces," said the master carpenter. "It'll not hold the bear, not if he goes to break it."

"It's not work to be done in a day," growled Baltis. "No, not in three days. A cage to hold a bear? I was the first to see Lord Shardik come ashore yesterday morning, barring that poor devil Lukon and his mate—"

"How's the bear to be brought to the cage?" interrupted the carpenter.

"Ah, that's more than we know—"

"You are here to obey Lord Ta-Kominion," said Kelderek. "It is the will of God that Lord Shardik is to conquer Bekla, and that you will see with your own eyes. Make the roof of wood if it must be so, and bind the whole cage round with rope, twisted tight."

The work was finished at last by torchlight and Kelderek,

161

when he had dismissed the men to eat, remained alone with Sheldra and Neelith, peering and probing, kicking at the wheels, fingering the axle pins and finally testing each of the six bars set aside to close the still-open end.

"How is he to be released, my lord?" asked Neelith. "Is there to be no door?"

"The time is too short to make a door," answered Kelderek. "When the hour comes to release him, we shall be shown the way."

"He must be kept drugged, my lord, as long as possible," said Sheldra, "for neither that nor any other cage will hold Lord Shardik if he is minded otherwise."

"I know it," said Kelderek. "We might as well have made a cart to put him in. If only we knew where he is—"

He broke off as Zilthé came limping into the torchlight, raised her palm to her forehead and at once sank to the ground.

"Forgive me, lord," she said, drawing her bow from her shoulder and laying it beside her. "We have been following Lord Shardik all day and I am exhausted—with fear even more than with fatigue. He went far—"

"Where is he?" interrupted Kelderek.

"My lord, he is sleeping on the edge of the forest, not an hour from here."

"God be praised!" cried Kelderek, clapping his hands together. "I knew it was His will!"

"It was Rantzay, my lord, who brought him back," said the girl, staring up at Kelderek as though even now afraid. "We came upon him at noon, fishing in a stream. He lay down near the bank and we dared not approach him. But after a long time, when it seemed that there was nothing to be done, Rantzay, without telling us what she intended, suddenly stood up and went out into the open where Lord Shardik could see her. She called him. My lord, as I live, she called him and he came to her! We all fled in terror, but she spoke to him in a strange and dreadful voice, rebuking him and telling him to return, for he should never have come so far, she said. And Shardik obeyed her, my lord! He passed by her, where she stood. He made his way back at her command."

"God's will indeed," said Kelderek with awe, "and all that we have done is right. Where is Rantzay now?"

"I do not know, my lord," said Zilthé, almost weeping. "Nito told us we were to follow Lord Shardik and that Rantzay would overtake us. But she did not, and it is many hours now since we last saw her."

Kelderek was about to send Sheldra up the valley when a challenge and answer sounded from farther along the road. After a pause they heard footsteps and Numiss appeared. He, too, was exhausted and did not ask Kelderek for leave to sit before flinging himself to the ground.

"I've come from beyond Gelt," he said. "We took Gelt easy —set it on fire—not much fighting but we killed the chief and after that the rest of 'em were willing enough to do what Lord Ta-Kominion told 'em. He talked to some of 'em alone and I dare say he asked them what they knew about Bekla—how to get there and all the rest of it. Anyway, whatever it was—"

"If he gave you a message, tell me that," said Kelderek sharply. "Never mind what you heard or suppose."

"This is the message, sir. 'I expect to fight the day after to-morrow. The rains can be no later and now the hours are more precious than stars. Bring Lord Shardik no matter what the cost.'"

Kelderek jumped up and began pacing to and fro beside the cage, biting his lip and smiting his clenched fist into his palm. At length, recovering himself, he told Sheldra to go and find Rantzay and, if Shardik had been drugged, to bring back word at once. Then, fetching some brands to start a fire, he sat down by the cage with Numiss and the two girls to wait for news. None spoke, but every now and again Kelderek would look up, frowning, to mark the slow time from the wheeling stars.

When at last Zilthé started and laid a hand on his arm, he had heard nothing. He turned to meet her eyes and she stared back at him, holding her breath, her face half firelit, half in shadow. He too listened, but could hear only the flames, the fitful wind and a man coughing somewhere in the camp behind them. He shook his head but she nodded sharply, stood up and motioned him to follow her along the road. Watched by Neelith and Numiss they set off into the darkness, but had gone only a little way when she stopped, cupped her hands and called, "Who's there?"

The reply "Nito!" was faint but clear enough. A few moments later Kelderek caught at last the girl's light tread and went forward to meet her. It was plain that in her haste and agitation she had fallen—perhaps more than once. She was begrimed, disheveled and scratched across the knees and one forearm. Her breath came in sobs and they could see the tears on her cheeks. He called to Numiss and together they supported her as far as the fire.

The camp was astir. Somehow the men had guessed that news was at hand. Several were already waiting beside the cage and one spread his cloak for the girl across a pile of leftover planks, brought a pitcher and knelt down to wash her bleeding scratches. At the touch of the cold water she winced and, as though recalled to herself, began speaking to Kelderek.

"Shardik is lying insensible, my lord, not a bowshot from the road. He has been drugged with theltocarna—enough to kill a strong man. God knows when he will wake."

"With theltocarna?" said Neelith, incredulously. "But—"

Nito began to weep again. "And Rantzay is dead—dead! Have you told Lord Kelderek how she spoke to Shardik beside the stream?

Zilthé nodded, staring aghast.

"When Shardik had passed her and gone, she stood for a time stricken, it seemed, as though, like a tree, she had called lightning down to her. Then we were alone, she and I, following the others as best we might. I could tell—I could tell that she meant to die, that she was determined to die. I tried to make her rest but she refused. It is not two hours since we returned at last to the edge of the forest. All the girls could see her death upon her. It was drawn about her like a cloak. None could speak to her for pity and fear. After what we had seen by the stream at noon, any one of us would have died in her place; but it was as though she were already drifting away, as though she were on the water and we on the shore. We stood near her and she spoke to us, yet we were separated from her. She spoke and we were silent. Then, as she ordered, I gave her the box of theltocarna, and she walked up to Lord Shardik as though he were a sleeping ox. She cut him with a knife and mingled the theltocarna with his blood; and then, as he woke in anger, she stood before him yet again, with no more fear than she had shown at noon.

And he clutched her, and so she died." The girl looked about her. "Where is the Tuginda?"

"Get the long ropes on the cage," said Kelderek to Baltis, "and set every man to draw it. Yes, and every woman too, except for those who carry torches. There is no time to be lost. Even now we may be too late to reach Lord Ta-Kominion."

Less than three hours later the enormous bulk of Shardik, the head protected by a hood made from cloaks roughly stitched together, had been dragged with ropes down the slope and up a hastily piled ramp of earth, stones and planks into the cage. The last bars had been hammered into place and the cage, hauled in front and pushed behind, was jolting and rocking slowly up the valley toward Gelt.

20 *Gel-Ethlin*

It could surely be no more than a day—two days at the most—thought Gel-Ethlin, to the breaking of the rains. For hours the thundery weather had been growing more and more oppressive, while rising gusts of warm wind set the dust swirling over the Beklan plain. Santil-kè-Erketlis, commander of the northern army of patrol, being taken sick with the heat, had left the column two days previously, returning to the capital by the direct road south and entrusting Gel-Ethlin, his second in command, with the task of completing the army's march to Kabin of the Waters, down through Tonilda and thence westward to Bekla itself. This would be a straightforward business—a fortification to be repaired here, a few taxes to be collected there, perhaps a dispute or two to be settled and, of course, the reports to be heard of local spies and agents. None of these matters was likely to be urgent and, since the army was already a day or two behind time for its return to Bekla, Santil-kè-Erketlis had told Gel-Ethlin to break off as soon as the rains began in earnest and take the most direct route back from wherever he happened to find himself.

"And high time too," thought Gel-Ethlin, standing beside his command banner with the falcon emblem, to watch the column go past. "They've marched enough. Half of them are in no sort of condition. The sooner they get back to rain-season quarters the better. If the stagnant water fever hit them now they'd go down in cursing rows."

He looked northward, where the plain met the foothills rising to the steep, precipitous ridges above Gelt. The skyline, dark and threatening, with cloud hiding the summits, appeared to Gel-Ethlin full of promise—the promise of early relief. With luck their business could be decently cut short in Kabin and one forced march, with the rains and the prospect of homecoming to spur them on, would see them safely in Bekla within a couple of days.

The two Beklan armies of patrol—the northern and the southern—customarily remained in the field throughout the summer, when the risk was greatest of rebellion or, conceivably, of attack from a neighboring country. Each army completed, twice, a roughly semicircular march of about two hundred miles along the frontiers. Sometimes detachments saw action against bandits or raiders, and occasionally the force might be ordered to make a punitive raid across a border, to demonstrate that Bekla had teeth and could bite. But for the most part it was routine stuff—training and maneuvers, intelligence work, tax collection, escorting envoys or trade caravans, road and bridge mending, and most important of all, simply letting themselves be seen by those who feared them only less than they feared invasion and anarchy. Upon the onset of the rains, the northern army returned to winter in Bekla, while the southern took up its quarters in Ikat Yeldashay, sixty miles to the south. The following summer the roles of the armies were reversed.

No doubt the southern army was already back in Ikat, thought Gel-Ethlin enviously. The southern army had the easier task of the two; their route of march was less exhausting and the dry season was less trying a hundred miles to the south. Nor was it only a question of work and conditions. Although Bekla was, of course, a city beyond compare, he himself had found, last winter, an excellent reason—in fact, for a soldier, a most time-honored and attractive (if somewhat expensive) reason—for preferring Ikat Yeldashay.

The Tonildan contingent, a particularly sorry-looking lot, were marching past now, and Gel-Ethlin called their captain out to explain why the men looked dirty and their weapons ill cared for. The captain began his explanation—something about having had the command wished on him two days ago in place of an officer ordered to return with Santil-kè-Erketlis—and while he continued, Gel-Ethlin, as was often his way, looked him sternly in the eye while thinking about something completely different.

At least this summer they had not had to go traipsing over the hills of Gelt and into the backwoods. Once several years ago, when he was still a junior commander, he had served on an expedition to the south bank of the Telthearna, and a dismal, uncomfortable business it had been, camping among the gloomy forests, or commandeering flea-ridden quarters from some half-savage tribe of islanders living like frogs in the river mists. Fortunately the practice of sending Beklan troops as far as the Telthearna had almost ceased since their intelligence reports from the island—what the devil was it called? Itilga? Catalga? —had become so regular and reliable. One of the less apelike barons was secretly in the pay of Bekla and apparently the High Baron himself was not averse to a little diplomatic bribery, provided a show was made of respecting his dignity and position, such as they were. During the recent summer marches Santil-kè-Erketlis had received two reports from this place. The first, duly passed on to headquarters at Bekla, had resulted in instructions being returned to the army that once again there was no need to send troops into inhospitable country so far afield. It had, in fact, contained nothing worse than news of an exceptionally widespread forest fire that had laid waste the farther bank of the Telthearna. The second report had included some tale of a new tribal cult which it was feared might boil over into fanaticism, though the High Baron seemed confident of keeping it under control. Bekla's reactions to the second report had not yet found their way back to the northern army, but anyway, thank God, it was now too late in the season to think of sending even a patrol over the hills of Gelt. The rains were coming any day—any hour.

The officer had finished speaking and was now looking at him in silence. Gel-Ethlin frowned, gave a contemptuous snort, suggesting that he had never heard such unconvincing nonsense in his life, and said he would inspect the contingent himself next morning. The officer saluted and went off to rejoin his men.

At this moment a messenger arrived from the governor of Kabin, sixteen miles to the east. The governor sent word that he was worried lest the rains should begin and the army withdraw to Bekla before reaching him. During the past ten or twelve days the level of the Kabin reservoir, from which water was brought by canal sixty miles to Bekla, had sunk until the lower walls had become exposed and a section had cracked in the heat. If a disaster were to be prevented the repair work ought to be carried out at once, before the rains raised the level again; but to complete the job in a matter of a day or two was beyond local resources.

Gel-Ethlin could recognize an emergency when he was faced with one. He sent at once for his most reliable senior officer and also for a certain Captain Han-Glat, a foreigner from Terekenalt, who knew more than anyone in the army about bridges, dams and soil movement. As soon as they appeared he told them what had happened and gave them a free hand to select the fittest troops, up to half the total strength, for a forced march to Kabin that night. As soon as possible after getting there they were to make a start on repairing the reservoir. He himself, with the rest of the men, would join them before evening of the following day.

By late afternoon they were gone, the soldiers grumbling but at least not mutinous. There was a good deal of limping and their pace was slow. Still, that was less worrying than the thought of the probable condition they would be in when they got to Kabin. Presumably, however, Han-Glat would need a few hours to survey the reservoir and decide what needed to be done, and this in itself would give them some rest. At any rate he, Gel-Ethlin, could hardly be criticized by headquarters in Bekla for the way he had gone about the matter. As night fell he went the rounds of the sentries and bivouacs—a shorter task than usual, with his command down to half strength—heard the casualty reports and authorized a handful of genuinely sick men to be sent back to Bekla by oxcart; ate his supper, played three games of *wari* with his staff captain (at which he lost fifteen *meld*) and went to bed.

168

The following morning he was up so early that he had the satisfaction of rousing some of his officers in person. But the low spirits of the men gave him much less satisfaction. The news had got round that they were in for not only a forced march to Kabin, rains or no rains, but also for plenty of work when they got there. Even the best troops are apt to take it hard when ordered to do something arduous after having been led to believe that their work is virtually finished, and Gel-Ethlin had deliberately retained his second-best. Himself a sturdy, energetic man, staunch in adversity, he could hardly contain his annoyance at the stupidity of the soldiers in being unable to realize the serious nature of the news from Kabin. It was only with difficulty that three or four of his senior officers were able to convince him that it was hardly to be expected that they would.

"It's a curious thing, sir," said Kapparah—a leathery fifty-five-year-old who had survived a lifetime's campaigning and prudently turned all the loot that had stuck to his fingers into farmland on the borders of Sarkid—"it's always struck me as a curious thing, that when you're asking men to give a little extra, the amount they're genuinely able to give depends on the reason. If it's defending their homes, for instance, or fighting for what they believe is theirs by right, they'll find themselves able to do almost anything. In fact, if it's a matter of any sort of fighting, they're nearly always able to give a good deal. They can understand that, you see, and no one wants his mates to think he's a coward, or that he dropped out while they went on. Those kinds of thoughts are like keys to a secret armory. A man doesn't know what he's got inside until the key opens it. But to repair the reservoir at Kabin—no, they can't grasp the importance of that, so it's a key that doesn't fit the lock. It's not *won't*, sir, it's *can't*, you know."

The camp had been struck, the columns were drawn up ready to march and the pickets, who had been fed and inspected at their posts, were being called in last of all, when the guard commander brought in a limping, blood-stained hill man. He was little more than a boy, openmouthed and wide-eyed, staring about him and continually raising one hand to his mouth as he licked the bleeding gash across his knuckles. Two soldiers had him under the armpits or he might well have turned tail.

"Refugee, sir," said the guard commander, saluting Bekla-fashion, with his right forearm across his chest, "from the hills. Talking about some sort of trouble at Gelt, sir, as near as I can make him out."

"Can't stop for that sort of thing now, guard commander," said Gel-Ethlin. "Turn the fellow loose and get your men fallen in."

Released by the soldiers, the hill man at once fell on his knees in front of Kapparah, whom he probably took for the senior officer present. He had babbled a few words in broken Beklan—something about "bad men" and "fire"—when Kapparah stopped him by speaking to him in his own language. There followed a swift dialogue of question and answer so incisive and urgent that Gel-Ethlin thought it better not to interrupt. Finally Kapparah turned to him.

"I think we'd better get the whole story out of this man before we set off for Kabin, sir," he said. "He keeps saying Gelt's been taken and burned by an invading army and he will have it that they're on their way down here."

Gel-Ethlin threw out his hands with a questioning look of mock forbearance and the other officers, who did not particularly like Kapparah, smiled sycophantically.

"You know what we're up against at Kabin, Kapparah. This is hardly the time—" He broke off and began again. "Some terrified peasant lad from the hills who'll say anything—"

"Well, that's just it, sir; he's not a peasant lad. He's the chief's son, run for his life, it seems. Says the chief's been murdered by fanatics in some religious war they've started."

"How do we know he's the chief's son?"

"By the tattooing on his arms, sir. He'd never dare to have that done just to deceive people."

"Where are these invaders supposed to have come from?"

"From Ortelga, sir, he says."

"From *Ortelga*?" said Gel-Ethlin. "But at that rate we should have heard—"

Kapparah said nothing and Gel-Ethlin thought the problem over quickly. It was an awkward one. In spite of there having been no recent report from Ortelga, it was just possible that some sort of tribal raid really was going to be made on the

170

Beklan plain. If it took place after he had marched away to Kabin, ignoring a tribesman's warning uttered in the hearing of his senior officers—and if lives were lost— He broke off this train of thought and started another. If the great reservoir were breached and ruined in the rains for lack of an adequate labor force, after he had marched away toward Gelt on the strength of a hysterical report made by a native youth in the hearing of his senior officers— He stopped again. They were all looking at him and waiting.

"Bring the boy to that shed over there," said Gel-Ethlin. "Let the men fall out, but see that they stay in their companies."

Half an hour later he had concluded that the story was one that he could not ignore. Washed and fed, the youth had recovered himself and spoken with restraint and dignity of his own loss, and with consistency of the danger that was threatening. It was a curious and yet convincing tale. An enormous bear, he said, had appeared on Ortelga, probably fugitive from the fire beyond the Telthearna. Its appearance was believed by the islanders to herald the fulfillment of a prophecy that Bekla would one day fall to an invincible army from the island and had started a rising, led by a young baron, in which the previous ruler and certain others had been either killed or driven out. Gel-Ethlin perceived that this, if true, would account for the failure of the Beklan army's normal flow of intelligence. Yesterday afternoon, the youth continued, the Ortelgans had suddenly appeared in Gelt, set it on fire and murdered the chief before he could organize any defense of the town. Fanatical and undisciplined, they had swept through the place and apparently subdued the townspeople altogether. Several of the latter, their homes and means of livelihood destroyed, had actually joined the Ortelgans for what they could get. Surely, said the young man, there could never have been men more eager than the Ortelgans to go upon their ruin. They believed that the bear was the incarnation of the Power of God, that it was marching with them, invisibly, night and day, that it could appear and disappear at will and that it would in due course destroy their enemies as fire burns stubble. On the orders of their young leader —who was evidently both brave and able, but appeared to be ill —they had thrown a ring of sentries around Gelt to prevent any news getting out. The youth, however, had climbed down a sheer precipice by night, escaping with no more than a badly gashed hand, and then, knowing the passes well, had come over twenty miles during six hours of darkness and daybreak.

"What a damned nuisance!" said Gel-Ethlin. "Which way does he think they're likely to come, and when?"

The young man apparently thought it certain that they would come by the most direct route and as quickly as they could. Indeed, it was probable that they had already started. Setting aside their eagerness to fight, they had little food with them, for there was virtually none to be commandeered in Gelt. They would have to fight soon or be forced to disperse for supplies.

Gel-Ethlin nodded. This agreed with all his own experience of rebels and peasant irregulars. Either they fought at once or else they fell to pieces.

"They don't sound likely to get far, sir," said Balaklesh, who commanded the Lapan contingent. "Why not simply go on to Kabin and leave them to fall apart in the rains?"

As is often the way, the wrong advice immediately cleared Gel-Ethlin's mind and showed him what had to be done.

"No, that wouldn't do. They'd wander about for months, parties of brigands, murdering and looting. No village would be safe and in the end another army would have to be sent to hunt them down. Do you all believe the boy's telling no more than the truth?"

They nodded.

"Then we must destroy them at once, or the villages will be saying that a Beklan army fell down on its job. And we must reach them before they get down the hill road from Gelt and out on the plain—partly to stop them looting and partly because once they're on the plain they may go anywhere. We might lose track of them altogether and the men are in no state to go marching about in pursuit. There's even less time to be lost now than if we were going to Kabin. Kapparah, hang on to the lad— we'll need him as a guide. You'd all better go and tell your men that we've got to get to the hills by the afternoon. Balaklesh, you take a hundred reliable spearmen and start at once. Find us a good defensive position in the foothills, send back a guide and then push on and try to find out what the Ortelgans are doing."

Within an hour the sky had clouded over from one horizon to the other and the west wind was blowing steadily. The red dust filled the soldiers' eyes, ears and nostrils and mingled grittily, beneath their clothes, with the sweat of their bodies. They marched with cloths or leather bound over mouths and noses, continually screwing up their eyes, unable to see the hills ahead, each company following that in front through the thick helter-skelter of dust which piled itself like snow along the windward sides of rocks, of banks, of the few sparse trees and huts along the way—and of men. It got into the rations and even into the wineskins. Gel-Ethlin marched behind the column on the lee-ward flank, whence he could check the stragglers and keep them in some sort of order. After two hours he called a halt and re-formed the column in echelon, so that when they set out again each company was marching downwind of that immediately behind it. This, however, did little to relieve their discomfort, which was due less to the dust they raised themselves than to the storm blowing over the whole plain. Their pace diminished and it was not until a good three hours after noon that the lead-ing company reached the edge of the plain and, having recon-noitered half a mile in either direction, found the road to Gelt where it wound up through the myrtle and cypress groves on the lower slopes.

About a thousand feet above the plain the road reached a level green spot where the ghost of a waterfall trickled down into a rock pool, and here, as they came up, the successive companies fell out, drank and lay down in the grass. Looking back, they could see the dust storm on the plain below and their spirits rose to think that at least one misery was left behind. Gel-Ethlin, grudging the delay, urged his officers to get them on their feet again. The afternoon had set in dark and the wind over the plain was dropping. They stumbled on wearily, their footsteps, the clink of their arms and the occasional shouts of orders echoing from the crags about them.

It was not long before they came to a narrow gorge, where two officers of the advance party were awaiting them. Balaklesh, the officers reported, had found an excellent defensive position about a mile farther up the road, beyond the mouth of the gorge, and his scouts had been out ahead of it for more than an hour.

Gel-Ethlin went forward to meet him and see the position for himself. It was very much the sort of thing he had had in mind, an upland plateau about half a mile wide, with certain features favorable to disciplined troops able to keep ranks and stand their ground. Ahead, to the north, the road came curving steeply downhill around a wooded shoulder. On the right flank was thick forest and on the left a ravine. Through this bottleneck the advancing enemy must needs come. At the foot of the shoulder the ground became open and rose gently, among scattered crags and bushes, to a crest over which the road passed before entering the gorge. Balaklesh had chosen well. With the crags as natural defensive points and the slope in their favor, troops in position would take a great deal of dislodging and it would be extremely difficult for the enemy to fight their way as far as the crest. Yet unless they did so they could not hope to pursue their march down to the plain.

Gel-Ethlin drew up his line on the open slope, with the road running at right angles through his center. There would be no need for his weary men to break ranks or advance until the enemy had shattered themselves against his front.

Under the still thickening clouds, the lowest vapors of which were swirling close above them, they waited on through the clammy twilit afternoon. From time to time there were rolls of thunder and once lightning struck in the ravine half a mile away, leaving a long red streak like a weal down the gray rock. Somehow the men had got wind of the magic bear. The Yeldashay spearmen had already produced a doggerel ballad about its hyperbolical (and increasingly ribald) exploits; while at the other end of the line some regimental buffoon seized his chance, capering and growling in an old ox hide, with arrowheads for claws on his fingers' ends.

At last Gel-Ethlin, from his command post on the road halfway down the slope, caught sight of the scouts returning down the hill among the trees. Balaklesh, running, reached him quickly. They had, he reported, come very suddenly upon the Ortelgans, who were advancing so fast that they themselves, already tired, had barely been able to get back ahead of them. As he spoke, Gel-Ethlin and those about him could hear, from the woods above, the growing hubbub and clatter of the approaching rabble. With a last word about the supreme importance of not breaking ranks until ordered, he dismissed his officers to their posts.

Waiting, he heard drops of rain beating on his helmet but at first could feel none on his outstretched hand. Then, filling all the distance, an undulating gauze of rain came billowing over the edge of the ravine from the left. A moment later the view below became blurred and a kind of growling sigh rose from the lines of soldiers on either side. Gel-Ethlin took half a dozen steps forward, as though to see better through the moving mist of rain. As he did so a band of shaggy-haired men, half-savage in appearance and carrying various weapons, came tramping together around the curve of the road below and stopped dead at the sight of the Beklan army confronting them.

21 *The Passes of Gelt*

To BURN GELT had been no part of Ta-Kominion's intention. Nor could he find out who had done it, each of the barons denying all knowledge of how or where the fire had begun. Ta-Kominion, with his personal followers, had reached the wretched little square in the center of the town to find two sides already ablaze, the body of the chief lying with a spear in the back and a crowd of Ortelgans looting and drinking. He and Zelda, with a handful of the steadier men, beat some sort of order into them and—there being no water in the place except what could be scooped from two wells and one shrunken mountain brook—checked the fire by breaking up the huts downwind and dragging away the posts and straw. It was Zelda who pointed out that at all costs they must prevent any of the townspeople from carrying the news down to the plain. Guards were set on all roads and paths leading out of the town, while a young man named Jurit, to whom Ta-Kominion had that morning given Fassel-Hasta's command, led a reconnoitering force down the steep southward road to find out what lay before them.

Ta-Kominion sat on a bench in one of the dim, fly-buzzing huts, trying to convince four or five frightened, speechless town elders that he meant them no harm. From time to time he broke off, frowning and groping for words as the walls swam before his eyes and the sounds from outside rose and fell in his ears like talk from beyond a door continually opening and closing. He moved restlessly, feeling as though his body were wrapped in stiff ox hides. His wounded forearm throbbed and there was a tender swelling in his armpit. Opening his eyes, he saw the faces of the old men staring at him, full of wary curiosity.

He spoke of Lord Shardik, of the revealed destiny of Ortelga and the sure defeat of Bekla, and saw the dull disbelief and fear of reprisal and death which they could not keep from their eyes. At last one of them, shrewder perhaps than the rest, who must have been calculating the probable effect of what it had occurred to him to say, replied by telling him of the northern army of patrol under General Santil-kè-Erketlis which, if he were not mistaken—as well he might be, he added hastily, his cunning peasant's face assuming an expression of humility and deference —was due at this time to cross the plain below on its circuit to Kabin and beyond. Did the young lord mean to fight that army or would he seek to avoid it? Either way, it seemed best not to remain in Gelt, for the rains were due, were they not, and—he broke off, acting the part of one who knew his place and would not presume to advise the commander of so fine an army.

Ta-Kominion thanked him gravely, affecting not to be aware that it mattered little to those standing before him whether he went forward or back, so long as he left Gelt. If the old man had meant to frighten him, he had reckoned without the blazing faith in Shardik that filled every heart in the Ortelgan army. Probably the elders supposed that he intended only to raid one or two villages in the plain and then escape back over the hills with his booty—weapons, cattle and women—covered from pursuit by the onset of the rains.

Ta-Kominion, however, had never from the outset intended other than to seek out and destroy all enemy forces, whatever their strength, that might lie between himself and Bekla. His followers, he knew, would be content with nothing less. They meant to fight as soon as possible, since they knew that they

176

could not be defeated. Shardik himself had already shown them what became of his enemies, and to Shardik it would make no difference whether his enemies were treacherous Ortelgan barons or patrolling Beklan soldiers.

The thought of the Beklan army, with which the crafty elder of Gelt had thought to dismay him, filled Ta-Kominion only with a fierce and eager joy, restoring to him the will power to drive on his sick body and feverish mind.

Bowing to the old men, he left the hut and paced slowly up and down outside, heedless of the stinking refuse and the scab-mouthed, mucous-eyed children begging among his soldiers. Not for one moment did it occur to him to deliberate whether or not he should fight. Lord Shardik and he himself had already decided upon that. But on him, as Shardik's general, fell the task of deciding when and where. Even this did not occupy him long, for all his thoughts led to one and the same conclusion—that they should march straight on toward Bekla and fight the enemy wherever they might meet him on the open plain. There was scarcely any food to be commandeered in Gelt and the events of the afternoon had shown him how little real control he had over his men. The rains might come at any hour and despite Zelda's cordon the news could not long remain secret that Gelt had fallen to the Ortelgans. More immediate than all these, because he felt it within his own body, was the knowledge that soon he might become incapable of leading the army. Once the battle was won his illness would matter little, but his collapse before they fought would bring to his men misgiving and superstitious dread. Besides, he alone must command the battle. How else to become lord of Bekla?

Where was the Beklan army and how soon could they hope to meet it? The elders had said that the distance to the plain was about a day's march, and he could expect the enemy to seek him out as soon as they had news of him. They would be as eager for battle as himself. In all probability, therefore, he could expect to fight on the plain not later than the day after tomorrow. This must be his plan. He could make no better, could only offer to Lord Shardik his courage and zeal to use as he would. And to Shardik it must remain to delay the rains and bring the Beklans in their path.

Where was Shardik and what, if anything, had Kelderek achieved since he left him? No two ways about it, the fellow was a coward: yet it mattered little, if only he could somehow or other contrive to bring the bear to the army before they fought. If they won—as win they would—if indeed they came at last to take Bekla itself—what would Kelderek's place be then? And the Tuginda—that futile yet disturbing woman, whom he had sent back to Quiso under guard—what was to be done with her? There could be no authority that did not acknowledge his own. Get rid of them both, perhaps, and in some way alter the cult of Shardik accordingly? Later there would be time to decide such things. All that mattered now was the approaching battle.

Feeling suddenly faint, he sat down upon the rubble of a burned hut to recover himself. If, he thought, the sickness had not left him by the time the battle was over, he would send for the Tuginda and offer to reinstate her on condition that she cured him. Meanwhile, he could only rely on Kelderek to exercise authority in her name. But it was important that the fellow should be urged on to complete his task.

He stood up, steadied himself against the still-standing door post until the surge of giddiness had passed off, and then made his way back to the hut. The elders had left and, calling his servant Numiss, he gave him a brief message to carry to Kelderek, stressing that he expected to fight within two days. As soon as he had made sure that the man had his words by heart, he asked Zelda to see to his safe conduct through the pickets and himself lay down to sleep, giving orders that all was to be ready for the march to continue at dawn next day.

He slept heavily, undisturbed by the looting, raping and drunkenness that broke out again at nightfall and continued unchecked, none of the barons caring to run the risk of trying to stop it. When at last he woke, he knew at once that he was not merely ill, but worse than he had been in his life before. His arm was so swollen that the bandage was pressing into the flesh, yet he felt that he could not bear to cut it. His teeth chattered, his throat was so sore that he could scarcely swallow and as he sat up pain throbbed behind his eyes. He got up and staggered to the door. Gusts of warm wind were blowing from the west and the sky was thick with low cloud. The sun was not to be seen, but nevertheless he knew that it must be well after dawn. He leaned against the wall, trying to summon the strength to go and rouse the men who should have been obeying his orders.

It was not until an hour before noon that the army at last set out. Their pace was slow, several of the soldiers having burdened themselves with such loot as they had been able to come by—cooking pots, mattocks, stools, the sorry and valueless possessions of men poorer than themselves. Many marched with aching heads and curdled stomachs. Ta-Kominion, no longer able to conceal his illness, walked in a confused and troubled dream. He scarcely remembered what had happened that morning, or what he had done to get the men on their feet. He could recall the return of Numiss, with his report that Shardik had been drugged at the cost of a priestess's life. Kelderek, so the message ran, hoped to overtake them by nightfall. The last nightfall, thought Ta-Kominion, before the destruction of the Beklan army. When that was done, he would rest.

The narrow road wound along the sides of steep, wooded ravines sheltered from the wind, against rock faces where the brown ferns drooped for rain. For a long time the sound of an invisible torrent rose up from below, through mists that swirled hither and back but dispersed no more than did the cloud above. All was solitude and echo, and soon the men ceased to sing, to jest or even to talk beyond a few words in low voices. One tattered fellow, loosing an arrow, hit a buzzard as it swooped above them and, proud of his marksmanship, slung the carcass around his neck until, as the parasites began to creep from the cooling body, he slung it over a precipice with a curse. Once or twice, looking out across the tops of trees, they caught glimpses of the plain below, and of tiny herds of cattle galloping among the windy dust clouds. In superstitious dread of these wild hills they pressed on, many glancing uneasily about them and carrying their weapons drawn in their hands.

The straggling horde covered more than two miles of the track and there were no means of passing orders save by word of mouth. Between two and three hours after noon, however, when they had descended below the mists and the higher hills, a halt took place without any order being given, the several companies and bands coming up to find the vanguard fallen

179

out and resting in an open wood. Ta-Kominion limped among the men, talking and joking with them as though in a trance, less to encourage than to let them see him and try to learn for himself what fettle they were in. Now that they had left the sheer solitudes which had disquieted and subdued them, their ardor was returning and they seemed as eager as ever to join battle. Yet Ta-Kominion—who as a lad of seventeen had fought beside Bel-ka-Trazet at Clenderzard and three years later commanded the household company which his father had sent to Yelda to fight in the slave wars—could sense how green and unseasoned was their fervor. In one way, he knew, this might be counted to the good, for in their first battle men spend what they can never recover to spend again, so that that battle—even for those for whom it is not the last—may well be their best. But the toll taken of such inexperienced fervor was likely to be high. From such troops little could be expected in the way of disciplined maneuver or steadiness under attack. The best way to use their rough, untrained quality would be simply to bring them quickly to the plain and let them assault the enemy in full strength and on open ground.

A spasm seized him and the trees before his eyes dissolved into circling shapes of yellow, green and brown. Somewhere far off, it seemed, rain was beating on the leaves. He listened, but then realized that the sound lay within his own ear, as full of pain as an egg is full of yolk. He had a fancy to break it open and watch the thick, fluid pain spill over the ground at his feet.

Someone was speaking to him. He opened his eyes yet once more and raised his head. It was Kavass, his father's fletcher, a decent, simple-minded man who had taught him his archery as a boy. With him were four or five comrades who—or so it seemed to Ta-Kominion—had prevailed upon Kavass to come and ask the commander to settle some difference among them. The fletcher, who was tall, as tall as himself, was looking at him with respectful sympathy and pity. In reply he grimaced and then managed to force a wry smile.

"Touch of the fever, sir, eh?" said Kavass deferentially. Everything about him—his stance, his look and the sound of his voice—tended to confirm Ta-Kominion in his leadership and at the same time to emphasize their common humanity.

"Seems like it, Kavass," he answered. His words boomed in his own head, but he could not tell whether in fact he was speaking loud or low. "It'll pass off." Clenching his teeth to stop them from chattering, he missed what Kavass said next, and was about to turn away when he realized that they were all waiting for him to reply. He remained silent but looked steadily at Kavass as though expecting him to say something more. Kavass seemed confused.

"Well, I only meant, sir—and no disrespect, I'm sure—when he came ashore that morning, when you was with him, whether he told you he'd appear again, like—that he'd be there to make sure we won the battle," said Kavass.

Ta-Kominion continued to stare at him, guessing at his meaning. The men became uneasy.

"Nothing to do with us," muttered one. "I said as 'twas nothing to do with us."

"Well, only it's like this, sir," pursued Kavass. "I was one of the first beside you that morning, and when Lord Shardik went over the water, you told us he knew Ortelga was as good as taken and he was off to Bekla—to show us the way, like. And what the lads was wondering, sir, was whether he's going to be there to win for us when we come to fight?"

"We're *bound* to win, aren't we, sir?" said another of the men. "It's the will of Shardik—the will of God."

"How do you know?" said a fourth, a surly, skeptical-looking fellow with blackened teeth. He spat on the ground. "D'you think a bear talks, eh? Think a bear talks?"

"Not to you," replied Kavass contemptuously. "Of course, he don't talk to the likes of you—or me either, for the matter of that. What I told you was that Lord Shardik had said we was to march on Bekla and that he was going there himself. So it stands to reason he's going to appear when we fight the battle. If you don't place no reliance on Lord Shardik, why are you here?"

"Well, it's all according, ain't it?" said the man with the blackened teeth. "He might be there and then again he might not. All I said was, Bekla's a strong place. There's soldiers—"

"Be quiet!" cried Ta-Kominion. He walked across to the man as steadily as he was able, took his chin in his hand and lifted his head as he tried to focus his eyes on his face. "You blas-

181

phemous fool! Lord Shardik can hear you now—and see you as well! But *you* will not see *him* until the appointed time, for he means to test your faith."

The man, twenty years older than Ta-Kominion at least, stared back at him sullenly without a word.

"You can be sure of this," said Ta-Kominion, in a voice that could be heard by everyone nearby. "Lord Shardik intends to fight for those that trust him. And he *will* appear when they fight—he will appear to those that deserve it! But not to those who deserve a wood louse for a God."

As he stumbled away he wondered yet again how long Kelderek would need to overtake them. If all went well it might be possible, while the army encamped that night, to discuss with Kelderek how best they could make use of Shardik. Whatever might be disclosed afterward by Baltis and the other men who were now with Kelderek, Shardik must appear to the enemy in awe-inspiring power—he must not be displayed insensible and drugged. Also, it would be better to keep him away from the men altogether until he was revealed at the proper time, which would presumably be immediately before the battle. Yet Ta-Kominion knew that he himself would not be able to retrace even a mile of the road tonight. If Kelderek did not reach the army he would have to send Zelda back to find him and speak with him. As for himself, he could not go on much longer without a rest. He must lie down and sleep. But if he did so, would he be able to get up again?

The march was resumed, the army following the road through the wood and down the hillside beyond. Ta-Kominion took up a place in the middle of the column, knowing that if he remained in the rear he would not be able to keep up. For a time he leaned on Numiss's arm until, perceiving that the wretched man was exhausted, he sent for Kavass to take his place.

They went on through the darkening, sultry afternoon. Ta-Kominion tried to estimate how far ahead the vanguard might be. The distance down to the plain could not now be more than a few miles. He had better send a runner to tell them to halt when they reached it. Just as he was about to call the nearest man he slipped, jolted his arm and almost fell down with the pain. Kavass helped him to the side of the track.

"I'll never get there, Kavass," he whispered.

"Don't worry, sir," replied Kavass. "After what you told the lads, they'd fight just as well, even if you did have to sit out, like. That's got round, you know, sir, what you said back there. Most of them never actually saw Lord Shardik when he came ashore on Ortelga, you see, and they're keen to fight just to be there when he shows up again. They know he's coming. So even if you *was* to have to lay down for a bit—"

Suddenly there reached Ta-Kominion's ears a confused, distant clamor, echoing up from the steep woods below—the familiar, guttural cries of the Ortelgans and, clearly distinguishable at rhythmic intervals, a higher, lighter sound of other voices, shouting together. Underneath all was the thudding, trampling noise of a tumultuous crowd.

Ta-Kominion knew now that he must be delirious, for evidently he could no longer tell reality from hallucination. Yet Kavass seemed to be listening too.

"Can you hear it, Kavass?" he asked.

"Yes, sir. Sounds like trouble. Part of that noise isn't our lads, sir."

Commotion was working back along the column like flood water flowing up a creek from the main river. Men were running past them down the hill, looking back to point and shout to those behind. Ta-Kominion tried to call out to them but none regarded him. Kavass flung himself at a running man, stopped him by main force, held him as he gabbled and pointed, flung him aside and returned to Ta-Kominion.

"Can't make it out altogether, sir, but there's some sort of fighting down there, or at least that's what he said."

"Fighting?" repeated Ta-Kominion. For a few moments he could not remember what the word meant. His vision had blurred and with this came the curious sensation that his eyes had melted and were running down his face, while still retaining, though in a splintered manner, the power of sight. He raised his hand to wipe away the streaming liquid. Sure enough, he could no longer see. Kavass was shouting beside him.

"The rain, sir, the rain!"

It was indeed rain that was covering his hands, blurring his eyes and filling the woods with a leafy sibilance that he had supposed to be coming from inside his own head. He stepped into the middle of the track and tried to make out for himself what was going on at the foot of the hill.

"Help me to get down there, Kavass!" he cried.

"Steady, sir, steady," replied the fletcher, taking his arm once more.

"Steady be damned!" shouted Ta-Kominion. "Those are Beklans down there—Beklans—and our fools are fighting them piecemeal, before they've even deployed! Where's Kelderek? The rains—it's that bitch of a priestess—she's cursed us, damn her!—help me down there!"

"Steady, sir," repeated the man, holding him up. Hobbling, hopping, stumbling, Ta-Kominion plunged down the steep track, the clamor growing louder in his ears until he could plainly discern the clashing of arms and distinguish the cries of warriors and the screams of the wounded. The woodland, he saw, ended at the foot of the hill and the fighting, which he still could not make out clearly, had been joined in the open, beyond. Men with drawn weapons were running back among the trees. He saw a great, fair-haired fellow pitch to the ground, blood oozing from a wound in his back.

Suddenly Zelda appeared through the leaves, calling to the men about him and pointing back into the open with his sword. Ta-Kominion shouted and tried to run toward him. As he did so, he felt a sharp, clutching sensation pass through his body, followed by a cold rushing, a crumbling and inward flow. He blundered into a tree trunk and fell his length in the road. As he rolled over he knew that he could not get up—that he would never get up again. The flood gates of his body had broken and very soon the flood would cover hearing, sight and tongue forever.

Zelda's face appeared above him, looking down, dripping rain on his own.

"What's happened?" asked Ta-Kominion.

"Beklans," answered Zelda. "Fewer than we, but they're taking no chances. The ground's in their favor and they're simply standing and blocking the road."

"The bastards—how did they get up here? Listen—everyone *must* attack at the same time," whispered Ta-Kominion.

"If only they would! There's no order—they're going for them all anyhow, just as they happen to come up. There's some have had enough already, but others are still out there. It'll be dark in less than an hour—and now the rain—"

"Get them—all back—under the trees—re-form attack again," gasped Ta-Kominion, contriving to utter the words with an enormous effort. His mind was drifting into a mist. It did not surprise him to find that Zelda had gone and that he was once more facing the Tuginda on the road to Gelt. She said nothing, only standing submissively, her wrists tied together with a soaked and filthy bandage. Her eyes were gazing past him at the hills and at first he thought that she must be unaware of his presence. Then, with a conclusive and skeptical glance, like that of some shrewd peasant woman in the market, she looked into his face and raised her eyebrows, as much as to say, "And have you finished now, my child?"

"You bitch!" cried Ta-Kominion. "I'll strangle you!" He wrenched at the bandage and the deep, suppurating wound along his sword arm, which for more than two days had been pouring poison into his body, burst open upon the rain-pitted dust of the track where he lay. For a moment he jerked his head up, then fell back and opened his eyes, crying, "Zelda!"

But it was Kelderek whom he saw bending over him.

22 *The Cage*

THROUGHOUT THE LATTER PART of the night and on into the dawn that appeared at last, gray and muffled, behind the clouds piled in the east, Baltis and his men slowly hauled the cage above the forests of the Telthearna. Behind and below them the miles of treetops—that secluded, shining haunt of the great butterflies—appeared, like waves seen from a cliff-top, to be creeping stealthily downwind. Far off, the line of the river shone in the cloudy light with a glint dull as a sword's, the blackened north bank dim in the horizon haze.

The bear lay inert as though dead. Its eyes remained closed, the dry tongue protruded, and with the jolting of the boards the head shook as a block of stone vibrates on the quarry floor at the thudding of rock masses falling about it. Some of the dusty, footsore girls clung to the ramshackle structure to steady it as it went, while others walked ahead, removing stones from the track or filling ruts and holes before the wheels reached them. Behind the cage plodded Sencred, the wheelwright, watching for the beginnings of play in the wheels or sagging in the axletrees, and from time to time calling up the rope-lines for a halt while he checked the pins.

Kelderek took his turn at the ropes with the others, but when at length they stopped to rest—the girls pushing heavy stones for blocks behind the wheels—he and Baltis left the men and walked back to where Sencred and Zilthé stood leaning against the cage. Zilthé had thrust her arm through the bars and was caressing one of the bear's forepaws, with its curved sheaf of claws longer than her own hand.

"Waken, waken to destroy Bekla,

"Waken, Lord Shardik, *na kora, na ro,*" she sang softly, rubbing her sweating forehead against the cool iron.

Full of sudden misgiving, Kelderek stared at the bear's corpselike stillness. There seemed not the least swell of breathing in the flank and the flies were settling about the ears and muzzle.

"What is this drug? Are you sure it has not killed him?"

"He is not dead, my lord," said Zilthé, smiling. "See!" She drew her knife, bent forward and held it under Shardik's nostrils. The blade clouded very slightly and cleared, clouded and cleared once more; she drew it back and held the flat, warm and moist, against Kelderek's wrist.

"Theltocarna is powerful, my lord, but she who is dead knew —none better—how it should be used. He will not die."

"When will he wake?"

"Perhaps this evening, or during the night. I cannot tell. For many creatures we know the dose and the effect, but his body is like that of no other creature and we can only guess."

"Will he eat then? Drink?"

"Creatures that wake from theltocarna are always dangerous.

186

Often there is a frenzy more violent than that before the trance, and then the creature will attack anything that it encounters. I have seen a stag break a rope as thick as one of these bars, and then kill two oxen."

"When?" asked Kelderek wonderingly.

She began to tell him of Quiso and the sacred rites of the spring equinox, but Baltis interrupted her.

"If what you're saying's true, then those bars won't hold him."

"The roof's not stout enough to hold him either," said Sencred. "He's only got to stand upright and it'll smash like a pie crust."

"We've been wasting our time," said Baltis, spitting in the dust. "He might as well not be the other side of those bars at all. He'll get up and go when he wants. But I'll tell you this, I'll go first."

"We shall have to drug him again, then," said Kelderek.

"That would certainly kill him, my lord," put in Sheldra. "Theltocarna is a poison. It cannot be used twice—no, not twice in ten days."

There was a murmur of agreement from the other girls.

"Where is the Tuginda?" asked Nito. "Is she with Lord Ta-Kominion? She would know what to do."

Kelderek made no answer but, walking back up the track, began getting the men to their feet again.

An hour later the going became easier as the ascent flattened off and the road grew less steep. As near as he could judge from the confused, murky sky, it was about noon when at last they came into Gelt. The square was littered as though after a riot. There was scarcely a living creature to be seen, but a smoldering reek hung in the air and a smell of garbage and ordure. A solitary ragged urchin loitered, watching them from a safe distance.

"Smells like a herd of bloody apes," muttered Baltis.

"Tell your men to eat and rest," said Kelderek. "I'll try to find out how long the army's been gone."

He crossed the square and stood looking about him in perplexity at the shut doors and empty alleys beyond. Suddenly he felt a sharp, momentary pain, like the sting of an insect, in the lobe of his left ear. He put his hand to the place and drew it away with blood between finger and thumb and in the same instant realized that the arrow that had grazed him was sticking in the door post across the way. He spun around quickly but saw only another deserted lane running between closed doors and shuttered windows. Without turning his head, he stepped slowly backward into the square and remained watching the blank, silent hovels for any sign of movement.

"What's up?" asked Baltis, coming up behind him. Kelderek touched his ear again and held out his fingers. Baltis whistled.

"That's nasty," he said. "Throwing stones, eh?"

"An arrow," said Kelderek, nodding at the door post. Baltis whistled again.

At that moment, with a grating sound upon the threshold, a nearby door opened and a bleary, dirty old woman appeared. She was hobbling and staggering beneath the weight of a child in her arms. As she came nearer Kelderek saw with a start that it was dead. The old woman tottered up to him and laid the child on the ground at his feet. It was a girl, about eight years old, blood matted in her hair and a conjunctive yellow discharge around the open eyes. The old woman, bent and muttering, remained standing before him.

"What do you want, grandmother?" asked Kelderek. "What's happened?"

The old woman looked up at him from eyes bloodshot with years of crouching over wood fires.

"Think no one sees. They think no one sees," she whispered. "But God sees. God sees everything."

"What happened?" asked Kelderek again, stepping over the child's body and grasping the stick-thin wrist beneath the rags.

"Ay, that's right, better ask them—ask them what happened," said the old woman. "You'll catch 'em if you're quick. They're not gone far—they're not gone long."

At this moment two men came striding side by side around the corner. They kept their eyes fixed before them and their faces bore the tense, resolute expression of those who knowingly run a risk. Without speaking to Kelderek they grasped the old woman's arms and began leading her away between them. For a moment she struggled, protesting shrilly.

"It's the governor-man from Bekla! The governor-man! I'm telling him—"

"Now just you come along, mother," said one of the men. "Just come along with us now. You don't want to be standing about here. Come along now—"

They shut the door behind them and a moment later came the sound of a heavy bar falling into place.

Kelderek and Baltis left the child's body on the ground and returned across the square. The men had formed a ring around the girls and were looking nervously about.

"I don't think we ought to stop here," said Sencred, pointing. "There's not enough of us to make it safe."

A crowd of men had gathered at the far end of a lane leading off the square, talking and gesticulating among themselves. A few were carrying weapons.

Kelderek took off his belt, laid his bow and quiver on the ground and walked toward them.

"Careful," called Baltis after him. Kelderek ignored him and walked on until he was thirty paces from the men. Holding his hands open on either side of him, he called,

"We don't want to hurt you. We're your friends."

There was a burst of jeering laughter and then a big man with gray hair and a broken nose stepped forward and answered,

"You've done enough. Let us alone or we'll kill you."

Kelderek felt less afraid than exasperated.

"Try and kill us, then, you fools!" he shouted. "Try it!"

"Ah, and have his friends come back," said another man. "Why don't you go and catch your friends up? They've not been gone an hour."

"I'd say take his advice," said Baltis, who had approached and was standing at Kelderek's shoulder. "No point in waiting till they work themselves up to rush us."

"But our people are tired," answered Kelderek angrily.

"They'll be worse than that, my boy, if we don't get out of here," said Baltis. "Come now—I'm no coward and neither are those lads of mine, but there's nothing to be gained by staying." Then, as Kelderek still hesitated, he called out to the men, "Show us the way, then, and we'll go."

At this, like a pack of pie-dogs, they all took a few wary steps forward, and then began shouting and pointing southward. As soon as he was sure of the way, Kelderek drew a line in the dust with his foot and warned them not to cross it until the Ortelgans were gone.

"Ay, we can leave Gelt without any help from you," shouted Baltis, laying hold of the ropes once more to encourage his weary men.

They plodded slowly away, the townspeople staring after them, chattering together and pointing at the huge brown body stretched behind the bars.

Outside the town the road fell away downhill. Soon it became so steep that their task was no longer to drag the cage after them but rather to control its downward course. Coming to a broad, level place above a long slope, they turned it about and took the strain on the ropes from behind. At least the ground, dry and gritty, gave good foothold and for a time they made better speed than during the morning. A mile or two below, however, the road narrowed and began to wind along the rocky side of a ravine, and here they were forced to let the cage down foot by foot, straining backward while Sencred and two or three of his men used poles to lever the front wheels this way and that. At one place, where the bend was too sharp, they had to set to work to broaden the track, prising out the rocks with hammers, iron bars and whatever came to hand, until at last they were able to shift an entire boulder and send it plummeting over the edge into long seconds of silence. Farther on, two of the men slipped and the rest, cursing and terrified, were jerked forward and nearly pulled off their feet.

Not long after this, Kelderek saw that play had increased in the wheels and that the whole structure had shifted and was no longer true on the frame. He consulted Baltis.

"It's not worth trying to right it," answered the smith. "The truth is, another hour or two of this is going to shake the whole damned thing to pieces. The frame's being ground like corn, d'ye see, between the road below and the weight of the bear above. Even careful work couldn't stand up to that forever, and this lot had to be done quick—like the loose girl's wedding. So what d'ye want, young fellow—are we going on?"

"What else?" replied Kelderek. And indeed for all their hardship and near exhaustion, not one of the men had complained or tried to argue against their going on to overtake the army. But when at last they had done with the precipices and the steep pitches and were resting at a place where the road broadened and entered an open wood, he allowed himself for the first time to wonder how the business would end. Apart from the girls, who were initiates of a mystery and in any case would never question anything he told them to do, no one with him had any experience of the strength and savagery that Shardik could put forth. If he were to waken in the midst of the Ortelgan army and burst, raging, out of the flimsy cage, how many would be slaughtered? And how many more, through this, would become convinced of his anger and disfavor toward Ortelga? Yet if Baltis and the rest, for their own safety, were told to abandon Shardik now, what could he himself say to Ta-Kominion, who had sent word that Shardik must be brought at all costs?

He decided to press on until they were close behind the army. Then, if Shardik were still unconscious, he would go forward, report to Ta-Kominion and obtain further orders.

But now it became a matter of finding men with enough strength left to pull on the ropes. After the past twelve hours some were scarcely able to put one foot before the other. Yet even in this extremity, their passionate belief in the destiny of Shardik drove them to stumble, to stagger, to hobble on. Others, in the very act of pulling, fell down, rolling out of the track of the wheels and gasping to their companions to give them a hand. Some set themselves to push behind the cage but as soon as it gathered a little speed, fell forward and measured their length on the road. Sencred cut himself a forked crutch and limped on beside his splayed wheels. Their pace was that of an old man creeping the street, yet still they moved—as a thaw moves up a valley, or flood water mounts in minute jerks to burst its banks at last and pour over the land. Many, like Zilthé, put their arms through the bars to touch Lord Shardik, believing and feeling themselves strengthened by his incarnate power.

Into this bad dream fell the rain, mingling with sweat, trickling salty over puffed lips, stinging open blisters, hissing through the leaves, quenching the dust in the air. Baltis lifted his head to the sky, missed his footing with the effort and stumbled against Kelderek.

"Rain," he grunted. "The rain, lad! What's to be done now?"

"What?" mumbled Kelderek, blinking as though the smith had woken him.

"The rain, I says, the rain! What's to become of us now?"

"God knows," answered Kelderek. "Go on—just go on."

"Well—but they can't fight their way to Bekla in the rain. Why not go back while we can—save our lives, eh?"

"No!" cried Kelderek passionately. "No!" Baltis grunted and said no more.

Many times they ground to a stop and as many times found themselves moving again. Once Kelderek tried to count their lessening numbers, but gave up in confusion. Sencred was nowhere to be seen. Of the girls, Nito was missing, Muni and two or three more. Those who were left still kept beside the cage, daubed from head to foot with rainy mud churned up by the wheels. The light was failing. In less than an hour it would be dark. There was no sign of the army and Kelderek realized with desperation that in all probability his band of fireless stragglers would be forced to spend the night in the wilderness of these foothills. He would not able to keep them together. Before morning they would be shivering, sick, mutinous, victims of panic fear. And before morning, if Zilthé were right, Shardik would awaken.

Baltis came up beside him again.

"It's a bad look-out, y'know, young fellow," he said between his teeth. "We'll have to stop soon: it'll be dark. And what's to be done then? You and I'd better go on alone—find the young baron and ask him to send back help. But if you ask me, he'll have to come back out of it himself if he wants to stay alive. You know what the rains are. After two days a rat can hardly move, let alone men."

"Hark!" said Kelderek. "What's that noise?"

They had come to the top of a long slope, where the road curved downhill through thick woodland. The men on the ropes stood still, one or two sinking down in the mud to rest. At first there seemed to be no sound except, all about them, the pouring of the rain in the leaves. Then, faintly, there came again to Kelderek's ears the noise he had heard at first—distant shouting, sharp and momentary as flying sparks, voices confusing and overlaying one another like ripples on a pool. He looked from one man to the next. All were staring back at him, waiting for him to confirm their single thought.

"The army!" cried Kelderek.

"Ay, but what's the shouting for?" said Baltis. "Sounds like trouble to me."

Sheldra ran forward and laid her hand on Kelderek's arm.

"My lord!" she cried, pointing. "Look! Lord Shardik is waking!"

Kelderek turned toward the cage. The bear, its eyes still closed, was hunched on the rickety floor in an unnatural, crouching position, suggesting not sleep but rather the grotesque posture of some gigantic insect—the back arched, the legs drawn up together under the body. Its breathing was uneven and labored and froth had gathered at its mouth. As they watched, it stirred uneasily and then, with an uncertain, stupefied groping, raised one paw to its muzzle. For a moment its head lifted, the lips curling as though in a snarl, and then sank again to the floor.

"Will he wake now—at once?" asked Kelderek, shrinking involuntarily as the bear moved once more.

"Not at once, my lord," answered Sheldra, "but soon—within the hour."

The bear rolled on its side, the bars clattered like nails on a bench and the near-side wheels lurched, splaying under the massive weight. The sounds of battle were plain now and through the shouting of the Ortelgans they could discern a rhythmic, intermittent cry—a concerted sound, hard and compact like a missile. *"Bek-la Mowt! Bek-la Mowt!"*

"Press on!" shouted Kelderek, hardly knowing what he said. "Press on! Shardik to the battle! Take the strain behind and press on!"

Fumbling and stumbling in the rain, they unfastened the wet ropes, hitched them to the other end of the rickety bars and pushed the cage forward down the slope, checking it as it gathered momentum. They had gone only a short distance when Kelderek realized that they were closer to the battle than he had supposed. The whole army must be engaged, for the din extended a long way to right and left. He ran a short distance ahead, but could see nothing for the thick trees and failing light.

Suddenly a little knot of five or six men came running up the hill, looking back over their shoulders. Only two were carrying weapons. One, a red-haired, raw-boned fellow, was ahead of the others. Recognizing him, Kelderek grabbed his arm. The man gave a cry of pain, cursed and aimed a clumsy blow at him. Kelderek let go and wiped his bloody hand on his thigh.

"Numiss!" he shouted. "What happened?"

"It's all up, that's what's happened! The whole damned Beklan army's down there—thousands of 'em. Get out of it while you can!"

Kelderek took him by the throat.

"Where's Lord Ta-Kominion, damn you? Where?"

Numiss pointed.

"There—lying in the bloody road. He's a goner!" He wrenched himself free and vanished.

The cage, following down the hill, was now close behind Kelderek. He called to Baltis, "Wait—hold it there till I come back!"

"Can't be done—it's too steep!" shouted Baltis.

"Wedge it, then!" answered Kelderek over his shoulder. "Ta-Kominion's here—"

"Too steep, I tell you, lad! It's too steep!"

Running down the hill, Kelderek glimpsed beyond the trees a rising slope of open, stony ground, over which Ortelgans were streaming back toward him. From farther away, steady as a drumbeat, came the concerted shouts of the enemy. He had not gone half a bowshot before he saw his man. Ta-Kominion was lying on his back in the road. The downhill flow of rain, with its flotsam of twigs and leaves, was dammed against his body as though beneath a log. Beside him, chafing his hands, crouched a tall, gray-haired man—Kavass the fletcher. Suddenly Ta-Kominion screamed some incoherent words and tore at his own arm. Kelderek ran up and knelt over him, his gorge rising at the smell of gangrene and putrefaction.

"Zelda!" cried Ta-Kominion. His white face was horribly convulsed, its shape that of the skull beneath and only more ghastly for the life that flickered in the eyes. He stared up at Kelderek, but said nothing more.

"My lord," said Kelderek, "what you required has been done. Lord Shardik is here."

Ta-Kominion uttered a sound like that of a mother beside a fretful child, like that of the rain in the trees. For an instant Kelderek thought that he was whispering him to silence.

"Sh! Sh-sh-ardik!"

"Shardik has come, my lord."

Suddenly a snarling roar, louder even than the surrounding din of battle, filled the tunnel-like roadway under the trees. There followed a clanging and clattering of iron, sharp cracks of snapped wood, panic cries and a noise of dragging and scraping. Baltis's voice shouted, "Let go, you fools!" Then again broke out the snarling, full of savagery and ferocious rage. Kelderek leapt to his feet. The cage had broken loose and was rushing down the hill, swaying and jumping as the crude wheels ploughed ruts in the mud and struck against protruding stones. The roof had split apart and the bars were hanging outward, some trailing along the ground, others lashing sideways like a giant's flails. Shardik was standing upright, surrounded by long white splinters of wood. Blood was running down one shoulder and he foamed at the mouth, beating the iron bars around him as Baltis's hammers had never beaten them. The point of a sharp, splintered stake had pierced his neck and as it swayed up and down, levering itself in the wound, he roared with pain and anger. Red-eyed, frothing and bloody, his head smashing through the flimsy lower branches of the trees overhanging the track, he rode down upon the battle like some beast-god of apocalypse. Just in time, Kelderek threw himself against the bank. Spongy and sodden, it gave way beneath his weight and he sank backward into the mud. The cage thundered past him, grinding over the very spot where he had been kneeling, and the three near-side wheels, each as thick as a man's arm, passed across Ta-Kominion's body, crushing a bloody channel through clothing, flesh and bone. Still further it went, driving through the Ortelgan fugitives like a demon's chariot until, striking head-on against a tree trunk, it tilted forward and smashed to pieces. For a few moments Shardik, thrown upon his back, thrashed and struggled for a footing. Then he stood up and, with the point of the stake still embedded in his neck, burst through the trees and onto the battlefield.

195

23 *The Battle of the Foothills*

GEL-ETHLIN LOOKED RIGHT AND LEFT through the falling dusk and rain. His line remained unbroken. For well over an hour the Beklan troops had simply stood their ground, repulsing the fierce but piecemeal attacks of the Ortelgans. At the first onslaught, delivered unhesitatingly and with fanatical courage by no more than two or three hundred men, he had concluded with relief that he was not opposed by a large force. Then, as more and still more of the Ortelgans emerged from the woods, jostling and pushing their way into a rough-and-ready battle line that spread to right and left until it was as long as his own, he saw that the youth from Gelt had spoken no more than the truth. This was nothing less than an entire tribe in arms, and altogether too numerous for his liking. Soon one attack after another was breaking upon his line, until the slope was covered with dead and crawling, cursing wounded. After some anxious time, however, it became clear that the enemy, who had come upon him as unexpectedly as he had intended, possessed no effective central command and were merely attacking under individual leaders, group by group as each baron might decide. He realized that although he was probably outnumbered by something like three to two, this would not in itself bring about his defeat as long as the enemy lacked all real coordination and discipline. He need do no more than defend and wait. All things considered, these remained the best tactics. His army was at half strength and that the weaker half; the poor condition of the men, after several days' marching in the heat, had been aggravated by their pummeling in the dust and wind that morning; and the slope below was becoming more muddy and slippery at every moment. As long as the Ortelgans continued to make sporadic attacks here and there along the line, it was an easy matter for the Beklan companies not engaged on either side to turn inward and help to break them up. By nightfall—soon, now—his troops might well have had enough, but what it would be best to do then would depend on the state each side was in.

His most prudent course might be to return to the plain. It was unlikely that these irregulars would be able to follow them or that they would even be able, now that the rains had broken, to keep the field. Their food supplies were probably scanty, whereas he had rations—of a sort—for two days and, unlike the enemy, would have the opportunity to commandeer more if he retreated into friendly country.

Stand firm until darkness, thought Gel-Ethlin, that's the style. Why risk breaking ranks to attack? And then come away, leaving the rain to finish the job. As he watched the enemy, among the trees below, re-forming for a fresh attack under the command of a dark, bearded baron with a gold torque on one arm, he thought the idea over and could see nothing wrong with it: and if he could not, presumably his superiors in Bekla would not. He ought not to risk his half-army, either by attacking unnecessarily or by keeping it out in these hills in the rains. His part should be that of a sound, steady commander, nothing flashy.

And yet—he paused. When they got back to Bekla, Santil-kè-Erketlis, that brilliant opportunist, would probably smile understandingly, sympathize with him for having been obliged to come away without destroying the enemy, and then point out how that destruction could and should have been effected. "You a commander-in-chief, Gel-Ethlin?" Santil-kè-Erketlis had once said, good-humoredly enough, while they were returning together from a drinking party. "Man, you're like an old woman with the housekeeping money. 'Oh, I wonder whether I might have beaten him down another meld—or perhaps if I'd gone to that other man round the corner—?' A fine army strikes like the great cats, my lad—swiftly and once. It's like the wheelwright's work—there comes a moment when you have to say, 'Now, hit it.' A general who can't see that moment and seize it doesn't deserve victory." Santil-kè-Erketlis, victor of a score of engagements, who had virtually dictated his own terms at the conclusion of the Slave Wars, could afford to be generous and warmhearted. "And how does one seize the moment?" Gel-Ethlin had asked rather tipsily, as they each seized something else and stood against the wall. "By never stopping to think of all the things that can go wrong," Santil-kè-Erketlis had replied.

Another attack came up the slope, this time straight toward his center. The Tonildan contingent, a second-rate lot if ever there was one, was breaking ranks with a kind of nervous anticipation and advancing uncertainly downhill to meet it. Gel-Ethlin ran forward, shouting, "Stand fast! Stand fast, The Tonilda!" At least no one could say that he had a thin word of command. His voice cut through the din like a hammer splitting a flint. The Tonilda fell back and re-formed line, the rain pouring off their shoulders. A few moments later the Ortelgan attack came rushing across the last few yards and struck like a ram against a wall. Weapons rang and men swayed back and forth, panting and gasping like swimmers struggling in rough water. There was a scream and a man stumbled out of the line clutching his stomach, pitched forward into the mud and lay jerking, resembling in his unheeded plight a broken fish cast up and dying on the shore. "Stand fast, the Tonilda!" shouted Gel-Ethlin again. A redheaded, raw-boned Ortelgan fellow burst through a gap in the line and ran a few steps uncertainly, looking about him and waving his sword. An officer thrust at him, missed his body as he moved unexpectedly and wounded him in the forearm. The man spun around, yelling, and ran back through the gap.

Behind the line Gel-Ethlin, followed by his pennant bearer, trumpeter and servant, ran to his left until he was beyond the point of attack. Then, pushing through the front rank of the Deelguy mercenaries, he turned and looked back at the fighting on his right. The din obliterated every noise else—the rain, his own movements, the voices of those about him and all sounds from the wood below. The Ortelgans, who had evidently now learned—or found a leader with enough sense—to protect the flanks of their assault, had broken through the Tonildan line in a wedge about sixty yards broad. They were fighting, as they had all the evening, with a kind of besotted ferocity, prodigal of life. The trampled, muddy ground which they had won was littered with bodies. His own losses, too, were mounting fast—that was only too plain to be seen. He could recognize some of the men lying on the ground, among them the son of one of Kapparah's tenants, a decent lad who last winter had acted as his go-between to the girl in Ikat. The attack had become a dangerous one, which would have to be halted and thrown back quickly before the enemy could reinforce it. He turned and made toward the nearest commander in the line—Kreet-Liss, that cryptic and reticent soldier, captain of the Deelguy mercenaries. Kreet-Liss, though anything but a coward, was always liable to turn awkward, an ally suddenly afflicted with difficulty in understanding plain Beklan whenever orders did not suit him. He listened as Gel-Ethlin, whom the noise obliged to shout almost into his ear, told him to withdraw his men, bring them across into the center and counterattack the Ortelgans.

"Yoss, yoss," he shouted back finally. "Bad owver ther, better trost oss, thot's it, eh?" The three or four black-ringleted young barons standing about him grinned at each other, slapped some of the rain out of their gaudy, bedraggled finery and went to get their men together. As the Deelguy fell back, Gel-Ethlin found himself unable, in the failing light, to attract the attention of Shaltnekan, the commander adjacent to their left, whom he wanted to close up and fill the gap. He sent his servant across with the order and as he did so thought suddenly, "Santil-kè-Erketlis would have sent the Deelguy out in front of the line, to attack the Ortelgans' rear and cut them off." Yes, but suppose they had proved not strong enough for the job and the Ortelgans had simply cut them to pieces and got out? No, it would have been too much of a risk.

Young Shaltnekan and his men were approaching now, their heads bent against the rain driving into their faces. Gel-Ethlin went to meet them, flailing his arms across his chest, for he was wet through to the skin.

"Can't we break ranks and attack them, sir?" asked Shaltnekan, before his commander could speak. "My lads are sick of standing on the defensive against that bunch of flea-bitten savages. One good push and they'll break up."

"Certainly not," answered Gel-Ethlin. "How do you know what reserves they may have down in those woods? Our men were tired when they got here and once we break ranks they could be fair game for anything. We've nothing to do but stand fast. We're blocking the only way down to the plain and once they realize they can't shift us they'll go to pieces."

"Just as you say, sir," answered Shaltnekan, "but it goes

against the grain to stand still when we might be driving the bastards over the hills like goats."

"Where's the bear?" shouted one of the men. It was evidently a newly invented catch phrase, for fifty voices took it up. " 'E isn't here!"

" 'E's in despair!" continued the joker.

" 'E wouldn't dare!"

"We'll comb 'is 'air!"

"They're still in good spirits, sir, you see," said Shaltnekan, "but all the same, there's one or two good men have been cut up today by those river-frogs and the boys are going to take it very hard if they're not allowed to have a cut at them before it gets too dark."

"And I say stand fast!" snapped Gel-Ethlin. "Get back into line, that man!" he shouted to the buffoon who was playing the part of the bear. "Dress the front rank—sword's length between each man and the next!"

"Stand and bloody shiver," muttered a voice.

Gel-Ethlin strode to the rear, feeling his wet clothes clammy against his body. The twilight was deepening and he was obliged to look about for some moments before he caught sight of Kreet-Liss. He ran toward him and arrived just as the Deelguy went forward into their attack. The concerted, rhythmic cry of "Bek-la Mowt! Bek-la-Mowt!" was taken up along the whole line, but broke off in the center as the Deelguy closed with the enemy. It was plain that the Ortelgans were ready to pay dearly to hold the gap they had made. Three times they repulsed the mercenaries, yelling as they stood astride the bodies of their fallen comrades. Many were brandishing swords and shields taken from the dead of the decimated Tonilda, and each time an enemy was cut down the Ortelgans opposing him would stoop quickly to snatch the foreign arms which he believed must be better than his own—though both, as like as not, had been forged from iron of Gelt.

Suddenly a fresh Beklan attack fell upon the Ortelgan right, and again the steady, beating cry of "Bek-la Mowt!" rose above the surrounding clamor. Gel-Ethlin, who had been about to order Kreet-Liss to attack once more, was peering to his left to make out what had happened when someone plucked his sleeve. It was Shaltnekan.

"Those are my boys attacking them now, sir," he said.

"Against orders!" cried Gel-Ethlin. "What do you mean by it? Get back—"

"They're going to break in a moment, if I know anything about it, sir," said Shaltnekan. "Surely you won't stop us pursuing them now?"

"You'll do no such thing!" replied Gel-Ethlin.

"Sir," said Shaltnekan, "if we let them off the field in any sort of order, what's going to be said back in Bekla? We'll never live it down. They've got to be routed—cut to bits. And now's the time to do it, or they'll be off in the dark."

The Ortelgans were running back out of the gap as Shaltnekan's attack drove in their right flank. Kreet-Liss and his men followed them, stabbing the enemy's wounded as they advanced. A few minutes later the original Beklan line was restored and Gel-Ethlin, peering, could make out to his left the gap where Shaltnekan's company had left their place. There could be no denying that it had been a fine stroke of initiative: and no denying, either, that there was a good deal of force in the argument that the enemy's escape, after the mauling they had suffered, would probably be ill received in Bekla. To destroy them, on the other hand, would establish his reputation and silence any possible criticism on the part of Santil-kè-Erketlis.

The Beklan officers, obedient to orders, had halted their men on the original defensive line and the Ortelgans were streaming down the slope unpursued, several supporting their wounded or carrying looted Beklan equipment. As Gel-Ethlin watched them, a voice spoke from the ground at his feet. He looked down. It was the tenant lad from Kapparah's farm near Ikat. He had raised himself on one elbow and was trying to stanch with his cloak a great gash in his neck and shoulder.

"Go on, sir, go on!" gasped the boy. "Finish them off! I'll take a letter down to Ikat tomorrow, won't I, just like old times? God bless the lady, she'll give me a whole sackful of gold!"

He pitched forward on his face and two of Shaltnekan's men dragged him back behind the line. Gel-Ethlin, his mind made up, turned to the trumpeter.

"Well, Wolf," he said, addressing the man by his nickname, "no good you standing there doing nothing! Break ranks—general pursuit. And blow hard, so that everyone can hear it!"

The trumpet had hardly sounded before the various Beklan companies began racing down the slopes, those on the wings scattering widely and trying to turn inward toward the road. Every man hoped to beat his comrades to the plunder—such as it might be. This was what they had marched through the wind for, withstood the attacks for, shivered obediently for in the rain. True enough, there would be little or nothing to take from these barbarians except their fleas, but a couple of slaves would fetch a good price in Bekla and there was always the sporting chance of a baron with gold ornaments, or even a woman among the baggage behind.

Gel-Ethlin ran too, among the foremost, his pennant bearer on one side of him and Shaltnekan on the other. As they reached the foot of the slope and came close to the edge of the woods, he could see, among the trees, the Ortelgans once more forming a line to meet them. Evidently they meant to go down fighting. For the first time he drew his sword. He might as well strike a blow or two on his own account before the business was done.

From close at hand, somewhere inside the woods, there came a loud grinding, rumbling sound which grew nearer and changed to a smashing and splintering of wood and a clashing of iron. Immediately after, there sounded above all the tumult a savage roaring, like that of some huge beast in pain. Then the boughs burst apart in front of him and Gel-Ethlin stood rigid with horror, bereft of every feeling but panic fear. The ordinary course of things seen and comprehended; the senses, that five-fold frame of the world; the unthinking human certainty of what can and cannot reasonably happen, upon which all rational living is based—these dissolved in an instant. If a rag-draped skeleton had come stalking out of the trees on bare, bony feet, invisible to all but himself, and made toward him with wagging head and grinning jaws, he could not have been more stupefied, more deeply plunged into terror and mental chaos. Before him, no more than a few yards away, there stood, more than twice as tall as a man, a beast which could have no place in the mortal world. Most like a bear it looked, but a bear created in hell to torment the damned by its mere presence. The ears were flattened like a cat's in rage, the eyes glimmered redly in the failing light and streaked, ochreous foam came frothing from between teeth like Deelguy knives. Over one shoulder—and this drove him almost mad with fear, for it proved that this was no earthly creature—it carried a great, pointed stake, dripping with blood. Blood, too, covered the claws curving from the one paw raised above its head as though in some horrible greeting of death. Its eyes—the eyes of a mad creature, inhabiting a world of cruelty and pain—looked down upon Gel-Ethlin with a kind of dark intelligence all too sufficient for its single purpose. Meeting that gaze, he let his sword drop from his hand; and as he did so the beast struck him with a blow that crushed his skull and drove his head down through his shoulders.

A moment later Shaltnekan fell across his body, his chest broken in like a smashed drum. Kreet-Liss, stumbling on the wet slope, made one thrust with his sword before his neck was ripped open in a fountain of blood. And this sword thrust, wounding it, drove the creature to such a frenzy of murderous destruction that every man ran shrieking as it ploughed its way up the crowded slope, seeking whom to tear and destroy. The men on the wings, halted and crying out to learn what had happened, felt their bowels loosen at the news that the bear-god, more dreadful than any imagined creature from the nether wastes of fever and nightmare, had indeed appeared and had recognized and killed of intent the general and two commanders.

From the wavering Ortelgan line there rose a triumphant shout. Kelderek, limping and staggering with exhaustion, was the first man to emerge from the trees, shouting "Shardik! Shardik the Power of God!" Then, with yells of "Shardik! Shardik!" which were the last sound in the ears of Ta-Kominion, the Ortelgans poured up the slope, hacking and thrusting anew through the broken Beklan center. A few minutes afterward, Kelderek, Baltis and a score of others reached the mouth of the gorge beyond the ridge and, heedless of their isolation, faced about to hold it against any who might try to force an escape. Of Shardik, vanished into the falling darkness, there remained neither sight nor sound.

Within half an hour, when night put an end to the bloodshed, all Beklan resistance had been quenched. The Ortelgans, following the terrible example which had redeemed them from defeat, showed no mercy, killing their enemies and stripping their bodies of weapons, shields and armor, until they were as well-found a force as had ever swept down upon the Beklan plain. A few of Gel-Ethlin's men succeeded in escaping toward Gelt. None found his way past Kelderek to regain the plain by the road up which they had marched that afternoon.

With the clouded, rainy moon rose the white smoke of fires coaxed into life by the victors to cook the plundered rations of the enemy. But before midnight the army, urged forward by Zelda and Kelderek so fervently that they stayed not even to bury the dead, were limping on toward Bekla, outstripping all news of their victory and of the total destruction of Gel-Ethlin's force.

Two days later, reduced to two-thirds of their strength by fatigue and the privations of their forced march, the Ortelgans, advancing by the paved road across the plain, appeared before the walls of Bekla; smashed in the carved and gilded Tamarrik Gate—that unique masterpiece created by the craftsman Fleitil a century before—after storming it for four hours with an im-provised ram at a cost of over five hundred men; overcame the garrison and the citizens, despite the courageous leadership of the sick Santil-kè-Erketlis; sacked and occupied the city and began at once to strengthen the fortifications against the risk of counterattack as soon as the rains should end.

Thus, in what must surely have been one of the most extraor-dinary and unpredictable campaigns ever fought, fell Bekla, the capital of an empire of subject provinces 20,000 square miles in extent. Of those provinces, the farthest from the city seceded and became enemies to its new rulers. The nearer, rather than face the rapine and bloodshed of resistance, put themselves under the protection of the Ortelgans, of their generals Zelda and Ged-la-Dan and their mysterious priest-king Kelderek, styled Crendrik—the Eye of God.

BOOK III

Bekla

24 *Elleroth*

Bekla, city of myth and conjecture, hidden in time as Tiahuanaco in the Andes fastness, as Petra in the hills of Edom, as Atlantis beneath the waves! Bekla of enigma and secrets, more deeply enfolded in its religious mystery than Eleusis of the reaped corn, than the stone giants of the Pacific or the Kerait lands of Prester John. Its gray, broken walls—across whose parapets only the clouds come marching, in whose hollows the wind sounds and ceases like the trumpeter of Krakow or Memnon's statue on the sands—the stars reflected in its waters, the flowers scenting its gardens, are become like words heard in a dream that cannot be recalled. Its very history lies buried, unresolved—coins, beads and gaming boards, street below street, shards below shards, hearth beneath hearth, ash under ash. The earth has been dug away from Troy and Mycenae, the jungle cut from about Zimbabwe; and caged in maps and clocks are the terrible leagues about Urumchi and Ulan Bator. But who shall disperse the moon-dim darkness that covers Bekla, or draw it up to view from depths more lonely and remote than those where bassogigas and ethusa swim in black silence? Only sometimes through tales may it be guessed at, those tokens riddling as the carved woods from the Americas floating centuries ago to the shores of Portugal and Spain; or in dreams, perhaps, it may be glimpsed—from the decks of that unchanging navy of gods and images that sails by night, carrying its passengers still in no bottoms else than those which bore, in their little time, Pilate's wife, Joseph of Canaan and the wise Penelope of Ithaca with her twenty geese. Bekla the incomparable, the lily of the plain, the garden of sculptured and dancing stone, appears from its mist and dusk, faint as the tracks of Shardik himself in forests long consumed.

Six miles around were the walls, rising on the south to encircle the summit of Mount Crandor, with its citadel crowning the sheer face of the stone quarries below. A breakneck flight of steps led up that face, disappearing, at a height of eighty feet, into the mouth of a tunnel which ran upward through the rock to emerge into the twilight of the huge granary cellar. The only other entry to the citadel was the so-called Red Gate in the south wall, a low arch through which a chalybeate brook flowed from its source within to the chain of falls—named the White Girls—that carried it down Crandor's gradual southern slope. Under the Red Gate, men long ago had worked to widen and deepen the bed of the brook, but had left standing, two feet beneath the surface of the water, a narrow, twisting causeway of the living rock. Those who had learned this path's sub-aqueous windings could wade safely through the deep pool and then—if permitted—enter the citadel by the stairway known as the Vent.

It was not Mount Crandor, however, which drew the gaze of the newcomer to Bekla, but the ridge of the Leopard Hill below, with its terraces of vines, flowers and citrous tendriona. On the crest, above these surrounding gardens, stood the Palace of the Barons, the range of its towers reflecting light from their balconies of polished, rose-colored marble. Twenty round towers there were in all, eight by the long sides of the palace and four by the short, each tapering, circular wall so smooth and regular that in sunlight not one stone's lower edge cast a shadow upon its fellow below, and the only blackness was that within the window openings, rounded and slitted like keyholes, which lit the spiral stairways. High up, as high as tall trees, the circular balconies projected like the capitals of columns, their ambulatories wide enough for two men to walk side by side. The marble balustrades were identical in height and shape, yet each was decorated differently, carved on each side in low relief with leopards, lilies, birds or fish, so that a lord might say to his friend, "I will drink with you tonight on the Bramba tower," or a lover to his mistress, "Let us meet this evening on the Trepsis tower and watch the sun set before we go to supper." Above these marvelous crow's nests the towers culminated in slender, painted spires—red, blue and green—latticed and containing gong-toned copper bells. When these were rung—four bells to each note of the scale—the wavering metallic sounds mingled with their own echoes from the precipices of Crandor and vibrated over the roofs below until the citizens, thus summoned to rejoice at festival, holiday or royal welcome, laughed to feel their ears confounded in sport as the eye is confounded by mirrors face to face.

The palace itself stood within its towers and separate by several yards from their bases. Yet—wonderful to see—at the height of the roof, that part of the wall that stood behind each tower sloped outward, supported on massive corbels, to embrace it and project a little beyond, so that the towers themselves, with their pointed spires, looked like great lances set upright at regular intervals to pierce the walls and support the roof as a canopy is supported at the periphery. The voluted parapets were carved in relief with the round leaves and flame-shaped flower buds of lilies and lotus; and to these the craftsmen had added, here and there as pleased them, the likenesses of insects, of trailing weeds and drops of water, all many times larger than the life. The hard light of noon stressed little of these fancies, accentuating rather the single, shadowed mass of the north front, grave and severe as a judge presiding above the busy streets. But at evening, when the heat of the day broke and the hard shadows fled away, the red, slanting light would soften the outline of walls and towers and emphasize instead their marvelous decoration, so that at this hour the palace suggested rather some beautiful, pleasure-loving woman, adorned with jewels and flowers, ready for a joyous meeting or homecoming beyond compare. And by the first light of day, before the gongs of the city's two water clocks clashed one after the other for sunrise, it had changed yet again and become, in the misty stillness, like a pool of water lilies half-opened among the dragonflies and sipping, splashing swallows.

Some way from the foot of the Leopard Hill was the newly excavated Rock Pit, immediately above which stood the House of the King, a gaunt square of rooms and corridors surrounding a hall—once a barracks for soldiers, but now reserved for another use and another occupant. Close by, grouped about the north side of the cypress gardens and the lake called the Barb, were stone buildings resembling those in Quiso, but larger and more numerous. Some of these were used as dwellings by the Ortelgan leaders, while others were set aside for hostages or for delegations from the various provincial peoples, whose comings

BEKLA

at the time of the Ortelgan conquest

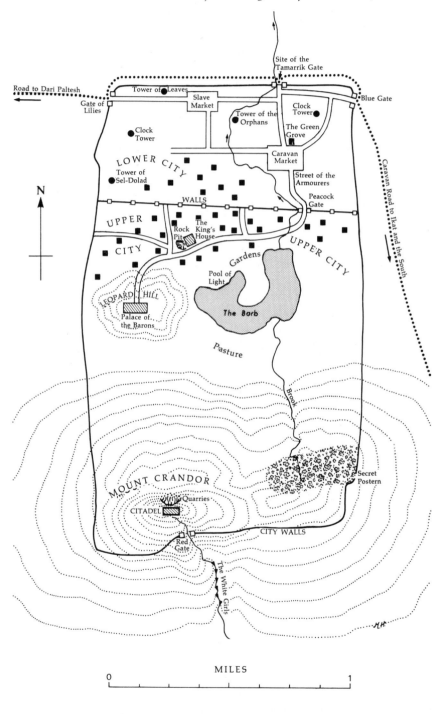

MILES

and goings, with embassies to the king or petitions to lay before the generals, were incessant in this empire at war on a debatable frontier. Beyond the cypress gardens a walled road led to the Peacock Gate, the only way through the fortified rampart dividing the upper from the lower city.

The lower city—the city itself, its paved streets and dusty alleys, its odors and clamor by day, its moonlight and jasmine by night, its cripples and beggars, its animals, its merchandise, its traces everywhere of war and pillage, doors hacked and walls blackened with fire—does the city too return out of the dark? Here ran the street of the money changers and beyond, on either side of a narrow avenue of ilex trees, stood the houses of the jewel merchants—high, barred windows and a couple of strong fellows at the gate to inquire a stranger's business. The torpid flies about the open sweet-stalls, the smells of leather and dung and spices and sweat and herbs, the fruit market's banks of gaudy panniers, the rostra, barracoons and blocks of the slave market with its handsome children, its cozening foreigners and outlandish tongues, the shoemakers sitting absorbed at their tapping and stitching in the midst of the hubbub, the clinking streetwalkers strolling nowhere in particular with their stylized gait and sidelong glances, the colored flowers in the water, the shouting across a street of the news of a sale or an offer, in cryptic words revealing nothing except to their intended hearer; the quarrels, the lies, the promises, the thieves, the long-drawn crying of wares on notes that the years have turned into songs, the streets of the stonemasons, carpenters, weavers, of the astrologers, doctors and fortune-tellers. The scuttling lizards, the rats and dogs, the fowls in coops and the pretty birds in cages. The cattle market had been burned to the ground in the fighting and on one of the sagging, open doors of the temple of Cran someone had daubed the mask of a bear—two eyes and a snarling muzzle, set between round ears. The Tamarrik Gate, that wonder second only to the Palace, was gone forever—gone the concentric filigree spheres, the sundial with its phallic gnomon and nympholeptic spiral of hours, the incredible faces peering through the green leaves of the sycamore, the great ferns and the blue-tongued lichens, the wind harp and the silver drum that beat of itself when the sacred doves alighted at evening to be fed. The fragments of Fleitil's masterpiece, constructed in an age when none conceived it possible that war could approach Bekla, had been gleaned from the rubble secretly and with bitter tears, during the night before Ged-la-Dan and his men supervised the building, by forced labor, of a new wall to close the gap. The two remaining gates, the Blue Gate and the Gate of Lilies, were very strong and entirely suited to Bekla's present and more dangerous role of a city that scarcely knew friend from foe.

On this cloudy spring morning the surface of the Barb, ruffled by the south wind, had the dull, broken shine of an incised glaze. Along the lonelier, southeastern shore, from which pasture land, enclosed within the city walls, stretched away up the slopes of Crandor, a flock of cranes were feeding and squabbling, wading through the shallows and bending their long necks down to the weeds. On the opposite side, in the sheltering cypress gardens, men were strolling in twos and threes or sitting out of the wind in the evergreen arbors. Some were attended by servants who walked behind them carrying cloaks, papers and writing materials, while others, harsh-voiced and shaggy as brigands, broke from time to time into loud laughter or slapped each other's shoulders, betraying, even while they tried to hide it, the lack of ease which they felt in these trim and unaccustomed surroundings. Others again clearly wished to be known for soldiers and, though personally unarmed, in deference to the place and the occasion, had instructed their servants to carry their empty scabbards conspicuously. It seemed that a number of these men were strangers to each other, for their greetings as they passed were formal—a bow, a grave nod or a few words: yet their very presence together showed that they must have something in common. After a time a certain restlessness—even impatience—began to show among them. Evidently they were waiting for something that was delayed.

At length the figure of a woman, scarlet-cloaked and carrying a silver staff, was seen approaching the garden from the King's House. There was a general move in the direction of the gate leading into the walled road, so that by the time the woman reached it, forty or fifty men were already waiting there. As she entered some thronged about her; others, with an air of detachment, idled, or pretended to idle, within earshot. The woman, dour and stolid in manner, looked around among them, raised in greeting her hand with its crimson wooden rings, and began to speak. Although she spoke in Beklan, it was plain that this was not her tongue. Her voice had the slow, flat cadence of Telthearna province and she was, as they all knew, a priestess of the conquerors, an Ortelgan.

"My lords, the king greets you and welcomes you to Bekla. He is grateful to each of you, for he knows that you have the strength and safety of the empire at heart. As you all know, it was—"

At this moment she was interrupted by the stammering excitement of a thickset, lank-haired man who spoke with the accent of a westerner from Paltesh.

"—Madam Sheldra—säiyett—tell us—the king—Lord Crendrik—no harm has befallen him?"

Sheldra turned toward him unsmilingly and stared him into silence. Then she continued,

"As you all know, he intended to have received you this morning in audience at the Palace, and to have held the first meeting of the Council this afternoon. He has now been obliged to alter this intention."

She paused, but there was no further interruption. All were listening with attention. The distant idlers came closer, glancing at each other with raised eyebrows.

"General Ged-la-Dan was expected to reach Bekla last night, together with the delegates from eastern Lapan. However, they have been unexpectedly delayed. A messenger reached the king at dawn with the news that they will not be here until this evening. The king therefore asks your patience for a day. The audience will be held at this time tomorrow and the Council will commence in the afternoon. Until then you are the guests of the city, and the king will welcome all who may wish to sup with him in the Palace an hour after sunset."

A tall, beardless man, wearing a fox-fur cloak over a white, pleated kilt and purple damask tunic blazoned with three corn sheaves, came strolling elegantly along the terrace and turned his eyes toward the crowd as though he had just noticed them for the first time. He stopped, paused a moment and then addressed Sheldra across their heads in the courteous and almost apologetic tone of a gentleman questioning someone else's servant.

"I wonder what might have delayed the general? Perhaps you can be so kind as to tell me?"

Sheldra made no immediate reply and it seemed that her self-possession was not altogether equal either to the question or to the questioner. She appeared to be not so much considering the question as hoping that it might go away, as though it were some kind of pestering insect. She betrayed no actual confusion but at length, keeping her eyes on the ground, she turned, avoiding the tall man's gaze in the manner of some governess or duenna in a wealthy house, out of countenance to find herself required to respond graciously to unsought attention from friends of the family. She was about to leave when the newcomer, inclining his sleek head and persisting in his kindly and condescending manner, stepped smoothly through the crowd to her side.

"You see, I am most anxious to learn, since if I am not mistaken, the general's army is at present in Lapan province, and any misfortune of his would certainly be mine as well. I am sure that in the circumstances you will excuse my importunity."

Sheldra's muttered answer seemed appropriate less to a royal messenger than to some gauche and sullen waiting-woman in a yeoman's kitchen.

"He stayed with the army, I think—I heard, that is. He is coming soon."

"Thank you," replied the tall man. "He had some reason, no doubt? I know that you will wish to help me if you can."

Sheldra flung up her head like a mare troubled by the flies.

"The enemy in Ikat—General Erketlis—General Ged-la-Dan wished to leave everything secure before he set out for Bekla. And now, my lords, I must leave you—until tomorrow—"

Almost forcing her way past them, she left the garden with clumsy and less than becoming haste.

The man with the corn-sheaves tunic strolled on toward the shrubbery by the lake, looking across at the feeding cranes and toying with a silver pomander secured to his belt by a fine gold chain. He shivered in the wind and drew his cloak closer about

214

him, lifting the hem above the damp grass with a kind of stylized grace almost like that of a girl on a dance floor. He had stopped to admire the mauve-stippled, frosty sparkle on the petals of an early-flowering *saldis*, when someone plucked his sleeve from behind. He looked over his shoulder. The man who had attracted his attention stood looking back at him with a grin. He had a rugged, somewhat battered appearance and the skeptical air of a man who has experienced much, gained advancement and prosperity in a hard school and come to regard both with a certain detachment.

"Mollo!" cried the tall man, opening his arms in a gesture of welcome. "My dear fellow, what a pleasant surprise! I thought you were in Terekenalt—across the Vrako—in the clouds—anywhere but here. If I weren't half frozen in this pestilential city I'd be able to show all the pleasure I feel, instead of only half of it."

Thereupon he embraced Mollo, who appeared a trifle embarrassed but took it in good part, and then, holding him by the hand at arm's length as though they were dancing some courtly measure, looked him up and down, shaking his head slowly and continuing to speak as he had commenced, in Yeldashay, the tongue of Ikat and the south.

"Wasting away, wasting away! Obviously full of tribesmen's snapped-off arrowheads and rot-gut booze from the barracks of beyond. One wonders why the holes made by the former wouldn't drain off some of the latter. But come, tell me how you happen to be here—and how's Kabin and all the jolly water boys?"

"I'm the governor of Kabin now," replied Mollo with a grin, "so the place has come down in the world."

"My dear fellow, I congratulate you! So the water rats have engaged the services of a wolf? Very prudent, very prudent." He half-sang a couple of lines.

> A jolly old cattle thief said to his wife,
> (*San, tan, tennerferee*)
> "I mean to live easy the rest of my life—"

"That's it," said Mollo with a grin. "After that little business of the Slave Wars we got mixed up in—"

"When you saved my life—"

"When I saved your life (God help me, I must have been out of my mind), I couldn't stay in Kabin. What was there for me? My father sand-blind in the chimney corner and my elder brother taking damned good care that neither Shrain nor I got anything out of the estate. Shrain raised forty men and joined the Beklan army, but I didn't fancy that and I decided to go further. Arrowheads and rot-gut—well, you're right, that's about it."

"Boot, brute and loot, as it were?"

"If you can't steal it, you've got to fight for it, that's it. I made myself useful. I finished up as a provincial governor to the king of Deelguy—honest work for a change—"

"In Deelguy, Mollo? Oh, come now—"

"Well, fairly honest, anyway. Plenty of headaches and worries —too much responsibility—"

"I can vividly imagine your feelings on discovering yourself north of the Telthearna, in sole command of Fort Horrible—"

"It was Klamsid province, actually. Well, it's one way of feathering your nest, if you can survive. That was where I was when I heard of Shrain's death—he was killed by the Ortelgans, five years ago now, at the battle of the Foothills, when Gel-Ethlin lost his army. Poor lad! Anyway, about six months back a Deelguy merchant comes up before me for a travel permit— a nasty, slimy brute by the name of Lalloc. When we're alone, 'Are you Lord Mollo,' says he, 'from Kabin of the Waters?' 'I'm Mollo the governor,' says I, 'and apt to come down heavy on oily flatterers.' 'Why, my lord,' says he, 'there's no flattery.'"

"Flottery, you mean."

"Well, flottery, then. I can't imitate their damned talk. 'I've come from spending the rainy season at Kabin,' he says, 'and there's news for you. Your elder brother's dead and the property's yours, but no one knew where to find you. You've three months in law to claim it.' 'What's that to me?' I thought to myself; but later I got to thinking about it and I knew I wanted to go home. So I appointed my deputy as governor on my own authority, sent the king a message to say what I'd done—and left."

"The inhabitants were heartbroken? The pigs wept real tears in the bedrooms?"

"They may have—I didn't notice. You can't tell them from the inhabitants, anyway. It was a bad journey at that time of year. I nearly drowned, crossing the Telthearna by night."

"It had to be by night?"

"Well, I was in a hurry, you see."

"Not to be observed?"

"Not to be observed. I went over the hills by way of Gelt—I wanted to see where Shrain died—say a few prayers for him and make an offering, you know. My God, that's an awful place! I don't want to talk about it—the ghosts must be thicker than frogs in a marsh. I wouldn't be there at night for all the gold in Bekla. Shrain's at peace, anyway—I did all that's proper. Well, when I came down the pass to the plain—and I had to pay toll at the southern end, that was new—it was late afternoon already and I thought, 'I shan't get to Kabin tonight—I'll go to old S'marr Torruin, him that used to breed the prize bulls when my father was alive, that's it.' When I got there—only myself and a couple of fellows—why, you never saw a place so much changed: servants by the bushel, everything made of silver, all the women in silk and jewels. S'marr was just the same, though, and he remembered me all right. When we were drinking together after dinner I said, 'Bulls seem to be paying well.' 'Oh,' says he, 'haven't you heard? They made me governor of the Foothills and warden of the Gelt pass.' 'How on earth did that come about?' I asked. 'Well,' says he, 'you've got to watch out to jump the right way in a time of trouble—it's a case of win all or lose all. After I'd heard what happened at the battle of the Foothills, I knew these Ortelgans were bound to take Bekla: it stood to reason—they were meant to win. I could see it plain, but no one else seemed able to. I went straight to their generals myself—caught 'em up as they were marching south across the plain to Bekla—and promised them all the help I could give. You see, the night before the battle the best half of Gel-Ethlin's army had been sent to Kabin to repair the dam—and if that wasn't the finger of God, what was? The rains had just begun, but all the same, those Beklans at Kabin were in the Ortelgans' rear as they marched south. It's not the sort of risk any general can feel happy about. I made it impossible for them to move—took my fellows out and destroyed three bridges, sent false information to Kabin, intercepted their messengers—' 'Lord,' says

I to S'marr, 'what a gamble to take on the Ortelgans!' 'Not at all,' says S'marr. 'I can tell when lightning's going to strike, and I don't need to know exactly where. I tell you, the Ortelgans were meant to win. That half-army of poor old Gel-Ethlin's simply broke up—never fought again. They marched out of Kabin in the rain, turned back again, went on half-rations—then there was mutiny, wholesale desertion. By the time a messenger got through from Santil-kè-Erketlis, a mutineers' faction was in command and they nearly hanged the poor fellow. A lot of that was my doing, and didn't I let this King Crendrik fellow know it, too? That was how the Ortelgans came to make me governor of the Foothills and warden of the Gelt pass, my boy, and very lucrative it is.' All of a sudden S'marr looks up at me. 'Have you come home to claim the family property?' he asks. 'That's it,' I said. 'Well,' says he, 'I never liked your brother— griping, hard-fisted curmudgeon—but you're all right. They're short of a governor in Kabin. There was a foreigner there until recently—name of Orcad, formerly in the Beklan service. He understood the reservoir, you see, and that's more than the Ortelgans do—but he's just been murdered. Now you're a local lad, so you won't get murdered, and the Ortelgans like local men as long as they feel they can trust them. After what's happened they trust me, naturally, and if I put in a word with General Zelda you'll probably be appointed.' Well, the long and short of it was, I agreed to make it worth S'marr's while to speak for me, and that's how I come to be governor of Kabin."

"I see. And you commune with the reservoir from the profound depths of your aquatic knowledge, do you?"

"I've no idea how to look after a reservoir, but while I'm here I mean to find someone who has and take him back with me, that's it."

"And is he up here now for the Council, your charming old bull-breeding chum?"

"S'marr? Not he—he's sent his deputy. He's no fool."

"How long have you been governor of Kabin?"

"About three days. I tell you, all this happened very recently. General Zelda was recruiting in those parts, as it happened, and S'marr saw him the next day. I'd not been back home more than one night when he sent an officer to tell me I was appointed governor and order me to come to Bekla in person. So here I am, Elleroth, you see, and the first person I run into is you!"

"Elleroth Ban—bow three times before addressing me."

"Well, we *have* become an exalted pair, that's it. Ban of Sarkid? How long have you been Elleroth Ban?"

"Oh, a few years now. My poor father died a while back. But tell me, how much do you know about the new, modern Bekla and its humane and enlightened rulers?"

At this moment two of the other delegates overtook them, talking earnestly in Katrian Chistol, the dialect of eastern Terekenalt. One, as he passed, turned his head and continued to stare unsmilingly over his shoulder for some moments before resuming his conversation.

"You ought to be more careful," said Mollo. "Remarks like that shouldn't be made at all in a place like this, let alone overheard."

"My dear fellow, how much Yeldashay do you suppose those cultivated pumpkins understand? Their bodies scarcely cover their minds with propriety. Their oafishness is indecently exposed."

"You never know. Discretion—that's one thing I've learned and I'm alive to prove it."

"Very well, we will indulge your desire for privacy, chilly though it may be to do so. Yonder is a fellow with a boat, yo ho, and no doubt he has his price, like everyone in this world."

Addressing the boatman, as he had Sheldra, in excellent Beklan, with scarcely a trace of Yeldashay accent, Elleroth gave him a ten-meld piece, fastened his fox-fur cloak at the throat, turned up the deep collar round the back of his head and stepped into the boat, followed by Mollo.

As the man rowed them out toward the center of the lake and the choppy wavelets began to set up a regular, hollow slapping under the bow, Elleroth remained silent, staring intently across at the grazing land that extended from the southern side of the king's house, around the western shore of the lake and on to the northern slopes of Crandor in the distance.

"Lonely, isn't it?" he said at last, still speaking in Yeldashay.

"Lonely?" replied Mollo. "Hardly that."

"Well, let us say relatively unfrequented—and that ground's

nice and smooth—no obstacles. Good." He paused, smiling at Mollo's frowning incomprehension.

"But to resume where we were so poignantly interrupted. How much do you know about Bekla and these bear-bemused river boys from the Telthearna?"

"I tell you—next to nothing. I've had hardly any time to find out."

"Did you know, for example, that after the battle in the Foot-hills, five and a half years ago, they didn't bury the dead—neither their own nor Gel-Ethlin's? They left them for the wolves and the kites."

"I'm not surprised to hear it. I've been on that field, as I told you, and I've never been so glad to leave anywhere. My two fellows were almost crazy with fear—and that was in daylight. I did what had to be done for Shrain's sake and came away quick."

"Did you *see* anything?"

"No, it was just what we all felt. Oh, you mean the remains of the dead? No—we didn't stray off the road, you see, and that was cleared soon after the battle by men who came down from Gelt to do it, so I heard."

"Yes. The Ortelgans, of course, didn't bother. But it wasn't really to be expected that they would, was it?"

"By the time the battle was won the rains had set in and night was falling, wasn't that it? They were desperate to get on to Bekla."

"Yes, but no Ortelgan did anything after Bekla had fallen either, although there must have been plenty of coming and going between Bekla and their Telthearna island. I find that terribly tedious as a subject for contemplation, don't you? It bores me to distraction."

"I hadn't considered it before in quite that way."

"Start now."

The boat, turning, had followed first the southern and then the eastern shore of the Barb and as it approached them the cranes flew up in a clattering, white-winged flock. Elleroth bent his head over the bow, idly running one finger through the water along the outline of his own shadow as it moved across the surface. After some time Mollo said, "I've never understood why the city fell. They took it by surprise and smashed in the Tamarrik Gate. Well, all right, so the Tamarrik Gate was military nonsense. But what was Santil-kè-Erketlis doing? Why didn't he try to hold the citadel? You could hold that place forever."

He pointed back at the sheer face of the quarry, three-quarters of a mile away, and the summit of Crandor above.

"He *did* hold it," answered Elleroth, "right through the rains and after—getting on for four months altogether. He was hoping for some relief from Ikat, or even from the troops at Kabin —the ones your trusty bull-breeding friend attended to. The Ortelgans let him alone for a long time—they'd come to have a healthy respect for him, I dare say—but when the rains were over and he was still there they began to worry. They needed to put an army in the field toward Ikat, you see, and there was no one to spare to keep Santil contained in the citadel. So they got rid of him."

"Got rid of him—just like that? What do you mean? How?"

Elleroth struck the surface lightly with the edge of his hand, so that a thin, pattering crescent of water drops flew backward along the side of the boat.

"Really, Mollo, you don't seem to have learned much about military methods during your travels. There were plenty of *children* in Bekla, even if all of them weren't children of the citadel garrison. They hanged two children every morning in sight of the citadel. And of course there were plenty of mothers too, at liberty to go up to the citadel and beg Erketlis to come to terms before the Ortelgans became even more inventive. After some days he offered to go, provided he was allowed to march out fully armed and proceed unmolested to Ikat. Those terms the Ortelgans accepted. Three days later they tried to attack him on the march, but he'd been expecting something of the sort and succeeded in discouraging them quite effectively. That happened near my home in Sarkid, as a matter of fact."

Mollo was about to reply when Elleroth, seated at the boatman's back, spoke again, without any alteration in his quiet tone.

"We are about to run into a large floating log, which will probably stave in the bow."

The boatman stopped rowing at once and turned his head.

"Where, sir?" he asked, in Beklan. "I don't see anything."

"Well, *I* see that you understand *me* when I am speaking Yeldashay," replied Elleroth, "but that is not a crime. It seems to have turned even more chilly, and the wind is fresher than it was. You had better take us back, I think, before we catch the Telthearna ague. You have done very well—here are another ten meld for you. I'm sure you never gossip."

"God bless you, sir," said the boatman, pulling on his right oar.

"Where now?" asked Mollo, as they stepped ashore in the garden. "Your room—or mine? We can go on talking there."

"Come, come, Mollo—the arrangements for eavesdropping will have been completed days ago. Dear me, those amateur instructors of yours in Deelguy! We will have a stroll through the town—hide a leaf in the forest, you know. Now that priestess woman who addressed us this morning—the one with a face like a nightjar—would you say that she—"

They made their way downhill, by way of the walled lane, to the Peacock Gate, and were shut into the little enclosed chamber called the Moon Room while the porter, unseen, operated the counterpoise that opened the postern. There was no way between the upper and lower cities except through this gate and the porters, vigilant and uncommunicative as hounds, opened for none whom they had not been instructed to recognize. As Elleroth followed Mollo out into the lower city, the gate closed behind them, heavy, smooth and flat, its iron flanges overlapping the walls on either side. For a few moments they stood alone above the din of the town, grinning at each other like two lads about to plunge together into a pool.

The Street of the Armorers led downhill into the colonnaded square called the Caravan Market, where all the goods coming into the city were weighed and checked by the customs officers. On one side stood the city warehouses, with their loading and unloading platforms, and Fleitil's brazen scales, which could weigh a cart and two oxen as easily as a sack of flour. Mollo was watching the weights being piled against forty ingots of Gelt iron when a grimy-faced, ragged boy, limping on a crutch, stumbled against him, stooped quickly sideways with a kind of clumsy, sweeping bow, and then began to beg from him.

"No mother, sir, no father—a hard life—two meld nothing to a gentleman like you—generous face—easy to see you're a lucky man—you like to meet a nice girl—be careful of rogues here— many rogues in Bekla—many thieves—perhaps one meld—need a fortuneteller—you like to gamble perhaps—I meet you here tonight—help a poor boy—no food today—"

His left leg had been severed above the ankle and the stump, bound in dirty cloth, hung a foot above the ground. As he shifted his weight the leg swung limply, as though there were no strength from the thigh down. He had lost a front tooth, and as he lisped out his monotonous, inexpressive offers and entreaties, red betel-stained spittle crept over his lower lip and down his chin. He had a shifty-eyed, wary look and kept his right arm slightly bent at his side, the hand open, the thumb and fingers crooked like claws.

Suddenly Elleroth stepped forward, gripped the boy's chin in his hand and jerked up his face to meet his own eyes. The boy gave a shrill cry and tried to back away, pouring out more words, distorted now by Elleroth's grip on his jaw.

"Poor boy, sir, no harm, gentleman won't hurt a poor boy, no work, very hard times, be of service—"

"How long have you followed this life?" asked Elleroth sternly.

The boy stammered with eyes averted.

"Don't know, sir, four years, sir, five years, done no wrong, sir, six years perhaps, whatever you say—"

Elleroth, with his free hand, pulled up the boy's sleeve. Bound round the forearm was a broad leather band and thrust beneath it by the blade was a handsome, silver-hilted knife. Elleroth pulled it out and handed it to Mollo.

"Didn't feel him take it, did you? That's the worst of wearing one's knife in a sheath on the hip. Now stop howling, my boy, or I'll see you flogged before the market warden—"

"I'll see him flogged, howling or no," interrupted Mollo. "I'll—"

"Wait a moment, my dear fellow." Elleroth, still grasping the boy's chin, turned his head to one side and with his other hand thrust back his dirty hair. The lobe of the ear was pierced by a round hole about as big as an orange pip. Elleroth touched it with his finger and the boy began to weep silently.

"*Genshed u arkon lowt tha?*" said Elleroth, speaking in Terekenalt, a tongue unknown to Mollo.

The boy, who was unable to speak for his tears, nodded wretchedly.

"*Genshed varon, shu varon il pekeronta?*" The boy nodded again.

"Listen," said Elleroth, reverting to Beklan. "I am going to give you some money. As I do so I shall curse you and pretend to hit you, for otherwise a hundred wretches will come like vultures from every hole in the market. Say nothing, hide it and go, you understand? Curse you!" he shouted, gripping the boy's shoulder and pushing him away. "Be off, get away from me! Filthy beggars—" He turned on his heel and walked away, with Mollo beside him.

"Now what the devil—?" began Mollo. He broke off. "Whatever's the matter, Elleroth? You're surely not—not *weeping*, are you?"

"My dear Mollo, if you can't observe a knife vanishing from its sheath on your own hip, how can you possibly expect to observe accurately the expression on a face as foolish as mine? Let us turn in and have a drink—I feel I could do with one, and the sun's become rather warmer now. It will be pleasant to sit down."

25   *The Green Grove*

THE NEAREST TAVERN IN THE COLONNADE, whose sign proclaimed it to be "The Green Grove," was out of the wind but warmed nevertheless, at this early time of the year, by a charcoal brazier, low enough to keep floor drafts from chilling the feet. The tables were still damp from their morning scrubbing and the settle, facing toward the square, was spread with brightly colored rugs which, though somewhat worn, were clean and well brushed. The place appeared to be frequented chiefly by the better kind of men having work or business in the market—buyers, household stewards, caravan officers, merchants and one or two market officials, with their uniform green cloaks and round leather hats. There were pumpkins and dried tendrionas hanging in nets against the walls and pickled aubergines, cheeses, nuts and raisins set out in dishes. Through a door at the back could be caught a glimpse of the courtyard, with white doves and a fountain. Elleroth and Mollo sat down at one end of the settle and waited without impatience.

"Well, Death, don't come along just yet," cried a long-haired young caravaneer, flinging back his cloak to free his arm as he drank and looking over the top of his leather can as though half-expecting that unwelcome personage to make a sudden appearance round the corner. "I've got a bit more profit to make down south and a few more jars to empty here—haven't I, Tarys?" he added to a pretty girl with a long black plait and a necklace of silver coins, who set down before him a plate of hard-boiled eggs in sour cream.

"Ay, likely," she answered, "without you get yourself killed int' south one trip. Profit, profit—happen you'd go to Zeray for profit."

"Ay—happen!" he mimicked, teasing her and spreading out a row of foreign coins, one under each finger, for her to take whatever was due in payment. "Help yourself. Why don't you take *me* now, instead of the money?"

"I'm not that hard up yet," retorted the girl, taking three of the coins and coming across to the settle. Her eyelids were stained with indigo and she had pinned a bunch of red-flowering *tectron* in her bodice. She smiled at Mollo and Elleroth, a little unsure how to address them, since on the one hand they were strangers and clearly gentlemen, while on the other they had been an audience for her little flirtation with the caravaneer.

"Good morning, my dear lass," said Elleroth, speaking as though he were her grandfather and at the same time looking her up and down with an air of open admiration which left her more confused than ever. "I wonder whether you have any *real* wine, from the south—Yeldashay, perhaps, or even just Lapan? What we need to drink on a morning like this is sunshine."

"There's none come in a long while, sir, more's t' pity," answered the girl " 'Tis the war, y'see. We can't get it."

"Now I'm sure you're underrating the resources of this splendid establishment," replied Elleroth, putting two twenty-meld pieces quietly into her hand. "And you can always pour it into a jug, so that no one else knows what it is. Ask your father. Just bring the best you've got, as long as it's—er—well, pre-bear, you know, pre-bear. We shall recognize it all right, if it's from the south."

Two men came through the chain-curtained entrance and called to the girl in Chistol, smiling across at her.

"I suppose you have to learn a lot of languages, with so many admirers?" asked Mollo.

"Nay, they've to learn mine or I'm doon with them," she smiled, nodding, as she left, to Elleroth, to show that she would do as he had asked.

"Ah, well, I suppose the world still takes a lot of stopping," said Elleroth, leaning back on the settle, snapping a pickled aubergine and throwing half into his mouth. "What a pity so many furious boys persist in trying! Will it suit you if we go on talking Yeldashay, by the way? I'm tired of speaking Beklan, and Deelguy is beyond me, I fear. One advantage of this place is that no one would think it unduly odd, I believe, if we were to converse by coughing down each other's necks or tapping the table with very large toothpicks. A little Yeldashay will be all in the day's work to them."

"That boy," said Mollo, "you gave him money, after he'd stolen my knife. And what was that hole in his ear? You seemed to know what you were looking for, all right."

"You have no inkling, provincial governor?"

"None."

"Long may you continue to have none. You met this man Lalloc, you told me, in Deelguy. I wonder, did you ever hear tell of one Genshed?"

"No."

"Well, curse the war, then!" shouted a man who had just come in, evidently in reply to some remark of the landlord standing before him with compressed lips, shrugged shoulders and hands held out on either side. "Bring us any damn' thing, only be quick. I'm off south again in half an hour."

"What's the news of the war?" called Elleroth across the room.

"Ah, it's going to get rough again now the spring's here, sir," answered the man. "There'll be nothing coming up from the south now—no, not for some months, I dare say. General Erketlis is on the move—likely to drive up east of Lapan, so I've heard."

Elleroth nodded. The girl returned with a plain earthenware jug, leather beakers and a plate of fresh radishes and watercress. Elleroth filled both cans, drank deeply and then looked up at her openmouthed, with an exaggerated expression of astonishment and delight. The girl giggled and went away.

"Better than we might have expected," said Elleroth. "Well, never mind about the poor boy, Mollo. Put it down to eccentricity on my part. I'll tell you one day. Anyway, it's got nothing to do with what we were talking about on the lake."

"How did they get their bear back?" asked Mollo, crunching a radish and spreading out his legs toward the brazier. "What I heard—if it's true it frightens me, and no one's ever told me it's not—was that the bear smashed through the Beklan line and killed Gel-Ethlin as if it knew who he was. That's one thing they can all tell you in Deelguy, because there was a Deelguy contingent in the Beklan army and the bear killed their commander at the same time—tore his throat out. You must admit it's all very strange."

"Well?"

"Well, then the bear disappeared as night was falling. But you know where it is now—there, up the hill." He jerked his thumb over his shoulder.

"This man Crendrik—the king—he spent the whole of the following summer tracking it down," replied Elleroth. "As soon as the rains ended he went out with his priestesses or whatever they call them and worked over the whole country from Kabin to Terekenalt and from Gelt to the Telthearna. He used to be a hunter, I believe. Well, whether he was or not, he found the bear at last in some very inaccessible part of the hills and he fired the whole hillside, including two wretched villages, to force it down to the plain. Then he made it insensible with some kind of drug, hobbled it with chains—"

"*Hobbled* it?" interrupted Mollo. "How on earth do you hobble a bear?"

"They'd learned that no cage could hold it, so I was told, so while it was drugged they fastened its legs to a choke-chain around its neck, so that the more it kicked the more it throttled itself. Then it was dragged to Bekla on an open wheeled platform in less than two days—something like sixty miles. They had relays of men to take over from one another and never stopped at all. Even so it nearly died—didn't terribly care for the chains, you see. But it only goes to show, my dear Mollo, how much importance the Ortelgans attach to the bear and to what lengths they're prepared to go in anything that concerns it. Telthearna diving boys they may be, but they're evidently inspired to great heights by that animal."

"They call it the Power of God," said Mollo. "Are you sure it isn't?"

"My dear Mollo, what *can* you mean? (Let me fill up that leather thing you have there. I wonder whether they have any more of this?)"

"Well, I can't account for all that's happened in any other way. Old S'marr feels the same—he said they were meant to win. First the Beklans fail to get any sort of news of what's happened, then they go and split their army in two, then the rains break, then the bear kills Gel-Ethlin just when he's got them beaten and no one in Bekla has the least warning until the Ortelgans are down on them—are you really saying that all that's mere coincidence?"

"Yes, I am," replied Elleroth, dropping his whimsical manner and leaning over to look straight into Mollo's face. "An over-civilized people grow complacent and careless and leave the door open for a tribe of fanatical savages, through a mixture of luck, treachery and the foulest inhumanity, to usurp their place for a few years."

"A few years? It's five years already."

"Five years *are* a few years. Are they secure? You know they're not. They're opposed by a brilliant general, with a base as near as Ikat. The Beklan empire is reduced to half of what it was. The southern provinces have seceded—Yelda, Belishba, arguably Lapan. Paltesh would like to secede and daren't. Deelguy and Terekenalt are both enemies, so far as they can spare time from their own troubles. The Ortelgans could be overthrown this summer. That Crendrik—he'll end in Zeray, you mark my words."

"They're reasonably prosperous—there's plenty of trade still in Bekla."

"Trade? Yes, what sort of trade, I wonder? And you've only to look around you to see how badly even a place like this is affected. What used to bring more prosperity to Bekla than anything else? Building, masonry, carving—all that sort of craftsmanship. That trade is ruined. There's no labor, the big craftsmen have quietly gone elsewhere and these barbarians know nothing of such work. As for the outer provinces and the neighboring kingdoms, it's only a very occasional patron who sends to Bekla now. Plenty of trade? What sort of trade, Mollo?"

"Well, the iron comes in from Gelt, and the cattle—"

"What sort of trade, Mollo?"

"The slave trade, is that what you're getting at? Well, but there's slave trading everywhere. People who lose wars get taken prisoner—"

"You and I fought together once to keep it at that. These men are desperate for trade to pay for their war and feed the subject peoples they're holding down—desperate for any sort of trade. So it's no longer kept at that. What sort of trade, Mollo?"

"The children, is that what you're getting at? Well, if you want my opinion—"

"Excuse me, gentlemen. I don't know whether you're interested, but I'm told the king is approaching. He'll be crossing the market in a few moments. I thought as you gentlemen seem to be visitors to the city—"

The landlord was standing beside them, smiling obsequiously and pointing out through the entrance.

"Thank you," replied Elleroth. "That's very good of you. Perhaps—" he slid another gold piece into the landlord's hand—"if you could contrive to find some more of this excellent stuff—charming girl, your daughter—oh, your niece? Delightful—we'll return in a few minutes."

They went out into the colonnade. The square had become hotter and more crowded and the market servants, carrying pitchers and long aspergilla of bound twigs, were walking hither and thither, laying the glittering, sandy dust. At a distance above, the north front of the Barons' Palace stood in shadow, the sun, behind it, glinting here and there upon the marble balustrades of the towers and the trees on the terraces below. As

Mollo stood gazing in renewed wonder, the gongs of the city clocks sounded the hour. A few moments afterward he heard, approaching by the street down which he and Elleroth had come that morning, the ringing of another gong, softer and of a deeper, more vibrant pitch. People were drawing aside, some leaving the square altogether or slipping into the various doorways around the colonnade. Others, however, waited expectantly as the gong drew nearer. Mollo edged his way between those nearest to him and craned his neck, peering over the beam of the Great Scales.

Two files of soldiers were coming down the hill, pacing slowly on either side of the street. Although they were armed in the Beklan style, with helmet, shield and short sword, their dark eyes, black hair and rough, unkempt appearance showed them to be Ortelgans. Their swords were drawn and they were looking vigilantly about them among the crowd. The man bearing the gong, who walked at the head of and between the two files, was dressed in a gray cloak edged with gold and a blue robe embroidered in red with the mask of the Bear. The heavy gong hung at the full extent of his left arm, while his right hand, holding the stick, struck the soft, regular blows which both announced the king's approach and gave their step to the soldiers. Yet the beat was not that of marching men, but rather of solemn procession, or of a sentinel pacing on some terrace or battlement alone.

Behind the man with the gong came six priestesses of the Bear, scarlet-cloaked and adorned with heavy, barbaric jewelery —necklaces of ziltate and penapa, belts of inlaid bronze and clusters of carved wooden rings so thick that the fingers of their folded hands were pressed apart. Their grave faces were those of peasant girls, ignorant of gentle ways and accustomed to a narrow life of daily toil, yet they carried themselves with a dark dignity, withdrawn and indifferent to the staring crowd on either side. At their center walked the solitary figure of the priest-king.

It had not occurred to Mollo that the king would not be carried—either in a litter or on a chair—or drawn in a cart, perhaps, by caparisoned and gilt-horned oxen. He was taken unawares by this curious lack of state, by this king who walked through the dust of the marketplace, who stepped aside to avoid a coil of rope lying in his path and a moment after tossed his head, dazzled by a flash of light reflected from a pail of water. In his curiosity he climbed precariously on the plinth of the nearest column and gazed over the heads of the passing soldiers.

The train of the king's long cloak of blue and green was raised and held behind him by two of the priestesses. Each blue panel bore in gold the mask of the Bear and each green panel the emblem of the sun as a lidded and radiant eye—the Eye of God. His long staff, of polished zoan wood, was bound about with golden filigree; and from the fingers of his gauntlets hung curving silver claws. His bearing, that neither of a ruler nor a warrior, possessed nevertheless a mysterious and cryptic authority, stark and ascetic, the power of the desert-dweller and the anchorite. The dark face, haggard and withdrawn, was that of a man who works in solitude, the face of a hunter, a poet or a contemplative. He was young, yet older than his years, going gray before his time, with a stiffness in the movement of one arm which suggested an old injury ill-healed. His eyes seemed fixed on some inward scene which brought him little peace, so that even as he looked about him, raising his hand from time to time in somber greeting to the crowd, he appeared preoccupied and almost disturbed, as though his thoughts were struggling in disquiet with some lonely anxiety beyond the common preoccupations of his subjects—beyond riches and poverty, sickness and health, appetite, desire and satisfaction. Walking like other men through the dusty marketplace in the light of morning, he was separated from them by more than the flanking soldiers and the silent girls: by arcane vocation to an ineffable task. As Mollo watched, there came into his mind the words of an old song:

> What cried the stone to the chisel?
> "Strike, for I am afraid!"
> What said the earth to the ploughman?
> "Ah, the bright blade!"

The last soldiers were receding at the far end of the square, and as the sound of the gong died away, the business of the market resumed. Mollo rejoined Elleroth and together they returned to The Green Grove and their place on the settle. It was now less than an hour to noon and the tavern had become more crowded but, as is often the way, this added to their seclusion rather than otherwise.

"Well, what did you think of the kingly boy?" enquired El-leroth.

"Not what I expected," answered Mollo. "He didn't strike me as the ruler of a country at war, that's the size of it."

"My dear fellow, that's merely because you don't understand the dynamic ideas prevalent down on the river where the reeds all shiver. Matters there are determined by resort to hocus-pocus, mumbo jumbo and even, for all I know, jiggery-pokery—the shades of distinction being fine, you understand. Some bar-barians slit animals open and observe portents revealed in the steaming entrails, yum yum. Others scan the sky for birds or storms. Ebon clouds, oh *dear*! These are what one might term the blood-and-thunder methods. The Telthearna boys, on the other hand, employ a bear. It's all the same in the end—it saves these people from having to think, you know, which they're not terribly good at, really. Bears, dear creatures—and many bears are among my best friends—have to be interpreted no less than entrails and birds, and some magical person has to be found to do it. This man Crendrik—you are right, he could neither com-mand an army in the field nor administer justice. He is a peasant —or at all events he is not of noble birth. He is the wonderful What-Is-It who stepped out of the rainbow—a familiar figure, dear me, yes! His monarchy is a magical one: he has taken it upon himself to mediate to the people the power of the bear—the Power of God, as they believe."

"What does he do, then?"

"Ah, a good question. I am glad you asked it. What, indeed? Everything but think, we may be sure. I have no idea what methods he employs—possibly the bear piddles on the floor and he observes portents in the steaming what-not. How would I know? But a crystal ball of some kind there must surely be. One thing I know about the man—and this is genuine enough, for what it's worth. He possesses a certain curious ability to go near the bear without being attacked; apparently he has been known even to touch it and lie down beside it. As long as he can go on doing that, his people will believe in his power and therefore in their own. And that no doubt accounts, my dear Mollo, for his having the general air of one finding himself in a leaking canoe with a vivid realization that he cannot swim."

"How so?"

"Well, one day, sooner or later, the bear is fairly sure to wake up in a bad temper, yes? Growl growl. Biff biff. Oh dear. Applications are invited for the interesting post. That, in one form or another, is the inevitable end of the road for a priest-king. And why not? He doesn't have to work, he doesn't have to fight: well, obviously he has to pay for it somehow."

"If he's the king, why does he walk through the streets on his own two feet?"

"I confess I'm not sure, but I conceive that it may be something to do with his being different in one respect from others of his kind. As a rule, among these roughs, the priest is himself the manifestation of God. They kill him now and then, you know, just to keep him in mind of it. Now here, the bear is the divine creature and the gentleman we have just been admiring represents, as long as he can keep on going near it, a proof that the bear means him, and therefore his people, good and not harm. The bear's savagery is working on their side and against their enemies. They have cornered it until it, as it were, corners him. It may well be the whole point that he is plainly vulnerable and yet remains unharmed—a magic trick. So he takes pains to show that he is indeed a real and ordinary human being, by walking through the city every day."

Mollo drank and pondered in silence. At last he said, "You're like a lot of men from Ikat—"

"I come from Lapan, from Lapan, jolly man: from Sarkid, actually; but not from Ikat."

"Well, like a lot of the southerners. You think everything out, trust in your minds and in nothing else. But people up here aren't like that. The Ortelgans have established their power in Bekla—"

"They have not."

"They have, and principally for one reason. It's not just that they've fought well, and it's not that there's already been a great deal of intermarriage with Beklan girls—those are just things that follow from the real reason, which is Shardik. How is it that they've succeeded against all probability, unless Shardik is really the Power of God? Look what he did for them. Look what they've achieved in his name. Everyone who knows what happened—"

"It's lost nothing in the telling—"

"Everyone feels now what S'marr felt from the outset—they're meant to win. We don't reason it all out like you; we see what's before our eyes, and what's before our eyes is Shardik, that's it."

Elleroth leaned forward with his elbows on the table and bent his head, speaking earnestly and low.

"Then let me tell *you* something, Mollo, that you evidently *don't* know. Are you aware that the whole worship of Shardik, as carried on here in Bekla, is knowingly contrary to the Ortelgans' traditional and orthodox cult, of which this man they call Crendrik is not and never has been the legitimate head?"

Mollo stared. "*What?*"

"You don't believe me, do you?"

"I'm not going to quarrel with you, Elleroth, after all we've been through together, but I hold authority under these people —they've made my fortune, if you like, that's it— and you want me to believe that they're—"

"Listen." Elleroth glanced around quickly and then continued.

"This is not the first time that these people have ruled in Bekla. Long ago they did so; and in those days, too, they worshiped a bear. But it was not kept here. It was kept on an island in the Telthearna—Quiso. The cult was controlled by women—there was no priest-king, no Eye of God. But when at last they lost Bekla and fell from power, their enemies were careful to see that no bear remained to them. The chief priestess and the other women were allowed to stay on their island, but without a bear."

"Well, the bear's returned at last. Isn't that a sure sign?"

"Ah, but wait, good honest Mollo. All is not told. When the bear returned, as you put it—when they acquired this new model—there was a chief priestess on the island—a woman with the reputation of being no fool. She knows more about disease and healing than any doctor south of the Telthearna—or north of it either, I should think. There's no doubt that she's effected a great many remarkable cures."

"I think I've heard something about her, now you mention it, but not in connection with Shardik."

"At the time when this bear first appeared, five or six years ago, she was the recognized and undisputed head of the cult, her office having descended regularly for God only knows how long. And this woman would have nothing to do with the attack on Bekla. She has consistently maintained that that attack was not the will of God but an abuse of the cult of the bear; and consequently she has been kept in virtual imprisonment, with a few of her priestesses, on that Telthearna island, even though the bear—her bear—is being kept in Bekla."

"Why hasn't she been murdered?"

"Ah, dear Mollo, the penetrating realist—always straight to the point. Why, indeed, has she not been murdered? I don't know, but I dare say they fear her as a sorceress. What she has undoubtedly retained is her reputation as a healer. That was why my brother-in-law traveled a hundred and fifty miles to consult her at the end of last summer."

"Your brother-in-law? Ammar-Tiltheh is married, then?"

"Ammar-Tiltheh is married. Ah, Mollo, do I see a slight shadow cross your face, stemming, as it were, from old memories? She has the kindest memories of you, too, and hasn't forgotten nursing you after that wound which you were so reckless as to get through saving me. Well, Sildain is a very shrewd, sensible fellow—I respect him. About a year ago he got a poisoned arm. It wouldn't heal and no one in Lapan could do it any good, so at last he took it into his head to go and see this woman. He had a job to get on the island—she's kept pretty well incommunicado, it seems. But in the end they let him, partly because he bribed them and partly because they saw he'd probably die if they didn't. He was in a bad way by that time. She cured him, all right—quite simply, apparently, by applying some sort of mold; that's the trouble about doctors, they always make you do something revolting, like drinking bats' blood— have some more wine?—but while he was there he learned a little—not much—about the extent to which these Ortelgans have abused the cult of the bear. I say not much, because apparently they're afraid that the priestess's very existence may stir up trouble against them and she's watched and spied on all the time. But Sildain told me more or less what I've told you—that she's a wise, honorable and courageous woman; that she's the rightful head of the cult of the bear; that according to her interpretation of the mysteries there was no sign that they were divinely intended to attack Bekla; and that this man Crendrik and that other fellow—Minion, Pinion, whatever he called himself—appropriated the bear by force for their own purposes and that everything that's been done since then has been nothing but blasphemy, if that is the right term."

"I wonder still more why they haven't murdered her."

"Apparently it's rather the other way round—they feel the lack of her and they haven't yet given up hope of persuading her to come to Bekla. In spite of all he's done, the Crendrik man still feels great respect for her, but although he's sent several times to beg her to come, she always refuses. Unlike you, Mollo, *she* won't be a party to their robbery and bloodshed."

"It still doesn't alter their extraordinary success and the confidence with which they fight. I've got every reason to support them. They've made me governor of Kabin and if they go, I go."

"Well, they've left me as Ban of Sarkid, if it comes to that. Nevertheless, the number of hoots I give for them is restricted to less than two. Do you think I'd sell the honor of Sarkid for a few meld from these dirty, murderous—"

Mollo laid a hand on his arm and glanced quickly sideways without moving his head. The landlord was standing just behind the settle, apparently absorbed in trimming the wick of a lamp fixed to the wall.

"Can we have some bread and cheese?" said Elleroth in Yeldashay.

The landlord gave no sign that he understood.

"We have to go now, landlord," said Elleroth, in Beklan. "Do we owe you anything further?"

"Nothing at all, good sirs, nothing at all," said the landlord, beaming and presenting each of them with a small model, in iron, of the Great Scales. "Allow me—a little souvenir of your visit to The Green Grove. A neighbor makes them—we keep them for our special customers—greatly honored—hope we shall have the pleasure on another occasion—my poor house—always glad—"

"Tell Tarys to buy herself something pretty," said Elleroth, putting ten meld on the table.

"Ah, sir, too kind, most generous—she'll be delighted—a charming girl, isn't she? No doubt if you wished—"

"Good morning" said Elleroth. They stepped out into the colonnade. "Do you think he may perhaps make a point of hiding his linguistic abilities from the common light of day?" he asked, as they strolled once more across the market.

"I'd like to know," answered Mollo. "I can't help wondering why he trims lamps at noon. Or why he trims lamps at all, if it comes to that, seeing it's women's work and he has that girl to help him."

Elleroth was turning the ugly little model over in his hands.

"I feared it—I feared it. He must take us for utter fools. Does he think we can't recognize the Gelt iron-mark when we see it? So much for his neighbor who makes them—weighed in the Great Scales and found nonexistent."

He placed the model on a windowsill overlooking the street and then, as an afterthought, bought some grapes from a nearby stall. Having put a grape carefully into each scale, he handed half the remainder to Mollo and they walked on, eating grapes and spitting out the pips.

"But does it really matter whether the fellow understood you or not?" asked Mollo. "I know I warned you when I saw him standing there, but that's become second nature after all these years. I can hardly believe you could be accused on his evidence, let alone convicted of anything serious. It'd be his word against mine, anyway, and of course *I* can't remember hearing you say anything whatever against the Ortelgans."

"No, I'm not afraid of being arrested for that sort of thing," answered Elleroth, "but all the same, I've got my reasons for not wanting these people to know my true feelings."

"Then you'd better be more careful."

"Indeed, yes. But I'm rash, you know—such an impetuous boy!"

"I know that," replied Mollo, grinning. "Haven't changed, have you?"

"Hardly at all. Ah, now I recall where we are. This brook is the outfall of the Barb, which runs down to what was once the Tamarrik Gate. If we follow it upstream along this rather pleasant path, it will bring us back close to the Peacock Gate, where that surly fellow let us out this morning. Later on, I want to stroll out beyond the Barb as far as the walls on the east side of Crandor."

"What on earth for?"

"I'll tell you later. Let's talk of old times for the moment. Ammar-Tiltheh will be delighted to hear that you and I have met again. You know, if ever you had to leave Kabin, you'd always be welcome in Sarkid for as long as you liked to stay."

"Leave Kabin? I'm not likely to be able to do that for at least a year or two, though you're very kind."

"You never know, you never know. It's all a question of what you can—er—bear, as it were. How straight the smoke is going up; and the swifts are high, too. Perhaps the weather is going to be kinder during our stay than I dared to hope."

26 *The King of Bekla*

THE BARE HALL, BUILT AS A MESS for common soldiers, was gloomy and ill-ventilated, for the only windows were at clerestory level, the place having been intended for use principally at evening and after nightfall. It was rectangular and formed the center of the barracks building, its four arcades being surrounded by an ambulatory, off which lay the storerooms and armories, the lockup, lavatories, hospital, barrack rooms and so on. Almost all the bays of the arcades had been bricked up by the Ortelgans nearly four years ago and the raw, unrendered brickwork between the stone columns not only added to the ugliness of the hall but imparted also that atmosphere of incongruity, if not of abuse, which pervades a building clumsily adapted for some originally unintended purpose. Across the center of the hall, alternate flagstones of one course of the floor had been prised up and replaced by mortar, into which had been set a row of heavy iron bars with a gate at one end. The bars were tall—twice as high as a man—and curved at the top to end in downward-pointing spikes. The tie bars, of which there were three courses, overlapped one another and were secured by chains to ringbolts set here and there in the walls and floor. No one knew the full strength of Shardik, but with time and the full resources of Gelt at his disposal, Baltis had been thorough.

At one end of the hall the central bay of the arcade had been left open and from each side of it a wall had been built at right angles, intersecting the ambulatory behind. These walls formed a short passage between the hall and an iron gate set in the outer wall. From the gate a ramp led down into the Rock Pit.

Between the gate and the bars the floor of the hall was deep in straw and a stable-smell of animal's manure and urine filled the air. For some days past, Shardik had remained indoors, listless and eating little, yet starting suddenly up from time to time and rambling here and there, as though goaded by pain and seeking some enemy on whom to avenge it. Kelderek, watching nearby, prayed continually in the same words that he had used more than five years ago in the forest darkness, "Peace, Lord Shardik. Sleep, Lord Shardik. Your power is of God. Nothing can harm you."

In the fetid twilight he, the priest-king, was watching over the bear and waiting for news that Ged-la-Dan had reached the city. The Council would not begin without Ged-la-Dan, for the provincial delegates had been assembled first for the purpose of satisfying the Ortelgan generals about contributions of troops, money and other supplies required for the summer campaign, and secondly to be told as much as was considered good for them about Ortelgan plans for the enemy's defeat. Of these plans Kelderek himself as yet knew nothing, although they had already, no doubt, been formulated by Zelda and Ged-la-Dan with the help of some of the subordinate commanders. Before the commencement of the Council, however, and certainly before any step was taken to put the plans into effect, the generals would seek his agreement in the name of Lord Shardik; and anything which, in his prayer and pondering, he might dislike or doubt, he could if he wished require them to alter in Shardik's name.

Since that day when Shardik had struck down the Beklan

THE KING'S HOUSE

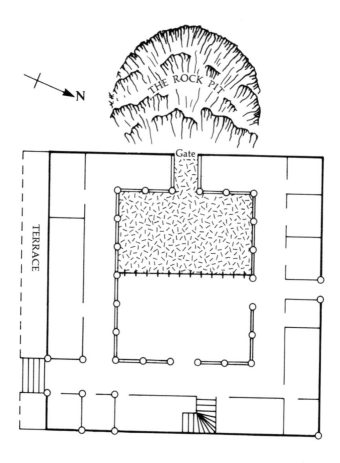

Bars	┼┼	Brick walls closing arcading	
Strawed area			
Columns	○ ○	Steps	

commanders and disappeared into the rainy nightfall of the
Foothills, Kelderek's authority and influence had become greater
than Ta-Kominion's could ever have been. In the eyes of the
army it was plainly he who had brought about the miracle of the
victory, he who had first divined the will of Shardik and then
acted in obedience to it. Baltis and his men had told everywhere
the tale of his apparent folly in insisting upon the construction
of the cage and of the single-mindedness with which he had
conducted the desperate march over the hills, completed by less
than half of those who had begun it. The breach broken through
the Tamarrik Gate could hardly have been carried against a
leader like Santil-kè-Erketlis, had it not been for the fanatical
belief of every Ortelgan that Shardik, in mystic communion
with Kelderek, was invisibly present, leading the assault and
striking unseen at the hearts and arms of Bekla. Kelderek himself had known beyond doubt that he and none other was the
elect of Shardik, whom he was ordained to bring to the city of
his people. On his own authority he had ordered Sheldra and
the other girls to set out with him, as soon as spring should
come, to seek Shardik until he was found. The Ortelgan barons,
while they did not dispute this authority, had vehemently opposed the idea of his magical presence leaving the city as long
as Santil-kè-Erketlis remained undefeated in the citadel on
Crandor; and Kelderek, impatient of delay as the warm days
returned, had suppressed his personal revulsion at the methods
by which Zelda and Ged-la-Dan had compelled the Beklan general to vacate his stronghold. Such revulsion, he considered,
while it might be natural enough to the common man that he
had once been, was altogether unworthy of a king, whose contempt and lack of pity for the enemy was a necessity for his
own people, or how could wars be won? In any case the matter
was below the sphere of his authority, for he was a magical and
religious king, concerned with the perception and interpretation
of the divine will; and certainly no religious question was involved in Ged-la-Dan's decision to erect a gallows within view
of the citadel and to hang two Beklan children every day until
Santil-kè-Erketlis should agree to leave it. Only when Ged-la-
Dan had told Kelderek that he ought to attend each hanging in
the name of Shardik had he exercised his own will in the matter,

replying curtly that it was he and not Ged-la-Dan who had been appointed by God to discern where and on what occasions there might be a need for his presence and for the manifestation of the power conferred on him by Shardik. Ged-la-Dan, secretly fearing that power, had said no more and Kelderek, for his part, had profited by what had been done without having to witness it. After some days the Beklan general had agreed to march south, leaving Kelderek free to seek Shardik in the hills west of Gelt.

From that long and arduous search neither the bear nor the king had returned unchanged. Shardik, snarling and struggling in his chains till he lay exhausted and half-strangled, had been drawn into the city by night and under an enforced curfew, lest the people should see what might appear to them as the humiliation of the Power of God. The chains had inflicted wounds on one side of his neck and beneath the joint of the left foreleg; and these healed slowly, leaving him with something of a limp and with an awkward, unnatural carriage of his great head which, in walking, he now moves slowly up and down, as though still feeling the pressure of the chain that was no longer there. Often during the first months he was violent, battering at the bars and walls with enormous blows that thudded through the building like a smith's hammer. Once the new brickwork closing one of the bays split and collapsed under his anger and for a time he wandered in the ambulatory beyond, beating, until he was weary, at the outer walls. Kelderek had divined from this a portent of success for an attack toward Ikat; and in fact the Ortelgans, following his divination, had forced Santil-kè-Erketlis to retreat southward through Lapan, only to be compelled once more to halt their advance on the borders of Yelda.

In less than a year, however, Shardik had grown sullen and lethargic, afflicted with worms and plagued by a canker which caused him to scratch dolefully at one ear until it was ragged and misshapen. Lacking both Rantzay and the Tuginda, and hampered by the confined space and the continual gloomy savagery of the bear, Kelderek abandoned the hope he had once entertained of recommencing the Singing worship. Indeed all the girls, though assiduous in feeding Shardik, ministering to his needs and cleaning and tending the building that had become

242

his dwelling, now feared him so greatly that little by little it became accepted that to come near him, unless protected by the bars, no longer formed any part of their services. Only Kelderek, of all their company, still knew in his heart that he must stand before him, offering his life for no reward and uttering again and again his prayer of self-dedication, "*Senandril*, Lord Shardik. Accept my life. I am yours and ask nothing of you in return." Yet even as he prayed he answered himself, "Nothing —except your freedom and my power."

During the long months of searching, in the course of which two girls had died, he had contracted a malarial fever, and this returned from time to time, so that he lay shivering and sweating, unable to eat and—particularly when the rains were beating on the wooden roof above—seeming to himself, in confused dreams, to be once more following Shardik out of the trees to destroy the appalled and stricken hosts of Bekla; or again, he would be seeking Melathys, plung down the Ledges in the starlight toward a fire which receded before him, while from among the trees the voice of the Tuginda called, "Commit no sacrilege, now of all times."

He came to know the days when he could be sure that Shardik would make no move—the days when he could stand beside him as he lay brooding and speak to him of the city, of the dangers that beset it and its need of divine protection. At times, unpredictably, there would return upon him the inward sense of being elevated to some high plane beyond that of human life. But now, instead of attaining to that pinnacle of calm, shining silence from which he had once looked down upon the outskirts of the Ortelgan forest, it seemed that he joined Lord Shardik upon the summit of some terrible, cloud-swirling mountain, a place of no-life, solitary and distant as the moon. Through the darkness and icy vapor, from the pit of stars flaring in the black sky, there would sound rolling thunder, the screaming of birds, half-heard voices—unintelligible cries of warning or fierce triumph. These were borne to him crouching on the edge of a visionary and dreadful precipice, enduring this world of suffering without refuge. From pole to pole there was none left in the world to suffer but he; and always, in this trance, he was powerless to move—perhaps no longer human, but changed to a rock buried under snow or split by lightning, an anvil hammered by a cold power in regions unendurable to human life. Usually his sense of this awful sphere was mercifully dulled—superimposed, as it were, upon a continuing recollection of fragments of his lucid self, like reflections upon the visible bed of a river: as that he was king of Bekla, that sharp blades of straw were pricking the flesh of his legs, that the open gate to the Rock Pit was forming a square of bright light at the far end of the dark hall. Once or twice, however, he had become enclosed and locked altogether, like a fish in ice, among the gulfs of time where the mountains lived out their lives and crumbled and the stars, in millennia, were consumed away to darkness; and, falling to the ground, had lain oblivious beside the shaggy body of Shardik until at last, hours later, waking with a profound sense of grief and desolation, he had limped his way out of the hall to stand in the sun with the exhausted, undemanding relief of one cast up from shipwreck.

Unable to comprehend whatever truth might lie hidden in this terrible place to which, as by a compass needle, he was guided by his unaltered devotion to Shardik, he would nevertheless seek, clumsily and conscientiously, to derive from what he suffered some meaning, some divine message applicable to the fortunes of the people and the city. Sometimes he knew in himself that these soothsayings were contrived, all but mendacious, the very stuff of a mountebank. Yet often, those which he knew most surely to have been cobbled out of incomprehension, self-reproach and a mere sense of duty would appear later to have been fulfilled, to have borne actual fruit, or at all events were received by his followers as evident truth, while the nebulous searchings of his integrity to compass in words what lay, like a half-remembered dream, beyond his power to recall or express would evoke only shaken heads and shrugged shoulders. Worst of all, in its effect on others, was the honest silence of humility.

Shardik absorbed him night and day. The spoils of Bekla—to the barons, the soldiers and even to Sheldra and her companions so precious and gratifying an end in themselves—were no lure to him. The honor and state devised for the king he accepted, and the role which gave heart and assurance to barons and people he fulfilled with a profound sense both of their need and his own fitness through election by God. And yet, musing in the gaunt, echoing hall, watching the bear in its fits of rage and of torpor, he was filled with the conviction that, after all, what he had accomplished—all that seemed miraculous and near-divine in human terms—was of no importance in contrast to what remained to be revealed. Once, in the days when he had been concerned with no more than to get his hunter's living, he had thought only of what was necessary to that narrow purpose, like a peasant leaving unconsidered the whole world beyond his own strip of land. Then the power of Shardik had touched him and in the eyes of himself and others he had entered upon the world as an emissary of God, seeing plainly and certainly, through the knowledge divinely imparted to him, both the nature of his task and what was needed for its performance. As the instrument of Shardik he had been accorded a unique perception, self-sufficient and free from all ignorance and uncertainty. In the light of that perception everything had been found by others to have the value which he himself attached to it: and everything had fallen into the place to which he had appointed it. The High Baron of Ortelga had proved to be of small moment, yet all-important his own apparently suicidal determination to carry to Quiso the news of Shardik's coming. But now, though Shardik was lord in Bekla, this perception no longer seemed, to himself, sufficient. Continually, he was haunted by an intuitive sense that all that had happened as yet had scarcely touched the fringe of the truth of God, that he himself was still blind and that some great disclosure remained to be sought and found, to be prayed for and granted—a revelation of the world in the light of which his own state and monarchy would signify as little to himself as to the huddled creature in the cage, with its staring pelt and evil-smelling dung. Once in a dream he found himself robed and crowned for the festival of victory held every year upon the onset of the rains, but paddling his hunter's raft along the southern shore of Ortelga. "Who is Shardik?" called the beautiful Melathys, walking among the trees. "I cannot tell," he called back. "I am only an ignorant, simple man." At this she laughed, took off her great golden collar and tossed it easily to him across the reeds; but he, in the act of catching it, knew it to be worthless and let it fall into the water. Waking to see Shardik rambling back and forth beyond the bars, he rose and, as the dawn lightened, stood a long while in prayer. "Take back all else, Lord Shardik, my power and kingdom if you will. But give me fresh eyes to perceive your truth—that truth to which I cannot yet attain. *Senandril*, Lord Shardik. Accept my life if you will, but grant, at whatever cost, that I may find what I still seek."

It was this all-demanding austerity of preoccupation which, more than his readiness to confront the bear, more than prophecy or any other attribute, maintained his power and authority over the city and established the awe felt for him not only by the people but also by those very barons who could not forget that he had once been nothing but an Ortelgan hunter. There was none to whom it was not plain that he was in truth the prisoner of his own all-consuming integrity, that he took no pleasure in the jewels and wine, the girls and flowers and feasting of Bekla. "Ah, he speaks with Lord Shardik!" they said, watching as he paced through the streets and squares to the soft beat of the gong. "We live in the sun, for he takes the darkness of the city on himself." "Gives me the cold shivers, he does," said the courtesan Hydraste to her pretty friend as they leaned from her window in the hot afternoon. "*You* couldn't do even that much, to him," replied the friend, flicking a ripe cherry down upon a young man passing below, and leaning a little farther over the sill.

To himself, his integrity was unforced, rooted in the compulsion to seek, to discover a truth which he felt to lie far beyond the fortune he had made for Ortelga, far beyond his own role of priest-king. In his prophecies and interpretations he was less betraying this integrity than compounding with necessity in the face of his need for more time if he was to attain to what he sought—just as a doctor, feeling himself on the brink of discovering at last the true cause of a disease, may nevertheless continue to treat it by accepted methods, not from any intention to deceive or exploit, but because until he succeeds in his great aim there is nothing better. Kelderek, who might have drugged Shardik to be sure of standing safely before him on appointed days in the presence of the people, who might have introduced human sacrifice or elaborate forms of compulsory worship, so great was the veneration in which he was held, endured instead the danger of death and the twilit solitude of the hall where he prayed and meditated continually on an uncomprehended mystery. Something there was to be discovered, something attainable only at great cost, the one thing worth attaining, beside which all older religious notions would appear pathetic fragments of superstition, an esotericism as shallow as the whispered secrets of children. This it was that would constitute Shardik's supreme gift to men. And thus he himself knew that his priesthood, which seemed to others incapable of further magnification and therefore essentially procedural and unchanging in its nature, a matter of service and rites performed in due season, was in reality an all-demanding search, during which time was always passing and his steps never covered the same ground twice. This it was which by its tremendous nature would transcend—even justify—all wrong done in the past, all violence to the truth, even—even—and here the trend of his thoughts would fail, giving place to the picture of the road to Gelt at moonset and himself standing silent while Ta-Kominion led his prisoner away down the valley. Then he would groan and fall to striding up and down outside the bars, beating fist on palm as he strove to break his train of thought, and tossing his head as though in imitation of the afflicted Shardik.

For the memory of the Tuginda gave him no peace, even though the event had made it plain that Ta-Kominion must have been right and that she would have thwarted the miraculous gift of victory and frustrated the conquest of Bekla. After Shardik had been brought to the city and all but the southerly provinces around Ikat had recognized the rule of the conquerors, the barons had decided, with Kelderek's full agreement, that it would be both magnanimous and prudent to send messengers to assure the Tuginda that her error of judgment had been forgotten and that the time was now ripe for her to take her place beside them; for notwithstanding all that Kelderek had come to signify, no Ortelgan could lose that numinous awe for Quiso with which he had been instilled from birth, and not a few were uneasy that in their new prosperity their leaders should evidently have set aside the Tuginda. It was known that two priestesses had been killed between the coming of Shardik and the battle of the Foothills, and as long as the conquest of Bekla remained to be consolidated by subduing the provinces, the barons had been able to tell their followers that they had begged the Tuginda to remain in Quiso for her own safety. Many had expected that Shardik, once recovered, would be taken to Quiso, as in days long ago. Kelderek, however, from the time when he had set out from Bekla to find the bear, had never intended this; for if he were to go with Shardik to the Tuginda's island he must forfeit his supremacy as priest-king, while without the actual presence of Shardik he could not expect to reign in Bekla. With Shardik in Bekla and the northerly provinces subdued, there could no longer be any plausible reason for the Tuginda's absence except her own refusal to come, and the messengers— of whom Neelith had been one—had been instructed to stress to her the harm that might well be done to the people's confidence and to the fighting power of the army were she to continue to grudge Kelderek his superior power of divining the will of Shardik, and to show petty spite by sulking in Quiso and thereby depriving the people of all she meant to them.

"And this we can now put to her strongly," said Ged-la-Dan to the other members of the baronial council, "for make no mistake, she is no longer the figure we once feared in the days of Bel-ka-Trazet. She was wrong about the will of Lord Shardik, while Ta-Kominion and Kelderek were not. Her honor is as great and no greater than we are ready to accord to her, and will be commensurate with the extent of her use to us. But since many of the people still accord her honor, it will be prudent to add to our own security by bringing her here. In fact, if she will not come I will bring her myself."

Kelderek had said nothing in dissent from this harsh assessment, since he felt sure that the Tuginda would be glad to accept her offered reinstatement, and that once she was in Bekla he would be able to help her to restore her former standing in the eyes of the barons.

The messengers had returned without Neelith. It seemed that on Quiso she had broken off her prepared speech to kneel at the Tuginda's feet in tears, begging her forgiveness and crying passionately that she would never leave her again as long as she lived. After hearing what the rest had to say, the Tuginda had merely reminded them that she had been sent back to Quiso as a prisoner. She had, she said, no more liberty than that now accorded to Shardik to determine for herself whether or not she would go to one place or another.

"But," she added, "you may tell them in Bekla that when Lord Shardik takes that liberty once again, I will take mine too. And you may also tell Kelderek that whatever he may think to the contrary, I am bound as he, and he is bound as I. And that he will one day discover."

With this reply they had been obliged to return.

"The bitch!" said Ged-la-Dan. "Does she think she is in any position to disguise her sulky mood with impudent speeches—she in the wrong of it and we in the right? I will be as good as my word, and I shall not be long about it either."

Ged-la-Dan was absent for a month, which cost the army a serious tactical reverse in Lapan. He returned without the Tuginda and remained silent about the reason, until the tale told by his servants, under questioning from the other barons, began to make him a laughingstock behind his back. It turned out that he had made two separate and unsuccessful attempts to land on Quiso. On each occasion a stupor had fallen upon himself and those with him and his canoe had drifted below the island. On the second occasion it had struck a rock and sunk, and he and his companions had barely escaped with their lives. Ged-la-Dan lacked neither pride nor courage, but for his second attempt he had been forced to make use of fresh servants, the original paddlers having utterly refused to go a second time. Kelderek, shuddering at his own memories of the night journey to Quiso, could only marvel at the baron's stubbornness. It was plain that it had cost him dear indeed. For many months afterward, even in the field, he contrived to avoid sleeping alone and would never again travel by water.

Was it, then, to expiate the memory of the Tuginda that Kelderek cared little what he ate and drank, remained chaste and left to others the spending of the wealth considered proper to the king's grandeur? Often he felt that this was indeed the reason, even while he wondered for the thousandth time what he could have done to help her. To have intervened on her behalf would have been to declare himself against Ta-Kominion. But despite his reverence for the Tuginda, he had passionately supported Ta-Kominion and been ready to follow him into any hazard. The Tuginda's conception of Shardik's power he had never understood, while Ta-Kominion's was plain. And yet he knew that at bottom to vindicate his own courage in Ta-Kominion's eyes he had thrown in his lot with what must surely have been the most desperate campaign that had ever proved successful. Now he was priest-king of Bekla, and he and not the Tuginda was the interpreter of Shardik. Yet how much understanding did he truly possess, and how much of the Ortelgan conquest was really due to him as Shardik's elect?

The thought of the Tuginda was never far from his mind. As, after a few years of marriage, a childless woman cannot be free from her disappointment, reflecting, "What a beautiful morning—but I am childless," or "Tomorrow we go to the wine festival—but I am childless," so Kelderek's thoughts were troubled continually by the recollection of himself standing silent while the Tuginda was bound and led away. She had known her own mind as he had not known his: and he had deceived himself in believing that she would ever consent to become a party to Shardik's captivity in Bekla. Sometimes he felt ready to renounce his crown and return to Quiso to entreat, like Neelith, her forgiveness. Yet this would be to give up both his power and his search for the great revelation, of the imminence of which he was sometimes almost sure. Besides, he suspected that if he attempted the journey the barons would not suffer one so disloyal to themselves to live.

From this dilemma his one retreat was to Shardik. Here was no undeserved reward of luxury, flattery or compliant, whispering pleasure by night, no riches or adulation—only solitude, ignorance and danger. While he served Lord Shardik in fear and suffering of mind and body, at least he could not accuse himself of having betrayed the Tuginda for his own gain. Often, during the years that had passed, he had half-hoped that Shardik would put an end to his perplexity by taking the life which was so continually offered to him. But once only had Shardik attacked him, striking suddenly as he stepped through the gate in the bars and breaking his left arm like a dry stick. He had fainted with the pain, but Sheldra and Nito, who had been at his back, had saved his life, dragging him away on the instant. The arm had set crooked, though he still had the use of it. Yet although, setting aside the pleadings of the girls and the warnings of the barons, he had continued, as soon as he was able, to stand from time to time before Shardik, the bear had never again shown him violence. Indeed, he seemed indifferent to Kelderek's approach and often, having raised his head as though to assure himself that it was he and none other, would continue merely to mope in the straw. At these times Kelderek would stand beside him, deriving comfort, as he prayed, from the knowledge that in spite of all that had passed, he and only he remained the human companion and mediator of Shardik. And thus, out of his unaccountable safety, were born his terrible visions of desolation, his conviction that he was still far wide of the mark and his belief that Shardik had some great secret to reveal.

Yet despite his hours of solitude and austerity he was no mere recluse, brooding always upon the ineffable. During the four years since his return to Bekla with Shardik, he had played a full part in the counsels of the Ortelgans and maintained not only a number of intelligence agents, but also his own body of advisers with special knowledge of the various provinces, their features and resources. Much of the information that reached him was of military importance. A year before, he had received warnings of a daring plan to damage the iron workings at Gelt, so that Ged-la-Dan had been able to arrest the Yeldashay agents on their way north through Thettit, disguised as traders from Lapan. More recently, not three months ago, there had come from Dari Paltesh the disturbing news that a force of more than two thousand Deelguy irregulars, whose leaders had evidently realized the impossibility of crossing the mountains by the strongly guarded Gelt pass, had made their way along the north bank of the Telthearna, crossed into Terekenalt (whose king, no doubt being well paid, had done nothing to stop them), and then, by a swift march through Katria and Paltesh, succeeded in reaching the rebel province of Belishba, there being no provincial force strong enough to dispute their passage before they were gone. At this setback the Ortelgan leaders had shaken their heads, seeing at work the long and resourceful arm of Santil-kè-Erketlis and speculating on the use to which he would put this cleverly won reinforcement.

In matters relating to trade, customs and taxation, however,

Kelderek had quickly come to feel that his own insight, though faulty and inexperienced, was essentially surer than the barons'. It was, perhaps, precisely because he had never been either a baron or a mercenary living on tenants' dues and the plunder of war, but had made his rough living as a hunter and had known what it was to be dependent on iron, leather, wood and yarn for the artifacts of his craft that he perceived more plainly than they the vital importance to the empire of trade. For months he had argued, against the indifference of Zelda and Ged-la-Dan, that neither the life of the city nor the war against the southern provinces could be maintained solely by spoil and that it was essential to keep open the recognized trade routes and not impress into military service every able-bodied young craftsman, merchant and caravaneer within the empire's boundaries. He had proved to them that in a year, two prosperous cattle breeders and their men, thirty tanners or twenty shoemakers could not only earn their own living but pay a tax large enough to keep in the field twice their own number of mercenaries.

And yet trade had declined. Santil-kè-Erketlis, an adversary more shrewd and experienced than any of the Ortelgan leaders, had taken steps to see that it did. Bridges were broken and caravans attacked by paid bandits. Warehouses and their contents were mysteriously destroyed by fire. The finest craftsmen —builders, masons, jewelers, armorers, even vintners—were secretly approached and persuaded, sometimes at a cost equal to that of a year's pay for ten spearmen, that it would be in their best interests to travel south. The king's son of Deelguy was invited to Ikat, treated as befitted a prince and, perhaps not altogether fortuitously, found himself in love with a noble lady of that city, whom he married. The resources of the rebel provinces were less than those of Bekla, but Santil-kè-Erketlis possessed a flair for perceiving where a little extraordinary expenditure would prove effective. As time went on, merchants and traders became less and less ready to hazard their wealth in a realm so subject to the uncertainties and fluctuations of war. Taxes became increasingly difficult to collect from a people feeling the pinch and Kelderek was hard put to it to pay the contractors and craftsmen who supplied the army.

It was in this difficulty that he had had recourse to a wide extension of the slave trade. A slave trade of sorts had always existed in the Beklan empire, but for about ten years before the Ortelgan conquest it had been restricted, having been allowed to get out of control to the point of provoking reaction throughout the provinces. It was traditionally accepted that prisoners taken in war, unless they could pay a ransom, might be sold as slaves. Sometimes these men would succeed in gaining their liberty, either returning home or else making a new life in the country to which they had been brought. Despite the harshness and suffering involved, this practice was regarded, in a hard world, as fair between peoples at war. During the latter days of Bekla's high prosperity, however, the number of large estates, households and businesses had increased and consequently the demand for slaves had grown until it became worthwhile for men to turn professional dealers and cater for it. Kidnaping and even breeding had become widespread, until several of the provincial governors had felt themselves driven to protest in the name of towns and villages living in fear—not only from raiding dealers but also from escaped slaves turned brigands—and of respectable citizens outraged. The slavers, however, had not been without their supporters, for the trade could not only afford to pay heavy taxes but also provided work for such craftsmen as clothiers and blacksmiths, while buyers visiting Bekla brought money to the innkeepers. The issue had come to the boil in the civil conflict known as the Slave Wars, when half a dozen independent campaigns had been fought in as many provinces, with and without the help of allies and mercenaries. From this confusion Santil-kè-Erketlis, formerly a Yeldashay estate owner of ancient family but no great wealth, had emerged as the most able leader on either side. Having defeated the slave trade supporters in Yelda and Lapan, he had sent help to other provinces and finally succeeded in settling matters in Bekla itself to the entire satisfaction of the Heldril ("old-fashioned people"), as his party was called. The cost to the state of extraditing the dealers and freeing all slaves who could prove themselves native to the empire had been met partly by fresh encouragement of the builders', masons' and carvers' trades for which Bekla had always been famous and partly by measures (of which the construction of the great Kabin reservoir had been one) to increase the prosperity of the peasants and small farmers.

Nevertheless there remained, not only in Bekla itself but also in several of the towns in the western provinces, influential men who regretted the Heldril victory. It was these that Kelderek had sought out and put into local power, the bargain being that they should support the war in return for a revival of the unrestricted slave trade. This policy he defended to his own barons —some of whom could remember slave raids on the mainland country near Ortelga fifteen and twenty years before—partly as one of "needs must" and partly by emphasizing that the country was not being laid open to a totally uncontrolled trade. A fixed number of dealers were granted licenses each year to "take up" not more than their permitted quotas of women and children in particular provincial districts. Where a quota of able-bodied men was granted to any particular dealer, a fifth had to be surrendered to the army. There were, of course, no troops to spare to see that these consents were not abused and enforcement had to be left to the provincial governors. To all who complained of what he had done, Kelderek had one answer—"We will restrict the slave trade again when the war is over, so help us to win it."

"Many of those who get taken up as slaves are local ne'er-do-wells and criminals that the dealers buy out of the jails," he had assured the barons, "and even of the children, many would otherwise have been neglected and ill-treated by mothers who never wanted them. A slave, on the other hand, always has a chance to prosper, with luck and ability." Han-Glat, an ex-slave from Terekenalt who was now in charge of the army's pioneering and construction troops, gave powerful support to Kelderek, letting it be known that any slave under his command had as good a chance of promotion as a free man.

The profit from the trade was high, especially as it became known that Bekla once more had a state-protected slave market with a wide range of goods, and agents from other countries found it worth their while to travel there, pay the market dues and spend their money. Despite his arguments in defense of what he had done—the best argument being the public accounts —Kelderek found himself keeping away not only from the market but also from the streets by which the slave consignments commonly came and went. For this he despised himself; yet setting aside the involuntary pity which he knew to be a weakness in a ruler, he had also the uneasy feeling that there might be in his policy some flaw which he was not seeking over-hard to detect. "The kind of disrupting, shortsighted expedient that one might expect to occur to a common man and a bar-barian," the former Heldril governor of Paltesh had written, in a letter resigning his appointment before deserting to Yelda. "Does he think I don't know as well as he that it's an expe-dient?" Kelderek commented to Zelda. "We can't afford to be benevolent and generous until we've captured Ikat and defeated Erketlis." Zelda had agreed, but then added, "And equally, of course, we can't afford to alienate too many of our own people, even if they're not Ortelgans. Be careful it doesn't get out of hand." Kelderek felt himself like a man in dire need who takes care not to probe too closely the specious assurances of an affable moneylender. Though inexperienced as a ruler, he had never lacked common sense and had learned early in life to dis-trust fair appearances and any prize that came too easily. "But when we have taken Ikat," he told himself, "then we'll be able to cease these shifts and hand-to-mouth methods. O Lord Shar-dik, bring us one more victory! *Then* we will put an end to the slave trade and I will be free to seek nothing but your truth." Sometimes, at the thought of this great day, the tears would spring to his eyes as readily as to those of any enslaved child at the memory of home.

27   *Zelda's Advice*

KELDEREK LOOKED ABOUT HIM at the shadowy, cavernous hall—as grim and barbaric a temple of blood as had ever housed the trophies of a tyranny. Because of the dimness of the light from above, torches, fixed in iron brackets, burned continually, and these had discolored the brickwork and the stone columns with irregular, cone-shaped streaks of black. In the still air the thick yellow flames lolled hither and yon, sluggish as lobworms dis-turbed in winter-dug earth. Now and then a spurt of resin flared sideways or a knot exploded with a crack. The smoke, eddying in the roof and mingling its pine scent with the smell of the bear, seemed like the rustling sound of the straw made visible. Between the torch brackets, panoplies were fixed to the walls— short swords and ear-flapped helmets of Belishba, the round, leather shields of Deelguy mercenaries and the spike-and-ball spears which Santil-kè-Erketlis had first brought north from Yelda. Here, too, was the ripped and bloody banner of the Chalice of Deparioth, which Ged-la-Dan himself had taken two years before at the battle of Sarkid, cutting his way through the enemy's hurdle-palisades at the head of twelve followers, not one of whom had remained unwounded at the fight's end. The Canathron of Lapan, with its serpent's head and condor's wings arching to stoop, stood wreathed with vine shoots and red blossoms, for it had been brought to Bekla as an enforced (though dubious) surety for the loyalty of Lapan, by hostage-priests who were permitted to continue its rites in attenuated form. Along the farther wall, domed and yellow in the torchlight, were ranged the skulls of enemies of Shardik. Little they differed one from another, save in the patterns formed by the grinning teeth, though two or three were cracked like old plaster and one was faceless, mere splinters surrounding a jagged hole from forehead to jawbone. The shadows of their eye sockets moved in the torchlight, but Kelderek had long ceased to pay any attention to these unburied remains. To him, indeed, the display was tedious —nothing more than a sop to the vanity of subordinate commanders in the field, one or another of whom would from time to time claim that he had killed enemies of rank and hence deserved the distinction of presenting the skulls to Shardik. The girls kept them in trim, oiling and wiring, as once they had busied themselves with their hoes on the Ledges of Quiso. Yet for all the accumulated mementos of this victory and that (thought Kelderek, pacing slowly down the hall and turning at the sound of a sudden, plunging movement behind the bars), the place was still what it had always been—disordered, impermanent, a repository rather than a shrine—perhaps because the life of the city itself had become that of a base behind an army, a society with few young men and too many lonely women. Had not Shardik been better served among the scarlet flowers of the trepsis beside the pool, and in the dry, twilit forest whence he himself had first stepped forward to offer him his life?

"When a fish is caught and lies in the net," he thought, "one sees the luster dying slowly out of its scales. And yet—how else to eat the fish?"

He turned once more, this time at the sound of approaching footsteps in the corridor. The gong of the clock near the Peacock Gate had not long struck the tenth hour and he had not expected Ged-la-Dan's arrival so soon. Zilthé, older now but still trim, quick and light-stepping, came into the hall, raising her palm to her forehead with the smile of a friend. Of all the girls who had come from Quiso or had since entered the service of Shardik, Zilthé alone possessed both grace and a light heart, and Kelderek's somber mood softened as he returned her smile.

"Has Lord Ged-la-Dan come so soon?"

"No, my lord," replied the girl. "It is General Zelda who wishes to see you. He says that he hopes the time is convenient, for he needs to speak with you soon. He did not say so, my lord, but I believe that he wants to see you before General Ged-la-Dan arrives."

"I will go out to him," said Kelderek. "Watch by Lord Shardik —you or another. He must not be left alone."

"I will feed him, my lord—it is time."

"Then put the food in the Rock Pit. If he will go out there for a while, so much the better."

Zelda was waiting on the sun terrace that ran along the south side of the hall, his dark red cloak drawn close against the chilly breeze. Kelderek joined him and together they walked across the gardens and on into the fields lying between the Barb and the Leopard Hill.

"You have been watching with Lord Shardik?" asked Zelda.

"For several hours. He is disturbed and fretful."

"You speak as though he were a sick child."

"At these times we treat him as such. It may be nothing—but I would be happier if I were sure that he is not sick."

"Perhaps—could it be—" Zelda paused, but then said only, "much sickness is ended by the coming of summer. He will soon be better."

They rounded the western shore of the Barb and began to cross the pasture slope beyond. Before them, about three quarters of a mile away, lay that part of the city walls that ran uphill to encircle Crandor's eastern spur.

"Who's that fellow coming down toward us?" asked Zelda, pointing.

Kelderek looked. "Some nobleman—a stranger. It must be one of the provincial delegates."

"A southerner by the look of him—too dandified for any northern or western province. Why is he walking here alone, I wonder?"

"He's free to do so if he wishes, I suppose. Many who visit the city like to be able to say that they've walked entirely around the city walls."

The stranger came on, bowed graciously with a rather affected sweep of his fur cloak, and passed by.

"Do you know him?" asked Zelda.

"Elleroth, Ban of Sarkid—a man about whom I've found out a good deal."

"Why? Isn't he safe?"

"Possibly—possibly not. It's strange that he should have come himself as delegate. He was with Erketlis in the Slave Wars—in fact he's been a noted Heldro in his time. There's no particular reason why he should have changed his ideas, but all the same I was advised that it would be safer to leave him alone than to try to get rid of him. He has a lot of influence and standing with his own people, and as far as I can learn he's never done us any actual harm."

"But has he helped us?"

"Lapan's been fought over so much that it's hard to say. If a local ruler takes care to keep in with both sides, who's to blame him? There's nothing known against him except his record before we came."

"Well, we'll see what he has to offer us at the Council."

Still Zelda seemed hesitant to talk of whatever had led him to seek out Kelderek, and after a little Kelderek spoke again.

"Since we're talking of the delegates, I ought to mention another to you—the man you recently appointed as governor of Kabin."

258

"Mollo? What about him? By the way, that man is staring after us—I wonder why."

"Strangers not uncommonly stare after me," replied Kelderek with a faint smile. "I've become accustomed to it."

"That's it, no doubt. Well, what about Mollo? S'marr Torruin of the Foothills recommended him—says he's known him for years. He seems an excellent man."

"I've learned that until a short time ago he was a provincial governor in Deelguy."

"In Deelguy? Why did he leave?"

"Exactly. To take up his patrimony of a small estate in Kabin? I'm inclined to doubt it. Our present relations with Deelguy are strained and difficult—we don't know what they may be intending. I wonder whether we ought to risk this appointment of yours—we might be walking into a trap. A knife in the back from Kabin would be bad just at the moment."

"I think you're right, Kelderek. I knew nothing of this. I'll speak to Mollo myself tomorrow. We can't afford any risk in Kabin. I'll tell him we've decided that after all we ought to have a man with special knowledge of the reservoir."

He fell silent again. Kelderek veered a little downhill to the left, thinking that by thus seeming to commence their return he might loosen the baron's tongue.

"What do you think of the war now?" asked Zelda suddenly.

"Ask the kites and crows, they're the ones that knows," replied Kelderek, quoting a soldiers' proverb.

"Seriously, Kelderek—and entirely between ourselves?"

Kelderek shrugged his shoulders. "You mean its prospects? You know more of those than I."

"You say Lord Shardik seems ill at ease?" persisted Zelda.

"Not every mood or ailment of Lord Shardik is a portent of the war. If that were so, a child could read the omens."

"Believe me, Kelderek, I don't question your insight as priest of Shardik—nor you my generalship, I hope."

"Why do you say that?"

Zelda stopped and looked around at the open, rough pasture about them. Then he sat down on the ground. After a few moments' hesitation Kelderek joined him.

"To sit here may not become our dignity," said Zelda, "but I prefer to speak where none can overhear. And I warn you, Kelderek, that if need be I shall deny that I ever spoke at all."

Kelderek made no reply.

"More than five years ago we took this city; and there's not a man who fought in that campaign but knows that we did so by the will of Shardik. But what's his will now? I wonder whether I'm the first to feel perplexed on that score."

"I dare say you're not."

"You know what my men were singing after we took Bekla? 'Now Lord Shardik's battle's won, We'll squeeze the girls and lie in the sun.' They don't sing that any more. Four years up and down the marches of the southern provinces have knocked all that out of them."

Three-quarters of a mile away on the Serpent Tower—the southeastern tower of the Barons' Palace—Kelderek could see a soldier leaning over the balustrade. No doubt he had been ordered to watch for the approach of Ged-la-Dan, but it was plain from his attitude that he had seen nothing as yet.

"What was Shardik's will in restoring us to Bekla? Was it what the men supposed—to make us strong and prosperous for the rest of our lives? If so, why is Erketlis still in the field against us? What have we done to displease Lord Shardik?"

"Nothing that I know."

"Shardik killed Gel-Ethlin—he struck the blow himself—and after we had taken Bekla, you and I and everyone supposed that by his will we should soon defeat Erketlis and capture Ikat. Then there would be peace. But that hasn't happened."

"It will happen."

"Kelderek, if you were anyone other than the king of Bekla and the priest of Shardik—if you were a provincial governor or a subordinate commander promising me something—I should answer 'Then it had better happen damned quickly.' I'll be plain. For several years my men have been fighting and dying. They're just preparing to do so for another summer, and in no very good frame of mind. The truth is that, leaving aside the will of Shardik and speaking purely as a general, I can see no military reason why we should ever win this war."

Someone below seemed to be calling to the man on the tower. He leaned out over the parapet, looked down for a few moments and then resumed his watch.

"It was Lord Shardik who gave us the victory over Gel-Ethlin," went on Zelda. "If it hadn't been for what he did, we could never have defeated a Beklan army—an irregular force like ours."

"No one ever said otherwise. Ta-Kominion himself knew it before the battle. Yet we did win, and we took Bekla."

"Now we're doing well merely to contain Erketlis. We can't defeat him—certainly not conclusively. There are several reasons why. I suppose when you were a boy you wrestled, ran races and so on. Can you remember times when you knew for certain that the other lad was better than you were? As a general, Erketlis is quite out of the ordinary, and most of his men were in the former southern army of patrol. Many of them feel that they're fighting for their homes and families, and that makes them ready to put up with very hard conditions. They're not like us, invaders disappointed in hopes of quick profits. Our men have felt for a long time now that something's slipped through their net. Food of some sort or other is easy to come by down in the south. We can't deprive Erketlis' army of food, and they don't look for much more than that. But their very existence makes difficulties for us. As long as they remain undefeated, they're a focus for disaffection and trouble anywhere in the empire from Gelt to Lapan—old Heldril sympathizers and so on. Erketlis has only got to maintain himself in the field, but we've got to do more than that; we've got to defeat him before we can restore to Beklan people the peace and prosperity of which we've deprived them. And the plain truth is, Kelderek, that I have no grounds—no military grounds—for thinking that we can do it."

The man on the Serpent Tower suddenly began waving his arms and pointing southeastward. Then he cupped his hands, shouted something down and disappeared from the balcony.

"Ged-la-Dan will be here in less than an hour," said Kelderek. "Have you said any of this to him?"

"No, but I've no reason to suppose that he's any happier with our military prospects than I am."

"What about the help we're expecting from the Council delegates tomorrow?"

"Whatever it is, it won't be enough. It never has been in the past. You must understand that at present we're holding on in

Lapan as best we can. It's not we but Erketlis that means to attack."

"Can he?"

"As you know, he has recently received a force from Deelguy, led by a baron of whose actions their king pretends to be ignorant. There's a rumor that Erketlis now believes himself strong enough both to cover Ikat and to attack us as well, and that he's planning to march farther north than ever before."

"On Bekla?"

"That would depend on his success once he'd started, I dare say. But my own belief is that he may go wide of Bekla and try to show his power in the country northeast of it. Suppose, for example, that he simply told the Deelguy that he'd lead them north on their march home, doing all the damage he could on the way? Suppose they set themselves to destroy the Kabin reservoir?"

"Could you not stop them?"

"I don't know. But what I'm proposing, Kelderek—and what I have never proposed at all if you receive it ill—is one of two courses. The first is that we should negotiate a peace with Erketlis at once. Our terms would be that we retain Bekla, with the northern provinces and as much land to the south as we can get. That would mean ceding certainly Yelda, Belishba and probably Lapan, with Sarkid, of course. But we should have peace."

"And the second?"

For the first time Zelda turned and looked full at Kelderek, his dark eyes and beard framed in the red cloak-collar. Gently he drew out his knife, held it suspended a moment between finger and thumb, and then let it fall, hilt-upward, to stick quivering in the ground. Wrinkling his nose and sniffing, as though at the smell of burning, he drew out the knife and returned it to its sheath. The allusion was not lost upon Kelderek.

"I knew from the beginning—yes, that very night—that in some way you were carrying the destiny of Ortelga. Even before you and Bel-ka-Trazet set out for Quiso, I was sure that you had been sent to bring us luck and power. Later, when the first rumors reached Ortelga, I believed in Shardik's return because I had seen you withstand Bel-ka-Trazet's anger and realized that only the truth could have enabled you to do so. It was I who advised Ta-Kominion to risk his life by crossing the Dead Belt by night to seek you out; and I was the first baron to join him the next morning, when he came ashore behind Lord Shardik. At the battle of the Foothills, before ever Ta-Kominion reached the field, I led the first attack on Gel-Ethlin's army. I have never doubted Lord Shardik—nor do I doubt him now."

"What then?"

"*Loose* Lord Shardik! Loose him, and await what may befall. Perhaps it is not his will that we should continue the war. He may have another, perhaps an altogether different purpose. We should be ready to trust him, even to admit that we may have mistaken his will. If we loose him, he may reveal some unknown thing. Are you sure, Kelderek, that we may not be, after all, denying his purpose by keeping him here in Bekla? I have come to believe that that purpose cannot be the continuation of the war, for if it were, we should by now be at least within sight of the end. Somewhere we have lost the thread of our destiny. Loose him, and pray that in this darkness where we are wandering, he will put it back into our hand."

"*Loose* Lord Shardik?" said Kelderek. He could imagine nothing less favorable either to the continuance of his reign or to the divine secret still to be discovered by himself. At all costs he must steer Zelda away from this rash, superstitious idea, the consequences of which were quite unpredictable. "*Loose* Lord Shardik?"

"And then follow him, simply trusting in what will befall. For if indeed we have failed him, then since it cannot be in courage or resolution in the field, it can be only in not trusting him enough."

It was on the tip of Kelderek's tongue to reply that the Tuginda had once spoken in this way and that Ta-Kominion had known how to deal with it. As he paused, pondering how best to begin the delicate task of discussion, they both saw in the distance a servant running toward them across the pasture. They stood up and awaited him.

"Tomorrow night is the spring fire festival," said Kelderek.

"I had not forgotten."

"I will say nothing of this to anyone, and we will speak of it again after the festival. I need time to think."

The servant reached them, raised his palm to his bent brow and waited, trying to control his panting breath.

"Speak," said Kelderek.

"My lord, Lord Ged-la-Dan is almost here. He has been sighted on the road and will reach the Blue Gate within this half-hour."

In the city below, the gongs sounded once more for the hour, the further following immediately upon the nearer like an echo. Kelderek perceived that to retain the servant would put an end to their talk for the time being.

"Accompany us," he said; and then to Zelda, as the man took up his place behind them, "I and the priestess Sheldra will go out to meet Ged-la-Dan on the road. Will you not come with us."

28 *Elleroth Shows His Hand*

"—And to have left all I had in Deelguy—"

"Compose yourself, Mollo."

"I'll not live inside their damned boundaries—not within ten days' journey of them—that blasted bear-priest—whatever he calls himself—Kildrik, that's it—"

"Be reasonable, Mollo. Calm yourself. You didn't leave Deelguy with the least idea of becoming governor of Kabin, let alone with any promise from Bekla. You left because you wanted to succeed to the family estate, or so you told me. No one's deprived you of that and you're no worse off than you were on the night when you dined with your bull-breeding friend."

"Don't be ridiculous. Everyone in Kabin knows that General Zelda appointed me on S'marr's recommendation. I had a long meeting with the elders, before I set out, about Kabin's contribution to the summer campaign. It was little enough they meant to give, too—we're not a rich province—never have been. 'Don't worry,' I said, 'I'll convince them in Bekla—I'll see you're not ruined to pay for the war.' What do you think they're going to

264

say now? They'll say I've been kicked out because I couldn't screw enough out of the province—"

"Perhaps you have."

"But damn it, no one here's even asked me yet what we were going to contribute, so how can it be that? But whatever it is, the Kabin landowners will be convinced that I let them down somehow or other—played my cards wrong, that's it—and now I'm to be replaced by someone who isn't even a local man, someone who'll have no scruples about fleecing them for more. Who's going to believe me when I say I haven't the least idea why the appointment wasn't confirmed? I'll be lucky if no one seeks my life one way or another. It's not that I care about, though. Do you know a better way to make a man really angry than to promise him something and then to take it away?"

"Offhand, no. But my dear Mollo, what did you expect when you took up with this bunch of bruin boys? I'm surprised the possibility didn't occur to you at the outset."

"Well, didn't *you* take up with them?"

"By no means—rather the reverse, actually. At the time when they burst upon an astonished world I was already Ban of Sarkid and it was they, when they arrived, who took a good, long look at me and decided on balance to leave it at that—though whether they were wise to do so remains to be seen. But to go to them cap in hand, as you did, and actually ask for a nice, lucrative appointment; to offer, in effect, to help with the defeat of Santil and the furtherance of the slave trade— And besides, they're so frightfully boring. Do you know, last night, down in the city, I was inquiring about the drama. 'Oh no,' says the old fellow I asked, 'that's all been stopped for as long as the war lasts. They tell us it's because there's no money to spare, but we're sure it's because the Ortelgans don't understand the drama, and because it used to be part of the worship of Cran.' I really felt most frightfully bored when he told me that."

"The fact remains, Elleroth, that your position as Ban of Sarkid has been confirmed in the name of Shardik. You can't deny it."

"I don't deny it, my dear fellow."

"Is the slave trade any better under Shardik, then, than it was ten years ago, when you and I were fighting alongside Santil?"

"If that's a serious question, it certainly doesn't deserve a serious answer. But you see, I'm not a humanitarian—just an estate owner trying to live a reasonably peaceful life and make enough to live on. It's awfully difficult to get people to settle down and work properly when they think that they or their children may be required to form part of a slave quota. It seems to bother them, oddly enough. The real trouble with slavery is that it's such a terribly shortsighted policy—it's bad business. But one can hardly go the length of leaving one's ancestral homestead just because a dubious bear has taken up residence round the corner."

"But why are you actually here, in person, on the bear's business?"

"Like you, perhaps, to make the best deal I can on behalf of my province."

"Kabin's in the north; it's got to stay in with Bekla. But Lapan's a southern province—a disputed province. You could declare openly for Erketlis—secede, and take half Lapan with you."

"Dear me, yes, so I could. Now I wonder why I never thought of that?"

"Well, you make fun of the business, but I don't find it so damned amusing, I'll tell you. It's not the loss of the governorship I mind. What I can't stand is that they've made me look a fool with everyone I've known since I was a lad. Can't you imagine it? 'Here he comes, look; thought he was going to be governor and tell us all what to do. Come home with his tail between his legs, that's it. Oh, good *morning*, Mr. Mollo, sir, lovely weather, isn't it?' How can I go back to my estate now? I tell you, I'd do anything to harm these blasted Ortelgans. And whatever I did, they'd deserve it, if they can't run an empire better than that. I'm like you—it's bad business methods I object to."

"Do you mean what you say, Mollo?"

"Yes, I damned well do. I'd risk anything to harm them."

"In that case—er, let us just step outside for a stroll in some nice, lonely place with no propinquitous walls or bushes—what a pleasant morning! You know, every time I see the Baron's Palace it seems to express something fresh, original and delightfully un-Ortelgan—where was I?—ah, yes; in that case, I may

266

perhaps be able to lead you step by step to the highest pitch of quivering excitement—or somewhere like that, anyway."

"What do you mean?"

"Well, you see, I am not, alas, the good, simple fellow that you suppose. Beneath this well-washed exterior there beats a heart as black as a cockroach and fully half as brave."

"Well, you've evidently got something you mean to say. Tell me plainly—I'll be as secret as you like."

"Perhaps I will. Well then, you must know that at one time, about five years ago, when Santil came through Sarkid on his march from Bekla to Ikat, I was seized with a foolish desire to take some of my fellows and join him."

"I wonder you didn't. I suppose you jibbed at the idea of losing the estate and everything else?"

"Oh, I jibbed practically without stopping—I was jibbering, in fact. However, I had managed to get myself more or less to the point of departure when Santil himself came to see me. Yes —at the outset of a desperate campaign, with everything to be organized and Ikat to be turned into a military supply base, that remarkable man found time to come twenty miles to talk to me and then return by night. I dare say he knew I wouldn't have obeyed anyone else."

"You *obeyed* him? What did he come to say?"

"He wanted me to stay where I was and put on a convincing act of benevolent neutrality to Bekla. He thought that if it were skillfully done, it would be more useful to him than leaving Sarkid to be controlled by some nominee of the enemy. He was quite right, of course. I've always hated people thinking I'd decided not to go and fight, but the advantages to Santil have been greater than anything he could expect from my shouting 'Yah!' at an Ortelgan spearman. He gets to hear a great deal about the movements of Master Ged-la-Dan and the other man, Zelda; and they find themselves in all sorts of difficulties whenever they're operating in the neighborhood of Sarkid. You know— couriers disappear, funny accidents happen, commandeered rations seem to disagree with people and so on. Any little larks we can think of. In fact, I honestly believe that if it weren't for Sarkid, Santil's western flank would have been turned long ago and he might never have been able to hold Ikat at all. But it needs very delicate handling indeed. Ged-la-Dan's a tough, ugly customer and I've had to go to great lengths to convince him that I prefer his side to the other. For years I've kept him thinking that on balance, and because of my local influence and knowledge, it would be better to keep me than to replace me. Little does he know that my love of boyish mischief leads me to grease his stairs from time to time."

"I see; and I suppose I might have guessed."

"Now this next bit is the sensation of a lifetime. Your pulse will tingle with a thousand thrills—well, say five hundred. About a month ago Santil paid me another nocturnal visit, disguised as a wine merchant, incidentally. And what he told me was that this spring, for the first time, he is strong enough both to cover Ikat and to attack northward in force. In fact, he may at this moment have begun a march that will take him north of Bekla before he's done."

"Not to Bekla?"

"That'll depend on the support he gets. Initially, he probably won't try to attack Bekla, but simply march into the north and see whether any of the provinces will rise for him. Of course, he may come upon a good opportunity to defeat an Ortelgan army, and if so, he's not the man to waste it."

"And where do you come in? For obviously you do."

"Well, as a matter of fact, I am that despicable creature, a secret agent."

"Get away!"

"I trust I may in due course. Does it occur to you that if something really nasty were to happen in Bekla just as Santil begins his attack, these superstitious fellows would be most upset? Anyway, it did to Santil. So I came as a delegate to the Council."

"But what do you mean to try to do? And when?"

"Something reckless, I fancy, will be appropriate. I had considered the possibility of causing the king or one of the generals to cease to function, but I don't think it can be done. I missed rather a good chance yesterday afternoon, due to being unarmed, and I doubt whether another will present itself. But I have been considering. The destruction of the King's House and the death of the bear itself—*that* would have a calamitous effect. It might well tip the scale, in fact, when the news reached the army."

268

"But it can't be done, Elleroth. We could never succeed in that."

"With your help I believe we might. What I intend to do is to set fire to the roof of the King's House."

"But the place is built of stone!"

"Roofs, my dear Mollo? Roofs are made of wood. You couldn't span a hall that size with stone. There will be beams and rafters supporting tiles. Look for yourself—there is even some thatch at the far end—you can see it from here. A fire should do well if only it can get a little time to itself."

"It'll be seen at once—and anyway the place will be guarded. How can you possibly climb up to the roof carrying a torch or whatever you're going to need? You wouldn't get near the place before you were stopped."

"Ah, but this is where *you* will be so invaluable. Listen. To-night happens to be the spring fire festival. Have you never seen it? At nightfall they extinguish every flame in the city, until there is total darkness. Then the new fire is kindled and every householder comes to light a torch from it. After that the whole place goes mad. There will be a brazier or at least a torch burning on every accessible roof in the city. They have a procession of boats on the Barb, full of lights and made to look like fiery dragons—the water reflects them, you know. Very pretty. There'll be a torchlight procession—any amount of smoke in people's nostrils, and their eyes dazzled. Tonight, if ever, a fire on the roof of the King's House won't be noticed until it's too late."

"But they don't leave the bear unguarded."

"Of course not. But this we can deal with, if you are as angry and revengeful as you say. I've already marked a place where I think I can climb to the roof; and to make sure, I've risked buying a rope and grapnel. After dark you and I light torches and set out for the festival—armed under our cloaks, of course, and rather late. We make for the King's House and there we silently deal with any sentries we may find. Then I'll climb to the roof and start the fire. There'll almost certainly be a priestess left in the hall to attend upon the bear—perhaps more than one. If they're not silenced they'll spot the fire from below. So you'll have to go in and tackle whomever you find in the hall."

"Why not just go in and kill the bear?"

"Have you ever seen the bear? It's stupendously large—unbelievable. Nothing but several heavy arrows could do it. We haven't got a bow and we can't risk attracting attention by trying to get one."

"When the fire gets a grip, won't the bear simply go out into the Rock Pit?"

"If it's already in by nightfall, they drop the gate between the hall and the pit. It's in at the moment."

"I don't fancy the idea of using a sword on a woman—even an Ortelgan priestess."

"Neither do I; but my dear Mollo, this is war. You need not necessarily kill her, but at the least you'll have to do enough to stop her raising the alarm."

"Well, suppose I do. The roof's burning and about to fall in on the bear and you've climbed down and joined me. What do we do then?"

"Vanish like ghosts at cockcrow."

"But where? The only access to the lower city is through the Peacock Gate. We'll never get away."

"There's quite a fair chance, actually. Santil advised me to look into it and I did, yesterday afternoon. As you know, the city walls run south and completely encircle Crandor; but high up, near the southeast corner, there's a disused postern in the wall. Santil told me it was made by some king long ago, no doubt for some unspeakable purpose of his own. Yesterday afternoon I walked up there, as Santil suggested, and had a look at it. It was all overgrown with brambles and weeds, but bolted only on the inside. I shouldn't think anyone's touched it for years. I oiled the bolts and made sure it can be opened. If anyone's gone there since and seen what I've done, that's too bad, but I doubt they will have. I had a nasty moment coming back, when I met the so-called king and General Zelda walking in that direction, but they turned back soon after I'd passed them. Anyway, that's our best chance and we can't do better than take it. If we can get as far as the upper slopes beyond the Barb without being caught, we may very well get through that gate and reach Santil's army in two or three days. No pursuit will go faster than I shall, I promise you."

"I call it a thin chance. The whole thing's more than risky. And if we're caught—"

"Well, if you now feel that you'd prefer not to take part, my dear Mollo, by all means say so. But you said you'd risk anything to harm them. As far as I'm concerned, I haven't kept my skin whole these five years just to come here and risk nothing. Santil wants a resounding crash—I must try to provide one."

"Suppose, after all, I did kill the woman, couldn't we simply dive into the crowd and pretend complete ignorance? No one would be able to identify us, and the fire might have been an accident—blown sparks on the wind."

"You can certainly try that if you prefer, but they are bound to find out that the fire was no accident—I shall have to rip up the roof to get it to take properly. Suspicion will certainly fall on me—do you think it won't on you, after the motive you've been given today? Can you trust yourself to resist suspicion and inquiry convincingly for days on end? Besides, if the bear dies, the Ortelgans will be beside themselves. They are quite capable of torturing every delegate in the city to get a confession. No, on balance, I think I prefer my postern."

"Perhaps you're right. Well, if we succeed and then manage to reach Erketlis—"

"You will certainly not find him ungrateful, as no doubt you realize. You will do very, very much better for yourself than you would as governor of Kabin."

"I believe that, certainly. Well, if I don't turn coward or think of any other stumbling block before nightfall, I'm your man. But thank God there isn't long to wait."

29 *The Fire Festival*

As DUSK FELL ALONG THE TERRACES of the Leopard Hill, with a green, yellow-streaked sky in the west and flutterings of bats against the last light, the new moon, visible all afternoon, began to gleam more brightly, seeming, as it moved toward its early setting, so frail and slender as almost to be insubstantial, no more than a ripple of the surrounding air catching the light like water undulating over a submerged rock. Small and lonely it looked, despite the nearby stars; fragile and fine as a greenfinch in spring, assailable as the innocence of a child wandering alone in a field of summer daisies. All below lay in silence and starlit darkness, the city quieter than midnight, every fire extinguished, every voice silent, not a light that gleamed, not a girl that sang, not a flame that burned, not a beggar that whined for alms. This was the hour of the Quenching. The streets were deserted; the sandy squares, raked smooth at close of day, stood empty, ribbed and void as wind-frozen pools. Once the distant howl of a dog broke off short, as though quickly silenced. So still at last grew the moon-faint night that the sound of a boy's weeping, in a barracoon of the slave market, carried as far as the Peacock Gate, where a single guard stood in the shadows, his arms folded, his spear leaning against the wall at his back. Above this expectant quiet, still as the spring fields outside the city, the wan crescent of light moved slowly on, like one compelled to travel toward a dark destination, of which he knows only that it will end his youth and change his life beyond foreseeing.

High on the Serpent tower, Sheldra, cloaked against the night air, stood gazing westward, waiting for the lower horn of the declining moon to align itself with the pinnacle of the Bramba tower at the opposite corner. When at last it did so, the mile-wide silence was broken by her long, ululant cry of "Shardik! Lord Shardik's fire!" A moment after, a streaking, dusky tongue of flame leapt up the thirty feet of the pitch-coated pine trunk erected on the palace roof, appearing from the city below as a column of fire in the southern sky. From along the walls dividing the upper from the lower city, the priestess's wailing call was answered and repeated, as five similar but lesser flames rose, one after another, from the roofs of the equidistant guard turrets, like serpents from their baskets at the reedy note of the snake charmer. Then, from the lower city, there followed in appointed order the flames of the various gates and towers—the Blue Gate, the Gate of Lilies, the towers of the great clocks, the tower of Sel-Dolad, the tower of the Orphans and the tower of Leaves. Each flame soared into the night with the speed of a gymnast climbing a rope, and the poles burned in long, blazing waves, the fire rippling like water along their sides. So for a little they stood alone, indicating the length and breadth of the city where it lay upon the plain like a great raft moored under the steep of Crandor. And as they burned, their crackling alone breaking the silence that returned upon the ceasing of the cries from the towers, the streets began to fill with growing numbers of people emerging from their doors; some merely standing, like the sentry, in the dark, others groping slowly but purposefully toward the Caravan Market. Soon many were assembled there, all unspeaking, all standing patiently in a moonset, flame-flecked owl-light almost too dim for any to recognize his neighbor.

Then, far off against the Leopard Hill, appeared the flame of a single torch. Quickly it moved, bobbing, descending, racing down through the terraces toward the Barb, through the gardens and on toward the Peacock Gate, which stood ready open for the runner to enter the Street of the Armorers and so come down to the market and the reverent, waiting crowd. How many were gathered there? Hundreds, thousands. Very many men and some women also, each one the head of a household: justices and civic officers, foreign merchants, tally-keepers, builders and carpenters, the respectable widow side by side with Auntie from the jolly girls' house, hard-handed cobblers, harness-makers and weavers, the keepers of the itinerant laborers' hostels, the landlord of The Green Grove, the guardian of the provincial couriers' hospice and more, many more, stood shoulder to shoulder in silence, their only light the distant glinting of the tall flames which had summoned them from their homes, each carrying an unlit torch, to seek, as the gift of God, the blessing of the renewal of fire. The runner, a young officer of Ged-la-Dan's household, honored with this task in recognition of courageous service in Lapan, carried his torch, lit from the new fire on the Palace roof, to the plinth of the Great Scales and there at last halted, silent and smiling, waiting a few moments to collect himself and to be sure of his effect before holding out the flame to the nearest suppliant, an old man wrapped in a patched, green cloak and leaning on a staff.

"Blest be the fire!" called the officer in a voice that carried across the square.

"Blest be Lord Shardik!" replied the old man quaveringly, and as he spoke lit his torch from the other's.

Now a handsome middle-aged woman stepped forward, carrying in one hand her torch and in the other a yellow-painted wand, in token that she was deputizing for a husband absent at the war. There were many such in the crowd.

"Blest be the fire!" cried the young officer again, and "Blest be Lord Shardik!" she answered, looking him in the eye with a smile that said, "And blest be you too, my fine fellow." Holding her lit torch aloft, she turned and set out for home, while a rough, heavily built man dressed like a drover took her place before the plinth.

There was no jostling or haste but a measured and joyous solemnity as torch after torch was lit. None might speak until the gift of fire had been bestowed upon him. Not all waited to receive fire from the actual torch carried from the Palace. Many, eager, took it as it was offered by those who were moving away across the square, until on all sides resounded the happy shouts of "Blest be the fire!" and "Blest be Lord Shardik!" Gradually the square became full of more and more points of light, like sparks spreading across the back of a hearth or the surface of a smoldering log. Soon the tossing, dancing flames were flowing out in every direction along the streets, while loosened tongues chattered like birds at first light and the rekindled lamps began to shine in one window after another. Then, on the roofs of the houses up and down the city, smaller fires began to burn. Some were poles, in imitation of those already lit on the gates and towers, others braziers full of wood or clearer fires of scented gums and incense-sprinkled charcoal. Feasting began and music, drinking in the taverns, dancing in the squares. Everywhere, the gift of light and warmth by night manifested the power over cold and darkness bestowed by God on man and man alone.

Beside the Barb, in the upper city above the Peacock Gate, another, graver messenger had arrived with his torch—none other than General Zelda, his full armor dully reflecting the smoky light as he strode toward the ripples lapping on the shore. Here, too, suppliants were waiting, but fewer and less fervent, their emotions modified by that detachment and self-conscious restraint which characterizes the aristocratic, wealthy or powerful participating in popular customs. Zelda's invocatory "Blest be the fire" was spoken indeed with raised voice but in a formal, level tone, while the responding, "Blest be Lord Shardik," though uttered sincerely, lacked the hearty ring of flower girls or market porters in the lower city, breaking two hours' darkness and silence with the words appointed to commence one of the great frolics of the year.

Kelderek, robed in saffron and scarlet and attended by the priestesses of Shardik, stood waiting on the highest terrace of the Leopard Hill, surveying the city below: the torches spreading through the streets like water flowing from a sluice along dry irrigation channels; the multitudinous shapes of doors and windows emerging in light out of the darkness, as though called into existence by the new fires kindled within them; and nearer, the lines of flames lengthening, extending farther along the shore of the Barb. So sometimes may news actually be seen to spread through a crowd, wind across a dusty plain, or sunrise down the western slope of a valley. About him burned the salts and gums and oils prepared for the fire festival, mysterious and splendid in combustion—kingfisher blue, cinnabar, violet, lemon and frost-green beryl—each transparent, gauzy fire, in its bronze bowl, carried upon rods between the shoulders of two women. The gonglike bells of the Palace towers were ringing, their shuddering harmonies vibrating over the city, fading and returning like waves upon a shore. As he watched, the slip of the new moon sank at last below the western horizon and upon the lake appeared the gliding shape of a great dragon, a grinning monster all of fire, green-eyed and clawed, its jaws spouting a plume of white smoke that trailed behind it as it gathered way. Shouts of admiration and excitement broke out, young men's battle cries and the stylized calls of the chase. Then, as the dragon reached the center of the Barb, there sprang into being upon the farther shore another fiery shape, erect upon its hind legs, thirty feet tall, round-eared, long-muzzled, snarling, one clawed forepaw raised aloft. As the cries of "Shardik! Lord Shardik's fire!" rose higher and echoed from the walls about the garden, the figure of a naked man, bearing a torch in each hand, appeared in the bear's jaws. One moment he paused on that high, bright platform, then he leapt out above the water. Secured to his shoulders and unrolling behind him was a long strip of tarred canvas which, burning, made it appear as though the bear were salivating fire. The leaper, plunging into the water below, slipped out of his harness and swam to the shore. Another followed, and now it was the shape of a fiery arrow which fell from the bear's mouth to the water. Quicker and quicker came the leapers, so that the flaming shapes of swords, spears and axes poured from between the bear's teeth to hurtle down over the lake. At length, as the dragon, belching smoke, glided beneath the towering effigy of Shardik, a burning noose dropped to encircle the prow forming its throat. The lights of its hot eyes went out and amid shouts of triumph its smoky breath died away as it floated captive at the glowing, ember-shaggy feet.

Meanwhile, Kelderek and his train had already begun to descend the terraces in slow procession. The chanting of the priestesses rose about him with a sound that wrung his heart, for it was that same antiphony that he had first heard in the forests of western Ortelga. Then, the voices of Rantzay and the Tuginda had formed part of a wall of sound encircling a summit of the spirit, sublime above the mortal world of fear and ignorance. Yet of this memory his grave, lean face showed no outward sign. His clasped hands were untrembling and his body, beneath the heavy robes, moved firmly on toward the appointed destination. The plant-scents of the night, thin and evanescent in the early spring air, mingled with the resinous odors of the colored fires and the drift of torch smoke on the breeze; and bemused, perhaps, by these and by his fast since sunrise, by his memories and the sound of the Singing, he imagined first one and then another companion to be walking beside him toward the torch-lit garden and the dragon-reflecting lake: a dark girl wearing a broad golden collar, who laughed and plunged the point of an arrow into her white arm before turning to him a face wan with fear; a tall, gaunt woman, limping exhausted on a staff, her sweating hands clutching a box where bladders lay packed in moss; and an old, red-eyed hag, who tottered at his elbow in filthy rags, bearing in her arms a dead child and imploring his help in mumbled words beyond his understanding. So real did they seem that dread and foreboding came upon him, pacing on. "Shardik," he prayed, "*Senandril*, Lord Shardik. Accept my life. Redeem the world, and begin with me."

And now he is come to the garden, where the lords and ladies fall back before him and the barons raise their swords in salutation of the power entrusted by God to the priest-king. The priestesses' singing dies away, the copper bells are silent, the fiery bear and the dragon have done their strife and burn low with none to regard. The people about the shore cease their shouts and cheering, so that the distant sound of the lower city's riot rises up from below the walls. The priest-king walks forward alone, before the eyes of armed barons and of the envoys of his vassal provinces, toward the brink of a deep inshore pool —the Pool of Light. Here, unhelped by man or woman, he must divest himself of his heavy robes and crown and stand naked, in the sharp night air, to thrust his feet into sandals of lead placed ready for him on the verge. Below him, deep in the pool, there burns amidst the darkness and water a single light—a light enclosed in a hollow crystal sphere secured to a rock, fanned with air and emitting its heat and smoke through hidden vents. This is the fire of Fleitil, devised long ago for the worship of Cran, but now made a part of the fire festival of Shardik. Down the flight of underwater steps the king will go, his feet weighted to carry him to the floor of the pool, and thence release himself and rise through the water, bearing that miraculous globe of light. Already he has moved forward, feeling for each stone step wtih ponderous feet and slowly descending in a silence broken only by the water lapping about his knees, his loins, his neck.

But hark! What dreadful sound is that, breaking the reverent hush of Ortelgan warriors and Beklan lords, slicing like a sword across the crowded garden and the empty lake? Heads turn, voices break out. A moment's silence and it is repeated—the roar of a great animal in rage, in fear and pain, so loud, so fierce and savage that women clutch the arms of their men, as at the sound of thunder or of fighting, and young boys feign unconcern, ill-concealing their involuntary fear. The lady Sheldra, waiting close to the king at the water-steps, turns about and stands tense, raising one hand to shield her eyes from the torchlight as she tries to see across the garden to the dark outline of the King's House beyond. The roaring ceases and is followed by heavy, vibrating thuds, as though some soft but massive object were striking against the wall of that cavernous, echoing place.

Kelderek, who had already drawn breath to submerge and drop from the lowest step to the bed of the pool, gave an inarticulate cry and struggled to release himself from the weighted sandals. A moment more and he drew the pins, pulled himself out of the water and stood dripping on the paved verge. The murmurs about him grew louder, unfriendly and fearful. "What has happened?" "What is he about?" "To break off—unlucky!" "An unlucky act—no good will come of it!" "Sacrilege!" In the crowd nearby, a woman began to weep with quick, nervous whimperings of fear.

Kelderek, paying them no heed, bent down, as though to dress himself again in the stiff, heavy vestments lying at his feet. In his haste his hands fumbled with the fastenings, the robe fell sideways and, flinging it down, he began to push his way, naked as he was, through the group of priestesses about him. Sheldra put her hand on his arm.

"My lord—"

"Get out of the way!" answered Kelderek, roughly flinging her off.

"What's the matter, Kelderek?" said Zelda, coming forward and speaking low and quickly at his shoulder. "Don't be foolish, man! What are you about?"

"Shardik! Shardik!" shouted Kelderek. "Follow me, for God's sake!"

He ran, twigs and stones piercing his bare feet. Bleeding, his naked body shoved and forced its way between men in armor and shrieking, scandalized women, whose brooches and belt buckles scratched his flesh. A man tried to bar his path and he felled him with a blow of his fist, yelling again, "Shardik! Get out of the way!"

"Stop! Come back!" called Zelda, pursuing and trying to clutch him. "The bear's only frightened of the fire, Kelderek! It's the noise and smell of the smoke's upset it! Stop this blasphemy! Stop him!" he shouted to a group of officers a little way ahead.

They stared irresolutely and Kelderek broke through them, tripped and fell, got up and again dashed forward, his wet body smeared from head to foot with dirt, blood and the leafy fragments of the garden. Grotesque in appearance, as dirty and lost

278

to dignity as some wretched butt of the barrack room, stripped, pelted and chased by his loutish comrades for their mean sport, he ran on, heedless of everything but the noise from the hall now close in front of him. As he reached that same terrace on which he had joined Zelda the day before, he stopped and turned to those following him.

"The roof! The roof's on fire! Get up there and put it out!"

"He's out of his mind!" cried Zelda. "Kelderek, you fool, don't you realize there's a fire burning on every roof in Bekla tonight? For God's sake—"

"Not up there! Do you think I don't know? Where are the sentries? Get them up there—send men to search around the far side!"

Alone, he rushed through the south door, along the ambulatory and into the hall. The place was dim, lit by no more than five or six torches fixed along the smoke-streaked walls. By the cage bars in the center of the hall Zilthé was sprawled face down, her head lying in a puddle of blood that oozed over the stones. From the roof above came sounds of crackling and burning, and something heavy shifted and slipped with a rending noise. A sudden spurt of flame came and went and sparks floated down, dying as they fell.

Shardik, swaying from side to side like a fir tree when woodmen rock it at the base to loosen the roots, was standing erect at the farther end of the hall, beating with his huge paws on the closed gate and roaring with rage and fear as the fire burned more strongly above him. In his back was a jagged gash as long as a man's forearm and near him lay a bloody spear which, evidently torn from one of the panoplies on the wall, must have fallen out of the wound as he rose on his hind legs.

Before the bars, with his back to Kelderek, stood a man armed with a bow. This also he must have snatched from the wall, for from either end still dangled the broken leather thongs by which it had been fastened. A heavy-headed arrow lay on the string and the man, no doubt unaccustomed to the weapon, was fumbling as he drew it. Kelderek, naked and unarmed as he was, rushed forward. The man, turning, dodged quickly, drew his dagger and stabbed him in the left shoulder. The next moment Kelderek had flung himself upon him, biting, kicking and clawing, and borne him to the ground. He did not feel whatever wounds he received, nor the pain in his thumbs as he pressed them, almost to breaking, into the man's throat and beat the back of his head against the floor. He sank his teeth in him like a beast, released his hold an instant to batter him, then clutched him once more and tore him, as a savage guard-hound tears a robber whom he has caught in his master's house.

When Zelda and those with him entered the hall, bearing the dead body of a sentry and holding under guard Elleroth, Ban of Sarkid and envoy of Lapan, whom they had overpowered in the act of climbing down from the roof, they found the king, covered from head to foot in blood and dirt, bleeding from five or six stab wounds and weeping as he bent over the young priestess on the floor. The lacerated body beside him was that of Mollo, envoy of Kabin, who had been actually torn and battered to death at the king's bare hands.

30 *Elleroth Condemned*

WITH A FLOW OF RELIEF like that felt by a child when light is brought into the dark room where he is lying afraid, Kelderek realized that he had been dreaming. The child desists from frightening himself with the fancy that the oak chest might be a crouching animal, and accepts that the grotesque face peering down upon him is nothing but a pattern of lines in the rafters; and at once other, true proportions, not actually revealed by, but nevertheless consequent upon, the bringing of the light are plain. The distant sound outside the window, though unaltered from a few moments before, is now, clearly, not faint, evil laughter but the croaking of frogs, while by a subtle shift of emphasis, the smell of new-sawn wood, of penned cattle or of drying skins, which just now seemed so menacing, the very smell of fear, alters in its effect as it becomes linked with familiar people and bright, diurnal things. But with those things return almost at once the shadows which they cast. Will he be scolded because he cried out in his fear? Or has someone perhaps discovered that yesterday he did what he should not? He has only exchanged one kind of anxiety for another.

In Kelderek's wakening mind, the misty topography of thought seemed to turn as though upon a pivot; dream and reality took up their proper places and he recognized the true aspect and features of his situation. He had not, he realized, been summoned to the presence of Bel-ka-Trazet—that was a dream —and therefore, thank God, he need no longer try to devise how best to defend himself. The aching pain in his body was certainly real, but was due not to blows received from the High Baron's men, but to his fight with the intruder in the hall. He was not, after all, in danger of death, yet instead there now returned to him the recollection of all that he had forgotten in sleep—the wounding of Shardik, the burning hall, Zilthé lying on the stones and his own injuries. How long had he been asleep? Suddenly, as a wall crumbles at the point where it is most vulnerable, the drowsy, undiscriminating progress of his awakening was broken by the realization that he did not know what had become of Shardik. At once he cried "Shardik!," opened his eyes and tried to start up.

It was daylight and he was lying on his own bed. Through the southern window, with its view over the Barb, a pale sun was shining. It seemed an hour or two after dawn. His left hand was bound up—his shoulder too, he could feel, and the opposite thigh. Biting his lip with pain, he sat up and put his feet to the floor. As he did so, Sheldra came into the room.

"My lord—"

"Shardik! What has become of Lord Shardik?"

"My lord, General Zelda has come to speak with you. He is in haste. He says it is important."

She hurried out, while he shouted feebly after her, "Shardik! Shardik!" She returned with Zelda, who was cloaked and booted as though for a journey.

"Shardik!" he cried, and tried to stand, but stumbled back on the bed. "Is he alive? Will he live?"

"Like master, like man," replied Zelda with a smile. "Shardik is alive, but it's a deep wound and he needs rest and care."

"How long have I been asleep?"

"This is the second day since you were hurt."

"We gave you a drug, my lord," said Sheldra. "The knife blade broke off short in your thigh, but that we were able to take out."

"Zilthé? What of Zilthé?"

"She is alive, but her brain is damaged. She tries to speak, but can find no words. It will be long, or never, before she can serve Lord Shardik again."

Kelderek put his head in his hands, thinking with anguish of the quicksilver lass who had once mistaken him for the quarry and shot an arrow between his arm and body; she who, standing alone in the waning moonlight, had seen Lord Shardik strike down the treacherous messenger on the road to Gelt.

"Kelderek," said Zelda, interrupting his thoughts, "no doubt you need to rest; but nevertheless you must listen to me, for time is very short and I have to be gone. There are things to be done, but the ordering of them I must leave in your care. That should do well enough, for the whole city desires only to serve and obey you. They know that it was you alone who saved Lord Shardik's life from those villains."

Kelderek raised his head and looked at him in silence.

"Yesterday, at dawn," went on Zelda, "a messenger reached Bekla from the army in Lapan. His news was that Santil-kè-Erketlis, after sending a force to distract our attention with a pretended attack west of Ikat, had himself passed us on the east flank and was marching north through Tonilda."

"What does he intend?"

"That we don't know—he may not have any preconceived aim, apart from seeking support in the eastern provinces. But he will probably form an aim in the light of whatever support he gets. We've got to follow and try to contain him, that's certain. A general like Erketlis wouldn't begin a march unless he felt sure he could make something of it. Ged-la-Dan left yesterday morning. I've stayed to see to the raising of three more companies and some extra supplies—the city governor will tell you the details. I'm off now, with every man I've been able to impress: they're waiting for me in the Caravan Market, and a cheap lot they are, I'm afraid."

"Where are you making for?"

"Thettit-Tonilda. Our army's coming north after Erketlis, so somewhere between here and Thettit I'm bound to strike their line of march. The trouble is that Erketlis achieved so much surprise—he must be nearly two days ahead of them."

"I wish I could come with you."

"I wish it too. Would to God Lord Shardik could join us for a new battle! I can see it all—darkness falling and Erketlis struck down with one blow of his paw. Heal him, Kelderek; restore him, for all our sakes! I'll see you get news—every day, if possible."

"But one thing more I must learn at once. What happened two nights ago? It was Mollo of Kabin, wasn't it, who wounded Lord Shardik? But who fired the roof of the hall, and why?"

"I'll tell you," answered Zelda, "and fools we were not to foresee it. It was Elleroth, Ban of Sarkid—he who passed us when we were walking that day above the Barb. If you'd not acted as you did in leaping from the pool, Lord Shardik would have died at the hands of that precious pair. The roof would have fallen in on him and on Zilthé, and both the traitors would have escaped."

"But Elleroth—is he dead too?"

"No. He was taken alive as he came down from the roof. It will be your task to see him executed."

"To see him executed? I?"

"Who else? You are the king, and the priest of Shardik."

"I have little relish for it, even when I think what he tried to do. To kill in battle is one thing; an execution is another."

"Come, Kelderek Play-with-the-Children, we can't afford to have you turn squeamish. The man's murdered an Ortelgan sentry and attempted a sacrilegious crime, wicked beyond belief. Obviously he must be executed before you and in the presence of every baron and provincial delegate in Bekla. Indeed, you will have to require the attendance of all Ortelgans of any rank or standing whatever—there are so few left in the city and the Ortelgans ought to outnumber the provincial delegates by at least three to one."

Kelderek was silent, looking down and picking at the blanket. At length, ashamed of his weakness, he asked hesitantly, "Must —must he be tortured? Burned?"

283

Zelda turned toward the window overlooking the Barb and stood gazing out across the water. After a little he said, "This is not a question either of indulging mercy or of gratifying revenge, but simply of achieving an effect for political reasons. People have got to see the man die and to be convinced, by what is done, that we are right and he is wrong. Now if a man—a bandit, say—is to be executed to impress the poor and ignorant and deter them from lawbreaking, it is best if he dies a cruel death, for such people have no imagination and lead hard, rough lives themselves. A quick death seems little hardship to them. It is necessary that the man should be humiliated and deprived of his dignity before their mean minds can take in the lesson. But with men of the better sort, it's another matter. If we torture a man like Elleroth of Sarkid, his courage is likely to excite admiration and pity and many of the delegates, who are men of rank, may even end by feeling contempt for us. We would do better to aim at arousing respect for our mercy. Although it is only just that he should die, it is with regret that we kill such a man—that is what we must give out. It is your affair, Kelderek, but since you ask me, I would advise you to have him beheaded with a sword. It will be enough, with a man of Elleroth's standing, that we put him to death at all."

"Very well. He shall be executed in the hall, in the presence of Lord Shardik."

"I should have told you. The fire did much harm before we could quench it. Baltis says the roof is in a bad state and will take some time to repair."

"Is he the best judge? Has no one else been up to see it?"

"I cannot tell, Kelderek. You forget the news I told you of the war. All is at sixes and sevens, and you must see to this yourself. Lord Shardik is your mystery, and one which you have shown that you understand. Of the roof, I can tell you only what the man told me. Order the matter as you think best, so long as Elleroth is executed before all the delegates. And now, goodbye. Only keep the city as well as you have kept Lord Shardik, and all may yet be well. Pray for the defeat of Erketlis, and wait for news."

He was gone and Kelderek, full of pain and tired to exhaustion, could remain awake hardly long enough for his wounds to be dressed before lying down to sleep again.

The next day, however, already troubled by the delay in commencing his task and anxious to have it done and finished, he sent for the city governor and the garrison commander and set about the arrangements. He was determined that the execution should take place in the hall and in the presence of Shardik, since he felt it to be just and right that Elleroth should die upon the scene of his crime. Also, he thought, there, more than anywhere else, he himself would be seen as the agent of Shardik, invested with the implacable and divine authority proper to one putting to death an aristocrat and the hereditary lord of a province twice as large as Ortelga.

The roof of the hall, he was informed, though in a precarious state and unable to be repaired until some heavy lengths of timber could be brought in to replace the two central tie beams, was nevertheless safe enough for an assembly.

"The way we see it, my lord," said Baltis, half-turning for corroboration to the Beklan master builder standing at his elbow, "it's sound enough unless there was to be any real violence —rioting or fighting or anything the like of that. The roof's supported by the walls, d'ye see, but the tie beams—that's to say, the crossbeams—they've been that much burned that there's some might not stand up to a heavy shaking."

"Would shouting be dangerous?" asked Kelderek, "or a man struggling, perhaps?"

"Oh, no, my lord, it'd need a lot more than that to make it go —like the old woman's ox. Even if the beams wasn't to be repaired, they'd still stand up for months very like, although the rain'd be in through the holes, of course."

"Very well," replied Kelderek. "You have leave to go." Then, turning to the governor, he said, "The execution will take place tomorrow morning, in the hall of the King's House. You will see to it that not less than a hundred and fifty Ortelgan and Beklan lords and citizens are present—more if possible. No one is to carry arms, and the provincial delegates are to be separated and dispersed about the hall—no more than two delegates to be seated together. The rest I leave in your hands. The lady Sheldra, however, will be caring for Lord Shardik and you are to meet her early tomorrow and take account of her wishes. When all is ready to your satisfaction, she will come here to summon me."

285

31 *The Live Coal*

THE NIGHT TURNED COLD, near to frost, and soon after midnight a white fog began to fill all the lower city, creeping slowly higher to cover at last the still waters of the Barb and thicken about the Palace and the upper city until there was no seeing from one building to the next. It muffled the coughing of the sentries and the stamping of their feet for warmth—or was it, thought Kelderek, standing cloaked in the bitter draft at the window of his room, that they slapped themselves and stamped rather to break the close, lonely silence? The fog drifted into the room and thickened his breathing; his sleeves, his beard felt chill and damp to the touch. Once he heard swans' wings overhead, flying above the fog, the rhythmic, unhindered sound recalling to him the far-off Telthearna. It faded into the distance, poignant as the whistling of a drover's boy to the ears of a man in a prison cell. He thought of Elleroth, without doubt awake like himself, and wondered whether he too had heard the swans. Who were his guards? Had they allowed him to send any message to Sarkid, to settle his affairs, to appoint any friend to act for him? Ought he not himself to have inquired about these things—to have spoken with Elleroth? He went to the door and called "Sheldra!" There was no reply and he went into the corridor and called again.

"My lord!" answered the girl drowsily, and after a little came toward him carrying a light, her sleep-bleared face peering from the hood of her cloak.

"Listen!" he said. "I am going to see Elleroth. You are to—"

He saw her startled look as the sleep was jolted from her brain. She fell back a step, raising the lamp higher. In her face he saw the impossibility of what he had said, the head-shakings behind his back, the soldiers' speculations, the later questions of Zelda and Ged-la-Dan; the icy indifference of Elleroth himself to the ill-timed solicitude of the Ortelgan medicine man; and the growth and spread among the common people of some misconceived tale.

"No," he said. "It's no matter. I spoke what I did not intend—it was some remnant of a dream. I came to ask whether you have seen Lord Shardik since sunset."

"Not I, my lord, but two of the girls are with him. Shall I go down?"

"No," he said again. "No, go back to bed. It's nothing. Only the fog troubles me—I have been imagining some harm to Lord Shardik."

Still she paused, her heavy face expressing her bewilderment. He turned, left her and went back to his room. The flame of the lamp shed a cheerless nimbus on the fog hanging in the air. He lay prone upon the bed and rested his head on his bent forearm.

He thought of all the blood that had been shed—of the battle of the Foothills and the crying of the wounded as the victorious Ortelgans mustered in the falling darkness; of the smashing of the Tamarrik Gate and the cacophonous, smoking hours that followed; of the gallows on Mount Crandor and the skulls in the hall below. Elleroth, a nobleman of unquestioned courage and honor, bending all his endeavors to the task, had almost succeeded in burning to death the wounded Shardik. And soon, when he was laid across a bench like a pig and the blood came spurting from his neck, few of those about him would feel the horror and sorrow natural to the heart of any peasant's child.

He was unaccountably seized with misgiving, by a premonition so vague and undefined that he could make nothing of it. No, he thought, this could be no divination on his part. The plain truth was that, despite his horror of Elleroth's deed, he had little stomach for this cold-blooded business. "They should have killed him as he came down from the roof," he said aloud, shivered in the cold, and huddled himself under the rugs.

He drowsed fitfully, woke, drowsed and woke again. Thought dissolved into fantasy and, not dreaming yet not awake, he imagined himself stepping through his embrasured window as from the fissured opening of a cave and, emerging, saw again under starlight the Ledges descending between the trees of Quiso. He was about to bound away down their steep pitch but, pausing at a sound from behind him, turned and found himself face to face with the old, muttering hag of Gelt, who stooped and laid at his feet—

He cried out and started up. The fog still filled the room, but it was murky daylight and in the corridor he could hear the voices of the servants. His bound wounds throbbed and ached. He called for water and then, robing himself without help and laying his crown and staff ready on the bed, sat down to wait for Sheldra.

Soon there came from the terrace below sounds of footsteps and low voices. Those who were to attend the execution must be converging on the hall. He did not look out, but remained on the edge of the bed, staring before him, the dark robe covering him from his shoulders to the ground. Elleroth, he thought, must also be waiting; he did not know where: perhaps not far away—perhaps near enough to hear the footsteps and voices diminish and silence return—a waiting, expectant silence.

When he heard Sheldra's step in the corridor, he rose at once and went to the door before she could reach it. He realized that he wished to prevent the need for him to hear her voice, that voice which would sound no different had she come to tell him that Lord Shardik had raised the dead to life and established peace from Ikat to the Telthearna. As he stepped across the threshold she was waiting and looked at him impassively, her face expressing neither dread nor excitement. He nodded gravely and she, unspeaking, turned about to precede him. Beyond her, the other women were waiting, their stiff robes filling the narrow corridor from wall to wall. He raised his hand to silence their whispering and asked,

"Lord Shardik—what is his mood? Is he disturbed by the crowd?"

"He is restless, my lord, and looks fiercely about him," answered one of the girls.

"He is impatient to see his enemy brought before him," said another. She gave a quick laugh and at once fell silent, biting her lip as Kelderek turned his head and stared coldly at her.

At his word they began to file slowly along the corridor, preceded by the beat of the gong. Looking down as he reached the head of the stairway, he saw the fog trailing through the open doorway and the young soldier at the entrance shifting his feet and gazing up at them. One of the girls stumbled, recovering herself with a hand that slapped against the wall. An officer appeared, looked up at Sheldra, nodded and went out through the door. She turned her head and whispered, "He has gone to fetch the prisoner, my lord."

Now they were entering the hall. He would scarcely have recognized it, so much closer and smaller did it seem to have grown. This was no longer the echoing space of flame-shot dusk where he had kept watch so many nights in solitude and where he had leapt empty-handed upon the Kabin envoy at his evil task. Except along the line of a narrow path extending before him between two ropes, men stood pressed together from wall to wall. There was a confusion of heads, robes, cloaks, armor, and of faces turned toward him, swaying and bobbing as each sought to catch a glimpse of him over and around his neighbor. Above them the fog hung like the smoke of bonfires in the cold air. The charred, irregular gaps in the roof showed only as lighter patches of fog. Though the clothes of the spectators were of every hue—some gaudy and barbaric as nomads' or brigands' garb—yet in this dank gloom their brightness and variety seemed soaked away, like the colors of sodden leaves in autumn.

The floor had been covered with a mixture of sand and saw-dust, so that no sound came from his footsteps or from those of the women pacing before him. At the center of the hall an open space had been left in front of the bars and here, in an attempt to clear and warm the air, a brazier of charcoal had been set. The light smoke and fume drifted one way and another. Men coughed, and patches of the heaped fuel glowed as the draft blew them brighter. Close to the brazier stood a heavy bench, on which the three soldiers who were to carry out the execution had laid their gear—a long sword with a two-handed hilt, a sack of bran to soak up the blood and three cloaks, neatly folded, with which to cover the head and body as soon as the blow had been struck.

In the center of the space a bronze disc had been placed on the floor, and upon this Kelderek, with the women flanking him on either side, took up his position, facing the bench and the waiting soldiers. For an instant his teeth chattered. He clenched them, raised his head—and found himself looking into the eyes of Shardik.

Insubstantial, the bear appeared—monstrous, shadowy in the

smoky, foggy gloom, like some djinn emergent from the fire and brooding darkly above it in the half-light. He had come close to the bars and, rising on his hind legs, stood peering down, his forepaws resting on one of the iron ties. Seen through the heat and fume from the brazier his outline wavered, spectral and indistinct. Looking up at him, Kelderek was momentarily bemused, overcome by that dreamlike state, experienced sometimes in fever, in which the mind is deceived as to the size and distance of objects, so that the shape against the light of a fly on a windowsill is supposed that of a house on the skyline, or the falling of a distant torrent is mistaken for the rustle of wall hangings or curtains. Across a great distance Shardik, both bear and mountain summit, inclined his divine head to perceive his priest, minute upon the plain below. In those far-off, gigantic eyes Kelderek—and he alone, it seemed, for none else moved or spoke—could discern unease, danger, impending disaster grim and foreboding as the rumbling of a long-silent volcano. Pity, too, he saw, for himself, as though it were he and not Elleroth who was the victim condemned to kneel at the bench, and Shardik his grave judge and executioner.

"Accept my life, Lord Shardik," he said aloud, and as he uttered the familiar words, awoke from the trance. The heads of the women on either side turned toward him, the illusion dissolved, the distance diminished to a few yards and the bear, more than twice his own height, dropped on all fours and resumed its uneasy rambling up and down the length of the bars. He saw the oozing scab of the half-healed spear wound in its back and heard its feet stumbling through the thick, dry straw.

"He is not well," he thought and, oblivious of all else, would have stepped forward even then had not Sheldra laid a hand on his arm, motioning with her eyes toward the opening from the ambulatory on his right.

To the low, steady beat of a drum, two files of Ortelgan soldiers were entering the hall, their feet on the sand as soundless as his own had been. Between them walked Elleroth, Ban of Sarkid. He was very pale, his forehead sweating in the cold, his face drawn and streaked with sleeplessness, but his step was firm, and as he turned his eyes here and there he contrived to appear to be observing the scene in the hall with a detached and condescending air. Beyond him, Shardik had begun to prowl more violently, with a restless, dominating ferocity of which none in the hall could remain unaware; but Elleroth ignored him, affecting interest only in the packed mass of spectators to his left. Kelderek thought, "He has already considered how best to keep his dignity and determined upon this part to act." He remembered how once he himself, sure of immediate death, had lain waiting for the leopard to spring from the bank above and thought, "He is so much afraid that his sight and hearing are misted over. But he knew it would be so, and he has rehearsed these moments." He called to mind the plot of which Elleroth was guilty and tried to recover the anger and hatred which had filled him on the night of the fire festival, but could feel only a mounting sense of dread and apprehension, as though some precarious tower of wrong piled upon wrong were about to topple and fall. He closed his eyes, but at once felt himself swaying and opened them again as the drum ceased, the soldiers drew apart and Elleroth stepped forward from among them.

He was dressed plainly but finely, in the traditional style of a nobleman of Sarkid—much as he might have dressed, Kelderek supposed, to feast his tenants at home or to entertain friends at a dinner party. His *veltron*, pleated saffron and white, was of new cloth, embroidered with silk, and the slashed gores of his breeches were cross-stitched with an intricate, diapered pattern in silver filigree, a month's work for two women. The long pin at his shoulder was also silver, quite plain, such as might have belonged to any man of means. Kelderek wondered whether it might be a keepsake from some comrade of the Slave Wars— from Mollo himself, perhaps? He wore no jewels, no neck chain, bracelet or ring; but now, as he stepped out from among the soldiers, he drew from his sleeve a gold pendant and chain, slipped it over his head and adjusted it at his neck. As it was recognized, murmurs arose among the spectators. It represented a couchant stag, the personal emblem of Santil-kè-Erketlis and his entourage.

Elleroth came to the bench and paused, looking down at what was on it. Those nearest saw him brace himself against a quick tremor. Then, stooping, he felt the edge of the blade with one finger. As he straightened, his eyes met those of the executioner with a tense, forced smile and he spoke for the first time.

"No doubt you know how to use that thing or you wouldn't

be here. I shall give you little trouble and I hope you'll do as much for me."

The fellow nodded awkwardly, evidently at a loss to know whether he should reply. But as Elleroth handed him a small leather bag, murmuring, "That's among yourselves," he drew the strings, looked into it and, wide-eyed, began to stammer out his thanks in words so banal and out of place as to seem both shameful and macabre. Elleroth checked him with a gesture, stepped forward to face Kelderek and inclined his head with the coldest suggestion of a formal greeting.

Kelderek had already instructed the governor that a herald was to describe the crime committed by Elleroth and Mollo and conclude by announcing the sentence of death. There was no interruption as this was now done, the only sounds to be heard besides the herald's voice being the intermittent growling of the bear and its rough, spasmodic movements among the dry straw. "He is still feverish," thought Kelderek. "This disturbance and the crowd have unsettled him and will delay his recovery." Each time he looked up, it was to meet the cold, contemptuous gaze of the condemned man, one side of his face cast into shadow by the light from the brazier. Whether it was assumed or real, he could not out-stare that indifference and finally bent his head, pretending abstraction as the herald described the burning roof, the founding of Shardik and his own frenzied onslaught upon Mollo in the hall. Whisperings of foreboding seemed all about him, intermittent and impalpable as the bitter draft from the ambulatory and the thin streams of fog trailing like cobwebs down the walls.

The herald ceased at length and silence fell. Sheldra touched his hand and, recollecting himself, Kelderek began to utter to Elleroth, in imperfect Beklan, the words which he had prepared.

"Elleroth, formerly Ban of Sarkid, you have heard the recital of your crime and the sentence passed upon you. That sentence, which must now be carried out, is a merciful one, as becomes the power of Bekla and the divine majesty of Lord Shardik. But in further token of that mercy and of the might of Lord Shardik, who has no need to fear his enemies, I now grant you consent to speak if you so desire: after which, we wish you a courageous, dignified and painless death, calling upon all to witness that cruelty is no part of our justice."

Elleroth remained silent so long that at length Kelderek looked up, only to encounter once more his stare and realize that the condemned man must have been waiting for him to do this. Yet still he could feel no anger, even while he once more dropped his eyes and Elleroth began to speak in Beklan.

His first words came high and thin, with little gasping pauses, but he quickly checked himself, resuming in a strained but firmer tone, which gathered strength as he continued.

"Beklans, delegates of the provinces, and Ortelgans. To all of you assembled here today, in this northern cold and fog, to see me die, I am grateful for hearing me speak. Yet when a dead man speaks you must look to hear nothing but plain words."

At this moment Shardik came once more to the bars, rising on his hind legs directly behind Elleroth and looking intently out across the hall. The glow from the brazier threw an amber light up the length of his shaggy pelt, so that Elleroth appeared to be standing before some high, firelit doorway fashioned, larger than life, in the shape of a bear. Two or three of the soldiers looked over their shoulders, flinching, and were checked by a low word from their officer; but Elleroth neither turned his head nor paid them attention.

"I know that there are those here who would not hesitate to acknowledge their friendship with me if they did not know that to do so would avail me nothing; but I fear that some of you are secretly disappointed and perhaps—a few—even ashamed to see me, the Ban of Sarkid, led here to die as a criminal and conspirator. To you I say that what may seem a shameful death is not felt as such by me. Neither Mollo, who is dead, nor I, who am about to die, broke any oath given to our enemies. We told no lies and used no treachery. The man I killed was a soldier, armed and on duty. The worst that can be said of us is that a poor girl, watching in this hall, was struck down and badly injured, and for this, though I did not strike the blow, I am most sincerely sorry. But I must tell you, and tell you all plainly, that what Mollo and I undertook was an act of war against rebels and robbers—and against a superstitious, cruel and barbarous cult, in the name of which evil deeds have been committed."

"Silence!" cried Kelderek, above the murmurs and muttering from behind him. "Speak no more of this, Lord Elleroth, or I shall be forced to bring your speech to an end."

"It will end soon enough," replied Elleroth. "If you doubt it, bear-magician, ask the inhabitants of Gelt, or those who can remember that decent, honest fellow Gel-Ethlin and his men—ask them. Or you can seek nearer home and ask those who built gallows for children on the slopes of Crandor. They will tell you how soon your Ortelgans can stop the breath that a man—or a child—needs for speaking. Nevertheless, I *will* say no more of this, for I have said what I intended; my words have been heard and there is another matter of which I must speak before I end. This is a thing which concerns only my own home and family and that house of Sarkid of which I am about to cease to be the head. For that reason I will speak in my own tongue—though not for long. From those who will not understand me, I beg for patience. From those who understand, I beg their help after my death. For even though it may seem the least likely of possibilities, it may be that somewhere, somehow, the chance will be granted to one of you to help me when I am dead, and to mend as bitter a sorrow as ever darkened the heart of a father and brought grief to an old and honorable house. Many of you will have heard the lament called the "Tears of Sarkid." Listen, then, and judge whether they may not fall for me, as for the Lord Deparioth long ago."

As Elleroth began speaking in Yeldashay, Kelderek wondered how many of those in the hall understood his words. It had been an error to allow him to address them. Yet in Bekla this privilege had always been accorded to any nobleman condemned to die, and to have withheld it would have undone much of the effect of granting him a merciful death. However he had gone about the business, he reflected bitterly, nevertheless a man like Elleroth, with his self-possession and aristocratic assurance, would have been bound to make his mark and to contrive to show the Ortelgans as harsh and uncivilized.

Suddenly his attention was caught by an alteration in the tone of the voice. Looking up, he was astonished at the change that had come over the proud, haggard figure before him. Elleroth, with a look of the most earnest supplication, was leaning forward, speaking in a tone of passionate intensity and gazing from one to another about the hall. As Kelderek looked at him in amazement, he saw tears in his eyes. The Ban of Sarkid was weeping: yet clearly not for his own misfortune, for here and there, at his back, Kelderek could hear answering murmurs of sympathy and encouragement. He frowned, mustering his smattering of Yeldashay in an effort to understand what Elleroth was saying.

"—misery no different from that suffered by many common men," he made out, but lost the thread and could not distinguish the next words. Then "cruelty to the innocent and helpless—" "long searching to no avail—" After an interval he discerned "—the heir of a great house—" and then, spoken with a sob— "the vile, shameful Ortelgan slave trade."

To his right Kelderek saw Maltrit, the captain of the guard, lay his hand on the hilt of his sword, looking quickly around as the murmuring grew throughout the hall. He nodded to him and gestured quickly with his hand twice, palm upward. Maltrit picked up a spear, hammered the butt on the floor and shouted, "Silence! Silence!" Once more Kelderek forced himself to look Elleroth in the eye. "You must needs have done now, my lord," he said. "We have been generous to you. I ask you now to repay us with restraint and courage."

Elleroth paused, as though collecting himself after his passionate words, and Kelderek saw return to his gray face the look of one striving to master fear. Then, in a tone in which controlled hysteria mingled oddly with stinging contempt, he said in Beklan, "Restraint and courage? My dear riparian witch doctor, I fear I am short on both—almost as short as you. But at least I have one advantage—*I* haven't got to go any further. You see, it's going to be such a terribly long way for you. You can't realize how far. Do you remember how you came up from the Telthearna, all slippity-slop for a spree? You came to Gelt— they remember it well, I'm told—and then you went on. You went to the Foothills and laid about you in the twilight and the rain. And then your meaty boys smashed the Tamarrik Gate— do you remember that, or did you perhaps fail to notice what it looked like? And then, of course, you got mixed up in a war with people who quite unaccountably felt that they didn't like you. What a long, long way it's been! Thank goodness I shall be having a rest now. But *you* won't, my dear waterside wizard. No, no—the sky will grow dark, cold rain will fall and all trace of the right way will be blotted out. You will be all alone. And still you will have to go on. There will be ghosts in the dark and voices in the air, disgusting prophecies coming true, I wouldn't wonder, and absent faces present on every side, as the man said. And still you will have to go on. The last bridge will fall behind you and the last lights will go out, followed by the sun, the moon and the stars; and still you will have to go on. You will come to regions more desolate and wretched than you ever dreamed could exist, places of sorrow created entirely by that mean superstition which you yourself have put about for so long. But still you will have to go on."

Kelderek stared back at him, frozen by the intensity and conviction of his words. His own premonition had returned upon him, closer now, its outline more distinct—a sense of loneliness, danger and approaching calamity.

"The thought makes me feel quite cold," said Elleroth, controlling his trembling with an effort. "Perhaps I should warm myself for a short spell before the man with the chopper interrupts these joyous, carefree moments."

He turned quickly. Two paces took him to the side of the brazier. Maltrit stepped forward, uncertain of his intention yet ready to forestall any irregular or desperate act; but Elleroth merely smiled at him, shaking his head as easily and graciously as though declining the advances of Hydraste herself. Then, as Maltrit stood back, responding instinctively to his smooth and authoritative manner, Elleroth, with a selective air, deliberately plunged his left hand into the brazier and drew out a burning coal. Holding it up in his fingers, as though displaying for the admiration of friends some fine jewel or crystal artifact, he looked once more at Kelderek. The appalling pain had twisted his face into a sickening travesty of relaxed good humor and his words, when they came, were distorted—grotesque mouthings, an approximation to speech which was nevertheless clear enough to be understood. The sweat ran from his forehead and he shook with agony, yet still he held up the live coal in his hand and aped horribly the manner of one at ease among his comrades.

"You see—bear king—you holding live coal—" (Kelderek could smell burning flesh, could see his fingers blackening and supposed that he must be burned to the bone: yet still, transfixed by the white eyes writhing in his face, remained where he stood.) "How long you a'le go on? Burn you up, hobble pain, carrying burning fire."

"Stop him!" cried Kelderek to Maltrit. Elleroth bowed.

"No need— 'blige you all. Come now, little pain"—he staggered a moment, but recovered himself—"little pain—nothing some 'flicted by 'telgans, 'sure you. Let's make haste."

With assumed carelessness and without looking behind him, he tossed the coal high over his shoulder, waved his hand to the crowd in the hall, strode quickly to the bench and knelt down beside it. The coal, fanned brighter by its course through the air, flew steeply over the bars and fell into the straw close to where Shardik had paused a moment in his restless prowling. In seconds a little nest of fire had appeared, the small, clear flames between the blades of straw seeming, at first, as still as those trailing mosses that grow among the branches of trees in a swamp. Then they began to climb, fresh smoke joined that already in the foggy air, and a crackling sound was heard as the fire spread across the floor.

With an unnatural, high-pitched cry of fear, Shardik sprang backward, arching the huge ridge of his back like a cat facing an enemy. Then, in panic, he fled across the breadth of the hall. Blindly, he ran full tilt against one of the columns on the opposite side and as he recoiled, half-stunned, the wall shook as though from the blow of a ram.

The bear got up, rocking dizzily, looked about it and then once more ran headlong from the now fast-spreading fire. It struck the bars with its full weight and remained struggling as though among the strands of a net. As it rose once more on its hind legs, one of the ties running from the bars to the wall was pressed against its chest and in frenzy it beat at it again and again. The bolted end of the tie pulled out of the wall, dragging with it the two countersunk stones into which it was mortised.

At this moment Kelderek heard overhead a heavy, grinding movement and, looking up, saw a patch of light in the roof slowly narrowing before his eyes. Staring at it, he suddenly realized that the great beam above him was moving, tipping, slowly turning like a key in a lock. A moment more and one end, no longer supported by the wall, began to scrape and splinter its way down the stonework like a giant's finger.

As the beam fell, Kelderek flung himself across the floor,

away from the bars. It dropped obliquely across the line of the ironwork, smashing down a quarter of its length to a depth of three or four feet. Then it settled, one end suspended in that iron tangle and the other canted against the opposite wall, and the bars bent and drooped beneath it like blades of grass. Slowly, the whole mass of wreckage continued to subside downward. Behind it, the fire still spread through the straw and the air grew thicker with smoke.

Shouting and tumult filled the hall. Many were looking around for the nearest way out, others trying to keep order or to call their friends together. At the doors the soldiers stood uncertainly, waiting for orders from their officers, who could not make themselves heard above the din.

Only Shardik—Shardik and one other—moved with unhesitating certainty. Out of the burning straw, over the broken bars came the bear, clawing at the iron with a noise like the storming of a breach.

As when a dam gives way in some high valley of the hills the water falls in a thunderous mass through the gap and pours on in obedience not to any will of its own but simply to inanimate, natural law, overwhelming or sweeping aside all that hinders it, changed in an instant from a controlled source of gain and power to a destructive force, killing as it runs to waste and devastating as it escapes from the restraint of those who supposed that they had made it safely their own—so Shardik, in the savagery of his fear, made his way, smashing and clambering, over the broken bars.

As those below the dam, dwelling or working in the very path of the water, perceive with terror that a disaster which none envisaged is even now upon them, indeflexible and leaving no recourse but immediate headlong flight—so those in the hall realized that Shardik had broken loose and was among them.

And as those farther away from the dam, hearing, whatever they may be, the rumble of the collapsing wall, the roaring of water and the unexpected tumult, stand still, looking at one another wide-eyed, recognizing the sounds of disaster but as yet ignorant that what they have heard imports nothing less than the work of years ruined, the destruction of their prosperity and the discredit of their name—so those in the upper city, outside the hall, the peering sentinels on the wall, the gardeners and cattlemen coughing and shivering at their work along the shores of the Barb, the delegates' servants loitering at their masters' doors, the youths abandoning archery practice for the morning, the court ladies muffled against the cold, looking southward from the roof of the Barons' Palace for the sun to clear the shoulder of Crandor and disperse the fog—all heard the fall of the beam, the clang of the bars and the uproar that followed. Each in his own manner realized that some calamity must have befallen and, fearful but not yet suspecting the truth, began to move toward the House of the King, questioning those whom he met on the way.

As Shardik came clambering over the pile of wreckage, fragments of iron and wood were scattered and it shifted and sank beneath his weight. He mounted on the tie beam and for a moment crouched there looking down into the hall, dire as a cat in a loft to the mice who run squeaking. Then, as the beam began to tilt under him, he leapt clumsily down, landing on the stones between the brazier and the execution bench. All about him men were clamoring and pushing, striking and tearing at one another in their effort to escape. Yet at first he went no further but remained ramping from side to side—a movement frighteningly expressive of fury and violence about to break forth. Then he rose on his hind legs, looking, above the heads of the fugitives, for a way out.

It was at this terrible moment, before more than a few had succeeded in forcing their way through the doors and while Shardik still stood towering above the crowd like some atrid ogre, that Elleroth leapt to his feet. Snatching up the executioner's sword from the bench before him, he ran across the empty, deserted space around the bear, passing within a foot of it. A dozen men, pressed and jostling together, were blocking the northern entrance to the ambulatory and through these he cut his way, slashing and thrusting. Kelderek, still lying where he had flung himself to avoid the falling beam, saw his sword arm striking and the shriveled left hand hanging at his side. Then he was gone through the arch and the crowd closed behind him.

Kelderek rose to his knees and was instantly knocked to the

floor. His head struck the stone and he rolled over, dazed by the blow. When he looked up it was to see Shardik clawing and cuffing his way toward that same door by which he himself, with the women, had entered the hall half an hour before. Already three or four bodies lay in the bear's wake, while on either side men clamored hysterically and trampled one another, some actually beating with their hands against the columns or trying to climb the sheer brickwork that closed the arcades.

Shardik came to the doorway and peered around it, resembling grotesquely some hesitant wayfarer about to set out on a stormy night. At the same moment the figure of Elleroth appeared for an instant beyond him, running from left to right past the opening. Then Shardik's bulk closed the entire aperture, and as he passed through it there came from beyond a single, terrified scream.

When Kelderek reached the door, the first object that met his eyes was the body of the young soldier who had stared up at him as he descended the staircase that morning. It was lying face down, and from the almost-severed neck a stream of blood was pouring across the floor. Through this the bear had trodden, and its bloody tracks led out to the terrace and across the grass. Following them into the gardens, Kelderek came almost face to face with Shardik as he emerged from the thick mist along the shore. The bear, running in a lumbering canter around the western end of the Barb, passed him and disappeared up the pasture slope beyond.

BOOK IV

Urtah, and Kabin

32 *The Postern*

THEY TELL—AH! they tell many things of Shardik's passing from Bekla, and of the manner of his setting out upon his dark journey to that unforeseeable destination appointed by God. Many things! For how long, then, was he at large within the walls of Bekla, under Crandor's summit? For as long, perhaps, as a cloud may take, in the eyes of a watcher, to pass across the sky? A cloud passes across the sky and one sees a dragon, another a lion, another a towered citadel or blue promontory with trees upon it. Some tell what they saw and then others tell what they were told—many things. They say that the sun was darkened as Lord Shardik departed, that the walls of Bekla opened of their own accord to let him pass, that the trepsis, once white, has bloomed red since that day when the prints of his feet bloodied its flowers in passing. They say that he wept tears, that a warrior raised from the dead went before him with a drawn sword, that he was made invisible to all but the king. They tell many, shining things. And of what value is the grain of sand at the heart of a pearl?

Shardik, shouldering through the fog and scattering the terrified cattle as a seaward-running bramba disturbs lesser fish in crossing a pool, left the southern shore of the Barb and began to ascend the slope of the rough pasture beyond. Kelderek followed, hearing behind him the hubbub and clamor spreading across the city. To his right the Barons' Palace loomed indistinct and irregular, like an island of tall rocks at nightfall; and as he paused, uncertain of the direction taken by Shardik, a single bell began ringing, light and quick, from one of the towers. Coming upon the bear's tracks in a patch of soft ground, he was puzzled to see fresh blood beside them, though the prints themselves were no longer bloody. A few moments later, through a chance rift in the fog, he caught sight of Shardik again, almost a bowshot ahead on the slope, and glimpsed between his shoulders the red gash of the reopened wound.

This was a piece of ill fortune that would make his task more difficult, and he considered it as he went cautiously on. Shardik's recapture could be only a matter of time, for the Peacock Gate and the Red Gate of the citadel were the only ways out of the upper city. Elleroth, too, wherever he might be, was unlikely to be able to climb the walls, lacking the use of one hand. It would be best now if he were found and killed without recapture. His guilt had appeared as manifestly as could well be. Had he not himself spoken of a deliberate act of war? As a fugitive within the walls he could not remain at large for long. No doubt Maltrit, that competent and reliable officer, was already searching for him. Kelderek looked around to see whether there was anyone within hail. The first person he fell in with could be sent to Maltrit with a message that Elleroth, when found, was to be killed at once. But what if those who were hunting for him were to encounter Shardik in the fog? In his frightened and confused state, and enraged by the pain of the wound Mollo had inflicted, the bear would be deadly dangerous—far too dangerous for any immediate attempt at recapture. The only possible way would be to remove all cattle from the upper city, together with anything else which might provide food, and then, leaving the Rock Pit open and baited, wait for hunger to compel Shardik to return. Yet the Power of God could not be left to wander alone, unwatched and unattended, while all his people took refuge from him. The priest-king must be seen to have the matter in hand. Besides, Shardik's condition might well grow worse before he came back to the pit. In this unaccustomed cold, wounded and unfed, he might even die on the lonely eastern heights of Crandor, for which he appeared to be making. He would have to be watched—by night as well as by day—a task with which scarcely anyone now remaining in the city could be reliably entrusted. If it were to be performed at all, the king would have to set an example. And his very knowledge of Shardik, of his cunning and ferocity and the ebb and flow of his savage anger, brought home to him the danger involved.

Higher on the slope, where the pasture land merged into rough, rocky hillside, the air became somewhat clearer and Kelderek, looking back, could see the thicker mist white and level below him, blotting out the city save for the towers that rose through it here and there. Beneath it, with never a soul to be seen, the noises of alarm were spreading far and wide, and as he listened to them he realized that it was from this frightening tumult that the bear was climbing to escape.

Almost a thousand feet above Bekla a shoulder ran eastward from the summit of Crandor. The line of the city wall, exploiting the crags and steep places along the mountain's flank, surmounted the eastern declivity of this ridge before turning westward toward the Red Gate of the citadel. It was a wild, overgrown place, revealing little to the eye of one approaching from below. Kelderek, sweating in the cold air and flinging back the heavy robe that encumbered him, halted below the ridge, listening and watching the thicket where he had seen Shardik disappear among the trees. A little way to his left ran the wall, twenty feet high, the cloudy sky showing white here and there through the narrow loopholes that overlooked the slope outside. On his right, a stream pattered down a rocky gully out of the thicket. It was the last place into which any man in his senses would follow a wounded bear.

He could hear nothing beyond the natural sounds of the mountainside. A buzzard, sailing sideways above him, gave its harsh, mewing cry and disappeared. A breeze rustled through the trees and died away. The unceasing water close by became at last the sound of the silence—that, and the noise still audible from the city below. Where was Shardik? He could not be far off, bounded as he was by the curve of the wall. Either he was already on the other side of the ridge and moving west toward the Red Gate or else, which seemed more likely, he had taken refuge among the trees. If he were there now, he could hardly move away without being heard. There was nothing to be done but wait. Sooner or later one of the soldiers, searching, would come within earshot and could be sent back with a message.

Suddenly, from among the trees above came sounds of splintering wood and the grinding and knocking of falling stones. Kelderek started. As he listened, there followed the same cry that he had heard across the cypress gardens by night—a loud growling of pain, utterable by none but Shardik. At this, trembling with fear and moving as in a trance, he stumbled his way up the track which the bear had already broken through the bushes and creepers, and peered into the half-light among the trees.

The grove was empty. At its eastern end, where the trees and bushes grew closely up to the sheer wall, was a ragged, irregular opening, bright with daylight. Approaching cautiously, he saw with astonishment that it was a broken doorway. Several lining-stones on both sides had been forced out of the jambs and lay tumbled about. The heavy wooden door, which opened outward, must have been left open by one who had passed through, for there seemed to be no latch and the bolts were drawn. The upper hinge had been dragged from its setting in the jamb and the splintered door sagged, its lower corner embedded in the ground outside. The stone arch, though damaged, was still in place, but the downward-pointing central cusp was covered with blood, like a weapon withdrawn from a wound.

On the inner side of the doorway, just where a man might have stood to draw the bolts, Kelderek caught sight of something bright half-trodden into the ground. He stooped and picked it up. It was the golden stag emblem of Santil-kè-Erketlis, the pendant still threaded on the fine, snapped chain.

He stepped through the doorway. Below him, the mist was lifting from the great expanse of the Beklan plain—a shaggy, half-wild country from which rose here and there the smoke of villages—stretching southward Lapan, east to Tonilda, north-ward to Kabin and the mountains of Gelt. A mile away, at the foot of the slope, plainly visible through the clearing air, ran the caravan road from Bekla to Ikat. Shardik, his back and shoulders covered with blood from the wound gored yet again by the cusp of the door, was descending the mountainside some two hundred feet below.

As he followed once more, picking his way and steadying himself with his hands against the crags, Kelderek began to realize how unfit he was for any long or arduous undertaking. Mollo, before he died, had stabbed or gashed him in half a dozen places and these half-healed wounds, which had been bearable enough as long as he kept to his room, were now beginning to throb and to send sharp twinges of pain through his muscles. Once or twice he stumbled and almost lost his balance. Yet even when his uncertain feet sent dislodged stones rattling down the slope, Shardik, below him, never once looked back or paid him any attention, but having reached the eastern foot of Crandor continued in the same direction. For fear of robbers, the scrub on either side of the caravan road had been roughly cut back to the length of almost a bowshot. This open place the bear crossed without hesitation and so entered upon the wilderness of the plain itself.

Kelderek, approaching the road, stopped and looked back at the eastern face he had descended. It puzzled him that, although so many traveled this road, he had never heard tell of the postern on the east ridge. The wall, he now perceived, ran by no means straight in its course and in the view from below was masked here and there by crags. The postern must lie—and had no doubt been deliberately sited—in some oblique angle of the wall, for he could not see it even now, when he knew whereabouts to look. As he turned to go on, wondering for what devious purpose it had been made and cursing the ill turn of fortune of which it had been the means, he caught sight of a man approaching up the road from the south. He waited: the man drew nearer and Kelderek saw that he was armed and carrying the red staff of an army courier. Here at last was the opportunity to send his news back to the city.

He now recognized the man as an Ortelgan a good deal older than himself, a certain master fletcher formerly in the service of Ta-Kominion's family. That he should be on active service at his age was somewhat surprising, though in all probability it was at his own wish. In the old days on Ortelga the boys had altered his name, Kavass, to "Old Kiss-me-arse," on account of the marked deference and respect with which he always treated his superiors. An excellent craftsman and an irritatingly child-like, simple and honest man, he had appeared to take a positive delight in asserting that those above him (whatever their origins) must know better than he and that faith and loyalty were a man's first duties. Now, recognizing the king, disheveled and alone by the roadside, he at once raised his palm to his forehead and fell on one knee without the least show of surprise. He would no doubt have done so if he had come upon him festooned with trepsis and standing on his head.

Kelderek took his hand and raised him to his feet. "You're

old for a courier, Kavass," he said. "Wasn't there a younger man they could send?"

"Oh, I volunteered, my lord," replied Kavass. "These young fellows nowadays aren't so reliable as an older man, and when I set out there was no telling whether a courier would be able to get through to Bekla at all."

"Where have you come from, then?"

"From Lapan, my lord. Our lot were detached on the right of General Ged-la-Dan's army, but it seems he had to march in a hurry and didn't stop to tell us where. So the captain, he says to me, 'Well Kavass,' he says, 'since we've lost touch with General Ged-la-Dan, and seem to have an open flank on the left as far as I can tell, you'd better go and get us some orders from Bekla. Ask whether we're to stay here, or fall back, or what.' "

"Tell him from me to start marching toward Thettit-Tonilda. He should send another courier there at once to learn where General Ged-la-Dan is and get fresh orders. General Ged-la-Dan may have great need of him."

"To Thettit-Tonilda? Very good, my lord."

"Now listen, Kavass." As simply as he could, Kelderek explained that both Shardik and an escaped enemy of Bekla were at large on the plain, and that searchers must be summoned at once, both to look for the fugitive and to take over from himself the task of following the bear.

"Very good, my lord," said Kavass again. "Where are they to come?"

"I shall follow Lord Shardik as best I can until they find me. I don't think he'll go either fast or far. No doubt I shall be able to send another message from some village."

"Very good, my lord."

"One other thing, Kavass. I'm afraid I must borrow your sword and whatever money you have. I may very well need them. I shall have to exchange clothes with you, too, like an old tale, and put on that jerkin and those breeches of yours. These robes are no good for hunting."

"I'll take them back to the city, my lord. My goodness, they're going to wonder what I've been up to until I tell 'em! But don't you worry—you'll follow Lord Shardik all right. If only there were more that would simply trust him, my lord, as you and I do, and ask no questions, then the world would go right enough."

"Yes, of course. Well—tell them to make haste," said Kelderek, and at once set off into the plain. Already, he thought, he had delayed too long and might not easily recover sight of Shardik. Yet, thinking unconsciously in terms of the forest where he had learned his craft, he had forgotten that this was different country. Almost immediately he caught sight of the bear, a good half-mile to the northeast, moving as steadily as a traveler on a road. Except for the huts of a distant village, away to the right, the plain stretched empty as far as the eye could see.

Kelderek was in no doubt that he must continue to follow. In Shardik lay the whole power of Ortelga. If he were left to wander alone and unattended, it would be plain to the eyes of peasants—many no doubt still secretly hostile to their Ortelgan rulers—that something was wrong. News of his whereabouts might be falsified or concealed. Someone might wound him again or even, perhaps, succeed in killing him as he slept. It had been hard enough to trace him five years before, after the fall of Bekla and the retreat of Santil-kè-Erketlis. Despite his own pain and fatigue and the danger involved, it would in the long run be easier not to lose track of him now. Besides, Kavass was reliable and the searchers could hardly fail to find them both before nightfall. Weak though he was, he should be equal to that much.

33 *The Village*

ALL THAT DAY, while the sun moved round the sky at his back, Kelderek followed as Shardik plodded on. The bear's pace varied little. Sometimes he broke into a kind of heavy trot, but after a short distance would falter, throwing up his head repeatedly, as though trying to rid himself of irritant pain. Although the wound between his shoulders was no longer bleeding, it was clear from his uneasy, stumbling gait and his whole air of discomfort that it gave him no peace. Often he would rise on his hind legs and gaze about him over the plain; and Kelderek, afraid in that open place without cover, would either stand still or drop quickly to his knees and crouch down. But at least it was easy to keep him in sight from a distance; and for many hours, remaining a long bowshot or more away, Kelderek moved quietly on over the grass and scrub, holding himself ready to run if the bear should turn and make toward him. Shardik, however, seemed unaware of being followed. Once, coming to a pool, he stopped to drink and to roll in the water; and once he lay for a while in a grove of myrtle bushes, planted for a landmark around one of the lonely wells used time out of mind by the wandering herdsmen. But both these halts ended when he started suddenly up, as though impatient of further delay, and set off once more across the plain.

Two or three times they came within sight of cattle grazing. Far-off though they were, Kelderek could make out how the beasts turned and raised their heads all together, uneasy and suspicious of whatever unknown creature it might be that was coming. He hoped for the chance to call to one of the herd boys and send him with a message, but always Shardik passed very wide of the herds and Kelderek, considering whether to leave him, would decide to await a better opportunity.

Late in the afternoon he saw by the sun that Shardik was no longer moving northeast but north. They had wandered deep into the plain—how far he could not tell—perhaps ten miles east of the road that ran from Bekla to the Gelt foothills. The bear showed no sign of stopping or turning back. Kelderek, who had expected that he would wander until he found food and then sleep, had not foreseen this steady journeying, without pause either to eat or rest, by a creature recently wounded and confined for so long. He now realized that Shardik must be impelled by an overwhelming determination to escape from Bekla —to stop for nothing until he had left it far behind, and to avoid on his way all haunts of man. Instinct had turned him toward the mountains and these, if it were his intention to do so, he might well reach in two to three days. Once in that terrain he would be hard to recapture—last time it had cost lives and the burning of a tract of partly inhabited country. Yet if enough men could only be mustered in time he might be turned and then, dangerous though it would be, perhaps driven with noise and torches into a stockade or some other secure place. It would indeed be a desperate business but whatever the outcome, the first need was to check him in his course. A message must be sent and helpers must come.

As the sun began to sink, the greens and browns of the long, gentle slopes changed first to lavender and then to mauve and gray. A cool, damp smell came from the grass and scrub. The lizards disappeared and small, furry animals—coneys, mice and some kind of long-tailed, leaping rat—began to come from their holes. The hard shadows softened and a thin, light dusk rose, as though out of the grounds, in the lower parts of the shallow combes. Kelderek was now very tired and nagged by pain from the stab wound in his hip. Concentrating on remaining alert to Shardik, he became aware only gradually, like a man awakening, of distant human voices and the lowing of cattle. Looking about him, he saw in a hollow, a long way to his left, a village—huts, trees and the gray-shining dot of a pond. He could easily have overlooked it altogether, for the low, inconspicuous dwellings, irregular in outline and haphazard as trees or rocks, seemed, with their mixture of dun, gray and earth-brown colors, almost a natural part of the landscape. All that obtruded upon his weary sight and hearing were a little smoke, the movement of cattle and the far-off cries of the children who were driving them home.

At this moment Shardik, a quarter of a mile ahead, stopped and lay down in his tracks, as though too tired to go farther. Kelderek waited, watching the faint shadow of a blade of grass beside a pebble. The shadow reached and crossed the pebble, but still Shardik did not get up. At length Kelderek set off for the village, looking behind him continually to be sure of the way back.

Before long he came to a track, and this led him to the cattle pens on the village outskirts. Here all was in turmoil, the herd boys chattering excitedly, rebuking one another, raising sudden cries, whacking, poking and running here and there as though cattle had never before been driven into a stockade since the world began. The thin beasts rolled their eyes white, slavered, lowed, jostled and thrust their heads over each other's backs as they crowded into the pens. There was a flopping and smell of fresh dung, and a haze of dust floated glittering in the light of the sunset. No one noticed Kelderek, who stood still to watch for a few moments and to take comfort and encouragement from the age-old, homely scene.

Suddenly one of the boys, catching sight of him, screamed aloud, pointed, burst into tears and began jabbering in a voice distraught with fear. The others, following his gaze, stared wide-eyed, two or three backing away, knuckles pressed to open mouths. The cattle, left to themselves, continued to enter the pens of their own accord. Kelderek smiled and walked forward, holding out both hands.

"Don't be afraid," he said to the nearest child, "I'm a traveler, and I—"

The boy turned and ran from him; and thereupon the whole little crowd took to their heels, dashing away among the sheds until not one was to be seen. Kelderek, bewildered, walked on until he found himself fairly among the dusty houses. There was still nobody to be seen. He stopped and called out, "I'm a traveler from Bekla. I need to see the elder. Where is his house?" No one answered and, walking to the nearest door, he beat on the timbers with the flat of his hand. It was opened by a scowling man carrying a heavy club.

"I am an Ortelgan and a captain of Bekla," said Kelderek quickly. "Hurt me and this village shall burn to the ground."

Somewhere within, a woman began to weep. The man answered, "The quota's been taken. What do you want?"

"Where is the elder?"

The man pointed silently toward a larger house a little way off, nodded and shut the door.

The elder was gray, shrewd and dignified, a taker of his time, a user of convention and propriety to size up his man and gain opportunity to think. With impenetrable courtesy he greeted the stranger, gave orders to his women and, while they brought first water and a thin towel, and then food and drink (which Kelderek would not have refused if they had tasted twice as sour), talked carefully of the prospects for the summer grazing, the price of cattle, the wisdom and invincible strength of the

present rulers of Bekla and the prosperity which they had undoubtedly brought upon the land. As he did so, his eyes missed
nothing of the stranger's Ortelgan looks, his dress, his hunger
and the bound wounds on his leg and forearm. At last, when he
evidently felt that he had found out as much as he could and
that no further advantage was to be gained from avoiding the
point (whatever it might be), he paused, looked down at his
folded hands and waited in silence.

"Could you spare a couple of lads for a trip to Bekla?" asked
Kelderek. "I'll pay you well."

The elder continued silent for a little, weighing his words. At
last he replied, "I have the tally-stick, sir, given to me by the
provincial governor when we provided our quota last autumn.
I will show you."

"I don't understand. What do you mean?"

"This is not a large village. The quota is two girls and four
boys every three years. Of course, we give the governor a present of cattle, to show our gratitude to him for not fixing it
higher. We are not due again for two and a half years. Have
you a warrant?"

"Warrant? There's some mistake—"

The elder looked up quickly, smelling a rat and not slow to
be after it.

"May I ask if you are a licensed dealer? If so, surely it is your
business to know what arrangements are in force for this
village?"

"I'm not a dealer at all. I—"

"Forgive me, sir," said the elder crisply, his manner becoming
somewhat less deferential, "I cannot help finding that a trifle
hard to believe. You are young, yet you assume an air of authority. You are wearing the ill-fitting and therefore probably—
er—acquired clothes of a soldier. You have clearly walked far,
probably by some lonely way, for you were very hungry: you
have been recently wounded in several places—the wounds suggest to me a scuffle rather than battle—and if I am not wrong,
you are an Ortelgan. You asked me for two boys for what you
called a trip to Bekla and said you would pay me well. Perhaps,
when you say that, there are some elders who reply, "How
much?" For my part, I hope to retain my people's respect and

to die in my bed, but setting that aside, I don't care for your kind of business. We are all poor men here, but nevertheless these people are my people. The Ortelgans' law we are forced to obey, but as I told you, we are quit for two autumns to come. You cannot compel me to deal with you."

Kelderek sprang to his feet.

"I tell you I'm no slave trader! You've completely misunderstood me! If I'm an unlicensed slave trader, where's my gang?"

"That is what I would very much like to know—where and how many. But I warn you that my men are alert and we will resist you to the death."

Kelderek sat down again.

"Sir, you must believe me—I am no slave trader—I am a lord of Bekla. If we—"

The deep twilight outside was suddenly filled with clamor—men shouting, trampling hooves and the bellowing of terrified cattle. Women began to scream, doors banged and feet ran past on the track. The elder stood up as a man burst into the room.

"A beast, my lord! Like nothing ever seen—a gigantic beast that stands erect—three times the height of a man—smashed the bars of the big cattle pen like sticks—the cattle have gone mad—they've stampeded into the plain! Oh, my lord, the devil —the devil's upon us!"

Without a word and without hesitation, the elder walked past him and out through the door. Kelderek could hear him calling his men by name, his voice growing fainter as he made his way toward the cattle pens on the edge of the village.

34   The Streels of Urtah

FROM THE DARKNESS OF THE PLAIN beyond the village, Kelderek watched the turmoil as a man in a tree might look down upon a fight below. The example set by the elder had had little effect upon his peasants and no concerted action had been organized against Shardik. Some had barred their doors and plainly did not mean to stir out of them. Others had set out—or at least had shouted in loud voices that they were setting out—in an attempt to recover, by moonlight, as many of the cattle as they could find. A crowd of men with torches were jabbering around the well in the center of the village, but showed no sign of moving away from it. A few had accompanied the elder to the pens and were doing what they could to repair the bars and prevent the remaining cattle from breaking down the walls. Once or twice, momentarily, Kelderek had seen the enormous outline of Shardik moving against the flickering torchlight as he wandered on the village outskirts. Evidently he had little fear of these flames, so similar to those to which he must have become accustomed during his long captivity. There seemed no likelihood whatever of the villagers attacking him.

When at last the half-moon emerged from behind clouds, not so much enabling him to see for any distance as restoring his awareness of the great expanse of the misty plain, Kelderek realized that Shardik was gone. Drawing Kavass's short sword and limping forward to an empty, broken pen, he came first upon the body of the beast which the bear had been devouring and then upon a trembling, abandoned calf, trapped by the hoof in a split post. During the past hour this helpless little creature had been closer to Shardik than any living being, human or animal. Kelderek freed the hoof, carried the calf bodily as far as the next pen and set it down near a man who, with his back turned, was leaning over the rails. No one took any notice of him and he stood for a few moments with one arm around the calf, which licked his hand as he steadied it on its feet. Then it ran from him and he turned away.

A confused shouting broke out in the distance and he made toward it. Where there was fear and clamor, the likelihood was that Shardik would not be far away. Soon three or four men passed him, running back toward the village. One was whimpering in panic and none stopped or spoke to him. They were hardly gone before he made out, in the moonlight, the shaggy blackness of Shardik. Possibly he had been pursuing them—perhaps they had come upon him unexpectedly—but Kelderek, sensing his mood and temper with the familiarity of long years, knew by nothing he could have named that the bear had been disturbed rather than roused to rage by these hinds. Despite the danger, his pride revolted against joining their flight. Was he not lord of Bekla, the Eye of God, the priest-king of Shardik? As the bear loomed closer in the moon-dim solitude, he lay down prone, eyes closed, head buried in his arms, and waited.

Shardik came down upon him like a cart and oxen upon a dog asleep in the road. One paw touched him; he felt the claws and heard them rattle. The bear's breath was moist upon his neck and shoulders. Once more he felt the old elation and terror, a giddy transport as of one balanced above a huge drop on a mountain summit. This was the priest-king's mystery. Not Zelda, not Ged-la-Dan nor Elleroth, Ban of Sarkid, could have lain thus and put their lives in the power of the Lord Shardik. But now there was none to see and none to know. This was an act of devotion more truly between himself and Shardik than any which he had performed either on Ortelga or in the King's House at Bekla. "Accept my life, Lord Shardik," he prayed silently. "Accept my life, for it is yours." Then, suddenly, the thought occurred to him, "What if it were to come now, the great disclosure which I sought so long in Bekla, Lord Shardik's revelation of the truth?" Might it not well be now, when he and Shardik were alone as never since that day when he had lain helpless before the leopard?

But how was he to recognize the secret and what was he to expect? How would it be imparted—as an inspiration to his inward mind, or by some outward sign? And would he then die, or be spared to make it known to mankind? If the price were his life, he thought, then so be it.

The huge head was bent low, sniffing at his side, the breeze was shut off, the air was still as under the leeward wall of a house. "Let me die if it must be so," he prayed. "Let me die— the pain will be nothing—I shall step out into all knowledge, all truth."

Then Shardik was moving away. Desperately, he prayed once more. "A sign, Lord Shardik—O my lord, at the least vouchsafe some sign, some clue to the nature of your sacred truth!" The sound of the bear's low, growling breath became inaudible before its tread ceased to shake the ground beneath him. Then, as he still lay half-rapt in his trance of worship and supplication, there came to his ear the weeping of a child.

He got to his feet. A boy, perhaps seven or eight years old, was standing a short distance off, evidently lost and beside himself with fear. Perhaps he had been with the men until they ran from Shardik, leaving him alone to save himself as best he could. Kelderek, trembling and confused now with the passing of the ecstatic fit, stumbled across the ground toward him. Bending down, he put an arm around the boy's shoulder and pointed to the distant flames of the torches round the cattle pens. The boy could hardly speak for his tears, but at last Kelderek made out the words, "The devil-creature!"

"It's gone—gone," said Kelderek. "Go on, don't be frightened, you'll be safe enough! Run home as quick as you can! That's the way, over there!"

Then, like one picking up once more a heavy burden, he set out to follow Shardik by night across the plain.

Still northward the bear went—north and somewhat to the west, as Kelderek could see by the stars. They moved across the sky all night, but nothing else moved or changed in that loneliness. There was only the light, steady wind, the *thrip, thrip* of the dry stalks round his ankles, and here and there a faintly shining pool, at which he would kneel to drink. By first light, which crept into the sky as gradually and surely as illness steals upon the body, he was tired to exhaustion. When he crossed a slow-moving brook and then found his feet resting upon smooth, level stones, the meaning did not at first pierce his cloud of fatigue. He stopped and looked about him. The flat stones stretched away to right and left. He had just waded the conduit that ran from the Kabin reservoir to Bekla, and was now standing on the paved road to the Gelt foothills.

Early as it was, he looked into the distance in the faint hope of seeing some traveler—a merchant, perhaps, bound for the Caravan Market and the scales of Fleitil; an army contractor from a province; or an Ortelgan messenger returning from the country beyond Gelt—anyone who could carry word to Bekla. But in each direction there was no one to be seen; nor could he make out even a hut or the distant smoke of a wayfarers' encampment. For much of its length, as he knew, the road ran through frequented country; might he, perhaps, be near one of the camping stations for drovers and caravans—a few huts, a well and a tumbledown shelter for cattle? No, he could see nothing of the kind. It was bad luck to have reached the road at such an hour and to have struck so lonely a stretch. Bad luck—or was it the cunning of Shardik to have kept away from the road until he sensed that he could cross it unseen? Already he was some distance beyond it and climbing the opposite slope. Soon he would be across the ridge and out of sight. Yet still Kelderek lingered, hobbling and peering one way and the other in his disappointment and frustration. Long after he had realized that even if someone were now to appear in the distance, he could not hope both to speak with him and to recover the trail of the bear, he still remained upon the road, as though there were some part of his mind that knew well that never again would he set eyes upon this great artifact of the empire which he had conquered and ruled. At last, with a long, sighing groan, like one who, having looked for help in vain, cannot tell what will now befall, he set off for the point where Shardik had disappeared over the crest.

An hour later, having limped painfully to the top of yet another ridge, nearly two miles to the northwest, he stood looking down upon a startlingly different land. This was no lonely plain of sparse herbage, but a great, natural enclosure, tended and frequented. Far off, round hillocks marked its farther edge and between himself and these lay a rich, green vale several miles across. This, he realized, was nothing less than a single, enormous meadow or grazing ground upon which, distant one from another, three or four herds were already at pasture in the sunrise. He could make out two villages, while on the horizon traces of smoke suggested others that drew their substance from this verdurous place.

Not far below him, in a low-lying dip, the ground was broken —riven, indeed—in a most curious manner, so that he stared at it in wonder, as a man might stare at a sheer cliff or chain of waterfalls, or again, perhaps, at some rock to which chance and the weather of centuries have given an uncanny likeness—a crouching beast, say, or a skull. It was as though, ages gone, a giant had scored and scratched the surface of the plain with a pronged fork. Three clefts or ravines, roughly parallel and of almost equal length, lay side by side within the space of half a mile. So abrupt and narrow were these strange gorges that in each, the branches of the trees extending from either steep slope almost touched one another and closed the opening. Thus roofed over, the depths of the ravines could not be perceived. The sun, shining from behind the ridge on which he was standing, intensified the shadows which, he supposed, must lie perpetually within those almost subterranean groves. All about their edges the grass grew taller and no path seemed to approach them from any direction. As he stood gazing, the breeze stiffened for a moment, the cloud shadows on the plain rippled in long undulations and in the ravines the leaves of the topmost branches, barely rising above the surrounding grass, shook all together and were still.

At this, Kelderek felt a quick tremor of dread, a gaingiving of some menace which he could not define. It was as though something—some spirit inhabiting these places—had awakened, observed him and quickened at what it perceived. Yet there was nothing to be seen—except, indeed, the arched bulk of Shardik making his way toward the nearest of the three clefts. Slowly he trampled through the long grass and paused on the verge, turning his head from side to side and looking down. Then, as smoothly as an otter vanishing over the lip of a river bank, he disappeared into the concealment of the chasm.

He would sleep now, thought Kelderek; it was a day and a night since his escape, and even Shardik could not wander from Bekla to the mountains of Gelt without rest. No doubt if the plain had offered the least cover or refuge he would have stopped before. To Shardik, a creature of hills and forests, the plain must seem an evil place indeed, and his new liberty as comfortless as the captivity from which he had escaped. The ravines were clearly lonely, perhaps even avoided by the herdsmen, for no doubt they were dangerous to cattle and like enough their very strangeness made them objects of superstitious dread. The tangled twilight, smelling neither of beast nor man, would seem to Shardik a welcome seclusion. Indeed, he might well be reluctant to leave it, provided he were not forced to seek food.

The more Kelderek pondered, the more it seemed to him that the ravine offered an excellent chance of recapturing Shardik before he reached the mountains. His very spirits rose as he began to plan what was best to be done. This time he must at all costs convince the local people of his good faith. He would promise them substantial rewards—whatever they asked, in effect: freedom from market tolls, from the slave quotas, from military service—always provided that they could keep Shardik in the ravine until he was recaptured. It might not prove unduly difficult. A few goats, a few cows—water might already be there. A messenger could reach Bekla before sunset and helpers should be able to arrive before evening of the following day. Sheldra must be told to bring with her the necessary drugs.

If only he himself were not so much exhausted! He, too, would have to sleep if he were not to collapse. Should he simply lie down here and trust that Shardik would still be in the ravine when he woke? But the message to Bekla must be sent before he slept. He would have to make his way to one of the villages; but first he must find some herdsman and persuade him to keep watch on the ravine until he returned.

Suddenly he caught the sound of voices a little way off and turned quickly. Two men, who had evidently come up the slope before he had heard them, were walking slowly away from him along the ridge. It seemed strange that they should apparently not have seen him or, if they had, that they should not have spoken to him. He called out and hastened toward them. One was a youth of about seventeen, the other a tall, elderly man of solemn and authoritative appearance, wrapped in a blue cloak and carrying a staff as tall as himself. He certainly did not look like a peasant and Kelderek, as he stopped before him, felt that his luck had turned at last, to have met someone able both to understand what he needed and to see that he got it.

"Sir," said Kelderek, "I beg you not to judge me by appearances. The truth is, I am worn out by wandering for a day and a night on the plain and I am in great need of your help. Will you sit down with me—for I don't think I can stand any longer —and let me tell you how I come to be here?"

The old man laid his hand on Kelderek's shoulder.

"First tell me," he said gravely, pointing with his staff to the ravines below, "if you know it, the name of those places below us."

"I don't know. I was never here before in my life. Why do you ask me?"

"Let us sit down. I am sorry for you, but now that you are here you need wander no more."

Kelderek, so much dazed with fatigue that he could no longer weigh his words, began by saying that he was the king of Bekla. The old man showed neither surprise nor disbelief, only nodding his head and never averting his eyes, which expressed a kind of severe, detached pity, like that of an executioner, or a priest at the sacrificial altar. So disturbing was this look that after a little Kelderek turned his own eyes away and spoke gazing out over the green vale and the strange ravines. He said nothing of Elleroth and Mollo, or of the northward march of Santil-kè-Erketlis, but told only of the collapse of the roof of the hall, of the escape of Shardik and of how he himself had followed him, losing his companions in the mist and sending back a chance-found messenger with orders to his soldiers to follow and find him. He told of his journey over the plain and, pointing down the hill, of how Shardik—whose recapture was all-important—had taken cover in the cleft below, where no doubt he was now sleeping.

"And be sure of this, sir," he ended, meeting the unwavering eyes once more and forcing himself to return their gaze. "Any harm done to Lord Shardik or myself would be most terribly revenged, once discovered—as discovered it would certainly be. But the help of your people—for I take you to be a man of some standing here—in restoring Lord Shardik to Bekla—that will be acknowledged with the greatest generosity. When that task is done, you may name any reasonable reward and we will grant it."

The old man remained silent. To Kelderek, puzzled, it seemed that although he had heard him with attention, he was nevertheless unconcerned either with the dread of revenge or the hope of reward. A quick glance at the youth showed only that he was waiting to do whatever his master might require.

The old man rose and helped Kelderek to his feet.

"And now you need sleep," he said, speaking kindly but firmly, as a parent might speak to a child after hearing his little tale of the day's adventures. "I will go with you—"

Impatience came upon Kelderek, together with perplexity that such slight importance should apparently have been attached to his words.

"I need food," he said, "and a messenger must be sent to

Bekla. The road is not far away—a man can reach Bekla by nightfall, though I assure you that long before that he will be bound to meet with some of my soldiers on the road!"

With no further word the old man motioned to the youth, who stood up, opened his scrip and put it into Kelderek's hands. It contained black bread, goat's cheese and half a dozen dried tendrionas—no doubt the end of the winter's store. Kelderek, determined to retain his dignity, nodded his thanks and laid it on the ground beside him.

"The message—" he began again. Still the old man said nothing and from behind his shoulder the youth replied, "I will carry your message, sir. I will go at once."

While Kelderek was making him repeat two or three times both the message and his instructions, the old man stood leaning on his staff and looking at the ground. His air was one less of abstraction than of a detached, self-contained patience, like that of some lord or baron who, during a journey, waits while his servant goes to ask the way or question an innkeeper. When Kelderek paid the youth, emphasizing how much more he would receive, first when he delivered the message and secondly when he had brought the soldiers back, he did not look at the money, expressed his thanks only with a bow and then at once set off in the direction of the road. Kelderek, suspicious, sat watching until he had gone a long way. At last he turned back to the old man, who had not moved.

"Sir," he said, "thank you for your help. I assure you I shall not forget it. As you say, I need sleep, but I must not go far from Lord Shardik, for if by chance he should wander again, it will be my sacred duty to follow him. Have you a man who can watch beside me and rouse me if need should be?"

"We will go down to that eastern cleft," replied the old man. "There you can find a shady place and I will send someone to watch while you sleep."

Pressing one hand over his aching eyes, Kelderek made a last attempt to break through the other's grave reserve. "My soldiers —great rewards—your people will bless you—I trust you, sir—" he lost the thread of this thought and faltered in Ortelgan, "lucky I came here—"

"God sent you. It is for us to do His will," replied the old man. This, Kelderek supposed, must be some idiomatic reply to the thanks of a guest or traveler. He picked up the scrip and took his companion's offered arm. In silence they went down the slope, among the small domes of the anthills, the grassy tussocks and coneys' holes, until at length they came to the tall grass surrounding the ravines. Here, without a word, the old man stopped, bowed and was already striding away before Kelderek had grasped that he was going.

"We shall meet again?" he called, but the other gave no sign that he had heard. Kelderek shrugged his shoulders, picked up the scrip and sat down to eat.

The bread was hard and the juice long gone from the fruit. When he had eaten all there was, he felt thirsty. There was no water—unless, indeed, there might be a pool or spring in one of the ravines; but he was too tired to go and search all three. He decided to look into the nearest—it seemed unlikely that Shardik would be alert or attack him—and if he could neither see nor hear water he would simply do without until he had slept.

The tangled grass and weeds grew almost to his waist. In summer, he thought, the place must become almost impassable, a veritable thicket. He had gone only a few yards when he stumbled over some hard object, stooped and picked it up. It was a sword, rusted almost to pieces, the hilt inlaid with a pattern of flowers and leaves in long-blackened silver—the sword of a nobleman. He swung idly at the grass, wondering how it came to be there, and as he did so the blade tore across like an old crust and flew into the nettles. He tossed the hilt after it and turned away.

Now that he saw it at close quarters, the lip of the ravine looked even more sharp and precipitous than from a distance. There was indeed something sinister about this place, unhusbanded and yieldless in the midst of the abundant land all about. There was something strange, too, about the sound of the breeze in the leaves—an intermittent, deep moaning, like that of a winter wind in a huge chimney, but faint, as though far off. And now, to his sleep-starved fancy, it seemed that the sides of the cleft lay apart like an open wound, like the edges of a deep gash inflicted by a knife. He reached the edge and looked over.

The tops of the lower trees were spread beneath him. There

was a hum and dart of insects and a glitter of leaves. Two great butterflies, newly awakened from winter, were fanning their blood-red wings a yard below his eyes. Slowly his gaze traveled across the uneven expanse of the branches and back to the steep slope at his feet. The wind blew, the boughs moved and suddenly—like a man who realizes that the smiling stranger with whom he is conversing is in fact a madman who means to attack and murder him—Kelderek started back, clutching at the bushes in fear.

Below the trees there was nothing but darkness—the darkness of a cavern, a darkness of sluggish air and faint, hollow sounds. Beyond the lowest tree trunks the ground, bare and stony, receded downward into twilight and thence into blackness. The sounds that he could hear were echoes—like those in a well, but magnified in rising from some greater, unimaginable depth. The cold air upon his face carried a faint, dreadful odor —not of decay, but rather of a place which had never known either life or death, a bottomless gulf, unlit and unvisited since time began. In a fascination of horror, lying upon his stomach, he groped behind him for a stone and tossed it down among the boughs. As he did so, some dim memory came rising toward the surface of his mind—night, fear and the bringer of an unknown fate moving in the dark; but his present terror was too sharp, and the memory left him like a dream. The stone tore its way down through the leaves, knocked against a branch and was gone. There was no other sound. Soft earth—dead leaves? He threw another, pitching it well out into the center of the concave leaf-screen. There was no sound to tell when it struck the ground.

Shardik—where was he? Kelderek, the palms of his hands sweating, the soles of his feet tingling with dread of the pit over which he lay, peered into the gloom for the least sign of any ledge or shelf. There was none.

Suddenly, half in prayer, half in desperation, he cried aloud, "Shardik! Lord Shardik!" And then it seemed as though every malignant ghost and night-walking phantom pent in that blackness were released to come rushing up at him. Their abominable cries were no longer echoes, they owed nothing to his voice. They were the voices of fever, of madness, of hell. At once deep and unbearably shrill, far-off and squealing into the nerves of his ear, pecking at his eyes and clustering in his lungs like a filthy dust to choke him, they spoke to him with vile glee of a damned eternity where the mere spectacle of themselves in the gloom would be torment unbearable. Sobbing, his forearms wrapped about his head, he crawled backward, cowered down and covered his ears. Little by little the sounds died away, his normal perceptions returned and as he grew calmer he fell into a deep sleep.

For long hours he slept, feeling neither the spring sun nor the flies settling upon his limbs. The amorphous forces active in sleep, profound and inexpressible, moving far below that higher, twilight level where their fragments, drifting upward, attract to themselves earthly images and become released in the bubbles called dreams, caused in him not the least bodily movement as, without substance, form or mass they pursued their courses within the universe of the solitary skull. When at last he woke, it was to become aware, first, of daylight—the light of late afternoon—and then of a confused blaring of human cries, which faintly resembled the terrible voices of the morning. Yet, whether because he was no longer lying over the chasm or because it was not he himself who had cried out, these voices lacked the terror of those others. These, he knew, were the shouts of living men, together with their natural echoes. He raised himself cautiously and looked about him. To his left, out of the southerly end of the ravine, where Shardik had disappeared that morning, three or four men were clambering and running. Little, shaggy men they were, carrying spears—one cast his spear away as he ran—and plainly they were in terror. As he watched, another tripped, fell and rose again to his knees. Then the bushes along the lip were torn apart and Shardik appeared.

As when villagers have taken away the calf from a strong cow she bellows with rage, breaks the rails of the stockade and tramples her way through the village, afraid of none and filled only with distress and anger at the wrong she has suffered; the villagers fly before her and in her fury she smashes through the mud wall of a hut, so that her head and shoulders appear suddenly, to those within, as a grotesque, frightening source of destruction and fear—so Shardik burst through the tall weeds and bushes on the edge of the ravine and stood a moment, snarling, before he fell upon the kneeling man and killed him even as he cried out. Then, at once, he turned and began to make his way along the verge, coming on toward the place where Kelderek was lying. Kelderek lay prostrate in the long grass, holding his breath, and the bear passed not ten feet away. He heard its breathing—a liquid, choking sound like that made by a wounded man gasping for air. As soon as he dared, he looked up. Shardik was plodding away. In his neck was a fresh, deep wound, a jagged hole oozing blood.

Kelderek ran back along the edge of the ravine to where the men were gathered about the body of their comrade. As he approached, they picked up their spears and faced him, speaking quickly to each other in a thick argot of Beklan.

"What have you done?" cried Kelderek. "By God's breath, I'll have you burned alive for this!" Sword in hand, he threatened the nearest man, who backed away, leveling his spear.

"Stand back, sir!" cried the man. "Else tha'll force us—"

"Ah, kill him now, then!" said another.

"Nay," put in the third quickly. "He never went into the Streel. And after what's come about—"

"Where's your damned headman, priest, whatever he calls himself?" cried Kelderek. "That old man in the blue cloak? He set you on to this. It was him I trusted, the treacherous liar! I tell you, every village on this cursed plain shall burn— Where is he?"

He broke off in surprise as the first man suddenly dropped his spear, went to the edge of the ravine and stood looking back at him, pointing downward.

"Stand away, then," said Kelderek. "No—right away—over there. I don't trust you murderous dirt-eaters."

Once more he knelt on the edge of the pit. But here the first yards of the slope below him inclined gently. Not far down, half-concealed among the trees, was a level, grassy ledge with a little pool. Shardik, lying there, had flattened and crushed the grass. Half in the pool, face down, lay a man's body, wrapped about with a blue cloak. The back of the skull was smashed open to the brains and nearby lay the bloody head of a spear. The shaft was nowhere to be seen. It might, perhaps, have fallen into the abyss.

Hearing a movement behind him, Kelderek leapt about. But the man who had returned was still unarmed.

"Now ye must go, sir," he whispered, staring at Kelderek and trembling as at the supernatural. "I never seen the like of this before, but I know what's appointed if ever they comes alive from the Streel. Now that ye've seen, ye'll know that the creature's passed beyond us and our power. It's the will of God. Only, in His name, sir, spare us and go!"

Upon this all three fell to their knees, clasping their hands and looking at him with such patent fear and supplication that he could not tell what to make of it.

"There's none will touch ye now, sir," said the first man at last, "neither we nor any others. If ye wish, I'll go with you, any way ye please, as far as the borders of Urtah. Only go!"

"Very well," replied Kelderek, "you *shall* come with me, and if any more of you dung-bred bastards try to betray me, you'll be the first to die. No—leave your spear and come."

But after some three miles he turned loose his wretched, abject hostage, who seemed to fear him as he would a risen ghost, and once more went on alone, following warily the distant form of Shardik wandering northward across the vale.

35 Shardik's Prisoner

LITTLE BY LITTLE THE KNOWLEDGE GREW upon Kelderek that he was a vagabond in strange country, without friends, far from help, straitened by need and moving in danger. It was not until later still that he realized also that he had become the prisoner of Shardik.

It was plain that the bear had been further weakened by its latest wound. Its pace was slower, and although it continued toward the hills—now clearly visible on the northern horizon—with the same resolution, it stopped to rest more often and from time to time showed its distress by sudden wincings and unnatural, sharp movements. Kelderek, who now feared less the sudden onset of its swift, inescapable charge, followed it more closely, sometimes actually calling, "Courage, Lord Shardik!" or "Peace, Lord Shardik, your power is of God!" Once or twice it seemed to him that Shardik recognized his voice and even took comfort from it.

The night came on sharp and although Shardik rested for several hours, lying in full view on the open ground, Kelderek for his part could not remain still, but paced about, watching from a distance until, when the night was nearly over, the bear suddenly got up, coughing pitifully, and set off once more, its labored breathing clearly audible across the silence.

Kelderek's hunger grew desperate and later that morning, seeing in the distance two shepherds setting a fold of hurdles, he ran half a mile to them, intending to beg anything—a crust, a bone—while still keeping Shardik in sight. To his surprise they proved friendly, simple fellows, plainly pitying his want and fatigue and ready enough to help him when he told them that, although bound by a religious vow to follow the great creature which they could see in the distance, he had desperate need to send a message to Bekla. Encouraged by their goodwill, he went on to tell them of his escape the day before. As he finished, he looked up to see them staring at one another in fear and consternation. "The Streels! God have mercy!" muttered one. The other put half a loaf and a little cheese on the ground and backed away, saying, "There's food!" and then, like the man with the spear, "Do us no harm, sir—only go!" Yet here, indeed, they were more prompt than Kelderek, for thereupon both of them took to their heels, leaving their trimming knives and mallets lying where they were among the hurdles.

That night Shardik made for a village and through this Kelderek passed unchallenged and seen of none, as though he had been some ghost or cursed spirit of legend, condemned to wander invisible to earthly eyes. On the outskirts Shardik killed two goats, but the poor beasts made little noise and no alarm was raised. When he had eaten and limped away Kelderek ate too, crouching in the dark to tear at the warm, raw flesh with fingers and teeth. Later he slept, too tired to wonder whether Shardik would be gone when he woke.

The singing of birds was in his ears before he opened his eyes, and at first this seemed natural and expected, the familiar sound of daybreak, until he recalled, with an instant sinking of the heart, that he was no more a lad in Ortelga, but a wretched man alone and lying on the Beklan plain. Yet on the plain, as well as he knew, there were scarcely any trees and therefore no birds, save buzzards and larks. At this moment he heard men talking nearby and, without moving, half-opened his eyes.

He was lying near the track down which he had followed Shardik in the night. Beside him the flies were already crawling on the goat leg which he had wrenched off and carried away with him. The country was no longer plain-land, but an arboreous wilderness interspersed with small fields and fruit orchards. At a little distance, the wooden rails of a bridge showed where the track crossed a river, and beyond lay a thick, tangled patch of woodland.

Four or five men were standing about twenty paces off, talking together in low voices and scowling in his direction. One was carrying a club and the others rough, hoe-like mattocks, the farming peasant's only tool. Their angry looks were mixed with a kind of uncertainty, and as it came to Kelderek that these were no doubt the owner of the goats and his neighbors, he realized also that he must indeed have become a figure of fear—armed, gaunt, ragged and filthy, his face and hands smeared with dried blood and a haunch of raw flesh lying beside him.

He leapt up suddenly and at this the men started, backing quickly away. Yet peasants though they were, he had still to reckon with them. After a little hesitation they advanced upon him, halting only when he drew Kavass's sword, set his back against a tree and threatened them in Ortelgan, caring nothing whether they understood him, but taking heart from the sound of his own voice.

"You just put that sword down, now, and come with us," said one of the men gruffly.

"Ortelgan—Bekla!" cried Kelderek, pointing to himself.

"It's a thief you are," said another, older man. "And as for Bekla, it's a long way off and they'll not help you, for they've trouble enough of their own, by all accounts. You're in the wrong, now, whoever you are. You just come with us."

Kelderek remained silent, waiting for them to rush him, but still they hesitated, and after a little he began to retreat watchfully down the track. They followed, shouting threats in their patois, which he could barely understand. He shouted angrily back and, feeling with his left hand the rails of the bridge close behind him, was about to turn and run when suddenly one of them pointed past him with a triumphant laugh. Looking quickly round, he saw two men approaching the bridge from the other side. Evidently there had been a wide hunt for the goat thief.

The bridge was not high and Kelderek was about to vault the parapet—though this could have done little more than prolong the hunt—when all the men, both those in front of him and those close behind, suddenly cried out and ran, pelting away in all directions. Unassailable and conclusive as nightfall on a battlefield, Shardik had come from the wood and was standing near the track, peering into the sunlight and miserably fumbling at his wounded neck with one huge paw. Slowly and as though in pain, he made his way to the edge of the stream and drank, crouching not more than a few paces from the far end of the bridge. Then, dull-eyed, with dry muzzle and staring coat, he limped away into the cover of the thicket.

Still Kelderek stood on the bridge, oblivious of whether or not the peasants might return. At the commencement of this, the fourth day since he had left Bekla, he felt an almost complete exhaustion, beyond that merely of the body—a total doubting of the future and a longing like that which comes upon the hard-pressed soldiers of an army which is losing, but has not yet lost, a battle, at any cost to desist from further struggle for the moment, to rest, let come what may, although they know that to do so means that the fight can be renewed only at greater disadvantage. The calf muscle of his right leg was strained and painful. Two of Mollo's stab wounds, those in his shoulder and hip, throbbed continually. But more dispiriting even than these was the knowledge that he had failed in his self-appointed task, inasmuch as Shardik could not now be recaptured before he reached the hills. Looking northward over the trees, he could see clearly the nearer slopes, green, brown and shadowy purple in the morning light. They might perhaps be six, eight miles away. Shardik too must have seen them. He would reach them by nightfall. Weeks—perhaps months—would now have to be spent in hunting him through that country—an old bear, grown cunning and desperate by reason of earlier capture. There was no remedy but that the Ortelgans would have to undertake the most wearisome of all labor—that which has to be performed in order to put right what should never have gone amiss.

That morning he had escaped certainly injury, possibly death, for it was unlikely that the rough justice of the peasants would have spared an Ortelgan; and who now would believe that he was the king of Bekla? An armed ruffian, forced to beg or rob in order to eat, could pursue his way only at the risk of life and limb. Of what use, indeed, was it for him now to continue to follow Shardik? The paved road could not be more than half a day's journey to the east—perhaps much less. The time had come to return, to summon his subjects about him and plan the next step from Bekla. Had Elleroth been caught? And what news had come from the army in Tonilda?

He set off southward, deciding to follow the stream for a time and turn east only when he was well away from the village. Soon his pace grew slower and more hesitant. He had gone perhaps half a mile when he stopped, frowning and slashing at the bushes in his perplexity. Now that he had actually left Shardik, he began to see his situation in a different and daunting light. The consequences of return were incalculable. His own monarchy and power in Bekla were inseparable from Shardik. If it was he who had brought Shardik to the battle of the Foothills, it was Shardik who had brought him to the throne of Bekla and maintained him there. More than that, the fortune and might of the Ortelgans rested upon Shardik and upon the continuance of his own strange power to stand before him unharmed. Could he safely return to Bekla with the news that he had deserted the wounded Shardik and no longer knew where he was or even whether he was dead or alive? With the war in its present state, what effect would this have on the people? And what would they do to him?

Within an hour of leaving the bridge, Kelderek had returned to it and made his way upstream to the northern end of the wood. There were no tracks and he concealed himself and waited. It was not until afternoon, however, that Shardik appeared once more and continued upon his slow journey—encouraged now, perhaps, by the smell of the hills on the northwest wind.

36 *Shardik Gone*

By afternoon of the next day Kelderek was on the point of collapse. Hunger, fatigue and lack of sleep had worked upon his body as beetles work upon a roof, rust on a cistern or fear on the soldier's heart—always taking a little more, leaving a little less to oppose the forces of gravity, of weather, of danger and fear. How does the end come? Perhaps an engineer, arriving at last to inspect and check, discovers that he can pierce with his finger the pitted, paper-thin plates of iron. Perhaps a comrade's jest or a missile narrowly missing its mark causes him who was once an honest soldier to bury his head in his hands, weeping and babbling, just as rotten purlins and rafters become at last no more than splinters, wormholes and powder. Sometimes nothing occurs to precipitate the catastrophe and the slow decay, unhastened from without—of the water tank in the windless desert or the commander of the lonely, precarious garrison —continues without interruption, till nothing is left that can be repaired. Already the king of Bekla was no more, but this the Ortelgan hunter had not yet perceived.

Shardik had reached the edge of the Foothills a little after dawn. The place was wild and lonely, the country increasingly difficult. Kelderek clambered upward through dense trees or among tumbled rocks, where often he could not see thirty paces ahead. Sometimes, following an intuitive feeling that this must be the way the bear had taken, he would reach a patch of open ground only to conceal himself as Shardik came stumbling from the forest behind him. At almost any time he might have lost his life. But a change had come upon the bear—a change which, as the hours passed, became more plain to Kelderek, piercing his own sufferings with pity and at last with actual fear of what would befall.

As in the splendid house of some great family, where once lights shone in scores of windows at night and carriages bearing relatives, friends and news came and went, the very evidence and means of grandeur and authority over all the surrounding countryside, but where now the lord, widowed, his heir killed in battle, has lost heart and begun to fail; as in such a house a few candles burn, lit at dusk by an old servant who does what he can and must needs leave the rest, so fragments of Shardik's strength and ferocity flickered, a shadow suggesting the presence that once had been. He wandered on, safe indeed from attack—for what would dare to attack him?—but almost, or so it seemed, without strength to fend for himself. Once, coming upon the body of a wolf not long dead, he made some sorry shift to eat it. It seemed to Kelderek that the bear's sight was weaker, and of this, after a time, he began to take advantage, following closer than he or the nimblest of the girls would have dared in the old days on Ortelga; and thus he was able to prolong his endurance even while his hope diminished of finding, in this wilderness, any to help him or carry his news to Bekla.

In the afternoon they climbed a steep valley, emerging on a ridge running eastward above the forests, and along this they continued their slow and mysterious journey. Once Kelderek, rousing himself from a waking fancy in which his pains seemed torpid flies hanging upon his body, saw the bear ahead of him on a high rock, clear against the sky and gazing over the Beklan plain far below. It seemed to him that now it could go no farther. Its body was hunched unnaturally and when at length it moved, one shoulder drooped in a kind of crippled limping. Yet when he himself reached the rock, it was to see Shardik already crossing the spur below and as far away as before.

Coming to the foot of the ridge, he found himself at the upper end of a bleak waste, bounded far off by forest like that through which they had climbed the day before. Of Shardik there was no sign.

It was now, as the light began to fail, that Kelderek's faculties at last disintegrated. Strength and thought alike failed him. He tried to look for the bear's tracks, but forgot what ground he had already searched and then what it was that he was seeking. Coming upon a pool, he drank and then, thrusting his feet for ease into the water, cried out at the fierce, stinging pain. He found a narrow path—no more than a coney's track—between the tussocks and crept down it on hands and knees, muttering, "Accept my life, Lord Shardik," though the meaning of the words he could not recall. He tried to stand, but his sight grew clouded and sounds filled his ears, as of water, which he knew must be unreal.

The path led to a dry ravine and here for a long time he sat with his back against a tree, gazing unseeingly at the black streak of an old lightning flash that had marked the rock opposite with the shape of a broken spear.

Dusk had fallen when at last he crawled up the farther side. His physical collapse—for he could not walk—brought with it a sense of having become a creature lacking volition, passive as a tree in the wind or a weed in the stream. His last sensation was of lying prostrate, shivering and trying to drag himself forward by clutching the fibrous grasses between his fingers.

When he woke it was night, the moon clouded and the solitude stretching wide and indistinct about him. He sat up, coughing, and at once suppressed the sound with an arm across his mouth. He was afraid—partly of attracting some beast of prey, but more of the empty night and of his new dreadful loneliness. Following Shardik, he had feared Shardik and nothing else. Now Shardik was gone; and as when some severe and demanding leader, whom his men both respected and feared, is reported lost, they loiter silently, addressing themselves with assumed diligence to trivial or futile duties in attempts to evade the thought that none will utter—that they are now without him whom they trusted to stand between them and the enemy—so Kelderek rubbed his cold limbs and coughed into the crook of his elbow, as though by concentrating on the ills of his body he could make himself immune to the silence, the desolate gloom and the sense of something hovering, glimpsed in the tail of his eye.

Suddenly he started, held his breath and turned his head, listening incredulously. Had he indeed heard, or only imagined, the sound of voices, far off? No, there was nothing. He stood up, and found that he could now walk, though slowly and with pain. But which way should he go, and with what purpose? Southward, for Bekla? Or should he try to find some refuge and remain until daylight, in the hope of coming once more upon Shardik?

And then beyond all doubt he heard, for no more than an instant, a distant clamor of voices in the night. It was come and gone; but that was no wonder, for it had been far off, and what had reached his ear might well have been some momentary, louder outcry. If the distance or his own weakness had not deceived him, there had been many voices. Could the noise have come from a village where some gathering was being held? There was no light to be seen. He was not even sure from which direction the sound had come. Yet at the thought of shelter and food, of resting in safety among fellow men and of an end to his loneliness and danger, he began to hasten—or rather, to stagger —in any direction and in none until, realizing his foolishness, he sat down once more to listen.

At length—after how long he could not tell—the sound reached him again, perceived and then dying on the ear, like a wave, spent among tall reeds, that never breaks upon the shore. Released and at once quenched, it seemed, as though a door far off had opened for a moment and as suddenly closed upon some concourse within. Yet it was a sound neither of invocation nor of festival, but rather of tumultuous disorder, of riot or confusion. To him, this in itself mattered little—a town in uproar would be nevertheless a town—but what town, in this place? Where was he, and could he be sure of help once it was known who he was?

He realized that he was once more groping his way in what now seemed to him the direction of the sound. The moon, still obscured among clouds, gave little light, but he could both see and feel that he was going gently downhill, among crags and bushes, and approaching what seemed a darker mass in the near-darkness—woodland it might be, or a confronting hillside.

His cloak caught on a thornbush and he turned to disentangle it. At this moment, from somewhere not a stone's throw away in the dark, there came an agonized cry, like that of a man dealt some terrible wound. The shock, like lightning striking close at hand, momentarily bereft him of reason. As he stood trembling and staring into the dark, he heard a quick, loud gasp, followed by a few choking words of Beklan, uttered in a voice that ceased like a snapped thread.

"She'll give me a whole sackful of gold!"

At once the silence returned, unbroken by the least noise either of struggle or of flight.

"Who's there?" called Kelderek.

There was no answer, no sound. The man, whoever he might be, was either dead or unconscious. Who—what—had struck him down? Kelderek dropped on one knee, drew his sword and waited. Trying to control his breathing and the loosening of his bowels, he crouched still lower as the moon gleamed out a moment and vanished again. His fear was incapacitating and he knew himself too weak to strike a blow.

Was it Shardik who had killed the man? Why was there no noise? He looked up at the dimly luminous cloud bank and saw beyond it a stretch of open sky. Next time the moon sailed clear he must be ready on the instant to look about him and act.

Below, at the foot of the slope, the trees were moving. The wind among them would reach him in a few moments. He waited. No wind came, yet the sound among the trees increased. It was not the rustling of leaves, it was not the boughs that were moving. *Men* were moving among the trees! Yes, their voices—surely—but they were gone—no, there they were once more—the voices he had heard—beyond all doubt now, human voices! They were the voices of Ortelgans—he could even catch a word here and there—Ortelgans, and approaching!

After all his dangers and sufferings, what an unbelievable stroke of good fortune! What had happened, and where was this place that he had reached? Either in some inexplicable way he had come upon soldiers of the army of Zelda and Ged-la-Dan—which might, after all, have marched almost anywhere during the past seven days—or else, more probably, these were men of his own guard from Bekla, searching for him and for Shardik as they had been ordered. Tears of relief came to his eyes and his blood surged as though at a lovers' meeting. As he stood up, he saw that the light was increasing. The moon was nearing the edge of the clouds. The voices were closer now, descending the hill through the trees. With a shout he stumbled down the slope toward them, calling, "I am Crendrik! I am Crendrik!"

He was on a road, a trodden way leading down toward the woods. Plainly, the night-marching soldiers were also on this road. He would see their lights in a moment, for lights they must surely be carrying. He tripped and fell, but struggled up at once and hastened on, still shouting. He came to the foot of the slope and stopped, looking up, this way and that, among the trees.

There was silence: no voices, no lights. He held his breath and listened, but no sound came from the road above. He called at the top of his voice, "Don't go! Wait! Wait!" The echoes faded and died.

From the open slope behind him came a surge of voices shouting in anger and fear. Strangely unimmediate they were, fluctuating, dying and returning, like the voices of sick men trying to tell of things long gone by. At the same moment the last veil of cloud left the moon, the ground before him started up into misty light and he recognized the place where he was.

In nightmare a man may feel a touch upon his shoulder, look around and meet the glazed but hate-filled eyes of his mortal enemy, whom he knows to be dead; may open the door of his own familiar room and find himself stepping through it into a pit of graveworms; may watch the smiling face of his beloved wither, crumble and putrefy before his eyes until her laughing teeth are surrounded by the bare yellow skull. What if such as these—so impossible of occurrence, so ghastly as to seem descried through a window opening upon hell—were found no dreams but, destroying as a stroke every fragment of life's proved certainty, were to carry the mind, as the crocodile its living prey, down to some lower, unspeakable plane of reality, where sanity and reason, clutching in frenzy, feel all holds give way in the dark? There in the moonlight ran the road from Gelt, up the bare, sloping plateau, among scattered crags and bushes, to the crest over which showed faintly the rocks of the gorge beyond. To the right, in shadow, was the line of the ravine that had protected Gel-Ethlin's flank, and behind him lay those woods from which, more than five years before, Shardik had burst like a demon upon the Beklan leaders.

Dotted about the slope were low mounds, while some way off appeared the dark mass of a larger tumulus, on which grew two or three newly sprung trees. Beside the road stood a flat, squared stone, roughly carved with a falcon emblem and a few symbols of script. One of these, common in inscriptions about the streets and squares of Bekla, carried the meaning "At this place—" All about, with never a man to be seen, faint sounds of battle swelled and receded like waves, resembling the noises of day and life as a foggy dawn resembles clear noon. Shouts of anger and death, desperate orders, sobbing, prayers for mercy, the ring of weapons, the trampling of feet—all light and half-sensed as the filamentary legs of a swarm of loathsome insects upon the face of a wounded man lying helpless in his blood. Kelderek, his arms clutched about his head, swayed, uttering cries like the blarings of an idiot—speech enough for converse with the malignant dead, and words enough in which to articulate madness and despair. As a leaf that, having lived all summer upon the bough, in autumn is plucked off and swept through the turbulent, roaring air toward the sodden darkness below, so severed, so flung down, so spent and discarded was he.

He fell to the ground, babbling, and felt a rib cage of unburied bones snap beneath his weight. He lurched in the white light, over graves, over rusty, broken weapons, over a wheel covering the remains of some wretch who once, years before, had crept beneath it for vain protection. The bracken that filled his mouth was turned to worms, the sand in his eyes to the stinking dust of corruption. His capacity to suffer became infinite as, rotting with the fallen, he dissolved into innumerable grains suspended among the wave-voices, sucked back and rolled forward to break again and again upon the shore of the desolate battlefield where, upon him more dreadfully than upon any who had ever strayed there, unwarned to shun it, the butchered dead discharged their unhoused misery and malice.

Who can describe the course of suffering to the end where no more can be endured? Who can express the unendurable vision of a world created solely for horror and torment—the struggling of the half-crushed beetle glued to the ground by its own entrails; the flapping, broken fish pecked to death by gulls upon the sand; the dying ape full of maggots, the young soldier, eviscerated, screaming in the arms of his comrades; the child who weeps alone, wounded for life by the desertion of those who have gone their selfish ways? Save us, O God, only place us where we may see the sun and eat a little bread until it is time to die, and we will ask nothing more. And when the snake devours the fallen fledgling before our eyes, then our indifference is Thy mercy.

In the first gray light, Kelderek stood up a man newborn of grief—lost of memory, devoid of purpose, unable to tell night from morning or friend from foe. Before him, along the crest, translucent as a rainbow, stood the Beklan battle line, sword, shield and axe, the falcon banner, the long spears of Yelda, the gaudy finery of Deelguy: and he smiled at them, as a baby might laugh and crow, waking to see about her cot rebels and mutineers come to add her murder to those of the rest. But as he gazed, they faded like pictures in the fire, their armor transformed to the first glitter of morning on the rocks and bushes. So he wandered away in search of them, the soldiers, picking as he went the colored flowers that caught his eye, eating leaves and grass and stanching, with a strip torn from his ragged garments, a long gash in his forearm. He followed the road down to the plain, not knowing his whereabouts and resting often, for though pain and fatigue now seemed to him the natural condition of man, yet still it was one that he sought to ease as best he could. A band of wayfarers who overtook him threw him an old loaf, relieved to perceive that he was harmless, and this, when he had tried it, he remembered to be good to eat. He cut himself a staff which, as he went, tapped and rattled on the stones, for the cold of extreme shock was upon him all day. Such sleep as he had was broken, for he dreamed continually of things he could not entirely recall—of fire and a great river, of enslaved children crying and a shaggy, clawed beast as tall as a rooftree.

How long did he wander, and who were they who gave him shelter and helped him? Again, they tell tales—of birds that brought him food, of bats that guided him at dusk and beasts of prey that did him no harm when he shared their lairs. These are legends, but perhaps they scarcely distort the truth that he, capable of nothing, was kept alive by what was given him unsought. Pity for distress is felt most easily when it is plain that the sufferer is not to be feared, and even while he remained armed, none could fear a man who limped his way upon a stick, gazing about him and smiling at the sun. Some, by his clothes, thought him to be a deserting soldier, but others said no, he must be some three-quarter-witted vagabond who had stolen a soldier's gear or perhaps, in his necessity, stripped the dead. Yet none harmed him or drove him away—no doubt because his frailty was so evident and few care to feel that denial on their part may hasten a man to his death. One or two, indeed, of those who suffered him to sleep in sheds or outhouses—like the gatekeeper's wife at the stronghold of S'marr Torruin, warden of the Foothills—tried to persuade him to rest longer and then perhaps find work, for the war had taken many. But though he smiled, or played awhile with the children in the dust, he seemed to understand but little, and his well-wishers would shake their heads as at length he took his staff and went haltingly on his way. Eastward he went, as before, but each day only a few miles, for he sat much in the sun in lonely places and for the most part kept to less-frequented country along the edge of the hills, feeling that here, if at all, he might happen once more upon that mighty, half-remembered creature which, as it seemed to him, he had lost and with whose life his own was in some shadowy but all-important respect bound up. Of the sound of distant voices he was greatly afraid and seldom approached a village, though once he allowed a tipsy herdsman to lead him home, feed him and take from him, either in robbery or payment, his sword.

Perhaps he wandered for five days, or six. Longer it can hardly have been when one evening, coming slowly over a shoulder of the lower hills, he saw below him the roofs of Kabin—Kabin of the Waters—that pleasant, walled town with its fruit groves on the southwest and, nearer at hand on the north, the sinuous length of the reservoir running between two green spurs, the surface wrinkling and sliding under the wind, suggesting some lithe animal caged behind the outfall dam with its complex of gates and sluices. The place was busy—he could see a deal of movement both within and outside the walls; and as he sat on the hillside, gazing down at a cluster of huts and the smoke that filled the meadows outside the town, he became aware of a party of soldiers—some eight or nine—approaching through the trees.

At once he jumped to his feet and ran toward them, raising one hand in greeting and calling, "Wait! Wait!" They stopped, staring in surprise at the confidence of this tattered vagrant, and turning uncertainly toward their *tryzatt*, a fatherly veteran with a stupid, good-natured face, who looked as though, having risen as high as he was likely to get in the service, he was all for an easy life.

"What's this, then, tryze?" asked one, as Kelderek stopped before them and stood with folded arms, looking them up and down.

The tryzatt pushed back his leather helmet and rubbed his forehead with one hand.

"Dunno," he replied at length. "Some beggar's trick, I suppose. Come on, now," he said, laying one hand on Kelderek's shoulder, "you'll get nothing here, so just muck off, there's a good lad."

Kelderek put the hand aside and faced him squarely.

"Soldiers," he said firmly. "A message—Bekla—" He paused, frowning as they gathered about him, and then spoke again.

"Soldiers—*Senandril*, Lord Shardik—Bekla, message—" He stopped again.

"Havin' us on, ain't he?" said another of the men.

"Don't seem that way, not just," said the tryzatt. "Seems to know what he wants all right. More like he knows we don't know his language."

"What language is it, then?" asked the man.

"That's Ortelgan," said the first soldier, spitting in the dust. "Something about his life and a message."

"Could be important, then," said the tryzatt. "Could be, if he's Ortelgan, and come to us with a message from Bekla. Can you tell us who you are?" he asked Kelderek, who met his eye but answered nothing.

"I reckon he's come from Bekla, but something's put things out of his mind, like—shock and that," said the first soldier.

"That'll be it," said the tryzatt. "He's an Ortelgan—been working secretly for Lord Elleroth One-Hand maybe; and either those swine in Bekla tortured him—look what they did to the Ban, burned his bloody hand off, the bastards—or else his wits are turned with wandering all this way north to find us."

"Poor devil, he looks all in," said a dark man with a broad belt of Sarkid leatherwork bearing the corn-sheaves emblem. "He must have walked till he dropped. After all, we couldn't be much farther north if we tried, could we?"

"Well," said the tryzatt, "whatever it is, we'd better take him along. I've got to make a report by sunset, so the captain can sort him out then. Listen," he said, raising his voice and speak-

ing very slowly, in order to make sure that the foreigner standing two feet away from him could understand a language he
did not know, "you—come—with us. You—give—message—
captain, see?"

"Message," replied Kelderek at once, repeating the Yeldashay.
"Message—Shardik." He stopped and broke into a fit of coughing, leaning over his staff.

"All right, now don't you worry," said the tryzatt reassuringly, buckling his belt, which he had slackened for the purpose
of talking. "We"—he pointed, miming with his hands—"take—
you—town—captain—right? You'd better lend him a hand," he
added to the two men nearest him. "We'll be 'alf the mucking
night else."

Kelderek, his arms drawn over the soldiers' shoulders for
support, went with them down the hill. He was glad of their
help, which was given respectfully enough—for they were uncertain what rank of man he might be. He for his part understood hardly a word of their talk and was in any case preoccupied in trying to remember what message it was that he had to
send, now that he had at last found the soldiers who had
vanished so mysteriously in the dawn. Perhaps, he thought, they
might have some food to spare.

The main part of the army was encamped in the meadows
outside the walls of Kabin, for the town and its inhabitants were
being treated with clemency and in such dwellings as had been
commandeered there was room for no more than the senior
officers, their aides and servants and the specialist troops, such
as scouts and pioneers, who were under the direct control of the
commander in chief. The tryzatt and his men, who belonged to
these, entered the town gates just as they were about to be shut
for the night and, ignoring questions from comrades and by-
standers, conducted Kelderek to a house under the south wall.
Here a young officer wearing the stars of Ikat questioned him,
first in Yeldashay and then, seeing that he understood very
little, in Beklan. To this Kelderek replied that he had a message.
Pressed, he repeated "Bekla" but could say no more; and the
young officer, unwilling to browbeat him and pitying his starved
and filthy condition, gave orders to let him wash, eat and sleep.

Next morning, as one of the cooks, a kindly fellow, was again

342

washing his gashed arm, a second, older officer came into the room, accompanied by two soldiers, and greeted him with straightforward civility.

"My name is Tan-Rion," he said in Beklan. "You must excuse our haste and curiosity, but to an army in the field time is always precious. We need to know who you are. The tryzatt who found you says that you came to him of your own accord and told him that you had a message from Bekla. If you have a message, perhaps you can tell me what it is."

Two full meals, a long and comfortable night's sleep and the attentions of the cook had calmed and to some extent restored Kelderek.

"The message—should have gone to Bekla," he answered haltingly, "but the best chance—is lost now."

The officer looked puzzled. "To Bekla? You are not bringing a message to us, then?"

"I—have to send a message."

"Is your message to do with the fighting in Bekla?"

"Fighting?" asked Kelderek.

"You know that there has been a rising in Bekla? It began about nine days ago. As far as we know, fighting is still going on. Have you come from Deelguy, or where?"

Confusion descended again upon Kelderek's mind. He was silent and the officer shrugged his shoulders.

"I am sorry—I can see that you are not yourself—but time may well be very short. We shall have to search you—that for a start."

Kelderek, who had become no stranger to humiliation, stood unresisting as the soldiers, not ungently and with a kind of rough courtesy, set about their task. They placed their findings on the window ledge—a stale crust, a strip of cobbler's leather, a reaper's whetstone which he had found lying in a ditch two days before, a handful of dried aromatic herbs which the gate-keeper's wife had given him against lice and infection, and a talisman of red-veined stone which must once have belonged to Kavass.

"All right, mate," said one of the soldiers, handing him back his jerkin. "Steady, now. Nearly done, don't worry."

Suddenly the other soldier whistled, swore under his breath

and then, without another word, held out to the officer on the palm of his hand a small, bright object which glittered in the sunlight. It was the stag emblem of Santil-kè-Erketlis.

37 Lord One-Hand

THE OFFICER, STARTLED, TOOK THE EMBLEM and examined it, drawing the chain through the ring and fastening the clasp carefully, as though to allow himself time to think. At length, with an uncertainty that he had not shown before, he said, "Will you be good enough to—to tell me—I am sure you will understand why I have to know—whether this is your own?"

Kelderek held out his hand in silence but the officer, after a moment's hesitation, shook his head.

"Have you come here in search of the commander in chief himself? Perhaps you are a member of his household? If you can tell me it will make my task easier."

Kelderek, to whom the memory was now beginning to return of much that had befallen him since leaving Bekla, sat down upon the bed and put his head in his hands. The officer waited patiently for him to speak. At last Kelderek said, "Where is General Zelda? If he is here, I must see him immediately."

"General Zelda?" replied the officer in bewilderment.

One of the soldiers spoke to him in a low voice and together they went to the far end of the room.

"This man's an Ortelgan, sir," said the soldier, "or else I'm one myself."

"I know that," replied Tan-Rion. "What of it? He's some agent of Lord Elleroth who's lost his wits."

"I doubt he is, sir. If he's an Ortelgan, then clearly he's not a household officer of the commander in chief. You heard him ask for General Zelda. I agree it's plain that some shock's confused his mind, but my guess is that he's made his way into the middle of the wrong army without realizing it. If you come to think of it, he'd hardly be expecting to find us here in Kabin."

Tan-Rion considered.

"He could still have come by that emblem honestly. In his case it might be no more than a token to prove who he was working for. Nobody knows what strange people may have been reporting direct to General Erketlis or carrying his messages these last few months. Suppose, for instance, that Lord Elleroth made use of this man while he was in Bekla? When is General Erketlis expected to return, have you heard?"

"Not until the day after tomorrow, sir. He got wind of a big slave column on the move west of Thettit-Tonilda and heading for Bekla; to reach it in time meant some very hard going, so the general took a hundred men from the Falaron regiment and said he'd do the job himself."

"Very like him. I'm only afraid he may try that sort of thing once too often. Well, at that rate I suppose we'll have to keep this man until he gets back."

"I suggest we might ask Lord One-Hand—Lord Elleroth—to see him, sir. If he recognizes him, as I gather you yourself think may be possible, then at least we shall know where we are, even if the man doesn't come round enough to tell us anything."

After a few more fruitless questions to Kelderek, Tan-Rion, together with his two soldiers, conducted him out of the house and up on the town walls. Here, walking in the spring sunshine, they looked down upon the town on one side and on the other upon the huts and bivouacs of the camp in the fields outside. The smoke of fires was drifting on the breeze and in the market-place a crowd was gathering in response to the long-drawn, stylized summons of a red-cloaked crier.

"Must have made his fortune since we came here, eh?" said a sentry on the wall to one of Tan-Rion's soldiers, jerking his thumb to where the crier below was already climbing on his rostrum.

"I dare say," answered the soldier. "I know I've done well enough out of him. He hangs about our place and offers to pay for anything we can tell him."

"Well, just be careful how much you do tell him," snapped Tan-Rion, turning his head.

"You bet, sir. We all want to stay alive."

They descended from the wall by a flight of steps near the

gate at which Kelderek had entered the town the night before and, passing through a square, came to a large stone house where a sentry stood before the door. Kelderek and his escort were taken to a room which had formerly been that of the household steward, while Tan-Rion, after a few words with the captain of the guard, accompanied that officer through the house and into the garden.

The garden, green and formal, was shady with ornamental trees and shrubs—*lexis*, purple *cresset* and sharp-scented *planella* already opening its tiny, mauve-speckled flowers to the early sun. Through their midst, murmuring along its gravel bed, ran a brook channeled down from the reservoir. Along the verge, Elleroth was walking in conversation with a Yeldashay officer, a Deelguy baron and the governor of the town. He was gaunt and pale, his face haggard with pain and recent privation. His left hand, carried in a sling, was encased to the wrist in a great, padded glove of birch bark that covered and protected the dressings beneath. His sky-blue robe, a gift from the wardrobe of Santil-kè-Erketlis (for he had reached the army in rags), had been embroidered across the breast with the corn sheaves of Sarkid, while the silver clasp of his belt was fashioned in the stag emblem. He walked leaning on a staff and those beside him carefully suited their pace to his. He nodded courteously to Tan-Rion and the guard commander, who stood deferentially aside, waiting until he should be ready to hear them.

"Of course," Elleroth was saying to the governor, "I cannot tell you what the commander in chief will decide. But clearly, whether the army remains here and for how long will depend not only on the movements of the enemy but also on the state of our own supplies. We're quite a long way from Ikat"—he smiled—"and we shan't be loved up here much longer if we eat everybody out of house and home. The Ortelgan army are in the middle of their own country—or what they call their own country. I dare say we may decide to seek them out and fight them soon, before the balance begins to tip against us. I can assure you that General Erketlis has all this very much in mind. At the same time, there are two excellent reasons why we should like to stay here a little longer, provided you can bear with us— and I assure you that you would not, in the long run, be losers.

In the first place, we are doing what we intended—what the enemy supposed we could never do and what we could not have done without help from Deelguy." He bowed slightly to the baron, a heavy, swarthy man, showy as a macaw. "We think that if we continue to hold the reservoir, the enemy may feel driven to attack us at a disadvantage. He for his part is probably waiting to see whether we shall stay here. So we want to look as though we shall."

"You are not going to destroy the reservoir, my lord?" asked the governor anxiously.

"Only in the very last resort," answered Elleroth cheerfully. "But I'm sure with your help we shall never come to that, shall we?" The governor replied with a wry smile and after a few moments Elleroth continued.

"The second reason is that we are anxious, while we are here, to hunt down as many slave traders as we can. We have already caught not only several who hold warrants from the so-called king of Bekla, but also one or two of those who do not. But as you know, the country beyond the Vrako, right across to Zeray and up as far as the gap of Linsho, is wild and remote. Here, we are on its doorstep: Kabin is the ideal base from which to search it. If only we can gain the time, our patrols will be able to comb out the whole of that area. And believe it or not, we have received a reliable offer of help from Zeray itself."

"From *Zeray*, my lord?" said the governor incredulously.

"From Zeray," answered Elleroth. "And you told me, didn't you," he went on, turning with a smile to Tan-Rion, who was still waiting nearby, "that you had information about at least one unlicensed slave trader who is believed to be either beyond the Vrako at this moment or else making toward it from Tonilda?"

"Yes, my lord," replied Tan-Rion. "The child-dealer, Genshed —a most cruel, evil man, from Terekenalt. But Trans-Vrako will be difficult country to search and he might very well give us the slip, even now."

"Well, we shall have to do the best we can. So you see—"

"Any news of your own trouble, my lord?" broke in the Yeldashay officer impulsively.

Elleroth bit his lip and paused a moment before answering.

"I'm afraid not—for the time being. So you see," he resumed quickly to the governor, "we are going to need all the help you can give us; and what I would like to learn from you is how we can best feed and supply the army while we stay here a little longer. Perhaps you will be so good as to think about it and we will have a talk with the commander in chief when he returns. We sincerely want to avoid making your people suffer, and as I said, we will pay honestly for your help."

The governor was about to withdraw when Elleroth suddenly added, "By the way, the priestess from the Telthearna island—the wise woman—you gave her a safe-conduct, as I asked you?"

"Yes, my lord," replied the governor, "yesterday at noon. She has been gone these twenty hours."

"Thank you."

The governor bowed and went away through the trees. Elleroth stood still, watching a trout that hung on the edge of the current, motionless save for the flickering of its tail. It darted upstream and he sat down on a stone bench, easing his hand in the sling and shaking his head as though at some thought that preoccupied and distressed him. At length, recalling Tan-Rion, he looked up with a questioning smile.

"Sorry to bother you, sir," said Tan-Rion briskly. "Yesterday evening one of our patrols brought in a wandering Ortelgan who kept talking about a message to or from Bekla. This morning we found this on him and I thought best to come and show it to you at once."

Elleroth took the stag emblem, looked at it, started, frowned and then examined it more closely.

"What does he look like, this man?" he asked at length.

"Like an Ortelgan, my lord," replied Tan-Rion, "spare and dark. It's hard to say much more—he's pretty well exhausted—half-starved and worn out. He must have had a very bad time."

"I will see him immediately," said Elleroth.

38 *The Streets of Kabin*

AT THE SIGHT OF ELLEROTH KELDEREK'S MEMORY, by this time half-restored—like the safety of a swimmer whose limp feet, as he drifts, have already touched bottom here and there; or the consciousness of an awakening sleeper whose hearing has caught but, who has not yet recognized for what they are, the singing of the birds and the sound of rain—cleared as immediately as the misted surface of a mirror wiped by an impatient hand. The voices of the Yeldashay officers, the starred banner floating on the walls above the garden, the cognizances worn by the soldiers standing about him—all these assumed on the instant a single, appalling meaning. So might an old, sick man, smiling as his son's wife bent over his bed, grasp in a moment the terrible import of her look and of the pillow poised above his face. Kelderek gave a quick, gasping cry, staggered and would have fallen if the soldiers had not caught him under the arms. As they did so, he struggled briefly, then recovered himself and stood staring, tense and wide-eyed as a bird held in a man's hand.

"How do you come to be here, Crendrik?" asked Elleroth.

Kelderek made no reply.

"Are you seeking refuge from your own people?"

He shook his head mutely and seemed about to faint.

"Let him sit down," said Elleroth.

There was no second bench and one of the soldiers ran to bring a stool from the house. As he returned, two or three of the guards off duty followed him and stood peering from among the trees, until their tryzatt ordered them sharply back to the house.

"Crendrik," said Elleroth, leaning toward him where he sat hunched upon the stool, "I am asking you again. Are you here as a fugitive from Bekla?"

"I—I am no fugitive," replied Kelderek in a low voice.

"We know that there has been a rising in Bekla. You say that that has nothing to do with your coming here, alone and exhausted?"

"I know nothing of it. I left Bekla within an hour of yourself —and by the same gate."

"You were pursuing me?"

"No."

Kelderek's face was set. The guard commander seemed about to strike him, but Elleroth held up his hand and waited, looking at him intently.

"I was following Lord Shardik. That is my charge from God," cried Kelderek with sudden violence and looking up for the first time. "I have followed him from Bekla to the hills of Gelt."

"And then—?"

"I lost him, and later came upon your soldiers."

The sweat was standing on his forehead and his breath came in gasps.

"You thought they were your own?"

"It's no matter what I thought."

Elleroth searched for a moment among a bundle of scrolls and letters lying beside him on the bench.

"Is that your seal?" he asked, holding out a paper.

Kelderek looked at it. "Yes."

"What is this paper?"

Kelderek made no reply.

"I will tell you what it is," said Elleroth. "It is a license issued by yourself in Bekla to a man called Nigon, authorizing him to enter Lapan and take up a quota of children as slaves. I have several similar papers here."

The hatred and contempt of the men standing nearby was like the oppression of snow unfallen from a winter sky. Kelderek, hunched upon the stool, was shaking as though with bitter cold. The scent of the planella came and went, evanescent as the squeaking of bats at twilight.

"Well," said Elleroth briskly, getting up from the bench, "I have recovered this trinket, Crendrik, and you have nothing to tell us, it seems; so I can resume my work and you had better return to your business of seeking the bear."

Tan-Rion drew in his breath sharply. The young Yeldashay officer started forward.

"My lord—"

Again Elleroth raised his hand.

"I have my reasons, Dethrin. Surely if anyone has the right to spare this man, it is I?"

"But, my lord," protested Tan-Rion, "this evil man—the priest-king of Shardik himself— Providence has delivered him into our hands—the people—"

"You may take my word for it that neither he nor the bear can harm us now. And if it is merely a matter of retribution that is troubling you, perhaps you will persuade the people to forgo it, as a favor to me. I have certain information which leads me to conclude that we should spare this man's life."

His mild words were spoken with a firm directness which plainly admitted of no further argument. His officers were silent.

"You will go eastward, Crendrik," said Elleroth. "That will suit us both, since not only is it the opposite direction from Bekla, but it also happens to be the direction your bear has taken."

From the square outside could now be heard a growing hubbub—murmuring broken by angry shouts, raucous, inarticulate cries and the sharper voices of soldiers trying to control a crowd.

"We will give you food and fresh shoes," said Elleroth, "and that is as much as I can do for you. I can see well enough that you are in poor shape, but if you stay here you will be torn to pieces. You will not have forgotten that Mollo came from Kabin. Now understand this plainly. If ever again you allow yourself to fall into the hands of this army, you will be put to death. I repeat, you will be put to death. I should not be able to save you again." He turned to the guard commander. "See that he has an escort as far as the ford of the Vrako, and tell the crier to give out that it is my personal wish that no one should touch him."

He nodded to the soldiers, who once more grasped Kelderek by the arms. They had already begun to lead him away when suddenly he wrenched himself about.

"Where is Lord Shardik?" he cried. "What did you mean— he cannot harm you now?"

One of the soldiers jerked back his head by the hair, but Elleroth, motioning them to let him go, faced him once more.

"We have not hurt your bear, Crendrik," he said. "We had no need."

Kelderek stared at him, trembling. Elleroth paused a moment. The noise of the crowd now filled the garden and the two soldiers, waiting, looked at one another sidelong.

"Your bear is dying, Crendrik," said Elleroth deliberately. "One of our patrols came upon it in the hills three days ago and followed it eastward until it waded the upper Vrako. They were in no doubt. Other news has reached me also—never mind how —that you and the bear came alive from the Streels of Urtah. Of what befell you at the Streels you know more than I, but that is why your life is spared. I have no part in blood required of God. Now go."

In the steward's room, one of the soldiers threw back his head and spat in Kelderek's face.

"You dirty bastard," he said, "burned his mucking hand off, did you?"

"And now he says we're to let you go," said the other soldier. "You damned, rotten Ortelgan slave trader! Where's his son, eh? *You* saw to that, did you? You're the one that told Genshed what he had to do?"

"Where's his son?" repeated the first soldier, as Kelderek made no reply but stood with bent head, looking down at the floor.

"Didn't you hear me?" Taking Kelderek's chin in his hand, he forced it up and stared contemptuously into his eyes.

"I heard you," mouthed Kelderek, his words distorted by the soldier's grip, "I don't know what you mean."

Both the soldiers gave short, derisive laughs.

"Oh, no," said the second soldier. "You're not the man who brought back slave trading to Bekla, I suppose?"

Kelderek nodded mutely.

"Oh, you admit that much? And of course you don't know that Lord Elleroth's eldest son disappeared more than a month ago, and that our patrols have been searching for him from Lapan to Kabin? No, you don't know anything, do you?"

He raised his open hand, jeering as Kelderek flinched away.

"I know nothing of that," replied Kelderek. "But why do you blame the boy's disappearance on a slave trader? A river, a wild beast—"

The soldier stared at him for a moment and then, apparently convinced that he really knew no more than he had said, answered, "We know who's got the lad. It's Genshed of Terekenalt."

"I never heard of him. There's no man of that name licensed to trade in Beklan provinces."

"You'd make the stars angry," replied the soldier. "Everyone's heard of him, the dirty swine. No, like enough he's not licensed in Bekla—even you wouldn't license him. I dare say. But he works for those that are licensed—if you call that work."

"And you say this man has taken the Ban of Sarkid's heir?"

"Half a month ago, down in eastern Lapan, we captured a trader called Nigon, together with three overseers and forty slaves. I suppose you'll tell us you didn't know Nigon either?"

"No, I remember Nigon."

"He told General Erketlis that Genshed had got the boy and was making north through Tonilda. Since then patrols have searched up through Tonilda as far as Thettit. If Genshed was ever there, he's not there now."

"But how could you expect me to know this?" cried Kelderek. "If what you say is true, I don't know why Elleroth spared my life any more than you do."

"He spared you, maybe," said the first soldier. "He's a fine gentleman, isn't he? But we're not, you slave-trading bastard. I reckon if anyone knows where Genshed is, it's you. What were you doing in these parts, and how else could he have got clean away?"

He picked up a heavy tally-stick lying on the steward's table and laughed as Kelderek flung up his arm.

"Stop that!" rapped the guard commander, appearing in the doorway. "You heard what One-Hand said. You're to let him alone!"

"If they will let him alone, sir," answered the soldier. "Listen to them!" He pulled a stool to the high window, stood on it and looked out. The noise of the crowd had if anything increased, though no words were distinguishable. "If they *will* let him alone, One-Hand's the only man they'd do it for."

Sitting down apart, Kelderek shut his eyes and tried to collect his thoughts. A man may by chance overhear words which he knows to have been spoken with no malice toward himself, perhaps not even with reference to his own affairs, but which nevertheless, if they are true, import his personal misfortune or misery—words, perhaps, of a commercial venture foundered, of an army's defeat, of another man's fall or a woman's loss of honor. Having heard, he stands bewildered, striving by any means to set aside, to find grounds for disbelieving the news, or at least for rejecting the conclusion he has drawn, like an unlucky card, for his own personal fortune. But the very fact that the words did not refer directly to him serves more than anything else to corroborate what he fears. Despite the desperate antics of his brain, he knows how more than likely it is that they are true. Yet still there is a faint possibility that they may not be. And so he remains, like a chess player who cannot bear to lose, still searching the position for the least chance of escape. So Kelderek sat, turning and turning in his mind the words which Elleroth had spoken. If Shardik were dying—but Shardik could not be dying. If Shardik were dying—if Shardik were dying, what business had he himself left in the world? Why did the sun still shine? What was now the intent of God? Sitting so rapt and still that at length his guards' attention wandered and they ceased to watch him, he contemplated the blank wall as though seeing there the likeness of a greater, incomprehensible void, stretching from pole to pole.

Elleroth's son—his heir—had fallen into the hands of an unlicensed slave dealer? He himself knew—who better?—how possible it was. He had heard of these men—had received many complaints of their activities in the remoter parts of the Beklan provinces. He knew that within the Ortelgan domains slaves were captured illegally who never reached the market at Bekla, being driven north through Tonilda and Kabin or west through Paltesh to be sold in Katria or Terekenalt. Although the prescribed penalties were heavy, as long as the war lasted the probability of an unlicensed dealer's capture was remote. But that this man Genshed, whoever he might be, should have taken the son and heir of the Ban of Sarkid! No doubt he meant to demand a ransom if ever he got him safe to Terekenalt. But for what conceivable reason, with such a grief in his heart and such a wrong to lay to the charge of the hated priest-king of Bekla, had Elleroth insisted on sparing his life? For a while he pondered this riddle but could imagine no answer. His thoughts returned to Shardik, but at last he almost ceased to think at all, drowsing where he sat and hearing, sharper than the noise of the crowd, the plangent drip of water into a butt outside the window.

The guard commander returned and with him a burly, black-bearded officer, armed and helmeted, who stared at Kelderek, slapping his scabbard against his leg with nervous impatience.

"Is this the man?"

The guard commander nodded.

"Come on, then, you, for God's sake, while we've still got them under some sort of control. I want to live, if you don't. Take this pack—shoes and two days' food—that's the Ban's orders. You can put the shoes on later."

Kelderek followed him down the passage and through the courtyard to the gatekeeper's lodge. Under the arch behind the shut gate, some twenty soldiers were drawn up in two files. The officer led Kelderek to a central place between them and then, taking up his own position immediately behind him, gripped him by the shoulder and spoke in his ear.

"Now you do as I say, do you see, or you'll never even have the chance to wish you had. You're going to walk across this blasted town to the east gate, because if you don't, I don't, and that's why you're going to. They're quiet now because they've been told it's the Ban's personal wish, but if anything provokes them, we're as good as dead. They don't like slave traders and child butchers, you see. Don't say a word, don't wave your bloody arms, don't do any damned thing; and above all, keep moving, do you understand? Right!" he shouted to the tryzatt in front. "Get on with it, and God help us!"

The gate opened, the soldiers marched forward and Kelderek stepped at once into dazzling sunlight shining directly into his eyes. Blinded, he stumbled, and instantly the captain's hand was in his armpit, supporting and thrusting him on.

"You stop and I'll run you through."

Colored veils floated before his eyes, slowly dissolving and vanishing to disclose the road at his feet. He realized that he was bowed, neck thrust forward, peering down like a beggar on a stick. He straightened his shoulders, threw back his head and looked about him.

The unexpected shock was so great that he stopped dead, raising one hand before his face as though to ward off a blow.

"Keep moving, damn you!"

The square was packed with people—men, women and children, standing on either side of the road, crowded at the windows, clinging to the roofs. Not a voice spoke, not a murmur was to be heard. All were staring at him in silence, each pair of eyes following only him as the soldiers marched on across the square. Some of the men scowled and shook their fists, but none uttered a word. A young girl, dressed as a widow, stood with folded hands and tears unwiped upon her cheeks, while beside her an old woman shook continually as she craned her neck, her fallen-in mouth working in a palsied twitching. His eyes met for a second the round, solemn stare of a little boy. The people swayed like grass, unaware of their swaying as they moved their heads to keep him in their gaze. The silence was so complete that for a moment he had the illusion that these people were far away, too far to be heard from the lonely place where he walked between the soldiers, the only sound in his ears their regular tread that crunched upon the sand.

They left the square and entered a narrow, stone-paved street, where their footsteps echoed between the walls. Trying with all his will to look nowhere but ahead, he still felt the silence and the gaze of the people like a weapon raised above him. He met the eyes of a woman who threw up her arm, making the sign against evil, and dropped his head once more, like a cowering slave who expects a blow. He realized that he was breathing hard, that his steps had become more rapid than the soldiers', that he was almost running to keep his place among them. He saw himself as he must appear to the crowd—haggard, shrinking, contemptible, hastening before the captain like a beast driven up a lane.

The street led into the marketplace and here, too, were the innumerable faces and the terrible silence. Not a woman was haggling, not a trader crying his wares; as they approached the fountain basin—Kabin was full of fountains—the jet faltered and died away. He wondered who it was that had timed it so surely, and whether he had had orders to do so or had acted of his own accord; then tried to guess how far it might now be to the east gate, what it would look like when they reached it and what orders the captain would give. The cheek of the soldier beside him bore a long, white scar and he thought, "If my right foot is the next to dislodge a stone, he got it in battle. If my left, then he got it in a fight when he was drunk."

Not that these thoughts could come for an instant between his horror of the silence and of the eyes which he dared not meet. If it were not some sick fancy of his own fear and anguish, there was in this crowd a mounting tension, like that before the breaking of the rains. "We must get there," he muttered. "At all costs, Lord Shardik, we must get there before the rains break."

A cloud of flies flew up before his face, disturbed from a piece of offal lying in the road. He thought of the gylon fly, with its transparent body, hovering among the reeds along the Telthearna. "I have become a gylon fly—their eyes pass through me —through and through me—meeting those of others that pass through me from the other side. My bones are turning to water. I shall fall.

> He came, he came by night,
> Silence lay all about us.
> A sword passed through me, I am changed for ever.
> *Senandril na kora, senandril na ro.*"

His thoughts, like a deserted child's, returning to the memory of loss and grief, came back to Elleroth's words in the garden.

"Your bear is dying, Crendrik—"

"Shut up and get on," said the officer between his clenched teeth.

He did not know that he had spoken aloud. The dust whirled up in a sudden flurry of wind, yet of all the eyes around him not one seemed to close against it. The road was steeper now; they were climbing. He bent forward, dropping his head like an ox drawing a load uphill, looking down at the ground as he dragged himself on. They were leaving the marketplace, yet the silence was pulling him backward, the silence was a spell which held him fast. The weight of the thousands of eyes was a load he could never drag up this hill to the east gate. He faltered and then, stumbling backward against the captain, turned his head and whispered, "I can't go on."

He felt the point of the captain's dagger thrust against his back, just above the waist.

"Ban of Sarkid or no Ban of Sarkid, I'll kill you before my men come to any harm. Get on!"

Suddenly the silence was broken by the cry of a child. The sound was like the flaring of a flame in darkness. The soldiers, who when he stumbled had stopped uncertainly, gathering about him and the captain, started as though at a trumpet and every head jerked around toward the noise. A little girl, perhaps five or six years old, running to cross the road before the soldiers came, had tripped and fallen headlong and now lay crying in the dust, less from pain, perhaps, than from the grim appearance of the soldiers at whose feet she found herself sprawling. A woman stepped out of the crowd, picked her up and bore her away, the sound of her voice, reassuring and comforting the child, carrying plainly back along the lane.

Kelderek raised his head and drew a deep breath into his lungs. The sound had broken the invisible but dreadful web in which, like a fly bound about with sticky thread, he had almost lost the power to struggle. As when men break open at last a dry trench by the river, in which they have been repairing a canoe, the water comes flooding in, bringing back to the craft its true element and lifting it until it floats, so the sound of the child's voice restored to Kelderek the simple will and determination of common men to endure and survive, come what may. His life had been spared, no matter why; the sooner he was away from this town the better. If the people hated him, then he had the answer—he would be gone.

Without further words to the captain he took up his pace once more, spurning the soft sand with his heels as he trudged up the hill. The people were pressing close now, the soldiers keeping them off with the shafts of their spears, the captain shouting, "Back! Keep back!" Ignoring them, he turned a corner at the top and at once found himself before the gate tower, the gate standing open, the guard turned out and drawn up on either side to prevent anyone following them out of the town. They tramped under the echoing arch. Without looking around he heard the gate grind and clang to and the bolts shot home.

"Don't stop," said the captain, close behind him as ever.

Marching down a hill between trees, they came to a rocky ford across a torrent that swept down from the wooded hills on the left. Here the men, without waiting for orders, broke ranks, kneeling to drink or flinging themselves on the grass. The officer once again gripped Kelderek's shoulder and turned him about, so that they stood face to face.

"This is the Vrako—the boundary of Kabin province, as I dare say you know. The east gate of Kabin is shut for an hour by the Ban's orders and I shall be keeping this ford closed for the same length of time. You're to cross by this ford and after that you can go where you please." He paused. "One more thing. If the army gets orders to patrol east of the Vrako, we shall be looking out for you, and you'll not escape again."

He nodded to show that he had no more to say; and Kelderek, hearing behind him the growling curses of the soldiers—one threw a stone which struck a rock close by his knee—stumbled his way across the ford and so left them.

BOOK V

Zeray

39 *Across the Vrako*

IN BEKLA HE HAD HEARD OF THE COUNTRY east of Kabin—the midden of the empire, one of his provincial governors had called it —a province with no estates and no government, without revenue and without one city. Forty miles below Ortelga the Telthearna turned, in a great bend, to flow southward past the eastern extremity of the Gelt Mountains. South of these mountains and west of the Telthearna lay a remote wilderness of wooded ridges, of marshes, creeks and forest, without roads and with no settlements except a few miserable villages where the inhabitants lived on fish, half-wild pigs and whatever they could scratch from the soil. In such a region, to seek and find a man was all but impossible. Many a fugitive and criminal had disappeared into its wastes. There was a proverb in Bekla, "I would kill So-and-So, were it worth the journey to Zeray." Rough, unruly boys would be told by their mothers, "You'll end in Zeray." It was rumored that from this isolated place—for town it could not be called—where the Telthearna narrowed to a strait less than a quarter of a mile wide, a man who could pay might be taken across to the eastern shore and no questions asked. In the old days, even the northern army of patrol had fixed the eastern limit of its march at Kabin, and no tax collectors or assessors would cross the Vrako for fear of their lives. Such was the country which Kelderek had now entered and the place in which, by Elleroth's mercy, he was free to remain alive for as long as he could.

Having taken the fresh shoes from his pack and put them on, he walked fast for some while down the narrow, overgrown track. What more likely, he thought, than that once the gate and ford were open, some might follow in the hope of overtaking and killing him? For although he knew well enough that he was likely to die in this country and indeed could find in himself little desire to save his life, yet he was determined not to lose it at the hands of any Yeldashay or other enemy of

Shardik. Within an hour he came to a place where an even wilder path branched northward to his left, and this he followed, clambering for a time through the undergrowth beside it to avoid leaving traces on the track itself.

At last, a little before noon, having heard and seen no one since his crossing of the Vrako, he sat down by the bank of a creek and, when he had eaten, fell to considering what he should do. Underlying all his thoughts, like a rock submerged in a swirling pool, was the conviction that he had passed some mysterious but nonetheless real spiritual boundary, over which he could never return. What was the meaning of the adventure at the Streels of Urtah, the news of which the shepherds had heard with so much awe and fear? What had befallen him in his oblivion on the battlefield, while he lay at the mercy of the unavenged dead? And why had Elleroth spared the life of one whose rule had brought about the loss of his own son? Pondering these inexplicable happenings, he knew that they had quenched the strength and faith that had burned in the heart of the priest-king of Bekla. Little more than a ghost he now felt himself to be, a drained thing haunting a body wasted with hardship.

Deepest bell of all that tolled in his heart was Elleroth's news of Shardik. Shardik had crossed the Vrako and was believed to be dying—in that there could have been no deceit. And if he, Kelderek, still set any value on his life, his best course would be to accept it. In a country of this nature, to look for Shardik would be only to invite such danger and hardship as neither his mind nor his body were capable of withstanding. Either he would be murdered, or he would die in the forests of the hills. Shardik, whether alive or dead, was irrecoverable; and for the least chance of life he himself ought to head south, contrive somehow to make his way into northern Tonilda and then reach the Ortelgan army.

Yet an hour later he was once more climbing northward, holding, with no attempt at concealment or self-protection, to the track as it wound into the lower hills. Elleroth, he thought bitterly, had rated him accurately enough. "Take my word for it, neither he nor the bear can harm us now." No indeed, for he was the priest of Shardik and nothing else besides. Afraid of

Ta-Kominion's contempt, and influenced by him to believe that the will of God could be none other than that Shardik should conquer Bekla, he had stood by while the Tuginda was bound and led away like a criminal, and had then gone on to set himself up as the mediator of Shardik's favor to his people. Without Shardik he would be nothing—a rainmaker mumbling in a drought, a magician whose spells had failed. To return to Zelda and Ged-la-Dan with the news (if they did not already know it) that Elleroth was with the Yeldashay and Shardik lost forever would be to sign his own death warrant. They would scarcely lose a day in getting rid of such a figure of defeat. Elleroth knew this. Yet he knew more. He had understood, as many an enemy would not, Kelderek's passionate faith and the integrity of his belief in Shardik. As an experienced master, though privately entertaining contempt for a servant's personal values and beliefs, can nevertheless perceive that by his own lights that servant is capable of sincerity, even, perhaps, of courage and self-denial, so Elleroth, hating Shardik, had known that Kelderek, whatever gleams of hope fortune might tempt him with, would be unable to separate his own fate from that of the bear. And this was why, since he also knew—or supposed that he knew, thought Kelderek with a sudden spurt of forlorn defiance—that Shardik was dying, he had seen no harm in sparing the priest-king's life. But why had he actually gone about to impose his will in this matter upon those surrounding him? Could it be, Kelderek wondered, that he himself had become visibly marked with some sign, perceptible to such as Elleroth, of being accursed, of having passed through merited sufferings to a final inviolability in which he was now to remain, to await the retribution of God? At this thought, shuffling slowly on through the solitude, he sighed and muttered under the burden of his misery, for all the world like some demented old woman in a desolated town, bearing in her arms the weight of a dead child.

Even in this notorious no-man's-land he had not expected so complete an emptiness. All day he met never a soul, heard no voice, saw no smoke. As afternoon turned to evening he realized that he would be forced to pass the night without shelter. In the old days, as a hunter, he had sometimes spent nights in the forest, but seldom alone and never without fire or weapons. To send him across the Vrako without even a knife and with no means of making a fire—had this perhaps been intended, after all, as nothing but a cruel way of putting him to death? And Shardik—whom he would never find—was Shardik already dead? Sitting with his head in his hands, he passed into a kind of waking oblivion that was not sleep, but rather the exhaustion of a mind unable any longer to grip thought, slipping and sliding like wheels in the mud of the rains.

When at last he lifted his head he at once caught sight, among the bushes close by, of an object so familiar that although it had been carefully concealed, he felt surprise not to have noticed it earlier. It was a trap—a wooden block-fall such as he himself had often set in days gone by. It was baited with carrion and dried fruit, but these had not been touched and the trip peg was still supporting the block.

The evening wanted no more than two hours to nightfall and, as well he knew, those who leave traps unvisited overnight are apt to find the next day that scavenging beasts have reached them first. He scratched out his footprints with a broken branch, climbed a tree and waited.

In less than an hour he heard the sounds of someone approaching. The man who appeared was dark, thickset and shaggy-haired, dressed partly in skins and partly in old, ragged garments. A knife and two or three arrows were stuck in his belt and he was carrying a bow. He bent down, peered at the trap under the bushes and was already turning away when Kelderek called to him. At this he started, drew his knife in a flash and vanished into the undergrowth. Kelderek realized that if he were not to lose him altogether he must take a risk. He scrambled to the ground, calling, "I beg you, don't go! I need help."

"What you want, then?" answered the man, invisible among the trees.

"Shelter—advice too. I'm a fugitive, exile—whatever you like. I'm in trouble."

"Who isn't? You're this side the Vrako, aren't you?"

"I'm unarmed. Look for yourself." He threw down the pack, raised his arms and turned one way and the other.

"Unarmed? Then you're mad." The man stepped out from

the bushes and came up to him. He was indeed a ruffian of frightening appearance, swarthy and scowling, with a yellow, mucous discharge of the eyes and a scar from mouth to neck which reminded Kelderek of Bel-ka-Trazet.

"I'm in no state to play tricks or drive a bargain," said Kelderek. "This pack's full of food and nothing else. Take it and give me shelter for tonight."

The man picked up the pack, opened and looked into it, tossed it back to Kelderek and nodded. Then, turning, he set off in the direction from which he had come. After a time he said,

"No one after you?"

"Not since the Vrako."

They walked on in silence. Kelderek was struck by the complete absence of that friendly curiosity which usually finds a place in strangers' meetings. If the man wondered who he was, whence he had come and why, he evidently did not intend to ask; and there was that about him which made Kelderek think better of putting any questions on his own account. This, he realized, must be the nature of acquaintance in this country of shame for the past and hopelessness for the future—the courtesy of the prison and the madhouse. However, some kinds of question were apparently permissible, for after a time the man jerked out, "Thought what you're going to do?"

"Not yet—die, I dare say."

The man looked sharply at him and Kelderek realized that he had spoken amiss. Here men were like beasts at bay—defiant until they were torn to pieces. The whole country, like a brigands' cave, was divided into bullies and victims—the last place in which to speak of death, whether in jest or acceptance. Confused, and too weary to dissimulate, he said,

"I was joking. I've got a purpose, though I dare say that to you it may seem a strange one. I'm looking for a bear that's believed to be in these parts. If I could find it—"

He stopped, for the man, his mouth and jaw thrust forward, was staring at him from his oozing eyes with a mixture of fear and rage—the rage of one who attacks whatever he does not understand. He said nothing, however, and after a moment Kelderek stammered, "It—it's the truth. I'm not trying to make a fool of you—"

"Better not," answered the man. "So you're not alone, then?"

"I've never been more alone in my life."

The man drew his knife, seized him by the wrist and forced him to his knees. Kelderek looked up into the snarling, violent face.

"What's this about the bear, then? What you up to—what you know about the other one—the woman, eh?"

"What other one? For God's sake, I don't know what you mean!"

"Don't know what I mean?"

Panting, Kelderek shook his head and after a moment the man released him.

"Better come and see, then: better come and see. You mind now, I don't take to tricks."

They went on again, the man still clutching his knife and Kelderek half minded to run from him into the woods. Only his exhaustion held him back, for the man would probably pursue, overtake and perhaps kill him. They crossed a ridge and descended steeply toward a dreary, stagnant creek. Smoke hung in the trees. A patch of ground along the shore, cleared after a fashion, was littered with bones, feathers and other rubbish. At one side, too near the water, stood a lopsided, chimneyless hovel of poles, branches and mud. There were clouds of flies. Three or four skins were pegged out to dry, and some black birds—crows or rooks—were huddled in a wooden pen on the marshy ground. The place, like a song out of tune, seemed an offense against the world, for which the only possible remedy was obliteration.

The man again grasped Kelderek's wrist and half-led, half-dragged him toward the hut. A curtain of dusty skins hung across the entrance. The man jerked his head and gestured with his knife but Kelderek, stupid with fatigue, fear and disgust, did not understand that he was to enter first. The man, seizing his shoulder, pushed him so that he stumbled against the curtain. He pulled it aside, ducked his head and went in.

The walls surrounded a single, evil-smelling space, at the farther end of which a fire was smoldering. There was little light, for apart from the curtained door and a hole in the roof, through which some of the smoke escaped, there was no opening; at the farther end, however, he made out a human shape, wrapped in a cloak and sitting, back toward him, on a rough bench beside the fire. As he peered, bending forward and flinching from the knife at his back, the figure rose and turned to face him. It was the Tuginda.

40 Ruvit

SUDDENLY TO BE CONFRONTED with a shameful deed from the past, a deed accomplished yet uneffaced, like the ruins of a poor man's house destroyed by some selfish lord to suit his own convenience, or the body of an unwanted child cast up by the river on the shore: to stumble unexpectedly upon an accusation that no bravado can defy nor glib tongue turn aside; an accusation made not aloud, to the ears of the world, but quietly, face to face, without anger, perhaps even without speech, to one unprepared for the surge of his own confusion, guilt and regret. The harp of Binnorie named its murderess, and the two pretty babes in the ballad answered the cruel mother under her father's castle wall. Stones have been known to move and trees to speak. Yet never a word said Banquo's ghost. Though few can have touched a murdered corpse and seen the wounds burst open and bleed, yet many, coming alone upon old letters thrust into a drawer, have reread them weeping for pardon; or again, burning with self-contempt, have learned from chance remarks how unforgotten has been the misery, how crushing the disappointment brought by themselves upon those who never spoke of it. The deeply wronged, like ghosts, have no need to speak to their oppressors or accuse them before crowds. More terrible by far is their unexpected and silent reappearance in some secluded place, at some unguarded hour.

The Tuginda stood beside the bench, her eyes half-closed against the smoke. For some moments she did not recognize him. Then she started, jerking up her head. At the same instant Kelderek, with a sudden, sharp sob, thrust his hand between his teeth, turned and was already halfway through the entrance when he was pushed violently backward and fell to the ground. The man, knife in hand, was staring down at him, gnawing his lip and panting with a kind of feral excitement. This, Kelderek realized on the ghastly instant, was one to whom murder must once have been both trade and sport. In his clouded mind violence hung always, precarious as a sword by a hair; by another's fear or flight it was excited as uncontrollably as a cat by the scuttling of a mouse. This was some bandit survivor with a price on his head, some hired assassin who had outlived his usefulness to his employers and run for the Vrako before the informer could turn him in. How many solitary wanderers had he killed in this place?

The man, bending over him, was breathing in low, rhythmic gasps. Kelderek, supporting himself on one elbow, tried in vain to return the maniac glare with a look of authority. As his eyes fell, the Tuginda spoke from behind him.

"Calm yourself, Ruvit! I know this man—he is harmless. You are not to hurt him."

"Hiding in the woods, talked about the bear. 'Up to tricks,' I thought, 'up to tricks. Make him go in, don't tell him anything, ah, that's it. Find out what he's up to, find out what he's up to—' "

"He won't hurt you, Ruvit. Come and make up the fire, and after supper I'll bathe your eyes again. Put your knife away."

She led the man gently to the fire, talking as though to a child, and Kelderek followed, not knowing what else to do. At the sound of her voice the tears had sprung to his eyes, but he brushed them away without a word. The man took no further notice of him and he sat down on a rickety stool, watching the Tuginda as she knelt to blow the fire, put on a pot and stirred it with a broken spit. Once she looked across at him, but he dropped his eyes; and when he looked up again she was busy over a clay lamp, which she trimmed and then lit with a kindled twig. The wan, single flame threw shadows along the floor and as darkness fell seemed less to brighten the squalid hut than to serve, with its guttering and wavering in the drafts that came through the ill-made walls, as a reminder of the defenselessness of all who might have the misfortune to be, like itself, solitary and conspicuous in this sad country.

She had aged, he thought, and had the look of one who had endured both loss and disappointment. Yet she was unextinguished—a fire burned low, a tree stripped by a winter gale. In this horrible place, beyond help or safety, alone with one man who had betrayed her and another who was half-crazy and probably a murderer, her authority asserted itself quietly and surely, in part as mundane as that of some shrewd, honest farmer talking with those whom he makes feel that it will be better not to try to cheat him. But beyond this open foreground of the spirit he could perceive, as he had perceived long ago—as he knew that even poor, murderous Ruvit could sense, in the same way that a dog is aware of the presence of joy or grief in a house—the deeper, more mysterious country of her strength. She was possessed of the immunity not only of priestess, pilgrim and doctor, but also of that conferred by the mystery whose servant she was—by the power which he had felt before ever he met her, when he had sat slumped in the canoe drifting down to Quiso in the dark. No wonder, he thought, that Ta-Kominion had died. No wonder that the headlong, fiery ambition which had blinded him to the strength in her had also poisoned him beyond recovery.

He began to consider the manner of his own death. Some, or so he had heard, had dragged out their lives beyond the Vrako until the prices on their heads and even the nature of their crimes had been forgotten and nothing but their own despair and addled wits prevented their return to towns where none was left who could recall what they had done. Such survival was not for him. Shardik, if only he could find him, would at last take the life which had been so often offered to him—would take his life before the contemptible desire to survive on any terms could transform him into a creature like Ruvit.

Lost in these thoughts, he heard little or nothing of whatever passed between Ruvit and the Tuginda as she finished preparing the meal. Vaguely, he was aware that although Ruvit had become quiet he was nevertheless afraid of the fall of darkness, and that the Tuginda was reassuring him. He wondered how long the man had lived here, facing nightfall alone, and what it was that had made this life—a hard one, surely, even for a fugitive beyond the Vrako—the only one he dared to live. After a time the Tuginda brought him food, and as she gave it to him, laid her hand for a moment on his shoulder. Still he said nothing, only nodding wretchedly, unable to meet her eyes. Yet when he had eaten, as is the way, some shreds of spirit involuntarily returned to him. He sat closer to the fire, watching as the Tuginda swabbed the discharge from Ruvit's eyes and bathed them with some herbal infusion. With her he was quiet and amenable, and at moments almost resembled what he might have been if evil had not consumed him—a decent, stupid drover, perhaps, or the hard-handed tapster of an inn.

They slept clothed, on the ground, as needs they must, the Tuginda making no complaint of the dirt and discomfort, or even of the vermin that gave them no peace. Kelderek slept little, mistrusting Ruvit on both his own account and the Tuginda's; but it seemed rather that the poor wretch welcomed the chance of a night's sleep free from his superstitious fears, for he never moved till morning.

Soon after first light Kelderek blew up the fire, found a wooden pail and, glad to get into the fresh air, made his way to the shore, washed and then returned with water for the Tuginda. He could not bring himself to rouse her, but went outside again into the first sunlight. His resolve was unchanged. Indeed, he now saw in himself a gulf like that into which he had gazed from the plain of Urtah. The blasphemous wrong, in which he had participated, inflicted by Ta-Kominion upon the Tuginda, was but a part of that wider, far-reaching evil of his own committing—the sacrilege against Shardik himself and all that had followed from it. Rantzay, Mollo, Elleroth, the children sold into slavery in Bekla, the dead soldiers whose voices had flickered about him in the dark—they came thrusting, jagged and sharp, into his mind as he stood beside the creek. When the Tamarrik Gate had finally collapsed, he remembered, there had been a great central breach, from which had radiated splintered fissures and rifts, fragments of exquisitely carved wood, shards of silver sagging inward, shattered likenesses no longer recognizable in the ruin. The Ortelgans had cheered and shouted, smashing their way forward through the wreckage with cries of "Shardik! Shardik!"

His tears fell silently. "Accept my life, Lord Shardik! O God, only take my life!"

He heard a step behind him and, turning, saw that his prayer was answered. A few feet away Ruvit stood looking at him, knife in hand. He knelt down, offering his throat and heart and opening his arms as though to a guest.

"Strike quickly, Ruvit, before I have time to feel afraid!"

Ruvit stared at him a moment in astonishment; then, sheathing his knife, he stepped forward with a shifty, lopsided grin, took Kelderek's hand and pulled him to his feet.

"Ay, ay, old feller, mustn't take it that way, ye know. Comes hard to start with, eels get used to skinning, know what they say, never look back across the Vrako, drive ye crazy. Just on me way to kill a bird. Some wrings their necks, I always cuts their heads off." He looked over his shoulder toward the door behind him and whispered, "You know what? That's a priestess, that is. Ever gets back, she's going to put in a word for me. Thought yesterday she wanted you dead, but she don't. Ah—put in a word for me, she says. That the truth, think that's the truth, eh?"

"It's the truth," answered Kelderek. "She could get you a pardon in any city from Ikat to Deelguy. It's for me she can't."

"Got to forget it here, lad, forget it, that's it. Five year, ten year, call the lice your friends after ten year, ye know."

He killed the bird, plucked and drew it, left the guts lying on the ground and together they returned to the hovel.

Two hours later Kelderek, having given to Ruvit what was left of the food he had brought from Kabin, set out with the Tuginda along the shore of the creek.

41 *The Legend of the Streels*

STILL HE COULD NOT BRING HIMSELF to speak of the past. At last he said,

"Where are you going, säiyett?"

She made no immediate answer, but after a little asked,

"Kelderek, are you seeking Lord Shardik?"

"Yes."

"With what purpose?"

He startled, remembering her strange power of discerning more than had been spoken. If she had perceived the intention which he had formed, she would no doubt try to dissuade him, though God knew she of all people had little reason to wish to prolong his life. Then he realized of what it was that she must be thinking.

"Lord Shardik will never return to Bekla," he said. "That's certain enough—and neither shall I."

"Are you not king of Bekla?"

"No longer."

They left the creek and began to follow a track leading eastward over the next ridge. The Tuginda climbed slowly and more than once stopped to rest. "She has no strength now for this life," he thought. "Even were there no danger, she ought not to be here." He began to wonder how he could persuade her to return to Quiso.

"Säiyett, why have you come here? Are you also seeking Shardik?"

"I received news in Quiso that Lord Shardik was gone from Bekla and then that he had crossed the plain to the hills west of Gelt. Naturally I set out in search of him."

"But why, säiyett? You should not have undertaken such a journey. The hardship—"

"You forget, Kelderek." Her voice was hard. "As Tuginda of Quiso I am bound to follow Lord Shardik while that is possible —that is, while the Power of God is not subjected to the power of men."

He was silent, full of shame; but later, as she was leading the way downhill, he asked,

"But your women—the other priestesses—you did not leave Quiso alone?"

"No, I received news also of the advance north of Santil-kè-Erketlis. I had known already that he meant to march in the spring and that he intended to take Kabin. Neelith and three other girls set out for Kabin with me. We planned to seek Lord Shardik from there."

"Did you speak with Erketlis?"

"I spoke with Elleroth of Sarkid, who told me how it came about that he escaped from Bekla. He was well-disposed toward me because some time ago I cured his sister's husband of a poisoned arm. He told me also that Lord Shardik had crossed the Vrako in the foothills north of Kabin, not two days before."

"You say Elleroth treated you as a friend—and yet he allowed you to go alone and unescorted across the Vrako?"

"He does not know that I have crossed the Vrako. Elleroth was friendly to me, but on one thing I could not move him. He would lend me no help to find Lord Shardik or save his life. To him and his soldiers Shardik means nothing but the god of their enemies and of all that they are fighting against." She paused and then, with a momentary tremor in her voice, added, "He said—the god of the slave traders."

Kelderek had not thought that he could suffer more bitterly.

"He told me of his son," went on the Tuginda, "and after that I asked nothing more of him. He told me, too, that some of his soldiers had come upon Lord Shardik in the hills and felt sure that he was dying. I asked him why they had not killed him and he replied that they had been afraid to attempt it. So I do not myself believe that Lord Shardik is dying."

At this he was about to speak, but she went on,

"I had hoped that Elleroth might give me some soldiers to conduct us across the Vrako, but when I saw that it was useless to ask, I let him believe that we meant to return to Quiso, for he would certainly have stopped me from crossing the Vrako alone."

"But would none of the girls come with you, säiyett?"

"Do you think that I would bring them into this country—the thieves' kitchen of the world? They begged to come. I told them to return to Quiso, and since they are bound by oath to obey me, they went. After that I bribed the guards at the ford and once across the river I turned north, as you did."

"Säiyett, where do you mean to go now?"

"I believe that Shardik is trying to return to his own country. He is making for the Telthearna and will cross it if he can. Therefore I am going to Zeray, to seek help in watching for him along the western shore. Or if he has already swum the Telthearna, we may learn of it in Zeray."

"Elleroth, perhaps, was right. Shardik may indeed be dying, for since leaving Bekla he has once more been wickedly and cruelly wounded."

She stopped, turned and stared up at him. "Did Elleroth tell you that?"

He shook his head.

She sat down but said no more, only continuing to look at him with eyes full of uncertainty and questioning. Seeking for further words, he burst out,

"Säiyett, the Streels of Urtah—what is their mystery and their meaning?"

At this she gave a quick, low gasp, as it were of dread and consternation; but then, recovering herself, answered, "You had better tell me what you know yourself."

He told her how he had followed Shardik out of Bekla and of their crossing of the plain. She listened silently until he came to the adventure at Urtah, but as he spoke of his awakening and of the wounded Shardik climbing from the Streel to scatter his attackers, she began to weep bitterly, sobbing aloud, as women mourn for the dead. Appalled by this passionate grief in one whom he had hitherto thought of as stretching out her scepter over all ills besetting the heart of man, he waited with a hopeless, leaden patience, not presuming to intrude upon her sorrow, since he perceived that it flowed from some bitter knowledge which he, too, must presently possess.

At length, becoming calmer, she began to speak; her voice was like that of a woman who, having learned of some terrible bereavement, understands that henceforth her life will be a waiting for death.

"You asked me, Kelderek, about the Streels of Urtah. I will tell you what I know, though that is little enough, for the cult is a close secret inherited by each generation, and such is the fear of it that I never heard of any who dared to pry into those mysteries. But though, thank God, I have never seen the Streels, a little I know—the little I have been told because I am the Tuginda of Quiso.

"How deep the Streels are no one knows, for none has ever descended into their depths and returned. Some say they are the mouths of hell, and that the souls of the wicked enter them by night. They say, too, that only to look down and cry aloud into the Streels is sufficient to awaken a torment that will drive a man mad."

Kelderek, his eyes on her face, nodded. "It is true."

"And how old the cult is no one knows, or what it is they worship. But this I can tell you. Always, for hundreds of years, their mystery at Urtah has been the bringing of retribution upon the wicked—those, that is, for whom such retribution has been ordained by God. Many are wicked, as well you know, yet not all the wicked find their way to the Streels. This—or so I have always understood—is the way of that dreadful business. The evildoer is one whose crime cries out to heaven, beyond restitution or forgiveness; one whose life, continuing, defiles the very earth. And it is always by some accident that he appears to come to Urtah: he is in ignorance of the nature of the place to which his journey has led him. He may be attended or he may be alone, but always he himself believes that it is chance, or some business of his own, which has brought him to Urtah of his own free will. Yet those who watch there—those who see him come—*they* recognize him for what he is and know what they have to do.

"They speak him fair and treat him courteously, for however foul his crime it is none of their duty to hate him, any more than the lightning hates the tree. They are but the agents of God. And they will not trick him either. He must be shown the place and asked whether he knows its name. Only when he answers 'No' do they persuade him toward the Streels. Even then he must—"

She stopped suddenly and looked up at Kelderek.

"Did you enter the Streel?"

"No, säiyett. As I told you, I—"

"I know what you told me. I am asking you—are you sure that you did not enter the Streel?"

He stared at her, frowning, then nodded. "I am sure, säiyett."

"He must enter the Streel of his own accord. Once he has done that, nothing can save him. It becomes their task to kill him and cast his body into the depths of the Streel.

"Some who have died there have been men of rank and power, but all have been guilty of some deed whose vileness and cruelty prey upon the very minds of those who hear it. You will have heard of Hypsas, for he came from Ortelga."

Kelderek closed his eyes, beating one hand upon his knee.

"I remember. Would to God I did not."

"Did you know that he died in the Streels? He intended to escape to Bekla or perhaps to Paltesh, but it was to Urtah that he came."

"I didn't know. They say only that he vanished."

"Very few know what I have told you—priests and rulers for the most part. There was King Manvarizon of Terekenalt, he that was grandfather of King Karnat the Tall. He burned alive his dead brother's wife, together with her little son, his nephew, the rightful king, whose life and throne he had sworn to defend. Five years later, being on the plain of Bekla at the head of his army, he came to Urtah with a few followers, his purpose, so he thought, being to spy out that land for himself. He ran screaming into the Streel, flying from none but a little herd-boy who was driving sheep—or perhaps from some other little boy that no one else could see. They saw him draw his sword, but he flung it to the ground as he ran, and there no doubt it lies to this day, for no possession of a victim is ever taken, buried or destroyed."

"You say that all who enter the Streels must die?"

"Yes, from that moment their death is certain. One respite only there may be, but it is very rare—almost unknown. Once in a hundred years, perhaps, it may happen that the victim comes alive from the Streel: and then they will not touch him, for that is a sign that God has sanctified him and intends to make use of his death for some blessed and mysterious purpose of His own. Long, long ago, there was a girl who fled with her lover across the Beklan plain. Her two brothers—hard, cruel men—were following, for they meant to kill them both, and she saw that her lover was afraid. She was determined to save him and she stole away by night and came upon her brothers as they slept; and for his sake, because she dared not kill them, she blinded them both in their sleep. Later—how, I do not know—she came alone to Urtah and there she was stabbed and thrown down as she lay in the Streel. But that night she climbed out alive, though wounded almost to death. They let her go, and she died in giving birth to a boy. That boy was the hero U-Deparioth, the liberator of Yelda and the first Ban of Sarkid."

"And that is why Elleroth knows what you have told me?"

"He would know that and more besides, for the House of Sarkid has been honored by the priests of Urtah from that day to this. He would certainly have received news of what befell Lord Shardik and yourself at Urtah."

"How is it that I never learned of the Streels in Bekla? I knew much, for men were paid to tell me all; yet this I never knew."

"Few know, and of them none would tell you."

"But you have told me!"

She began to weep once more. "Now I believe what Elleroth said to me at Kabin. I know why his men did not hurt Lord Shardik and why he spared your life also. No doubt he was not told that you yourself had not entered the Streel. He would indeed be insistent that your life must be spared, for once he knew that Lord Shardik—and you, as he supposed—had come alive from the Streels, he would know, too, that neither must be touched on pain of sacrilege. Shardik's death is appointed by God, and it is certain—certain!" She seemed exhausted with grief.

Kelderek took her hand.

"But säiyett, Lord Shardik is guilty of no evil."

She lifted her head, staring out over the dismal woods.

"Shardik has committed no evil." She turned and looked full into his eyes. "Shardik—no: Shardik has committed no evil!"

42 The Way to Zeray

WHERE THE TRACK WAS LEADING he did not know, or even whether it still ran eastward, for now the trees were thick and they followed it in half-light under a close roof of branches. Several times he was tempted to leave altogether the faint thread of a path and simply go downhill, find a stream and follow it—an old hunter's trick which, as he knew, often leads to a dwelling or village, though it may be with difficulty. But the Tuginda, he saw, would not be equal to such a course. Since resuming their journey she had spoken little and walked, or so it seemed to him, like one going where she would not. Never before had she appeared to him subdued in spirit. He recalled how, even on the Gelt road, she had stepped firmly and deliberately away down the hillside, as though undaunted by her shameful arrest at the hands of Ta-Kominion. She had trusted God then, he thought. She had known that God could afford to wait, and therefore so could she. Even before he himself had caged Shardik at the cost of Rantzay's life, the Tuginda had known that the time would come when she would be called once more to follow the Power of God. She had recognized, when it came, the day of Shardik's liberation from the imprisonment to which he himself had subjected him. What she had not foreseen was Urtah—the destination ordained for the bloody beast-god of the Ortelgans, in whose name his followers had—

Unable to bear these thoughts, he flung up his head, striking one hand against his brow and slashing at the bushes with his stick. The Tuginda seemed not to notice his sudden violence, but walked slowly on as before, her eyes on the ground.

"In Bekla," he said, breaking their silence, "I felt many times that I was close to a great secret to be revealed through Lord Shardik—a secret which would show men at last the meaning of their lives on earth, how to safeguard the future, how to be secure. We would no longer be blind and ignorant, but God's servants, knowing how He meant us to live. Yet though I suffered much, both waking and sleeping, I never learned that secret."

"The door was locked," she answered listlessly.

"It was I who locked it," he said, and so fell silent once more.

Late in the afternoon, emerging at last from the woods, they came to a miserable hamlet of three or four huts beside a stream. Two men who could not understand him, but muttered to each other in a tongue he had never heard, searched him from head to foot but found nothing to steal. They would have handled and searched the Tuginda also had he not seized one by the wrist and flung him aside. Evidently they thought that whatever chance of gain there might be was not worth a fight, for they stood back, cursing, or so it seemed, and gesturing to him to be off. Before the Tuginda and he had gone a stone's throw, however, a gaunt, ragged woman came running after them, held out a morsel of hard bread and, smiling with blackened teeth, pointed back toward the huts. The Tuginda returned her smile, accepting the invitation with no sign of fear and he, feeling that it mattered little what might befall him, made no objection. The woman, scolding shrilly at the two men standing a little distance off, seated her guests on a bench outside one of the huts and brought them bowls of thin soup containing a kind of tasteless gray root that crumbled to fibrous shreds in the mouth. Two other women gathered and three or four rickety, potbellied children, who stared silently and seemed to lack the energy to shout or scuffle. The Tuginda thanked the woman gravely in Ortelgan, kissing their filthy hands and smiling at each in turn. Kelderek sat as he had sat the night before, lost in his thoughts and only half-aware that the children had begun to teach her some game with stones in the dust. Once or twice she laughed and the children laughed too, and by and by one of the surly men came and offered him a clay bowl full of weak, sour wine, first drinking himself to show there was no harm. Kelderek drank, gravely pledging his host; then watched the moon rise and later, invited into one of the huts, once more lay down to sleep upon the ground.

Waking in the night, he went out and saw another man sitting cross-legged beside a low fire. For a time he sat beside him without speaking, but at length, as the man bent forward to thrust one end of a fresh branch into the glow, he pointed toward the nearby stream and said, "Zeray?" The man nodded and, pointing to him, repeated, "Zeray?" and, when he nodded in his turn, laughed shortly and mimicked one in flight looking behind him for pursuers. Kelderek shrugged his shoulders and they said no more, each sitting by the fire until daybreak.

There was no path beside the stream and the Tuginda and he followed its course with difficulty through another tract of forest, from which it came out to plunge in a series of falls down a rocky hillside. Standing on the brow, he looked out over the plain below. Some miles away on their left the mountains still ran eastward. Following the chain with his eye he glimpsed, far off in the east, a thin, silver streak, dull and constant in the sunlight. He pointed to it.

"That must be the Telthearna, säiyett."

She nodded, and after a few moments he said, "I doubt whether Lord Shardik will ever reach it. And if we cannot trace him when we get there, I suppose we shall never know what became of him."

"Either you or I," she answered, "will find Lord Shardik again. I saw it in a dream."

After gazing intently for a little toward the southeast, she began to lead the way downhill among the tumbled boulders.

"What did you see, säiyett?" he asked when next they rested.

"I was looking for some trace of Zeray," she replied, "but of course there is nothing to be seen from so far." And he, acquiescing in the misunderstanding—whether deliberate on her part or otherwise—questioned her no further of Shardik.

From the foot of the hillside there stretched a wide marsh that mired them to the knees as they continued to follow the stream among pools and reed-clumps. Kelderek began to entertain a kind of fancy that he, like one in an old tale, was bewitched and changing, not swiftly, but day by day, from a man to an animal. The change had begun at the Vrako and continued imperceptibly until now, when he wandered like a beast in a field, pent within land not of his own choosing and where neither places nor people had names. The power of speech was gradually leaving him too, so that already he was able through long, waking hours, not only to be silent, but also actually to think nothing, his human awareness retracted to the smallest of points, like the pupil of a cat's eye in sunlight; while his life, continued by the sufferance of others, had become a meaningless span of existence before death. And more immediate to him now than any human regret or shame were simply the sores and other painful places beneath the sweat-stiffened hide of his clothes.

Crossing the marsh after some hours, they came at last upon a track and then to a village, the only one he had seen east of the Vrako, and the poorest and most wretched he could remember. They were resting a short distance outside it when a man carrying a faggot of brushwood passed them and Kelderek, leaving the Tuginda sitting beside the track, overtook him and asked once more the way to Zeray. The man pointed southeastward, answering in Beklan, "About half a day's journey: you'll not get there before dark." Then, in a lower tone and glancing across at the Tuginda, he added, "Poor old woman—the likes of her to be going to Zeray!" Kelderek must have glanced sharply at him for he added quickly, "No business of mine—she don't look well, that's all. Touch of fever, maybe," and at once went on his way with his burden, as though afraid that he might already have said too much in this country where the past was sharp splinters embedded in men's minds and an ill-judged word a false step in the dark.

They had hardly reached the first huts, the Tuginda leaning heavily upon Kelderek's arm, when a man barred their way. He was dirty and unsmiling, with blue tattoo marks on his cheeks, and the lobe of one ear pierced by a bone pin as long as a finger. He resembled none that Kelderek could remember to have seen among the multiracial trading throngs of Bekla. Yet when he spoke it was in a thick, distorted Beklan, one word making do for another.

"You walk from?"

Kelderek pointed northwestward, where the sun was beginning to set.

"High places trees? All through you walk?"

"Yes, from beyond the Vrako. We're going to Zeray. Let me save you trouble," said Kelderek. "We've nothing worth taking, and this woman, as you can see, is no longer young. She's exhausted."

"Sick. High places trees much sick. Not sit down here. Go away."

"She's not sick, only tired. I beg you—"

"Not sit down," shouted the man fiercely. "Go away!"

The Tuginda was about to speak to him when suddenly he turned his head and uttered a sharp cry, at which other men began to appear from among the huts. The tattooed man shouted, "Woman sick," in Beklan, and then broke into some other language, at which they nodded, responding, "Ay! ay!" After a few moments the Tuginda, relinquishing Kelderek's arm, turned and began walking slowly back up the track. He followed. As he reached her side a stone struck her on the shoulder,

383

so that she staggered and fell against him. A second stone pitched into the dust at their feet and the next struck him on the heel. Shouting had broken out behind them. Without looking around, he bowed his head against the falling stones, put his arm around the Tuginda's shoulders and half-dragged, half-carried her back in the direction from which they had come.

Helping her to a patch of grass, he sat down beside her. She was trembling, her breath coming in gasps, but after a few moments she opened her eyes and half-rose to her feet, looking back down the road.

"Damn and blast the bastards!" whispered the Tuginda. Then, meeting his stare, she laughed. "Didn't you know, Kelderek, that there are times when everyone swears? And I had brothers once, long ago." She put her hand over her eyes and swayed a moment. "That brute was right, though—I'm not well."

"You've eaten nothing all day, säiyett—"

"Never mind. If we can find somewhere to lie down and sleep, we shall reach Zeray tomorrow. And there I believe we may find help."

Wandering over the ground nearby, he came upon a stack of turves, and of these made a kind of shelter in which they huddled side by side for warmth. The Tuginda was restless and feverish, talking in her sleep of Rantzay and Sheldra and of autumn leaves to be swept from the Ledges. Kelderek lay awake, tormented by hunger and the pain in his heel. Soon, now, he thought, the change would be complete and as an animal he would suffer less. The stars moved on and at length, watching them, he also fell asleep.

Soon after dawn, for fear of the villagers, he roused the Tuginda and led her away through a ground-mist as white and chill as that through which Elleroth had been brought to execution. To see her reduced to infirmity, catching her breath as she leaned upon him and compelled to rest after every stone's throw walked at the pace of a blind beggar, not only wrung his heart but filled him also with misgiving—the misgiving of one who observes some portent in the sky, and fears its boding. The Tuginda, like any other woman of flesh and blood, was not equal to the hardship and danger of this land; like any other woman, she could sicken, and perhaps die. Contemplating this possibility, he realized that always, even in Bekla, he had unconsciously felt her to be standing, compassionate and impervious, between himself and the consuming truth of God. He, the impostor, had stolen from her everything of Shardik—his bodily presence, his ceremony, the power and adulation—all that was of men: everything but the invisible burden of responsibility borne by Shardik's rightful mediator, the inward knowledge that if she failed there was none other. She it was and not he who for more than five years had borne a spiritual load made doubly heavy by his own abuse of Shardik. If now she were to die, so that none remained between him and the truth of God, then he, lacking the necessary wisdom and humility, would not be fit to step into her place. He was found out in his pretensions, and the last action of the fraudulent priest-king should be, not to seek death from Shardik, of which he was unworthy, but rather to creep, like a cockroach from the light, into some crevice of this country of perdition, there to await whatever death might befall him from sickness or violence. Meanwhile the fate of Shardik would remain unknown: he would vanish unwatched and unattended, like a great rock dislodged from a mountainside, that smashes its way downward, coming to rest at last in trackless forests far below.

Afterward, of all that took place during that day he could recall only one incident. A few miles beyond the village, they came upon a group of men and women working in a field. A little distance away from the others, two girls were resting. One had a baby at the breast and both, as they laughed and talked, were eating from a wicker basket. Half a mile farther on he persuaded the Tuginda to lie down and rest, told her he would return soon and hastened back to the field. Approaching unseen, he crept close to the two girls, sprang suddenly upon them, snatched their basket and ran. They screamed but, as he had calculated, their friends were slow to reach them and there was no pursuit. He was out of sight, had wolfed half the food, thrown away the basket and rejoined the Tuginda almost before they had decided that a silly girl's few handfuls of bread and dried fruit were not worth the loss of an hour's work. As he limped away on his bruised heel, coaxing the Tuginda to swallow the crusts and raisins he had brought back, he reflected that starvation and misery made an apt pupil. Ruvit himself could hardly have done better, unless indeed he had silenced the girls with his knife.

Evening was falling once more when he realized that they must at last be approaching Zeray. They had seen few people all day and none had spoken to or molested them, due no doubt partly to their destitution, which showed them, clearly enough, to be not worth robbing, and partly to the evident sickness of the Tuginda. There had been no more woodland and Kelderek had simply gone southeast by the sun through an open wilderness, broken here and there by sorry pastures and small patches of ploughed land. Finally they had come once more to reeds and sedges, and so to the shore of a creek which he guessed to be an inlet of the Telthearna itself. They followed it a little way inland, rounded the head and so came to the southern bank, along which they made their way. As it grew broader he could see, beyond the creek's mouth, the Telthearna itself, narrower here than at Ortelga and running very strongly, the eastern shore rocky in the distance across the water. Even through his despair a kind of dull, involuntary echo of pleasure stole upon him, a subdued lightening of the spirit, faint as a nimbus of the moon behind white clouds. That water had flowed past Ortelga's reeds, had rippled over Ortelga's broken causeway. He tried to point it out to the Tuginda, but she only shook her head wearily, scarcely able to follow even the direction of his arm. If she were to die in Zeray, he thought, his last duty would be to ensure that somehow the news was carried upstream to Quiso. Despite what she had said, there seemed little hope of their finding help in a remote, squalid settlement peopled almost entirely (or so he had always understood) by fugitives from the justice of half a dozen lands. He could see the outskirts now, much like those of Ortelga—huts and wood smoke, circling birds and in the evening air, from which the sunlight was beginning to fade, the glitter of the Telthearna.

"Where are we, Kelderek?" whispered the Tuginda. Almost her whole weight was upon his arm and she was gray-faced and sweating. He helped her to drink from a clear pool and then supported her to a little grassy mound nearby.

"This is Zeray, säiyett, as I suppose."

"But here—this place?"

He looked about him. They were in what seemed a kind of wild, untended garden, where spring flowers were growing and trees stood in bloom. A melikon hung over the water, the peasants' False Lasses covered with the blossoms which would later turn to golden berries dropping in the still summer air. Everywhere were low banks and mounds like the one on which they were sitting; and now he saw that several of these had been roughly marked with stones or pieces of wood stuck in the ground. Some looked new, others old and dilapidated. At a little distance were four or five mounds of newly turned earth, ungrassed and strewn with a few flowers and black beads.

"This is a graveyard, säiyett. It must be the burial ground of Zeray."

She nodded. "Sometimes in these places they have a watchman to keep off animals at night. He might—" She broke off, coughing, but then resumed, with an effort, "He might tell us something of Zeray."

"Rest here, säiyett. I will go and see."

He set off among the graves and had not gone far when he saw at a little distance the figure of a woman standing in prayer. Her back was toward him and both she and the raised grave-pile beside which she was standing were outlined against the sky. The sides of the grave had been faced with boards, carved and painted, giving it something of the appearance of a large, decorated chest; and, by contrast with the neglected humps all around, it possessed a kind of grandeur. At one end a pennant had been thrust upright in the soil, but the cloth hung limp, unstirred by the least wind, and he could not see the device. The woman, dressed in black and bareheaded like a mourner, appeared to be young. He wondered whether the grave to which she had come alone was that of her husband and whether he had died a natural or a violent death. Slim and graceful against the pale sky, her arms extended and hands raised palm forward, she was standing motionless, as though for her the beauty and dignity of this traditional posture constituted in themselves a prayer as devout as any words or thoughts that could proceed from her mind.

"This," he thought, "is a woman to whom it is natural to express her feelings—even grief—through her body as well as through her lips. If Zeray contains even one woman of such grace, perhaps it cannot be altogether vile."

He was about to go up to her when the sudden thought of how he must appear made him hesitate and turn away. Since leaving Bekla he had not once seen his own reflection, but he remembered Ruvit, like some shambling, red-eyed animal, and the ragged, stinking men who had first searched and then befriended him. Why this woman was here alone, he could not tell. Perhaps young women in Zeray commonly went about alone, though from all that he had ever heard of the place this seemed unlikely. Could she perhaps be some courtesan mourning a favorite lover? Whatever the reason, the sight of himself would probably alarm her and might even put her to flight. But she would feel no fear of the Tuginda and might even take pity on her.

He retraced his steps to the water.

"Säiyett, there is a woman praying not far away—a young woman. For me to approach her alone would only frighten her. If I help you, and we go slowly, can you come with me?"

She nodded, licking her dry lips and stretching out both hands for his. Helping her to her feet, he supported her faltering steps among the graves. The young woman was still standing motionless, her arms raised as though to draw down peace and blessing upon the dead friend or lover earth-wrapped at her feet. The posture, as well he knew, became a strained one in no long while, yet she seemed heedless of discomfort, of tormenting flies and the loneliness of the place, absorbed in her self-contained, silent sorrow.

"She needs neither to weep nor to utter words," he thought. "Perhaps loss and regret fill her life as they have come to fill mine, and she can add nothing except her presence in this place. No doubt there are many such in Zeray."

As they approached the tomb the Tuginda coughed again and the woman, startled, turned quickly around. The face was young and, though still beautiful, thin with hardship and marred, as he had guessed, by the lines of a settled sorrow. Seeing her eyes widen with surprise and fear, he whispered urgently, "Speak, säiyett, or she will fly."

The woman was staring as though at a ghost; the knuckles of her clenched hands were pressed to her open mouth and suddenly, through her rapid breathing, came a low cry. Yet she neither ran nor turned to run, only staring on and on in incredulous amazement. He, too, stood still, afraid to move and trying to recall of what her consternation reminded him. Then, even as he saw her tears begin to flow, she sank to her knees, still gazing fixedly at the Tuginda, with a look like that of a child unexpectedly found by a searching mother and as yet uncertain whether that mother will show herself loving or angry. Suddenly, in a passion of weeping, she flung herself to the ground, grasping the Tuginda's ankles and kissing her feet in the grass.

"Säiyett," she cried through her tears, "oh, forgive me! Only forgive me, säiyett, and I will die at peace!"

Lifting her head, she looked up at them, her face agonized and distorted with crying. Yet now Kelderek recognized her, and knew also where he had seen before that very look of fear. For it was Melathys who lay prostrate before them, clasping the Tuginda's feet.

A quick gust of wind from the river ran through the trees and was gone, tossing and opening the pennant as some passer-by might idly have spread it with his hand and let it fall again. For a moment the emblem, a golden snake, showed plainly, rippling as though alive; then drooped and disappeared once more among the folds of the dark, pendent cloth.

43 *The Priestess's Tale*

"WHEN HE CAME," SAID MELATHYS, "when he came, and Ankray with him, I had already been here long enough to believe that it could be only a matter of time before I must die by one chance or another. During the journey down the river, before ever I reached Zeray, I had learned what I had to expect from men when I sought food or shelter. But the journey—that was an easy beginning, if only I had known. I was still alert and confident. I had a knife and knew how to use it, and there was always the river to carry me farther down." She stopped, looking quickly across at Kelderek, who, replete with his first full meal since leaving Kabin, was sitting beside the fire, soaking his lacerated feet in a bowl of warm water and herbs. "Did she call?"

"No, säiyett," said Ankray, huge in the lamplight. He had entered the room while she was speaking. "The Tuginda is asleep now. Unless there's anything more you need, I'll watch beside her for a time."

"Yes, watch for an hour. Then I will sleep in her room myself. Lord Kelderek's needs I leave to you. And remember, Ankray, whatever befell the High Baron on Ortelga, Lord Kelderek has come to Zeray. That journey settles all scores."

"You know what they say, säiyett. In Zeray, Memory has a sharp sting and the wise avoid her."

"So I have heard. Go, then."

The man went out, stooping at the doorway, and Melathys, before she resumed, refilled Kelderek's wooden beaker with rough wine from the goatskin hanging on the wall.

"But there is no going on from Zeray. All journeys end here. Many, when they first come, believe that they will be able to cross the Telthearna, but none, so far as I know, has ever done so. The current in midstream is desperately strong and a mile below lies the Gorge of Bereel, where no craft can live among the rapids and broken rocks."

"Does no one ever leave by land?"

"In Kabin province, if they find a man who is known to have crossed the Vrako from the east, he is either killed or compelled to return."

"That I can believe."

"Northward from here, thirty or forty miles upstream, the mountains come down almost to the shore. There is a gap— Linsho, they call it—no more than half a mile wide. Those who live there make all travelers pay a toll before they will let them pass. Many have paid all they possess to come south; but who could pay to go north?"

"Could none?"

"Kelderek, I see you know nothing of Zeray. Zeray is a rock to which men cling for a last little while until death washes them away. They have no homes, no past, no future, no hope, no honor and no money. We are rich in shame and in nothing else. I once sold my body for three eggs and a glass of wine. It should have been two eggs, but I drove a hard bargain. I have known a man murdered for one silver piece, which proved worthless to the murderer because it could be neither eaten, worn nor used as a weapon. There is no market in Zeray, no priest, no baker and no shoemaker. Men catch crows alive and breed them for food. When I came, trade did not exist. Even now it is only a trickle, as I will tell you. The sound of a scream at night goes unremarked and the possessions a man has he carries with him and never puts down."

"But this house? You have food and wine; and the Tuginda, thank God, is in a comfortable bed."

"The doors and windows are strongly barred—have you noticed? But yes, you are right. Here we have a little comfort— for how long is another matter, as you will see when I have finished my tale."

She poured more hot water into Kelderek's foot-bowl, sipped her wine and was silent for a little, bending toward the fire and stretching her beautiful arms and body this way and that, as though bathing herself in its warmth and light. At length she continued.

"They say women delight to be desired, and so perhaps they do—some, and somewhere else. I have stood screaming with fear while two men I hated fought each other with knives to decide which of them should force himself upon me. I have been dragged out of a burning hut at night by the man who had killed my bed-mate in his sleep. In less than three months I belonged to five men, two of them were murdered, while a third left Zeray after trying to stab me. Like all those who leave, he went not because he wished to reach somewhere else, but because he was afraid to remain.

"I am not boasting, Kelderek, believe me. These were not matters to boast of. My life was a nightmare. There was no refuge at all—nowhere to hide. There were not forty women in Zeray all told—hags, drabs, girls living in terror because they knew too much about some vile crime. And I came to it a virgin priestess of Quiso, not twenty-one years old." She paused a moment, and then said, "In the old days on Quiso, when we fished for bramba we used live bait. God forgive me, I could never do that again. Once I tried to burn my face in the fire, but for that I found no more courage than I had had to encounter Lord Shardik.

"One night I was with a man named Glabron, a Tonildan who was feared even in Zeray. If a man could only make himself feared enough, a band would form around him to kill and rob, to put food in their stomachs and stay alive a little longer. They would frighten others away from the fishing places, keep watch for newcomers to waylay and so on. Sometimes they would set out to raid villages beyond Zeray, though usually it was little enough they got for their trouble. It's very small pickings here, you see. Men fought and robbed for a bare living. A man who could neither fight nor steal could expect to live perhaps three months. Three years is a good life for the hardest of men in Zeray.

"There's a tavern of sorts, down near the shore at this end of the town. They call it 'The Green Grove' after some place in Ikat, I believe—or is it Bekla?"

"Bekla."

"Ikat or Bekla, I never heard that the drink there could turn men blind, nor yet that the landlord sold rats and lizards for food. Glabron exacted some wretched pittance in return for not destroying the place and for protecting it from others like himself. He was vain—yes, in Zeray he was vain—and must needs have the pleasure of others' envy: that they should watch him eat when they were hungry and hear him insulting those whom they feared; oh yes, and he must be tormenting their lust with the sight of what he kept for himself. 'You'll take me there once too often,' I said. 'For God's sake, isn't it enough that I'm your property, and Keriol's body's floating down the Telthearna? Where's the sport in waving a bone at starving dogs?' Glabron never argued with anyone, least of all with me. I wasn't there for talk, and he himself was about as ready with words as a pig.

"They'd had a success that evening. Some days before, a body had been washed ashore with a little money on it, and two of Glabron's men had gone inland and come back with a sheep. Most of it they ate themselves, but a part they exchanged for drink. Glabron grew so drunk that I became more afraid than ever. In Zeray a man's life is never so much in danger as when he's drunk. I knew his enemies and I was expecting to see one or more of them come in at any moment. It was dim enough in the room—lamplight's a scarce luxury here—but suddenly I noticed two strangers who'd entered. One had his face almost buried in the top of a great fur cloak and the other, a huge man, was looking at me and whispering to him. They were only two to Glabron's six or seven, but I knew what could happen in that place and I was frantic to get away.

"Glabron was singing a foul song—or thought he was singing it—and I plucked at his sleeve and interrupted him. He looked round for a moment and then hit me across the face with the back of his hand. He was just going on when the muffled stranger walked across to the table. His cloak was still held across his face and only one of his eyes showed over the top. He kicked the table and rocked it, so that they all looked up at him.

" 'I don't like your song,' he said to Glabron, in Beklan. 'I don't like the way you treat this girl; and I don't like you either.'

"As soon as he spoke I knew who he was. I thought, 'I can't bear it.' I wanted to warn him, but I couldn't utter a word. Glabron answered nothing for a few moments, not because he was particularly taken aback, but because it was always his way to go slowly and calmly about killing a man. He liked to make an effect—that was part of the fear he inspired—to let people see that he killed deliberately and not in a fit of rage.

" 'Oh, don't you, I say,' he said at length, when he was sure the whole room was listening. 'I wonder whom I have the honor of addressing, don't you know?'

" 'I'm the devil,' says the other man, 'come for your soul, and not a moment too soon either.' And with that, he dropped his arm. They'd never seen him before, of course, and in that dim light the face which he disclosed was not the face of a human being. They were all superstitious men—ignorant, with evil consciences, no religion and a great fear of the unknown. They leapt away from him, cursing and falling over each other. The Baron already had his sword out under his cloak, and in that moment he ran Glabron through the throat, grabbed me by the arm, cut down another man who was in his way and was out in the dark with me and Ankray before anyone had had time even to draw a knife.

"I won't tell you all the rest of the story—or not tonight. Later there'll be time. But I suppose you can well believe that nothing like Bel-ka-Trazet had ever been seen here before. For three months he and I and Ankray never slept at one and the same time. In six months he was lord of Zeray, with men at his back whom he could trust to do his bidding.

"He and I lived in this house, and people used to call me his queen—half in jest and half in earnest. No one dared to show me anything but respect. I don't think they would have believed the truth—that Bel-ka-Trazet never touched me. 'I doubt whether you've learned a very good opinion of men,' he said to me once, 'and as for me, it's little enough I've got left in the way of self-respect. At least while I'm alive I can still honor a priestess of Quiso, and that will be better for us both.' Only Ankray knows that secret. The rest of Zeray must believe that we were fated to be childless, or else that his injuries—

"But though I was never in love with him, and was grateful for his self-restraint, yet still I honored and admired him, and I would have consented to be his consort if he had wished. Much of the time he was dour and brooding. Pleasures here are meager enough, but always he had little zest for any—as though he were punishing himself for the loss of Ortelga. He had a sharp, mordant tongue and no illusions."

"I remember."

" 'Don't ask me to come out drinking with you,' he said once to his men. 'I might get chased downstream by a bear.' They knew what he meant, for although he'd never told them the story, news had reached Zeray of the battle in the foothills and the fall of Bekla to the Ortelgans. When anything went wrong he used to say, 'You'd better get yourselves a bear—you'll do better then.' But though they feared him, they always trusted and respected him and they followed him without hesitation. As I said, there was no one here who was the least match for him. He was too good for Zeray. I suppose any other baron, forced to fly as he was, would have crossed to Deelguy or made for Ikat or even Terekenalt. But he—he hated pity as a cat hates water. It was his pride, and the bitter streak in him, that sent him to Zeray like a murderer on the run. He actually enjoyed pitting himself against the misery and danger of the place. 'There's a lot one could do here,' he said to me one evening, while we were fishing inshore. 'There's some passable land on that bit of plain around Zeray, and plenty of timber in the forests. It could never be a rich province, but it could be reasonably well off, if only the peasants weren't frightened to death and there were roads to Kabin and Linsho. Law and order and some trade—that's all that's needed. If I'm not mistaken, it's here that the Telthearna runs closest to Bekla. Before we're done we'll have two good, stout ropes stretched across these straits and a raft ferry running along them. I'm not an Ortelgan for nothing—I know what can be done with rope, and how to make it, too. Easier than contriving the Dead Belt, I assure you. Think of opening a trade route to the east—Bekla would pay any money for the use of that.'

" 'They'd come and annex the province,' I said.

" 'They could try,' he answered, 'but it's more secure than Ortelga ever was. Forty miles from the Vrako to Zeray, and twenty miles of it thick forest and hills, difficult going unless someone builds a road—which we could destroy whenever we liked. I tell you, my girl, we'll have the last laugh on the bear yet.'

"Now the truth was that not even Bel-ka-Trazet could bring prosperity to a place like Zeray, because he had no barons or men of any quality, and could not be everywhere himself. What could be done, he did. He punished murder and robbery and stopped raiding inland, and he persuaded or bribed a few peasants to bring in wood and wool and do their best to teach carpentry and pottery, so that the town could start bartering what it made. We bartered dried fish too, and rushes for thatching and matting—anything we could. But compared even with Ortelga it was very thin-flowing, rickety business, simply because of the sort of men who come here—criminals can't work, you know—and the lack of even one road. Bel-ka-Trazet realized this, and it was less than a year ago now that he resolved on a new scheme.

"We knew what had been happening in Ikat and Bekla—there

395

were fugitives here from both cities. Bel-ka-Trazet had been impressed by what he had heard of Santil-kè-Erketlis and finally he decided to try to drive a bargain with him. The difficulty was that we had so terribly little to offer. As the Baron said, we were like a man trying to sell a lame ox or a lopsided pot. Who would trouble to come and take Zeray? Even to a general not facing an enemy army in the field, it would hardly be worth the march from Kabin. We discussed it between ourselves again and again and at last Bel-ka-Trazet devised an offer which he thought might appeal both to Santil and to our own followers. His idea was to tell Santil that if ever he were to march north, whether or not he succeeded in taking Bekla he was welcome to annex Zeray. We would help him in any way he wished. In particular, we would help him to close the gap of Linsho in the north and then to round up all slave traders who might have fled east of the Vrako to escape him. We would also tell him that we believed that with skilled rope-makers and carpenters, and the labor of his own pioneers working to their orders, it would be possible to construct a raft-ferry across the Telthearna narrows. Then, if all went well, he could build a road from Kabin to Zeray, and these enterprises too, if they appealed to him, we would assist in every way we could. Finally, if he were not afraid to enlist men from Zeray, we would send him as many as possible, provided that he would grant them pardons.

"The five or six men whom the Baron called his councilors agreed that this offer was our best hope of remaining alive, either in Zeray or out of it, if only the Yeldashay would agree to come. But to get a message to Santil would be difficult. There are only two ways out of this country east of the Vrako. One is northward through the gap of Linsho; the other is west across the Vrako in the neighborhood of Kabin. Below Kabin the Vrako is impassable, all along the Tonilda border to its confluence with the Telthearna. Desperate men find their way to Zeray, but even more desperate men cannot contrive a way out.

"It might well prove impossible, we thought, for anyone to reach Ikat Yeldashay, but at least we had a man who was ready to try. His name was Elstrit, a lad of about seventeen who, rather than abandon his father, had joined him in his flight from Terekenalt. What his father had done I don't know, for he died

396

before I came to Zeray and Elstrit had been living on his wits ever since, until he had the sense to throw in his lot with Bel-ka-Trazet. He was not only strong and clever, but he had the advantage of not being a known criminal or a wanted man. Clever or not, he still had to attempt the Vrako crossing at Kabin. It was the Baron who hit on the idea of forging him a Beklan slave-dealer's warrant. In Kabin he was to say that he was working for Lalloc, a known dealer in children, and had the protection of the Ortelgans in Bekla; that on Lalloc's instructions he had entered Zeray province by way of Linsho Gap and traveled through it to see whether the country offered any prospects for a slave raid. He was now returning to report to Lalloc in Bekla. Then, later, as soon as he approached the province of Yelda, he could destroy the forged warrant. It was a thin enough story, but the seal on the warrant was a very good imitation of the bear seal of Bekla (it was made for us by a notorious forger) and we could only hope for good luck. Elstrit crossed the Vrako about three months ago, soon after the rains, and what became of him after that we don't know—not even so much as whether he ever reached Ikat.

"It was a month after that that the Baron fell sick. Many fall sick in Zeray. It's no wonder—the filthiness of the place, rats, lice, infection, continual strain and fear, the burden of guilt and the loss of hope. The Baron had had a hard life and in spite of himself he was failing. You can guess how we nursed him, Ankray and I. We were like men in a wilderness of wild beasts, who tend a fire in the night and pray for dawn. But the fire went out—it went out."

The tears stood brimming in her eyes. She brushed them sharply away, hid her face in her hands a moment and then, with a deep sigh, went on.

"Once he spoke of you. 'That fellow Kelderek,' he said, 'I'd have killed him if the Tuginda hadn't sent for us that night. I don't wish him ill any longer, but for Ortelga's sake I only hope he can finish what he's started.' It was a few days later that he spoke to our men as best he could—for by that time he was very weak. He advised them to spare no pains to get news of Santil's intentions and if there seemed the least hope, at all costs to keep order in Zeray until he came. 'Otherwise you'll all be dead in less than a year,' he said, 'and the place will be worse than ever it was before we started.' After that, only Ankray and I were with him until he died. He went very hard. You'd expect that, wouldn't you? The last thing he said was, 'The bear—tell them the bear—' I bent over him and asked, 'What of the bear, my lord?' but he never spoke again. I watched his face—that terrible face—guttering down like the wax of a spent candle. When he was gone, we did what we had to do. I covered his eyes with a pad of wet cloth, and I remember how, as we were laying the arms straight, the cloth slipped, so that the dead eyes opened and I saw them staring into mine.

"You have seen his grave. There were heavy hearts—and frightened hearts—at the time when that was made. It was over a month ago, and every day since then Zeray has slipped a little further between our hands. We have not lost it yet, but I will tell you what it is like. I remember that once, when I was a little girl, I stood watching a miller driving his ox round and round to grind corn. Two men who thought he had cheated them began quarreling with him, and at last they dragged him away and beat him. The ox went on plodding round, first at the same speed, then slower, until at last—and anxiously, as my clear child's eye could see—it dared to try what would happen if it stopped. Nothing happened, and it lay down. Half the men in Zeray are wondering whether they dare to defy us. Any day now some will try. I know our men—the Baron's men. Without him they will never hold together. It's only a matter of time.

"Every evening I have gone to his tomb and prayed for help and deliverance. Sometimes Ankray comes with me, or perhaps another, but often I go alone. There's no modesty in Zeray, and I'm past being afraid. As long as none dares insult me, I take it as a sign that we still have some grip on the place; and it does no harm to behave as though I believed we had. Sometimes I have prayed that Santil's army may come, but more often I use no words, simply offering to God my hope and longing, and my presence at the grave of the man who honored and respected me.

"On Quiso, the Tuginda used to teach us that real and actual trust in God was the whole life of a priestess. 'God can afford to wait,' she used to say. 'Whether to convert the unbelieving, to reward the just or to punish the wicked—God can afford to wait. With Him, everything comes home in the end. Our work is not only to believe that, but to show that we believe it by everything that we say and do.' "

Melathys wept quietly and continuously as she went on. "I had put out of my mind how I came to Zeray and the reason why. My treachery, my cowardice, my sacrilege—perhaps I thought that my sufferings had blotted them out, had dug a ditch between me and that priestess who broke her vows, betrayed Lord Shardik and failed the Tuginda. Tonight, when I turned and saw who was standing behind me, do you know what I thought? I thought, 'She has come to Zeray to find me, either to renounce or forgive me, either to condemn me or take me back to Quiso'—as though I were not defiled forty times over. I fell at her feet to implore her forgiveness, to tell her I was not worth what I believed she had done, to beg her only to forgive me and then let me die. Now I know it's true what she said. God—" and, letting her head fall forward on her arms across the table, she sobbed bitterly—"God can afford to wait. God can afford to wait."

Kelderek put his hand on her shoulder. "Come," he said, "we'll talk no more tonight. Let's put these thoughts aside and simply do the immediate tasks before us. Very often, in perplexity, that's best, and a great comfort in trouble. Go and look after the Tuginda. Sleep beside her, and we'll meet again tomorrow."

As soon as Ankray had made up his bed, Kelderek lay down and slept as he had not slept since leaving Bekla.

44 *The Heart's Disclosure*

SPECK BY SPECK, THE NOONDAY SUNLIGHT moved along the wall and from somewhere distant sounded the slow *chunk, chunk* of an axe in wood. The Tuginda, her eyes closed, frowned like one tormented by clamor and tossed from side to side, unable, as it seemed, to be an instant free from discomfort. Again Kelderek wiped the sweat from her forehead with a cloth dipped in the pitcher by the bed. Since early morning she had lain between sleep and waking, recognizing neither Melathys nor himself, from time to time uttering a few random words and once sipping a little wine and water from a cup held to her lips. An hour before noon Melathys, with Ankray in attendance, had set out to confer with the former followers of the Baron and acquaint them with her news, leaving Kelderek to bar the door and watch alone against her return.

The sound of the axe ceased and he sat on in the silence, sometimes taking the Tuginda's hand in his own and speaking to her in the hope that, waking, she might become calmer. Under his fingers her pulse beat fast; and her arm, he now saw, was swollen and inflamed with weeping scratches which he recognized as those inflicted by the trazada thorn. She had said nothing of these, nor of the deep cut in her foot, which Melathys had found and dressed the night before.

Slow as the sunlight, his mind moved over all that had befallen. The days that had passed since his leaving Bekla were themselves, he thought, like some Streel of time into which he had descended step by step and whence he had now emerged for a short time before death. There was no need for him, after all, to expiate his blasphemy by seeking that death, for however events might turn out it seemed certain. If Erketlis were victorious but nevertheless sent no troops east of the Vrako, either because he had never received Bel-ka-Trazet's message or because it had found no favor with him, then sooner or later he himself would die from violence or sickness, either in Zeray or in the attempt to escape from it. But if Erketlis's troops, crossing the Vrako, were to come upon him in Zeray or elsewhere—and it was likely enough that they would be keeping their eyes open for him—he had Elleroth's word for it that they would put him to death. If Erketlis were defeated, it was possible that Zelda and Ged-la-Dan, coming to Kabin, might send soldiers across the Vrako to seek Shardik. But once Shardik was known to be dead, they would not trouble themselves about his former priest-king. And if the discredited priest-king were to attempt to return from Zeray, whether to Bekla or to Ortelga, he would not be suffered to live.

400

Never again would he posture and ape the part of Shardik's mediator to the people. Nor ever again could he become the single-hearted visionary who, fearless in his divinely imparted elation, had walked and slept beside Shardik in the woods of Ortelga. Why, then, despite his resolve four days ago in Ruvit's hovel, despite his unlessened shame and remorse, did he now find in himself the will to live? Mere cowardice, he supposed. Or perhaps it was that some remaining streak of pride, which had encouraged him to entertain the thought of a deliberate death of atonement, resented the prospect of dying on an Ikat sword or a Zeray criminal's knife. Whatever the reason, he found himself considering whether he might not attempt—however desperate the odds against him—first to bring the Tuginda back to Quiso, and then perhaps to escape to some country beyond the Telthearna. Yet mere survival, he realized as he pondered, was not the whole of the motive which had changed his earlier resolve to die.

Into his mind returned the picture of the beautiful, white-robed girl who had paced by night across the flame-lit terrace above the Ledges of Quiso, the girl whose craven fear in the woods of Ortelga had aroused in himself nothing but pity and the wish to protect and comfort her. She, like him, had found unexpectedly the self-deceit and cowardice in her own heart and, having once, no doubt, believed of herself that Shardik had no more loyal and trustworthy servant, had learned with bitter shame that the truth was otherwise. Since then she had suffered still more. Abandoning Shardik and throwing herself upon the world, she had found the world's misery but never the world's pleasure. Guilt, cruelty and fear must almost have destroyed in her the natural power to love any man or to look for any security or joy from a man's love. But—and here, releasing the Tuginda's hand, he sprang up and began striding back and forth across the room—perhaps that power was not beyond saving, not drowned beyond hope of recovery by one ready to show that he valued it above all else?

The Tuginda moaned, her face twisted as though in pain. He crossed to the bed and knelt to support her with one arm around her shoulders.

"Rest, säiyett. You are among friends. Be at peace."

She was speaking, very low, and he put his ear to her lips.

"Shardik! To find—Lord Shardik—"

She ceased, and again he sat beside her.

His love for Melathys, he knew now, had lain dormant in his heart from the first. The girl on the terrace, her great, golden collar glinting in the flame-light; the girl who had played, immune, with the point of the arrow and the edge of the sword, as a goddess might play with cataracts or lightning; who, uninstructed and unquestioning, had divined the importance of his coming to Quiso—this memory had never left him. Of his admiration and awe for her he had certainly been conscious, but how could he, the ragged, dirty hunter who had fallen senseless to the ground for fear of the magic of Quiso, possibly have suspected, then, that desire also had sown its seed in his heart? To desire a priestess of Quiso—the very thought, entertained, was sacrilege. He recalled the events of that night—the anger of Bel-ka-Trazet, the bewitched landing on Quiso in the dark, the crossing of the swaying bridge over the ravine, the sight of Rantzay and Anthred walking among the glowing embers, and, weighing heavier than all, the burden of the news which he bore. Small wonder that he had not dwelled much upon the nature of his feeling for Melathys. And yet, unregarded, as though germinating its own life independently and alone, deep below his consuming preoccupation with Shardik, his cryptic love had taken root. In his pity for Melathys, he now realized, there had lain an unrecognized satisfaction in finding that human weakness had its part even in her; that she, like any other mortal, could stand in need of comfort and encouragement. Lastly, he recalled the night when the High Baron and he had discovered her flight. "That girl had some sense," the Baron had said. At the sardonic words he himself had felt not only resentment, but also anguish that Melathys, like the golden berries of the melikon, should have proved worthless, have drifted away with the river, to be seen no more. And yet another feeling he recalled which had come into his heart—and how, he wondered, could he possibly have failed to perceive the significance of this? —a sense of personal loss and betrayal. Already, even at that time, he had unconsciously begun to think of her as in some sense his own and, though strong then and confident in his own integrity, had felt neither contempt nor anger at her flight, but only disappointment. Since that night, neither she nor anyone had betrayed him so thoroughly as he had betrayed himself. If she had wept for forgiveness in the graveyard, what was his need?

He thought, too, of his unforced chastity in Bekla; of his indifference to both the luxury at his command and the outward grandeur of his kingship; of his continual sense that there was some truth that he still lacked. The great secret to be imparted through Shardik, the secret of life which he had never found—this, he still knew, was no figment. This he had not confused with his unrecognized love for Melathys. Yet—and now he frowned, puzzled and uncertain—in some mysterious way the two were connected. With the help of the second he might, perhaps, have succeeded, after all, in finding the first.

Just as the Tuginda had warned, the conquest of Bekla had proved to have nothing to do with the truth of Shardik, had served only to impede the search and hinder the divine disclosure of that truth. Now that Shardik was lost forever, he himself had awoken, like a drunkard in a ditch, to the recollection of folly, while the magic girl among the bowls of fire had become a disgraced fugitive, familiar with fear, with lust and violence. Error and shame, he reflected, were the inescapable lot of mankind; yet still it comforted him to think that Melathys too had a part in this bitter inheritance. If, somehow, he could save her life and bring her and the Tuginda to safety, then perhaps he might at last beg the Tuginda's forgiveness and, if Melathys would consent to come with him, journey far away and forget the very name of Shardik, of whom he had proved himself so unworthy.

Hearing Melathys call from beyond the courtyard, he went out and unbarred the door. The girl's news was that Farrass and Thrild, those followers of the Baron whom she herself felt were most to be trusted, were ready to speak with him if he would go to meet them. Asking Ankray to make the journey once again as his guide, he set out to cross Zeray.

Despite all that he had heard, he was unprepared for the squalor and filth, the sullen, half-starved faces peering as he went by, the miasma of want, fear and violence that seemed to rise out of the very dirt underfoot. Those whom he passed on the waterfront were hollow-cheeked and gray-faced, sitting or lying listlessly as they stared out at the choppy water racing down the midstream channel and the deserted eastern shore beyond. He saw no shops and no one plying a trade, unless indeed it were a shivering, potbellied child with a basket, who waded knee-deep in the shallows, stooping and searching—for what, Kelderek could not tell. Upon arriving at his destination, like one awaking from a dream, he could recall few details, retaining only an undifferentiated impression of menace sensed rather than observed, and of hard glances which he had found himself unwilling to meet. Once or twice, indeed, he had stopped and tried to look about him, but Ankray, without presuming in so many words to warn him, had contrived to convey that they would do better to keep on their way.

Farrass, a tall, thin-faced man, dressed in torn clothes too small for him and carrying a club at his belt, sat lengthwise, with one foot up, on a bench, looking warily at Kelderek and continually dabbing with a rag at an oozing sore on his cheek.

"Melathys says you were the Ortelgan king of Bekla."

"It's true, but I'm seeking no authority here."

Thrild, dark, slight and quick-moving, grinned where he leaned against the window ledge, biting a splinter of kindling wood between his teeth.

"That's as well, for there's little to be had."

Farrass hesitated, reluctant, like everyone east of the Vrako, to ask questions about the past. At length, shrugging his shoulders like a man deciding that the only way to have done with an awkward job is to get on with it, he said, "You were deposed?"

"I fell into the hands of the Yeldashay army at Kabin. They spared my life but sent me across the Vrako."

"Santil's army?"

"Yes."

"They're at Kabin?"

"They were six days ago."

"Why did they spare you?"

"One of their principal officers persuaded them. He had his reasons."

404

"And you chose to come to Zeray?"

"I fell in with an Ortelgan priestess in the forest, a woman who was once my friend. She was seeking—well, seeking Bel-ka-Trazet. She's lying sick now at the Baron's house."

Farrass nodded. Thrild grinned again. "We're in distinguished company."

"The worst," replied Kelderek. "I want only to save my life and the priestess's—by helping you, perhaps."

"How?"

"That's for you to say. I've been assured of death if I fall into the hands of the Yeldashay army a second time. So if Santil accepts Bel-ka-Trazet's offer and sends troops to Zeray, it's likely to turn out badly for me unless you can persuade them to give me a safe-conduct out of here. That's the bargain I'm hoping to drive with you."

Farrass, chin on hand, looked at the floor, frowning and pondering, and again it was Thrild who spoke.

"You mustn't overestimate us. The Baron had some authority when he was alive, but without him we've less and less. We're safe ourselves for the time being and that's about as far as it goes. It's little regard the Yeldashay would be likely to have for any request we made of them."

"You've already done us a good turn," said Farrass, "by bringing news that Santil's at Kabin. Did you hear whether he ever received the Baron's message?"

"No. But if he thinks that there are fugitive slave traders this side of the Vrako it's quite possible that Yeldashay troops have already crossed it. Whether or not, I think you should send him another messenger at once, and at all costs try to hold things together here until you get an answer."

"If he's at Kabin," replied Farrass, "our best hope, though it may not be yours, will be to go there ourselves, with Melathys, and ask him to let us go on to Ikat."

"Farrass here never really believed in the scheme for Santil to come and take Zeray," said Thrild. "Now the Baron's dead I agree with him. The Baron would have had the place ready to offer—we haven't. We'd do better to get out now and go and meet the Ikats at Kabin. You must understand our position. We don't pretend to keep law and order. A man in Zeray is free to murder and steal as long as he doesn't become so dangerous that it's safer for us to kill him than let him alone. All but a few of the men in this place have committed some serious crime. If they were to learn that we'd invited Ikat soldiers to come and take the town, they'd up and go for us like cornered rats. It's not worth our while to try to carry on with the Baron's plan."

"But there's no wealth in Zeray. Why do they kill and steal here?"

Thrild threw up his hands. "Why? For food, what else? In Zeray, men starve. The Baron once hanged two Deelguy for killing and eating a child. In Zeray, men eat caterpillars—dig mud-skapas out of the river to boil for soup. Do you know the gylon?"

"The glass-fly? Yes. I grew up on the Telthearna, you know."

"Here, at midsummer, the swarms cover the river inshore. People scoop them up in handfuls and eat them thankfully."

"It's only because those of us who supported the Baron know that we must either keep together or die," said Farrass, "that none of us has so far tried to take his woman. A quarrel among ourselves would mean the end of all of us. But that can't last. Someone's bound to try soon. She's pretty."

Kelderek shrugged his shoulders, keeping his face expressionless.

"I suppose she can choose for herself when she's ready?"

"Not in Zeray. But anyway that problem's solved now. We must set off for Kabin and she'll come with us, no doubt. Your Ortelgan priestess too, if she wants to live."

"How soon? She's in a high fever."

"Then we can't wait for her," said Thrild.

"I'll take her north when she recovers," said Kelderek. "I've told you why it's impossible for me to go to Kabin, either now or later."

"If you went north you'd wander until you were killed. You'd never get through the gap at Linsho."

"You said I'd brought you good news. Isn't there anything you can do to help me?"

"Not by staying here. If the Ikats will listen to us, we'll try to persuade them to send for your Ortelgan priestess, and you can try your luck with them when they come. What more do you expect? This is Zeray."

406

45 *In Zeray*

"THE DAMNED COWARDS," said Melathys, "and the Baron not forty days in his grave! If I were General Santil I'd send them back to Zeray and hang them on the shore. They could perfectly well hold this place for six days. That would be more than enough time for someone to get through to Kabin and come back with a hundred soldiers. But no, they'd rather run."

Kelderek stood with his back to her, staring out into the little courtyard. He said carefully, "As things are, you ought to go with them."

She did not answer and after some moments he turned around. She was standing smiling, waiting to meet his eyes. "Not I. It's seldom indeed that a second chance is offered to someone as undeserving as I. I don't intend to desert the Tuginda a second time, believe me."

"If you reach Kabin with Farrass and Thrild you'll be safe. Once they're gone you won't be safe here. You must think of that very seriously."

"I don't want safety on those terms. Did you think that what I said at the Baron's tomb was hysterical?"

He was about to speak again when she went to the door and called for Ankray.

"Ankray, the Baron's men are leaving Zeray for Kabin tonight or tomorrow. They're hoping to reach the army of General Santil-kè-Erketlis. I think you should go with them, for your own safety."

"You're going, then, säiyett?"

"No, Lord Kelderek and I will be staying with the Tuginda."

Ankray looked from one to another and scratched his head.

"Safety, säiyett? The Baron always said that General Erketlis would be coming here one day, didn't he? That's why he sent that young fellow Elstrit—"

"General Erketlis may still come here, if we're lucky. But Farrass and the rest prefer to go now and seek him wherever he is. You're free to go with them and it will probably be the safest thing to do."

407

"If you'll excuse my saying so, säiyett, I doubt it, among those men. I'd rather stay here, among Ortelgan people, if you understand me. The Baron, he always used to say that General Santil would come, so I reckon he will."

"It's as you like, Ankray," said Kelderek. "But if he doesn't, then Zeray's going to become even more dangerous for all of us."

"Why, sir, the way I see it, if that happens, we'll just have to set out for Kabin on our own account. But the Baron, he wouldn't want me to be leaving Ortelgan priestesses to shift for themselves, like, even with you to help them."

"You're not afraid to stay, then?"

"No, sir," answered Ankray. "The Baron and me, we was never afraid of anyone in Zeray. The Baron, he always used to say, 'Ankray, you just remember you've got a good conscience and they haven't.' He usually—"

"Good," said Kelderek, "I'm glad that's what you want. But do you think," he asked, turning to Melathys, "that they may try to *force* you to join them?"

She stared at him solemnly, wide-eyed, so that he saw again the girl who had drawn Bel-ka-Trazet's sword and asked him what it was.

"They can try to *persuade* me if they like, but I doubt they will. You see, I've caught the Tuginda's fever, haven't I, which shows that it must be very infectious? That's what they'll be told, if they come here."

"Pray God you won't catch it in all earnest," said Kelderek. He realized with a blaze of passionate admiration that, despite all she knew of Zeray, her decision to remain, taken with delight rather than determination, was affording her not fear, but an elated joy in the recovery of her self-respect. To her, the appearance of the Tuginda in the graveyard had seemed first a miracle, then an act of incredible love and generosity; and though she now knew the true story of the Tuginda's journey, nevertheless she still attributed it to God. Like a disgraced soldier whose commander has suddenly called him out of the lockup, given him back his arms and told him to go and retrieve his good name on the battlefield, she was soaring upon the realization that enemies, danger and even death were of small account compared with the misery of guilt which, against all expectation, had been removed from her. Despite what Kelderek had seen at the Baron's tomb, he had not until now believed that all she had suffered in Zeray had caused her less grief than the memory of her flight from Ortelga.

The Tuginda seemed no better, being still tormented by a continual restlessness. As evening fell Ankray remained with her, while Melathys and Kelderek used the last of the daylight to make sure of the locks and shutter bars and to check food and weapons. The Baron, Melathys explained, had had certain sources of supply which he had kept secret even from his followers, either he or Ankray going now and then by night to bring back a goat or half a sheep from a village up river. The house was still fairly well supplied with meat. There was also a good deal of salt and a certain amount of the rough wine.

"Did he pay?" asked Kelderek, looking with satisfaction at the haunches in the brine tubs and reflecting that he had never expected to feel gratitude toward Bel-ka-Trazet.

"Chiefly by guaranteeing that the villagers would not be molested from Zeray. But he was always very ingenious in finding or making things we could trade. We made arrows, for instance, and needles out of bone. I have certain skills, too. Every postulant on Quiso has to carve her own rings, but I can carve wood still better now, believe me. Do you remember this? I've taken to using it."

It was Bel-ka-Trazet's knife. Kelderek recognized it instantly, drew it from the sheath and held the point close before his eyes. She watched, puzzled, and he laughed.

"I've reason to remember it almost better than any man on Ortelga, I dare say. I saw both it and Lord Shardik for the first time on one and the same day—that day when I first saw you. I'll tell you the story at supper. Had he a sword?"

"Here it is. And a bow. I still have my bow too. I hid it soon after I reached Zeray, but I recovered it when I joined the Baron. My priestess's knife was stolen, of course, but the Baron gave me another—a dead man's, I dare say, though he never told. It's rough workmanship, but the blade's good. Now over here, let me show you—"

She was like a girl looking over her trousseau. He remembered how once, years before, having built a cage trap for birds, he had found a hawk in it. There was no market for hawks—the factor from Bekla had wanted bright feathers and cageable birds —and, having no use for it himself, he had released it, watching as it flashed up and out of sight, full of joy at the recovery of its hard, dangerous life. Having walked through Zeray that afternoon, he now believed all that he had been told of sudden, unpredictable danger, of lust and murder moving below the surface of half-starved torpor like alligators through the water of some fetid creek. Yet Melathys, who had better reason than any to know of these things, plainly felt herself in a state of grace so immune that they had for the moment, at all events, no power to make her afraid. It must be for him to see that she took no foolish risks.

The Tuginda still lay in her arid sleep; a sleep comfortless as a choked and smoking fire, of which she seemed less the beneficiary than the victim. Her face was passive and sunken as Kelderek had never seen it, the flesh of her arms and throat slack and wasted. Ankray boiled a salt meat soup and cooled it, but they could do no more than moisten her lips, for she did not swallow. When Kelderek suggested that he should go out and find some milk, Ankray only shook his head without raising his eyes from the ground.

"There's no milk in Zeray," said Melathys, "nor cheese, nor butter. I've seen none in five years. But you're right—it's fresh food she ought to have. Salt meat and dried fruit are no cure for a fever. We can do nothing tonight. You sleep first, Kelderek. I'll wake you later."

But she did not wake him, evidently content to watch—with a little sleep, perhaps, for herself—beside the Tuginda until morning. It was Ankray, returned from some early expedition of his own, who woke him with the news that Farrass and his companions had left Zeray during the night.

"There's no doubt of it?" asked Kelderek, spluttering as he splashed cold water over his face and shoulders.

"I don't reckon so, sir."

Kelderek had not expected that they would go without some attempt to force Melathys to join them, but when he told her the news she was less surprised.

"I dare say each of them may have thought of trying to make

me his property," she said. "But to have me with them across the kind of country that lies between here and Kabin, slowing them down and causing quarrels—I'm not surprised that Farrass decided against that. He probably expected that as soon as I'd learned from you what they meant to do I'd come back and beg him to take me. When I didn't, he thought he'd show me how little I meant to them. They always felt resentment, you know, because they naturally supposed the Baron was my lover, but they feared him and needed him too much to show it. All the same, I wondered yesterday whether they might not try to force me to go with them. That was why I left it to you to tell them that Santil was at Kabin. I wanted to be well out of the way when they learned that."

"Why didn't you warn me to conceal it from them? They might have come here for you."

"If they'd learned it from someone else—and one never knows what news is going to reach Zeray—they'd have had strong suspicions that we had concealed it. They'd probably have turned against us then, and that could have been nasty."

She paused, kneeling down before the fire. After a time she said, "Perhaps I wanted them to go."

"Your danger's greater now they're gone."

She smiled and went on staring into the fire. At length she answered, "Possibly—possibly not. You remember what you told me Farrass said—"Someone's bound to try soon." Anyway, I know where I'd rather be. Things have changed very much with me, you know."

Later, he persuaded her to keep to the house so that people, no longer seeing her, might suppose that she had gone with Farrass and Thrild. Ankray, when told, nodded approvingly.

"There's sure to be trouble now, sir," he said. "It'll likely take a day or two to come to the boil, but when a wolf moves out, a wolf moves in, as they say."

"Do you think we may be attacked here?"

"Not necessarily, sir. It might come to that and it might not. We'll just have to see how things turn out. But I dare say we'll still be here all right when General Santil comes."

Kelderek had not told Ankray what he himself had to expect in this eventuality; nor did he do so now.

Later that afternoon, taking with him a knife and some fish-

411

ing tackle—two hand-lines of woven thread and hair, three or four small, fire-hardened wooden hooks, and a paste of meat fat and dried fruit kneaded together—he went down to the shore. He could observe no change from the previous day in the lackluster movements and aimless loitering of the men whom he saw. Although some had cast lines from a kind of spit running out into deeper water, the place did not look to him a likely one for a catch. After watching them for a time, he made his way unobtrusively upstream, coming at length to the graveyard and its creek. Here, too, there were a few fishermen, but none who struck him as either skilled or painstaking. He was surprised, for from what he had heard the town to a large extent depended for food on catching fish and birds.

Retracing his steps of two days before, he went inland, up the shore of the creek, until he found a spot where, with the help of an overhanging tree, he was able to scramble across. Half an hour later he had regained the Telthearna bank and come upon what he had been seeking—a deep pool close inshore, with trees and bushes giving cover.

It was satisfying to find that he had not lost his old skill. As a man tormented by a lawsuit, by money troubles or anxiety about a woman, can nevertheless derive pleasure and actual solace from a game skillfully played or a plant which he has nurtured into bloom (so accurate, despite all the mind's attempts to mislead it, is the heart's divination of where true delight is to be found), so Kelderek, despite his conviction that he would die in Zeray, despite his fears for the Tuginda, his grief for the evil he had done and the hopelessness of his longing for Melathys (for what possibility could there now be, in the time left to him in this evil place, of healing the wounds inflicted by all she had undergone at the hands of men?), still found comfort in the windless, cloudy afternoon, in the light on the water, the silence broken only by the faint breeze and river sounds and in his own ability, where a man lacking it would have wasted the time idling at one end of a motionless line. Here at least was something he could do—and a pity, he thought bitterly, that he had ever left it. Would he not, if Shardik had never appeared on Ortelga, have remained a contented hunter and fisher, Kelderek Play-with-the-Children, looking no further than his solitary, hard-acquired skill and evening games on the shore? He put these thoughts aside and set to work in earnest.

After lying prone and hidden for some time, ground-baiting the pool and fishing each part of it with watchful attention, he hooked a fish which he was obliged to play with great care on the light handline before at last it broke surface and proved to be a good-sized trout. A few minutes more and he contrived to snatch it with a finger and thumb thrust into the gills. Then, sucking his bleeding scratches, he cast out again.

By the early evening he had taken three more trout and a perch, lost a hook and a length of line and run out of bait. The air was watery and cool, the clearing sky feathered with light cloud, and he could neither hear nor smell Zeray. For a time he sat beside the pool, wondering whether their best course, when the Tuginda had recovered, might not be to leave Zeray altogether and, now that the summer was approaching, live and hunt in the open, as they had lived on Ortelga during the days of Shardik's cure and first wanderings. From murder they would be safer than in Zeray, and with Ankray's help he should be able to forage for them well enough. As for his own life, if Erketlis's troops came his chances of escape, even if they put a price on his head, would be better than if he were to await them in Zeray. Deciding that he would put the idea to Melathys that evening, he wound the lines carefully, threaded his fish on a stick and set out to return.

It was twilight when he crossed the creek but, peering toward Zeray through the mist which already covered the shoreward ground and now seemed to be creeping inland, he could see not one lamp shining. Filled with a sudden and more immediate fear than he had hitherto felt of this cinder pit of burnt-out rogues, he cut a cudgel from a tree before continuing on his way. He had not been alone outdoors and after dark since the night on the battlefield and now, as the twilight deepened, he became more and more nervous and uneasy. Unable to face the graveyard, he turned short to his right and was soon stumbling among muddy pools and tussocks of coarse grass as big as his head. When at last he came to the outskirts of Zeray he could not tell in which direction the Baron's house might lie. Houses and hovels stood haphazard as anthills in a field. There were no definable streets or alleys, as in a true town: neither loiterers nor passers-by; and although he could now see, here and there, faint streaks of light showing through the chinks of doors and shutters, he knew better than to knock. For an hour—or less than an hour, perhaps, or more—he wandered gropingly in the dark, starting at every noise and hastening to set his back against the nearest wall and, as he crept on, expecting each moment a blow on the back of the head. Suddenly, as he stood looking up at the few stars visible through the mist and trying to make out which way he was facing, he realized that the roof outlined faintly against the sky was that of the Baron's house. Making quickly toward it, he tripped over something pliant and fell his length in the mud. At once a door opened nearby and two men appeared, one carrying a light. He had just time to scramble to his feet before they reached him.

"Fell over the cord, eh?" said the man without the light, who had an axe in one hand. He spoke in Beklan and, seeing that Kelderek understood him, continued, "That's what the cord's for, to be sure. Why you hanging round here, eh?"

"I'm not—I'm going home," said Kelderek, watching them closely.

"Home?" The man gave a short laugh. "First time I heard it called that in Zeray."

"Good night," said Kelderek. "I'm sorry I disturbed you."

"Not so fast," said the other man, taking a step to one side. "Fisherman, are you?" Suddenly he started, held up his light and looked more searchingly at Kelderek. "God!" he said. "I know you. You're the Ortelgan king of Bekla!"

The first man peered in his turn. "He mucking is, too," he said. "Aren't you? The Ortelgan king of Bekla, him as used to talk to the bear?"

"Don't be ridiculous," said Kelderek. "I don't even know what you mean."

"We was Beklans once," said the second man, "until we had to run for knifing an Ortelgan bastard that mucking well deserved it. I reckon its your turn now. Lost your bear, have you?"

"I was never in Bekla in my life and as for the bear, I've never even seen it."

"You're an Ortelgan all right, though," said the second man.

414

"D'you think we can't tell that? You talk the same as the mucking lot of them—"

"And I tell you I never left Ortelga until I had to come here, and I wouldn't know the bear if I saw it. To hell with the bear!"

"You bloody liar!" The first man swung up his axe. Kelderek hit him quickly with his cudgel, turned and ran. The light went out as they followed and they stopped uncertainly. He found himself before the courtyard door and hammered on it, shouting, "Ankray! Ankray!" At once they were after him. He shouted again, dropped the fish, gripped his cudgel and faced about. He heard the bolts being drawn. Then the door opened and Ankray was beside him, jabbing with a spear into the dark and cursing like a peasant with a bull on the pole. The oncoming footsteps faltered and Kelderek, sufficiently self-possessed to pick up his fish, pulled Ankray through the door into the courtyard and bolted it behind them.

"Thank God it was no worse, sir," said Ankray. "I've been out here waiting for you since nightfall. I thought like enough you might run into some kind of trouble. The priestess has been very anxious. It's always dangerous after dark."

"It's lucky for me you did wait," answered Kelderek. "Thanks for your help. Those fellows don't seem to like Ortelgans."

"It's not a matter of Ortelgans, sir," said Ankray reproachfully. "No one's safe in Zeray after dark. Now the Baron, he always—"

Melathys appeared at the inner door, holding a lamp above her head and staring out in silence. Coming close, he saw that she was trembling. He smiled, but she looked up at him unsmilingly, forlorn and pallid as the moon in daylight. On an impulse, and feeling it to be the most natural thing in the world, he put one arm around her shoulder, bent and kissed her cheek. "Don't be angry," he said. "I've learned my lesson, I promise you, and at least I've got something to show for it." He sat down by the fire and threw on a log. "Bring me a pail, Ankray, and I'll gut these fish. Hot water too, if you've got it. I'm filthy." Then, realizing that the girl had still said not a word, he asked her, "The Tuginda—how is she?"

"Better. I think she's begun to recover."

Now she smiled, and at once he perceived that her natural

415

anxiety, her alarm at the sound of the scuffle outside, her impulse to anger with him, had been no more than clouds across the sun. "So have you," he thought, looking at her. Her presence was instinct with a new quality at once natural, complementary and enhancing, like that imparted by snow to a mountain peak or a dove to a myrtle tree. Where another might have noticed nothing, to him the change was as plain and entire as that of spring branches misted green with the first appearing leaves. Her face no longer looked drawn. Her bearing and movements, the very cadence of her voice, were smoother, gentler and more assured. Looking at her now, he had no need to call upon his memories of the beautiful priestess of Quiso.

"She woke this afternoon and we talked together for a time. The fever was lower and she was able to eat a little. She's sleeping again now, more peacefully."

"It's good news," replied Kelderek. "I was afraid she must have taken some infection—some pestilence. Now I believe it was no more than shock and exhaustion."

"She's still weak. She'll need rest and quiet for some time; and fresh food she must have—but that, I hope, we can get. Are you a sorcerer, Kelderek, to catch trout in Zeray? They're almost the first I've ever seen. How was it done?"

"By knowing where to look and how to go about it."

"It's a foretaste of good luck. Believe that, won't you, for I do. But stay here tomorrow—don't go out again—for Ankray's off to Lak. If he's to get back before nightfall he'll need all day."

"Lak? Where is Lak?"

"Lak's the village I told you of, about eight or nine miles to the north. The Baron used to call it his secret cupboard. Glabron once robbed Lak and murdered a man there, so when the Baron had killed him I took care that they should learn of it. He promised them they should never again be troubled from Zeray and later, when he'd got control—or as much control as we ever had —he used to send them a few men at harvest and in the hut-building season—any he felt he could trust. In the end, one or two were actually allowed to settle in Lak. It was part of another scheme of the Baron's for settling men from Zeray throughout the province. Like so many of our schemes, it never got far for lack of material; but at least it achieved something—it gave us a private larder. Bel-ka-Trazet never asked for anything from Lak, but we traded, as I told you, and the elder thought it prudent to send him gifts from time to time. Since he died, though, they must have been waiting on events, for we've had no message, and while I was alone I was afraid to send Ankray so far. Now you're here, he can go and try our luck. I've got a little money I can give him. He's known in Lak, of course, and they might let us have some fresh food for the sake of old times."

"Wouldn't we be safer there than in Zeray—all four of us?"

"Why, yes—if they would suffer us. If Ankray gets the chance tomorrow, he's going to tell the chief about the flight of Farrass and Thrild and about the Tuginda and yourself. But Kelderek, you know the minds of village elders—half ox, half fox, as they say. Their old fear of Zeray will have returned; and if we show them that we are in haste to leave it, they will wonder why and fear the more. If we could take refuge in Lak, we might yet find a way out of this trap; but everything depends on showing no haste. Besides, we can't go until the Tuginda has recovered. The most that Ankray will be able to do tomorrow is to see how the land lies. Are your fish ready? Good. I'll cook three of them and put the other two by. We'll feast tonight, for to tell you the truth—" she dropped her voice in a pretense of secrecy and leaned toward him, smiling and speaking behind her hand—"neither Ankray nor the Baron ever had the knack of catching fish!"

When they had eaten and Ankray, after drinking to the fisherman's skill in the sharp wine, had gone to watch by the Tuginda while he wove a fresh length of line out of thread from an old cloak and a strand of Melathys' hair, Kelderek, sitting close to the girl so that he could keep his voice low, recounted all that had happened since the day in Bekla when Zelda had first told him of his belief that Erketlis could not be defeated. Those things which had all but destroyed him, those things of which he was most ashamed—the elder who had thought him a slave trader, the Streels of Urtah, the breaking of his mind upon the battlefield, Elleroth's mercy, the reason for it and the manner of his leaving Kabin—these he told without concealment, looking into the fire as though alone, but never for a moment losing his sense of the sympathy of this listener, to whom defilement, regret and shame had long been as familiar as they had become to himself. As he spoke of the Tuginda's explanation of what had happened at the Streels and of the ordained and now inevitable death of Shardik, he felt Melathys' hand laid gently upon his arm. He covered it with his own, and it was as though his longing for her broke in upon and quenched the flow of his story. He fell silent, and at length she said, "And Lord Shardik —where is he now?"

"No one knows. He crossed the Vrako, but I believe he may be already dead. I have wished myself dead many times, but now—"

"Why then did you come to Zeray?"

"Why indeed? For the same reason as any other criminal. To the Yeldashay I'm an outlawed slave trader. I was driven across the Vrako; and once across it, where else can a man go but Zeray? Besides, as you know, I fell in with the Tuginda. Yet there is another reason, or so I believe. I have disgraced and perverted the divine power of Shardik, so that all that now remains to God is his death. That disgrace and death will be required of me, and where should I wait but in Zeray?"

"Yet you have been speaking of saving our lives by going to Lak?"

"Yes, and if I can I will. A man on the earth is but an animal and what animal will not try to save its life while there remains a chance?"

Gently she withdrew her hand. "Now listen to the wisdom of a coward, a murderer's woman, a defiled priestess of Quiso. If you try to save your life you will lose it. Either you can accept the truth of what you have told me and wait humbly and patiently upon the outcome—or else you can run up and down this land, this rats' cage, like any other fugitive, never admitting to what is past and using a little more fraud to gain a little more time, until both run out."

"The outcome?"

"An outcome there will surely be. Since I turned and saw the Tuginda standing at the Baron's grave, I have come to understand a great deal—more than I can put into words. But that is why I am here with you and not with Farrass and Thrild. In the sight of God there is only one time and only one story, of which all days on earth and all human events are parts. But that can only be discovered—it cannot be taught."

Puzzled and daunted by her words, he nevertheless felt comforted that she should think him worth her solicitude, even while he grasped—or thought he grasped—that she was advising him to resign himself to death. Presently, to prolong the time of sitting thus close beside her, he asked, "If the Yeldashay come, they may well help the Tuginda to return to Quiso. Shall you return with her?"

"I am—what you know. I can never set foot on Quiso again. It would be sacrilege."

"What will you do?"

"I told you—wait upon the outcome. Kelderek, you must have faith in life. I have been restored to faith in life. If only they would understand it, the task of the disgraced and guilty is not to struggle to redeem themselves but simply to wait, never to cease to wait, in the hope and expectation of redemption. Many err in setting that hope aside, in losing belief that they are still sons and daughters."

He shook his head, gazing into her smiling, wine-flushed face with such a look of bewilderment that she burst out laughing; and then, leaning forward to stir the fire, half-murmured, half-sang the refrain of an Ortelgan lullaby which he had long forgotten.

> Where does the moon go every month
> And where have the old years fled?
> Don't trouble your poor old head, my dear,
> Don't trouble your poor old head.

"You didn't know I knew that, did you?"

"You're happy," he said, feeling envy.

"And you will be," she answered, taking his hands in her own. "Yes, even though we die. There, that's enough of riddling for one night; it's time to sleep. But I'll tell you something easier, and this you *can* understand and believe." He looked at her expectantly, and she said with emphasis, "That was the best fish I've ever eaten in Zeray. Catch some more!"

46　*The Kynat*

OPENING HIS EYES NEXT MORNING, Kelderek knew at once that he
had been woken by some unusual sound. Uncertain, he lay as
still as though in wait for a beast. Suddenly the sound came
again, so close that he started. It was the call of the *kynat*—two
smooth, fluting notes, the second higher than the first, followed
by a chirring trill cut suddenly short. On the instant he was
back in Ortelga, with the gleam from the Telthearna reflected on
the inside of the hut roof, the smell of green-wood smoke and
his father whistling as he sharpened his knife on a stone. The
beautiful, gold-and-purple bird came to the Telthearna in spring
but seldom remained, continuing its passage northward. Despite
its marvelous plumage, to kill it was unlucky and ill-omened,
for it brought the summer and bestowed blessing, announcing
its good news to all—"Kynat! Kynat churrrrr—ak!" ("Kynat,
Kynat will tell!") Welcome and propitious hero of many songs
and tales, it would be heard and blessed for a month and then
be gone, leaving behind it, like a gift, the best season of the
year. Biting his lower lip in his stealth, Kelderek crept to the
window, noiselessly lifted the stout bar, opened the shutter a
crack and looked out.

The kynat, not thirty feet away, was perched on the roof
ridge on the opposite side of the little courtyard. The vivid
purple of its breast and back glowed in the first sunlight, more
magnificent than an emperor's banner. The crest, purple inter-
plumed with gold, was erect, and the broad flange of the tail,
each feather bordered with gold, lay open upon the gray slope
of the tiles, brilliant as a butterfly on a stone. Seen thus at close
quarters, it was inexpressibly beautiful, with a splendor beyond
description to those who had never seen it. The river sunset, the
orchid pendent in mossy shade, the translucent, colored flames
of temple incenses and gums wavering in their copper bowls—
none could surpass this bird, displayed in the morning silence
like a testament, a visible exemplar of the beauty and humility
of God. As Kelderek gazed, it suddenly spread its wings, dis-

playing the soft, saffron-colored down of the undersides. It opened its bill and called again, "Kynat! Kynat will tell!" Then it was gone, eastward toward the river.

Kelderek flung back the shutter and stood dazzled in the sun that had just cleared the wall. As he did so, another shutter opened on his left and Melathys, in her shift, her arms bare and her long hair loose, leaned out, as though trying to follow with her eyes the flight of the kynat. She caught sight of him, started for a moment and then, smiling, pointed silently after the bird, like a child to whom gestures come more naturally than words. Kelderek nodded and raised one hand in the sign used by Ortelgan messengers and returning hunters to signify good news. He realized that she, like him, felt the accident of his seeing her half-naked simply as something acceptable between them; not that it was no matter, as it might have been in the commotion of a fire or some other disaster, but rather that its significance was altered, as though in a time of festival, from immodesty to a happy extravagance becoming the occasion. To use plain terms, he thought, the kynat had taken her out of herself, because that was the kind of lass she was. And as this thought crossed his mind, he realized also that he had ceased to think of her as either the one-time priestess of Quiso or the consort of Bel-ka-Trazet. His understanding of her had outgrown these images, which had now opened, like doors, to admit him to a warmer, undissembling reality within. Henceforth, in his mind, Melathys would be a woman whom he knew, and whatever front she might present to the world he, like herself, would look through it from the inside, aware of much, if not all, that it concealed from others. He found that he was trembling. He laughed and sat down on the bed.

What had taken place, he knew, involved a contradiction. After all she had suffered, she no doubt felt impatient of conventional ideas of modesty. Nevertheless, what she had done sprang from sensitivity and not from shamelessness. Carried away by her delight in the kynat, she had yet known well enough that he would understand that this was no invitation, in the sense that Thrild or Ruvit would receive it. She had been sure that he would accept what he saw simply as part of their common delight in the moment. She would not have behaved before another man in this way. So in fact there was an invitation—to a deeper level of confidence, where formality and even propriety could be used or set aside entirely as they might be felt to help or hinder mutual understanding. In such a framework, desire could wait to find its allotted place.

So much, though it was new to him and outside any experience that he had had of the dealings between men and women, Kelderek understood. His excitement grew intense. He longed for Melathys, her voice, her company, her mere presence, to the exclusion of all else. He became determined to save her life and his own, to take her away from Zeray, to leave behind forever the wars of Ikat and Bekla, the sour vocation that had fallen upon him unsought and the fruitless hope which he had once entertained of discovering the great secret to be imparted through Shardik. To reach Lak and from there, somehow, to escape with this girl who had restored to him the desire to live— if it could be done, he would do it. If it were possible for her to love a man, he would win her with a fervor and constancy beyond any in the world. He stood up, stretched out his hands and began to pray with passionate earnestness.

A stick tapped gently upon the courtyard paving and he turned with a start to see Ankray standing outside the window, cloaked and hooded, carrying a sack over his shoulder and armed with a sword at his belt and a kind of rough javelin or short spear. He was holding one finger to his lips, and Kelderek went over to him.

"Are you off to Lak?" he asked.

"Yes, sir. The priestess has given me some money and I'll make it go far enough. You'll be wanting to bolt the gate behind me. I just thought I'd tell you without letting the priestess know —there's a dead man lying in the road—a stranger, I reckon— some newcomer, maybe: they're the ones that catch it soonest here, as often as not. You'll want to be very careful while I'm gone. I wouldn't go out, sir, or leave the women at all, not if I was you. Anything could happen in the town just now."

"But aren't you the one that needs to be careful?" replied Kelderek. "Do you think you ought to go?"

Ankray laughed. "Oh, they're no match for me, sir," he said. "Now the Baron, he always used to say, 'Ankray,' he used to say, 'you knock 'em down, I'll pick 'em up.' Well, after all, you don't have to pick 'em up, sir, now do you? So if I just go on knocking 'em down, it'll all be the same, you see."

Apparently highly satisfied with this piece of incontrovertible logic, Ankray leaned comfortably against the wall. "Yes, sir," he said, "the Baron always used to say, 'Ankray, you knock 'em down—' "

"I'll come and see you off," said Kelderek, leaving the window. At the courtyard gate he drew the bolts and stepped out first into the empty lane. The dead man was lying on his back about thirty yards away, eyes open and arms spread wide. The flesh of his face and hands had a fixed, pale, waxen look. His sprawling, untidy posture, together with the few torn clothes left on the body, made him look less like a corpse than like rubbish, something broken and thrown away. One finger had been severed, no doubt to remove a ring, and the stump showed as a dull red circle against the pallid hand.

"Well, you see how it is, sir," said Ankray. "I'll just be getting along now. If you take my advice, you'll leave it alone. There's others will take it away—you can be sure of that. If by any chance I shouldn't be back before dark, perhaps you'd be so kind as to wait in the courtyard, same as I did for you last night. But I shan't be loitering."

He swung up his sack and set off, looking sharply about him as he went.

Kelderek bolted the door and returned to the house. Ankray had cleared and swept the kitchen hearth but lit no fire, and he was washing in cold water when Melathys came in, carrying a dark red robe and some other garments. Kelderek, head bent over the pail, smiled up at her, shaking the water out of his eyes and ears.

"These were the Baron's," she said, "but that's no reason to leave them folded away forever. They'll fit quite as well as your soldier's clothes and be far more comfortable." She laid them down, filled a pitcher for the Tuginda and took it away.

As he dressed, he wondered whether this might be the very robe which Bel-ka-Trazet had been wearing when he fled from Ortelga. If it were not, he could only have taken it from some enemy killed since, for it was inconceivable that such a garment

423

could have been traded in Zeray. Elleroth himself, he thought wryly, might have sported it with confidence. It was of excellent cloth, evenly dyed a clear, dark red, and the workmanship was so fine that the seams were almost invisible. It was, as Melathys had said, very comfortable, being yielding and smooth, and the very act of wearing it seemed to remove him a step further from his dismal wanderings and the sufferings he had undergone.

The Tuginda, thinner and hollow-eyed, was sitting up, propped against the wall behind the bed while Melathys combed her hair. Kelderek, taking one of her hands between his own, asked whether she would like him to bring her some food. She shook her head.

"Later," she answered. Then, after a little, "Kelderek, thank you for helping me to reach Zeray—and I must ask your forgiveness for deceiving you in one matter."

"For deceiving me, säiyett? How?"

"I knew, of course, what had become of the Baron. All news reaches Quiso. I expected to find him here, but I did not tell you. I could see that you were badly shocked and exhausted, and I thought it better not to trouble you further. But he would not have harmed you, neither you nor me."

"You don't need to ask forgiveness of me, säiyett, but since you have, it's given very willingly."

"Melathys has told me that now that the Baron is gone there's no possibility of our finding help in Zeray."

She sighed deeply, staring down at her sunlit hands on the blanket with a look so disappointed and hopeless that he was moved, as people are apt to be by pity, to say more than he could be sure of.

"Don't distress yourself, säiyett. It's true enough that this is a place of rogues and worse, but as soon as you're well enough we shall leave—Melathys, you and I and the Baron's man. There's a village not far to the north where I hope we may find safety."

"Melathys told me. The servant has set out to go there today. Will the poor man be safe?"

Kelderek laughed. "There's one person who's sure of it and that's himself."

The Tuginda closed her eyes wearily and Melathys put down the comb.

"You should rest again now, säiyett," she said, "and then try to eat something. I'll be off to the kitchen, for there's a fire to be lit before I can cook."

The Tuginda nodded without opening her eyes. Kelderek followed Melathys out of the room. When he had laid the fire, she lit it with a fragment of curved glass held in a sunbeam. He was content to stand and watch as she busied herself with the food, only speaking a word occasionally or trying to anticipate her need of this or that. The room seemed as full of calm and reassurance as of sunlight, and for the time being, the future caused no more anxiety to him than to the joyous insects darting in the brightness outside.

Later, as the day, moving toward noon, filled the courtyard with a heat like that of summer, Melathys drew water from the well, washed the household clothes and laid them in the sun to dry. Coming back into the shade of the house, she sat down in the narrow window seat, wiping her neck and forehead with a rough cloth in place of a towel.

"Elsewhere, women can go and wash clothes in the river and take it for granted," she said. "That's what rivers are for— laundry and gossip: but not in Zeray."

"On Quiso?"

"On Quiso we were often less solemn than you may suppose. But I was thinking of any town or village where ordinary, decent people can go about the business of life without fear: yes, and without dragging shame behind them like a chain. Wouldn't it be fine—wouldn't it seem like a miracle—just to go to a market, to bargain with a stall-keeper, to loiter in the road eating something that you'd bought fair and honestly, to give some of it away to a friend while you gossiped by the river? I remember those things—the Quiso girls came and went a good deal on the island's business, you know. In some ways we were freer than other women. To be deprived of little, common pleasures that honest people take for granted—that's imprisonment, that's retribution, that's grief and loss. If people valued such things at their worth, they'd give themselves more credit for the common trust and honesty on which those things depend."

425

"You've got some compensation. Most women can't use words like that," answered Kelderek. "It's a narrow life for a village girl—cooking, weaving, children, pounding clothes on the stones."

"Perhaps," she said. "Perhaps. Birds sing in the trees, find their food, mate, build nests. They don't know anything else." She looked up at him, smiling and drawing the cloth slowly from side to side across the back of her neck. "It's a narrow life for birds. But you catch one and put it in a cage and you'll soon find out whether it values what it's lost."

He longed to take her in his arms so strongly that for a few moments his head swam. To conceal his feelings he bent over his knife and half-finished fishhook.

"You sing, too," he said. "I've heard you."

"Yes. I'll sing now, if you like. I sometimes used to sing for the Baron. He liked to hear old songs he remembered, but really it was all the same to him who sang them—Ankray would do. By the Ledges, you should hear him!"

"No—you. I can wait to hear Ankray."

She rose, peeped in at the Tuginda, left the room and returned with a plain, unornamented *hinnari* of light-colored *sestuaga* wood, much battered along the fingerboard. She put it into his hands. It was warped and more than a little out of true.

"Don't you say a word against it," she said. "As far as I know, it's the only one in Zeray. It was found floating down the river and the Baron put his pride in his pocket and begged the strings from Lak. If they break there aren't any more."

Sitting down again in the window seat, she plucked the strings softly for a while, adjusting and coaxing the hard-toned hinnari into such tune as it possessed. Then, looking into her lap as though singing to herself alone, she sang the old ballad of U-Deparioth and the Silver Flower of Sarkid. Kelderek remembered the tale—still told as true in that country—how Deparioth, abandoned by traitors in the terrible Blue Forest, left to wander till he died and long given up for lost by friends and servants, had been roused from his despair by a mysterious and beautiful girl, dressed like a queen in that desolate wilderness. She tended his hurts, found him fruits, fungus and roots fit to eat, restored his courage and guided his limping steps day by

426

day through the maze of the woods, until at last they came to a place that he knew. But as he turned to lead her toward the friends running to meet them, she vanished and he saw only a tall, silver lily blooming where she had been standing in the long grass. Heartbroken, he sank weeping to the ground, and ever after longed only to recover those days of hardship that he had spent with her in the forest.

> Give back the miry solitude,
> The thorns and briars outstretched to bless.
> There lay my kingdom, past compare:
> This court's the desert wilderness.

Ending, she was silent, and he too said nothing, knowing that there was no need for him to speak. She plucked the strings idly for a while and then, as though on impulse, broke into the little song "Cat Catch a Fish," that generations of Ortelgan children had known and played on the shore. He could not help laughing with delight to be taken thus by surprise, for he had neither heard nor thought of the song since he himself had left Ortelga.

"Have you lived on Ortelga, then?" he asked. "I don't remember you when I was a child."

"On Ortelga—no. I learned that song as a child on Quiso."

"You were a *child* on Quiso?" He had no recollection of what Rantzay had once told him. "Then when—"

"You don't know how I came to Quiso? I'll tell you. I was born on a slave farm in Tonilda and if I ever knew my mother, I can't remember her. That was before the Slave Wars and we were simply goods to be prepared for sale. When I was seven the farm was taken by Santil-kè-Erketlis and the Heldril. A wounded captain was making the journey to Quiso to be healed by the Tuginda, and he took me and a girl called Bria, to offer us to be brought up as priestesses. Bria ran away before we reached the Telthearna and what became of her I never knew. But I became a child of the Ledges."

"Were you happy?"

"Oh, yes. To have a home and wise, good people to love you and look after you, after being part of the stock of a slave farm —you can't imagine what that meant. It's not incurable, you know—the harm done to an ill-treated child. Everyone was kind

427

—I was spoiled. I got on well—I was clever, you see—and I grew up to believe that I was God's gift to Quiso. That was why, when the time came, I wasn't fit for any real self-sacrifice, as poor Rantzay was." She was silent for a little and then said, "But I've learned since then."

"Are you sorry that you'll never go back to Quiso?"

"Not now. I told you, it's been made plain to me—"

He interrupted her. "Not too late?"

"Oh, yes," she answered, "it's always too late." She got up and, passing close to him on her way to the Tuginda's room, bent down so that her lips just brushed his ear. "No, it's never too late." A few moments afterward she called to him to come and help the Tuginda to a seat by the fire, while she made the bed and swept the room.

During the latter part of the afternoon the sun became cooler and the courtyard shady. They sat outside, near the fig tree by the wall, Melathys on a bench under the Tuginda's open window, Kelderek on the coping of the well. After a time, disturbed in memory by the low chuckling and whispering sounds deep in the shaft, he rose and began to gather up the clothes she had spread during the morning.

"Some of these haven't dried, Melathys."

She stretched lazily, arching her back and lifting her face to the sky.

"They will."

"Not by tonight."

"M'mm. Fuss, fuss."

"I'll spread them on the roof for you, if you like. It's still sunny there."

"No way up."

"In Bekla every house had steps up to the roof."

"In Bekla town the pigs all fly, and the wine in the river goes gurgling by—"

Looking up the fifteen or sixteen feet of the wall, he picked a way, scrambled up the rough stonework, got both hands on the parapet and pulled himself over. Inside there was a drop of about a foot to the flat, stone roof. He tried it cautiously, but it was solid enough and he stepped down. The stones were warm in the sun.

"Throw the clothes up and I'll spread them."

"It must be dirty."

"A broom, then. Can you—"

He broke off, looking toward the river.

"What is it?" called Melathys, with a touch of anxiety. Kelderek did not answer and she asked again, more urgently.

"Men on the opposite side of the river."

"*What?*" She stared up at him incredulously. "That's a desert shore, no village for forty miles, or so I've always been told. I've never seen a man there since I've been here."

"Well, you can now."

"What are they doing?"

"I can't make out. They look like soldiers. People this side seem just as much surprised as you."

"Help me up, Kelderek."

After a little difficulty she climbed high enough for him to grasp her wrists and pull her up. Stepping on the roof, she immediately knelt down behind the parapet and motioned him to copy her.

"A month ago we might have stood openly on a roof in Zeray. I don't think I would now."

Together they looked eastward. Along the Zeray waterfront the rabble of loiterers had gathered in groups, talking together and pointing across the river. On the far shore, about half a mile from where they were kneeling on the roof, a band of perhaps fifty men could be seen, intent on some business of their own among the rocks.

"That man on the left—he's giving orders, do you see?"

"But what is it they're carrying?"

"Stakes. Look at that nearer one—it must be as long as the center-pole of an Ortelgan hut. I suppose they're going to build a hut—but whatever for?"

"Heaven knows—but one thing's certain, it can't be anything to do with Zeray. No one's ever yet crossed that strait. The current's far too strong."

"They're soldiers, aren't they?"

"I think so—or else a hunting expedition."

"In a desert? Look, they've started digging. And those are two great mauls they've got there. So when they've sunk those stakes deep enough to be able to get at the heads, they must be going to drive them in further."

"For a hut?"

"Well, let's wait and see. They'll probably—"

He stopped as she laid a hand on his arm and drew him back from the parapet.

"What is it?"

She lowered her voice. "Possibly nothing. But there was a man watching us from below—one of your friends of last night, I dare say. It might be better to go down now, in case he has ideas of breaking in. Anyway, the less attention we attract the better, and out of sight out of mind's a good maxim in this place."

After he had helped her down, he closed and secured the shutters of the few windows on the outer wall, brought Ankray's heavy spear into the courtyard and remained listening for some time. All was quiet, however, and at length he returned indoors. The Tuginda was awake and he sat down near the foot of the bed, content to listen while she and Melathys talked of old days on Quiso. Once the Tuginda spoke of Ged-la-Dan, but though Melathys evidently understood well enough the terms she used in describing his fruitless attempts to reach the island, Kelderek could make nothing of them.

Nor, he thought, was there any reason why he should. Melathys had said that she would never return there and certainly he would not. Magic, mysticism, the fulfillment of prophecies and the search for meanings beyond those of hearth and home— it was little enough he had gained from them, unless indeed he could count his hard-won experience. But though he himself was disillusioned, it seemed from what she had said that Melathys was not. It was clear enough, too, that the Tuginda thought of her as healed or redeemed—if those terms had any meaning—in some sense that did not apply to himself. No doubt, he thought, this was because Melathys had begged her forgiveness. Why had he been unable to do so?

Soon it would be dusk. Still deep in his thoughts, he left the women together and went out into the courtyard to wait for Ankray.

He was leaning against the bolted gate, listening for any

sound of approach and wondering whether he should climb once more to the roof when, looking up, he saw Melathys standing in the doorway. The flame-light of evening covered her from head to foot and showed the long fall of her hair as a smooth, glowing shadow, like the curved trough of a wave. As a man, having stopped to gaze at a rainbow, continues on his way but then, turning to look at it once more, is immediately enraptured yet again by its marvelous beauty, as though he had never seen it in his life before, so Kelderek was moved by the sight of Melathys. Arrested by his fixed look and catching, as it were, the echo of herself in his eyes, the girl stood still, smiling a little, as though to tell him that she was happy to oblige him until he should find himself able to release her from his gaze.

"Don't move," he said, at once bidding and entreating, and she showed neither confusion nor embarrassment, but a dignity joyous, spontaneous and unassuming as a dancer's. Suddenly, with an illusion like that which, in the hall of the King's House at Bekla, while he stood awaiting the soldiers bringing Elleroth, had shown him Shardik as both bear and distant mountain summit, he saw her as the tall zoan tree on the shore of Ortelga—an enclosing arbor of ferny boughs by the waterside. Without taking his eyes from hers, he crossed the courtyard.

"What do you see?" asked Melathys, looking up at him with a little spurt of laughter; and Kelderek, recalling the power of the priestesses of Quiso, wondered whether she herself had called the image of the zoan into his mind.

"A tall tree by the river," he answered. "A landmark for a homecoming."

Taking her hands in his own, he raised them to his lips. As he did so, there fell upon the courtyard door a rapid, urgent knocking. This was followed immediately by an ugly sound of jeering and Ankray's voice calling, "Now then, be off with you, and look sharp about it!"

431

47 *Ankray's News*

KELDEREK, SNATCHING UP THE SPEAR, ran and drew the bolts and Ankray, his sword drawn in his hand, ducked his head and stepped backward into the courtyard, slipping his sack from his shoulder as Kelderek shut the gate.

"I hope all's well, sir, with you and the priestesses," he said, drawing the javelin from his belt and sitting down on the coping of the well to pull off his muddy leggings. "I did my best to get back as quick as I could, but it's a fair step over that rough country."

Kelderek, unable at once to find words, merely nodded but then, unwilling to seem churlish to this good fellow who had risked his life for their sakes, laid a hand on his shoulder and smiled.

"No, no trouble here," he said. "You'd better come in and have a wash and a drink. Let me take your sack—that's it. By God, it's heavy! You haven't been too unlucky, then?"

"Well, yes and no, sir," replied Ankray, stooping to enter the doorway. "I was able to pick up a few things, true enough. I've got some fresh meat, if the priestess could fancy a bit of it this evening."

"I'll cook it," said Melathys, bringing a bowl of hot water and crushing herbs into it as she put it down on the floor. "You've done enough for one day. No, don't be stupid, Ankray: of course I'm going to wash your feet. I want to have a look at them. There's a cut, for a start. Keep still."

"There are three full wineskins in this sack," said Kelderek, looking into it, "as well as the meat and these two cheeses and some loaves. Here's some oil, and what's this—lard? And some leather. You must be as strong as five oxen to have carried this lot nine miles."

"Mind the fishhooks and the knifeblades, sir," said Ankray. "They're loose, but then I know where I put them, you see."

"Well, whatever your news is, let's eat first," said Kelderek. "If this is the *Yes*, we may as well make the most of it before you start on the *No*. Come on, drink some of this wine you've brought, and here's your good health."

It was well over an hour before the meal had been cooked and eaten. Ankray and Kelderek, after going out of the gate to look round the house, test the barred shutters from outside and make sure all was quiet, returned to find that Melathys had taken two lamps from the kitchen to add to that already in the Tuginda's room. The Tuginda welcomed Ankray and thanked him, praising his strength and courage and questioning him so warmly and sincerely that he soon found himself giving her an account of the day's adventures with as little constraint as he might have related it to the Baron. She told him to fetch a stool and sit down, and he did so without embarrassment.

"Do they still remember the Baron kindly in Lak?" asked Melathys.

"Oh yes, säiyett," answered the man. "There was two or three of them asked me whether I thought it would be safe if they was to come here, to pay their respects, like, at the grave. I said I'd fix a day to meet them, to make sure of them finding the right spot. They've got a great opinion of the Baron, have the folk in Lak."

"Did you get any chance to tell them about what's happened, or to find out whether we may be able to go there?"

"Well, that's just it, säiyett: I can't say as I was able to get far there. You see, I couldn't talk to the chief or any of the elders. It seems they're all greatly taken up with this business of the bear. They were holding some sort of meeting about it, and 'twas still going on when I had to start back."

"The bear?" asked Kelderek sharply. "What bear? What do you mean?"

"There's no one knows what to make of it, sir," replied Ankray. "They say it's witchcraft. There's not a man of them but he's frightened, for never a bear's been known before in those parts and by all I can make out this one's no natural creature."

"What did they tell you?" asked Melathys, white to the lips.

"Well, säiyett, seems 'twas about ten days ago now that the cattle began to be attacked in the night—pens broken and beasts killed. A man was found one morning with his head beaten in and another time a tree trunk that three men couldn't have

433

moved had been lifted out of a gap it had been set to block. They found tracks of some big animal, but no one knew what they were and everyone was afraid to search. Then about three days ago some of the men were out fishing, upstream and just a little way off shore, when the bear came down to drink. 'Seems it was that big they couldn't believe their eyes. Thin and sick it looked, they said, but very savage and dangerous. It stared at them from the bank and they went off quick. The men I talked to were all sure it's a devil, but myself, I wouldn't fear it, because I reckon it stands to reason who it is."

Ankray paused. None of his listeners spoke and he went on, "It was a bear hurt the Baron when he was a young fellow; and when we left Ortelga after the fighting—that was all to do with sorcery and a bear, or so I've always understood. The Baron's often said to me, 'Ankray,' he'd say, 'I'd have done better if I'd a been a bear, that I would. That's the way to make a kingdom out of nothing, believe me.' Of course, I reckoned he was joking, but now—well, säiyett, if any man was to come back as a bear, that man would be the Baron, don't you reckon? Them that saw it said 'twas terrible scarred and wounded, disfigured-like, round the neck and shoulders, and I reckon that proves it. There's no one in Lak ventures far now and all the cattle are penned together and fires kept burning at night. There's none of them dares go out and hunt the bear. There's even some kind of strange rumor that it's come alive out of hell."

The Tuginda spoke. "Thank you, Ankray. You did very well and we quite understand why you couldn't talk to the chief. You've earned a good night's sleep. Don't do any more work tonight, will you?"

"Very good, säiyett. No trouble, I'm sure. Good night, säiyett. Good night, sir."

He went out, taking the lamp which Melathys silently handed to him. As his footsteps receded Kelderek sat motionless, staring down at the floor like a man who, in an inn or shop, hopes by averting his face to avoid recognition by some creditor or enemy who has unexpectedly entered. In the room beyond, a log fell in the fire and faintly through the shutters came the distant, rattling sound of the night-croaking frogs. Still he sat, and still none spoke. As Melathys moved across the room and sat down on the bench beside the bed, Kelderek realized that his posture had become unnatural and constrained, like that of a dog which, for fear of a rival, holds itself rigid against the wall. Still looking directly at neither of the women, he stood up, took the second lamp from the shelf at his elbow and went to the door.

"I—I'll come back—something—a little while—"

His hand was on the latch and for an instant, in an unintended glance, he saw the Tuginda's face against the shadowy wall. Her eyes met his and he looked away. He went out, crossed the room beyond and stood for a little beside the fire, watching as its caves and cliffs and ledges were consumed away, crumbled and gave place to others. Now and then the sound of the women's voices, speaking seldom and low, reached his ears and at length, wishing to be still more alone, he went to the room where he slept and, once there, put down the lamp and stood still as an ox in a field.

What hold, what power over him did Shardik retain? Was it indeed of his own will or of Shardik's that he had slept beside him in the forest, plunged headlong into the Telthearna deeps and at last wandered from Bekla and his kingdom, through none would ever know what terror and humiliation, to Zeray? He had thought Shardik dead; or if not already dead, then dying far away. But he was not dead, not far away; and news of him had now reached—was it by his will that it had reached?—the man whom God had chosen from the first to be broken to fragments, just as the Tuginda had foretold. He had heard tell of priests in other lands who were the prisoners of their gods and people, remaining secluded in their temples or palaces until the day of their ritual, sacrificial death. He, though a priest, had known no such imprisonment. Yet had he been deluded in supposing himself free to renounce Shardik, to fly for his life, to seek to live for the sake of the woman whom he loved? Was he in truth like a fish trapped in a shrinking, landlocked pool in time of drought, free to swim wherever he could, yet fated, do what he might, to lie gasping at last on the mud? Like Bel-ka-Trazet, he had supposed that he had done with Shardik, but Shardik, or so he now suspected, had not done with him.

He started at the sound of a step and the next moment Mela-thys came into the dim room. Without a word he took her in

435

his arms and kissed her again and again—her lips, her hair, her eyelids—as though to hide among kisses, as a hunted creature among the green leaves. She clung to him, saying nothing, responding by her very choice of acquiescence, like one bathing in a pool who chooses for her own delight to remain standing breathlessly under the cascade that fills it. At length he grew calmer and, gently caressing her face between his hands, felt on his fingers the tears which the lamplight had not revealed.

"My love," he whispered, "my princess, my bright jewel, don't weep! I'll take you away from Zeray. Whatever may happen, I'll never, never leave you. We'll go away and reach some safe place together. Only believe me!" He smiled down at her. "I have nothing in the world, and I'll sacrifice all for your sake."

"Kelderek." She kissed him in her turn, gently, three or four times, and then laid her head on his shoulder. "My darling. My heart is yours until the sun burns out. Oh, can there ever have been so sorry a place and so wretched an hour for declaring love?"

"How else?" he answered. "How else could two such as we discover ourselves to be lovers, except by meeting at the end of the world, where all pride is lost and all rank and station overthrown?"

"I will school myself to have hope," she said. "I will pray for you every day that you are gone. Only send me news as soon as you can."

"Gone?" he replied. "Where?"

"Why, to Lak—to Lord Shardik. Where else?"

"My dear," he said, "set your mind at rest. I promised I would never leave you. I'm done with Shardik."

At this she stood back and, spreading her two arms wide behind her, palms flat against the wall on either side, looked up at him incredulously.

"But—but you heard what Ankray said—we all heard him! Lord Shardik is in the forest near Lak—wounded—perhaps dying! Don't you believe it is Lord Shardik?"

"Once—ay, and not long ago—I meant to seek death from Shardik in atonement for the wrong I had done both to him and to the Tuginda. Now I mean to live for your sake, if you'll have me. Listen, my darling. Shardik's day is done forever, and for all I know Bekla's and Ortelga's day as well. These things ought not to concern us now. Our task is to preserve our lives—the lives of this household—until we can get to Lak, and then to help the Tuginda to return safely to Quiso. After that we shall be free, you and I! I'll take you away—we'll go to Deelguy or Terekenalt—farther, if you like—anywhere where we can live a quiet, humble life, live like the plain folk we were meant to be. Perhaps Ankray will come with us. If only we're resolute, we'll have the chance to be happy at last, away from such loads as men's spirits were never meant to bear and such mysteries as they were never meant to pry into."

She only shook her head slowly as the tears fell and fell from her eyes.

"No," she whispered. "No. You must set out for Lak at dawn tomorrow and I must stay here with the Tuginda."

"But what am I to do?"

"That will be shown you. But above all you must keep a humble, receptive heart and the readiness to listen and obey."

"It's nothing but superstition and folly!" he burst out. "How can I, of all people, still remain a servant of Shardik—I that have abused and harmed him more than any man—more even than Ta-Kominion? Only think of the peril to yourself and the Tuginda in remaining here with none but Ankray! The place is alive with danger now. At any moment it may become as though fifty Glabrons had risen from the grave—"

At this she cried out and sank to the floor, sobbing bitterly and covering her face with her arms as though to ward off his unbearable words. Sorry, he knelt beside her, stroking her shoulders, speaking reassuringly as though to a child and trying to lift her up. At length she rose, nodding her head with a kind of weary hopelessness, as though in acceptance of what he had said of Glabron.

"I know," she said. "I'm sick with fear at the thought of Zeray. I could never survive that again—not now. But still you must go." Suddenly she seemed to take heart, as though by a forced act of her own will. "You won't be alone for long. The Tuginda will recover and then we'll come to Lak and find you. I believe it! I believe it! Oh, my darling, how I long for it—how I shall pray for you! God's will be done."

"Melathys, I tell you I'm not going. I love you. I won't leave you in this place."

"Each of us failed Lord Shardik once," she answered, "but we won't do so again—not now. He's offering us both redemption, and by the Ledges we'll take it, even if it means death!" Giving him her hands, she looked at him with the authority of Quiso in her face, even while the single, wan lamp-flame showed the tear streaks down her cheeks.

"Come, my dear and only beloved, we'll return now to the Tuginda and tell her that you're going to Lak."

For a moment he hesitated, then shrugged his shoulders.

"Very well. But be warned, I shall speak my mind."

She took up the lamp and he followed her. The fire had sunk low and as they passed the hearth he could hear the minute, sharp, evanescent tinkling of the cooling stones and dying embers. Melathys tapped at the door of the Tuginda's room, waited a few moments and then went in. Kelderek followed. The room was empty.

Pushing him to one side in her haste, Melathys ran to the courtyard door. He called, "Wait! There's no need—" But she had already drawn the bolts and when he reached the door he saw her lamp-flame on the other side of the courtyard, steady in the still air. He heard her call and ran across. The latch of the outer door was in place, but the bolts had been drawn back. On the wood, hastily traced, as it appeared, with a charred stick, was a curving, starlike symbol.

"What is it?" he asked.

"It's the sign carved on the Tereth stone," she whispered, distraught. "It invokes the Power of God and His protection. Only the Tuginda may inscribe it without sacrilege. Oh God! She couldn't help leaving the bolts drawn, but this she could do for us before she went."

"Quickly!" cried Kelderek. "She can't have gone far." He ran across the courtyard and beat on the shutters, shouting, "Ankray! Ankray!"

The moon gave light enough and they had not far to search. She was lying where she had fallen, in the shadow of a mud wall about halfway to the shore. As they approached, two men who were stooping over her made off as silently as cats. There was a broad, livid bruise at the back of her neck and she was bleeding from the mouth and nose. The cloak which she had been wearing over her hastily donned clothes was lying in the mud a few feet away, where the men had dropped it.

Ankray picked her up as though she had been a child and together they hastened back, Kelderek, his knife ready in his hand, repeatedly turning about to make sure they were not being followed. But none molested them and Melathys was waiting to open the courtyard door. When Ankray had laid the Tuginda on her bed the girl undressed her, finding no grave injuries except the blow at the base of the skull. She watched beside her all night, but at dawn the Tuginda had not recovered consciousness.

An hour later Kelderek, armed and carrying money, food and the seal ring of Bel-ka-Trazet, set out alone for Lak.

BOOK VI

Genshed

48 *Beyond Lak*

IT WAS AFTERNOON of the following day—hot enough, even during this season of early spring, to silence the birds and draw from the forest a steamy, humid fragrance of young leaves and sprouting vegetation. The Telthearna glittered, coiling swiftly and silently down toward Lak and on to the strait of Zeray below. From a little north of Lak, a region of forest several miles across stretched northward as far as the open country around the gap of Linsho, which divided it from the foothills and mountains beyond. It was from the southern extremities of this forest, dense and largely trackless, that the bear had been attacking the sheds and herds of Lak.

The shore hereabout was broken and indeterminate, undulating in a series of knoll-like promontories. Between these, the river penetrated up creeks and watery ravines, some of which ran almost half a mile inland. The promontories, grassy mounds on which grew trees and bushes, extended back from the waterside until, among thicker undergrowth, they ended abruptly in banks standing like little cliffs above the interior swamps. Frogs and snakes were numerous and at twilight, when the wading birds ceased their feeding, great bats would leave the forest to swoop for moths over the open river. It was a desolate place, seldom visited except by fishermen working offshore in their canoes.

Kelderek was lying at the foot of an *ollaconda* tree, almost concealed among the thick, exposed roots curving all about him like ropes. There was no breeze and except for the hum of the insects no sound from the forest. The opposite shore, bare and rocky, showed hazy in the sunlight, almost as distant as he remembered seeing it from Ortelga. Nothing but birds moved on the river's surface.

In the hot shade, the silence and solitude, he was deliberating upon an exploit so desperate that even now, when he had determined to attempt it, he was still half-hoping that it might be delayed or frustrated by the sudden appearance of fishermen or of some traveler along the shore. If fishermen came, he thought, he would take it as an omen—would call to them and ask to return to Lak in their canoe. None would be the wiser, for no one had been told what he intended. Indeed, it was essential to his purpose that none should know.

If the Tuginda were still alive Melathys, he knew, would never leave her. She would remain in Zeray, enduring the dangers of that evil place; and if the Tuginda were later to recover, she would accompany her to Lak—not now to escape from Zeray, but solely in order to be nearer to Shardik—perhaps even to seek him herself. But if the Tuginda were to die—if she were already dead—Melathys, though no longer a priestess of Quiso, would be indissuadable from the belief that she herself must now assume the Tuginda's duty to find Shardik: yes, he reflected bitterly, to seek to divine God's will from whatever accidents might attend the last days of a savage, dying animal. This remnant of an arid, meaningless religion, which had already brought him to grief, now stood between him and any chance he might have of escape from Zeray with the woman he loved.

And such an animal! Could there ever, in truth, have been a time when he had loved Shardik! Had he indeed defied Bel-ka-Trazet for his sake, believed him to be the incarnation of the Power of God and prayed to him to accept his life? Lak, which he had reached at noon of the previous day and where he had spent the night, was as full of hatred for Shardik as a fire is full of heat. There was no talk but of the mischief, craft and savagery of the bear. It was more dangerous than flood, more unpredictable than pestilence, such a curse as no village had ever known. It had destroyed not only beasts but, wantonly, the patient work of months—stockades, fences, pens, rock pools built for fish traps. Most believed it to be a devil and feared it accordingly. Two men, experienced hunters, who had ventured into the forest in the hope of trapping or killing it, had been found mauled to death, having evidently been taken by surprise. The fishermen who had seen it on the shore were all agreed that they had been frightened by the sense of something evil in its very presence, like that of a serpent or a poisonous spider.

Kelderek, showing the seal of Bel-ka-Trazet but saying of

himself only that he had been sent from Zeray to seek help in planning a journey north for the survivors of the Baron's household, had talked with the elder, an aging man who clearly knew little or nothing of Bekla, its Ortelgan religion or its war with the far-off Yeldashay. To Kelderek, as to a follower of Bel-ka-Trazet, he had shown a guarded courtesy, inquiring as closely as he felt he could about the state of affairs in Zeray and what was thought likely to happen there. Plainly, he took the view that now that the Baron was dead there was little to be gained from helping the Baron's woman.

"As for a journey to the north," he said, grimacing as he scratched between his shoulders and signaling to a servant to pour Kelderek more of his sharp, cloudy wine, "there's no attempting it as long as we are so afflicted. The men won't stir into the forest or up the shore. If the beast were to wander away, perhaps, or even to die—" He fell silent, looking down at the floor and shaking his head. After a little he went on, "I have thought that in full summer—in the heat—we might perhaps fire the forest, but that would be dangerous. The wind—often the wind goes into the north." He broke off again and then added, "Linsho—you want to go to Linsho? The ones they let through Linsho are those who can pay. That is how they subsist, those who live there." There was a note of envy in his voice.

"What about crossing the river?" asked Kelderek, but the chief only shook his head once more. "A desert place—robbed and killed—" Suddenly he looked up, his eye sharp as the moon emerging from behind clouds. "If we started taking men across the river, it would become known in Zeray." And he threw the dregs of his wine across the dirty floor.

It was while he was lying awake before dawn (and scratching as nimbly as the elder) that his desperate and secret project entered Kelderek's mind. If Melathys were ever to become his alone, then Shardik must die. If he were simply to wait for Shardik to die, it was very possible that Melathys would die first. Shardik must be known to be dead—the news must reach Zeray—but he must not be known to have met a violent death. The chief alone must be taken into confidence before the killing was carried out. To him the condition would be secrecy and Kelderek's price, payable upon proof of success, an escort to

Linsho for himself, the two women and their servant, together with whatever help might be necessary toward paying for their passage through the Gap.

A few hours later, still pondering this plan and saying nothing of where he was going, he set out northward along the shore. Whatever traces Shardik might have left, they would have to be found without a guide. To kill him, if it were possible at all, would be the most difficult and dangerous of tasks, not to be attempted without prior knowledge of the forest outskirts and the places he frequented in his comings and goings near Lak. Arriving at the first of the inlets between the island-like hillocks, Kelderek began a careful search for tracks, droppings and other signs of Shardik's presence.

Not that as the lonely morning wore on he was free for one moment from a mounting oppression of both fear and dread: the first showing him clearly his bleeding, mutilated body, savaged by the bear's great claws; the second revealing nothing, but hanging like a mist upon the edges of thought and conferring an uneasy suspicion. As a thief or fugitive who cannot avoid passing some watchtower or guardhouse continues on his way, but nevertheless cannot keep from glancing out of the tail of his eye toward the walls on which there is no one actually to be seen, so Kelderek pursued his course, able neither to admit nor entirely to exclude the idea that he was observed and watched from some transcendental region inscrutable to himself.

Shardik's power was dwindling, sinking, melting away. His death was ordained, was required by God. Why then should not his priest hasten that which was inevitable? And yet, to approach him as an enemy—to intend his death— He thought of those who had done so—of Bel-ka-Trazet, of Gel-Ethlin, of Mollo, of those who kept the Streels of Urtah. He thought, too, of Ged-la-Dan setting out, high-stomached, to impose his will upon Quiso. And then, on the very point of turning back, of abandoning his resolve, he saw again Melathys' tear-stained face lifted to his in the lamplight, and felt her body clasped to his own—that vulnerable body which remained in Zeray like a ewe abandoned by herdsmen on a wild hillside. No danger, natural or supernatural, was too great to be faced if only, by that means, he could return in time to save her life and convince her that nothing was of greater importance than the love she felt for him. Fighting against his mounting sense of uneasiness, he continued his search.

A little before noon, reaching the far end of one of the island-like promontories, he saw below him a pool at the mouth of a creek. Scrambling down the bank, he knelt among the stones to drink, and on raising his head immediately saw before him, some yards away on the creek's muddy farther shore, a bear's prints, clear as a seal on wax. Looking about him, he felt almost sure that this must be the place spoken of by the fishermen. It was plainly an habitual drinking place, bear-marked so unmistakably that a child could have perceived the signs, and certainly visited at some time since the previous day.

To have seen the prints before his own feet had marked the mud was a stroke of luck which should make it simple, a mere matter of patience, to gain sight of the bear itself. All he needed was a safe place of concealment from which to watch. Splashing through the shallows, he made his way back as far as the next inlet, a long stone's throw from the pool where he had knelt to drink. From here he once more climbed the promontory to the ollaconda tree and, having made sure that he could observe the shore of the creek, lay down among the roots to wait. The wind, as the elder had said, was from the north, the forest on his left was so thick that nothing could approach without being heard, and in the last resort he could take to the river. Here he was as safe as he could reasonably hope to be.

While the slow time passed with the movement of clouds, the whine of insects and the sudden, raucous cries and scutterings of waterfowl on the river, he fell to reflecting on how the killing of Shardik might be accomplished. If he were right, and this was a drinking place to which the bear regularly returned, it should afford him a good opportunity. He had never taken part in killing a bear, nor had he ever heard of anyone, except the Beklan nobleman of whom Bel-ka-Trazet had spoken, who had attempted it. Certainly a solitary bow seemed altogether too dangerous and uncertain. Whatever the Beklan might have supposed thirty years ago, he himself did not believe that a bear could safely be killed by this means alone. Poison might have succeeded, but he had none. To try to construct any kind of trap was out of the question. The more he pondered his difficulties, the more he was forced to the conclusion that the business would be impossible unless the bear's alertness and strength had become so much weakened that he could hope to hold it with a noose long enough to pierce it with several arrows. Yet how to noose a bear? Other, bizarre ideas passed through his mind—to catch poisonous snakes and by some means drop them out of a sack from above while the bear was drinking; to suspend a heavy spear—he broke off impatiently. These childish plans were not capable of being effected. All he could do for the moment was to await the bear, observe its condition and behavior and see whether any scheme suggested itself.

It was perhaps three hours later, and he had somewhat relaxed his vigilance, leaning his sweating forehead upon his forearm and wondering, as he closed his eyes against the river glitter, how Ankray meant to set about getting more food when what was in the house was gone, when he heard the sounds of a creature approaching from the undergrowth beyond the creek. The next moment—so quietly and swiftly may the most fateful and long-awaited events materialize—Shardik was before him, crouching upon the brink of the pool.

After war has swept across some farm or estate and gone its way, the time comes when villagers or neighbors, their fears aroused by having seen nothing of the occupants, set out for the place. They make their way across the blackened fields or up the lane, looking about them in the unnatural quiet. Soon, seeing no smoke and receiving no reply to their calls, they begin to fear the worst, pointing in silence as they come to the barns with their exposed and thatchless rafters. They begin to search, and, at a sudden cry from one of their number, come running together before an open, creaking door, where a woman's body lies sprawling face down across the threshold. There is a quick scurry of rats and a youth turns quickly aside, white and sick. Some of the men, setting their teeth, go inside and return, carrying the dead bodies of two children and leading a third child who stares about him, crazed beyond weeping. As that farm then appears to those men, who knew it in former days, so Shardik appeared now to Kelderek: and as they look upon the ruin and misery about them, so Kelderek looked at Shardik drinking from the pool.

The ragged, dirty creature was gaunt as though half-starved. Its pelt resembled some ill-erected tent draped clumsily over the frame of the bones. Its movements had a tremulous, hesitant weariness, like those of some old beggar worn out with denial and disease. The wound in its back, half-healed, was covered with a great liver-colored scab, cracked across and closing and opening with every movement of the head. The open and suppurating wound in the neck was plainly irritant, inflamed and torn as it was from the creature's scratching. The bloodshot eyes peered fiercely and suspiciously about, as though seeking on whom to revenge its misery; but after a little the head, in the very act of drinking, sank forward into the shallows, as though to keep it raised were a labor too grievous to be borne.

At length the bear stood up and, gazing in one direction and another, stared for a moment directly up at the mass of roots among which Kelderek lay in hiding. But it seemed to see nothing and, as he still watched it through a narrow opening like a loophole, the belief grew in him that it was concerned less with what it could see than with scenting the air and listening. Although it had not perceived him in his hiding place, yet something else—or so it appeared—was making it uneasy, something not far off in the forest. If this were so, however, it was evidently not so much disturbed as to run off. For some while it remained in the shallows, more than once dropping its head as before, with the object, as Kelderek now perceived, of bathing and cooling the wound in its neck. Then, to his surprise, it began to wade from the pool into deeper water. He watched, puzzled, as it made toward a rock some little way out in the river. Its chest, broad as a door, submerged, then its shoulders and finally, though with difficulty, it swam to the rock and dragged itself out upon a ledge. There it sat, facing, across the river, the distant eastern shore. After a time it made as though to plunge into midstream, but twice stopped short. Then a listlessness seemed to come upon it. Scratching dolefully, it lay down upon the rock as some old, half-blind dog might crouch in the dust, and covered its face with its forepaws. Kelderek remembered what the Tuginda had said—"He is trying to return to his own country. He is making for the Telthearna and will cross it if he can." If such a creature could weep, then Shardik was weeping.

To see strength failing, ferocity grown helpless, power and

domination withered by pain as plants by drought—such sights give rise not only to pity but also, and as naturally, to aversion and contempt. Our sorrow for our dying captain is sincere enough, yet we must nevertheless make haste to leave this sunken fire before the increasing cold can overtake our own fortunes. For all his glorious past, it is only right that he should be abandoned, for we have to live—to thrive if we can— and setting aside all other considerations, the truth is that he has become irrelevant to the things that should now properly concern us. How odd it is that until now no one, apparently, should have perceived that after all he was never particularly wise; never particularly brave; never particularly honest, particularly truthful, particularly clean.

Upon Kelderek's inward eye flashed once more the figure of Melathys standing in the light of the sunset, she the once unattainable, who but two days before had held him in her arms and told him with tears that she loved him; she whose gay courage had made light of the foul danger and evil amidst which he had been compelled against his will to leave her to take her chance; she who in herself more than outweighed his lost kingdom and ruined fortunes. Hatred rose up in him against the mangy, decrepit brute on the rock, the very source and image of that superstition which had made of Melathys a brigands' whore and of Bel-ka-Trazet a fugitive; had brought the Tuginda close to death and now stood between him and his love. That this wretched creature should still have power to thwart him and drag him down together with itself! As he thought of all that he had lost and all that he still might lose—probably would lose—he shut his eyes and gnawed at his wrist in his angry frustration.

"Curse you!" he cried silently in his heart. "Curse you, Shardik, and your supposed Power of God! Why don't you save us from Zeray, we who've lost all we possessed for your sake, we whom you've ruined and deceived? No, you can't save us: you can't save even the women who've served you all their lives! Why don't you die and get out of the way? Die, Shardik, die, die!"

Suddenly there came to his ear what seemed like faint sounds of human speech from somewhere within the forest. Fear came upon him, for since the night on the battlefield there had remained with him a horror of the distant voices of persons unseen. Strange sounds were these, too, mysterious and hard to account for, resembling less the voices of men than of children —crying, it seemed, in pain or distress. He sprang up and as he did so heard, louder than the voices, a heavy splashing close at hand. Looking behind him, he recoiled in terror to see the bear wading ashore at the very foot of the bank below. It was glaring up at him, shaking the water from its pelt and snarling savagely. In panic he turned and began to force his way through the undergrowth, snatching and tearing at the bushes and creepers in his way. Whether the bear was pursuing him he could not tell. He dared not look back, but plunged on over the top of the hillock, scarcely feeling the grazes and scratches that covered his limbs. Suddenly, as he forced his way through a tangle of branches, he found no ground beneath his feet. He clutched at a branch which broke under his weight, lost his balance and pitched forward down the steep bank of the creek bounding the promontory on its landward side. His forehead struck a tree root and he rolled over and lay unconscious, supine and half-submerged in mud and shallow water.

49 *The Slave Dealer*

PAIN, THIRST, A GREEN DAZZLE of light and a murmur of returning sound. Kelderek allowed his half-opened eyes to shut again and, frowning as he did so, felt something tight and rough pressed round his head. Raising one hand, he found his fingers rubbing against a band of coarse cloth and followed it around one temple, above the eyebrow. He pressed it and pain blazed up like a flame behind his eyeballs. He moaned and let fall his hand.

Now he remembered the bear, yet felt no more fear of it. Something—what?—had already told him that the bear was gone. The daylight, what little he could endure beneath his eyelids, was older—it must be some time since he had fallen—but it was not this that had reassured him. His mind began to clear and as it did so he became aware once more of the roughness of the cloth upon his forehead. And as an ominous sound, heard first faintly at a distance and then more loudly nearby, at the moment of repetition thrusts its startling meaning upon him who originally heard it with indifference, so, as Kelderek's returning senses grew keener, the significance of the cloth forced itself upon him.

He turned his head, shaded his eyes and opened them. He was lying on the bank of the creek, close to the muddy shallow into which he had fallen. The impression of his body was still plain in the mud, and the furrows evidently made by his feet as he was dragged to the spot where he now lay. On his other, shoreward side a man was sitting, watching him. As Kelderek's eyes met his the man neither spoke nor altered his gaze. He was ragged and dirty, with bristling, sandy hair and a rather darker beard, heavy eyelids and a white scar on one side of his chin. His mouth hung a little open, giving him an abstracted, pensive air and showing discolored teeth. In one hand he was holding a knife, with the point of which he kept idly stroking and pressing the fingertips of the other.

Kelderek smiled and, despite the stabbing pain behind his eyes, raised himself on his elbows. Spitting out mud and speaking with some difficulty, he said in Beklan,

"If it was you who pulled me out of there and put this bandage on my head, thank you. You must have saved my life."

The other nodded twice, very slightly, but gave no other sign that he had heard. Although his eyes remained fixed on Kelderek, his attention seemed concentrated on pressing rhythmically with the knife point the ball of each finger in turn.

"The bear's gone, then," said Kelderek. "What brought you here? Were you hunting or are you on a journey?"

Still the man made no reply and Kelderek, recalling that he was beyond the Vrako, cursed himself for being so foolish as to ask questions. He still felt weak and giddy, but it might pass off once he was on his feet. His best course now would be to get back to Lak before sunset and see what he was fit for after a meal and a night's sleep. He held out one hand and said, "Will you help me up?"

452

After a few moments the man, without moving, said in broken but intelligible Ortelgan, "You're a long way from your island, aren't you?"

"How did you know I'm an Ortelgan?" asked Kelderek.

"Long way," repeated the man.

It now occurred to Kelderek to feel for the pouch in which he had been carrying the money he had brought from Zeray. It was gone and so were his food and his knife. This did not altogether surprise him, but certain other things did. Since he had robbed him, why had the man dragged him out of the creek and bound up his head? Why had he stayed to watch him and why, since he was clearly not an Ortelgan himself, had he spoken to him in Ortelgan? He said once more, this time in Ortelgan, "Will you help me up?"

"Yes, get up," said the man in Beklan, as though answering a different question. His previously half-abstracted interest seemed to have become more direct and he leaned forward alertly.

Kelderek, supporting himself on one hand and beginning to draw up his left leg, felt a sudden tug at his right ankle. He looked down. Both ankles were shackled and between them ran a light chain about the length of his forearm.

"What's this?" he asked, with a sudden spurt of alarm.

"Get up," repeated the man. He rose and took two or three steps toward Kelderek, knife in hand.

Kelderek got to his knees and then to his feet, but would have fallen if the man had not gripped him by the arm. Shorter than Kelderek, he looked up at him sharply, straddle-legged, knife held ready. After a few moments, without moving his eyes, he jerked his head to one side.

"That way," he said in Ortelgan.

"Wait," said Kelderek. "Wait a moment. Tell me—"

As he spoke the man seized his left hand, jerked it forward and with the point of his knife pierced him beneath one fingernail. Kelderek cried out and snatched his hand away.

"That way," said the man, jerking his head once more and moving the knife here and there before Kelderek's face, so that he flinched first to one side and then to the other.

Kelderek turned and, with the man's hand on his arm, began

to stumble through the mud. At each step, the chain, pulled taut between his ankles, checked the natural length of his stride. Several times he tripped and at length fell into a kind of shuffle, watching the ground for any protrusion that might throw him down. The man, walking beside him, kept up a tuneless whistling through his teeth, the sound of which, intensified suddenly at random moments, made Kelderek start in anticipation of some further attack. Indeed, had it not been for this he would probably have collapsed from weakness and the nausea induced by the wound under his fingernail.

What kind of man might this be? From his dress and ability to speak Ortelgan it seemed unlikely that he was a Yeldashay soldier. What was the explanation of his having taken the trouble to save from a swamp, in lonely country, a destitute stranger whom he had already robbed? Kelderek sucked his finger, which was oozing blood from beneath the severed nail. If the man were a maniac—and why not, beyond the Vrako? What else had Ruvit been?—all he could do was to keep alert and watch for any chance that might offer itself. But the chain would be a grave handicap and the man himself, despite his short stature, was plainly the ugliest of adversaries.

He raised his eyes at the sudden sound of voices. They could not have walked far—perhaps not much more than a bowshot from the creek. The ground was still marshy and the forest thick. Ahead was a glade among the trees and here he could make out people moving, though he could see no fire or any of the usual features of a camp. The man uttered a single, wordless cry—a kind of bark—but waited for no answer, merely guiding him forward as before. They had reached the glade when the chain again tripped him and Kelderek fell to the ground. The man, leaving him to lie where he had fallen, walked on.

Breathless and caked in mud, Kelderek rolled over and looked up sideways from where he lay. The place, he realized at once, was full of a considerable number of people, and in fear that after all he had once again fallen into the hands of the Yeldashay, he sat up and stared quickly about him.

Save for the man himself, now sitting a little distance away and rummaging in a leather pack, all those in the glade were children. None appeared to be more than thirteen or fourteen years old. A boy nearby, with a harelip and sores round his chin, was staring at Kelderek with vacant, sleepy attention, as though he had just awakened. Farther off, a child with a continuous twitching of the head gazed up wide-eyed, his mouth gaping in a kind of rictus of startled alarm. As Kelderek looked this way and that he realized that many of the children were blemished or deformed in one manner or another. All were thin and dirty and had about them an air of listless ill-being, like half-starved cats on a rubbish heap. Almost all, like himself, were chained at the ankles. Of the two he could see who were not, one had a withered leg, while above the ankles of the other the cracked weals left by the removed shackles were pustulant with sores. The children sat or lay silent on the ground, one asleep, one crouching to excrete, one shivering continually, one searching the grass for insects and eating them. They imparted to the green-lit place an eerie quality, as though it were a pool and they fishes in a world of silence, each occupied entirely with his own preservation and paying no more attention to others than this might require.

The man, then, must be a slave trader dealing in children. The number of these permitted to work in the Beklan empire had been fixed, each being authorized by Kelderek, after inquiries made of the provincial governors, to buy specified quotas at approved prices in this place and that, a second quota not being allowed to be taken from the same place until a stated period had elapsed. The traders worked through the provincial governors and under their protection, being required to satisfy them that they had taken no more than their quotas and paid the approved prices, and in return receiving, where necessary, armed escorts for their journeys to the markets at Bekla, Dari-Paltesh or Thettit-Tonilda. It seemed likely that this man, while journeying with a party of child slaves bound for Bekla, had been cut off by the Yeldashay advance and in view of the value of his stock had decided, rather than abandon them, to flee beyond the Vrako. That would account for the children's shocking condition. But which of the dealers was this? No great number of warrants had been issued and Kelderek, who, intent on learning as much as possible about the yield to be expected and the trade's taxable worth, had himself talked to most of the traders at one time or another, now tried to recall their individual faces. Of those he was able to remember, none corresponded to this man. At no time had more than seventeen authorizations been valid in the empire, and of these scarcely any, once granted, had been transferred to a second holder; for who, once he had got his hands on it, would surrender so lucrative an occupation? Out of twenty names at the most, he could not recall this man's. Yet surely he must be one or other of them? Or was he—and here Kelderek felt a sudden qualm of misgiving—could he be an unauthorized slaver, one of those he had been warned about and had declared liable to the heaviest penalties, who got their slaves where they could, sometimes by kidnaping, sometimes by bluff and terror in remote villages, or again by purchasing the half-witted, deformed or otherwise unwanted from those who were prepared to sell them; and, bringing them across country as little observed as possible, sold them secretly, either to the authorized dealers or else to anyone ready to buy? That such men had been operating in the empire he knew, and had known also their reputation for ruthlessness and cruelty, for unscrupulous double-dealing and taking what they could get wherever they might find it. "All slave traders are dealers in wretchedness," a captured Yeldashay officer had once said to him while being questioned, "but there are some—those of whom you pretend to know nothing—who creep about the land like filthy rats, scraping up the very dregs of misery for trifling profits; and for these, too, we hold you answerable, for he who builds a barn knows that rats will come." Kelderek had let him talk and later, becoming still more indignant, the officer had unintentionally revealed a good deal of useful information.

Suddenly Kelderek's recollections were broken by the most unexpected of sounds—the laughter of an infant. He looked up to see a little girl, perhaps five years old, unchained, running across the glade and looking back over her shoulder at a tall, fair-haired lad. This boy, in spite of his chain, was pursuing her, evidently in sport, for he was hanging back and pretending, as people do when playing with quite little children, that she was succeeding in escaping from him. The child, though thin and pale, looked less wretched than the boys among whom she was running. She had almost reached Kelderek when she tripped and fell forward on her face. The tall lad, overtaking her, picked her up, holding her in his arms and tossing her up and down to comfort her and distract her from crying. Thus occupied, he turned for a moment toward Kelderek and their eyes met.

He who catches suddenly the lilt of a song which he has not heard for years or the scent of the flowers that bloomed by the door where once he played in the dust, finds himself swept back, whether he will or no and sometimes with tears, into the depth of time past, recovering for a few moments the very feeling of being another person, upon whom life used to press with other, lighter fingers than those which he has since learned to endure. With no less a shock did Kelderek feel himself once more the Eye of God, Lord Crendrik the priest-king of Bekla, and recall on the instant the smells of fog and of smoldering charcoal, the sour taste in his mouth and the murmur from behind him as he faced the bars in the King's House, trying to gaze into eyes that he could not meet, the eyes of the condemned Elleroth. Then the fit was gone and he was staring in perplexity at a youth tossing a yellow-haired child in his arms.

At this moment the slave dealer stood up, calling, "Eh! Shouter! Bled! Get moving!" Leaving his pack on the ground, he strode down the length of the glade, snapping his fingers to bring the children to their feet and, without speaking again, hustling them into a group at the farther end. He stopped beside the tall youth, who stood looking at him with the little girl still held in his arms. She cowered away, hiding her face, and as she did so the youth put one hand on her shoulder.

After a few moments it became plain that the slave dealer meant to stare the boy down and subdue him without word or blow. Tense and wary, the boy returned his stare. At length, speaking in halting Beklan with a strong Yeldashay accent, he said, "She's not strong enough to stand this much longer and there's no profit to you if she dies. Why don't you leave her outside the next village?"

The dealer drew his knife. Then, as the boy still waited for his reply, he took from his belt an iron object in the shape of two half-circles, each bluntly barbed at either end and joined together by a short bar. The boy hesitated a moment, then lowered his eyes, pressed his lips together and, still carrying the little girl, walked away to join the other children.

At the same moment a scowling youth, a little older than the rest, with a cast in one eye and a birthmark across his face, came running up to Kelderek. He was dressed in a torn leather tunic and carried a pliant stick as long as his arm.

"Come on, you too," said the boy in a kind of savage bellow, like a peasant cursing a beast with which he has lost patience. "Mucking get up, come on."

Kelderek got to his feet and stood looking down at him.

"What do you want me to do?" he asked.

"Don't answer me back," shouted the boy, raising his stick. "Get on up there, and look sharp about it, too."

Kelderek shrugged his shoulders and went slowly toward the group of children at the far end of the glade. There must be, he reckoned, about twenty or twenty-five of them, all boys, their ages varying, as near as he could tell, from fourteen to nine or ten, though of this it was hard to be sure, their condition being so dreadful and their appearance so much more wretched than that of even the poorest children he had ever seen in Bekla or Ortelga. A smell of stale filth came from them and a cloud of flies darted back and forth above their heads. One boy, leaning against a tree trunk, coughed continually, doubling himself up while a mucous, dysenteric flux ran down the inside of his legs. A fly settled on his ear and he struck at it. Kelderek, following the movement, saw that the lobe was pierced by a ragged hole. He looked at another of the children. His ear, too, was pierced. Puzzled, he looked at the next and the next. In each case the lobe of the right ear was pierced.

The slave dealer, now carrying his pack, together with a heavy bow strapped to one side of it, passed him and made his way to the head of the gang. Here a second boy was waiting. He also, like the boy who had shouted at Kelderek, was carrying a stick and dressed in a leather tunic. Short and squat, he looked more like a dwarf than a child. His back was bent by some kind of curvature and his long hair covered his shoulders, perhaps to hide this deformity to some extent. As the children began to shuffle forward, following the dealer, Kelderek noticed that all lowered their eyes as they passed this dwarfish boy. The boy for his part stood staring at each in turn, leaning toward them, his body tense, his knees a little bent, as though scarcely able to restrain himself from leaping upon and striking them then and there. Feeling a touch on his back, Kelderek turned and met the eyes of the tall lad, who as he walked was holding the little girl's ankles and carrying her over his shoulder like a sack.

"Take care not to look at Bled as you pass," whispered the lad. "If he catches your eye he'll set upon you." Then, as Kelderek frowned in bewilderment, he added, "He's mad, or as good as mad."

Heads averted, they passed the hunched figure and followed the straggling children into the forest. The pace was so slow that Kelderek, as often as it caught, was at leisure to stoop and disentangle his chain. After a little the youth whispered again, "It's easier if you walk exactly behind the boy in front and put your feet down one directly in front of the other. The chain's less likely to catch then."

"Who is this man?" whispered Kelderek.

"Good God, don't you know?" answered the boy. "Genshed —you must have heard of him?"

"Once, in Kabin, I heard that name: but where is he from? He's not a Beklan slave dealer."

"He is—he's the worst of the lot. I'd heard of him long before I dreamed I'd ever see him, let alone fall into his hands. Did you see him threaten me with the flytrap just now, when I was trying to speak to him about Shara here?"

"The flytrap?" replied Kelderek. "What's that?"

"That thing he's got on his belt. It forces your mouth open —wide open—and you can't shut it. I know, it doesn't sound bad, does it? I thought that once. My father would be ashamed of me, I suppose, but I couldn't stand it again, not another two hours of it."

"But—"

"Careful, don't let Shouter hear you."

They fell silent as the scowling youth ran past them to disentangle the chain of a child who had tripped and was apparently too weak to release it for himself. A little later, as they began edging their way forward again, Kelderek said, "Tell me more about this man and how you came to fall into his hands. You're a Yeldashay, aren't you?"

"My name is Radu, heir of Elleroth, Ban of Sarkid."

Kelderek realized that he had known from the first who the

459

boy must be. He made no reply and after a little the boy said,
"Don't you believe me?"

"Yes, I believe you. You're very like your father."

"Why, do you know him?"

"Yes—that is, I've seen him."

"Where? In Sarkid?"

"In—Kabin."

"Kabin of the Waters? Why, when was he there?"

"Not long ago. In fact, he may be there now."

"With the army? You mean General Santil's in Kabin?"

"He was, a short time ago."

"If only my father were here, he'd kill this swine in a
moment."

"Steady," said Kelderek, for the boy's voice had risen hysterically. "Here, let me take the little girl. You've carried her
long enough."

"She's used to me—she may cry."

But Shara, half-asleep, lay as quietly on Kelderek's shoulder
as she had on Radu's. He could feel her bones. She was very
light. For the twentieth time they halted, waiting for the children in front to go on.

"I heard in Kabin," said Kelderek, "that you'd fallen into
this man's hands. How did it happen?"

"My father was away on a secret visit to General Santil—
even I didn't know where he'd gone. I heard from one of our
tenants that Genshed was in the province. I wondered what my
father would want me to do—what he might be glad to hear I'd
done when he came back. I decided not to tell my mother anything about Genshed—she'd have told me not to stir off the
estate. It seemed to me that the right thing would be to go and
talk to my uncle Sildain, my father's sister's husband. We
always got on well together. I thought he'd know what to do.
I took my own servant with me and set out." He paused.

"And you ran into the slave dealer?" asked Kelderek.

"I acted like a child. I can see that now. Toroc and I were
resting in a wood and keeping no lookout at all. Genshed shot
Toroc through the throat—he knows how to use that bow. I
was still on my knees beside Toroc when Shouter and Bled
rushed me and knocked me down. Genshed hadn't any idea who
I was—I hadn't bothered to put on any particular clothes, you

see. When I told them, Shouter was for releasing me at once, before the whole place came round their ears, but Genshed wouldn't have it. I suppose he means to get back to Terekenalt somehow and then demand a ransom. He'd get more that way than ever he could by selling me as a slave."

"But evidently he wasn't interested in capturing your servant."

"No, and it's strange that he's taken you. It's well known that he deals only in children. He has his market for them, you see."

"His market?"

"In Terekenalt. You know what he does? Even the other dealers won't touch the trade he goes in for. The boys are castrated and sold to—well, to people who want to buy them. And the girls—I suppose—I suppose it must be worse for the girls."

"But there are no girls here—only this little one with you."

"There were girls, earlier on. I'll tell you what happened after I was captured. Genshed went on eastward—he didn't turn back into Paltesh. We never heard why, of course, but I think probably the whole of Sarkid was up behind him, looking for me. All the routes into Paltesh must have been watched. By the time we got into eastern Lapan he had over fifty children altogether, boys and girls. There was a girl about my age, her name was Reva—a gentle, timid kind of girl who'd never been away from home in her life. I never learned how she came to be sold to Genshed. Shouter and Bled, they used to—you know."

"Genshed allowed that?"

"Oh, no. They weren't supposed to, of course. But he's not quite sure of them, you see. He can't do without them while he's on an expedition and besides, they know too much—they could probably find a way to turn him in if they wanted to. Genshed doesn't employ overseers, like other slave traders. He knows a trick worth two of that. He picks out any specially cruel or heartless boys and trains them as overseers. Once he's back in Terekenalt, I believe he often gets rid of them and picks fresh ones for the next trip. Anyway, that's what I heard."

"Why do they work for him, then?"

"Partly because it's better to be an overseer than a slave; but there's more to it than that. The boys he chooses are those he has power over, because they admire him and want to be like him."

"And the girl you were telling me about?"

"She killed herself."

"How?"

"It was while Bled was actually with her, one night. She managed to get his knife out of his belt. He was too busy to notice, and she stabbed herself."

"It's a pity she didn't stab him and then run for it."

"Reva would never have thought of that. She was helpless and beside herself."

"Where did you cross the Vrako?" asked Kelderek. "And how, if it comes to that?"

"We met with another slave trader in eastern Lapan—a man called Nigon, who had an Ortelgan warrant to trade. I heard Nigon warn Genshed that Santil's army was marching north at a great rate and he'd better get out while he could. Nigon himself meant to get back to Bekla."

"He didn't, though. He was taken by the Yeldashay."

"Was he? I'm glad. Well, there was no point in Genshed trying to make for Bekla. He had no warrant, you see. So he went the only way he could—into Tonilda. We went like a forest fire, but every time we stopped we heard that the Yeldashay were closer behind us."

"How did your little girl survive?"

"She would have died in a few days, but I've carried her almost every step—I and another boy we called the Hare. I've got a lord's sworn duty to her, you see. She's the daughter of one of our tenants at home. My father would expect me to look after her at all costs, and I have."

The boy Bled drew level with them and for a time they edged their way forward in silence. Kelderek could see the children in front plodding and stumbling with bowed heads, speechless and apathetic as beasts. When Bled walked farther up the line, making his stick whistle in the air, not one raised his eyes.

"When we got close to Thettit-Tonilda, Genshed learned that the Yeldashay were due west of us already and still going north. They'd as good as cut us off from Gelt and Kabin. At Thettit he sold all the girls except Shara. He knew they wouldn't be able to survive the journey he'd planned."

Shara stirred and whimpered on Kelderek's shoulder. Radu leaned forward, caressing her, and whispered in her ear—per-

462

haps some joke between them, for the little girl chuckled and, trying to repeat what he had said, at once returned into her light sleep.

"Have you ever been in northern Tonilda?" asked the boy.

"No—I know it's wild and lonely."

"There are no roads and it was bitterly cold at night. We had no blankets and Genshed wouldn't light fires for fear of Yeldashay patrols. All the same, we had some bread then, and dried meat too. Only one boy collapsed. It was in the evening, and Genshed hanged him from a tree and made us stand around it until he was dead. I don't know how much he could have got for that boy, but you'd have thought he'd have left him alone for a night's rest and waited to see whether he could go on in the morning. I tell you, it isn't the money with him. He'd give his life for cruelty, I believe."

"He got angry, I suppose—lost his temper?"

"There's no telling whether he loses his temper. His violence is like an insect's—sudden and cold, and you feel it's natural—natural to something that's less than human, something that waits quite still and then darts like lightning. Sh!"

They had come to the bank of a creek and here Shouter was urging the children one by one into the water. As each floundered forward, Genshed, standing up to his waist in the middle, caught him by the arm and pushed him toward the opposite bank, where Bled dragged him out. Kelderek, holding the little girl in his arms, slipped in the thick slime and would have fallen if Genshed had not gripped him. The boy overseers cursed and swore at the children almost without ceasing, but Genshed uttered neither word nor sound. When at length all were across he stretched out his hand to Bled, pulled himself out and looked around among the children, snapping his fingers. Those who had lain down struggled to their feet and after a few moments the slave dealer set off once more into the forest.

"When we actually saw the Vrako we were very much afraid. It was a raging torrent, half a bowshot across and full of great rocks. I couldn't believe Genshed meant to cross it with thirty exhausted children."

"But the Vrako's impassable below Kabin," said Kelderek. "That's common knowledge."

"He'd planned the crossing in Thettit. He'd sent Shouter

round by Kabin, dressed as a drover's boy, and given him money to bribe the guard at the ford; but apparently they just let him through. Shouter had been told to look out for us on the bend of the river, where it turns to the east, but even so it took Genshed half a day to find him. It's a very wild, desolate place, you see."

"But what was the plan?"

"Genshed had bought a great length of tarred twine in Thettit, and a furlong of Ortelgan rope. He cut the rope into lengths and we all had to carry them on the journey. He married the lengths together again himself—it took him a day and a half. He was very thorough. When everything was ready he shot an arrow across the river with one end of the twine fastened to it. Then he bound the rope to the twine and Shouter pulled it across and made it fast. It was as much as ever he could do, though, because of the current. They made the rope as taut as they could by twisting wooden stakes into it on either side and hammering them into the ground. What with the current and the weight of the rope, it wasn't anything like taut, but that was how we crossed the Vrako."

Kelderek said nothing, imagining the deafening sound of the torrent and the terrified, exhausted children stumbling down the bank.

"Seven of us were drowned. The Hare was drowned—he lost his hold and went under like a stone. I never saw him come up again. When I was halfway across I felt sure I was going to lose hold myself."

"Shara?"

"That was it. I had her wrists tied together round my neck. I'd made a sort of tube from a rolled-up strip of bark and put it in her mouth, to give her a chance of breathing if her head went under water. But of course she got frightened and began to struggle and that nearly finished us both. I'll take her back now."

Kelderek gave him the child and Radu rocked her in his arms, humming very quietly, his mouth close to her ear. After some time he went on,

"What I've learned—what I've learned is how strong an evil man becomes. Genshed's strong because he's evil. Evil protects him, so that he can do its work. In a few days you'll come to see what I mean." He paused, and then added, "But Genshed's not the only one to blame for our misery."

"Why—who else?"

"The enemy—the Ortelgans, who revived the slave trade."

"They didn't give Genshed a warrant."

"No, but what did they think would happen? If you let in dogs you let in fleas."

Kelderek made no reply and for a long time they continued their shuffling snail's pace behind the children, stooping every few yards to free their dragging chains. At last Radu said, "You're sure that General Santil's army's in Kabin?"

"Yes—I came from there."

"And you actually saw my father there?"

"Yes, I did."

They bent their heads to pass Bled, standing with knees bent and stick half-raised in his hand. It was not until he had overtaken them and was some way ahead that Kelderek spoke again.

"It must be near sunset. When does he halt as a rule?"

"Are you tired?" asked Radu.

"I'm still dizzy from this wound in my head, and my finger's very painful. Genshed drove his knife under the nail."

"I've seen him do that more than once," said Radu. "Let me have a look. That ought to be tied up." He tore a strip from his rags and bound it round Kelderek's finger. "We may have a chance to wash it later. I doubt he'll go much farther tonight."

"Have you any idea why Genshed should want to keep me?" asked Kelderek. "You told me he killed your servant and that he deals only in children. Has he taken any other grown men or women that you know of?"

"No, not one. But whatever his reason is, it will be a cunning and evil one."

Soon after, they halted in a muddy strip of open land extending as far as the shore of the Telthearna on their right. Kelderek reckoned that since his capture they might have covered perhaps six miles. He guessed that Genshed must be making for Linsho, and that when he had bought his way through the Gap he would turn west for Terekenalt, either by water or by land. If he himself could not contrive to escape before that journey was well under way, then Melathys would be lost to him forever and in all probability he would never even learn her fate or that of the Tuginda.

At the order to halt, almost all the children sank down wherever they happened to be. A few fell asleep immediately. One or two crouched, talking together in whispers. None except Shara showed the least energy or spirit. She had woken and was wandering here and there, picking up bright leaves and colored pebbles that took her fancy. When she brought these back to Radu he made a kind of collar of leaves, in the manner of a daisy chain, and hung it around her neck. Kelderek, sitting beside them, was trying to make friends with the little girl—for she seemed half-afraid of him—when suddenly, looking up, he saw Genshed approaching, with Shouter and Bled behind him. The slave dealer was carrying some kind of implement wrapped in a handful of rags. The three passed behind Kelderek and he had already turned back to Shara when he felt himself seized by the shoulders and thrown backward to the ground. His arms were pulled out on either side of his body and he cried out as Genshed and Bled knelt on the muscles. Bending over him, the slave dealer said, "Open your mouth or I'll knock your teeth out."

Kelderek obeyed, gasping, and as he did so caught a glimpse of Shouter, clutching his ankles and grinning up at Genshed. The slave dealer forced his handful of rags into Kelderek's mouth and pulled off the bandage tied round his head.

"Right, get on with it," he said to Bled. "Turn his head this way."

Bled twisted Kelderek's head to the left and immediately he felt the lobe of his right ear sharply pinched, then crushed and pierced. A spurt of excruciating pain shot down his neck and along his shoulder. His whole body convulsed, almost throwing off the two boys. When he came to himself, all three had released him and were walking away.

Kelderek pulled the rags out of his mouth and put his hand to his ear. His fingers came away bloody and blood was dripping over his shoulder. The lobe was pierced through. He bent his head, breathing deeply as the worst of the pain began to subside.

Looking up, he saw Radu beside him. The boy thrust aside his long, matted hair and showed him his own pierced ear.

"I didn't warn you," said Radu. "You're not a child and I wasn't sure whether he'd do it to you or not."

Kelderek, biting on his hand, recovered himself sufficiently to speak.

"What is it—a slave mark?"

"It's for sl—for sl—for sleeping," muttered a white-faced, blinking boy nearby. "Yer, yer, yer—for sleeping." He laughed vacantly, closed his eyes and laid his head on his folded hands in a foolish pantomime.

"Goin' home s-soon," he said suddenly, opening his eyes again and turning to Radu.

"All the way," replied Radu, in the tone of one who takes up a catch phrase.

"Underground," concluded the boy. "You hungry?" Radu nodded and the boy returned to his listless silence.

"At night they pass a chain through everyone's ears," said Radu. "Shouter told me once that every child who's ever been through Genshed's hands has a pierced ear."

He got up and went to look for Shara, who had run to hide in the bushes at the slave trader's approach.

Soon after, Shouter and Bled distributed to each child a handful of dried meat and one of dried fruit. Some of the children went as far as the river for water, but most merely drank from the dirty holes and reed patches round about. As Kelderek and Radu, together with Shara, were making their way toward the river, Shouter came up to them, stick in hand.

"Got to keep an eye on you," he said to Kelderek with a kind of malicious amiability. "Making yourself at home, are you? Enjoying yourself? That's right."

Kelderek had already noticed that while all the children went in terror of Bled, who was obviously deranged and almost a maniac, several seemed to be on some kind of uncertain terms with Shouter, who from time to time—whether or not he was actually engaged in cruelty—assumed a certain bluffness of manner not uncommon among bullies and tyrants.

"Can you tell me why I'm here?" he asked. "What use am I to Genshed?"

Shouter sniggered. "You're here to be mucking sold, mate," he said. "Without your balls, I dare say."

"What happened to the overseer you replaced?" asked Kelderek. "I suppose you knew him?"

"Knew him? I killed him," answered Shouter.

"Oh, did you?"

"He was all in when we got back to Terekenalt, wasn't he?" said Shouter. "He'd gone to pieces. One day a girl from Dari scratched his mucking face to bits. He couldn't stop her. That night, when Genshed was drunk, he said if anyone could fight him and kill him he could have the job. I killed him all right—strangled him in the middle of Genshed's yard, with about fifty kids watching. Old Genshed was tickled to death. That's how I kept *my* balls, mate, see?"

They reached the river bank and Kelderek, wading in to the knees, drank and washed. Yet his body remained full of pain. As he thought of his own situation and that of Melathys and the Tuginda, despair overcame him and during their return he could find no spirit for any further attempt at talk with Shouter. The boy himself also seemed to have grown pensive, for he said no more, except to order Radu to pick up Shara and carry her.

In the half-light and rising mist Genshed stood snapping his fingers to summon one boy and another. As each approached and stood in front of him the slave dealer examined eyes, ears, hands, feet and shackles, as well as any wounds and injuries that he came upon. Although many of the children were lacerated and two or three seemed on the point of collapse, none received any treatment and Kelderek concluded that Genshed was merely looking over his stock and assessing their capacity to go farther. The children stood motionless, heads bent and hands at their sides, anxious only to be gone as soon as possible. One boy who trembled continually, flinching at each movement of Genshed, was left to stand where he was while the dealer looked at others immediately behind his back. Another, who could not keep quiet, but kept muttering and picking at the sores on his face and shoulders, was silenced by means of the flytrap until Genshed had done with him.

Shouter and Bled, receiving the boys as they left the slave dealer, fastened them together in threes or fours by thin chains drawn through the lobes of their ears. Each chain was secured

468

at one end to a short metal bar, the other being hooked to the belt or wrist of an overseer. When these preparations were complete, all lay down to sleep where they were on the marshy ground.

Kelderek, chained like the rest, had been separated from Radu and lay between two much younger boys, expecting every moment that a movement by one or the other would pull the chain links through his wounded lobe like the teeth of a saw. Soon, however, he realized that his companions, more practiced than he in making misery bearable, were less likely to trouble him than he them. They stirred seldom and had learned the trick of moving their heads without tightening the chain. After a little he found that both had moved close to him, one on either side.

"Not used to this yet, are you?" whispered one of the children in a broad Paltesh argot that he could barely understand. "Buy you today, did he?"

"He didn't buy me. He found me in the forest—yes, it was today."

"Thought as much. You smell of fresh meat—new ones often do, doesn't last long." He broke off, coughing, spat on the ground between them and then said, "Trick's to lie close together. It's warmer, and it keeps the chain slack, see, then anybody moves it don't pull."

Both children were verminous and scratched continually at the sodden, filthy rags covering their thin bodies. Soon, however, Kelderek was no longer aware of their smell, but only of the mud in which he was lying and the throbbing of his wounded finger. To distract his thoughts he whispered to the boy, "How long have you been with this man?"

"Reckon nearly two months now. Bought me in Dari."

"*Bought* you? Who from?"

"My stepfather. Father was killed with General Gel-Ethlin when I was very small. Mother took up with this man last winter and he didn't like me, only I'm dirty, see? Soon as the dealers come he sold me."

"Didn't your mother try to stop it?"

"No," answered the boy indifferently. "Suppose you had food, had you, only he took it away?"

"Yes."

"Shouter said almost no bloody mucking food left," whispered the little boy. "Said they'd reckoned to buy some before this, only there's no mucking place to buy it here."

"Why did Genshed come into this forest, do you know?" asked Kelderek.

"Soldiers, Shouter said."

"What soldiers?"

"Don't know. Only he don't like soldiers. Thats why he put the rope across the river—get away from the soldiers. You hungry, are you?"

"Yes."

He tried to sleep, but there was no quiet. The children whimpered, talked in their sleep, cried out in nightmare. The chains rattled; something moved among the trees; Bled leaped suddenly to his feet, chattering like an ape and wrenching every chain fastened to him. Raising his head, Kelderek could see the hunched figure of the slave dealer a little distance off, his arms clasped about his knees. He did not look like a man seeking sleep. Was he—like Kelderek himself—conscious of the danger of wild animals, or was it, perhaps, possible that he had no need of sleep—that he never slept?

At length he fell into a doze, and when he woke—after how long he could not tell—realized that the child beside him was weeping, almost without noise. He put out his hand and touched him. The weeping stopped at once.

"There's a lot can happen yet," whispered Kelderek. "Were you thinking of your mother?"

"No," replied the boy, "'bout Sirit."

"Who's Sirit?"

"Girl was with us."

"What's happened to her?"

"Gone to Leg-By-Lee."

"Leg-By-Lee? Where's that?"

"Don't know."

"Then how do you know she's gone there?"

The boy said nothing.

"What is Leg-By-Lee? Who told you about it?"

"Where they go, see?" whispered the boy. "Only anyone goes, we say they've gone to Leg-By-Lee."

"Is it far away?"

470

"Don't know."

"Well, if I managed to run away and he brought me back tomorrow, would I have gone to Leg-By-Lee?"

"No."

"Why not?"

"Cause you don't come back from Leg-By-Lee."

"You mean Sirit's dead?"

"Don't know."

They fell silent. A man may be forced to set out into bitter cold, and in the very act of doing so be conscious that the future is desperate and his chance of survival small. Yet this mere reflection, coming at that moment, will not of itself be enough to break his spirit or penetrate his heart with despair. It is as though he still carried, wrapped about the core of his courage, a residue of protecting faith and warmth which must first be penetrated and dispelled, little by little, hour after hour, perhaps day after day, by solitude and cold, until the last remnants are dispersed and the dreadful truth, which at the outset he perceived only with his mind, he feels in his body and fears in his heart. So it was with Kelderek. Now, in the night, with the sharp, ugly noises of wretchedness all around him and the pain crawling about his body like cockroaches in a dark house, he seemed to step down, to review his situation from an even lower level, to feel more deeply and perceive more clearly its nature, devoid of all real hope. He believed, now, in the prospect before him—the passage of Linsho and the long journey up the Telthearna, actually passing Quiso and Ortelga, to Terekenalt; and then slavery, preceded perhaps by the vile mutilation of which Shouter had spoken. Worst of all was the loss of Melathys and the thought that they would remain ignorant forever of each other's fates.

It was Shardik who had brought him to this—Shardik who had pursued him with supernatural malevolence, avenging all that his priest-king had done to abuse and exploit him. He was justly accursed of Shardik, and in his punishment had involved not only Melathys but the Tuginda herself—she who had done all she could, in the face of every obstacle put in her way, to preserve the worship of Shardik from betrayal. With this bitter reflection he once more fell asleep.

471

50 *Radu*

WHEN HE WOKE IT WAS SUNRISE; and as he stirred, a centipede as long as his hand, dark red and sinuous, undulated smoothly away from beneath his body. Shouter was drawing out the chains and coiling them into his pack. The forest was raucous with the calling of birds. Already, where the sun shone, the ground was steaming, and everywhere flies buzzed about patches of night soil and urine. A boy close by coughed without ceasing and all around, the children raised their thin voices in foul language and oaths. Two boys lay quarreling over a fragment of leather which one had stolen from the other, until Bled's stick brought them cursing to their feet.

Shouter gave out small handfuls of dried fruit and watched while they were eaten, his stick ready against any snatching or fighting. He winked at Kelderek and slipped him a second handful.

"Mind you eat it yourself, too," he whispered, "mucking quick."

"Is that all until tonight?" answered Kelderek, appalled at the thought of the day's march.

"It's nigh all there is left anyway," said Shouter, still keeping his voice down. "He says there's no more to be had until we get to Linsho, and that's supposed to be tomorrow evening. I reckon he didn't know what this place was going to be like. We'll be lucky to get out alive."

Kelderek, looking quickly to either side, whispered, "I could get you out alive."

Without waiting for an answer, he shuffled away to where Radu was feeding Shara from his own handful.

"You can't afford to do that," he said. "You've got to keep up your own strength if you want to be able to look after her."

"I've done it before," answered Radu. "I'll be all right as long as she is." He turned back to the little girl. "We're going home soon, aren't we?" he said. "You're going to show me the new calf, aren't you, when we get home?"

"All the way, underground," said a boy standing near; but Shara only nodded and fell to making patterns with her stones.

Soon they began to move off, following Genshed toward the river bank. Once there the slave trader turned upstream, making his way along the open, pebbly shore.

Now that they were no longer among the close trees and he could see the whole column, Kelderek understood, as he had not on the previous day, why their progress was so much interrupted and so slow. What he saw was an exhausted rabble, which surely could not be far from complete disintegration. Continually, one child or another would stop, leaning face forward against a rock or bank and, when Bled or Shouter came up to threaten him, only staring back as though too much stupefied even to feel fear. From time to time a boy would fall and Genshed, Shouter or Bled would pull him to his feet and slap him or dash water in his face. The slave dealer himself seemed well aware of the perishable condition of his stock. He was sparing with blows and called frequent halts, allowing the children to drink and bathe their feet. Once, when Bled, in a frenzy of rage, set about a boy who was fumbling and hesitating at the foot of a pile of rocks, he cuffed him away with a curse, asking where he thought he could sell a dead slave.

Later, as he and Radu lay gazing out across the glittering, noonday river, Kelderek, carefully keeping his voice low, said, "Shouter must know that he's got all he ever can out of Genshed. Surely he must fear returning to Terekenalt? The best thing he could do would be to cut and run, and take us with him. I know how to survive in this sort of country. I could save his life and ours if only I could persuade him to trust me. Do you think Genshed's made him some promise?"

For a time Radu answered nothing, looking sideways into the shallows and stroking Shara's hands. At length he said, "Genshed means more to him than you think. He's converted him, you see."

"Converted him?"

"That's why I'm afraid of Genshed. I know we all fear his cruelty, but I fear more than that."

"You mustn't let him break your spirit," said Kelderek.

473

"He's nothing but a contemptible brute—a sneak thief—mean and stupid."

"He was once," answered Radu, "but that was before he got the power he prayed for."

"What do you mean? What power?"

"Where he's concerned, it's no longer a matter of thieves and honest men," said Radu. "He's gone beyond that. Once he was nothing but a cruel, nasty slum-creeper. But evil's made him strong. He'd paid its price, and in return he's been given its power. You don't feel it yet, but you will. He's been granted the power to make others evil—to make them believe in the strength of evil, to inspire them to become as evil as himself. What he offers is the joy of evil, not just money, or safety, or anything that you and I could understand. He can make some people want to devote their lives to evil. That's what he did to Bled, only Bled wasn't up to it and it drove him mad. Shouter—he was just a poor, deserted boy, sold away from his home. It's not a question of how long he'll last with Genshed or what he'll get. He admires him—he wants to give him everything he's got—he isn't thinking about rewards. He wants to spend his life beating and hurting and terrifying. He knows he's not much good at it yet, but he hopes to improve."

Their hunger was like a mist in the air between them. Kelderek, looking about him for Shara, caught sight of her kneeling beside a pool a little way off and pulling out long strips of bright yellow and dark red weed, which she laid side by side on the stones.

"All this is only your fancy, you know," he said. "You're lightheaded with hunger and hardship."

"I'm lightheaded, that's true enough," answered Radu. "But I can see more clearly for that. If you don't think it's true, you wait and see."

He nodded toward Shara. "It's for her sake that I've not given in," he said. "Genshed wanted me to become an overseer in place of Bled. Bled's become a nuisance to him—he can't be relied on not to cripple boys or kill them. He's killed three boys since Lapan, you know."

"If you became an overseer, mightn't it give you a chance to escape?"

"Perhaps—from anyone but Genshed."

"But did he only try to talk you into becoming an overseer? Didn't he threaten you? You told me he once used the flytrap on you."

"That was because I hit Shouter to stop him interfering with Shara. Genshed would never threaten a boy to make him become an overseer. A boy who's going to become an overseer has got to want to do it. He's got to admire Genshed of his own accord and want to live up to him. Of course Genshed wants the ransom money for me, but if he could persuade me to become an overseer, that would mean even more to him, I believe. He wants to feel he's had a hand in making a nobleman's son as evil as himself."

"But as long as he doesn't threaten you, surely there's no question of your giving in to him?"

Radu paused, as though hesitating before confiding in Kelderek. Then he said deliberately, "God's given in. Either that or He's got no power over Genshed. I'll tell you something that I shall never forget. Before Thettit there was a boy with us—a big, shambling lad called Bellin. He could never have crossed the Vrako; he was clumsy and a bit simple. Genshed put him up for sale along with the girls. The man who bought him told Genshed he wanted to make him a professional beggar. He kept several, he said, and lived off what they brought in. He wanted Bellin mutilated, to excite pity when he was begging. Genshed hacked off Bellin's hands and held his wrists in boiling pitch to stop the bleeding. He charged the man forty-three meld. He said that was his rate for that particular job."

Turning aside, he tore a handful of leaves from a bush and began to eat them. After a moment Kelderek copied him. The leaves were sour and fibrous and he chewed them voraciously.

"Come on! Come on!" bawled Shouter, slapping at the surface of the shallows with his stick. "Get on your mucking feet! Linsho—that's where the grub is, not here!"

Radu stood up, swayed a moment and stumbled against Kelderek.

"It's the hunger," he said. "It'll pass off in a moment." He called to Shara, who came running, with a long strip of colored weed wound like a torque around one thin arm. "If there's one thing I've learned, it's that hunger's a form of torture. If there's more food for overseers than slaves when we get to Linsho, I might become an overseer yet. Cruelty and evil—they're not very far down in anyone. It's only a matter of digging them up, you know."

51 *The Gap of Linsho*

LATER, IN THE AFTERNOON, they came to a wide bend in the river and Genshed once more struck inland to cut across the peninsula. The humid heat of the forest became a torment. The children, some of whom lacked energy even to brush the flies from their faces, were ordered to come close together and each to grasp his neighbor's shoulder, so that they inched onward like some ghastly pack of purblind cripples, many keeping closed their insect-blackened eyes. The boy in front of Kelderek kept up a low, rhythmic sobbing—"Ah-hoo! Ah-hoo!"—until at length Bled flew at him, uttering a stream of curses and jabbing at his legs with the point of his stick. The boy fell, bleeding, and Genshed was forced to call a halt while he stanched his wounds. This done, he sat down with his back against a tree, whistling through his teeth and rummaging in the depths of his pack.

On an impulse, Kelderek went up to him.

"Can you tell me why you've taken me prisoner and how much you hope to get out of it? I can promise you a large sum to release me—more than you'd get for selling me as a slave."

Genshed did not look up and made no reply. Kelderek bent down, stooping over the slave trader's sandy hair and speaking more urgently.

"You can believe what I say. I'm offering you more than you could get for me in any other way. I'm not what I seem. Tell me how much you want, to let me go."

Genshed closed his pack and rose slowly to his feet, wiping his sweating hands along his thighs. Some of the children nearby looked up, waiting apprehensively for the snap of his fingers. He did not look at Kelderek, who had the odd impression that he heard and did not hear him, as a man might ignore a dog's barking while deep in thoughts of his own affairs.

"You can believe me," persisted Kelderek. "At Ortelga, which I suppose you mean to pass, I—"

Suddenly, with the speed of a fish taking its prey, Genshed's hand shot upward and gripped the pierced lobe of Kelderek's ear between finger and thumb. As his thumbnail dug into the wound Kelderek shrieked and tried to clutch his wrist. Before he could do so, the slave dealer drove his knee into his groin, at the same time releasing his ear to allow him to double up and fall to the ground. Then, stooping, he picked up his pack, put his arms through the straps and hoisted it behind his shoulders.

Two or three of the children tittered uncertainly. One threw a stick at Kelderek. Genshed, still with an air of abstraction, snapped his fingers and, as the children began pulling one another up and Shouter set up his usual bawling, walked away to the head of the line and nodded for the first boy to lay hold of his belt.

Kelderek opened his eyes to find Shara looking down at him.

"He hurt you, didn't he?" she said, speaking in a kind of Yeldashay patois.

He nodded and climbed heavily to his feet.

"He hurts us all," she said. "One day he's going away. Radu told me."

Pain and hunger swirled in him as stirred mud clouds a pool.

"Radu told me," she repeated. "Here's a red stone, look, and I've got a blue one, kind of a blue one. Are you hungry? You find caterpillars, can you? Radu finds caterpillars."

Shouter came up, took hold of Kelderek's hand and put it on Radu's shoulder in front of him.

An hour later they regained the shore and halted for the night. Kelderek found that he could form little idea of how far they might have gone during the day. Ten miles at the most, he supposed. Tomorrow Genshed meant to pass the Gap of Linsho. Would there be food, and would they rest? Surely Genshed could see that they must rest. Hunger closed down upon his mind as rain blots out the view across a plain. His thoughts, sliding like wet fingers, could compass nothing. Would there be food at Linsho? Would there, for a time, be no more shuffling, no more stooping to free the chain? Genshed might refrain from hurting him at Linsho, the pain in his finger would grow less. These were things to hope for—but he must try to look beyond these—consider—must consider what was best to be done—

"What are you thinking?" asked Radu.

Kelderek tried to laugh, and tapped his head.

"Where I was born, they used to say, 'You can tap on the wood, but will the insects run out?' "

"Where was that?"

He hesitated. "Ortelga. But it doesn't matter now."

After a pause, Radu said, "If ever you get back there—"

"All the way, underground," said Kelderek.

"You know what we mean when we say that?"

Shara came running toward them along the bank. She took Radu's hand, chattering faster than Kelderek could understand and pointing in the direction she had come from. A little way off, a thick tangle of creepers, covered with gaudy, trumpetlike flowers, hung like a curtain between the shore and the forest. Looking where Shara pointed, they saw that the whole mass was tremulous, shaking slightly but rapidly, vibrant with some strange, unexplained energy of its own. There was no bird or beast to be seen, yet along an expanse as broad as a hut wall the leaves and blooms quivered spasmodically and the long tendrils undulated with a kind of light, quick violence. The little girl, frightened yet fascinated, stared from behind Radu's shoulder. One or two of the other children gathered about them, also gazing curiously. Radu himself was plainly uncertain whether some strange creature might not be about to appear.

Kelderek picked the little girl up in his arms.

"There's nothing to be afraid of," he said. "I'll show you, if you like. It's only a hunting mantis—several, probably."

Radu followed them along the bank. At close quarters the flowers of the creeper gave off a heavy fragrance and great moths, their dark blue wings broad as the palm of a man's hand, were coming and going in the dusky air. High up, beneath an open bloom, one of these was struggling in the grip of a mantis crouched for prey among the flowers. They could see the long, crural shape of the insect half-hidden in the leaves, its front legs clutching the moth, which it had evidently seized as it hovered at the bloom. Its head turned this way and that with an eerie suggestion of intelligence as it followed the frenzied tugging of its victim, so violent that both the mantis and the surrounding creeper to which it was clinging were shaken in a rhythm light and rapid as the beating of the wings themselves. As often as the moth weakened, the mantis would pull it toward its jaws and again the struggle would break out. As Kelderek and Shara watched, a second moth was caught beneath a bloom some yards away, but after a few seconds tore itself clear, the mantis, as its hold was broken, being jerked forward among the leaves below its perch. Meanwhile the first moth faltered, its beautiful wings ceased at last to beat and in an instant the mantis had pulled it in and begun to devour it. The severed wings, first one and then the other, fluttered to the ground.

"Come back out of there, damn you!" cried Shouter, striding toward them along the bank. "What the hell d'you think you're doing?"

"Don't worry," answered Radu, as they returned and joined the other children already crowding around Shouter for their handfuls of food. "We'd hardly get far, you know."

Darkness fell and the children, lying down for the night, were once more chained through the ears. Kelderek, separated from Radu as before, found himself at the inner end of a chain, on one side of him Shouter himself and on the other the child who had been savaged by Bled during the afternoon. In the dark the latter resumed his steady, monotonous sobbing, but Shouter, if he heard, presumably thought that no entertainment could be derived from trying to stop him. After a time Kelderek stretched out his hand to the boy, but he only shrank away and, after a few moments' silence, began to sob more loudly. Still Shouter said nothing and Kelderek, afraid of what he might do and too much exhausted and dispirited to persevere with his clumsy attempts at comfort, let his pity and the other fragments of his thoughts dissolve into sleep while the mosquitoes, unhindered, fastened on his limbs.

The old woman of Gelt came hobbling slowly up the shore, her rags speckled in the half-moon's light, her feet noiseless on the stones. Kelderek watched her approach, puzzled at first but then, recognizing her, acquiescent in the knowledge that she was the creature of a dream. Gently, she drew the chain from his ear and he even seemed to feel the pain as the links passed one by one through the inflamed, tender lobe. Then she remained kneeling above him, looking down and mumbling with her sunken mouth.

"Think no one sees, they think no one sees," she whispered. "But God sees."

"What is it, grandmother?" asked Kelderek. "What happened?"

She was carrying the dead child in her arms, as she had carried it years before, but now it was closely wrapped, muffled from head to foot. It was nothing but a shape under her cloak.

"I'm looking for the governor-man from Bekla," she said. "I'm going to tell him—only it's a long time now—"

"You can tell me," he said. "I'm the governor-man from Bekla and all this misery is my doing, all of it."

"Ah," she said. "Ah. Bless you, sir, bless you. Look here, sir, yes, at that rate you'll want to."

She laid her burden on the ground. The wrappings were fastened at the head with the chain from his ear, but this she unwound, coiling it away and drawing apart the covering round the face.

The eyes were closed, the cheeks lusterless and waxen; but the dead child lying on the stones was Melathys. Her lips were a little apart, but nothing stirred the leaf which the old woman held to them. Weeping, he looked up, and saw under her ragged hood that she was Rantzay.

"She's not dead, Rantzay!" he cried. "Wake her, Rantzay, you must wake her!"

Rantzay made no reply, and as her lean fingers grasped and shook his shoulder he understood that she too was dead. He writhed away from her, filled with a dreadful sense of loss and desolation.

"Wake! Come on, wake!"

It was Shouter's face above his own, whispering urgently, fetid breath stinking, itching of insect bites, stones sharp under the spine and the faint light of day stealing into the sky beyond the Telthearna. Whimpering of the children in sleep and clicking of chains against the stones.

"It's me, you mucking idiot. Don't make a noise. I've pulled the chain out your ear. If you don't want to go to Terekenalt, then come on, for God's sake!"

Kelderek got up. His skin felt a single sheet of irritant bites and the river swam before his eyes. Still half in his dream, he looked around for the dead body in the shallows, but it was gone. He took a step forward, slipped and fell on the stones. Someone else, neither Rantzay nor Shouter, was speaking.

"What were you doing, Shouter, eh?"

"Nothing," answered Shouter.

"Took his chain out, have you? Where were you going?"

"He wanted to shit, didn't he? Think I'm going to let him shit up against me?"

Genshed made no reply, but drew his knife and began pressing the point against the ball first of one finger and then of another. After a few moments he opened his clothes and urinated over Shouter, the boy standing still as a post while he did so.

"Remember Kevenant, do you?" murmured Genshed.

"Kevenant?" said Shouter, his voice cracking with incipient hysteria. "What's Kevenant got to do with it? Who's talking about Kevenant?"

"Remember what he looked like, do you, when we were finished with him?"

Shouter made no answer, but as Genshed took the lobe of his ear between one finger and thumb he was seized with an uncontrollable trembling.

"See, you're just a silly little boy, Shouter, aren't you?" said Genshed, twisting slowly, so that Shouter sank to his knees on the stones. "Just a silly little boy, aren't you?"

"Yes," whispered Shouter.

The point of the knife brushed along his closed eyelid and he tried to draw back his head, but was stopped by the twisting of his ear.

"See all right, Shouter, can you?"

"Yes."

"Sure you can see all right?"

"Yes! Yes!"

"See what I mean, can you?"

"Yes!"

"Only I get everywhere, don't I, Shouter? If you were over there, I'd be there too, wouldn't I?"

"Yes."

"Do your work all right, Shouter, can you?"

"Yes, I can! Yes, I can!"

"Funny, I thought perhaps you couldn't. Like Kevenant."

"No, I can! I can! I treat 'em worse than Bled does. They're all afraid of me!"

"Keep still, Shouter. I'm going to do you a favor. I'm just going to clean under your nails with the point of my knife. Only I wouldn't want my hand to slip."

The sweat ran down Shouter's face, over his upper lip, over his lower lip bitten between his teeth, over his slobbered chin. When at last Genshed released him and walked away, sheathing the knife at his belt, he pitched forward into the shallows, but he was up again in a moment. In silence he washed himself, threaded the chain back through Kelderek's ear, fastened it to his belt and lay down.

Half an hour later Genshed himself distributed the last of the food, crumbs and fragments shaken from the bottom of the pack.

"The next lot's in Linsho, understand?" said Shouter to Radu. "You see to it that they all understand that. Either we get to mucking Linsho today or we start eating each other."

Kelderek was combing Shara's hair between his fingers and searching her head for lice. Although he had eaten what he had been given, he now felt so faint and tortured with hunger that he could no longer collect his wits. The figure of Melathys lying dead seemed to hover continually in the tail of his eye, and as often as it appeared he turned his head quickly, fumbling and clutching with his hands, until Shara grew impatient and wandered away up the shore.

"Someone stole her colored stones after we were unchained this morning," said Radu.

Kelderek did not answer, having suddenly made the important discovery of the futility of wasting energy in speech.

482

Speech, he now realized, involved so much unprofitable effort—thinking of words, moving lips to utter them, listening to a reply and grasping what it meant—that it was an altogether foolish thing on which to squander one's strength. To stand upright, to walk, to disentangle the chain, to remember to avoid catching Bled's eye—these were the things for which energy needed to be stored.

They were moving again, to be sure, for that was his chain clicking on the stones. But this walking was not the same. How was it different? In what way had they all changed? In his mind's eye he seemed to look down on them from above as they wound their way along the shore. Hither and thither they went, like ants over a stone, but much slower, like torpid beetles in autumn, on their clambering journeys up and down the long miles of grass stems. And now indeed he perceived plainly, though without concern, what had befallen. They had become part of the insect world, where all was simple and from henceforth would simply be lived, untroubled by conscious volition. They needed no speech, no feelings, no hearing, no awareness one of another. For days at a time they would even require no food. They would not know whether they were ugly or beautiful, happy or unhappy, good or bad, for these terms had no meaning. Appetite and satiety, scuttling energy and motionless torpor, ferocity and helplessness—these were their poles. Their short lives would soon end, prey to winter, prey to larger creatures, prey to one another; but this too was a matter of no regard.

Still fascinated and preoccupied by this new insight, he found himself climbing over some obstacle that had almost tripped him. Something fairly heavy and smooth, though yielding. Something with sticks in it—a bundle of rags with sticks in it, no, his chain had caught; bend down, now it was free, yes, of course, the obstacle was a human body—that was the head, there—now he had climbed over it, it was gone and the stones had returned as before. He closed his eyes against the glitter of the river and set himself doggedly to the task of keeping upright and taking steps; one step, another step, another.

Suddenly a cry sounded from behind him.

"Stop! Stop!"

483

Like a bubble out of dark ooze, his mind rose slowly into the former world of hearing, of seeing, of comprehension. He turned, to perceive Radu, with Shara beside him, kneeling over a body on the stones. Several of the boys, startled as he had been by the cry, had stopped and were moving uncertainly toward them. From somewhere in front Shouter was yelling, "What the muck's happened?"

He limped back. Radu was supporting the boy's head on one arm and splashing water over his face. It was the boy whom Bled had savaged the day before. His eyes were closed and Kelderek could not make out whether he was breathing or not.

"You walked over him," said Radu. "You walked over his body. Didn't you feel it?"

"Yes—no. I didn't know what I was doing," answered Kelderek dully.

Shara touched the boy's forehead and tried to pull the rags together across his chest.

"Tumbled down, didn't he?" she said to Radu. "He hasn't got a chain," she went on, in a kind of song, "He hasn't got a chain, to go to Leg-By-Lee—" Then, breaking off as she saw Genshed coming toward them, "Radu, he's coming!"

Genshed stopped beside the boy, stirred him with his foot, dropped on one knee, rolled back one eyelid and felt the heart. Then he stood up, looked around at the other boys and jerked his head. They moved away and Genshed faced Kelderek and Radu across the body.

As fire is stopped by the bank of a river, as the growth of the vine's tendrils is halted by the onset of winter, so their compassion faltered and died before Genshed. He said nothing, his presence sufficient to focus, like a lens, in a single point, their sense of helplessness to aid or comfort the boy. How futile was their pity, for what could it effect? Genshed lay all about them: in their own exhaustion, in this forest wilderness lacking food or shelter, in the glittering river hemming them in, the empty sky. He said nothing, allowing his presence to lead them to their own conclusion—that they were merely wasting their tiny remaining store of energy. When he snapped his fingers their eyes fell and, with Shara beside them, they followed the boys; nor did they trouble to look back. They and Genshed were now entirely of one mind.

484

A short distance along the shore, Shouter had called a halt. They lay down among the children, but none questioned them. Genshed returned, washed his knife in the water and then, ordering Bled to remain in charge, took Shouter with him and disappeared upstream. Returning half an hour later, he at once led the way inland among the woods.

As evening began to fall they stumbled their way up a long, gradual slope, the forest around them growing more open as they went. Between the trees Kelderek could see a red, westering sun and this, he found, awoke in him a dull surprise. Pondering, he realized that since leaving Lak he had not once seen the sun after midday. They must now be upon the forest's northern edge.

At the top of the slope, Genshed waited until the last of the children had come up before beginning to push through the undergrowth on the forest outskirts. Suddenly he stopped, peering forward and shading his eye against the sun. Kelderek and Radu, halting behind him, found themselves looking out across the northern extremity of the evil land which they had now traversed from end to end, from the Vrako's banks to the Gap of Linsho.

The air was full of a dazzling, golden light, slow-moving and honey-thick. Myriads of motes and specks floated here and there, their minute glitterings seeming to draw the light down from the sky to the ground, there to fragment and multiply. The evening beams glanced off leaves, off the wings of darting flies and the surface of the Telthearna flowing a mile away at the foot of the slope. Directly before them, to the north, the distant prospect was closed by the mountains—jagged, iron-blue heights, streaked with steep wedges of forest rising out of the virid foothills. Looking at this tremendous barrier, Kelderek called to mind that once—how long ago?—he had possessed the strength to follow Shardik into such mountains as these. Now, he could not have limped over the intervening ground to their foot.

Clouds half-hid the easternmost peak, which rose above the Telthearna like a tower, its precipitous face falling almost sheer to the river. Between the water and the wooded crags at the mountain's foot there extended a narrow strip of flat land little more than a bowshot across—the Gap of Linsho. Huts he could make out, and wisps of evening smoke drifting toward the wilds of Deelguy on the farther shore. A track led out of the Gap, ran a short way beside the water, then turned inland to climb the slope, crossed their front less than half a mile away and disappeared southwestward beyond the extremity of the forest on their left. Goats were tethered on the open sward and a herd of cows was grazing—one had a flat-toned, cloppering bell at her neck—watched by a little boy, who sat fluting on a wooden pipe; and an old ox, at the full extent of his rope, pulled the greenest grass he could get.

But it was not at the golden light, at the cattle or the child playing his pipe that Genshed stood staring, his hanging face like a devil's, sick with the pain of loss. Beside the track, a patch of ground had been enclosed with a wooden palisade and a fire was burning in a shallow trench. A soldier in a leather helmet was crouching, scouring pots, while another was chopping wood with a billhook. Beside the stockade a tall staff had been erected and from it hung a flag—three corn sheaves on a blue ground. Nearby, two more soldiers could be seen facing toward the forest, one sitting on the turf as he ate his supper, the other standing, leaning on a long spear. The situation was plain. The Gap had been occupied by a Sarkid detachment of the army of Santil-kè-Erketlis.

"Bloody God!" whispered Genshed, staring over the pastoral, flame-bright quiet of the hillside. Shouter, coming up from behind, drew in his breath and stood stock-still, gazing as a man might at the burning ruins of his own home. The children were silent, some uncomprehending in their sickness and exhaustion, others sensing with fear the rage and desperation of Genshed, who stood clenching and unclenching his hands without another word.

Suddenly Radu plunged forward. His rags fluttered about him and he flung both arms above his head, jerking like an idiot child in a fit.

"Ah! Ah!" croaked Radu. "Sark—" He staggered, fell and got up knee by knee, like a cow. "Sarkid!" he whispered, stretching out his hands; and then, barely louder, "Sarkid! Sarkid!"

With deliberation, Genshed took his bow from the side of his pack and laid an arrow on the string. Then, leaning against a tree, he waited as Radu again drew breath. The boy's cry, when it came, was like that of a sick infant, distorted and feeble. Once

more he cried, bird-like, and then sank to his knees, sobbing
and wringing his hands among the undergrowth. Genshed, pulling Shouter back by the shoulder, waited as a man might wait
for a friend to finish speaking with a passer-by in the street.

"O God!" wept Radu. "God, only help us! O God, please help
us!"

On Kelderek's back Shara half-awoke, murmured, "Leg-By-
Lee! Gone to Leg-By-Lee!" and fell asleep again.

As a man led to judgment might halt to listen to the sound of
a girl singing; as the eye of one just told of his own mortal illness might stray out of the window to dwell for an instant upon
the flash of some bright-plumaged bird among the trees; as some
devil-may-care fellow might drain a glass and dance a spring on
the scaffold—so, it seemed, not only Genshed's inclination but
also his self-respect now impelled him in this, his own utter
disaster, to pause a few moments to enjoy the rare and singular
misery of Radu. He looked around among the children, as though
inviting anyone else who might wish to try his luck to see what
voice he might have left for calling out to the soldiers. Watching
him, Kelderek was seized by a deadly horror, like that of a child
facing the twitching, glazed excitement of the rapist. His teeth
chattered in his head and he felt his empty bowels loosen. He
sank down, barely in sufficient command of himself to slide the
little girl from his back and lay her beside him on the ground.

At this moment a hoarse voice was heard from among the
bushes nearby.

"Gensh! Gensh, I say! Gensh!"

Genshed turned sharply, peering with sun-dazzled eyes into
the dusky forest behind him. There was nothing to be seen, but
a moment later the voice spoke again.

"Gensh! Don't be going out there, Gensh! For God's sake give
us a hond!"

A faint wisp of smoke curled up from a patch of undergrowth,
but otherwise all was stiller than the grassy slope outside. Genshed jerked his head to Shouter and the boy went slowly and
reluctantly forward with the best courage he could summon. He
disappeared among the bushes and a moment later they heard
him exclaim, "Mucking hell!"

Still Genshed said nothing, merely nodding to Bled to join

Shouter. He himself continued to keep half his attention upon Radu and Kelderek. After some delay the two boys emerged from the bushes, supporting a fleshy, thick-lipped man with small eyes, who grimaced with pain as he staggered between them, trailing a pack behind him along the ground. The left leg of his once-white breeches was soaked in blood and the hand which he held out to Genshed was red and sticky.

"Gensh!" he said. "Gensh, you know me, don't you, you won't leave me here, you'll be gotting me away? Don't go out there, Gensh, they'll got you same as they did me; we can't stay here, either—they'll be coming, Gensh, coming!"

Kelderek, staring from where he lay, suddenly called the man to mind. This blood-drenched craven was none other than the wealthy Deelguy slave dealer Lalloc—fat, insinuating, dandified, with the manners, at once familiar and obsequious, of a presuming servant on the make. Overdressed and smiling among his miserable, carefully groomed wares, he had once been accustomed to publicize himself in Bekla as "The high-class slave dealer, purveyor to the aristocracy. Special needs discreetly catered for." Kelderek remembered, too, how he had taken to calling himself "U-Lalloc," until ordered by Ged-la-Dan to curb his impertinence and mind his place. There was little enough of the demimondain dandy about him now, crouching at Genshed's feet, dribbling with fear and exhaustion, his yellow robe smeared with dirt and his own blood clotted across his fat buttocks. The strap of his pack was twisted round his wrist and in one hand he was clutching the plaited thong of a clay thurible, or fire pot, such as some travelers carry on lonely journeys and keep smoldering with moss and twigs. It was from this that the thin smoke was rising.

Kelderek remembered how in Bekla Lalloc, coming once to the Barons' Palace to apply for the renewal of his license, had fallen to deploring the wicked deeds of unauthorized slave dealers. "Your gracious Mojesty will need no ashorrance that my colleagues and I, acting in the bost interosts of the trade, would never have to do with soch men. To oss, profit is a secondary motter. We regard ourselves as your Mojesty's servants, employed to move your own fixed quotas about the empire as may suit your convenience. Now may I soggest—" and his rings had

488

clicked as he placed his hands together and bowed, in the manner of the Deelguy. And whence, Kelderek had wondered, whence in truth had he obtained the pretty children who had stood on his rostrum in the market, tense and dry-eyed, knowing what was good for them? He had never inquired, for the taxes on Lalloc's turnover had produced very large sums, all duly rendered—enough to pay and equip several companies of spearmen.

For a moment, as Lalloc's eye traveled over the children, it rested on Kelderek: but his momentary surprise, Kelderek could perceive, was due to no more than observing a grown man among the slaves. He did not recognize—how should he?—the former priest-king of Bekla.

Still Genshed stood silent, looking broodingly at the bleeding Lalloc as though wondering—as no doubt he was—in what way he could turn this unexpected meeting to his advantage. At length he said, "Bit of trouble, Lalloc; been in it, have you?"

The other spread his bloody hands, shoulders shrugging, eyebrows lifting, head wagging from side to side.

"I was in Kabin, Gensh, when the Ikats come north. Thought I had plonty of time to gotting back to Bekla, but left it too late —you ever know soldiers go so fost, Gensh, you ever know? Cot off, couldn't gotting to Bekla" (one hand chopped downward in a gesture of severance) "no governor in Kabin—new governor, man called Mollo, been killed in Bekla, they were saying—the king kill him with his own honds—no one would take money to protect me. So I cross the Vrako. I think, 'I'll stay here till it's over, me and my nice lottle boys what I bought.' So we stay in some torrible village. I have to pay and pay, just not to be murdered. One day I hear the Ikat soldiers come over the Vrako, honting everywhere for the slave dealers. I go north— ow, what 'orrible journey—rockon buy my way through Linsho. But I don't go through the forest, I come straight up the trock, walk right in among the soldiers. 'Ow I'm to know the Ikats gotting there first? Dirty thieves—take my lottle boys, all what I pay for. I drop everything, run into the forest. Then arrow cotch me in the thigh, ow, my God, the pain! They honting for me, not long. No, no, they don't need hont, clever bastards." He spat. "They know there's no food here, no shelter, no way

489

to go onnywhere. O my God, Gensh, what we do now, eh? You go out through those trees they'll have you—they're waiting for oss—someone tell me Nigon they kill, Mindulla they kill—"

"Nigon's dead," said Genshed.

"Yoss, yoss. You help me away, Gensh? We gotting across the Telthearna, gotting to Deelguy? You remomber how many lottle boys and girls I buy off you, Gensh, always buying off you, and I don't tell where—"

Suddenly Shouter whistled and plucked Genshed by the sleeve. "Look at the bastards!" he said, jerking his thumb.

Half a mile away, across the sunlit slope where the guard-house stood, twenty or thirty soldiers were coming toward the forest, trailing their long spears behind them over the grass. At a signal from their officer they extended their line, opening out to right and left as they approached the outskirts.

Not to one child, and to neither Radu nor Kelderek, did it occur that they might, even now, call out or try to reach the soldiers. Had not Genshed just permitted them to prove to themselves that they could not?

His domination—that evil force of which Radu had spoken—lay all about them like a frost, unassailable, visible only in its effects, permeating their spirits with its silent power to numb and subdue. It lay within them—in their starved bodies, in their hearts, in their frozen minds. Not God Himself could melt this cold or undo the least part of Genshed's will. Kelderek, waiting until Bled was looking elsewhere and would not see his slow, fumbling struggle, lifted Shara once more in his arms, took the unresisting Radu by the hand and followed the slave dealer back into the forest.

Along the higher ground they went, along the crest of the low ridge they had ascended earlier that afternoon, Lalloc hobbling beside Genshed and continually entreating not to be left behind. While he babbled, albeit in whispers and in phrases disjointed by shortness of breath, Genshed made no reply. Yet though he might seem inattentive, both to the children and to the fat pur-veyor of nice little boys, it appeared to Kelderek that neverthe-less he remained most alert within himself, like a great fish that skulks below a ledge, at one and the same time watching for the least chance to dash between the legs of the wading netsmen and waiting motionless in the hope that its stillness may deceive them into believing it already gone.

52 *The Ruined Village*

AND NOW BEGAN among the children that final disintegration which only the fear of Genshed had delayed so long. Despite the fog of ignorance and dread that covered them, one thing was clear to them all. Genshed's plans had failed. Both he and his overseers were afraid and did not know what to do next. Bled walked by himself, hunched and muttering, his eyes on the ground. Shouter gnawed continually at his hand, while ever and again his head, with open mouth and closed eyes, dropped forward like that of an ox unable to pull its load. From all three, despair emanated as bats come fluttering from a cave, thicker as the light fails. The children began to straggle. Several, having fallen or lain down on the ground, remained where they were, for Genshed and his whippers-in, now sharing the same evil trance as their victims, had neither purpose nor spirit to beat them to their feet.

It was plain that Genshed no longer cared whether the children lived or died. He paid them no heed, but pressed on at his own pace, concerned only to outdistance the soldiers; and when some of those who had fallen, seeing him disappearing ahead of them, struggled to their feet and somehow contrived to catch up with him again, still he spared them not a glance. Only of Kelderek and Radu did he remain steadily watchful, ordering them, knife in hand, to walk in front of him and stop for nothing.

As when two animals have fought, the one that is beaten seems actually to grow smaller as it slinks away, so, since turning back from the edge of the forest, Radu had regressed from a youth to a child. The pride of bearing with which he had carried his rags and sores, as though they were honorable insignia of the House of Sarkid, had given place to an exhausted misery

like that of a survivor from some disaster. He moved uncertainly
here and there, as though unable to pick his way for himself,
and once, with hands covering his face, gave way to a fit of
sobbing which ceased only when breath failed him. As he lifted
his head his eyes met Kelderek's with a look of panic-stricken
despair, like that of an animal staring from a trap.

"I'm afraid to die," he whispered.

Kelderek could find no answer.

"I don't want to die," repeated Radu desperately.

"Get on," said Genshed sharply, from behind.

"Those were my father's soldiers!"

"I know," answered Kelderek dully. "They may find us yet."

"They won't. Genshed will kill us first. O God, he frightens
me so much! I can't hide it any more."

"If the soldiers find us, they'll certainly kill me," said Kelderek.
"I was your father's enemy, you see. It seems strange now."

Startled, Radu looked quickly at him; but at the same moment
Shara, awake at last, began to struggle on Kelderek's shoulders
and to set up a thin wail of misery and hunger.

"Keep her quiet," said Genshed instantly.

Radu, with some difficulty, took her from Kelderek, but as he
did so slipped, so that the little girl gave a sharp cry of fear.
Genshed covered the ground between them in four strides,
gripped Radu by the shoulder with one hand and silenced the
child with the other over her mouth.

"Once more and I'll kill her," he said.

Radu cringed from him, whispering to Shara urgently. She became silent, and again they limped on among the trees.

"I won't die," said Radu presently, with more composure.
"Not as long as she needs me. Her father's one of our tenants,
you know."

"You told me."

It was almost dark and there had been no sounds of pursuit.
Of how many children now remained with them Kelderek had
no idea. He tried to look about him, but first could not focus his
sight and then could not remember for what it was that he was
supposed to be looking. The faintness of hunger seemed to have
destroyed both sight and sound. His brain swam and a feverish
pain stabbed through his head. When first he glimpsed stone

492

walls about him, he could not tell whether they might be real or figments of his splintered mind.

Shouter was shaking him by the arm.

"Stop! Stop, damn you! You gone mucking deaf or something? He says stop! Here," said the boy, with something faintly resembling human sympathy, "you'd better sit down, mate, you need a rest, you do. Sit down here."

He found himself sitting on a ledge of stone. Around him was what had once been a clearing, stumps of trees overgrown with creeper and weeds. There were walls of piled boulders and stones without mortar, some tumbled, some still standing: steadings and pens, all doorless, the roofs fallen in, holes exposing the smoke-blackened flues of chimneys. Nearby rose a low cliff of rock, once, no doubt, quarried to build these same dwellings; and at its foot a spring trickled into a shallow pool, from which the water, flowing through an outfall in the enclosing stones, ran away downhill toward the distant Telthearna. On the opposite side of the pool, the stone surround was half-covered by the long tendrils of a trepsis vine, on which a few scarlet flowers were already blooming.

"Where are we?" asked Kelderek. "Shouter, where are we?"

"How the hell d'you expect me to know?" answered Shouter. "Deserted village or something, i'n't it? No one been here for mucking years. What's it matter?" went on the boy, with choking violence. "We're all good as dead now. Good as any other place to die, isn't it?"

"For me," said Kelderek. "It is for me. It's like another place I once knew—there was a pool, and trepsis—"

"He's gone," said Radu. "Yes, go and have a drink, Shara dear. I'll come over in a moment."

"Are we going home soon?" asked the little girl. "Said we'd go home, didn't you? I'm hungry, Radu. I'm hungry."

"Going home soon, dear," said Radu. "Not tonight, but quite soon. Don't cry. Look, the big boys aren't crying. I'll look after you."

Shara put her two hands on his forearm and looked up at him, her wan, dirty face grave amid her matted hair.

"It's dark," she said. "Dad used to light a lamp. I think he did. When it got dark he used to light a lamp."

"I remember the lamps," said Radu. "I'm hungry too. It'll be all right in the end, I promise you."

"Genshed's bad, isn't he? He hurts us. Will he go to Leg-By-Lee?"

Radu nodded, his finger to his lips. "The soldiers are coming," he whispered. "The soldiers from Sarkid. They'll take us home. But that's a secret between you and me."

"I feel bad," she said. "Feel ill. Want a drink." She kissed his arm with dry lips and stumbled across to the pool.

"I've got to look after her," said Radu. He passed his hand across his forehead and closed his eyes. "Her father's one of our tenants, you know. Oh, I told you. I feel ill too. Is it a pestilence, do you think?"

"Radu," said Kelderek, "I'm going to die. I'm sure of that. The pool and the trepsis—they're sent as a sign to me. Even if the soldiers come I shall still die, because they'll kill me."

"Genshed," said Radu, "Genshed means to make sure of killing us. Or the devil that's using his body now—he means to kill us."

"You're lightheaded, Radu. Listen to me. There's something I need to ask you."

"No, it's true about the devil. It's because I'm lightheaded that I can see it. If a man loves hell and does hell's work, then the devils take over his body before he dies. That's what our old gatekeeper told me once in Sarkid. I didn't know what he meant then, but I do now. Genshed's become a devil. He frightens me almost to death—the mere sight of him—I believe he could kill me with fear if he set about it."

Kelderek groped for his arm like a blind man.

"Radu, listen to me. I want to ask your forgiveness, and your father's, too, before I die."

"My father's? But you don't know my father. You're as lightheaded as I am."

"It's for you to forgive me in your father's name, and in Sarkid's name. I've been your father's greatest enemy. You never asked my name. My name is Kelderek of Ortelga, but you knew of me once as Crendrik."

"Crendrik, the priest-king of Bekla?"

"Yes, I was once the king of Bekla. Never mind how I come to be here. It's God's justice, for it was I that brought the slave

494

trade back to Bekla and licensed the slave dealers in return for money to pay for the war against Santil-kè-Erketlis. If it's true that death settles all debts and wrongs, then I beg you to forgive me. I'm no longer the man who committed those deeds."

"Are we really to die, are you sure? There's no help for it?" It was a frightened, staring child who looked up at Kelderek in the last light.

"My time has come to die—I know that now. The Ikat soldiers would have killed me in Kabin, but your father stopped them. When he sent me across the Vrako, he told me that if ever they found me again they'd kill me. So I shall die, either at the soldiers' hands or at Genshed's."

"If my father could forgive you then, Crendrik, I can forgive you now. Oh, what does it matter? That little girl's going to die! Genshed will kill her—I know it," cried the boy, weeping.

Before Kelderek could answer, Genshed was standing over them, silent in the darkness. He snapped his fingers and they both climbed slowly to their feet, trembling and shrinking like beasts from a cruel master. He was about to speak when Lalloc approached and he turned toward him, leaving them where they stood.

"You wouldn't have gotting moch for them, Gensh," said Lalloc. "So don't worry, no, no. Even I couldn't be guvving you moch for those. You'll lose vorry little, vorry little indeed."

"I'm keeping these two by me, all the same," answered Genshed.

"No good keep onny of 'em, Gensh, not now. You nover gotting 'em out and if we got caught with 'em, thot's it, eh? Hard enough we gotting out at all, but we got nothing to eat, Gensh, we got to try gotting out. We try to go across to Deelguy, other side, thot's all we gotting the chonce now."

Genshed sat down on the broken wall, staring listlessly before him. Lalloc's rings clicked as he rubbed his hands nervously together.

"Gensh, we can't try tonight. Morning we try it; soon what it's light. You come inside over there, that one got a bit of roof on. We make a fire—won't show outside. Losten, Gensh, I got some drink—good, strong drink. We stay there, by and by it's morning, then we gotting across the river, eh?"

Genshed rose slowly to his feet and stood pressing the point of his knife against the ball of one finger and then another. At length he jerked his head toward Radu and said, "I'm keeping him by me."

"Well, jost what you say, Gensh, yoss, yoss, but he's no good to you now, none of them's any good to you now. Jost leave them, eh, we don't want them ony more, they don't got away anywhere in the dark, they're all worn out, fonish. Morning we gotting away."

"I'm keeping him by me," repeated Genshed.

Shara came slowly up to Radu, one arm held across her face. As she put her hand in the boy's, Genshed stared down at her, his eyes, like those of a snake, full of a cold, universal malevolence. Radu stooped to pick her up but, too weak to lift her, dropped on one knee and in doing so encountered Genshed's stare. He half-rose, apparently about to run, but as Genshed seized him by the pierced ear he gasped, "No! No! I won't—"

"See, you're just a silly little boy, aren't you, Radu?" said Genshed, twisting slowly, so that Radu sank to his knees. "Just a silly little boy, aren't you?"

"Yes."

Genshed drew the point of his knife along Radu's eyelid but then, as though suddenly weary of what had begun, thrust it back into the sheath, dragged him to his feet and led him away toward the ruined cottage where Lalloc was already kneeling and blowing his smoldering fire pot into a flame. Shara tottered beside them, the sound of her weeping becoming inaudible as they entered the doorway. Left alone in the darkness, Kelderek sank down on the open ground; but later—how long afterward he could not tell—crept on his hands and knees into the nearest hut, and there he fell asleep.

53 Night Talk

HE HAD BEEN GIVEN a bundle of child slaves to take to the Barons' Palace, but they were so heavy that he could not carry them and had to drag them behind him step by step. The way lay up a mountain and he was following Lord Shardik, up through the steep, dreary forests where the ghosts of the dead soldiers flickered and cackled among the branches. At last the way became so steep and the weight so heavy that he had to crawl on his hands and knees, and in this manner he came at last to the top. The Barons' Palace stood on the extreme summit, but drawing nearer he realized that it was nothing but flat, painted wood upon a frame, and as he stood looking at it, it broke to pieces and fell away down the back of the mountain.

Waking, he crawled into the open air and tried to get a sight of the stars. Either leaves or clouds were obscuring them. As best he could, he considered. If it were now very late—the middle of the night or later—both Genshed and Lalloc might be asleep: if they were, he might just possibly be able to release Radu and Shara—might even, perhaps, be able to kill Genshed with his own knife.

The night was pitch black, but from one direction he could make out a distant glow of firelight, partly obscured, or so it seemed, by some kind of curtain. He took a few steps toward it and perceived that he had misjudged the distance, for it was close—close by. A cloak had been fastened across the doorless gap through which Genshed had led Radu at nightfall. He reached it, knelt and put his eye to one of the slits through which the glow was showing.

Dry stone walls and a floor of cobbles—nothing else—and a low fire burning in the fireplace opposite. Who had collected the wood, he wondered. The slave dealers must have got it for themselves while he lay asleep. In the farther corner Radu and Shara were sleeping on the bare stones. Radu was lying motionless, but Shara whimpered continually, fretful and evidently ill. Beside her, on the wall, her shadow jumped and leapt, exaggerating each movement of the sick child as echoes in a ravine magnify and hurl back the cry of a man standing upon its brink.

Genshed, a long stick in one hand, was sitting on his pack, gazing into the flames and scraping moodily at a cluster of insects that had run to the top of a burning log. The fancy returned to Kelderek that he never slept, or that, like an insect, he became dormant only at certain seasons. Opposite, Lalloc was perched awkwardly on a log, with his wounded leg supported on another. A leather wineskin was propped against Genshed's pack, and after a few moments the slave dealer picked it up, drank and passed it across to Lalloc. Kelderek, seeing that any idea of rescue was hopeless, was about to creep away when Lalloc spoke. Curious, despite his lightheaded, insect-devoured misery, he listened.

"You wasn't ollways in this line of business, was you?" asked Lalloc, bending forward to rub his leg. "How long I know you, Gensh—three years?"

"Not always," answered Genshed.

"What you done—soldier maybe?"

Genshed leaned forward and dislodged a beetle into the flames. "I was executioner's mate in Terekenalt."

"Thot's a good job? Good money?"

"It was a living," said Genshed.

There was a pause.

"Bit of sport, was it, eh?"

"Kids' stuff," answered Genshed. "Got tired of it. You learn it all quick enough and you're only allowed to do what you're told."

"Thot's not moch, eh?"

"Well, it's all right—watch their faces when they bring them out—you know, when they see it all laid out for their personal benefit—the clinders and the frags and that."

"Frags first, ain't it?"

"Can be either," answered Genshed, "long as the fingers are broken. But you can't let yourself go, only now and then."

"What's now and then?"

Genshed drank again, and considered.

"If a man's condemned, all you can do is carry out the sentence. That's all right, but it's no better than boys or animals, is it? That's what I came to see, anyway."

"Why, what more you can do, then?"

"Screaming and crying, you get tired of that," said Genshed. "There's a bit more to it when they want information. The real style's breaking a man's mind, so that he turns what you want and stays that way even when you've finished with him."

"You got you can do thot?"

"Needs brains," said Genshed. "Of course I could have done it, I got the brains, but the bastards wouldn't give me the chance. Job like that's sold to the one who can buy it, isn't it? They don't want quality. I knew what I was worth. I wasn't going to stay hot-iron man all my life, just for the bare living. I started taking what I could get from prisoners—you know, to let 'em off light—or just take the money and not let 'em off—what could they do? That was what lost me the job. After that I was in a bad way for a time. Most people don't want to employ you when you've been in that line of trade—more fools them."

Lalloc threw another branch on the fire and squinted into the neck of the wineskin. In the corner Shara twisted on the floor, babbled a few words and licked her dry lips without waking.

"Ortolgans give you chonce, eh, like me?"

"They wouldn't give me a license, the bastards. You know that."

"Why they don't?"

"Too many children injured, they said. More like I hadn't got the money to buy the license."

Lalloc chuckled, but broke off as Genshed looked sharply across at him.

"Well, I don't laugh, no, no, but you need style, Gensh, to be slave dealer, you know. Why you don't gotting proper overseers? Then don't lot your children die, don't hurt them where it shows. Make them look nice, you know, teach them act up a little for the costomers."

Genshed crashed his fist into his palm.

"All right for you, eh? I got to work on the cheap. You don't need overseers for kids. Pick out a couple of the kids themselves —get rid of them soon as they know more than you want them to know. You—you only buy from other dealers, don't you, got capital to work with? I got to go out and get 'em on the cheap, all the trouble, all the danger, no license, then you buy them off me and sell 'em for more, don't you?"

"Well, but you ollways spoil so monny, Gensh, ain't it?"

"You got to expect to spoil some—got to expect to lose some as well. You got to break their minds—make them so they can't even think of running away. Beat one or two to death if you have to—frighten the rest half silly. I don't have to do so much as I did once—not now I've got the trick. I've driven kids mad without even touching them—that's style, if you like."

"Bot you can't soll them if they're gone mad, Gensh."

"Not for so much," admitted Genshed. "But you can count on getting some sort of price for almost anything, and you've had a bit of sport for the difference. Loony ones, ugly ones, all the ones rich dealers like you don't take—I can still sell them to the beggar-masters. You know, chop their hands off, chop their feet off, something of that, send them out to beg. Man in Bekla used to live off eighteen or twenty, most of them he got from me. Used to send them out begging in the Caravan Market."

"Well, thot might be your style, Gensh, but it's not big money. You got to make them look pretty, jost ontil the costomer's bought them, you know. Then you got to stoddy what the rich costomer want, you got to talk to the children, tell them it's all for their good they tickle the costomer, you know, eh?"

His voice held a barely concealed note of condescension. Genshed slashed at the fire in silence.

"What you keeping the little girl for?" asked Lalloc. "You gotting rod all the girls in Tonilda, you told me. Why you not solling her?"

"Ah—to keep *him* in order, that's it," said Genshed, jerking his thumb at Radu.

" 'Ow's thot?"

"He's a funny one," said Genshed. "Smartest thing I ever did, biggest risk I ever took; if it comes off I'll make a fortune, and it still could. That's a young aristocrat, this is—ransom job, once I get him back to Terekenalt. Long as I keep *him* I can lose all the rest. I can't break him—not altogether—you never can tell with that sort, even when they think they've broken themselves. The baby—she's better than anything for keeping the likes of him in order. Long as he's set himself to look after her, he won't be trying anything on, will he? The joke was he came to me of

500

himself at Thettit and said we had to keep her—got her across the Vrako, too. That was a risk—he could have drowned—but it was worth it to have no trouble from him. That sort can make a lot of trouble. Pride—oh yes, he's too good for the likes of you and me. But I'll break him before I'm done, the fine young gentleman—I'll have him flogging boys to earn his supper and never have to raise a finger to force him—you see if I don't."

"Who is he?" asked Lalloc.

"Ah! Who is he?" Genshed paused for effect. "That's the Ban of Sarkid's heir, that is."

Lalloc whistled. "Oh, Gensh, woll, no wonder the place full of Ikats, eh? You done it right, now we know why they don't stop looking, eh? We got a lot to thonk you for, Gensh."

"Two hundred thousand meld," said Genshed. "Isn't that worth a risk? And you said we'd get over the river in the morning, didn't you?"

"Who's the other one, Gensh—the man? Thought you dodn't only go for boys and girls?"

"Don't you know?" replied Genshed. "You ought to, you oily, creeping, bribing bastard."

Lalloc paused in drinking, looking over the top of the wineskin with raised eyebrows and reflective eyes. Then the wine slopped in its hollow caverns as he shook his head and the skin together.

"That's King Crendrik, that is," said Genshed. "Him that used to be the priest-king of Bekla. Him with the bear."

Lalloc nearly dropped the wineskin, caught it just in time and lowered it in slow amazement.

"Found him lying senseless in a swamp thirty miles south of here," said Genshed. "Don't know how he came there, but I recognized him all right. Seen him in Bekla, same as you have. Well, he won't run. He knows the Ikats are out to kill him."

Lalloc stared questioningly.

"It's like this, you see," said Genshed, stabbing at the fire. "I'm sharp. I keep him and the boy—leave the rest, but keep those two at all costs. Well now, we know the Ban of Sarkid's fighting for the Ikats. If ever the Ortelgans was to catch me— I got no license, remember—I can tell them I've got the Ban's son, hand him over to them, very likely they'll be so pleased they'll let me go. But if the Ikats catch us, I can give them Crendrik. Same thing—they'd be glad to get him, might let us go. Crendrik's got no other value, of course, but the boy's got plenty if only we can get away. The way the luck's turned out, we look more like being caught by the Ikats than the Ortelgans, so I'm hanging on to Crendrik."

"But if the Ikats cotch you with the boy, Gensh?"

"They won't," said Genshed. "I'll see to that. They won't catch me with a single child—or find the bodies, either."

He stood up brusquely, broke two or three branches across his knee and fed the fire. Kelderek could hear the back of Shara's head thud against the cobbles as she tossed and cried in her sleep.

"What's the scheme, then?" asked Genshed presently. "How d'you reckon to cross the Telthearna?"

"Well, it's a big rosk, Gensh, but it's only chonce we got. We got to try it, else we're for the Ikats all right. Down below here there's a vullage—Tissarn they call it—fishing vullage—by the ruvver, you know."

"I know—I came inland yesterday to avoid it."

"Woll, vorry soon as day we leave ovvrything—go straight down there, we find some man, I pay him all I got, he govv us canoe, boat, something, before the Ikats come. We go across, gotting to Deelguy. Current's strong, we go down long way, all the same we gotting across. Onnyway we got to try it."

"Won't the village be watched? That's why I dodged it."

"We got to try it, Gensh."

"We'll take the boy."

"I don't like thot. I'm wanted man in Deelguy, you know. I don't want onnybody see oss, maybe they gotting to know who the boy is, find out we're slave dealers, you know? It's not legal in Deelguy."

Genshed said nothing.

"Gensh, I'm hurt drodful bad. You my friend, Gensh, you stick by me? You holp me?"

"Yes, of course I'll help you, don't worry."

"No, but you swear it, Gensh? Swear you're my friend, swear you stick by me, holp me always, yoss? Please swear it, Gensh."

Genshed stepped across and clasped his hand.

"I swear I'll be your friend, Lalloc, and I'll stand by you, so help me God."

"Oh, thonk God, Gensh, thonk God I meeting you. We gotting safe all right. We sleep a time now, eh, but roddy we go fost thing what it's daylight. No time to lose, you know."

He wrapped himself clumsily in his cloak, lay down beside the fire and seemed at once to drop, almost to disappear into sleep, like a stone thrown into a pool.

Kelderek turned to crawl away in the darkness, but the pupils of his eyes, contracted by the light of the fire, admitted not the least image from the night about him. He waited, and as he did so realized that not only did he not know where he could go, but that it mattered nothing. Genshed would not sleep—of this he felt sure. He could either crawl away, weaponless, into the forest, to starve until the soldiers found him, or remain to await the will of Genshed at daylight. Should an ox in the abattoir choose to go to the right or the left? "We'll take the boy." But Genshed would not take him, Kelderek, across the Telthearna—there would be no profit to him in doing so. If he did not kill him, he would leave him on the shore to await the soldiers.

A horrible despair seized him, as a beast its prey, and a panic fear—the fear of one who knows that all he has dreaded is even now at hand and inescapable, that the door is fast and the water rising. Standing up, he stretched out his arms, peering into the blackness as he tried to make out the shapes of the ruins about him. One he could perceive—a dark mass to his right, low but just discernible against what appeared to be a gap in the trees. He stooped, and then knelt, to try to see it more clearly against the sky. As he stared, it moved, and at the same moment there came to his nostrils a smell that brought back instantly the straw, the smoky torches and brick-filled arcades of the King's House in Bekla—the rank, fetid smell of the bear.

For long moments it seemed to Kelderek that he must be already dead. The pool and the trepsis he had accepted as a portent of his death. That Genshed knew who he was—had known him from the first—and meant, if occasion offered, to profit by delivering him up to death—this had struck him full of that sense of helplessness which always accompanies the discovery that what we thought was hidden has, in fact, been known all along to our enemy. Now, in this, his last extremity, unseen, unheard, Shardik had appeared out of the miles of forest— Shardik, whom he himself had seen far to the south three days before. To wonder whether he was come in vengeance or in pity did not occur to Kelderek. Simply the terror of the incredible flooded his broken mind.

Again the dark bulk moved against the sky, and now a low growl showed that it was close—closer than it had seemed— only a few strides away. Kelderek, starting back against the wall of the slave traders' shelter, covered his face with his hands, whimpering with dread.

As he did so, a terrible shriek came from within. Another followed, and another; curses, blows, the thudding of some heavy object knocked over, convulsive struggling and finally a long, choking moan. The cloak fastened across the opening was ripped aside and the firelight gleamed out, showing for a moment two red, glowing eyes in the darkness and a great, black shape that turned and shambled away, disappearing between the ruined walls. Then silence returned, broken only by a dragging, jerking sound that finally ceased, and the labored breathing of one who finished his work by fastening once more the cloak across the doorway. The firelight was shut in and Kelderek, conscious of nothing save that Shardik was gone and he himself alive, crept into the first crevice he found and lay there, not knowing whether he slept or woke.

54 *The Cloven Rock*

BENEATH THE FIRST LIGHT creeping into the sky, the river shone a dull, turbid gray, the surface smooth, its flow imperceptible from that height at which the migrant geese flew on their northward journey. South of Linsho Gap the forest lay motionless, clothing like a shaggy pelt the body of the earth from which it grew. As yet no darting of birds disturbed the stillness. No breeze moved, no reflection of light glittered from the trees. The wings of the great butterflies were folded close.

Here and there the forest pelt was matted brown with clusters of old, dead creeper that had twined and climbed, before dying, through even the topmost tiers; here and there, as though eaten away and mangy, it lay open, showing the dirty skin beneath, callused with rocks, suppurating with bog, scurfy with thorn and scrub, in its illness supporting, like a dying ape full of maggots, an ugly, wriggling life, futile in its involuntary course toward death. In one such open place the gray light revealed a scabby crust, the remains of older, deeper wounds: tumbled stones, broken walls, boulders encircling a pool at the foot of a rock bare as a protruding bone. This crust, too, was crawling with stumbling, filthy creatures—human children—creeping out of the scabs like bugs from wood, moving aimlessly here and there, disgusting in their torpor and misery, inviting cruelty, so plainly were they created helpless in order that they might be the more easily destroyed. Soon the huge creature upon whose body they crawled and fed would feel them as an irritation, scratch itself and crush out their meaningless lives.

The body of Lalloc lay prone outside the doorway from which he had staggered with Genshed's knife in his back. The feet had tripped upon the step and the knees, buckling, had been pressed into the soft earth by the force of the corpulent body's fall. The arms were stretched forward, one along the ground, palm down and fingers digging into the soil, the other sticking up like a swimmer's, but stiffened in death. The head was twisted sideways and the mouth open. Two stabs had almost cut away the left cheek, which hung down below the chin in a ragged flap, exposing the clenched and splintered teeth. The clothes were so much drenched in blood, old and new, that they retained scarcely any other color.

Genshed was kneeling beside the pool, rinsing his arms in the water and cleaning under his nails with the point of his knife. His pack lay open on the ground behind him and from it he had taken two or three ankle chains. These he retained, but various other pieces of gear he threw to one side, evidently meaning to abandon them. Having closed the lightened pack and slung it on his back, he strung his bow, stuck five or six arrows into his belt and then picked up the still-smoldering fire pot, which he replenished by poking in moss and green twigs.

His movements were silent and from time to time he paused uneasily, listening, in the half-light, to the sounds of the awakening forest. When at length he heard a faint noise of footsteps in the undergrowth beyond the pool, he at once moved quickly aside and, with an arrow on the string, was already waiting in concealment when Shouter stepped out from among the trees.

Genshed lowered his bow and walked across to where the boy stood staring at the dead body on the ground. Shouter turned, started and backed away, one hand raised to his mouth.

"Tried to have a walk in the night, Shouter, did you?" said Genshed, almost whispering. "See any soldiers, did you? See any soldiers, Shouter?"

It was plain that Shouter was half-stupefied, either with fear, hunger, lack of sleep, or all three. Though trying to reply, for some moments he uttered nothing intelligible. At length he said, "All right, then; but I come back, didn't I? I want to mucking live, don't I?"

"So that's why you came back?" said Genshed, looking at him with a kind of pausing curiosity.

"Course I come back," cried Shouter. "In the forest—out there—" He stopped, pointing. "That's no living creature," he burst out. "It's come for you—it's been sent for you—" He pitched forward to his knees. "It wasn't me that killed Kevenant. *You* did that." He broke off, looking quickly back over his shoulder. "That thing—that creature—if it is a creature and not a devil—it was bigger than that rock, I tell you. It shook the mucking ground walking. I nearly come against it in the dark. God, I ran!"

"So that's why you came back?" repeated Genshed, after a pause.

Shouter nodded. Then, getting slowly to his feet, he looked around at the body and said indifferently, "You killed *him*, then?"

"No good to us, was he?" said Genshed. "Get caught in *his* company, that'd finish everything, that would. I got his money, though. Come on, get them up, get them moving."

"You're taking *them*?" asked Shouter, surprised. "For God's sake, why don't we just run, wherever it is?"

"Get them up," repeated Genshed. "Get a chain on the lot of them, wrist to wrist, and keep them quiet while you're doing it."

His domination filled the place like floodwater, uprooting or drowning all other wills. Those children who, dizzy with hunger and privation, had spent the night in the ruins and now, unable to conceive of flight or hiding, obeyed Shouter as they had obeyed him for so long, felt pouring from Genshed, as they tottered into the open, a yet more evil power than he had yet displayed. Now, in the collapse of his fortunes, his cruelty released from the restraints formerly imposed by the hope of gain, he walked among them with an eager, bright-eyed excitement from which they shrank horrified. Kelderek, crawling from the crevice where he had lain, felt this same power draw him first to his feet and then, with faltering steps, to the edge of the pool, where Genshed stood awaiting him. Knowing Genshed's will, he stood silent while Shouter chained him, shackling him by the wrist to a lank-haired boy whose eyes went continually to and fro. This boy, in turn, was chained to another, and so on until all had been fastened together. Kelderek wondered neither why Shouter had returned nor how Lalloc had come to his end. Such things, he realized now, had no need of explanation. They and all else in the world—hunger, illness, misery and pain—came to pass by the will of Genshed.

Shouter looked up from fastening the last shackle, nodded and stepped back. Genshed, fingering the point of his knife, stood smiling in the broadening daylight.

"Well," said Shouter at length, "aren't we getting out now?"

"Fetch Radu," answered Genshed, pointing.

About them the sounds of the forest were increasing, cries of birds and humming of insects. One of the children swayed on his feet, clutched at the next and then fell, dragging two others with him. Genshed ignored them and the children remained on the ground.

Radu was standing beside Kelderek. Glancing sideways, Kelderek could see expressed in his whole posture the dread of which he had spoken on the previous day. His shoulders were bowed, his hands clenched at his sides and his lips pressed tightly together.

"Good morning, Radu," said Genshed courteously.

The common hangman, to whom has been delivered some

once-fine gentleman, now pallid with fear, broken and condemned, cannot reasonably be expected to exclude from his
work all personal relish and natural inclination for sport. Into
his hands has fallen a rarity, a helpless but still-sentient speci-
men of those whom he serves, envies, fears, flatters and cheats
when he can. The occasion is an exhilarating one, and to do it
justice calls for both deliberation and mockery, including, of
course, a little sardonic mimicry of the affected manners of the
gentry.

"Please go with Shouter, Radu," said Genshed. "Oblige me by
putting that body out of sight."

"Mucking hell, how much longer—" Shouter cried, met
Genshed's eye and broke off. Kelderek, turning his head by
Genshed's unspoken permission, watched the two boys struggling to lift the gross, blood-soaked corpse and half-carry, half-
drag it back across the threshold over which Lalloc had fallen
before he died. As they returned, Genshed stepped forward and
took Radu gently by the shoulders. "Now, Radu," he said, with
a kind of serene joy, "go and bring Shara here. Be quick, now!"

Radu stared back from between his hands.

"She can't be moved! She's ill! She may be dying!" He paused
a moment, and then cried, "You know that!"

"Quiet, now," said Genshed, "quiet. Go and get her, Radu."

In the clouded stupor of Kelderek's mind there were no
sounds of morning, no stone hovels, no surrounding forest. A
ruined, desolate country lay under deluge. The last light was
failing, the rain falling into the brown, all-obliterating water;
and as he gazed across that hopeless landscape the little island
that was Radu crumbled and vanished under lapping, yellow
foam.

"Go and fetch her, Radu," repeated Genshed, very quietly.

Kelderek heard the sound of Shara's weeping before he
caught sight of Radu bringing her in his arms. She was struggling and the boy could scarcely carry her. His voice, as he tried
to soothe and comfort her, was barely audible above her half-
delirious, frightened crying.

"Radu, Radu, don't, let me alone, Radu, I don't want to go to
Leg-by-Lee!"

"Hush, dear, hush," said Radu, clutching at her clumsily as he tried to hold her still. "We're going home. I promised you, remember?"

"Hurts," wept the child. "Go away, Radu, it hurts."

She stared at Genshed without recognition, her own filth covering her as débris covers the streets of a fallen town. Dirty saliva ran down her chin and she picked weakly at the flaking crust around her nostrils. Suddenly she cried out again, evidently in pain, and passed a thin stream of urine, cloudy and white as milk, over the boy's arms.

"Come along; give her to me, Radu," said Genshed, holding out his hands.

Looking up, Kelderek saw his eyes, bright and voracious as a giant eel's, staring on either side of his open mouth.

"She makes too much noise," whispered Genshed, licking his lips. "Give her to me, Radu."

In the moment that Kelderek tried to step forward, he realized that Radu had refused to obey Genshed. He felt the sharp jerk of the chain at his wrist and heard the cursing of the boy to whom he was fastened. Simultaneously Radu turned and, with Shara's head rolling limply on his shoulder, began to stumble away.

"No, no, Radu," said Genshed in the same quiet tone. "Come back here."

Radu ignored him, moving slowly on, his head bowed over his burden.

With a sudden snarl, Genshed drew his knife and threw it at the boy. It missed, and he rushed upon him, snatched the child out of his arms and struck him to the ground. For a moment he stood motionless, holding Shara before him in his two hands. Then he sank his teeth in her arm and, before she could shriek, flung her into the pool. Shouter, running forward, was pushed aside as Genshed leaped after her into the water.

Shara's body fell upon the surface of the pool with a sharp, slapping sound. She sank but then, lifting her head clear, raised herself and knelt in the shallow water. Kelderek saw her throw up her clenched hands and, like a baby, draw breath to scream. As she did so Genshed, wading across the pool, pulled her backward and trampled her under the surface. Planting one foot on her neck, he stood looking about him and scratching his shoulders as the commotion, first of waves and then of ripples, subsided. Before the water had settled Shara, pressed down among the gravel and colored pebbles on the bottom, had ceased to struggle.

Genshed stepped out of the pool and the body, face-upward, rose to the surface, the hair, darkened by the water, floating about the head. Genshed walked quickly across to where Radu still lay on the ground, jerked him to his feet, picked up the knife and then, snapping his fingers to Shouter, pointed downhill toward the river. Kelderek heard the boy panting as he hurried to the head of the line.

"Come on, come on," muttered Shouter, "before he kills the mucking lot of us. Move, that's all, move."

Of themselves, the children could not have walked a hundred paces, could not have sat upright on a bench or stripped themselves of their verminous rags. Lame, sick, famished, barely conscious of their surroundings, they yet knew well enough that they were in the hands of Genshed. He it was who had the power to make the lame walk, the sick rise up and the hungry to overcome their faintness. They had not chosen him, but he had chosen them. Without him they could do nothing, but now he abode in them and they in him. He had overcome the world, so that life became a simple matter, without distraction, of moving by his will to the end which he had appointed. The will of Genshed, animating to the extent necessary to its purpose, excluded hope and fear of anything but itself, together with all import from other sights and sounds—from recollections of the previous day, from the evident terror of Shouter, the curious absence of Bled and the body of the little girl floating among the trepsis at the edge of the pool. The children were hardly more aware of these things than were the flies already clustering upon the blood of Lalloc soaking the ground. It was not for them to know the times or the seasons which Genshed had put in his own power. It was enough for them to do his will.

Kelderek, shuffling downhill among the trees, could feel no more than the rest. "The child is dead," he thought. "Genshed killed her. Well, such things have become commonplace among us; and by that I can be certain that my own wickedness has completed its work in me. If I had any heart left, would I not cry out at this? But I want nothing, except to avoid more pain."

The body of Bled was lying half-concealed in the undergrowth. It was surrounded by signs of violence—trampled earth and broken branches. The eyes were open, but in death the manic glare had left them, just as the limbs no longer retained their feral, crouching posture. It was these which had increased Bled's apparent size, as a live spider is magnified, in the eyes of those who fear it, by its vigilant tension and the possibility that it will run, suddenly and very fast, on its arched legs. Now Bled looked like a spider dead—small, ugly and harmless; yes, and messy too, for one side of his head had been smashed in and his body was limp and crumpled, as though crushed in the grip of a giant. Along the left side, his jerkin was torn open and the exposed flesh was lacerated by five great, parallel scratches, wide apart and deep.

Had he been even more feverish and weak, Kelderek, of all men, could not have failed to recognize the tracks about the corpse. Faint they were, for the ground was covered with moss and creeper, but had they been fainter still he would have known them. The boy's death, he realized, must have been recent, not more than two hours ago, and in this knowledge he motioned the children to silence and himself stood listening intently.

There was, however, no silencing Shouter as he flung himself to the ground in superstitious terror. Genshed, coming up, with Radu chained to his belt, could hardly drag him to his feet.

"Mucking hell," wept the boy, struggling, "I told you, didn't I? It's the devil, Genshed, come for the lot of us! I saw it, I tell you, I saw it in the dark—"

Genshed slapped him across the face and he fell against Radu, who stood still as a post, staring sightlessly before him as Shouter blubbered and clutched at his hands. Kelderek, who felt it more than likely that Shardik was within hearing, watched Genshed to see whether he would pay any attention to the tracks or recognize them for what they were. He expected that he would not, and Genshed's first words proved him right.

"Looks like some animal got him," said Genshed. "Serves him right, eh, hiding and then trying to bugger off before daylight? Here, pull yourself together, Shouter; I'm giving you a chance.

I'm being good to you, Shouter. There's no devil, you're just a silly little bastard, it's Ikats you've got to look out for. We got to be quick now, see? You get out there to the left, far as you can go, that's where they'll be coming from. If you spot any coming, get back to that rock down there on the bank—the one with the crack in it, see?—I'll be there. If you feel like giving yourself up to the Ikats, don't try it. They'll hang you off a tree before you can squeal. Understand?"

Shouter nodded and at another push from Genshed slipped away to the left, taking a line parallel to the bank of the Telthearna, which was now in sight below them, the inshore water green with reflections of the overhanging trees.

Downhill, each throb of the pulse a stab of pain behind the eyeballs, hand pressed over one eye, links of chain cutting into the wrist, vision blurred, so hard the effort to focus sight. Stumbling downhill; a sound of weeping, like a girl's; that must be an illusion. Don't weep, Melathys; dear love, don't weep for my death. Where will you go now, what will become of you? And did the soldiers ever reach Zeray? A message—but he'll never leave me to the soldiers, he'll kill me himself. Lord Shardik —after all, I shall die before Lord Shardik—I shall never know the great purpose for which God required his death. I betrayed him—I meant to kill him. Melathys on Quiso, Melathys playing with the Baron's sword. We couldn't expect mercy, a common man and a girl thrust into things too high for them. If only I'd listened to the Tuginda on the road to Gelt. Säiyett, forgive me now; I shall be dead within the hour. If the little girl could die, then so can I. This cruel man, it was I that made his work possible, it was I that brought Lalloc and his like to Bekla.

Downhill, don't slip, don't drag on the chain. The sun must have risen, dazzling down there on the inshore water, glinting under the trees. How the pain runs up my hand from the wounded finger. I misled hundreds to misery and death; and the Tuginda could have saved them all. I was afraid of Ta-Kominion; but it's too late now. It's Radu, it's Radu weeping, Genshed's broken him in the end. He'll live to murder other children, he'll be across the river when the soldiers find the little girl in the pool. Did you see it, God? Do you see what children suffer? They used to call me Kelderek Play-with-the-Children.

Why did You manifest Lord Shardik to a man like me, who only betrayed him and defeated Your purpose?

The undergrowth grew thicker near the river. As Kelderek stopped, hesitating, Genshed overtook him, his bow held in one hand while with the other he gripped Radu by the shoulder. He had gagged the boy with a piece of rope. Radu's head had fallen forward on his chest and his arms were hanging at his sides. Genshed began moving through the undergrowth toward the river bank, gesturing to Kelderek and the children to follow him in silence.

Kelderek stepped out upon the bank. The sun glittered in his eyes across the water. He found himself immediately above a little bay, a half-circular inlet surrounded by a steep bank perhaps twice as high as a man. All round the verge, to a breadth of two or three paces, the undergrowth had been cut back to make a path which, on either side of the bay, led down to the water's edge. A few yards to their right, squarely across this path and half-blocking it, stood the tall, cloven rock which Genshed had observed from the forest above. On their left, moored to the bank at the upstream corner of the inlet, lay a canoe, with nets, spears and other tackle strewn aboard. There was not a soul to be seen, but some distance beyond the canoe could be glimpsed, through the trees, a cluster of huts, from some of which smoke was already rising.

"Mucking hell!" whispered Genshed, casting a quick glance around among the trees. "Easy as that!"

From the forest there sounded suddenly a loud, fluting call, almost human in its consonantal clarity. A moment afterward a swift flash of purple and gold darted through the trees. It was a bird, so vivid in the sunlight that even the famished, feverish children stared in wonder.

"Kynat!" called the bird, "Kynat chrrrr-ak! Kynat, Kynat will tell!"

Glowing like an alchemist's fire, the saffron undersides of its wings alternately revealed and hidden as it flew, it circled the little bay, hovered a moment, spreading the flanged gold of its tail, and then alighted on the stern of the moored canoe.

"Kynat will tell!" it called, looking, alert and bright-eyed, toward the emaciated wretches on the bank as though it had indeed come with intent to carry its message to them and to none else.

Kelderek, hearing the call, looked about for the bird, but could make out nothing but swirling grays and greens, stabbed through with the golden shafts of the sunlight. Then, as it called again, he saw the courtyard in Zeray, and Melathys leaning out between the shutters. Even as he watched, she faded, and he seemed to see himself shuffling away through the dark woods, while his tears, falling as though from cliff to cliff, disappeared at last into an extreme darkness older than the world.

"Kynat will tell!" called the bird, and Kelderek, coming to himself, saw it perched close above the water and Genshed standing with bow bent and arrow drawn to the head. Sudden and clumsy as a charred log falling in the fire, he lunged forward: the chain tautened and he fell against Genshed in the act of loosing. The deflected arrow slammed into the stern of the canoe, causing it to rock and turn at its mooring, so that ripples followed one another across the pool. The bird, opening its amazing wings, rose into the air and flew away down the river.

"Four hundred meld they fetch!" cried Genshed. Then, rubbing his left wrist where the loosed bowstring had whipped it, he said very quietly, "Oh, Mister Crendrik, I must keep a little time for you, mustn't I? I must do that."

There was now about him a confident elation more terrible even than his cruelty—the elation of the thief who realizes that there is none in the house but a helpless woman, whom he can therefore rape as well as rob; of the murderer watching as his over-trusting companion is led away to face the charge which, thanks to his supposed friend's cunning, he cannot now disprove. He had indeed the devil's own luck but, as he well knew, luck comes to the sharp man—to the man of ability and style. The craft lay ready to his hand, the morning was windless, the water smooth. Lalloc's money was secure in his belt and chained to his wrist was a hostage worth more than the proceeds of ten slaving expeditions. At his feet, helpless but happily not senseless, lay the man who had once refused him a Beklan trading license.

With the speed and dexterity of long use, Genshed loosed both Kelderek and Radu and, extending their chains with another which he passed through their pierced ears, secured them to a tree. Kelderek crouched, staring at the water and giving no sign that he knew what was being done. Then the slave dealer, snapping his fingers for the last time, led the children along the path to his left and down to the upstream extremity of the inlet.

The canoe lay against the bank, moored to a heavy stone with a hole through it—the kind often used by fishermen as an anchor. Genshed, stooping down, put aboard first his pack and after that two paddles lying close by on the shore. Finally, he passed a chain through the anchor stone and back to the wrist of the nearest child. His preparations now complete, he left the children and returned quickly up the slope.

At the moment when he reached Radu and Kelderek, Shouter came bursting out of the undergrowth. Looking wildly around, he ran up the path to where Genshed was standing, knife in hand.

"The Ikats, Genshed, the Ikats! Spread out in a line they are, coming through the woods! Must have started looking for us soon as it got light!"

"How soon will they be here?" asked Genshed coolly.

"Taking their time, searching the whole mucking place, beating the bushes; but they'll be here soon enough, don't worry!"

Genshed made no reply but, turning back to Kelderek and Radu, released them, at the same time unslinging the fire pot, which he still carried in one hand, and blowing its smoldering sticks and moss to a glow. Into this he thrust the point of his knife.

"Now, Radu," he said, "listen to me. First you're going to put this knife into Mister Crendrik's eyes—both of them. If you don't, I'll do the same for you, understand? After that, you'll go down there with me, unfasten the mooring rope and then pitch that stone into the water. That'll take care of the stock we've got to leave behind. After that you and me, and perhaps Shouter, if I don't change my mind, can make a start. Time's short, so hurry up."

Gripping Kelderek's shoulder, he forced him to his knees at Radu's feet. Radu, still gagged with the rope, dropped the knife which Genshed thrust into his hand. It stuck in the ground, sending up a wisp of smoke from some transfixed and smoldering fragment. Genshed, having retrieved and again heated it, once more gave it to Radu, at the same time twisting his left arm behind his back, pulling out his gag and tossing it down into the water below.

"For God's sake!" cried Shouter desperately, "I tell you there's no time for this kind of sport, Genshed! Can't you wait for a bit of fun till we get back to Terekenalt? The Ikats, the mucking Ikats are coming! Kill the bastard if you're going to, only let's get on!"

"Kill the mucking lot!" whispered Genshed ecstatically. "Come on, Radu, do it. Do it, Radu. I'll guide your hand if you want, but you're going to do it."

As though entranced and bereft of will, Radu had already raised the knife, when suddenly, with a convulsive movement, he twisted himself out of Genshed's grasp.

"No!" he cried. "Kelderek!"

As though wakened by the cry, Kelderek rose slowly to his feet. His mouth hung open and one hand, the split fingernail covered with a bulbous, dirty scab, was held before him in a feeble posture of defense. After a moment, looking at Genshed but speaking uncertainly and as though to someone else, he said, "It must be as God wills, my lord. The matter is greater even than your knife."

Snatching the knife from Radu, Genshed struck at him, and the blow opened a long gash in his forearm. He uttered no sound, but remained standing where he was.

"Oh, Crendrik," said Genshed, gripping his wrist and raising the knife again, "Crendrik of Bekla—"

"My name is not Crendrik, but Kelderek Play-with-the-Children. Let the boy alone."

Genshed struck him a second time. The point of the knife penetrated between the small bones of the elbow and dragged him once more to his knees, beating ineffectually at Genshed as he fell. At the same moment Shouter, with a cry, pointed back along the verge.

Halfway between the children chained to the stone and the higher point where Genshed stood above the center of the inlet, the undergrowth parted and a great branch fell forward across the path, overbalanced and slid slowly into the water. A moment

516

afterward the gap, open still wider, disclosed the body of some enormous, shaggy creature. Then Shardik was standing on the bank, peering up at the four human beings above him.

Ah, Lord Shardik: supreme, divine, sent by God out of fire and water: Lord Shardik of the Ledges! Thou who didst wake among the trepsis in the woods of Ortelga, to fall prey to the greed and evil in the heart of Man! Shardik the victor, the prisoner of Bekla, lord of the bloody wounds: thou who didst cross the plain, who didst come alive from the Streel, Lord Shardik of forest and mountain, Shardik of the Telthearna! Hast thou, too, suffered unto death, like a child helpless in the hands of cruel men, and will death not come? Lord Shardik, save us! By thy fiery and putrescent wounds, by thy swimming of the deep river, by thy drugged trance and savage victory, by thy long imprisonment and weary journey in vain, by thy misery, pain and loss and the bitterness of thy sacred death; save thy children, who fear and know thee not! By fern and rock and river, by the beauty of the kynat and the wisdom of the Ledges, O hear us, defiled and lost, we who wasted thy life and call upon thee! Let us die, Lord Shardik, let us die with thee, only save thy children from this wicked man!

That the bear was close to death was plain enough. Its huge frame, deformed and lank with privation, was nothing but staring bones and mangy fur. One claw hung split and broken, and this evidently formed part of some larger wound in the foot, for the paw was held awkwardly and lifted from the ground. The dry muzzle and lips were cracked and the face misshapen, suggesting a kind of melting or disintegration of the features. The gigantic frame, from which the life was so clearly ebbing, was like a ruined aviary from which the bright birds have flown, those few that remain serving only to heighten the sense of loss and grief in the hearts of those that see them.

The bear appeared to have been startled by some alarm in the forest behind it; for after turning its head this way and that, it limped along the verge of the pool, as though to continue what had evidently been a flight from intruders. As it approached the children they cowered away, wailing in terror, and at this it stopped, turned back, passed the spot where it had emerged and took a few hesitant, prowling steps up the slope. Shouter, frenzied with fear, began tearing at the thick creepers and thorns beside him, failed to force his way in and fell to the ground.

"Bloody thing!" said Genshed between his teeth. "It's half-dead already, that is. Go on!" he shouted, waving his arms as though driving cattle. "Go on! Get out of it!" He took a step forward, but at this the bear snarled and rose falteringly on its hind legs. Genshed fell back.

"Why don't we run?" moaned Shouter. "Get us out of here, Genshed, for God's sake!"

"What, for that thing?" said Genshed. "And leave the boat and any chance we've got? We'd run straight into the Ikats. We're not going to be buggered up by that bloody thing, not at this time of day. I tell you, it's half-dead now. We just got to kill it, that's all."

His bow still lay where he had put it down after shooting at the kynat and, picking it up, he drew an arrow from his belt. Kelderek, still on his knees, his arm streaming blood, caught him by the ankle.

"Don't!" he gasped. "It'll charge—it'll tear us all to pieces, believe me!"

Genshed struck him in the face and he fell on his side. At this moment there was a distant sound of voices in the forest—a man called an order and another answered.

"Don't be afraid," said Genshed. "Don't worry, my lad, I'll have three arrows in him before he can even think of charging. I know a trick or two, I'll tell you. He won't try to charge me."

Without taking his eyes from the bear, he groped backward and ripped a long strip from Radu's rags. This he quickly knotted around the shaft of the heavy arrow a little above the head, leaving the two ends hanging like those of a garland or a ribbon in a girl's hair.

At the sound of the voices the bear had dropped on all fours. For a few moments it ramped from side to side, but then, as though from weakness, ceased and once more stood still, facing the slave trader on the path.

"Shouter," said Genshed, "blow up that fire pot."

Shouter, realizing what he intended, blew the pot into a glow and held it up with trembling hands.

"Keep it still," whispered Genshed.

The arrow was already fitted to the string and he lowered the bow so that one end of the rag fell across and into the open fire pot. It took instantly; and as the flame burned up, Genshed bent the bow and loosed. The flame streamed backward and the whole shaft appeared to be burning as it flew.

The arrow pierced the bear deeply beneath the left eye, pinning the burning rag to its face. With an unnatural, wailing cry, it started back, clawing at its mask of fire. The dry, staring coat caught and burned—first the ears, then one flailing paw, then the chest, upon which fragments of the burning rag were clawed down. It beat at the flames, yelping like a dog. As it staggered back, Genshed shot it again, the second arrow entering the right shoulder close to the neck.

As though in a trance, Kelderek again rose to his feet. Once more, as it seemed to him, he was standing on the battlefield of the Foothills, surrounded by the shouting of soldiers, the trampling of the fugitives, the smell of the trodden ground. Indeed, he could now plainly see before him the Beklan soldiers, and in his ears sounded the roaring of Shardik as he burst out from among the trees. Shardik was a blazing torch which would consume them all, a charging fire from which there was no escape. The wrath of Shardik filled the earth and sky, the revenge of Shardik would burn the enemy up and trample him down. He saw Genshed turn, run back down the path and force his body into the cleft of the rock. He saw Shouter hurled to one side and Radu flung on top of him. Leaping forward, he shouted,

"Shardik! Shardik the Power of God!"

Shardik, the arrow jutting from his face, came to the rock into which Genshed had squeezed for refuge. Standing erect, he thrust one blackened paw into the cleft. Genshed stabbed it and the bear, roaring, drew it back. Then he struck and split the rock itself.

The top of the rock cracked across like a nutshell and then, as Shardik struck it again, broke into three great fragments, which toppled and fell into the deep water below. Once more he struck —a dying blow, his claws raking his enemy's head and shoulders. Then he faltered, clutching, shuddering, at the rock, and slowly collapsed across its splintered, broken base.

Watching, Kelderek and Radu saw a figure crawl out from the base of the cleft. Radu screamed, and for a moment the figure turned toward him, as though it could hear. Perhaps it could: yet it had no eyes, no face—only a great wound, a pulp of bloody flesh, stuck here and there with teeth and splinters of bone, in which no human features could be discerned. Thin, wailing cries came from it, like a cat's, yet no words, for it had no mouth, no lips. It stumbled into a tree and shrieked aloud, recoiling with fragments of bark and twigs embedded in its soft, red mask. Blindly, it raised both hands before it, as though to ward off the blows of some cruel tormentor; yet there was no one near it. Then it took three blundering steps, tripped, and without a sound pitched over the verge. The splash of the fall came up from below. Radu crawled forward and looked over the edge, but nothing rose to the surface. The scabbard of his knife floating in blood on the water, and the flytrap lying smashed beside the broken rock—these were all that remained of the wicked, cruel slave trader, who had boasted that he could drive a child mad with fear worse than blows.

Kelderek dragged himself to the rock and knelt beside it, weeping and beating upon the stone. One enormous forepaw, thick as a roof beam, hung down beside his face. He took it between his hands, crying, "O Shardik! Shardik, my lord, forgive me! I would have entered the Streel for you! Would to God I had died for you! O Lord Shardik, do not die, do not die!"

Looking up, he saw the teeth like stakes, the snarling mouth fixed open and unmoving, flies walking already on the protruding tongue, the blackened pelt burned to the skin, the arrow protruding from the face. The pointed muzzle jutted in a wedge against the sky. Kelderek beat his hands on the rock, sobbing with loss and despair.

He was roused by a hand that gripped his shoulder, shaking him roughly. Slowly lifting his head, he recognized the man standing beside him as an officer of the Yeldashay army, the corn sheaves of Sarkid blazoned upon one shoulder. Behind him stood his young, hard-bitten tryzatt, sword at the ready in case of trouble, in his wary eye a look of bewilderment and disdain as he stared uncomprehendingly at the huge carcass slumped over the rock and the three filthy vagabonds groveling round its base.

"Who are you?" said the officer. "Come on, answer me, man! What are you doing here and why are those children chained to that stone? What were you going to do?"

Following his gaze, Kelderek saw soldiers standing beside the children on the bank, while a little farther off, among the trees, a group of villagers stood staring and muttering.

The officer smelled like a clean butcher's shop—the smell of the meat-eater to him who eats none. The soldiers stood up as effortlessly as trees in spring. Their straps were oiled, their harness glittered, their eyes traveled quickly here and there, their controlled voices linked them like gods in smooth communication. Kelderek faced the officer.

"My name is Kelderek Play-with-the-Children," he said haltingly, "and my life—my life is forfeit to the Yeldashay. I am willing to die, and ask only to be allowed to send a last message to Zeray."

"What do you mean?" said the officer. "Why do you say your life is forfeit? Are you the slave trader who has committed these unspeakable crimes? Children we have found in the forest—sick —famished—dying, for all I know. Is this your doing?

"No," said Kelderek. "No, I'm not your slave trader. He's dead—by the Power of God."

"What are you, then?"

"I? I'm—I'm the governor-man from Bekla."

"Crendrik, king of Bekla? The priest of the bear?"

Kelderek nodded and laid one hand on the massive, shaggy pelt that rose like a wall above him.

"The same. But the bear—the bear will trouble you no more. Indeed, it was never he that troubled you, but misguided, sinful men, and I the worst of them. Tell your soldiers not to mock him dead. He was the Power of God, that came to men and was abused by men; and to God he has now returned."

The officer, contemptuous and bewildered, felt it best to avoid further talk with this bleeding, stinking scarecrow, with his talk of God and his expressed readiness to die. He turned to his tryzatt, but as he did so another figure plucked at his arm—a boy, his hair matted, his body emaciated, his blackened nails broken and a chain about his ankles. The boy looked at him with authority and said in native Yeldashay, "You are not to hurt that man, captain. Wherever my father may be, please send someone at once to tell him you have found us. We—"

He broke off and would have fallen had not the officer, his perplexity now complete, caught him with one arm about his shoulders.

"Steady, my boy, steady. What's all this, now? Who is your father—and who are you, if it comes to that?"

"I—am Radu, son of Elleroth, Ban of Sarkid."

The officer started and as he did so the boy slid from his grasp and fell to the ground, pressing his hands against the broken rock and sobbing, "Shara! Shara!"

BOOK VII

The Power of God

55 *Tissarn*

A DRY MOUTH. Glitter of water reflected from beneath a roof of reeds and poles. An evening light, red and slow. Some kind of woven covering rough against the body. A small, urgent, scratching sound—a mouse close by, a man farther off? Pain, many pains, not sharp, but deep and persistent, the body infused in pain, finger, ear, arm, head, stomach, the breath coming short with pain. Weary, a weariness to be conscious and to feel the pain. Drained away; void with hunger; mouth dry with thirst. And yet a sense of relief, of being in the hands of people who intended no harm. Where he was he did not know, except that he was no longer with Genshed. Genshed was dead. Shardik had destroyed him and Shardik was dead.

Those about him, those—whoever they were—who had been to the trouble of putting him into this bed, would no doubt be content to leave him there for the time being. He could think no further, could not think of the future. Wherever he was, he must be in the hands of the Yeldashay. Radu had spoken to the officer. Perhaps they would not kill him, not only because—and this was very vague, a kind of child's intuition of what was and was not possible—not only because Radu had spoken to the officer, but also because of his destitution and his sufferings. He felt himself invested with his sufferings as though with a kind of immunity. What they would do with him he could not tell, but he was almost sure that they would not put him to death. His mind drifted away—he lacked all strength to pursue thought further —a clamor of ducks on the river—he must be very near the waterside—a smell of wood smoke—the throbbing pain in the finger nail was the worst—his forearm had been bound up, but too tightly. All that was left of him was passive, fragments swept together and cast into a corner, Shardik dead, sounds, smells, vague memories, the coverlet rough at his neck, head rolling from side to side with pain, Shardik dead, the reflected evening light fading among the poles of the roof above.

Eyes closed, he moaned, licking his dry lips, tormented by his pain as though by flies. When he opened his eyes again—not from any deliberate wish to see, but for the momentary relief that the change would bring before the pain overtook it and once more crawled over his body—he saw an old woman standing beside the bed, holding a clay bowl in her two hands. Feebly he pointed to it and then to his mouth. She nodded, smiling, put one hand under his head and held the bowl to his lips. It was water. He drank it and gasped, "More," at which she nodded, went away and came back with the bowl full. The water was fresh and cold: she must have brought it straight from the river.

"Do you feel very bad, poor boy?" she asked. "You must rest."

He nodded and whispered, "But I'm hungry." Then he realized that she had spoken in a dialect like Ortelgan and that he had unthinkingly replied to her in that tongue. He smiled and said, "I'm from Ortelga." She answered, "River people, like us," and pointed, as he supposed, upstream. He tried to speak again but she shook her head, laying a soft, wrinkled hand on his forehead for a few moments before going away. He fell half-asleep —Genshed—Shardik dead—how long ago?—and after a time she came back with a bowl of broth made of fish and some vegetable he did not know. He ate feebly, as best he could, and she skewered the bits of fish on a pointed stick and fed him, holding his hand and clicking her tongue over his wounded finger. Again he asked for more, but she said, "Later—later—not too much at first—sleep again now."

"Will you stay here?" he asked, like a child, and she nodded. Then he pointed to the door and said, "Soldiers?"

She nodded once more and it was then that he remembered the children. But when he tried to ask her about them, she only repeated, "Sleep now," and indeed, with his thirst quenched and the hot food in his belly he found it easy to obey her, sliding away into the depths as a glimpsed trout slips from the fisherman's sight.

Once he woke in the dark and saw her sitting by a little, smoky lamp, its flame shining green through a lattice of thin rushes. Again she helped him to drink and then to relieve himself, brushing aside his hesitation and shame. "Why don't *you* sleep now?" he whispered. She answered, smiling, "Ay—happen you won't have the baby just yet," from which he guessed that she must be the village midwife. Her jest put him in mind once more of the children. "The children?" he begged her. "The slave children?" But she only pressed her old, soft hand once more upon his forehead. "You know, they used to call me Kelderek Play-with-the-Children," he said. Then his head swam —had she drugged him?—and he fell asleep again.

When he woke he could tell that it was afternoon. The sun was still out of sight, somewhere beyond his feet, but higher and farther to his left than when he had first woken the day before. His head was clearer and he felt lighter, cleaner and somewhat less in pain. He was about to call to the old woman when he realized that in fact someone was already sitting beside the bed. He turned his head. It was Melathys.

He stared at her incredulously and she smiled back at him with the look of one who has brought a costly and unexpected present to a lover or a dear friend. She laid a finger on her lips but a moment after, perceiving that this would be insufficient to restrain him, she slipped forward on her knees beside the bed and laid her hand upon his.

"I'm real," she whispered, "but you're not to excite yourself. You're ill—wounds and exhaustion. Can you remember how bad you've been?"

He made no reply, only holding her hand to his lips. After a little she said, "Do you remember how you came here?"

He tried to shake his head but desisted, closing his eyes in pain. Then he asked her, "Where am I?"

"It's called Tissarn—a fishing village, quite small—smaller than Lak."

"Near—near where—?"

She nodded. "You walked here—the soldiers brought you. You can't remember?"

"Nothing."

"You've slept over thirty hours altogether. Do you want to sleep again?"

"No, not yet."

"Is there anything you need?"

He smiled faintly. "You'd better send the old woman."

She rose. "If you like." But then, smiling back at him over her shoulder, she said, "When I arrived you were filthy—as if anyone in Tissarn would notice a thing like that. I stripped you and washed you from head to foot. All the same, I will send her if you prefer."

"I never woke?"

"She told me she'd drugged you. I bound your arm again, too. They'd done it much too tight."

Later, as the evening fell and the ducks began their splashing and scuttering in the roof reflections—the hut, he now realized, must almost overhang the water—she came again to feed him and then to sit beside the bed. She was dressed like a Yeldashay girl, in a long blue *metlan*, gathered below the bosom and falling to her ankles. The shoulder was fastened with a fine emblematic brooch—the sheaves of Sarkid, worked in silver. Following his gaze she laughed, unpinned it and laid it on the bed.

"No, I haven't changed my love. It's only another part of the story. How do you feel now?"

"Weak, but less in pain. Tell me the story. You know that Lord Shardik is dead?"

She nodded. "They took me to see his body on the rock. What can I say? I wept for him. We mustn't speak of that now—it's everything for you to rest and not distress yourself."

"The Yeldashay don't intend my death, then?"

She shook her head. "You can be sure of that."

"And the Tuginda?"

"Lie quiet and I'll tell you everything. The Yeldashay entered Zeray the morning after you left. If they'd found you there they'd undoubtedly have killed you. They searched the town for you. It was the mercy of God that you went when you did."

"And I—I cursed Him for that mercy. Did Farrass bring them, then?"

"No, Farrass and Thrild—they got what they deserved. They met the Yeldashay halfway to Kabin and were brought back under suspicion of being slave traders on the run. I had to go and speak for them before the Yeldashay would release them."

"I see. And yourself?"

"The Baron's house was commandeered by an officer from Elleroth's staff—a man called Tan-Rion."

"I had to do with him in Kabin."

"Yes, so he told me, but that came later. He was cold and unfriendly at first, until he learned that our sick lady was none other than the Tuginda of Quiso. After that he put everything he had at our disposal—goats and milk, fowls and eggs. The Yeldashay seem to do themselves very well in the field, but of course they'd only come from Kabin, which they seem to have milked dry, as far as I can make out.

"The first thing Tan-Rion told me was that an armistice had been agreed with Bekla and that Santil-kè-Erketlis was negotiating with Zelda and Ged-la-Dan at some place not far from Thettit. He's still there, as far as I know."

"Then—then why send Yeldashay troops over the Vrako? Why?" He was still afraid.

"Stop exciting yourself, my darling. Be quiet and I'll explain. There are only two hundred Yeldashay all told this side of the Vrako, and Tan-Rion told me that Erketlis knew nothing about it until after they'd left Kabin. It wasn't he who gave the order, you see."

She paused, but Kelderek, obedient, said not a word.

"Elleroth gave the order on his own initiative. He told Erketlis he'd done it for two reasons: first, to round up fugitive slave traders, particularly Lalloc and Genshed—the worst of the lot, he said, and he was determined to get them—and secondly to ensure that someone should meet the Deelguy if they succeeded in crossing the river. He knew they'd started work on the ferry."

Again she paused and again Kelderek remained silent.

"Elstrit *did* reach Ikat, you see. I might have known he would. He gave Erketlis the Baron's message, and it seems that the idea of the ferry appealed so much to the commander of the Deelguy with Erketlis that he immediately sent to the king of Deelguy suggesting that pioneers should be sent down the east bank to begin work opposite Zeray and try to get the ferry started. I suppose he had the notion that any reinforcements sent from Deelguy to join the army after it had marched north might be able to avoid crossing the Gelt mountains. Anyway, those were the men you and I saw that afternoon, when we were on the roof. They're still there, but when I left no one had crossed the strait. Actually, I don't yet see how they're going to.

"But Elleroth had a third and more important reason, as Tan-Rion told me—more important to himself, anyway. He was going to find his poor son; or if he couldn't, it wasn't going to be for want of trying. There were eight officers altogether with the Sarkid company that entered Zeray, and every one of them had sworn to Elleroth, before they left Kabin, that they'd find his son if they had to search every foot of grounds in the province. As soon as they'd been in Zeray twenty-four hours and found out all there was to learn—that is, that Genshed wasn't there and that no one had seen him or heard of him—they set out upstream. They'd already sent a detachment north on the way in, to close the Linsho Gap. That must have been closed two days after you left Zeray."

"It was only just in time, then," said Kelderek.

"I went north with the Yeldashay, and I went on the Tuginda's express order. She regained consciousness toward evening of the day you set out. She was very weak, and of course at that time we were still afraid that the house would be attacked by those ruffians who'd injured her. But as soon as the Yeldashay came and the fear of being murdered was off our minds, she began making her plans again. She's very strong, you know."

"I do know—who better?"

"The night before the soldiers left Zeray she told me what I had to do. She said that with Ankray and two officers staying behind she felt perfectly safe, and I was to go north. I reminded her that there was no other woman in the house.

" 'Then perhaps you or Tan-Rion will get me a decent girl from Lak,' she said, 'but north you must certainly go, my dear. The Yeldashay are not looking for Lord Shardik, they're looking for Elleroth's boy. Yet you and I know that both Shardik and Kelderek are wandering somewhere between here and Linsho. What holy and sacred death Lord Shardik is doomed to die none can tell, but come it must. As for Kelderek, he is in great danger; and I know what is between you and him as surely as though you had told me. The Yeldashay believe both him and Shardik to be their enemies. You are needed both as friend and as priestess, and if you ask me what you are to do, I reply that God will show you.'

" 'Priestess?' I said. 'You're calling me a priestess?'

" 'You *are* a priestess,' she answered. '*I* say you are a priestess and you have my authority to act as such. It is as my priestess that you are to go north with the soldiers and do what you find to do.' "

Melathys paused for some moments to regain command of herself. At length she went on,

"So I—so I set out, as a priestess of Quiso. We went to Lak and there I learned first of Shardik and next that you had been there and gone. Nothing more was known of you. The day after, the Yeldashay began moving north toward Linsho, searching the forest as they went. Tan-Rion had promised the Tuginda to look after me and it was he who gave me this Yeldashay *metlan*. He had the cloth with him—he bought it in Kabin, I believe—I wonder who for?—and a woman in Lak made it up to his orders. 'You'll be perfectly all right with the men as long as you look like a Yeldashay girl,' he said. 'They know who you are, but it'll give them the idea that they ought to respect you and look after you.' He gave me this emblem too."

She paused, smiling, and picked it up. "Popular girl. Would you like me to throw it in the river?"

He shook his head. "There's no need. Besides, it might excite me, mightn't it? Go on."

She put it back on the blanket.

"The second day after we'd left Lak, in the morning, we found the body of a child—a boy of about ten—cast up on the shore. He was dreadfully thin. He'd been stabbed to death. He had a pierced ear and chain marks on his ankles. The soldiers were wild with rage. That was when I began to wonder whether you might have been murdered by the slave traders. I was frantic with worry and God help me, I thought more of that than of Lord Shardik.

"About the middle of that afternoon I was walking up the shore with Tan-Rion and his tryzatt when two canoes came downstream, manned by a Yeldashay officer, two soldiers and two villagers from Tissarn. That was how we learned that Radu had been found and Genshed and Lalloc were dead. The officer told us how Lord Shardik had given his life to save Radu and the children, and of how he split the rock. It was like a miracle, he said, like an old tale beyond belief.

531

"The Yeldashay, of course, could think of nothing but Radu, but I questioned the officer until I found out that you had been with Genshed and that Shardik had saved you too. 'Wounded, feverish and half out of his mind,' the officer said, but they didn't think you would die.

"One of the canoes went on to Zeray, but I made Tan-Rion give me a place in the other that was going back. We traveled upstream all night, inshore against the current, and reached Tissarn soon after dawn. I went first to Lord Shardik, as I was in honor and duty bound. No one had touched him; and just as the Tuginda had said, I knew then what I had to do. Tan-Rion has already set about the preparations. He made no difficulty when I asked him. The Yeldashay feel very differently now about Lord Shardik, you see.

"But I've talked too long, my darling. I mustn't tire you any more tonight."

"One question," said Kelderek. "One only. What of Radu and the children?"

"They're still here. I've met Radu. He spoke of you as his friend and comrade. He's weak and very much distressed." She paused. "There was a little girl?"

Kelderek drew in his breath sharply and nodded.

"Elleroth has been sent for," she said. "The other children— I've not seen them. Some are recovering, but I'm told that several are in a very bad way, poor little things. At least they're all in good hands. Now you must sleep again."

"And you too, my dearest Travel-All-Night. We must both sleep."

"Good night, Kelderek Play-with-the-Children. Look, the daylight's quite gone. I'll ask old Dirion, bless her, to bring her lamp and sit with you until she's sure you're asleep."

56 *The Passing of Shardik*

ALTHOUGH IT WAS NOW QUITE DARK he could hear, some distance away, the sounds of men working—concerted, rhythmic shouts, as though heavy objects were being lugged into place; hammering, splintering and the knock of axes. A faint glow of torchlight was discernible from somewhere near the river. Once, when a deep splash was followed by a particularly loud shouting, Dirion, sitting by her lamp, clicked her tongue reprovingly. She said nothing in explanation, however, and after a little he ceased to wonder what urgent demand of war could have come upon the soldiers in this remote place where, so far as he knew, no enemy threatened. He fell asleep, waking to see moonlit ripples reflected in the roof and Melathys sitting by the lamp. Somewhere outside, a Yeldashay sentry called, "All's well," in the expressionless, stylized tone of one who observes routine.

"You should sleep," he whispered. She started, came over to the bed, bent and kissed him lightly and then nodded, smiling, toward the neighboring room, as though to say she would sleep there, and at that moment Dirion returned. Yet much later in the night, when he woke, crying and struggling, from a dream of Genshed, it was still Melathys who was with him. He had somehow struck his wounded fingernail. The pain was sickening and she comforted him as infants or animals are comforted, repeating the same phrases in a quiet, assured voice, "There, there; the pain will go soon, it will go soon; wait now, wait now," until he felt that it was indeed she who was making the pain subside. As the darkness began to melt into first light he lay awake, acquiescent, listening to the river and the growing sounds of morning—the birds, the clang of a pot and the snapping of sticks which someone was breaking across his knee.

He realized that for the first time since leaving Ortelga he was taking pleasure in these sounds and that they were filling him, as once long ago, with expectancy of the coming day. To eat a meal, to complete a day's work, to come home tired to a fire, to greet a girl, talk and listen—a man free to do these things, he thought, should wear his blessings like a garland.

Yet when he had eaten and Melathys had changed his dressings he fell asleep again, waking only a little before noon, when a random sunbeam touched his eyes. He felt stronger, in pain certainly, but no longer its helpless victim. After a time he put his foot to the floor, stood up dizzily, holding on to the bed, and looked about him.

His room and another comprised the upper story of a fairly large hut: plank floor and walls, with an Ortelgan-style roof of reed thatch over *zetlapa* poles. The eastern side, behind the head of his bed, was a gallery, half-walled and open to the river almost immediately below.

He hobbled to the gallery wall and leaned upon it, looking out across the Telthearna to the distant Deelguy shore. Far off, men were fishing, their net stretched between canoes. The midstream current glittered and close by, a little to his left, a few gaunt oxen stood drinking in the shallows. It was so quiet that after a time his ear caught the sound of breathing. He turned and, looking into the next room, saw Melathys lying asleep on a low, rough bed like his own. She was no less beautiful in sleep, lips closed, forehead smooth, her long eyelids curved, he thought, like waves lapping on her cheeks in dark ripples of lashes. This was the girl who for his sake had slept very little last night and not at all the night before. He had been restored to her by Shardik, whom he had once cursed and planned to destroy.

He turned back toward the river and for a long time remained leaning on the half-wall, watching the slow clouds and their mirrored images. The water was so smooth that when two ducks flew across a white cloud, wheeled in the sky and disappeared upstream, their reflections were plain as themselves. This he saw with a sense of having seen the like before, yet he could not remember where.

He stood up to pray, but could not raise his wounded arm and after a short time, his weakness overcoming him, was forced once more to support himself against the half-wall. For a long time his thoughts formed no words, dwelling only upon his own past ignorance and self-will. Yet strangely, these thoughts were kind to him, bringing with them no shame or distress, and turning finally to a flood of humility and gratitude. The mysterious gift of Shardik's death, he now knew, transcended all personal

534

shame and guilt and must be accepted without dwelling on his own unworthiness, just as a prince mourning his father's death must contain his grief and be strong to assume, as a sacred trust, the responsibilities and cares of state which have fallen upon him. In spite of mankind and of all folly, Shardik had completed his work and returned to God. For his one-time priest to be absorbed in his own sorrow and penitence would be only to fail him yet again, the nature of the sacred truth immanent in that work being a mystery still to be grasped through prayer and meditation. And then? he thought. What then?

Below him the stones lay clean on the empty shore. The world, he reflected, was very old. "Do with me what You intend," he whispered aloud. "I am waiting, at last."

The fishermen had left the river. There appeared to be no one below in the village. So much quiet seemed strange in the early afternoon. When he heard the soldiers approaching he did not at first recognize the sound. Then, as they drew nearer, what had been one sound resolved into many—the tramping of feet, the clink of accouterments, voices, a cough, a shouted order, a tryzatt's sharp admonition. There must be many soldiers—more than a hundred, he guessed—and by the sounds, armed and equipped. Melathys still slept as they passed by, unseen by him, on the landward side of the hut.

As their tramping died away he suddenly heard Yeldashay voices talking below. Then there was a knock; Dirion opened the door and spoke a few words, but too quietly for him to make out what she had said. Supposing that the soldiers must be leaving the village and wondering whether Melathys knew of it, he waited and after a little Dirion came clambering up the ladder into the far end of the gallery. When she was halfway across the room she suddenly saw him, started and began scolding him back to bed. Smiling, he asked, "What is it? What's happening?"

"Why, the young officer, to be sure," she answered. "He's here for the säiyett—to take her down to the shore. They're ready for the burning, and I must wake her. Now you go back to bed, my dear."

At this moment Melathys woke as silently and swiftly as the moon emerges from behind clouds, her eyes opening and looking toward them with no remaining trace of sleep. To his surprise she ignored him, saying quickly to Dirion, "Is it afternoon? Has the officer come?" Dirion nodded and went across to her. Kelderek followed more slowly, came up to the bed and took her hand.

"What's happening?" he repeated. "What do they want?"

She gazed gravely up into his eyes.

"It is Lord Shardik," she answered. "I have to do—what is appointed."

Understanding, he drew in his breath. "The body?"

She nodded. "The appointed way is very old—as old as Quiso. The Tuginda herself could not recall all the ceremony, but what has to be done is plain enough, and God will not refuse to accept the best that we are able to offer. At least Lord Shardik will have a fitting and honorable passing."

"How does he pass?"

"The Tuginda never told you?"

"No," replied Kelderek sadly. "No; that, too, I neglected to learn."

"He drifts down the river on a burning raft." Then, standing up, she took both his hands in her own and said, "Kelderek, my dear love, I should have told you of this, but it could not have been delayed later than today, and even this morning you still seemed too tired and weak."

"I'm well enough," he answered firmly. "I am coming with you. Don't say otherwise." She seemed about to reply, but he added, "At all costs I shall come."

He turned to Dirion. "If the Yeldashay officer is still below, greet him from me and ask him to come and help me down the ladder." She shook her head, but went without argument, and he said to Melathys, "I won't delay you, but somehow or other I must be dressed decently. What clothes do you mean to wear?"

She nodded toward a rough-hewn, unpolished chest standing on the other side of the bare room, and he saw lying across it a plain, clean robe, loose-sleeved and high-necked, dyed, somewhat unevenly, a dark red—a peasant girl's "one good dress."

"They're kind people," she said. "The elder's wife gave me the cloth—her own—and her women made it yesterday." She smiled. "That's two new dresses I've been given in five days."

"People like you."

"It can be useful. But come, my dearest, since I'm not going to try to cross you in your resolve, we have to be busy. What will you do for clothes?"

"The Yeldashay will help me." He limped to the head of the ladder as Dirion came struggling up it for the second time, lugging with her a wooden pail of cold water. Melathys said in Beklan, "The washing's like the clothes. But she's the soul of kindness. Tell the officer I shan't be long."

The Yeldashay officer had followed Dirion halfway up the ladder and now, looking down, Kelderek recognized Tan-Rion.

"Please give me your hand," he said. "I'm recovered sufficiently to come with you and the priestess today."

"I didn't know of this," replied Tan-Rion, evidently taken aback. "I was told you would not be equal to it."

"With your help I shall be," said Kelderek. "I beg you not to refuse. To me this duty is more sacred than birth and death."

For answer Tan-Rion stretched out his hand. As Kelderek came gropingly down the ladder, he said, "You followed your bear on foot from Bekla to this place?"

Kelderek hesitated. "In some sort—yes, I suppose so."

"And the bear saved Lord Elleroth's son."

Kelderek, in pain, gave way to a touch of impatience. "I was there." Feeling faint, he leaned against the wall of the dark, lower room into which he had climbed down. "Can you—could your men, perhaps—find me some clothes? Anything clean and decent will do."

Tan-Rion turned to the two soldiers waiting by the door and spoke in his own tongue. One answered him, frowning and evidently in some perplexity. He spoke again, more sharply, and they hurried away.

Kelderek fumbled his way out of the hut to the shore, pulled off the rough, sacklike shift he had been wearing in the bed and knelt down to wash, one-handed, in the shallows. The cold water pulled him together and he sat, clearheaded enough, on a bench, while Tan-Rion dried him with the shift for want of anything better. The soldiers returned, one carrying a bundle wrapped in a cloak. Kelderek tried to make out what they said.

"—whole village empty, sir," he heard—"decent people—can't just help ourselves—done the best we can—"

Tan-Rion nodded and turned back to him. "They've brought

some clothes of their own. They suggest you put them on and wear a sentry's nightcloak over the top. I think that's the best we can do at this short notice. It will look well enough."

"I'm grateful," said Kelderek. "Could they—could someone—support me, do you think? I'm afraid I'm weaker than I thought."

One of the soldiers, perceiving his clumsiness and evident fear of hurting his heavily bound left arm, had already, with natural kindliness, stepped forward to help him into the unfamiliar clothes. They were the regulation garments of a Yeldashay infantryman. The man fastened the cloak at his neck and then drew his sound arm over his own shoulders. At this moment Melathys came down the ladder, bowed gravely to Tan-Rion, touched Kelderek's hand for an instant and then led the way out into the village street.

She was wearing the plaited wooden rings of a priestess of Quiso. Were they her own, he wondered, hidden and kept safe throughout her wanderings, or had the Tuginda given them to her pardoned priestess when she left Zeray? Her long black hair was gathered round her head and fastened with two heavy wooden pins—no doubt the very best that Dirion could borrow. The dark red robe, which would otherwise have fallen straight from the shoulder like a shift, was gathered at the waist by a belt of soft gray leather with a crisscross pattern of bronze studs, and from below this the skirt flared slightly, falling to her ankles. Even at this moment Kelderek found himself wondering how she had come by the belt. Had she brought it with her from Zeray, or was it the gift of Tan-Rion or some other Yeldashay officer?

Outside, between the huts, a double file of Sarkid soldiers in full panoply stood waiting. Each wore the corn sheaves on his left shoulder. They were spearmen, and at the approach of the priestess of Quiso, followed by their own officer and the limping, pallid Ortelgan priest-king who had suffered in comradeship with the Ban's son, they saluted by beating the bronze-shod butts of their spears in succession with a dull, rolling sound on the hard-trodden earth. Melathys bowed to the tryzatt and took up her place at the head of and between the two files. Kelderek, still leaning on the soldier's shoulder, stationed himself a few paces behind her. After a moment she turned and came back to him.

"You are still of the same mind, my love?" she whispered.

"If we go slowly—I can manage it."

Giving his soldier a nod and smile of thanks, she returned to her place, looked quickly about her and then, leaving it to the tryzatt and his men to follow her lead, set off with the same solemn, gliding step. Kelderek came limping, breathing hard and leaning heavily on the soldier's shoulder. The Telthearna lay on their left and he realized that they were going southward out of the village, toward the place where Shardik had died. They passed patches of cultivated ground, a shed for oxen with a great pile of manure outside it, a frame on which nets hung drying and an upended canoe, patched and repaired, its new caulking shining black in the sun. Hobbling between the files of soldiers, he recalled how he had once paced the streets of Bekla with his scarlet-cloaked priestesses, the train of his paneled robe carried behind him. He could feel again the weight of the curved, silver claws hanging from the fingers of his gauntlets, hear the stroke of the gong and see about him the finery of his attendants. He felt no regret. That great city he would never, he knew, see again; and gone, too, was the false illusion which had carried him thither in bloodshed and drawn him thence, alone and friendless, to suffering and self-knowledge. But the secret—the great secret of life on earth—the secret that Shardik might perhaps have been able to impart to a humble, selfless, listening heart—must that, too, be lost forever? "Ah, Lord Shardik," he prayed silently, "the empire was pride and folly. I am sorry for my blindness, and sorry, too, for all that you suffered at my hands. Yet for others' sake, not mine, I entreat you not to leave us forever without the truth that you came to reveal. Not for our deserving, but of your own grace and pity for Man's helplessness."

His foot slipped and he stumbled, clutching quickly at his companion's shoulder.

"All right, mate?" whispered the soldier. "Hold on. Comin' up now, look."

He lifted his head, peering in front of him. The two files were opening out, moving apart, while ahead of him Melathys still paced on alone. Now he remembered where he was. They had come to that part of the shore which lay between the southern outskirts of the village and the wooded inlet where Shardik had died. That it was crowded he could see, but at first he could not make out the people who were surrounding the stony, open space into which he was following Melathys. A sudden fear came upon him.

"Wait," he said to the soldier. "Wait a moment."

He stopped, still leaning on the man, and looked about him. From all sides, faces were turned toward him and eyes were staring expectantly. He realized why he had felt afraid. He had known them before—the eyes, the silence. But as though to transform the curses which he had carried out of Kabin, everyone was looking at him with admiration, with pity and gratitude. On his left stood the villagers: men, women and children all in mourning, with covered heads and bare feet. Gathered behind the file of soldiers now halted and facing inward in extended order, they filled the shore to the water's edge. Although, from natural awe and sense of occasion, they did not press forward, yet they could not help swaying and moving where they stood as they pointed out to one another, and held up their children to see, the beautiful priestess of Quiso and the holy man who had suffered such bitter hardship and cruelty to vindicate the truth and Power of God. Many of the children were carrying flowers—trepsis and field lily, planella, green-blooming vine and long sprays of melikon blossom. Suddenly, of his own accord, a little boy came forward, stared gravely up at Kelderek, laid his bunch at his feet and ran quickly back to his mother.

On the right stood the Yeldashay troops—the entire Sarkid contingent who had marched from Kabin to close the Linsho Gap. Their line, too, extended to the water's edge, and their polished arms shone bravely in the light of the westering sun. In front, a young officer held aloft the corn sheaves banner, but as Melathys passed him he dropped on one knee, slowly lowering it until the blue cloth lay broad across the stones.

With an extraordinary sense of grave, solemn joy, such as he had never known, Kelderek braced himself to go forward over the shore. Still he could not see the river, for between it and Melathys a third group was facing him—a single line, parallel with the water's edge, extending between the villagers and the soldiers. At its center stood Radu, pale and drawn, dressed, like Melathys, in villager's clothes, his face disfigured wtih bruises and one arm in a sling. On each side of him were some five or six of the slave children—all, it seemed, who had been able to find the strength to stand and walk. Indeed, it appeared to Kelderek, looking at them, that there might be some who could scarcely do so much, for two or three, like himself, were leaning on companions—village boys, they looked to be—while behind the line were benches, from which they had evidently risen at the approach of the priestess. He saw the boy with whom he had talked in the night and who had told him about Leg-By-Lee. Then he suddenly started, recognizing, at one extremity of the line, Shouter, who caught his eye for a moment and looked quickly away.

As Melathys halted, soldiers took away the benches, the children moved apart in either direction, and now for the first time Kelderek saw the water's edge and the river beyond.

A small fire was burning on the stones, a little in front of the shoreward extremity of the soldiers' line. It was bright and clear, with hardly a trace of smoke, and above the fire the air wavered, distorting the distant view. Yet this he scarcely noticed, standing, like a child, with one hand raised to his open mouth, staring at what lay immediately before him.

In the shallows a heavy raft was moored—a raft bigger than the floor of a dwelling-hut, made of sapling trunks lashed together with creeper. It was covered with high-piled brushwood, logs and dry faggots, over which had been sprinkled flowers and green boughs. Upon this great bed, pressing it down as a fortress settles upon the ground where it is built, lay the body of Shardik. He was lying on one side, as naturally as though sleeping, one forepaw extended, the claws hanging down almost to the water. The eyes were closed—stitched, perhaps, thought Kelderek, observing with what care and pains the villagers and soldiers had carried out their work of preparing for his obsequies the Power of God—but the long wedge of the muzzle, if it had once been shut, had in some way burst its binding, so that now the lips snarled open around the pointed teeth. The poor, wounded face had been cleaned and tended, yet all that the soldiers had been able to do could not obliterate, to the eyes of one who had once seen them, the marks of Shardik's wounds and sufferings. Nor could the long, careful combing, the removal of briars and thorns and the brushing in of oil disguise the starved desolation of the body. It was not possible for Shardik to appear small, but less colossal he looked and, as it were, shrunken in the grip of death. There was a faint odor of carrion, and Kelderek realized that Melathys, from the moment that she heard the news, must have grasped the necessity of speed and known that she would barely have time to carry out all that the Tuginda would wish. She had done well, he thought, and more than well. Then, as he took yet a few more painful steps forward, his line of vision became direct and he saw what had been concealed from him before.

Between Shardik's front paws lay the body of Shara. The extended paw covered her feet, while her raised head rested upon the other. She was bareheaded and dressed in a white smock, her hands clasped about a bunch of scarlet trepsis. Her fair hair had been combed over her shoulders and around her neck had been fastened a string of pierced and colored stones. Although her eyes were closed, she did not look as though she were asleep. Her thin body and face were those of a dead child, drained and waxen, and cleaner, stiller and more tranquil than ever Kelderek had seen them in life. Dropping his head on the soldier's arm, he sobbed as uncontrollably as though the shore had been deserted.

"Steady now, mate, steady," whispered the kindly, decent fellow, ignoring everything but the poor foreigner clinging to him. "Why, they ain't there, you know. That ain't nothing, that ain't. They're off somewhere better, you can be sure of that. Only we got to do what's right and proper, 'aven't we?"

Kelderek nodded, bore down on the supporting arm and turned once more to face the raft as Melathys passed close to him on her way to speak to Tan-Rion. Despite their debt to the Yeldashay she spoke, as was right, out of the authority conferred upon her and not as one asking a favor.

"Captain," she said, "by the ancient rule of Quiso no weapons must be brought into any place sacred to Lord Shardik. I tell you this, but I leave you, of course, to order the matter as you think best."

Tan-Rion took it very well. Hesitating only a moment, he nodded, then turned his soldiers about and marched them back a little distance along the shore. There each man grounded his spear and laid beside it his belt, short sword and knife. As they returned, halted and dressed their line, Melathys stepped forward into the shallows and stood motionless before the raft, her arms outstretched toward Shardik and the dead child.

How many times has that scene been depicted—carved in relief on stone, painted on walls, drawn with brush and ink on scrolls, scratched with pointed sticks in the wet sand of the Telthearna shore? On one side the fishermen and peasants, on the other the unarmed soldiers, the handful of children beside the fire (first, the very first, of all those to bless the name of Lord Shardik), the Man supported on the soldier's arm, the Woman standing alone before the bodies on the floating pyre? The sculptors and the painters have done what was required of them, finding ways to reflect the awe and wonder in the hearts of people who have known the story since they were little children themselves. The fisherfolk—handsome, strong young men, fine old patriarchs and their grave dames—face the resplendent soldiers in their red cloaks, each a warrior to conquer a thousand hearts. The Man's unhealed wounds bleed red upon the stones; the Woman is robed like a goddess; light streams from Lord Shardik's body upon the kneeling children, and the little girl smiles as though in her sleep, nestling between the strong, protecting limbs. The fire burns lambent, the regular wavelets lap white as wool upon the strand. Perhaps—who can tell?—this is indeed the truth, sprung like an oak from an acorn long vanished into the earth: from the ragged, muttering peasants (one or two already edging away to the evening chores); the half-comprehending soldiers obeying orders, their clothes and armor, conscientiously mended and burnished, showing every sign of a hard campaign and a forced march; from Shouter, trying for dear life to squeeze out a few tears; from Kelderek's uncontrollable trembling, Melathys' weary, dark-ringed eyes and homespun robe; from the grubby village flotsam bobbing in the shallows and the sorry huddle on the raft. These things were not remarked or felt at the time and now they have long disappeared, mere grains succeeded by the massive trunk above and the huge spread of roots below. And lost too—only to be guessed at now—are the words which Melathys spoke.

She spoke in Ortelgan, a tongue largely unknown to the Yeldashay, though understood well enough by the Tissarn villagers. First she uttered the traditional invocation of Quiso to Lord Shardik, followed by a sequence of prayers whose archaic and beautiful periods fell from her lips without hesitation. Then, turning to face her listeners and changing her voice to an even tone of narration, she spoke of the finding of Shardik on Ortelga and the saving of his life by the priestesses of Quiso; of his coming alive from the Streel; of his ordained suffering; and of the sacred death by which he had saved the heir of Sarkid and the enslaved children from the power of evil. Kelderek, listening, marveled, less at her self-possession than at the authority and humility present together in her voice and bearing. It was as though the girl whom he knew had relinquished herself to become a vessel brimmed with words old, smooth and universal as stones; and by these to allow mankind's grief and pity for death, the common lot of all creatures, to flow not from but through her. Out of her mouth the dead, it seemed, spoke to the unborn, as sand pours grain by grain through the waist of an hourglass. The sand was run at last and the girl stood motionless, head bowed, eyes closed, hands clasped at her waist.

The silence was broken by the voice of the young flag officer beginning, like a precentor, the beautiful Yeldashay lament sometimes called "The Grief of Deparioth," but more widely known, perhaps, as "The Tears of Sarkid." This, which tells of the sacred birth and the youth of U-Deparioth, liberator of Yelda and founder of the House of Sarkid, is sung to this day, though perhaps it has altered through the centuries, just as they say the shapes of the constellations undergo change, no man living long enough to perceive it. The soldiers took up the lament, their solemn chanting growing louder and echoing from the Deelguy shore.

> Among the standing corn sheaves she lay down,
> In bitter grief the friendless girl lay down
> Wounded, alone, the curse of the Streel upon her,
> She bore the hero Deparioth, when Yelda lay in chains.

The soldier beside Kelderek was singing with the rest, the words, coming to him unthinkingly, expressing for him his sense of forming a part of things greater than himself, his people, his homeland and those memories, his and no other man's, that made up his little share of human life.

> He knew neither his father nor his mother,
> Among strangers he labored as a slave,
> An exile, in a country not his own,
> The Lord Deparioth, God's appointed sword.

The flag officer stepped forward, holding the corn sheaves banner before him, and was met from the opposite line by a villager carrying a fishing net in his arms. Together they turned riverward and walked toward Melathys, passed her on either side, waded into the shallows and placed their burdens on the raft. Radu, following them, laid his hand for a moment first on Shardik's gray claws and then on Shara's forehead. Returning up the shore, he drew a brand from the fire and stood waiting, holding it upright before him.

> If I could meet thee, thou mighty Lord Deparioth,
> If I could meet thee and clasp thy hand in mine,
> I'd tell thee thy deeds are not forgotten in Yelda,
> That the tears of Sarkid fall to honor thee still.

The chanting sank and died away. As it did so, Melathys raised her head with a long, ululating cry that recalled instantly to Kelderek the city of Bekla lying silent in sacred darkness, the weight of his heavy robes and the sudden, upward leap of flame into the night sky.

"Shardik! Lord Shardik's fire!"

"Lord Shardik's fire!" responded the villagers.

Radu approached slowly across the stones and held out to Kelderek the burning brand.

For a few moments Kelderek, confused by the vividness of his memories, stood hesitant, unable to grasp what it was that he was being asked to do. Then, as his mind cleared, he started and took a step backward, one hand raised as though in refusal. Radu dropped upon one knee, still offering the fire.

"Seems they think you're the one that's got to do it, sir," whispered the soldier. "Reckon you're up to it?"

In the silence Kelderek could hear only the crackling of the flame and, beyond, the lapping of the water. Fixing his eyes on the raft, he stepped forward, took the brand from Radu and so came down the shore to where Melathys still stood waiting, with bowed head.

Now he was standing alone in the water, none between him and the dead child, closer to Shardik than at any time since the day when he had come alive from the Streel. The bodies lay before him, the bear's, massive as a mill wheel seen against the wall of a mill, marked by the ropes with which it had been dragged into place and by the arrow's gash in the starved, pinched mask.

He wondered whether they expected him to speak or to pray: then saw that he had no time, for the brand had burned low and must be used at once.

"*Senandril*, Lord Shardik!" he cried. "Accept our lives, Lord Shardik Die-for-the-Children!"

Up to his waist in the water, steadying himself against the edge of the raft with his wounded left hand, he thrust the brand into the pile of twigs and shavings before him. It caught immediately, burning up in the opaque, yellow flames of kindling. Withdrawing the brand, he lit again and yet again among the logs and sticks. Finally, as the butt began to crumble and to scorch his fingers, he tossed it, in a shower of sparks, to the top of the pyre. It lodged, burning, a few feet above the spot where Shara lay.

The raft was pivoting slowly away from him. He let go of it clumsily, wincing to feel the pain shoot up his arm as he pushed himself upright. The soldiers behind him had released the mooring ropes, which now trailed past him on either side, rippling but invisible in the lurid shallows. For now the whole shoreward side of the pyre was burning, blazing in a wall of hot, translucent flames, green, red and black-flecked orange. The fire ran back into the heart of the pyre, disclosing its depth as sunlight shows the distance between forest trees; and as it burned higher, up into the green branches and flowers where Shardik lay, a thick, white smoke began to fume and drift to the shore, almost blinding Kelderek and those behind him.

He choked, and gasped for breath. His eyes smarted, pouring water, but still he stood where he was. "Let it be so," he thought.

"This is best, for I could not bear to see the bodies burn." Then, even as he felt himself about to faint in the smother, the heavy raft began to turn more swiftly, so that the bodies and the whole of the side along which he had lit the fire faced upstream. Four or five of the young fishermen had fastened the upstream mooring rope to a canoe and were drawing the raft out toward the center of the river.

As it began to gather way, a storm of flames poured backward through the pyre. The sound of crackling changed to a hot, windy roaring and sparks and cinders raced upward, wavering and dodging like escaping birds. Logs began to shift and fall, and here and there a burning fragment dropped hissing into the water. Presently, cleaving through the noise of dissolution like a ploughshare through heavy soil, there rose once again the sound of singing. The villagers upon the shore were encouraging and urging on the young men at the paddles, who were laboring now as they drew farther out and began to be carried downstream with the current-borne raft.

> At dawn we come to the shore and loose our boats.
> If luck is with us none will be hungry tonight.
> Who has his net and who has skill with a spear?
> Poor men must live by any means they can.

The raft was half a bowshot from land now and as far downstream from where Kelderek stood, but still the paddlers dug rhythmically into the water and the plume of smoke blew shoreward as they toiled to pull it farther out.

> Buying wisdom dear is the lot of men,
> And learning to make the most of what they've got.
> What I call luck's a fire and a bellyful,
> A girl for your bed and children to learn your craft.

They clapped and stamped as they sang, in the rhythm of the paddles, and yet it was a grave and not unfitting sound, of a minor cadence, homely and shrewd, the single music of folk whose solemnity is but their wit turned inside out to serve the occasion and mood of the day. The raft was a long way out now and far downstream, so far that the distant paddles could be seen striking behind the beat of the song. The young men had turned the bow half-upstream into the current, so that the raft was below them and the side on which the bodies had lain was once more turned toward the shore. Kelderek, gazing, could discern nothing on top of the burning pyre. It had fallen inward at the center, the two glowing halves spread on either side like the wings of a great butterfly. Shardik was no more.

"Twice," he cried, "I followed you into the Telthearna, Lord Shardik. Now I can follow you no longer."

> Returning at dusk we see the fires on shore.
> If one is yours then you're a lucky man.
> No one ought to be left alone in the dark.
> If you die, brother, your children shall share my fire.

The paddlers cast off the rope and turned away, making for the shore downstream and an easy return in slack water under the bank. The raft could no longer be seen, but far off, a point on the surface of the river itself seemed to be burning, emitting smoke and covering the watery expanse with a wide, drifting cloud.

> We gut the fish and the children spit them to cook.
> "Hullo, my son, my tall young zoan tree!
> What have you got to say to your dad tonight?"
> "When I'm a man, I'll paddle a boat like you!"

The pouring smoke was gone. Trees hid it from view. Kelderek, closing his eyes as he turned away, found his soldier beside him, felt his arm under his shoulders and allowed himself to be lifted almost bodily through the shallows to the shore. Tan-Rion called up his men and turned them about to recover their arms. Then they marched away; and the villagers, too, began to disperse, two matronly women shepherding Radu and the other children with them. Yet several, before they went, came forward—some a little hesitantly, for they stood in awe of Kelderek—to kiss his hands and ask his blessing. Any holy man may have the power to confer good luck, and a chance is not to be missed. He stood hunched and silent as a heron, but nodded back at them and looked in the eye each one that passed before him—an old man with a withered arm, a tall young fellow who raised his palm to his forehead, a girl who smiled shyly at the priestess standing nearby and gave her the flowers she was carrying. Last of all came a ragged old woman, with a child lying asleep in her arms. Kelderek started and almost backed away but she, showing neither hesitation nor surprise, took his hand in her own, kissed it, spoke a few words with a smile and was gone, hobbling away over the stones.

"What did she say?" he asked Melathys. "I couldn't catch it."

"She said, 'Bless me, young sir, and accept my blessing in return.' "

*

He lay on his bed in the upper room, watching the elastic reflections widening, merging and closing among the roof poles. Melathys sat beside him, holding his good hand in both her own. He was tired out and feverish again, shivering and numb-cold. There was nothing left remarkable in the world. All was empty and cold, stretching away to the horizon and the blank sky.

"Hope you didn't find our singing out of keeping, sir," said Tan-Rion. "The priestess said it would be all to the good if we could manage a song, but the job was to think of something suitable that the lads could sing. They all know 'The Tears,' of course."

Kelderek found some words of thanks and praise, and after a little the officer, seeing that he was exhausted, took his leave. Presently Radu came, wrapped in a cloak from throat to ankles, and sat for a time opposite Melathys.

"They say my father's on his way," he said. "I'd hoped he might be here before this. If only he'd known, he'd have wished to be on the shore this afternoon."

Kelderek smiled and nodded like an old man, only partly taking in what he said. But indeed Radu said little, sitting silent for long minutes and once biting on his hand to still the chattering of his teeth. Kelderek slipped into a half-doze and woke to hear him answering Melathys.

"—but they'll be all right, I think." And then, after a pause, "Shouter's ill, you know—quite badly, they say."

"Shouter?" asked Melathys, puzzled.

"Is he?" said Kelderek. "But I saw him on the shore."

549

"Yes, I dare say he thought he'd better be there at all costs—not that it makes any difference—but he's in a bad way this evening. I believe it's fear as much as anything. He's terrified: partly of the other children, but partly of the villagers as well. They know who he is—or who he was—and they won't do anything for him. He's lying by himself in a shed, but I think he'd run away if he could."

"Who's Shouter?" asked Melathys again.

"Will they kill him?" said Kelderek. Radu did not answer at once and he pressed him. "What do *you* want to do with him?"

"No one's actually said anything; but what would be the good of killing him?"

"Is that really what you feel—after all you've suffered?"

"It's what I feel I ought to feel, anyway." He was silent again for some time and then said, "No one's going to kill *you*. Tan-Rion told me."

"I'll—I'll come and talk to Shouter," said Kelderek, groping to get up. "Where is the shed?"

"Lie down, my love," said Melathys. "I'll go. Since no one tells me about him, I must see this Shouter for myself—or hear him."

57 *Elleroth's Dinner Party*

WHEN HE WOKE, his Yeldashay soldier was sitting nearby mending a piece of leather in the fading light. Seeing Kelderek awake, he grinned and nodded, but said nothing. Kelderek slept again and was next wakened by Melathys lying down beside him.

"If I don't lie down I'll *fall* down. I'll be off to bed soon, but it means so much to be alone with you again for a little. How are you?"

"Empty—desolate. Lord Shardik—I can't take it in." He broke off, but then said, "You did well today. The Tuginda herself could have done no better."

"Yes, she could: and she would have. But what happened was ordained."

"Ordained?"

"So I believe. I haven't told you something else the Tuginda said to me before I left Zeray. I asked her whether, if I found you, I should give you any message from her, and she said, 'He's troubled because of what he did years ago, at moonset on the road to Gelt. He hasn't been able to ask forgiveness, although he wants it. Tell him I forgive him freely.' And then she said, 'I'm guilty too—guilty of pride and stupidity.' I asked, 'How, säiyett? How could you be?' 'Why,' she said, 'you know, as I do, what we have been taught and what we have taught to others. We were taught that God would reveal the truth of Shardik through two chosen Vessels, a man and a woman, and that He would break those Vessels to fragments and Himself fashion them again to His purpose. I had supposed, in my stupid pride, that the woman was myself, and often I have thought that I was indeed suffering that breaking. I was wrong. It was not I, my dear girl,' she said to me. 'It was not I but another woman that He chose to be broken and whom He has now fashioned again.'"

Melathys was crying and he put his arm around her, unable to speak for the shock of surprise that filled him. Yet he was in no doubt and, as perception began to come upon him of all that her words imported, he felt like one looking out toward an unknown country half-hidden in the twilight and mist of early morning. Presently she said,

"We have to return to the Tuginda. She will need a message sent to Quiso and help with preparing for her journey. And Ankray—something must be done for him. But that wretched boy out there—"

"He's a murderer."

"I know. Do you want to kill him?"

"No."

"It's easier for me to pity him—I wasn't there. But he was a slave like the rest of them, wasn't he? I suppose he has no one at all?"

"I think we may find there are several like that. It's the un-loved and deserted who get sold as slaves, you know."

"I should know."

"So should I. God forgive me! O God, forgive me!"

She checked him with a finger held to his lips. "Fashioned again to His purpose. I believe I'm at last beginning to see."

They could hear Dirion climbing the ladder. Melathys got up, bent over him and kissed his lips. Still holding her hand, he said, "Then what are we to do?"

"Oh, Kelderek! My darling Kelderek, how many more times? It will be shown us, shown us, *shown* us what we are to do!"

Next day his wounds were once more inflamed and painful. He was feverish and kept to his bed, but the following morning felt well enough to sit looking out over the river in the sunlight while he soaked his arm in warm water with herbs. The herbal smell mingled with wood smoke from Dirion's fire, and some children below played and scuffled over their task of spreading nets to dry on the shore. Melathys had just finished binding his arm and tying a sling for it when suddenly they heard cheering break out some distance away on the edge of the village. There are as many kinds of cheering as of children's weeping; the sound tells plainly enough whether the cause be deep or shallow, great or small. These were not ironical cheers of derision, nor yet of sport nor of acclamation for a comrade or hero, but deep, sustained cries of joy, expressive of some long-held hope attained and relief conferred. They looked at each other, and Melathys went to the head of the ladder and called down to Dirion. The cheering was spreading through the village and they could hear feet running and men's voices shouting excitedly in Yeldashay. Melathys went down and he heard her calling to someone farther off. Noise and excitement were blazing round the house like a fire and he had almost determined to try to go down himself when she returned, climbing the ladder as lightly as a squirrel. She took his good hand and, kneeling on the floor beside him, looked up into his face.

"Elleroth's here," she said, "and the news is that the war's over: but I don't know what that means any more than you."

He kissed her and they waited in silence. Melathys laid her head on his knee and he stroked her hair, wondering to find himself so indifferent to his fate. He thought of Genshed, of the slave children, of Shara and her colored stones, of the death of Shardik and the burning raft. It seemed to matter little what might follow upon these, except that come what might he would not leave Melathys. At length he said, "Have you seen Shouter this morning?"

"Yes. At least he's no worse. Yesterday I paid a woman to look after him. She seems honest."

Some time later they heard men entering below, and then Tan-Rion speaking quickly in words they could not catch. A few moments afterward he appeared at the head of the ladder, followed by Radu. Both stood waiting, looking down at someone who was following them. There was a pause and then Elleroth climbed awkwardly into the room, stretching out his ungloved right hand for help before stepping off the rungs.

Kelderek and Melathys rose and stood side by side as the Ban of Sarkid and his companions came forward to meet them. Elleroth, who was as clean and impeccably dressed as when Kelderek had last seen him in Kabin, offered his hand and after a moment's hesitation Kelderek took it, though returning the other's look uncertainly.

"We meet as friends today, Crendrik," said Elleroth. "That is, if you are willing, as I am."

"Your son is my friend," replied Kelderek. "I can truly say that. We suffered much together and believed we had lost our lives."

"So he tells me. I have heard little about it as yet, but I know that you were wounded defending him and that you probably saved his life."

"What happened," replied Kelderek hesitantly, "was—was confused. But it was Lord Shardik who laid down his life—it was he who saved us all."

"That too Radu has told me. Well, I see that I have much still to hear; and perhaps something to learn as well." He smiled at Melathys.

"Lord Kelderek has been gravely ill," she said, "and is still weak. I think we should sit down. I am only sorry that these are such rough quarters."

"Mine have been worse these two nights past," answered Elleroth cheerfully, "and it seemed no hardship in the world, I can assure you. You are a priestess of Quiso, I take it?"

Melathys looked confused and it was Kelderek who replied.

"This is the priestess Melathys, whom the Tuginda of Quiso sent as her deputy to conduct the last rites of Lord Shardik. The Tuginda was injured in Zeray and is still lying sick there."

"I am sorry to hear it," said Elleroth, "for she is honored as a healer from Ikat to Ortelga. But even she was taking too much danger on herself when she crossed the Vrako. Had I known, when she came to see me in Kabin, that she meant to go to Zeray, I would have prevented it. I hope she will soon be recovered."

"Pray God she will." replied Melathys. "I left her out of danger and better than she had been."

They sat together on the rough benches, in the gallery overlooking the Telthearna, while one of Tan-Rion's soldiers brought nuts, black bread and wine. Elleroth, who looked tired almost to the point of collapse, expressed concern for Kelderek's wounds and went on to inquire about the last rites of Shardik.

"Your soldiers did everything they could to help us," answered Kelderek. "They and the village people." Then, wishing to avoid being questioned about the details of the ceremony, he said, "You've marched from Kabin? You must have made great speed. Surely this is only the fourth day since Lord Shardik died?"

"The news was brought down the river to Zeray that evening," replied Elleroth, "and reached me in Kabin before noon of the next day. To march sixty miles in two and a half days is slow for a man whose son and heir was dead and is alive again, but then it's rough country and heavy going, as you'll know yourself."

"But you have hardly been in Tissarn an hour," said Melathys. "You should have eaten a meal and rested before troubling yourself to come here."

"On the contrary," rejoined Elleroth, "I would have come here sooner, but such is my vanity that I'm afraid I stopped to wash and change my clothes, though I confess I did not know that I was going to meet one of the beautiful priestesses of Quiso."

Melathys laughed like a girl accustomed to be teased and to tease in return.

"Then why the haste? Are Yeldashay nobles always so punctilious?"

"Yeldashay, säiyett? I am from Sarkid of the Sheaves." Then, gravely, he said, "Well, I had a reason. I felt that you, Crendrik, deserved to receive my thanks and to hear my news as quickly as I could bring both to you."

He paused, but Kelderek said nothing and after a few moments Elleroth went on, "If you still feel any anxiety on your account, I hope you will set it aside. When I told you in Kabin that we should kill you if we came upon you again, we were not to know that you would share the misery of slavery with the heir of Sarkid and play a part in saving his life."

Kelderek rose abruptly, walked a few steps away and stood with his back turned, looking out at the river. Tan-Rion raised his eyebrows and half-rose, but Elleroth shook his head and waited, taking Radu's hand and speaking quietly to him, aside, until Kelderek should have recovered his composure.

Turning at length, Kelderek said roughly, "And do you bear in mind also that it is I who brought about your son's sufferings and the little girl's death?"

"My father has heard nothing yet of Shara," said Radu.

"Crendrik," said Elleroth, "if you feel contrition, I can only be glad for it. I know that you have suffered—probably more than you can ever recount, for true suffering is of the mind and regret is the worst of it. I, too, have suffered grief and fear—for long weeks I suffered the loss of my son and believed him lost to me. Now we are all three released—he, you and I—and whether or not it was indeed a miracle, I am not so mean-spirited as to withhold gratitude from the poor bear, who came alive from the Streel, like the Lord Deparioth's own mother, or to retain any grudge against a man who has befriended my son. I say all debts are cleared by Shardik's death—his sacred death, for this we must believe it to have been. But I have another reason also for friendship between us—a political reason, if you like. There is now peace between Ikat and Bekla and even while we speak all prisoners and hostages are returning home." He smiled. "So it really wouldn't be at all appropriate, would it, for me to feel vindictive toward you."

Kelderek sat down on the bench. From the shore outside came the cries of three or four young fishermen who were launching their canoes.

"At the time when you were in Kabin," went on Elleroth, trying rather unsuccessfully to stifle a yawn of sheer exhaustion,

"General Santil-kè-Erketlis was personally leading some of our troops to overtake and release a slave column traveling westward from Thettit. He succeeded, but it brought him very close to the Beklan army, which, as I dare say you know, had followed us north from the Yeldashay frontier. It was while General Erketlis was returning with the slaves he had freed that he came upon a party of Beklan officers, who were also making for Kabin —to negotiate with us. They were headed by General Zelda and their purpose was to propose an immediate truce and the discussion of terms of peace.

"Three days ago I was taking part with Erketlis in that discussion with the Ortelgans, when news arrived from Zeray of what had happened here. I left for Tissarn at once, but nevertheless I'm sure that the terms will have been agreed by now. I needn't weary you with all the details—not until later—but the main is that Yelda, Lapan and Belishba will become independent of Bekla. The Ortelgans are to retain Bekla and the remaining provinces in return for an undertaking to abolish the slave trade and to help in returning all slaves to their homes."

Kelderek nodded slowly, staring down into his wine cup and tilting it this way and that. At length he looked up at Elleroth and said,

"I'm glad the war's over and more than glad that they'll abolish the slave trade." He put a hand over his eyes. "It's good of you to have come here to tell us so promptly. If I can't make you any better answer, it's because I'm still weak and my mind's confused. I hope we can talk again—tomorrow, perhaps."

"I shall be here for some days yet," answered Elleroth, "and we'll certainly meet again, for I've one or two other notions in my head—just notions at the moment, but they might come to something. Dear me—" he craned his neck—"those piscatorial boys out there are certainly slicing up the Telthearna—I suppose it keeps them warm, poor fellows, in these bitter northern climes. And who knows? They might even catch a fish in a minute."

Soon after, he took his leave and Kelderek, finding that the meeting had left him tired, uncertain and disturbed, slept for several hours, not waking until the late afternoon.

556

After a few days he felt stronger and his wounded arm became somewhat less painful. He took to walking on the shore and about the village, once going almost a mile north, as far as the open country around the Gap. He had not realized what a poor village it was—thirty or forty hovels and twenty canoes clustered about a shady, unhealthy patch of shore below a wooded ridge—that same ridge down which he had tottered on the morning of Shardik's death. There was little cultivated land, the villagers living for the most part on fish, half-wild pigs, waterfowl and any forest beasts that they could kill. There was almost no trade, the place was largely isolated and the effects of years of inbreeding were all too plain. The villagers were friendly enough, however, and he took to dropping in to their homes and talking to them about their skills and needs and the troubles of their hard, rough lives.

One afternoon, as he and Melathys were walking together outside the village, they came upon five or six of the former slave children, who were idling about among the trees. They looked warily at Kelderek, but none approached or spoke. He called out to them, went closer and did his best to talk to them as comrades—for so indeed he felt them to be—but it was not that day nor for several days after that he had the least success. In their silence and curt, unsmiling answers they differed much from the children he remembered on Ortelga. Little by little he began to understand that for nearly all, their sufferings with Genshed had been only the most recent in miserable lives of desertion, neglect and abuse. Parentless, friendless and helpless, they had been enslaved before ever they met Genshed.

From Shouter, after one or two visits, he judged it best to keep away for the time being. The boy had been injured when Shardik charged upon Genshed and neglect of his hurts had brought on a delirious fever of which, until a few days ago, he had been expected to die. He was consumed with fear and convinced that the Yeldashay intended him some cruel death; and the sight of any of those whom he had himself ill-treated intensified his guilt and panic. Kelderek left him to Melathys and her village woman, but nevertheless found himself wondering more than once what would become of him. Would he, perhaps, succeed in wandering back to Terekenalt, there to shift for himself and find a new criminal master? Or would he, before that, as he himself so clearly expected, be killed in Tissarn by those who had cause enough to hate him?

The Sarkid contingent also remained, some quartered in Tissarn and some where he had first seen them, guarding the approaches to the Linsho Gap. Tan-Rion, asked the reason, explained that the Yeldashay were still patroling the province for fugitive slave traders, from the confluence of the Vrako and Telthearna to the Gap itself, the Sarkid troops forming the heel of the net. The following evening two more slave traders were brought in, each alone and in the last stages of want and exhaustion, having fled north for days before the advancing curtain of soldiers. Next morning the patroling troops themselves reached Linsho and the hunt was over.

A few days later Kelderek was returning with Melathys from an hour's fishing—he could manage no more—when they met Elleroth and Tan-Rion not far from the place where Shardik's funeral raft had lain. Despite what Elleroth had said at their last meeting, he and Kelderek had not talked together since. It had not occurred to Kelderek, however, to regard this as a lapse on Elleroth's part. The Ban of Sarkid had been absent for several days among his various outposts and bivouacs; but in any case Kelderek was well aware that he himself was in no position to expect warmth from Elleroth or any repetition of the punctilious courtesy shown on the morning of his arrival. By chance it had so happened that the ex-king of Bekla had suffered in company with Elleroth's son and helped to save his life. This had saved his own; but nevertheless he was now of no use or value whatever to the Ban of Sarkid, who had already done fully as much as anyone would consider incumbent upon him.

Elleroth greeted them with his usual urbanity, inquired after Kelderek's recovery and expressed his hope that Melathys did not find life in the village unduly rough and comfortless. Then he said, "Most of my men—and I too—are leaving for Zeray the day after tomorrow. I suppose you'll both wish to come? I personally am traveling by river and I'm sure we can find places for you."

"We shall be grateful," answered Kelderek, conscious, despite himself, of his sense of inferiority to this man and of his utter dependence on his goodwill. "It's time now that we were returning to Zeray, and I'm afraid I'm not strong enough to march with the troops. You say 'most of your men.' Aren't they all going?"

"I should have explained to you earlier," replied Elleroth. "Under the terms agreed with the Ortelgans, we are taking control of this province—all land east of the Vrako. That is perfectly just and reasonable, as Bekla certainly never controlled it and the last—indeed the only—Baron of Zeray, the Ortelgan Bel-ka-Trazet, specifically invited us to annex it only a few months ago. For some little while, until we have the place settled, there will be a force of occupation, with outposts at suitable places."

"I'm only surprised you think it's worth your while," said Kelderek, determined to express some view of his own. "Will there be any profit at all?"

"The profit we shall owe to Bel-ka-Trazet," answered Elleroth. "I never knew him, but he must have been a remarkable man. If I'm not mistaken, it was he who first conceived what I believe is going to prove an innovation of the greatest importance."

"He *was* a remarkable man," said Melathys. "He was a man who could pluck advantage from an acre of ashes."

"He advised us," said Elleroth, "that it would be practicable to construct a ferry across Zeray strait, and even outlined to us how it might be done—an idea entirely of his own devising, as far as I can make out. Our pioneers, together with men from Deelguy, are engaged on the work now, but we have sent to ask for the help of some Ortelgan rope-makers. That will be most important. No one understands the uses and qualities of ropes like Ortelgans. When the ferry is complete, Zeray is bound to become a commercial town of importance, for there will be a new and direct route, both for Ikat and for Bekla, across the Telthearna and on to the east. Whatever countries may lie there, the ferry is bound to open up entirely new markets." He paused. "If I recall, Crendrik, you were interested in trade, weren't you, when you were in Bekla? No, no—" he held up his hand "—I didn't intend any malice, or to wound your feelings, I assure you. Please don't think that. Isn't it true, though, that you played a large part in directing the empire's policy in commerce?"

"Yes, that's true," answered Kelderek. "I'm not an aristocrat,

559

as you know. I've never owned land; and to those who are neither farmers nor soldiers, trade's vital if they're to thrive at all. That was what I could understand about Bekla that our generals couldn't. It was from that that the evil came—" he paused "—but there was good as well."

"Yes, I see," said Elleroth rather abstractedly, and began to talk to Melathys about the probable needs of the Tuginda.

The villagers learned with regret that the soldiers were leaving, for on the whole they had behaved well and paid honestly enough for whatever they had had. Besides, they brought welcome change and excitement to the normal squalor of life in Tissarn. There was the usual bustle as arms and equipment were got together and inspected, quarters relinquished, loads apportioned and an advance party dispatched to prepare the first night's camp (for only Elleroth and a few other officers, with their servants, were to go by water, available canoes being scarce).

During the afternoon Kelderek, weary of the racket and commotion, took a line and some bait and set off along the waterside. He had not gone far when he came upon nine or ten of the slave children splashing about the shore. Joining them, he found them in rather better spirits than he had come to expect, and even began to derive some pleasure from their company, which now reminded him a little of old days on Ortelga. One of the boys, a dark, quick-moving lad about ten years old, was teaching them a singing game from Paltesh. This led to others, until at length Kelderek, being teased and challenged to contribute something, showed them the first Ortelgan game that came into his head.

> Cat catch a fish in the river in the foam;
> Cat catch a fish and he got to get it home.
> Run, cat, run, cat, drag it through the mire—

As he scratched out the lines with a stick and laid down a green branch for the fish, he felt once more, as he had not for years, the exhilaration of that spontaneity, directness and absorption that had once led him to call children "the flames of God."

> Take it to the pretty girl that's sitting by the *fire!*

And away he went, hobbling and shuffling slowly enough, for as he had told Elleroth, he was still far from healed; yet in his heart he went as once in the days when he had been a young simpleton who would rather play with the children than drink with the men.

When it was no longer his turn to be the cat, he dropped out. He was resting unobtrusively behind a rock when he realized that the boy loitering near him was Shouter, but so haggard and pale that at first he had not recognized him. He was playing no part in the game, but staring moodily at the ground, pacing one way and another and jabbing viciously at the stones with a stick. A second glance showed Kelderek that if he was not actually weeping, he was probably as close to it as was possible for any boy who had spent several months in the service of Genshed.

"Are you feeling better?" asked Kelderek as Shouter came a little nearer.

"—be mucking stupid," answered Shouter, barely turning his head.

"Come here!" said Kelderek sharply. "What's brought you out here? What's the matter?" The boy made no reply and he took him by the arm and said again, "Come on, tell me, what's the matter?"

"Glad to be going, aren't they?" said Shouter, in a kind of savage gasp. "Either they're lucky or they're too bloody stupid to know they're not."

"Why, aren't they going home?" asked Kelderek.

"Home? There's half of them's never had any home. If they had, they wouldn't have been here, would they?"

"Go on," said Kelderek, still gripping his arm. "Why wouldn't they?"

"You know's well as I do; kids whose mothers don't want 'em, fathers have mucked off, they live how they can, don't they, one day someone sells 'em for forty meld to get rid of 'em —same as they did me—best thing ever happened to some of them, next to being dead. Slaves—they was slaves all along, wasn't they?"

"Where do you think they'll go now, then?"

"How the hell should I know?" bawled Shouter, with something like a return to his old form. "Leg-By-mucking-Lee, I shouldn't wonder. Why don't you let me alone? I'm not afraid of you!"

Kelderek, forgetting his line and bait, left the boys and made his way back to Dirion's house. Melathys met him at the door, wearing her Yeldashay *metlan* with the corn-sheaves emblem.

"You missed Elleroth," she said. "The Ban in person. He's invited us to dine with him tonight and says he very much hopes you won't be too tired. There'll be no one else and he's looking forward to seeing you, which from him amounts to a pressing invitation, I should think." After a few moments she added, "He stayed here a little while, in case you returned, and I—I took the opportunity to tell him how things are between you and me. I dare say he knew already, for the matter of that, but he had the good manners to pretend he didn't. I told him how I came to be in Zeray and about Bel-ka-Trazet. He asked what we intended to do now and I explained—or tried to explain—what Lord Shardik's death had meant to us. I told him you were quite decided that there could be no question of your ever returning to Bekla."

"I'm glad you told him," said Kelderek. "You talk more easily to him and his like than ever I shall. He reminds me of Ta-Kominion, and *he* was too much for me. Elleroth might help us, I suppose, but I don't intend to ask him. I owe him my life, yet all the same I can't bring myself to give any of these Yeldashay the chance to tell me that I'm lucky to be alive. But—but—"

"But what, my darling?" she asked, raising her lips and kissing the pierced lobe of his ear.

"You said, 'It will be shown us what we are to do,' and I've a kind of inkling that something may happen before we leave Tissarn."

"What?"

"No," he said, smiling. "No, it's you that's the clairvoyante priestess from Quiso, not I."

"I'm not a priestess," answered the girl gravely.

"The Tuginda said differently. But you'll be able to ask her again tomorrow night, and Ankray too for that matter."

" 'Well, säiyett, the Baron, now he always used to say—' " It was an excellent imitation, but she broke off suddenly. "Never mind, here comes Dirion. Now let me change that bandage on your arm. Whatever have you been doing up the river? It's far too dirty to go out to dinner with Elleroth."

It was pleasant to have so much light in the room, thought Kelderek, watching Elleroth's servant renew the lamps and sweep up the hearth. Not since Bekla had he seen a room so bright after dark. True, the light served to reveal no finery or display—little, indeed, but the poverty of the place, for Elleroth's quarters were much like his own—a wooden, shedlike house near the waterside, with two bare rooms on each floor—but it also showed that Elleroth, as might be expected, liked to be generous, even lavish, to his guests, and that, too, without thought of return, for, as he had promised, no one was present besides himself, Melathys, Tan-Rion, another officer and Radu. The boy, though still pale and emaciated in appearance, had changed as a musician changes when he sets hand to his instrument. As in an old tale, the wretched slave boy had turned back into the heir of Sarkid, a young gentleman, brought up to be deferential to his father, gracious to his father's officers, silently attentive to the conversation of his elders and in every way equal to his station. Yet it was not all courtier, for he talked earnestly to Kelderek for some time about the slave children and also about the ceremony on the shore; and when Elleroth's servant, having cut up his one-handed master's meat, was about to do the same for Kelderek, Radu forestalled him, setting aside Kelderek's protest with the remark that it was less than Kelderek had done for him.

The dinner had been as good as competent soldier-servants could produce on active service—fish (he himself could have caught better), duck, stringy pork with watercress, hot bannock's and goat's cheese, and an egg sillabub with nuts and honey. The wine, however, was Yeldashay, southern, full and smooth, and Kelderek smiled inwardly as he thought of Elleroth, in desperate haste to start his forced march from Kabin in response to the news that his son was alive, finding time to give orders that plenty of it was to be brought along. That Elleroth, for all his aristocratic detachment, had a magnanimous and sincere heart he had had ample proof and indeed could be said to be alive to testify: nor was he himself so envious or mean as to suppose that wealth and style necessarily denoted indifference to the feelings of poorer men. If Elleroth was an aristocrat, he felt an aristocrat's obligations, and that a good deal more warmly than Ta-Kominion or Ged-la-Dan. His soldiers would have followed him into the Streels of Urtah. And yet Kelderek, for all his real gratitude to this man, who had set aside their former enmity and treated him as a friend and guest, still found himself out of accord with Elleroth's smooth self-possession, with the even, controlled tone of his voice and his capacity for deftly converting Kelderek's rather anecdotal manner of conversation into his own style of detached, impersonal comment. He had been most courteous and considerate, but to Kelderek his talk and bearing nevertheless contained more than a suggestion of the ambassador entertaining half-civilized foreigners in the way of duty. Had there, perhaps, been some unrevealed purpose behind his invitation? Yet what purpose could there be, now that all was resolved and settled? Radu was alive—and Shardik was dead. Ikat and Bekla were at peace and Melathys and he were free to go where they might. So were Shouter and the slave children—free as flies, free as autumn leaves or as wind-borne ashes. No, there could be no more strands to unravel now.

It was fortunate, he thought, that Melathys, at any rate, had some stomach for the party. Even remembering all that she had suffered, yet in one way she had been lucky, for despite her devotion to the Tuginda and her determination to vindicate her long-ago treachery to Shardik, she was not and never had been made for the seclusion of an island priestess. She was flirting with Tan-Rion at this moment—embroidering upon some banter of how she would visit Sarkid and reveal all that he had done while he had been on active service. Kelderek felt no jealousy, but only gladness. He knew her to be warm-hearted, mercurial, even passionate. She was working out her own way of overcoming the evil that had been done to her and meanwhile he could be patient, despite the kindling of desire which told him that his body at least was recovering.

Yes, he reflected, his body was recovering. His heart would hardly do so. He had seen into the depth of a Streel lower than Urtah, a devil's hole where Shara lay meaninglessly murdered and Shouter loitered cursing in the wasteland. That was the human world—the world which Elleroth saw primarily in terms of a ruler's problems of law and order—the world in which Lord Shardik had given his sacred life to save children condemned to slavery by human selfishness and neglect.

Elleroth was speaking again now, of the balance of power between Ikat and Bekla, of the prospects for peace and the need to overcome all remaining feelings of enmity between the two peoples. Prosperity, he was saying, was a great warmer of hearts and hearths, and to this self-evident truth Kelderek felt safe in nodding assent. Then, pausing, Elleroth gazed downward, as though deliberating with himself. He swirled the remains of his wine round and round his cup, but waved aside the attentive soldier who, misunderstanding, stepped forward to refill it, and a few moments later he gave him leave to go. As the man went out, Elleroth looked up with a smile and said,

"Well, Crendrik—or Kelderek Zenzuata, as Melathys tells me I ought to call you—you've given me a great deal to think about: or at all events I *have* been thinking, and you have much to do with it."

Kelderek, at something of a loss but fortified by the Ikat wine, made no reply, yet was at least able to return his host's gaze with courteous expectancy and some degree of self-possession.

"One of our problems—and that not the least—is going to be, first, establishing proper control over Zeray, and then developing this whole province. If you were ever right about one thing, Kelderek, it was when you spoke of the necessity of trade to the prosperity of ordinary people. Zeray is going to become an important trade route, both for Bekla and for Ikat. We couldn't monopolize it even if we wished, for the trade will have to come through Kabin as well and the Kabinese don't want to become independent of Bekla. So we're going to need someone to look after Zeray, preferably not a complete foreigner, but one who favors neither Bekla nor Ikat; someone who's keen on trade and understands its great importance."

"I see," said Kelderek politely.

"And then, of course, we really need someone with personal experience of the Telthearna," went on Elleroth. "You might not be aware of this, Kelderek, being so familiar with it yourself, but it's not everyone who knows how to pay the necessary attention and respect to the ways of a great river, its droughts and floods and fogs and currents and shoals—a river where a vital trade ferry crosses a swift and dangerous strait. That calls for experience, and knowledge that's become second nature."

Kelderek drained his wine. His cup was wooden, of peasant workmanship, almost certainly turned, he thought, here in Tissarn. In the bowl, someone had taken a good deal of trouble over a very passable likeness of a kynat in flight.

"Then, again, it would be highly desirable for this governor to have had some previous experience of ruling and exercising authority," resumed Elleroth. "Even with military help, Zeray's likely to be a tough business for a time, considering its present state and that of the whole province. And I think the appointment really calls for someone who knows something about fairly rough people at first hand—someone who's knocked about, as you might say, and knows how to rough it a bit himself. I doubt whether we'd find a landowning aristocrat, or even a professional officer, prepared to take the job on. They almost all despise trade, and anyway who would be ready to leave land and estates to go to Zeray? And what existing provincial governor would want to make the move? Difficult, Tan-Rion, isn't it?"

"Yes, sir," said Tan-Rion. "Very."

"The place needs colonizing, too," said Elleroth. "Willing hands, that's going to be the great need. I suppose we ought to look for young people with nothing much to lose—people who need to be given a chance in life and aren't going to be too particular. It wouldn't be any good just dumping them down in Zeray, though; they'd find it too much for them, and only add to the criminal population. They'll need an eye kept on them by a kindly sort of governor who feels sympathetic and knows how to get something out of people that nobody else has much use for. Someone who's suffered a bit himself, I suppose. Dear me, it *is* a problem. I really cannot imagine where we are likely to unearth a person who fulfills all these different requirements. Melathys, my dear, have you any notion?"

"Oddly enough," answered Melathys, her eyes bright in the lamplight, "I believe I have. It must be clairvoyance—or else this excellent wine."

"I will write to Santil-kè-Erketlis from Zeray," said Elleroth, "but I feel sure that he will accept my recommendation. Radu, my dear boy, it's time you were in bed; and Kelderek too, if I'm not presuming. You've both been ill and you look quite tired out. We ought to start several hours before noon tomorrow, if we possibly can."

58 *Siristrou*

"—THIS BEING NOW the commencement of the tenth day that we have been traveling westward from the western borders of Your Majesty's kingdom, through some of the most inhospitable country I have ever seen. At first, while we remained close to the shore of the river Varin (which our guide calls, in his tongue, 'Tiltharna') there was forest and rocky scrubland—a continuation, in fact, of the kind of country found on Your Majesty's western borders, but wilder and, as far as we have seen, uninhabited. There are, of course, no roads and we ourselves did not come upon a single track. For much of the way we were obliged to dismount and lead the horses together with the pack mules, so stony and treacherous was the ground. Neither did we see any craft upon the river; but this did not surprise us since, as Your Majesty knows, none has ever arrived in Zakalon from upstream. The guide tells us that below his country there lies a gorge (which he named Bereel), full of rapids and half-submerged rocks, so that it is not possible to travel thence to us by way of the river. That this man and his followers should have made the entire journey on foot, their nation being altogether ignorant of the use of horses, shows partly, I think, that this unknown country for which we are bound breeds a tough and resolute people and partly that the inhabitants—or some of them—must be most eager to develop trade with us.

"We forded two tributaries of the Varin, each—since we encountered both near the confluence—with some difficulty. Indeed, at the second crossing we lost a mule and one of our tents.

That was the day before yesterday, and soon afterward we left the forest wilderness and entered upon the desert through which we are now traveling. This is a country of thorn-scrub and fine, blowing sand—bad going for both horses and mules—and of black rocks, which give it a forbidding appearance. There is a kind of flat-bodied, spiny-legged creature, something between a crab and a spider, about as big as a man's fist, which crawls slowly over the sand. It does no harm that I can perceive, yet I could wish that I had not seen it. Drinking water of a sort we can get from the Varin, but it is sandy and warm, for the desert peters out into pools and flats and the true, flowing river is more or less inaccessible behind these. This country is said by our guide to form the southern extremity of a land called Deelguy—so far as I can understand, a semi-barbarian kingdom of warrior-bandits and cattle thieves, living among forests and hill-valleys. Inhabited Deelguy, however, lies a good fifteen leagues to the north. The truth seems to be that this desert, being land that nobody wants, is allowed to remain in name part of the territory of the king of Deelguy, a monarch whose frontiers (and authority) are in any case vague in extent.

"Your Majesty will recall that when the man Tan-Rion, who is now our guide, managed to convey in audience with you that he came from a country beyond the Varin possessing resources for trade, Your Majesty's councilors, including, I admit, myself, found it hard to believe that such a country could exist without our prior knowledge. However, the difficulty of this journey, together with the circumstance that the inhabitants have succeeded only during the past year in establishing a reliable crossing of the Varin at a point within reach of Zakalon, now make this more credible to me; and in short, I have become convinced that, as you yourself said, this may well prove to be a land with resources worth our attention. Tan-Rion has described—if I have followed him—the mining both of iron and of several kinds of gems; also the carving of wood and stone—though into precisely what kinds of artifact I confess I do not know. He has also talked of corn, wine and cattle. Much of the possible trade, I think, will have to await either the construction of a road, or else the development of a water route. (It has not escaped me that it might later prove practicable to bring goods across the Varin and then to embark them again from some suitable point on this shore, below the rapids.) As to what we may barter, I have only to remind Your Majesty that apparently the entire country knows nothing of horses and that none of these people has ever seen the sea.

"As to their language, I am happy to say that I seem to be making some little progress. In fact there are, it appears, two languages in general use beyond the Varin; the first, called Beklan, being commoner in the northern parts while the second, Yeldashay, is spoken more generally in the south. They have similarities, but I am concentrating on Beklan, in which I can now rub along after a fashion. Writing they use very little and it seems to fascinate my soldier-instructor when I write down the sound of what he says. He tells me that it is but three years since the end of a civil war—something to do with the invasion of Bekla by a foreign tribe who apparently went in for slavery— I confess that I could not altogether make it out. But now they are at peace, and since relations between north and south have improved, the prospects for our embassage seem very fair, coming at the present time.

"Today we shall—if I have not been deceived—actually cross the Varin to a town from which it will be possible to travel inland to Bekla. I shall, of course, continue to keep Your Majesty informed—"

Siristrou, son of Balko, son of Mereth of the Two Lakes, High Councilor of His Ascendant Majesty King Luin of Zakalon, glanced through the unfinished letter, gave it to his servant to pack with the rest of the baggage and made his way out of the tent to where the horses were picketed in a patch of scrub. Heaven only knew how or when the letter would get delivered anyway. It would, however, look well to have kept a fairly continuous record, as showing that he had the king and his interest constantly in mind. He had allowed himself a mention of the nasty drinking water, though saying nothing of his disordered stomach and of the flux which he daily feared might turn to dysentery. A discreet suggestion of hardship would be more telling than too much detail. He would not mention his blood blisters, and still less the nervous anxiety that grew upon him the farther they traveled from Zakalon toward the unknown country on the other side of the river. Knowing the king's own hopes, he had taken care to express confidence in the prospects for trade. Indeed, these now seemed reasonable, and even if they turned out otherwise it would do no harm to have seemed initially hopeful of better things. In his heart, however, he wished that the king had not selected him to lead this expedition. He was no man of action. He had been surprised to be chosen and, disguising his misgivings as modesty, had inquired the reason.

"Oh, we need a detached, prudent man, Siristrou," the king had answered, laying a hand on his arm and walking him down the length of the long gallery that overlooked the beautiful Terrace of the Bees. "The last thing I want is to send some quarrelsome soldier or greedy young adventurer on the make, who'd only upset these strangers by trying to grab all he could for himself. That would be the way to get bad blood at the outset. I want to send a learned man with no craving for personal gain, someone who can make a detached assessment and bring back the truth. Do that, and I assure you that you won't be a loser by me. Those people, of whatever kind they are— things ought to be handled so that they can trust and respect us. By the Cat, they've sent far enough to find us! I don't want to see them merely exploited."

And so, to the murmur of the bees in the golden rod, he had accepted his appointment.

Well, that was fair enough; and to give him his due, Luin was a man of just and sound judgment—if you like, a good king. The trouble lay, as usual, in giving practical effect to his excellent ideas. When it came to the point, quarrelsome soldiers and greedy young adventurers on the make would have been much better at crossing wildernesses and deserts and would have felt much less afraid than a detached, prudent councilor of forty-eight, a schoolman with a taste for metaphysics and the study of ethics. There'd be precious little in that line where he was going. The manners and customs of half-civilized peoples had a certain interest, to be sure, but this was ground which he had covered quite sufficiently as a younger man. Now he was primarily a teacher, a student of the writings of the sages, perhaps even shaping to be a sage himself—if he survived. It was all very well for the king to say that he would not be a loser. He did not really need anything which the king had to give. Luin, however, was not a man whom one disobliged and it would not have been safe to thwart his wishes by refusal or even by seeming too hesitant.

"I don't so much mind being cut to pieces by barbarians," he said aloud, slashing with his whip at a thornbush. "I *do* object to being *bored*" (slash), "*wearied*" (slash), "condemned to *tedium*" (slash)—

"Sir?" said his groom, appearing from the picket-lines. "Did you call?"

"No, no," said Siristrou hastily, feeling self-conscious as he always did when caught talking to himself. "No, no. I was just coming to see whether you're ready to start, Thyval. We're supposed to reach the crossing today, as I think I told you. I don't know how far it is, but I should prefer to reach the other side in daylight, so that we can get some idea of the place before darkness sets in."

"Yes, sir, I reckon that's sense right enough. The lads are just getting their things together now. How about the mare, sir? Lead her with the mules?"

"You'll have to, if she's still lame," answered Siristrou. "Come and tell me as soon as you're ready."

In fact they reached the east bank a little before noon, after no more than five hours' march. Upon setting out, they had at first struck almost due north, turning away altogether from the pools and flashes marking the southern confines of the desert and filling the broad, treacherous flat which comprised the shore of the river beyond. Tan-Rion, after struggling to be understood, at length took a stick and drew a plan on the ground. Pointing first to this and then southwestward over the sand, he managed to convey to Siristrou and his companions that in that direction the river made a great bend, so that its course helf-encircled them, lying not only to the south but also to the west of where they now stood. Some way above the bent on his plan he scratched a line to represent their intended crossing, and once more pointed, this time northwestward, to show the direction in which it lay.

In these parts spring had not yet turned to summer, but

nevertheless the day soon grew hot and the wind freshened enough to blow the sand about unpleasantly. Siristrou, trudging beside the lame mare, dropped his head, half-closed his eyes and, as the sand gritted between his teeth, tried to think about his metaphysics pupils in Zakalon. One had to count one's blessings. At least there was no lack of tepid water to wash the sand down. Tan-Rion was in excellent spirits at the prospect of return and led his men in singing Yeldashay songs. It was good, boisterous stuff, but hardly music to Siristrou's taste.

Suddenly he was aware—and felt pleased to have been the first to see them, for his eyes were not all they had been—of distant figures on the sand. He stopped and looked ahead more intently. The country, though still desert, was no longer flat. There were slopes and long, steep dunes, speckled with the shadows of the white stones lying on them, motionless and timeless in the sun as only desert hills can appear. At a point to the left was a cluster of huts—a kind of shantytown, raw and new in appearance—and it was here that the moving figures could be seen. Beyond, the ground fell away invisibly and there seemed to be a kind of reflected glitter in the air. Through the still more distant horizon-haze—and he screwed up his eyes, but could see no better—there loomed a greenness which might be forest.

An hour later they halted on the left bank of the river and looked across to the town on the western side which Tan-Rion called Zeray. About them gathered a wonder-struck crowd of soldiers and Deelguy peasants, inhabitants of the shantytown and labor force of the ferry on this bank. All evidently realized that these strangers had in truth come from a distant, unknown country, brought back by Tan-Rion, whom they had seen set out three months before. The shrill jabbering grew, and the shoving, and the pointing, and the exclamations of astonishment as it was grasped that the long-nosed beasts wore man-made harnesses and were obedient to men, like oxen.

Siristrou, determined to show no nervousness in the close-pressing hubbub, not one word of which he could understand, stood silently beside his horse's head, ignoring everything until Tan-Rion, approaching, requested him to follow and began literally beating his way through the crowd with the flat of his scabbard. They scattered, laughing and gabbling like children, in a fear that was half pretense and half real, and then fell in behind the newcomers, dancing and chanting as Tan-Rion led the way to a larger hut which did duty for the Deelguy officers' quarters. He gave a single bang on the door and strode inside. Siristrou heard him shout a name and then, himself wishing to show detachment as the crowd once more closed around him, turning to gaze across the river at the town on the other side.

It lay beyond a strait of turbid, yellowish water about a quarter of a mile across and running, as far as he could judge, too swiftly in the center for any craft. He watched a great, leafy branch go rocking downstream almost as fast as though it were sailing through the air. He could not see the lower end of the strait, but upstream, on the opposite side, the river bent back into a bay where he thought he could make out what looked like a graveyard among trees at the mouth of a creek. The town itself lay nearer, directly opposite him, filling a blunt promontory downstream of the bay. In all his life he had never seen a town with such an utterly Godforsaken appearance. It was clearly not large. There were several old houses, both of stone and of wood, but none of any size or of graceful or pleasing proportions. The newer houses, of which there seemed to be more than the old, both finished and half-finished, had a utilitarian, quickly-run-up look, and had certainly not been sited or designed in accordance with any plan. There were a number of trees, some thriving and some not, but clearly nothing like a public garden anywhere. Near the waterside, people—and even at this distance they looked oddly small people—were working on two nearly completed, larger buildings, which looked like warehouses. In front of these stood a landing stage and also, both in and beside the water, a complex of stout posts and ropes, the use of which he could not guess. The whole was framed in a gray sky and green, wild-looking country, dotted here and there with patches of cultivation.

Siristrou groaned inwardly and his spirits fell still further. It was worse than he had expected. Tan-Rion had struck him as an intelligent and reasonably cultivated man, the product at least of an ordered society with settled values. The town he was now looking at resembled something a giant's children might have

573

thrown together with sticks and stones in play. Setting aside that it was a safe bet that no book or civilized musical instrument could be found from one end to the other, would he and his men be even safe in such a place? However, fear was unworthy of a metaphysician and High Councilor of Zakalon, and after all, his death would matter little—except, he thought bitterly, to his wife and children, the youngest a little girl of five whom he loved dearly. A big workman stepped forward and began to finger the cloth of his sleeve. He drew it away with a frown and the man laughed disconcertingly.

Tan-Rion reappeared at the door, followed by two men with heavy black moustaches and long hair, who were dressed and armed as though they were going to take part in a play as wandering bandits. Perhaps that was approximately right, thought Siristrou, except that this was no play. They stood looking him up and down, hands on hips. Then one spat on the ground. Siristrou returned their stare, considered smiling and offering his hand, decided against both and bowed coldly. At this, the one who had not spat also bowed, then laid an enormous, dirty hand on his shoulder and said, in what he recognized as excruciating Beklan,

"Ho, yoss, yoss! Nover mind! Nover mind!" And then, with great emphasis, shaking a forefinger, "You—most—pay!"

Tan-Rion broke in, expostulating in an indignation too fast to be followed. "Envoys," Siristrou heard. "Trade mission—important foreigners—not to be insulted." And finally, more slowly and emphatically, so that he followed it fully, "Lord Kelderek will pay you, if you insist. You can cross with us and see him."

At this the two bandits shrugged their shoulders and conferred. Then one nodded and pointed, remarking, "Furry roddy," and both began to lead the way upstream, the native crowd trailing behind as before.

They left the shantytown and found themselves once more walking in the empty sand, but now along the waterline beside the river. Siristrou noticed how unnaturally straight and regular this waterline was, and saw also that the edge of the shore had been leveled and paved almost like a road—in some places with stones and elsewhere with thick, round wooden billets, laid and trodden in side by side. There were numerous prints of ox hooves. Pointing to these, he shook his head and smiled to Tan-Rion to convey his bewilderment, but the latter only nodded and smiled in reply.

They had not been going very long before they reached their destination. In slack water against the bank lay a flat raft of heavy logs topped with plank decking, some twelve or fourteen feet square and having a pointed bow or cutwater on the side facing out into the stream. There was no rail or parapet of any kind, but down the center three thick, upright posts were fastened into the logs with wooden struts and crude iron brackets. Bolted to the top of each post was a hinged iron ring and through all three of these a stout rope ran the length of the raft. From the stern it continued to the shore, where it was secured to an iron bar driven into the ground. Before reaching this, however, it passed through a kind of pen containing several free-ended stakes, around some of which it was hitched. A panel of this enclosure was open, and three men were straining as they twisted the stake inside to increase tension on the rope. Siristrou, watching as the dripping cable rose little by little out of the water beyond the raft and inched its way back through the rings, realized with something of a shock that it evidently stretched across and downstream to Zeray on the other side— not much less than three-quarters of a mile, as near as he could estimate. It was on this cable that their lives were about to depend. The raft was going to be warped across, with the force of the current at a highly acute angle behind it.

Thyval plucked at his sleeve. "Excuse me, sir, do they reckon they're going to take us over on that there thing?"

Siristrou looked him in the eye and nodded slowly and gloomily two or three times.

"Well, the horses won't stand for it, sir, and anyway there ain't the room for them."

"Not just one horse, do you think, Thyval? These people know nothing whatever of horses and I'd like to arrive with one, if we can."

"Well, sir, I'd chance it alone, but trouble is, if it's rough— and I reckon it looks real nasty out there—we're all crowded together and there's no rail nor nothing—"

"Yes, yes, of course," said Siristrou hurriedly, finding the picture too much for his already wambling stomach. "The best thing will be if you come with me, Thyval, and Baraglat here—you're not afraid, are you, Baraglat? No, of course not, excellent fellow—and the rest will have to stay here with the horses until tomorrow. I'll come back—heaven knows how, against that current, but I will—and see to everything. Now about the baggage—how can we best divide it?—and some of Tan-Rion's men must be told to stay with ours—we can't leave our people alone with those bandit fellows—and they'll have to be given a hut for stabling—we won't stand for any nonsense—Tan Rion, one moment, please—"

Metaphysician or no metaphysician, Siristrou was not lacking in decision and practical ability, and his men trusted him. There is much difference between being incapable of doing something and merely disliking having to do it, and King Luin had always been a good though somewhat unorthodox picker. In half an hour the baggage had been divided; Tan-Rion had acceded to demand and detailed three reliable Yeldashay, one of whom spoke Deelguy, to remain with Siristrou's men and the horses; the Deelguy officers had been told what they were to provide in the way of quarters; and those who were to cross had embarked.

In addition to the travelers there was a crew of six Deelguy laborers, whose task was to stand shoulder to shoulder and haul on the rope. This they set about, chanting rhythmically behind their shanty leader, and the raft, sidling out almost directly downstream, came little by little into the central race.

For Siristrou the crossing was a most nerve-racking experience. Apart from the rope and its ring-crowned stanchions, beside which there was room for only the crew to stand, there was nothing whatever to hold on to as the heavy raft, with the current almost full astern, danced like the lid of a boiling pot. He crouched on the baggage, holding his knees and trying to set a reassuring example to his men, who were plainly terrified. Tan-Rion stood beside him, legs astride, balancing himself as the deck tilted and swung. The water poured across the planking as though from overturned buckets. What with the chanting, which was maintained steadily, and the ceaseless knocking and blitter-blatter of the river under the timbers, talk was possible only intermittently and by shouting. As they got well out, a cold wind began to throw up spray. Siristrou, soaked, slapped himself with his arms to keep from shivering, in case anyone should think he was afraid—which he was. Even after it had become plain that they were going to complete the crossing safely and suffer nothing worse than discomfort, he could not keep himself from biting his lip and tensing at every lurch as he watched the shores moving up and down on either side, so horribly far away. One of the Zakalon party, a lad of sixteen, was sick but, with a boy's ashamed indignation, threw off Siristrou's comforting arm, muttering, "I'm all right, sir," between his chattering teeth.

"What is it they're singing?" Siristrou shouted to Tan-Rion.

"Oh, the shantyman just makes it up—anything that keeps them going. Actually I *have* heard this one before, I believe."

"Shardik a moldra konvay *gow!*" chanted the leader, as his crew bent forward and took a fresh grip.

"*Shar*-dik! *Shar*-dik!" responded the crew, giving two heaves.

"Shardik a lomda, Shardik a pronta!"

"*Shar*-dik! *Shar*-dik!"

"What does it mean?" asked Siristrou, listening carefully to the reiterated syllables.

"Well, let's see; it means 'Shardik gave his life for the children, Shardik found them, Shardik saved them'—you know, anything that suits their rhythm."

"Shardik—who's he?"

Another terrific lurch. Tan-Rion grinned, raised either hand in a gesture of helplessness and shrugged his shoulders. A few moments later he shouted, "Nearly there!"

Gradually they came into slack water. Over the last hundred yards the men stopped chanting and pulled the raft in more easily. A coiled rope was thrown from the landing stage and a few moments later they had touched. Siristrou gripped an offered hand and for the first time in his life stepped ashore on the right bank of the Varin.

The raft had been drawn into a kind of dock made of stout stakes driven into the shallows. It was the sight of this from the opposite bank which had perplexed him earlier that morning. As the Deelguy laborers clambered to shore, six or seven boys, the eldest no more than about thirteen years old, jumped aboard, unloaded the baggage and then, having opened the hinged rings, released the rope and began poling the raft down the dock toward a similar rope at the farther end. Siristrou, turning away, saw Tan-Rion pointing back at himself and his party. He was standing a little way off, talking to a black-haired youth who seemed to have some kind of authority on the landing stage, for he suddenly interrupted Tan-Rion to call out an order to the children aboard the raft. A crowd was gathering. Those working on the half-finished, warehouselike sheds nearby had apparently downed tools to come and stare. Siristrou stared back with a certain perplexity, for most of them were mere boys. However, he had no further opportunity to speculate, for Tan-Rion came up to him, together with the black-haired youth, who bowed rather formally and offered his hand. He was ugly, even forbidding, with a cast in one eye and a birthmark across his face; but his manner, as he uttered a few words of greeting, was courteous and welcoming enough. He was wearing some kind of badge or emblem—a bear's head between two corn sheaves— and Siristrou, unable to understand his Beklan (which did not sound native), smiled, nodded and touched it with his forefinger by way of a friendly gesture.

"This young fellow's in charge of the harbor lads," said Tan-Rion. "His name's Kominion, but most of us just call him Shouter. I've sent a man to tell the governor of your arrival and ask for a house to be put at your disposal. As soon as we know where it is, Shouter will get your baggage up there—you can leave it quite safely with him. It'll take a little while, of course, and I'm afraid you may find your quarters rather rough: this is a frontier town, you see. But at least I can make sure that you get a meal and a fire while you have to wait. There's quite a decent tavern up here, where you can be comfortable and private —a place called The Green Grove. Now come on, stand back, you lads," he shouted. "Leave the foreigners alone and get back to work!"

Glad at least of firm ground after the floodrace in the strait, Siristrou, walking beside his guide, led his men across the water-front and up toward the town, which looked as busy and ram-shackle as a rookery.

*

"—obliged to leave the horses on the eastern bank, and upon my recrossing intend to dispatch this letter by two or three horsemen—though I shall miss them, for all those with me have done well under hard conditions, and I commend them to Your Majesty's favor.

"For the Varin ferry crossing that these people have developed, it is ingenious and gives me hope that we may profit by commerce with so resourceful a people. The Varin here is relatively narrow, the strait being perhaps four and a half hundred yards directly across, from this town of Zeray to the opposite shore. The current, accordingly, flows very fast, too fast for navigation, while below lies the dangerous gorge known as Bereel, of which I have already written and which they greatly fear. Yet this current they have turned to account, for from Zeray they have contrived to stretch two ropes across the river, one to a point on the opposite bank some thousand yards upstream, while the other is secured a similar distance downstream. This, I am told, was effected with great difficulty in the first place by conveying one end of each rope across the river several miles upstream, in safer water, and then manhandling either end downstream along the banks, little by little, to their present anchoring points. Each rope is about twelve hundred yards long and took several months to make.

"There are three ferry rafts, each perhaps five or six paces square, which make a circuit of three journeys. First, the crossing-rope having been secured through iron rings, it is drawn from Zeray across the river, the opposite point being so far downstream that it goes almost with the current. Upon its arrival they release the raft from the rope and then, once unloaded, it is drawn upstream by oxen in the slack water under the shore. The distance must be about a mile and a quarter and over this whole length they have dredged and cleared the inshore water, straightened the shore and paved it for the beasts' hooves. At the upstream point, a thousand yards above Zeray, the raft is secured to the second rope and thus makes the return crossing, once more having the current behind it.

"The ropes, I am told, will need to be renewed once a year, and this means that a principal labor of upkeep is the making, each year, of well over a mile of stout rope. The rafts—the first they have made—are as yet clumsy and precarious, but serve their purpose. The main impediment, I learned, is from floating branches and the like which, drifting down river, foul the ropes and have to be disengaged or cut loose; but these can be avoided to some extent by leaving the ropes slack when not in use.

"We are now installed in a house here, poor enough, for the whole town is but a rough place, but at least sound and clean. Later this afternoon I am to meet the governor and shall, of course, present Your Majesty's message of goodwill. Soon after, I believe, we are to travel westward some thirty or forty miles to a town called Kabin, where, if I have understood correctly, there is a reservoir supplying the city of Bekla. It is here, and in another city which they call Igat or Ikat, that we hope to speak with the rulers about trade with Zakalon.

"There is one feature of this town which Your Majesty, I am sure, would find as puzzling as I, and that is the great number of children who seem to work, sometimes without any grown man in charge, and to carry out on their own account much of the business of the place. Where a task requires skilled direction as, for example, the building of the new warehouses on the waterfront, they work under the bidding of the masons; but in other, simple tasks they seem often to have their own foremen, older children who direct them without other supervision. Their work, though serviceable, is from what little I have seen, rough, but for this place it does well enough, and certainly the children seem for the most part in good spirits. In this house we are looked after by three grave lasses of no more than eleven or twelve years of age, who take their task very seriously and clearly feel it an honor to have been chosen to tend the foreign strangers. My men stare, but the girls are not to be put out of countenance. They speak an argot and I can understand little of what they say, but it is no matter."

There was a light knock at the door. Siristrou looked up and, not calling to mind the Beklan for "Come in," made a noise which he hoped was expressive of encouragement and assent. One of the serving-children opened the door, raised her palm to her forehead and stood aside to admit the biggest man Siristrou had ever seen. His leather jerkin, which bore the emblem of the bear and corn sheaves, seemed ready to split across his massive chest, and his skin breeches—apparently made for a man of more normal size—reached about halfway down his calves. Over one shoulder he was carrying easily a large and extremely full-looking sack. He grinned cheerfully at Siristrou, raised his palm to his forehead and said, "Crendro."

This word was unknown to Siristrou, but as it was evidently a greeting he replied, "Crendro," and waited expectantly. His visitor's next utterance, however, beat him altogether and he could only conclude that he must be speaking in some strange tongue or dialect.

"Can you speak Beklan?" he asked haltingly. "I understand —a little Beklan."

"Why, me too, my lord," answered the giant, dropping into mangled but comprehensible Beklan with another amiable smile. "Living here, you can't help picking it up after a fashion. Ah, it's a strange town, this is, and that's the truth. So you're the foreign prince, eh, that's come over on the ferry? Going to make all our fortunes, I dare say—or so they tell us. Best respects, my lord, sir."

By this time Siristrou had perceived that his visitor was evidently some kind of servant—from his manner, a privileged one, but one also who would need keeping in check if he were not to become garrulous to the point of presumption. Without a smile, therefore, and in a businesslike manner, he said, "You have a message for me?"

"Why, that's so, my lord," replied the man. "My name's Ankray—I look after the governor and his lady. Governor got back from Lak an hour or two after noon and heard you were here; so he says to me, 'Ankray,' he says, 'if you're going down to the waterfront you can just bring me back a sackful of those thick blocks they're using down there—the ones that came in from Tonilda the other day—and on your way home you can step in, like, to that there foreign prince gentleman and tell him I'll be happy to see him whenever it suits him to come.' So if it's quite convenient to you, my lord, you might just be stepping along with me now, as you don't know the way, and I'll take you up there."

"It sounds as though it's convenient to *you*, at all events," said Siristrou, smiling in spite of himself.

"My lord?"

"Never mind," answered Siristrou, who had now, with kindly shrewdness, grasped that his man was something of a simpleton. "I will be ready to come with you directly."

It was not the kind of summons to the governor that he had been expecting; but no matter, he thought; this was a small town; there was nothing of importance to be heard or done here; the real diplomacy would come later, in the cities to the west. Nevertheless, one must be courteous to this governor, who might even be the man responsible for designing and constructing the ferry. As he thought of the probable number of such interviews ahead of him—to say nothing of all the uncomfortable traveling—he sighed. King Luin, in his way, had paid philosophers a compliment in sending one to find out about trade. Yet for all the king's notions, it was not trade, but ideas, that truly advanced civilization: and of those, in this country, there were likely to be about as many as stars in a pond. He sighed again, folded and pocketed his unfinished letter to the king, and called to Thyval to bring him his good cloak and make ready to attend him to the governor's house.

The giant led the way, conversing easily in his atrocious Beklan without apparently worrying in the least whether Siristrou understood him or not, and carrying his bulging sack as lightly as if it had been a fisherman's keep-net.

"Ah, now, this town's changed a great deal, my lord, you see. Now, the Baron, he always used to say, 'Ankray,' he used to say, 'that ferry, once we get it put across the river, that ferry'll bring in a deal of foreigners, coming over for what they can find—' begging your pardon, my lord. 'They'll bring all manner of things with them and one will be our prosperity, you mark my words.' Of course, the Baron, very likely he'd be surprised out of his life to see all the children here now; though myself, I like them, and there's no denying they can often do very well with anything, once they understand what's to be done. I'd never have thought it possible, but it's these newfangled ideas, you see, of the governor's. Now only the other day, down at the waterfront—"

At this moment they became aware of a band of eight or nine

quite young children, who were running after them and calling out to attract their attention. Two were carrying thick, heavy wreaths of flowers. Siristrou stopped, puzzled, and the children came up, panting.

"U-Ankray," said one, a dark-haired girl of about twelve, putting her hand into the giant's, "is this the foreign stranger— the prince who's come over the river?"

"Why, yes, that's so," answered Ankray, "and what of it? He's on his way to see the governor, so just don't you be hindering of him, now, my dear."

The little girl turned to Siristrou, raised her palm to her forehead and addressed him in Beklan with a kind of confident joy, which both arrested and startled him.

"My lord," she said, "when we heard you were here we made wreaths, to welcome you and your servants to Zeray. We brought them to your house, but Lirrit told us you had just set out to see the governor. 'But you run,' she said, 'and you'll catch him,' so we came after you to give you the wreaths, and to say, 'Welcome, my lord, to Zeray.' "

"What are they saying, sir?" asked Thyval, who had been staring at the children in some bewilderment. "Are they trying to sell us these flowers?"

"No, they're a gift, or so it seems," answered Siristrou. Fond of children as he was, the situation was outside his experience and he found himself at something of a loss. He turned back to the dark-haired girl.

"Thank you," he said. "You're all very kind." It occurred to him that he had probably better try to discover a little more. Some further acknowledgment of this rather charming courtesy might well be expected of him later by whoever was behind it. "Tell me, who told you to bring the wreaths? Was it the governor?"

"Oh, no, my lord, we picked the flowers ourselves. No one sent us. You see, we were gardening not far from the waterfront and then we heard—" and she ran off into a chattering, happy explanation which he could not follow, while two of her companions stood on tiptoe to hang the wreaths round his neck and Thyval's. Most of the flowers were of one kind, small and lavender-colored, with a light, sharp scent.

"What do you call these?" he asked, smiling and touching them.

"Planella," she answered, and kissed his hand. "We call them planella. And these are trepsis, the red ones."

"Let's sing to them," shouted a limping, dark-skinned boy at the back of the little crowd. "Come on, let's sing to them!"

And thereupon he began and the others took up his song, rather breathlessly and in several different keys. Thyval scratched his head.

"What are they singing, sir, can you make it out?"

"Hardly at all," replied Siristrou. "They're singing in some other language, not Beklan—although a word or two here and there seems the same. 'Something or other—pulls out—a fish,' I think, 'along the river—' Oh, well, you know the kind of songs children sing everywhere."

"They'll be wanting some money in a moment, I suppose," said Thyval.

"Have you managed to get hold of any of their money yet?"

"No, sir."

But the song ended and the children, taking each other's hands, ran away, laughing and waving and carrying the lame boy along with them and leaving Siristrou staring after them in the sunshine, with the scent of the planella all about him from the wreath around his neck.

"Funny sort of a go," muttered Thyval, making to remove his wreath.

"Don't take it off," said Siristrou quickly. "We mustn't risk doing anything that might offend these people."

Thyval shrugged his scented shoulders and they set off again, Ankray pointing the way up the slope to a stone house at the top. Although newly built, it was not very large or imposing, thought Siristrou, looking at the upper story, visible over the surrounding wall. In Zakalon such a house might do well enough, perhaps, for a prosperous merchant, a market governor or some such man. It was not a nobleman's house. However, from what Ankray had said, it was plain that the town had begun to grow only recently, no doubt upon the completion of the ferry. The governor, perhaps, if not himself the ferry's designer, might be an old soldier or some similar kind of practical man appointed to get through the early, rough task of building up the working port. Whoever he was, he certainly had little idea of style.

The gate in the wall—a heavy, cross-ply affair studded with the broad heads of iron nails—was standing half-open and Siristrou, following Ankray as he turned in without ceremony, found himself in a courtyard half resembling that of a farmer and half that of a builder's merchant. Materials of one kind and another were stacked all around the place—sacks of what appeared to be seed corn, raised off the ground on slatted boards, several newly turned ox yokes and some leather straps, an iron rainwater tank half-full, two heaps of stones, sorted large and small, a plough, a stack of logs and another of long poles, ten or twelve rough-cut paddles and a mass of caulking material, some coils of rope and a pile of planks. On the north side of the courtyard, against the south wall of the house itself, stood a carpenter's bench, and here a grizzled, aging man, with something of the look of an old soldier, was holding up an arrow in one hand while with the other he carefully fixed a trimmed goose quill below the notch. A younger man and a small crowd of rather ragged-looking boys were standing around him and it was plain that he was instructing them in fletching, for he was both speaking and illustrating his meaning by thrusting forward the arrow held between his finger and thumb, to demonstrate the effect of this particular style of fixing the flights. One of the lads asked a question and the man answered him, pointing to some feature of the arrow and then patting the boy's shoulder, evidently in commendation.

As Siristrou came farther into the courtyard, still following Ankray and feeling uncommonly self-conscious with the great wreath tickling the lobes of his ears, they all looked around at him, and at once the younger man stepped out of the little group and approached, clapping sawdust off his hands and calling over his shoulder, "All right, Kavass, just carry on. When you've finished, have a look at those thick blocks that Ankray's brought, will you?"

Since Ankray did not seem to be going to say anything to announce their arrival, Siristrou, summoning his faulty Beklan, said carefully, "I am here to see the governor."

"I'm the governor," replied the man, smiling. He inclined his head, raised his hand to his forehead and then, as though a little nervous, wiped it on his sleeve before offering it to Siristrou, who took it instinctively but with a certain sense of bewilderment. Perhaps the word he had used for "governor" was the wrong one? He tried again.

"The—er—ruler—the ruler of the town."

"Yes, I'm the ruler of the town. Aren't I, Ankray?"

"Yes, my lord. I've brought the thick blocks and this here foreign prince, just like you said. And that young fellow Shouter, he says to tell you—"

"Well, tell me that later. Will you let the säiyett know that the prince is here and then ask Zilthé to bring some nuts and wine into the reception room? See everything's as it should be, and take the prince's servant with you and look after him."

"Very good, my lord."

Walking beside his host into the house, Siristrou murmured, "If I have the meaning of that word correctly, I ought to tell you that I am not a prince."

"Never mind," replied the governor cheerfully. "If the people here think you are, it will please them and help you as well."

For the first time in several days Siristrou laughed and, able now to look directly at his host without seeming over-curious or unmannerly, tried to size him up. At first glance he looked about thirty, but of this it was hard to be sure, for in spite of his cheerful demeanor there was in his manner a kind of gravity and responsibility which suggested that he might be older. Nor was it easy to guess whether he was primarily a practical or a thinking man, for his face suggested to the perceptive Siristrou experience both of danger and—if words must be found—of grief; of suffering, perhaps. To come down to less fanciful matters, he was almost certainly not a nobleman. To begin with, he was not, to tell the truth, particularly clean, although his roughened hands, his sweat and streaks of grime suggested the craftsman, not the oaf. But there was something else about him—a kind of grave ardor, an air suggesting that the world was not yet altogether as he wished it to be and meant to see it become —that was less aristocratic than any amount of dirt. Altogether, thought the diplomatic Siristrou, a somewhat cryptic and paradoxical character, who might need careful handling. The lobe of one of his ears was pierced by an ugly, ragged hole which contained no earring, and his left arm was carried stiffly, as though affected by an old injury. What might his past be and how had he become governor of Zeray? He seemed neither a rough man lining his pocket nor an ambitious man eager to rise. An idealist? The only man who could be found to take the job? Oh well, thought Siristrou, one knew nothing about this entire country anyway and the man, whatever his history, was too small a fish for the net King Luin had sent him to spread. Later there would be others who mattered more, though no doubt the impression he made here would precede him inland.

They entered a plain, clean room, stone-floored and rush-strewn, where a fire was palely burning, dimmed by the afternoon sunlight. The governor, with another smile, gently lifted the wreath from Siristrou's shoulders and put it on the table beside him. It had not been very soundly made, and was already beginning to fall to pieces.

"Some of your townspeople's children came up and gave that to me while I was on the way here," said Siristrou.

"Really—do you happen to know which children they were?" answered the governor.

"It was little Vasa, my lord," said a girl's voice, "so Ankray tells me, and some of her Ortelgan friends. Shall I pour the wine now?"

A young woman had entered, with silver cups and a flagon on a tray. As she set them down and, turning toward Siristrou, raised her palm to her forehead, he perceived, with a quickly concealed *frisson* of pity, that she was not entirely in her right mind. Her wide, smiling eyes, meeting his own with a disconcerting directness out of keeping both in a servant and in a woman, passed, without change of expression, first to a butterfly fanning its wings on the sunny wall and then to the governor, who reached out and took her two hands affectionately in his own.

"Oh, Vasa, was it? The prince was lucky, then, wasn't he? Thank you, Zilthé, yes, by all means pour the wine at once. But I'll delay mine for a while—I'm going to wash first, and change my clothes. You see, I mustn't disgrace your visit," he said, turning to Siristrou. "Your arrival in Zeray is of the greatest importance to all of us—to the whole country, in fact. I've already dispatched a messenger to Kabin with the news. Will you excuse me for a short time? As you can see—"and he spread out his hands"—I'm not fit to receive you, but my wife will look after you until I come back. She'll be here directly. Meanwhile, I hope you'll find this a good wine. It's one of our best, though you probably have better in your country. It comes from Yelda, in the south."

He left the room and the girl Zilthé turned away to mend the fire and sweep up the hearth. Siristrou stood in the sunlight, still smelling the sharp, herbal scent of the planella in the wreath and hearing for a moment, at a distance, the rather arresting call of some unknown bird—two fluting notes, followed by a trill cut suddenly short. It certainly was a surprisingly good wine, as good as any in Zakalon: no doubt King Luin would be delighted with any trade agreement that included a consignment. He must bear it in mind. He looked up quickly as a second young woman came into the room.

Middle-aged or not, Siristrou retained an eye for a girl and this one caught it sharply. Upon her entry he was aware only of her remarkable grace of movement—a kind of smooth, almost ceremonial pacing, expressive of calm and self-possession. Then, as she came closer, he saw that, though no longer in the first bloom of youth, she was strikingly beautiful, with great, dark eyes and a rope of black hair gathered loosely and falling over one shoulder. Her deep red, sheathlike robe bore across the entire front, from shoulder to ankle, the rampant figure of a bear, embroidered in gold and silver thread against a minutely stitched, pictorial background of trees and water. Forceful, almost barbaric in style, the design, coloring and workmanship were so arresting that for a moment Siristrou was in danger of forgetting the sword for the scabbard, as the saying goes. Work like that, imported to Zakalon, would beyond doubt find a more than ready market. Meanwhile, however, what might be the conventions of this country with regard to women of rank? Free, evidently, for the governor had sent his wife to keep him company alone and therefore no doubt expected him to converse with her.

Well, he was not complaining. Perhaps he had misjudged the country after all, though from what little he had seen of Zeray, it would be strange to find a cultured woman here.

The girl greeted him with grace and dignity, though her Beklan seemed a little halting and he guessed that she, like the gigantic servant, must speak some other as her native tongue. From the window embrasure where they were standing could be seen the sheds and landing stage a quarter of a mile below, fronting the swiftly undulant water of the strait. She asked him, smiling, whether he had felt afraid during the crossing. Siristrou replied that he certainly had.

"I'm a great coward," she said, pouring him a second cup of wine and one for herself. "However long I live here, they'll never get *me* across to the other side."

"I know this side is called Zeray," said Siristrou. "Has the place on the opposite side a name, or is it too new to have one?"

"It hardly exists yet, as you've seen," she answered, tossing back her long fall of hair. "I don't know what the Deelguy call it—Yoss Boss, or something like that, I expect. But we call it Bel-ka-Trazet."

"That's a fine-sounding name. Has it a meaning?"

"It's the name of the man who conceived the idea of the ferry and saw how it could be made to work. But he's dead now, you know."

"What a pity he couldn't have seen it complete. I drink to him."

"I, too," and she touched her silver cup to his, so that they rang faintly together.

"Tell me," he said, finding the words slowly and with some difficulty, "you understand I know nothing of your country, and need to learn as much as I can—what part do women play in—er—well, life; that is, public life? Can they own land, buy and sell, go to—to law and so on—or are they more—more secluded?"

"They do none of those things." She looked startled. "Do they in your country?"

"Why, yes, these things are certainly possible for a woman—say, one with property, whose husband has died—who wishes to stand on her rights and conduct her own affairs, you know."

"I've never heard of anything like that."

"But you—forgive me—I lack the word—your *way* suggests to me that women may have a good deal of freedom here."

She laughed, evidently delighted. "Don't go by me when you reach Bekla, or some husband will knife you. I'm a little unusual, though it would take too long to explain why. I was once a priestess, but apart from that I've lived a—very different sort of life from most women. And then again, this is still a remote, half-civilized province, and my husband can do with almost anyone, man or woman—especially when it comes to helping the children. I act freely on his behalf and people accept it, partly because it's me and partly because we need every head and every pair of hands we've got."

Could she once have been some kind of sacred prostitute? thought Siristrou. It did not seem likely. There was a certain delicacy and sensitivity about her which suggested otherwise.

"A priestess?" he asked. "Of the god of this country?"

"Of Lord Shardik. In a way I'm still his priestess—his servant, anyway. The girl you saw here just now, Zilthé, was also his priestess once. She was badly injured in his service—that's how she came to be as you see her now, poor girl. She came here from Bekla. She feels safer and happier with us."

"I understand. But Shardik—that's the second time today I've heard his name. 'Shardik gave his life for the children, Shardik saved them.'" Siristrou had always had an excellent phonetic memory.

She clapped her hands, startled. "Why, that's Deelguy you're speaking now! Wherever did you hear that?"

"The ferrymen were singing it on the raft this morning."

"The Deelguy? Were they really?"

"Yes. But who is Shardik?"

She stood back, faced him squarely and spread her arms wide. "This is Shardik."

Siristrou, feeling slightly embarrassed, looked closely at the robe. Certainly the workmanship was quite unusual. The huge bear, red-eyed and rippling like a flame, stood snarling before a man armed with a bow, while behind, a group of ragged children were crouching upon what appeared to be a tree-lined river bank. It was certainly a savage scene, but to its meaning there was no clue. Animal worship? Human sacrifice, perhaps? He feared he might be getting drawn into deep water—and his command of the language was still so deficient. One must at all costs avoid wounding the susceptibilities of this high-spirited girl, who no doubt had great influence with her husband.

"I hope to learn more about him," he said at length. "That is certainly a splendid robe—most beautiful workmanship. Was it made in Bekla, or somewhere nearer here?"

She laughed again. "Nearer here certainly. The cloth came from Yelda, but my women and I embroidered it in this house. It took us half a year."

"Marvelous work—marvelous. Is it—er—sacred?"

"No, not sacred, but I keep it for—well, for occasions of importance. I put it on for you, as you see."

"You honor me, and—and the robe deserves the lady. There —in a language I've been learning for only two months!" Siristrou was enjoying himself.

She answered nothing, replying to him only with a glance sharp, bright and humorous as a starling's. He felt a quick pang. Injured arm or no injured arm, the governor was younger than he.

"Robes like this—not so fine as yours, of course, but of this kind—could they be traded to my country, do you think?"

Now she was teasing him, rubbing her hands and bowing obsequiously, like some greasy old merchant flattering a wealthy customer.

"Why, surely, kind sir, not a doubt of it. Very most delighted. How many you like?" Then, seriously, "You'll have to ask my husband about that. You'll find he can talk to you most knowledgeably about anything that's made or sold from Ortelga to Ikat. He's mad about trade—he believes in it passionately—he calls it the blood that circulates in the body of the world; and many other terms he has for it—especially when he's drinking this Yeldashay wine. Have some more." And again she picked up the flagon. "What is the name of your country?"

"Zakalon. It's very beautiful—the cities are full of flower gardens. I hope one day you'll visit it, if only you can overcome your reluctance to crossing the strait."

"Perhaps. It's little enough traveling I've ever done. Why, I've never even been to Bekla, let alone to Ikat-Yeldashay."

"All the more reason to become the first woman to go to Zakalon. Come and make our ladies jealous. If you like ceremony, you must come for the great—er—*midsummer festival,* if those are the right words."

"Yes, they are. Well done! Well, perhaps—perhaps. Tell me, sir—"

"Siristrou—säiyett." He smiled. He had just remembered "säiyett."

"Tell me, U-Siristrou, do you intend to remain here for a few days, or are you going to press straight on to Kabin?"

"Why, that's really for the governor to say. But in the first place, obviously, I shall have to see to bringing my men and—and beasts over from—from—er—Belda-Brazet—"

"Bel-ka-Trazet."

"—from Bel-ka-Trazet. And then I myself am not altogether in the best of health after the journey. It will be a few days, I think, before we're ready to start for Kabin. The wilderness and desert were very trying and the men need rest and perhaps a little—I don't know the word—you know, play, drink—"

"Recreation."

"That's it, recreation. Excuse me, I'll write it down."

Smiling, she watched him write, shaking her head.

"Then if you are here five days from now," she said, "you and your men will be able to see our spring festival. It's a very happy occasion. There'll be any amount of—*recreation,* and a most beautiful ceremony on the shore—at least, it means a lot to us, especially to the children. Shara's Day—that's the time to see the flames of God burning bright as stars."

"The flames of God?"

"It's a kind of joke of my husband's. He calls the children 'the flames of God.' But I was speaking of the ceremony. They decorate a great wooden raft with flowers and green branches, and then it floats away down the river, burning. Sometimes there may be three or four rafts together. And the children make clay bears and stick them all full of flowers—trepsis and melikon, you know—and then at the end of the day they put them on flat pieces of wood and float them away downstream."

"Is it some kind of commemoration?"

"Why, yes—it commemorates Lord Shardik and Shara. This

year an old and dear friend of ours is making the journey to be here—if all goes well, she'll be arriving in two or three days' time. She taught me, long ago, when I was a child—"

"Not very long ago."

"Thank you. I like compliments, particularly now I have two children of my own. If you've not been well, I'd certainly advise you to stay, for then you can ask her help. She's the greatest healer in all this country. Indeed, that's partly why she's coming—not only for the festival, but to see our sick children—we always have a number by the end of the winter."

Siristrou was about to ask her more when the governor returned to the room. He had changed his rough clothes for a plain black robe, embroidered across the breast alone with the bear and corn sheaves in silver; and this, so severe by contrast with the brilliance of his wife's garment, emphasized his grave, lined features and almost mystic air of composure. Siristrou studied his face as he looked down to pour his wine. This, too, he realized suddenly, was a metaphysician by temperament, even though he might have no fluent speech, no articulate ideas. Curiously, there came into his mind those lines of the Zakalonian poet Mitran which are spoken by the hero Serat to his consort in the time after making love—"I desire nothing, I lack for nothing, I am at the center of the world, where sorrow is joy." In a moment, however, the governor looked up, the cups clattered and rang on the tray and the charm was snapped.

Siristrou made a complimentary remark about the wine. The lady excused herself and left them, and the governor, inviting him to sit, began at once to speak of trade prospects as a betrothed might speak of his approaching marriage. If Siristrou had expected little or nothing from the hickory constable of a frontier town, he now found himself compelled to think again. The governor's questions fell like arrows. How far away was Zakalon? How many permanent camps or staging forts would be needed to service a regular trade route? How could Siristrou be sure that there were no hostile inhabitants of the wilderness? Given that the Telthearna might be used for downstream transport, what about upstream? The language problem—he could, if desired, send forty older children to Zakalon to be educated as guides and interpreters. Children learned more quickly than men; some of his would jump at such a chance. What goods could Zakalon offer? Horses—what exactly were they? He looked puzzled as Siristrou began to explain, and they both became confused over language and ended by laughing as Siristrou tried to draw a horse with his finger in spilled wine. Then he promised the governor that the very next day, on one side of the river or the other, he should see a man ride a horse more than twice as fast as he could run. If that were true, replied the governor, then Zakalon need look no further for wares to offer for some years to come. But what did Siristrou think, quite non-committally, might be the trade value of these horses—making a fair allowance, of course, for the cost and effort of transporting them from Zakalon? They began trying to estimate the equivalent values of consignments of wine, of iron and of products of fine craftsmanship such as that of the robe which he had just admired.

The governor called for more wine and the deranged girl served them, sensing their excitement and smiling like an old friend to see the governor busy and happy. Siristrou drank to Zeray. The governor drank to Zakalon. They congratulated one another on their propitious meeting and went on to envisage fancifully a future in which men would travel as freely as the birds of the air and goods would pass through Zeray from the ends of the earth. The governor obliged Siristrou with a verse of the song which the children had sung, explaining that the tongue was actually his own—Ortelgan—and that the lines were part of a singing game about a cat that caught a fish.

"But as to your journey to Bekla," said the governor, coming back to reality with something of a bump, "the road between here and Kabin's not finished yet, you know. Twenty miles of it're sound enough, but the other twenty're still only a muddy track."

"We shall manage it, don't worry. But I'd like to stay for your festival first—Shara's Day, I believe you call it? Your wife was speaking of it. She told me about the burning raft—for Lord Shardik, isn't it? Also, I think I should benefit by meeting your friend, the wise woman—I've not been well during the journey, and your wife says she's a great healer."

"The Tuginda?"

594

"I don't think I heard her—her name. Or is it a title?"

"It's both, in her case."

"Will she come by the half-finished road you were speaking of?"

"No, by water. We're lucky in this town to have the river as a highway from the north. Much of the province is still half-wild, though not as wild as it was. We're making new settlements here and there, although we never risk children in the remoter parts. But there's a child village on the road to Kabin: you'll pass through it on your way to Bekla. It's not very big yet—ten old soldiers and their wives are looking after about a hundred children—but we mean to make it bigger as soon as the land's in any state to support more. It's in a safe place, you see."

"I'm puzzled by the children," said Siristrou, "what little I've seen of them. Your town seems full of children—I saw them working at the landing stage and on your new warehouses. Two-thirds of the inhabitants seem to be children."

"Two-thirds—that's about right."

"They're not all the children of people here, then?"

"Oh, no one's told you about the children?" said the governor. "No, of course, there's hardly been time. They come from many different places—Bekla, Ikat, Thettit, Dari, Ortelga—there are even a few from Terekenalt. They're all children who've lost parents or families for one reason or another. A lot of them have simply been deserted, I'm afraid. They're not compelled to come here, although for many it's better than destitution, I suppose. It's still a hard life, but at least they can feel that we need them and value them. That in itself helps them a great deal."

"Who sends them?"

"Well, I'm in touch with all manner cf people—people who worked for me and used to send me news and so on, in the days when I—er—lived in Bekla; and the Ban of Sarkid has helped us a great deal."

Siristrou could not help feeling a certain distaste. Apparently this young governor, in his enthusiasm for trade, was developing his province and building up Zeray as a port through the labor of destitute children.

"How long are they compelled to remain?" he asked.

"They're not compelled. They're free to go if they want to, but most of them have nowhere to go."

"Then you wouldn't say they were slaves?"

"They're slaves when they come here—slaves of neglect, of desertion, sometimes of actual cruelty. We try to free them, but often it's anything but easy."

Siristrou began to see a connection between this and certain things which the young woman had said to him in their earlier conversation.

"Has it something to do with Lord Shardik?"

"What have you heard, then, about Lord Shardik?" asked the governor with an air of surprise.

"Your wife spoke of him, and about the festival too. Besides, the ferrymen on the raft this morning had a chant—"Shardik gave his life for the children." I should be interested to hear a little more, if you would care to tell me, about the cult of Shardik. I have an interest in such matters and in my own country I have been a—well, a teacher, I think you might say."

The governor, who was gazing into his silver cup and swirling the wine in it, looked up and grinned.

"That's more than I am, or ever shall be. I'm not particularly handy with words, though fortunately I don't need them to serve Lord Shardik. The teaching, as you call it, is simply that there isn't to be a deserted or unhappy child in the world. In the end, that's the world's only security: children are the future, you see. If there were no unhappy children, then the future would be secure."

He spoke with a kind of unassuming assurance, as a mountain guide might speak to travelers of passes and peaks which, for all their lonely wildness, he knows well. Siristrou had not understood all that he said and, finding it difficult to formulate questions in the other's language, fell back on the repetition of words which he had heard him speak.

"You said slaves of neglect and desertion? What does that mean?"

The governor rose, paced slowly across to the window and stood looking out toward the harbor. His next words came hesitantly, and Siristrou realized with some surprise that apparently he had seldom or never had occasion to try to express himself on this subject before.

"Children—they're born of mutual pleasure and joy—or they ought to be. And God means them to grow up—well, watertight, like a sound canoe; fit to work and play, buy and sell, laugh and cry. Slavery—real slavery's being robbed of any chance of becoming complete. The unwanted, the deprived and deserted— they're slaves all right—even if they don't know it themselves."

Siristrou felt no wish to become too much involved. To show a polite interest in foreign beliefs and customs was one thing; to become a target for the fervor of an uncultivated man was another.

"Well, well—perhaps there are some deserted children who don't mind too much."

"Which one of them told you that?" asked the governor, with so droll a simulation of genuine interest that Siristrou could not help laughing. However, he was wondering, now, how best to bring this part of their conversation to an end. He had himself begun it by asking for information, and it would not be civil simply to change the subject. The better way would be first to move on to some other aspect of the matter and thence slide to less tricky ground. Diplomacy was largely a matter of not upsetting people.

"Shardik—he was a *bear*, you say?"

"Lord Shardik was a bear."

"And he was—er—coming from God? I'm afraid I don't know the word."

"Divine?"

"Ah, yes. Thank you."

"He was the Power of God, but he was an actual bear."

"This was long ago?"

"No—I myself was present when he died."

"*You?*"

The governor said no more and after a few moments Siristrou, now genuinely interested, hazarded, "A bear—and yet you speak of his teaching. How did he teach?"

"He made plain to us, by his sacred death, the truth we had never understood."

Siristrou, mildly irritated, refrained from shrugging his shoulders, but could not resist asking, though in a tone of careful sincerity and self-depreciation,

"Wouldn't it be possible for some foolish person to try to argue—of course it would be foolish, but perhaps it might be said—that what took place was all a matter of chance and accident—that the bear was not sent by God—?"

He broke off, somewhat dismayed. Certainly he had said more than he need. He really must be more careful.

The governor was silent for so long that he feared he must have given offense. To have done so would be a nuisance and he would have to set to work to repair the damage. He was just about to speak again when the governor looked up, half-smiling, like one who knows his mind but must needs laugh at his own difficulty in expressing it. At length he said, "Those beasts of yours that you spoke of—the one's we're going to buy from you —you sit on their backs and they carry you swiftly—"

"The horses. Yes?"

"They must be intelligent—cleverer than oxen, I suppose?"

"It's hard to say—perhaps a little more intelligent. Why?"

"If music were played in their hearing and in ours, I suppose their ears would catch all the actual sounds that yours and mine would catch. Yet for all that, it's little they'd understand. You and I might weep; they wouldn't. The truth—those who hear it are in no doubt. Yet there are always others who know for a fact that nothing out of the ordinary took place."

He stooped and threw a log on the fire. The afternoon light was beginning to fade. The wind had dropped and through the window Siristrou could glimpse that the river was now smooth inshore. Perhaps if tomorrow's crossing were to take place in the early morning it might be less hair-raising.

"I've wandered very far," said the governor after a little. "I've seen the world blasphemed and ruined. But I've no time nowadays to dwell on that. The children, you see—they need our time. Once I used to pray, 'Accept my life, Lord Shardik'; but that prayer's been answered. He has accepted it."

At this, Siristrou felt that at last he was on familiar ground. To remove the burden of guilt was in his experience the function of most, if not of all, religions.

"You feel that Shardik takes away—er—that he forgives you?"

"Well, I don't know about that," answered the governor. "But once you know what you have to do, forgiveness matters much less—the work's too important. God knows I've done much wrong, but it's all past now."

He broke off at a sound of movement near the door of the darkening room. Ankray had entered and was waiting to speak. The governor called him over.

"There's some of the children waiting to see you, sir," said the man. "One or two of them new ones that come in yesterday —Kavass brought them up here. And that young fellow down at the landing stage, that Shouter—"

"Kominion?"

"Well, there's some calls him that," conceded Ankray. "Now the Baron, he wouldn't have—"

"Anyway, what does he want?"

"Says he wants some orders for tomorrow, sir."

"All right, I'll come and see him, and the rest of them too."

As the governor turned toward the door, a little boy, aged perhaps six, came wandering uncertainly through it, looked around and came to a halt, staring gravely up at him. Siristrou watched in some amusement.

"Hullo," said the governor, returning the child's gaze. "What are you after?"

"I'm looking for the governor-man. The people outside said—"

"Well, I'm the governor-man, and you can come with me if you like." He swung the child up in his arms just as Melathys came back into the room. She shook her head, smiling.

"Haven't you any dignity, my dearest Kelderek Play-with-the-Children? What will the ambassador think?"

"He'll think I'm one of those swift animals he's going to sell us. Look!" And he ran out of the room with the child on his shoulders.

"You'll dine with us, won't you?" said Melathys, turning to Siristrou. "It'll be about an hour, and there's no need to leave us. How can we entertain you until then?"

"Why, madam, please don't trouble," answered Siristrou, happy to find himself once more in the company of this charming girl, whom privately he considered rather too good for her husband, however keen on trade he might be. "I have a letter to finish to the king of Zakalon. Now that we have really reached your country at last, I mean to send a messenger to-morrow, with an account of our arrival and of all that has befallen. It will be entirely convenient to me to occupy the time until dinner in finishing it. Our king will be anxious for news, you understand." He smiled. "I can sit anywhere you like and be in nobody's way."

She looked surprised.

"You're actually going to *write* the letter? You yourself?"

"Well—yes, madam—if I may."

"You may indeed—if we can find you anything to write on and with. And that I rather doubt. May I watch for a little while? The only people I ever saw write were the Tuginda and Elleroth, Ban of Sarkid. But where are we to find what you need?"

"Don't put yourself out, madam. My man is here. He can go to my lodgings."

"I'll see that he's sent in to you. It will be most comfortable for you to stay in this room, I think. It's turning cold outside and the only other fire's in the kitchen, though Zilthé will be lighting another later, in the far room. When there's company, you see, we can do quite as well as any old village elder. But you're going to make us all rich, aren't you?"—and again she smiled at him as though their lack of luxury were the best of jokes.

"You have children, madam, you told me?"

"Two—they're only babies yet. The eldest isn't three years old."

"Will you not take me to see them, while my man is on his errand?"

*

"—have been pleasantly surprised to find the young governor of the town most knowledgeable about our trade prospects. He assures me that the principal cities will be able to offer us several commodities: metals, certainly iron, and perhaps some gold also, if I have understood him correctly, together with their wine —which is excellent, if only it will travel—and, I rather think,

600

some kinds of jewels, but whether precious or semiprecious, I cannot be sure. In return we should, in my opinion, offer principally horses. For these, I am in no doubt, they will pay well, since they have none and as yet know nothing of them. Indeed it will, I rather think, be necessary to consider how best to regulate such a trade, for it is bound to effect a profound change in their way of life and there will be, for the foreseeable future, an almost unlimited demand.

"The people themselves, what little I have yet seen of them, I like rather than otherwise. They are, of course, semibarbaric, ignorant and illiterate. Yet their art, in some forms at all events, seems to me accomplished and striking. I have been told that Bekla has some fine buildings and this I can believe. Some of their artifacts—for example, the embroidered needlework which I have seen—would undoubtedly be in great demand if sold in Zakalon.

"Your Majesty is aware of my interest in religious and metaphysical matters, and you will understand me when I go on to tell you that I am not a little intrigued to have come upon an odd cult which has undoubtedly had a great influence, not only on the life of this province but also, as far as I can ascertain, on that of the more metropolitan lands to the west. I can best describe it as a mixture of superstition and visionary humanitarianism, which I would certainly have discounted were it not for the results which it seems to have achieved. These people, if I understand the governor correctly, worship the memory of a gigantic bear, which they believe to have been divine. There is, of course, nothing unique about barbaric worship of any large and savage animal, whether bear, serpent, bull or other creature, nor yet in the concept of benefit from a divine death. In their belief, however, the death of this bear somehow availed—I have not yet learned how—to free certain enslaved children, and on this account they consider the security and happiness of all children to be of importance to the bear, and their well-being a sacred duty. One might say that they regard children as a ripening crop, of which no part ought to be wasted or lost. For parents to harm a child, for example by separation from one another, by deserting it or in any other way damaging its security and power to respond to life, is regarded as a wrong equivalent to selling it into slavery. All adherents of Shardik, as they call the bear, have the duty to care for homeless or deserted children wherever they may find them. In this town there are many such children, orphans or derelicts brought from the provinces farther west and more or less conscientiously looked after. The governor —a capable fellow on the whole, I think, though of no great standing in his country and perhaps a little strange in his ways —and his young wife are both very forward in the cult, and have in effect organized the town around the children, who actually outnumber the men and women by about two to one. They work under the supervision partly of grown men or women and partly of their own leaders, and although much of their work is, as one might expect, unskillfully, partially or clumsily performed, that matters little in a province such as this, where the great demand is for quick results and polish comes a long way behind utility and the meeting of immediate needs. No one could deny that this astonishingly benevolent cult demands generosity and self-sacrifice, in which the governor and his household certainly set an example, for they seem to live almost as plainly as the rest. Conditions for the children are rough and ready, but the governor shares the like and certainly seems to do a good deal to promote a sense of comradeship. I cannot help feeling that despite the superstitious worship of the bear, there may well be value in this idea. It is interesting to observe reason emerging from legend, just as this community is itself emerging from the forests that surround it into a state faintly approaching that of your Majesty's own country, the lack of whose civilized comforts your Majesty will, I am sure, understand that I feel most keenly."

Siristrou paused, stretched his fingers and looked up. The light was almost gone. He got up, pushing back the bench on which he was sitting, walked across to the window and stood looking out toward the west. The governor's dwelling stood almost on the edge of the town, and between it and the open country beyond lay nothing except a narrow lane and a stockade that apparently did duty for a town wall. The yellow afterglow showed a land of forest and marsh stretching away into the darkening distance. Here and there in the foreground were small patches of ploughed land, a few irrigation channels, wide tracts of reeds and random strips of water shining with a yellow paler than the sky. It was turning cold. Inland, the wind must be rising again, for he could just make out the shaggy woods moving in the far-off, dreary solitude. Night was falling, bleak and shelterless, and in all the prospect he could see neither light nor smoke. He shivered and was about to turn back into the room when his ear caught the *slap-slapping* of feet approaching along the lane. In idle curiosity he waited, and after a few moments an old woman appeared, black-clad, with a bundle of sticks tied on her back. Her bare feet slapped the earth as she jogged homeward, the bundle tossing up and down on her shoulders. In her arms she was carrying a little, fair-haired girl, and Siristrou could hear her murmuring to the child in a quiet, unhurried rhythm, meaningless and reassuring as the sound of a mill wheel or the song of a bird. As they passed under the window the little girl looked up, caught sight of him and waved her hand. He waved back, and as he did so realized that someone was standing behind him in the room. A little embarrassed, he turned and saw the girl Zilthé, who came up to him and spoke a few words he could not understand. Seeing him at a loss, she smiled, held up the tray of unlighted lamps she was carrying and nodded toward the fire.

"Oh, yes, by all means light them," he replied. "You won't be disturbing me."

She took a burning twig and kindled the wicks one by one, trimming and placing several lamps until the room was bright and well lit. The rest she carried away and Siristrou, left once more alone, sat down before the fire, holding out his hands to the warmth and, just as when a boy, looking into its heart for pictures and shapes—an island, a glowing knife, a barred cage; the likeness of an old woman, a deep ravine, a shaggy bear. The fire flamed in its warmth with a gentle murmur and a wood knot popped sharply. The logs moved, the ash crumbled and fell, the pictures were gone.

Melathys came hurrying in, carrying a joint of pork on a spit, her fine robe changed for a long gray kitchen smock. As she approached he stood up and smiled.

"Can't I work too?" he asked.

"Later, perhaps—another evening, when you've become an

603

old friend, as you surely will. You see what a splendid occasion your visit gives us for a feast. U-Siristrou, are you warm enough? Shall I put on some more logs?"

"No, please don't trouble," answered Siristrou. "That's a beautiful fire."